PENGUIN BOOKS

THREE NOVELS

Elmore Leonard was born in 1925 in New Orleans. He lived in Dallas, Oklahoma City and Memphis before his family settled in Detroit in 1935. He served in the US Navy during the Second World War and afterwards studied English literature at the University of Detroit, graduating in 1950. From 1949 to 1961 he worked as a copywriter in various advertising agencies and, apart from a few book reviews, he has been writing only novels and screenplays since 1967. *La Brava* (which won the 1983 Edgar Allan Poe Award for the best mystery novel) and many other of his books are published by Penguin, including *Glitz*, *The Switch*, *The Hunted*, *Unknown Man No. 89*, *Cat Chaser*, *Split Images*, *City Primeval*, *Bandits*, *Gold Coast*, *Touch*, *Freaky Deaky*, *Killshot*, *Get Shorty*, *Maximum Bob*, *Rum Punch* and *Pronto*. Many of his books have also been filmed.

Elmore Leonard is a member of the Authors' Guild, the Writers' Guild of America, Western Writers of America and Mystery Writers of America.

ELMORE LEONARD

THREE NOVELS

SWAG
STICK
MR. MAJESTYK

PENGUIN BOOKS

PENGUIN BOOKS

Published by the Penguin Group
Penguin Books Ltd, 27 Wrights Lane, London W8 5TZ, England
Penguin Books USA Inc., 375 Hudson Street, New York, New York 10014, USA
Penguin Books Australia Ltd, Ringwood, Victoria, Australia
Penguin Books Canada Ltd, 10 Alcorn Avenue, Toronto, Ontario, Canada M4V 3B2
Penguin Books (NZ) Ltd, 182–190 Wairau Road, Auckland 10, New Zealand

Penguin Books Ltd, Registered Offices: Harmondsworth, Middlesex, England

Swag first published in the USA by Delacorte Press 1976
Published in Penguin Books 1984
Stick first published in the USA by Arbor House Publishing Company 1983
Published in Penguin Books 1984
Mr. Majestyk first published in the USA by Dell 1974
Published in Penguin Books 1986
This collection first published 1994
1 3 5 7 9 10 8 6 4 2

Swag has also been published under the title *Ryan's Rules*

Typeset by Datix International Limited, Bungay, Suffolk
Printed in England by Clays Ltd, St Ives plc

CONTENTS

SWAG

1

There was a photograph of Frank in an ad that ran in the *Detroit Free Press* and showed all the friendly salesmen at Red Bowers Chevrolet. Under his photo it said *Frank J. Ryan.* He had on a nice smile, a styled moustache, and a summer-weight suit made out of that material that's shiny and looks like it has snags in it.

There was a photograph of Stick on file at 1300 Beaubien, Detroit Police Headquarters. Under the photo it said *Ernest Stickley, Jr.*, 89037. He had on a sport shirt that had sailboats and palm trees on it. He'd bought it in Pompano Beach, Florida.

The first time they ever saw each other was the night at Red Bowers Chevrolet on Telegraph when Stick was pulling out of the used-car lot in the maroon '73 Camaro. Frank walked up to the side window as the car stopped before turning out on the street. He said, "You mind if I ask where you're going?"

The window was down. Stick looked at the guy who was stooped over a little, staring at him: nice-looking guy about thirty-five or so, long hair carefully combed, all dressed up with his suit and tie on. A car salesman. Stick could smell the guy's aftershave lotion.

Stick said, "I could be going home, I could be going to Florida." Which was his intention, the reason he was taking the car. He said, "What do you care where I'm going?"

Frank's first impression of Stick was a guy off the farm who'd come to town and somebody had sold him a genuine Hawaiian sport shirt, he wore with the collar spread open, showing a little bit of white T-shirt. Frank said, "Since you didn't buy the car, I mean pay for it yet, I wondered."

"Uh-unh," Stick said. "I come here to price a new one."

Frank kept staring at him. "You always shop for a car after the place's closed?"

"Yeah, that's what I found out. The showroom's all lit up but it's closed. Hey," Stick said, "maybe you think this is one of yours because you got one like it."

"Maybe that's it," Frank said. "Even down to the Indiana plates. It was parked over there where there's an empty space now." He said, "You say it's yours, you want to show me the registration?"

"Fuck no," Stick said, and took off, leaving Frank standing there in the drive.

Frank went into the used-car office, called the Detroit police, and gave them a description of the car. He didn't do it right away. He took his time, thinking the guy must be a real farmer to try and steal a car off a lot that was all lit up. The guy had been very cool about it, though. Slow-talking, relaxed, with the trace of a southern accent. But he might have been putting it on, acting sincere. Frank himself would give customers a little down-home sound every once in a while and grin a lot. It wasn't hard.

He didn't give a personal shit if the guy got away with it or not. The car belonged to the Red Bowers Chevrolet. He wasn't out anything. But there was something personal about it if the guy was driving down Telegraph grinning, thinking he'd aced him. That's why Frank called the police. Also he called to see how the police would handle it. To see if they were any good.

They weren't bad. A squad car turned on its flashers as soon as the Camaro was spotted on the Lodge Freeway. It took another twenty minutes, though, and three sideswiped cars on Grand River, before they got him. They found the wrinkled Camaro in a parking lot and Stick sitting in the bar next door with a bottle of Stroh's beer.

The next time Frank saw Stick was at Detroit Police Headquarters on Beaubien, looking through the one-way glass at him standing in line with the five plainclothes cops who stood patiently staring into the light glare. It was funny. Frank hesitated again before saying, "Second one on the left."

"You're sure he's the one?"

"I'm sure it isn't one of those cops," Frank said.

Out in the office he asked the detective sergeant about the guy, who he was and if he'd been arrested before, and learned the following:

Ernest Stickley, Jr. No aliases. Address: Zanzibar Motel, Southfield, Michigan. Born in Norman, Oklahoma, October 11, 1940. Occupation: truck driver, transit-mix operator. Marital status: divorced; ex-wife and seven-year-old daughter residing in Pompano Beach, Florida.

The sheet also listed previous arrests. The first time for joyriding; sentence suspended. Arrested two years later on a UDAA charge—unlawfully driving away an automobile—and received one-year probation. The final one, arrested for grand theft, auto—transporting a stolen motor vehicle across a state line—and convicted. Served ten months in the Federal Correctional Institution at Milan, Michigan.

Frank said to himself, Well well well well. An auto thief named Ernest, with a record. Maybe a hick but a fairly nice-looking guy. Mid-thirties. Had nerve. Didn't seem to get excited. Obviously knew how to steal cars. In fact, Frank was pretty sure, the guy had stolen a lot more cars than were listed on this sheet. Four arrests now and most likely another conviction.

The third time Frank saw Stick was at the pretrial examination on the fourth floor of the Frank Murphy Hall of Justice. It was an air-conditioned, wood-paneled courtroom with indirect lighting and enough microphones placed around so the people in the audience could hear the proceedings. There were a few cops in off-duty clothes, some cute young black ladies and skinny guys in modified pimp outfits who were either pimps or pushers or might be felony suspects—B and E, robbery or assault—out on bond. There were a few spectators, too: mostly retirees who came up to watch felony exams and murder trials because they were more fun than movies and they were free.

Frank was surprised when he saw the assistant prosecutor: a young black guy in a tight sport coat. Young and short and fat. He had thought all young black guys in Detroit were at least six-seven and went about a hundred and a half. Frank decided the black guy was very smart and had passed the bar in the top ten. He looked like he was enjoying himself, shuffling papers, moving around a lot to talk to the judge and the court clerk and the defense lawyers; then turning away from them, smiling at some inside remark, having fun being a prosecuting attorney.

Frank had a feeling the people watching the guy were probably thinking, Look at that little mother. Little kiss-ass with the big horn-rim glasses on to show how smart he is. Everybody in the courtroom was black except Frank, a couple of Jewish lawyers in their sixties, and the off-duty cops waiting to be called as witnesses.

Stick hadn't been able to make bond. They brought him in through a side door and sat him at the end of a table facing the witness stand as the judge, a black guy with graying hair and a neat gray moustache, called a number and read Stick's name from a big file folder he was holding. Then the prosecutor called Mr. Frank Ryan, and he went through the gate and over to the court clerk, who swore him in and told him to sit down in the witness chair, take the mike off its stand, and hold it in front of him. They didn't waste any time. The little prosecutor asked him if he would please tell what happened the night of May twenty-second in the used-car lot at Red Bowers Chevrolet.

Frank told it. Most of it.

Then he was asked if he had, the next day, identified the same man in a show-up at Detroit Police Headquarters.

Frank said yes, he had.

The little prosecutor said, "And do you see that same man in this courtroom?"

Frank said, "No, I don't."

"And would you point—" The little prosecutor stopped. "What'd you say?"

"I said no, I don't see him."

"You *iden*tified him. Didn't you point him out at a show-up?"

"I thought he was the one," Frank said. "But now I see him again, I'm not sure."

Ernest Stickley, sitting about fifteen feet away, was staring at him. Frank met his gaze and held it a moment before looking at the prosecutor again.

"I mean maybe it's the same person, but I have to tell you I've got a reasonable doubt it isn't. I can't *swear* it's the same person."

"You're sure one day," the little prosecutor said, "now today you're not?"

"I didn't say I was sure. The police officer asked me if he was the one and I said, I think so. I said, He's certainly not any of those other ones."

The little prosecutor didn't seem to be having fun anymore. He began trying to put words in Frank's mouth until Stick's lawyer, appointed by the court, felt he had better object to that and the judge sustained it. Then Stick's lawyer put a few words of his own in Frank's mouth the way he slanted his question and Frank repeated no, he could not positively identify anyone in the courtroom as the person who'd driven off in the '73 Camaro. The prosecutor wouldn't let go. He went at Frank again until the judge told him to please introduce a new line of questioning or else call another witness.

The prosecutor thanked the judge—Frank wasn't sure why—and the judge thanked Frank as he stepped down. The judge was quiet, very polite.

Watching all this, especially watching the guy from the

used-car lot, Frank Ryan, Stick kept thinking, What the hell is going on? He couldn't believe it. He sat very still in the chair, almost with the feeling that if he moved, this Frank Ryan would look at him again and squint and say, Wait a minute, yeah, that's the one.

The guy from the used-car lot went out through the gate. Stick didn't turn around, but he had a feeling the guy was still in the courtroom.

He watched the officer who had arrested him take the stand, wearing slacks and a black leather jacket that was open, his holstered police special on a direct line with Stick's gaze.

The patrolman recited in Official Police how he and his partner had noted the Indiana license plate on the alleged stolen vehicle and had pursued the suspect, witnessing how he had apparently lost control taking a corner upon entering Grand River Avenue and proceeded to sideswipe three cars parked along the west side of the street. Because of the traffic they were not able to keep the suspect in sight, but did locate the vehicle in a parking lot adjacent to the Happy Times Bar located at 2921 Grand River. Upon entering the premises the patrolman asked the bartender who, if anyone, had come in during the past few minutes. The bartender pointed to the person later identified as the suspect. When approached, the suspect said, "What seems to be the trouble, Officer?" The suspect was placed under arrest and informed of his rights.

"And is that person now in this courtroom?"

"Yes sir," the patrolman said to the smart little prosecutor. "He's sitting right there in front of me."

Stick didn't move; he stared back at the policeman. Finally his lawyer leaned toward him with his cigar breath and asked in a hoarse whisper if he would be willing to take the stand, tell what he was doing in the bar and how he got there, show them he had nothing to hide.

Stick whispered back to him, "You out of your fucking mind?"

He didn't have to go up there and testify to anything if he didn't want to. They'd have to prove he had gotten out of the '73 Camaro and walked into the Happy Times Bar, and there wasn't any way in the world they could do it.

The prosecutor tried for another few minutes, until the judge called both attorneys up to the bench and politely told the prosecutor to please quit mind-fucking the court, produce some evidence that would stand up in trial or else everybody was going to miss lunch today. That was how Stick got off.

2

After he was released he didn't see the guy from the used-car lot in the courtroom or in the hall. He saw him on the steps outside the building, lighting a cigarette, and knew the guy was waiting for him to come over.

"You want one?"

"I'm trying to quit," Stick said. He hesitated. "Yeah, I guess I will," he said then and took a Marlboro from a pack the guy offered.

Holding a lighted match, the guy said, "I'm Frank Ryan. I wasn't sure if you heard my name up there."

Stick looked at him. "I heard it." Neither of them offered to shake hands.

Frank said, "You're lucky. That judge seemed like a nice guy. No bullshit."

"I guess I was lucky, all right," Stick said, looking at the guy's neatly combed hair. He was an inch or so taller than Stick, about six feet even, slim build in his green, lightweight, shiny-looking summer suit, with the coat open. Stick had on the same yellow, green, and blue sport shirt he'd worn for almost a week. He said, "It's funny how sometimes you get lucky and other times everything goes against you."

"It is funny," Frank Ryan said. "You want to get a drink or something?"

"I wouldn't mind it. I was in that Wayne County jail six days and six nights and they didn't serve us any cocktails or anything. I guess that's when you were deciding I wasn't the guy after all."

"You were the guy," Frank said.

Looking at each other, squinting a little in the sunlight, they were both aware of the people passing them on the steps and could feel the Frank Murphy Hall of Justice rising above them with its big plate-glass windows. Stick said, "You got a place in mind?"

They walked down St. Antoine toward the river and over a side street through Greektown to the Club Bouzouki. Stick had never heard of the place or the drink Frank ordered once they were sitting at the bar. Ouzo. Frank said why didn't he try one; but Stick said he'd just as soon go with bourbon, it seemed to do the job. He looked around the place, a big, flashy bar, mirrors and paintings, a dance floor and bandstand, bartenders in red vests, but only a few customers in here at 11:30 in the morning. It was dim and relaxing. Stick wasn't in a hurry. It was up to Frank; it was his party. He didn't seem to be in a hurry either. He sipped his milky-looking drink and said to Stick he ought to try it sometime. It tasted like paregoric, so it ought to be good for the stomach. Here he was, after six days in jail, sitting in a bar shooting the shit with the guy who'd put him in then gotten him out. Even though it didn't make sense, Stick wasn't going to rush it.

"You know, the whole thing was," Frank said, "I had a feeling you thought I was a cluck. I catch you dead nuts in the middle of the act, you don't even act nervous or anything."

"What was I supposed to do?" Stick said. "You walk up to me—you think I'm going to get out and run? I got the thing in drive."

"I know, but it was what I felt. Like you're thinking I'm too dumb to do anything about it."

"I wasn't thinking so much of you as just getting out of there."

"See, I go to the show-up," Frank said, "and I'm still a little pissed off. So I identify you. As far as I know, the cops have you nailed down, so it doesn't make any difference. Then I find out I'm the only eyeball witness they got. Also I find out your name's Ernest."

"That's it," Stick said, "Ernest. But I didn't pick it."

"I started thinking about that old saying about being frank and earnest," Frank said. "You be frank and I'll be earnest."

Stick waited. "Yeah?"

"It seemed to fit."

"It seemed to fit what?"

"Also I learned a few things about your record, about doing time at Milan. You want a cigarette?"

"I got to buy some, I guess, if I'm going to keep smoking," Stick said.

Frank struck a match and held it for him. "Something I was wondering," he said. "If you got a gun. If you ever carried one."

"A gun?" Stick looked at him. "You don't need a gun to pick up a car. You don't *want* a gun."

"Well, I didn't know if that was all you did."

"I'll tell you something," Stick said, "since you'll probably ask me anyway. The other night—I hadn't picked up a car in over five years. That's a fact."

"But you picked up plenty before that, huh?"

"You could be a cop and I could give you places and dates, but it wouldn't do you any good. Time's run out."

"Well, you know I'm not a cop."

"That's about all I know," Stick said, "so I'll ask you a question if it's okay. What're you besides a used-car salesman and a sport that drinks a white Greek drink that looks like medicine?"

"I don't drink it all the time," Frank said. "Only when I come here."

"Is that your answer?"

"I'm not ducking the question. It's not so much what I am," Frank said, "as what I want to be."

"Yeah, and what's that?"

Frank hesitated, drawing on his cigarette, then took a sip of the milky-looking ouzo. "What do they call you? Ernie?"

"You call me that, I won't answer," Stick said. "No, I used to be Ernie, a long time ago. Still once in a while people call me Ernest. It's my name, I can't do anything about that. But usually they call me Stick. Friends, guys I work with."

"Because you stick up places?"

"Because of my name, Stickley, and I was skinny, like a stick in high school, when I was playing basketball."

"Yeah? I did, too," Frank said. "Was that down in Oklahoma you played?"

"Up here. I was born in Norman," Stick said, "but I guess you know that, huh?"

Frank nodded. "I don't detect much of an accent, though."

"I guess I lost most of what I had," Stick said, "moving around different places. We come up here, our family, my dad worked out at Rouge twenty-three years."

Frank seemed interested. "We got a lot in common. My old man worked at Ford Highland Park. I was born in Memphis, Tennessee, came to Detroit when I was four, and lived here, I guess, most of my life, except for three years I spent in L.A."

"You married?" Stick asked him.

"Twice. And I got no intention right now of going for thirds. Let's get back," Frank said. "I want to ask you, you never stuck up a place? Used a gun?"

Stick waited a moment, like he was trying to see beyond the question, then shook his head. "Not my style. But since we're opening our souls, how about you?"

"Uh-unh, me neither," Frank said. "Well, years ago I was into a little burglary, B and E. Me and another guy, we didn't do too bad. But then he went into numbers or something—he was a black guy—so I quit before I got in too deep. In and out, you might say."

"You never used a gun during that time?"

"We didn't have to. We only went into places there wasn't anybody home."

"But now you got a sudden interest in guns, it seems."

"Not a sudden interest." Frank came around on his stool, giving it a quarter turn. "I've been studying the situation for some time now, ever since I got back from L.A., reading up on all the different ways people break the law to make money. You know why most people get caught?"

"Because they're dumb."

"Right. Or they're desperate. Like a junkie."

"Stay away from junkies," Stick said. "Don't have any part of them."

Frank raised his eyebrows, impressed. "You believe that, huh?"

"It's the first rule of life," Stick said. He finished his drink, making sure he got it all, shaking the ice in the empty glass. "I'd buy a round," he said, "but I got eight bucks on me and it's got to last till I find out where I'm at."

Frank looked over at the bartender and made a circular motion for a couple of more. He said to Stick, "Don't worry about it. Listen, I was going to ask you what you had in mind. The cop I talked to said you were unemployed."

"Not in Florida. I can get all the work I want in Florida. Cement work. I was going back there to see my little girl."

"I understand you're divorced, too."

"Finally. Listen to this, you want to hear something? We're living in Florida, my wife starts bitching about the hot weather, how she doesn't see her old friends anymore, how her mom's driving her crazy? Her mom lives down there. Wonderful woman, old lady's never smiled in her life. She's watching television, that commercial used to be on a couple years ago about brotherhood, working together and all? It shows all these people standing in a field singing that song—I can't think of how it goes now. All these people singing, and in there you start to recognize some celebrities, Johnny Carson . . . lot of different ones. Her mom squints at the TV set and says, 'Is that niggers?' I'm taking her to the eye doctor's, the car radio's on. Every Friday I'd take her to the eye doctor's. She listens to this group playing some rock thing and says, 'Is that niggers?' We come back up here, sell this house we got that's right off the Intercoastal—come back, my wife's still bitching. Now it's the cold weather, busing, the colored situation, shit, you name it. We're arguing all the time, so finally we separate. Not legally, but we separate. Now what does she do? She goes back to Florida and moves in with her mom. Divorce was final last month."

"Listen, I believe it," Frank said. "Man, every word."

"I don't know what's going to happen there," Stick said, "but I like to see my little girl once in a while."

"Fortunately," Frank said, "neither of my wives had any children. Or any of my acquaintances, I mean that I know of."

Their drinks came and Frank stirred his, watching the clear liquid turn milky as it mixed with the ice cubes. Stick waited for whatever was next and Frank said, "It's funny you mentioned staying away from junkies as a *rule.* That's one of my rules. Don't have anything to do with them. Don't even go to a place where they're liable to hang out."

"You never get in trouble doing that," Stick said.

"I got some other rules, too," Frank said. "In fact, I've got ten rules. I mean, written down."

"What? How to live a happy life?"

"Sort of. How to be a success in a particular undertaking. Which could certainly lead to a happy life."

"You going to tell me," Stick said, "or I got to ask you what they are?"

The bartender rang up their tab and put it on the bar. Frank waited until he moved away.

"I told you I've been studying, well, different ways of making money. I'm not talking about anything tricky like embezzlement, you know, or checks. I've hung a little paper, not much, there's no excitement in it. Christ, it's like work. No, I'm talking about going out and picking up some dough. You know how many ways you can do that?"

"I don't know—auto theft, B and E, burglary, strong-arm—" Stick paused. "There's probably a hundred ways. Some that haven't even been thought up yet."

"What you mentioned, you're talking about things you can

take," Frank said. "Yes, cars, TVs, silverware, fur coats, household shit. But you got to convert it into money, right? You've got to sell it to somebody, and he knows you didn't get the stuff laying around your basement or out in the garage."

"It's unavoidable if you got to fence it."

"That's what I'm talking about," Frank said. "The thing you do first, you eliminate the secondary party. You only take money. And money you can get rid of anywhere. Man, you spend it."

"So then you're into mugging, strong-arm, I mentioned that." Stick paused. "Bank robbery—is that what you want to do, rob a bank?"

Frank looked around and then at Stick again. "I'll tell you something. Nobody's going to rob banks as a career and get rich *and* stay out of jail. Not both. Not with the time locks, the alarm systems. The teller doesn't even have to press a button. You lift the money out of the drawer and a bell rings at the Holmes Protection Agency. They got the TV cameras. You pull a gun, you're on instant replay. The odds are lousy, less than fifty-fifty. Like the average take on a bank job in New York City last year was eleven thousand two. Not bad. But those are the guys that got away. Half the clowns didn't make it."

Frank paused to draw on his cigarette and take a drink. "Let me ask you something. What do you think pays the most? Wait a minute, let me rephrase it. What do you think is the fastest and, percentagewise, safest way to make the most money?"

"Not the horses," Stick said. "I used to spend weekends I wasn't working at Gulfstream or Hialeah."

"No, not the horses," Frank said patiently. "Think about it. What's the fastest and relatively safest way to do it?"

Stick was thoughtful. "Big payoff? Maybe kidnapping."

Frank was losing some of his patience. "Christ no, not kidnapping. FBI, you don't have a fucking chance kidnapping."

"Are we talking about something I never heard of?"

"You heard of it."

"All right," Stick said, "you tell me. What's the best way to make a lot of money fast? Without working, that is."

Frank held up the palm of his hand, his elbow on the edge of the bar. "You ready for this?"

"I'm ready."

"Armed robbery."

"Big fucking deal."

"Say it again," Frank said, "and put it in capital letters and underline it. Say it backward, robbery comma armed. Yes, it can be a *very* big deal. Listen, last year there were twenty-three thousand and thirty-eight reported robberies in the city of Detroit. Reported. That's everything. B and E, muggings, banks, everything. Most of them pulled by dummies, junkies, and still a high percentage got away with it."

"Going in with a gun," Stick said, "is something else."

"You bet it is." Frank leaned in a little closer. "Ernie . . . Ernest—"

"Stick."

"Stick . . . I'm talking about simple everyday armed robbery. Supermarkets, bars, liquor stores, gas stations, that kind of place. Statistics show—man, I'm not just saying it, the *statistics* show—armed robbery pays the most for the least amount of risk. Now, you ready for this? I see how two guys who know what they're doing and're businesslike about it"—he paused, grinning a little—"who're frank with each other and earnest about their work, can pull down three to five grand a week."

"You can also pull ten to a quarter in Jackson," Stick said.

"Listen," Frank said, his voice low and very serious, "I read a true story about two guys who actually did it. Two, three hits a week, they had to keep getting a bigger safe-deposit box. Lived well, I mean *well*, had all the clothes, broads they wanted, everything. It was written by this psychologist or sociologist, you know? who actually interviewed them."

"They told him anything he wanted to know?"

"They trusted him."

"Where was this, where he talked to them?"

"Well, at the time they were in Lucasville, Southern Ohio Correctional, but they went three and a half, four years straight, without ever being arrested. Oh, they were picked up a couple of times, on suspicion, but not for anything nailed down. See, any business will fail if you fuck up. I agree the end result is slightly different here. You don't just go broke, you're liable to give up a few years of your life, confined, you might say. But I don't see any reason to get caught. And that's where my ten rules for success and happiness come in. I see this strictly as a business venture. What I'm wondering now, if you're the business partner I'm looking for."

3

Frank Ryan's ten rules for success and nappiness were written in blue ink on ten different cocktail napkins from the Club Bouzouki, the Lafayette Bar, Edjo's, and a place called the Lindell AC. Some of the rules, especially the last few, were on torn napkins with crossed-out words and were hard to read. The napkins said:

1. ALWAYS BE POLITE ON THE JOB. SAY PLEASE AND THANK YOU.
2. NEVER SAY MORE THAN IS NECESSARY.
3. NEVER CALL YOUR PARTNER BY NAME—UNLESS YOU USE A MADE-UP NAME.
4. DRESS WELL. NEVER LOOK SUSPICIOUS OR LIKE A BUM.
5. NEVER USE YOUR OWN CAR. (DETAILS TO COME.)

6. Never count the take in the car.
7. Never flash money in a bar or with women.
8. Never go back to an old bar or hangout once you have moved up.
9. Never tell anyone your business. Never tell a junkie even your name.
10. Never associate with people known to be in crime.

The angle of the venetian blinds gave Stick enough outside light. He sat by the window in his striped undershorts, placing the cocktail napkins on his bare leg as he read them again, one by one, concentrating on making out some of the blotted words. He was smoking a Marlboro and taking sips from a can of Busch Bavarian that sat on the metal radiator cover beneath the window. He didn't look up until the groaning sound came from the bed and he knew Frank was awake.

"What's that noise?"

"Air conditioning," Stick said. "You want a beer?"

"Jesus Christ." Frank got up on an elbow, looking at the window, squinting. "What time is it?"

"About nine-thirty. My watch's over on the TV." Stick took a swallow of beer as Frank got to his feet on the floor and finally stood up. He was wearing jockey shorts and black socks.

"Where'd you sleep?"

"Right there in bed with you," Stick said, "but I swear I never touched you."

He waited until Frank went into the bathroom, then reached over and pulled the cord on the venetian blinds, raising them and flooding part of the room in morning sunlight. He wanted to get Frank's reaction when he came out and saw the bright pink walls.

He didn't notice them right away. When he came out, he said, "There's four cans of beer in the washbasin."

"Three for you and one for me," Stick said. "I've already had a couple."

Frank was looking at the pink walls now. "Jesus, where in the hell are we?"

"Zanzibar Motel. You're about a mile and a half from where you work. You can walk it if you want."

Frank stooped over a little, squinting, looking across the room at the sunlight filling the window. There wasn't much to see: empty asphalt pavement, and beyond that, a four-lane highway with a grass median, Telegraph Road. A few cars and a semi went past. They could hear them above the humming sound of the air conditioning.

"Where's my car?"

"You couldn't remember where you parked it."

Frank went into the bathroom and came out with a Busch.

"Then how'd we get here?"

"You remember looking for your car?"

" 'Course I do." Frank took a drink of beer and let his breath out, feeling a little better.

"You lost your parking ticket," Stick said.

"I know, that's why I couldn't find the car. All those streets over there look alike. At night, shit, you can't tell."

"You remember trying to get that waitress to take her clothes off?"

Frank hesitated, then drank some more of the beer. "We had a pretty good time, didn't we?"

Stick said, "You remember standing in front of the J. L. Hudson Company, in the middle of Woodward Avenue, taking a leak?"

"I really had to go, didn't I?"

"Eileen sure got a kick out of that."

Frank looked at him. "Eileen, huh?"

"The one you picked up at the Lafayette Bar. Wasn't she a size?"

Frank managed to grin and shake his head. "Yeah, she sure was."

"I was surprised she didn't get sore, you started calling her Fatty."

"Just kidding around," Frank said. He went over to the dresser, opened his wallet, and fingered the bills inside. "Yeah, I guess we had a pretty good time." Looking at Stick he said, "I must have paid for the cab, huh?"

"Taxicab? We didn't take any cab anywhere."

"All right, you win," Frank said. "How'd we get here?"

"In a 1975 Mercury Montego." Stick watched Frank look toward the window again. "You remember we're standing in front of the Sheraton-Cadillac?"

Frank's expression began to open and show signs of life. "Yeah, they wouldn't let us in the bar because you didn't have a coat on."

"We're standing out in front," Stick said, "when the Merc pulls up and the guy gets out, looking around. You remember?"

Frank seemed happier as he began to recall it and could see the Mercury—dark brown, shiny—in front of the hotel and Stick walking over to the guy who got out, and now Frank was grinning. "Yeah, you went up to the guy and said something—"

"I said, 'Good evening, sir. Are you a guest at the hotel?' "

"Right. And he said he'd only be about an hour and handed you the keys."

"And a dollar tip," Stick said.

Frank was still grinning. "Sure, I remember it. Where's the car?"

"Up the street, in the Burger Chef parking lot. You go out, don't look at it. Don't even walk past it." Stick held up the ten cocktail napkins. "You remember these?"

"Sure I remember them. What do you keep asking me that for? I remember everything that happened." Frank took the napkins over to the dresser, spread them out, and stood there idly scratching his jockey shorts as he looked at them.

Stick watched him. After a moment he said, "I been reading your rules for success and happiness. And you know what?"

Frank kept scratching. "What?"

"I think you got an idea."

Frank looked over now. "Yeah? You think so, huh?"

"I think it might be worth looking into. It's a wild-ass idea—two guys who don't know shit going into the armed-robbery business. But you never know, do you?" He watched Frank go into the bathroom again and raised his voice. "I'm thinking maybe it's the way to make a stake. Be able to put a down payment on something that'll carry you. Instead of working all your life. That's what I been doing, working. What have I got? Eight bucks in my pants, nothing, not a cent in the bank."

"Working is for workingmen," Frank said, coming out with two cans of Busch. He walked over to Stick and handed him one, raising his own. "To our new business, huh? What do you say?"

"To the new business." Stick raised his beer and took a sip. "I'll tell you a secret, buddy, put your mind at rest."

Frank seemed interested. "What's that?"

"Last night, you didn't take a leak in the middle of Woodward Avenue."

"I didn't?"

"Uh-unh. I did."

First they had to find Frank's car, which wasn't actually his, it was a demo.

Frank called a friend of his at Red Bowers Chevrolet, a salesman, and got him to drive them downtown to look for it. On the freeway the friend kept asking, "But how can you lose a car? Not have it stolen, *lose* it. A car." Frank told him it could happen to anybody. Get turned around, forget exactly where you parked it. "See, this guy here had the ticket, with the address on it and everything, and he lost it." Stick didn't say anything. They found the car, paid six and a half to get it out, and Frank bought them a couple of drinks at the Greek place.

After the friend left, Frank said, while they were downtown, they might as well look up Sportree and see about the guns. Right?

Stick hesitated. This was the part he wasn't sure of.

"Look," Frank said, "you got to have a gun or it isn't armed robbery, is it? You don't have a gun, the guy says go fuck yourself and you're standing there, your hand in your pocket, pointing your finger at him."

"I'm not talking about the guns," Stick said. "I'm talking about the source." He'd been thinking about it and his idea was maybe they ought to run down to South Carolina or someplace.

"Buy them?" Frank said. "Fill out the papers? Registered in

whose name, yours or mine?" No, Frank said, the only way to do it was to talk to Sportree, his old B and E associate.

Stick said how did they know they could trust this guy Sportree? Where was he getting the guns? Were they used before? Get caught with the goddamn piece and they check it and find it killed some colored guy the week before. "I never dealt with a colored guy," Stick said, "on anything important, and I don't know if I want to."

Frank told him to quit thinking about it. Sportree wasn't going to sell them the guns. All he'd do was set it up so they could put their hands on a couple of clean pieces. Once they found him.

Frank hadn't seen Sportree in a few years. When he tried to call, he got an operator who told him the number was no longer in service. Stick said why didn't he look in the phone book. Frank said, Jesus, that'd be like looking up Gracie's Whorehouse. Stick said why didn't he try it anyway.

That was how they found the listing for Sportree's Royal Lounge on West Eight Mile.

In the late afternoon and early evening Sportree's offered semidarkness and a sophisticated cocktail piano and was a spot for Southfield secretaries who worked in the new modern glass office buildings for companies that had moved out of downtown Detroit. They'd stop in after five and let guys buy them drinks. Or a secretary might come in with her boss, or with a salesman who called on her boss. A good-looking black girl with red hair and horn-rimmed glasses played cocktail Cole Porter from five to eight, getting the secretaries and the executives in the mood. Then she'd cover the piano keys and take her sheet music upstairs to the apartment over the Lounge.

Also at eight the two white bartenders, who had come on at noon, went off, and two black bartenders took over. By nine, the executives and the secretaries were out of there. By ten, the clientele was solid black and the cute redheaded piano player came down without her sheet music and played soul on and off until 2:00 A.M.

When Frank and Stick got there a little before seven, it was cocktail time and the secretaries were sitting around in the moody dimness with bosses or salesmen or waiting for live ones to come in. Walking in, Frank liked the place right away. He said, "Hey, yeah." A few of the girls looked up and gave them a quick reading, without showing any interest. Nothing. A guy who slept in his clothes and a garage mechanic off duty—probably what they thought. It bothered Frank. He felt seedy and needed a shave and imagined he had rotten breath. He wanted to go home and change, come back later. He wasn't disappointed at all when the bartender told them Sportree wouldn't be in till around ten.

They drove out to Stick's motel, the Zanzibar, picked up the ten cocktail napkins, the can of Busch Bavarian left over, and Stick's suitcase that looked like it had been through a lot of Greyhound bus stations and held nearly everything he owned. After that they went to Frank's apartment on Thirteen Mile in Royal Oak.

Frank told Stick to unpack and make himself comfortable while he took a shower. Stick looked around; it was a small place, one bedroom, not much. He didn't unpack but took a pale-green sport coat out of the suitcase and draped it over the back of a chair. He wondered if Frank had an iron. Probably not, the place was pretty bare, a few magazines lying around and ashtrays that hadn't been emptied. The place didn't look lived in; it looked like a waiting room in a hospital.

Frank put on a clean shirt, a dark-blue shiny suit, and asked Stick if he was going to change.

"I already did," Stick said, "this morning." He had on a faded blue work shirt.

Frank looked at the sport coat on the chair. "I guess you couldn't wear it anyway till you had it cleaned."

"I haven't worn it in a month," Stick said. "What do I need to get it cleaned for?"

"I mean pressed," Frank said. "Let's get out of here."

They stopped for something to eat and got back to Sportree's a little after ten.

As soon as they were inside the door, Stick said, "What's going on?" He kept his voice low. "What the fuck is going *on?*"

He followed Frank over to an open space at the bar, seeing the young black guys with their hats and hairdos turning to look at them.

Frank said to the bartender, "Bourbon and a scotch, please. Splash of water."

He looked over his shoulder at the tables. There wasn't another white person in the place. The light was off where the redheaded black girl had been playing the piano. The heavy chugging beat of West Indian reggae was coming from a hi-fi. The place seemed darker.

Frank waited for the bartender to put their drinks down. He said, "Where's Sportree? Tell him Frank Ryan. He knows me."

The bartender looked at him, didn't say a word, and moved away.

Stick said, "What's going *on?*"

"I got an idea," Frank said. "I don't know, but I got an idea."

When Sportree approached a few minutes later, Frank saw him coming in the mirror behind the bar. He looked over his shoulder at Sportree, at his open body shirt and double string of Ashanti trading beads, and said, "Where you going, to a drag party?"

Frank could feel the people near them watching, and felt good seeing the warm, amused expression in the man's eyes. He hadn't changed; he still knew who he was, in control. A good-looking, no-age black man with straightened long hair glistening across his forehead, a full, curled-down moustache, a little bebop growth beneath his lower lip, and liquid, slow-moving eyes.

Sportree said, very quietly, "Frank, how you doing? It's been a while."

Frank said, "I'd like you to meet my business associate, Ernest Stickley, Jr., man, if you can dig the name. Stick Stickley. And this is Sportree in the Zulu outfit, in case anybody doesn't know he's a jig."

Sportree didn't change his expression. He said, "You come down to learn some new words? Don't know whether you're Elvis Presley or a downtown white nigger, do you?"

"Well, you know," Frank said, "it's hard to keep up with all that jive shit living with honkies. Actually what we're looking for is a cleaning lady."

Sportree's expression held, then began to relax more, and he almost smiled. "A cleaning lady. Yeah, why don't we go upstairs, be comfortable? Talk about it."

They went outside to the entrance and up a flight of stairs to the apartment over the Lounge. The good-looking young black girl with red hair was sitting on the couch smoking a homemade cigarette. Sportree said, "A bourbon and a scotch, little water." Stick could smell the cigarette. He watched the girl get up without a word and go into the kitchen: little ninety-six-pounder in a white halter top and white pants.

As they sat down Sportree said, "You all want to smoke?"

Frank said, "Hey, don't start my partner on any bad habits. He's straight and I want to keep him that way."

Stick didn't say anything. He listened to Frank ask the black guy how the numbers business was, and the black said numbers, numbers was for little children. He was in the saloon business now. You mean in front, Frank said, with a pharmacy in the rear. The black guy said well, maybe a little coke and hash, some African speed, but no skag, uh-unh, he wouldn't deal shit to a man he found in bed with his lady.

The redheaded black girl brought the drinks in and left the room again, still without a word or change of expression.

Stick listened to Frank talking about the car business, L.A., smog, traffic on the Hollywood Freeway, how he'd worked in a bar in North Hollywood, screwed a starlet once, and finally, after thinking a while, remembering the name of the picture she was murdered in, which Stick and the black guy had never heard of. Stick went out to the kitchen and made himself another drink. The red-headed black girl sitting at the table reading *Cosmopolitan* didn't look up. He went back into the living room, which reminded him of a Miami Beach hotel, waited until Frank got through saying no, he wasn't in jail out there, and said, "You having a nice visit?"

Frank gave him a deadpan look. "Why, you in a hurry?"

"I thought we were looking for a cleaning lady."

Sportree was watching them both with his lazy, amused expression. He said, "Yeah, I believe somebody mentioned that." His eyes held on Frank. "Your business associate know what he's doing?"

"Cars," Frank said. "He's very good with cars. Many, many years at it, one conviction."

"If that's your pleasure, what you need with a cleaning lady?"

"That's his credentials. I'm saying we're all friends," Frank said. "Kindred spirits. Birds of a feather."

"Man," Sportree said, "you do need some new words."

"I'll take a side order," Frank said, "but for the entree how about a nice cleaning lady with big brown eyes?"

"You going back in the business? It's hard work, man. For young, strong boys with a habit."

Frank shook his head. "No, we got something else in mind. But first we got to locate a couple of items."

"Like what items we talking about?"

"Well, what this cleaning lady should look for are, you know, color TVs—"

"Yeah."

"Fur coats."

"Yeah."

"Watches. Jewelry."

"Go on."

"Silverware maybe, you know, silver stuff. And firearms."

Sportree grinned. "You almost forgot to mention that. Any particular firearms you got in mind?"

"Well, like the kind you might find in the guy's top drawer," Frank said. "Underneath his jockeys."

"No hunting rifles, anything like that."

"No, I had more in mind the smaller models you can hold in one hand."

"Put in your pocket, or in your belt."

"Yeah, that kind."

"You remember my cousin LaGreta?"

"That's right, your cousin."

"She used to have big eyes. I can talk to her," Sportree said. "Seems to me the rate was twenty bucks a house. I mean a house, you know, there's goods in it. She give you the plan, where everything is, twenty bucks."

"That's fine," Frank said. "Twenty bucks, if that's the going rate, fine."

"She's with this Rent-A-Maid and also a catering service," Sportree said. "Work parties, weddings, you understand? And does some cleaning jobs, too. She don't do floors, though. I remember her saying she don't do floors."

"Long as she gets in the house," Frank said, "I don't care what the fuck she does in there."

"Nice thing," Sportree said, "she gets around. You know, doesn't work for the same people all the time. That wouldn't be so good."

"Listen, that sounds fine," Frank said. "In fact it's exactly what we're looking for. If LaGreta's got the eyes you say she has."

"Nice big eyes," Sportree said.

"Can I ask you if she's on anything?"

"She smoke a little, that's all. Vacuum that big house, clean the oven, polish the furniture, she like to visit friends and have a little something. But what she make you know, she ain't on any hard shit."

"You think you can set it up?"

"I'll talk to her. You give me your telephone number."

Frank hesitated. "I better call you. We're in and out a lot. Maybe we're not there when you call."

Sportree said, "Frank, I hope you still the same person I used to be associated with." His gaze moved to Stick. "Just as I hope your friend here is pure."

"I'll tell you something," Stick said to him. "I enjoyed the drinks, but I don't know a rat's ass about you either, do I?"

It was the quiet way he said it that jolted Frank. He couldn't believe it—the first time Stick even opened his mouth. Frank said, "Hey, let's not have any misunderstandings," and looked over at Sportree.

"It's all right," Sportree said, his tone a little cooler than before. "You call me in a couple of days. Maybe I'll have something for you, maybe I won't."

When they were outside Frank said, "What're you trying to

prove? The guy's doing us a favor, you come on like you're some dangerous character."

"All I said was I didn't know him very well."

"But I do." Frank was tense. "I've known him a hell of a lot longer'n I've known you. You don't like the way I'm handling it, go back working cement, maybe I'll see you around."

"You're handling it," Stick said. "You made up the rules. It seems to me one of them, it says don't even tell a junkie your name. The first guy we talk to, it happens, runs a dope store."

"You don't know anything about him."

They got in the car and drove off and didn't say anything for a while, each feeling the other's presence. Finally Frank said, "Listen, this is kind of dumb. We got something going or we haven't. We don't blow it over a few words."

"I'll tell you the truth," Stick said. "I thought the guy was all right. I probably wasn't talking so much to him as I was to you."

Frank looked over. "I don't follow you."

"There you are," Stick said. "And I don't follow you around either, you say go pee-pee, I do it. You don't say to the guy I don't want a smoke. If I don't want it, I'll tell him."

Frank glanced away from the windshield again. "Is that all that's bothering you?"

"That's all," Stick said. "I thought I might as well mention it."

4

They spent the weekend on a slow tour of some of Detroit's industrial suburbs on the northeast side—Clawson, Madison Heights, Warren, Roseville—Stick driving, Frank taking notes, writing down the names and locations of bars, supermarkets, liquor stores, with a few words to describe the traffic and the fastest way out of each area. There was a liquor store in Warren that Frank especially liked and said maybe ought to be the first one. The liquor store was on a four-lane industrial street that was lined with machine and sheet-metal shops, automotive supply houses. Hit the place on a Friday, payday. How'd that sound? Stick said if they were going to start, the liquor store was probably as good a place as any.

Monday, Frank went back to Red Bowers Chevrolet and told the sales manager he was leaving the end of the week. The sales manager didn't seem too upset about it. Frank looked around the used-car lot and gave himself a good deal on a tan '72 Plymouth Duster that needed a ring job and some transmission work. If they had any luck at all, they wouldn't have the car very long.

After he got home he drove Stick around downtown Royal Oak until Stick spotted Al's Plumbing & Heating on South Main and said, "There. I think I like that one." He liked the way they parked the panel trucks behind the building with no fence or spotlight to worry about.

Tuesday, Stick took his green sport coat to the cleaner's, then stopped at an auto parts store and had some clips made for shorting and hooking up electric wires. The guy at the place didn't ask him any questions. He bowled and drank beer most of the afternoon, rolling a 186 he felt pretty good about.

Wednesday, Frank called Sportree, who told him to come down, he had something they might like.

What it was: a sheet of Ace tablet paper, lined, with the addresses of two homes in Bloomfield Hills and a list of the goods they'd find in each place. The words looked like they'd been written by a child, in pencil, but that was all right. They could read the words without any trouble. Especially the one that said *guns.*

"This one place, LaGreta say the man's got a gun collection in his recreation room, down in the basement," Sportree explained. "The whole family's out to the lake for the summer. Sometime the man stop off home, but usually he drive out there from his work. How's that sound to you for forty dollars? Whole mother collection to pick from."

Thursday night, they went to a ten o'clock show in Royal Oak, watched Clint Eastwood kill some people, and at twelve walked out of the movie theater, across the street, and down two blocks to Al's Plumbing & Heating. Frank waited on the corner while Stick went around the back. A few minutes later a panel truck with Al's name on the side stopped at the corner and Frank got in.

"That was pretty quick."

"It used to take me less than a minute," Stick said, "but with these newer models, I got to figure things out."

"You jump the wires?"

"Not under the hood." Stick patted the dashboard. "All the work's done underneath here. You look, you see some clips I had made."

Driving out to the gun collector's house in Bloomfield Hills, he told Frank what he used to do when he spotted a certain car he liked that had the dealer's name on it. Get the serial number off the car, then go to the dealer and tell them you lost the key and have one made. Simple.

They found the address and Stick pulled into the side drive of the big Colonial.

It was Frank's turn now. "They all do the same thing," he said, "leave two lights on downstairs and one up, and you're supposed to think somebody's home."

Stick sat in the truck while Frank rang the bell at the side door and waited. He rang it again and waited almost a minute before he broke a pane of glass in the door, reached in, and unlocked it. Stick got out of the truck and went inside, down a hallway past the kitchen to the family room, where a lamp was on. Frank was looking at the TV set, a big Motorola that was like a piece of furniture.

"What do you think?" Frank said. "Use the top for a bar, get rid of that little black-and-white I got. Except it's a big mother, isn't it?" He looked at Stick. "You think we can handle it?"

"If I remember right," Stick said, "we come here for guns."

There was a locked cabinet full of them down in the recreation room. Three rifles, three shotguns, and an assortment of handguns: several new-looking revolvers, a couple of Lugers, a Japanese automatic, and a Frontier model Colt .44, the kind Clint Eastwood had carried in the movie.

Stick had a feeling Frank would pick it up first. He did—pulled the hammer back and sighted and clicked the trigger, then hefted it in his hand, feeling the weight and looking at it from different angles. Frank held the Colt .44 against his hip, then threw it out in front of him and did it again.

"Fastest gun in Royal Oak," Stick said. "You know how to shoot?"

"Pull the trigger," Frank said. "Isn't that what you do?"

Stick considered a P-38 Walther, it looked pretty good, but

chose a Smith & Wesson .38 chief's special with a two-inch barrel. After Frank finished fooling around, he picked a big Colt Python 357 with a ventilated rib over its six-inch barrel. They found boxes of cartridges for both revolvers and got out of there.

The next day, Friday, Frank bought the Deluxe Anniversary Edition of *Gun Digest* and read off the vital statistics of his two revolvers, his forty-seven-ounce number and Stick's stubby little fourteen-ouncer. The Colt Python listed for a hundred and ninety-nine dollars and ninety-five cents new. Stick's little Smith only cost ninety-six. Stick said, "But I don't have to carry four pounds of metal around in my pants, do I?"

At noon Frank reported in at Red Bowers Chevrolet for the last time, sold two late-model used cars and made eighty-six bucks in commission. A good sign, everything was working. Stick got his sport coat from the cleaner's and had it on with a starched white shirt and a green-and-yellow-print tie when Frank got home. Frank didn't say anything about the coat or the tie. He changed and they each had a couple of drinks. At 6:30 they couldn't think of anything else they had to do, so they went out to hold up the liquor store.

Stick got a car from a movie theater parking lot in Warren, a '74 Olds Cutlass Supreme, drove it up the street to where Frank was waiting in the Duster, and picked him up. Frank asked if he had any trouble and Stick said, "What'd it take me, two minutes?"

Frank felt pretty good, anxious and a little excited, until they were approaching the liquor store. Then he wasn't sure. They came even with the building that was in a block of storefronts. There was plenty of parking space. Stick slowed down but kept going, his eyes on the rearview mirror.

"I wanted to look at it again," Stick said.

They went around the block, past vacant lots and plant-equipment yards.

"What we have to consider," Frank said, "what if we don't get much? Like fifty, sixty bucks, something like that. The guy could have most of his dough locked up somewhere, hidden. Then what do you do, he refuses to tell you where it is, shoot him?"

Stick was looking around. His eyes kept going to the rear-view mirror. "Or try another place," he said. "There's plenty around."

"What I mean is," Frank said, "maybe it's more trouble than it's worth. Nobody's forcing us. We go in a place because we want to. We try it or we don't. What're we out? Nothing. We could sell the guns. Maybe even the car, dump it off on somebody."

They were on the four-lane street again, with very little traffic going either way. A quiet, daylight-saving-time early evening in the summer. A car pulled away from the liquor store, leaving the curb empty for at least sixty feet.

"Well," Frank said, "what do you think?"

Stick swung the Olds in to the curb. "What do I think about what?" he said. "Let's do it."

He pulled up a little past the store entrance and put the lever in park, then accelerated to make sure the engine was idling.

As Stick opened his door, Frank said, "What's Rule Number One?"

Stick paused. "Always be polite. Say please and thank you."

Frank said, "You know, when I worked at the dealership a man came in to teach us how to sell cars over the phone. Call up people, find out if they're in the market. He says to me, 'What's your name?' I tell him Frank Ryan. He says, 'No, it's not.' He says, 'Not over the phone. You call a prospect, you say, "Hi, I'm Frank Duffy of Red Bowers Chevrolet." Duff-*ee*. You always use a name that ends in *y* or *i-e*. Because when you say it you got a smile on your face.' "

Stick waited, staring at Frank for a moment before he got out of the car.

The counter and shelves of liquor ran along the left wall. Down the middle of the store were wine bins and displays of party supplies. Along the right-hand wall the beer and soft drinks were in coolers with sliding glass doors. Two guys were standing over there.

Frank and Stick walked up to the liquor counter. The guy behind it was about sixty but big, over two hundred, with tight curly gray hair. He laid his cigarette in a chrome ashtray and said, "Can I help you?"

Frank wanted to look around, but he didn't. He hesitated and said, "Yes sir, you can," unbuttoned his suit coat, took out the Colt Python, and rested the butt on the counter so that the gun was pointing directly at the man's wide expanse of stomach. The man closed and opened his eyes and seemed tired.

"You can empty your cash register," Frank said. "But sir? I see anything in your hand's not green and made of paper, I'll blow you right through the fucking wall."

It was happening. Frank watched the guy punch open the cash register without a word. Maybe it had happened to him before. He held the gun on him and his hand was steady. He motioned with his head then.

Stick walked around the rack of potato chips and Fritos to the two guys standing by the beer cooler. They were hunched over, trying to decide, one of them reaching in then for a six-pack of Stroh's.

Opening his sport coat, Stick said, "Excuse me, gents." When they looked at him he said, "You see what I got here?" They didn't right away, until they saw he was holding his coat open.

The one with the six-pack said, "Jesus," and dropped it on the floor. Stick kept himself from jumping back.

The other one didn't say a word, his eyes on the butt of the .38 special sticking out of the waistband.

"You don't want to get hurt," Stick said, "and I certainly don't want to hurt you. So let's march to the rear, see what's in back."

Past the potato-chip rack he could see Frank holding open a paper bag and the man behind the counter dropping bills into it.

There was a young clerk in the storeroom, sitting on a stack of beer cases holding a sandwich and eating from a half-pint container of coleslaw. He looked surprised to see three men coming in, but he was also polite. He said, "Can I help you?"

Stick spotted the big walk-in reefer and said, "No thanks, I guess I can handle it myself."

He walked over, opened the door to the refrigerator, and nodded for the two customers to go inside.

The clerk said, "Hey, you can't go in there. What do you want?"

"You, too," Stick said. He held open his coat again. "Okay?"

When he came out into the store he thought the place was empty and got an awful feeling in his stomach for a moment. Then, near the cash register, Frank rose up from behind the counter with the paper bag.

As he came over the counter, the bag in one hand—the top of it rolled tightly closed—and the Python in the other, Stick said, "Where's the guy?"

"On the floor." Frank looked over the counter and said, "Stay down there, if you will please. Because if you raise up too soon, if you see me again, then I'll see you, won't I? And if I see you again, I won't hesitate to shoot and probably kill you."

Stick said, "Tell him the other people're in the icebox."

"You hear that, sir?" Frank looked over the counter again. "In the icebox."

"Tell him much obliged," Stick said.

"Yeah, much obliged. Maybe we'll see you again sometime."

Neither one of them wanted to look anxious. They walked out, taking their time.

In the car Stick put the gear into drive and waited, looking at the rearview mirror, until he saw the big guy with the gray curly hair appear suddenly in the doorway and stop dead. Stick got out of there then, tires squealing as he peeled away from the curb.

Frank turned around to look straight ahead again. "He saw the car, I'm sure. Maybe even the license."

"You bet he did," Stick said. "Now I drop you off at your car, head back to the picture show, and you pick me up there."

"It seems like a lot of trouble," Frank said.

"Yes, it does," Stick said. "But it sure keeps the police busy, looking for a '74 Cutlass Supreme, doesn't it? How much we get?"

Frank held the bag on his lap, the top tightly folded. "Rule Number Six," he said.

As soon as they were in the apartment Stick took off his sport coat. He was sweating. The Duster didn't have air conditioning. He looked at Frank, who was sitting on the couch lighting a cigarette like he had his lunch in the bag and there wasn't any hurry getting to it.

Stick said, "You going to count it or you want me to?"

"Why don't you make us a couple of drinks?" Frank said.

Stick went out to the kitchen. He poured scotch in one glass and bourbon in another, then got a tray out of the refrigerator and began filling the glasses with ice. It was all right that Frank counted it, but he wanted to watch, at least. He put a splash of water on the drinks and went back out to the living room.

"I don't believe it," Frank said.

He was hunched over the coffee table, looking down at the neatly stacked piles of bills, like a guy playing solitaire. He laid a twenty on one pile, a fifty on another. As Stick approached he was peeling off tens from the wad he held in his hand.

"Jesus," Stick said. "How much?"

"Don't talk, I'll have to start over."

Stick put the drinks down carefully, got a cigarette and lit it, and walked over to the window that looked out on the parking area behind the building. It was quiet back there, sunlight on the cars and long shadows, the end of the day. The cars looked hot. The tan Duster without air conditioning was parked there. A VW and a Pinto wagon and a Chevy pickup and a bike, a big Harley that made a racket every morning at seven fifteen—

"All right, how much you think?"

Stick turned from the window. "Why don't you tell me?"

Frank was sitting back with the scotch in his hand, all the bills stacked in front of him, now in five neat piles.

"How about six grand?" Frank said. "How about six thousand two hundred and forty-eight fucking dollars, man? Tax free?"

Stick came over to the table and stared at the money.

"Six, comma, two four eight," Frank said. "Most of it was in a box under the counter."

"Jesus, what a business," Stick said. "One day he makes that much?"

"You mean one day *we* make that much. No, what it is," Frank said, "the guy cashes paychecks."

"Yeah?"

"See, to get the hourly guys to come in, working in the shops. So he's got to have a lot of cash on hand payday. Keeps it in the box with the checks he cashes, from all different companies around there."

Stick looked up at him. "Endorsed? I mean the checks were signed?"

"I thought of that," Frank said, "but I figure it's not worth all the trouble, unless you know somebody likes to buy checks."

"Yeah, I guess so," Stick said. "Then you're dealing with somebody else."

"I figure we hit him earlier, we could've gotten even more. You know? Around three thirty or so, before the first-shift guys start coming in."

"You complaining?" Stick said. "First time, Christ. I don't believe it."

Frank started to grin. "Guy took one look at the Python—you see him?—I thought he was going to shit. I say to him, very polite, 'You can empty the cash register, sir. But I see anything in your hand isn't green or made of paper, I'm going to blow you right through the fucking wall.' "

Stick was grinning, too, shaking his head. He said, "I gave the two guys over by the beer cooler a flash of the Smith. I didn't take it out, I just showed it to them. I said, 'Hey, fellas, you see what I got here?' Just the grip sticking out. The guy drops his six-pack. The fella out in back's eating his lunch. He says, 'Can I help you?' "

"We're home counting our wages," Frank said, "they're still looking for the car. Or they got it staked out. The guy comes out of the show and they bust him."

"It's the only way to do it," Stick said. "Takes a little longer, but you keep your car clean, off the sheet. Yeah, it's a very good rule. In fact, that told me right away you had it pretty well thought out."

"You think it's worth it then, huh, all the trouble?"

"What trouble?"

"That's the way I see it," Frank said. "If they're all this easy, I believe we found our calling."

5

Frank would stand at the bar in the living room with one leg over a bamboo stool, pick up his scotch, and say, "Well, here we are."

Stick would say, "You sure?"

And Frank would say, "You look out and see if the broads are still there. I'll go count the suits."

It was a ritual after three months in the business and twenty-five armed robberies—after they'd bought the clothes and the new car and moved into the apartment building where nearly half the occupants were single young ladies. Frank liked to strike his pose at the bar and say, "Well, here we are."

During the first few weeks, when they were still in the small, one-bedroom place, he'd say, "You believe it?" He'd finish laying out the stacks of bills on the coffee table, look up at

Stick, and say, "You believe it? They're sitting out there waiting for us. Like they want to get held up, dying for it." Going in, Frank had told himself over and over it would be easy—if they observed the rules and didn't take chances—but he never thought it would be this easy.

After the first few weeks he began to take it in stride. They were pros, that's why it was easy. They knew exactly what they were doing. Look at the record: twenty-five armed robberies, twenty-five stolen cars, more money coming in than they could spend, and they had yet to get on a police sheet, even as suspects.

Frank would say, "Partner, what do you want? Come on, anything. You want it, buy it."

Frank didn't waste any time getting five new suits, a couple of sport outfits, slacks, shirts, and a safari jacket. Stick bought a suit, a sport coat, and three pairs of off-the-shelf pants for sixteen dollars each, studied the pants in the mirror—clown pants, they looked like—and had the store cut off the big bell-bottom cuffs before he'd buy them. They traded the Duster in on a white '75 Thunderbird with white velour upholstery, air, power everything, and went looking for a bigger apartment.

The third place they looked at was the Villa Monterey, out in Troy: a cream-colored stucco building with dark wood trim, a dark wood railing along the second-floor walk, a Spanish tile roof, and a balcony with each apartment overlooking the backyard where shrubbery and a stockade fence enclosed the patio and swimming pool. There was also an ice machine back there, a good sign.

Stick said he thought it looked like a motel. Frank said no, it was authentic California. He told the manager, the lady who showed them the apartment, okay, gave her the deposit and three months in advance to get out of signing a lease, and that was it. They got two bedrooms, bath, bar in the living room with bamboo stools, orange-and-yellow draperies, off-white shag carpeting, off-white walls with chrome-framed graphics, chrome gooseneck lamps, chrome-and-canvas chairs, an off-white Naugahyde sectional sofa, and three dying plants for four and a half a month, furnished. Stick didn't tell Frank but he thought the place looked like a beauty parlor.

The first Saturday they were in, Frank went out on the balcony. He looked down at the swimming pool and said, "Holy shit." He said it again, reverently, "Holy shit. Come here and look."

There were five of them lying around the pool in their skimpy little two-piece outfits. Nice-looking girls, none of them likely to be offered a screen test—except one, who turned out to be a photographer's model—but all of them better than average, and they were right there, handy. Frank and Stick went to the pool just about every afternoon they weren't working—Frank in a tank suit with his stomach sucked in, and Stick in a new pair of bright blue trunks—and got to know the regulars pretty well. Frank called them the career ladies.

There was a nurse, Mary Kay something, an RN who worked nights on the psychiatric floor at Beaumont Hospital. Dark hair, very clean-looking. Also very skinny, but with wide hips. A generous pelvic region, Frank said. Mary Kay was a possible. Stick said, Maybe, if you looked sincere and told her you loved her.

There was a redheaded girl, frizzy red hair and bright brown eyes, who wore beads and seven rings with her bikini. Arlene. She was a little wacky and laughed at almost everything they said, whether it was supposed to be funny or not. Somebody was paying Arlene's rent, a guy in a silver Mark IV who came twice a week, Tuesday and Thursday, at six, and was usually out by 10:30. Arlene said he was a good friend.

There were several Jewish career ladies. Frank was glad to see that. He told Stick he liked good-looking Jewish girls because they had a lot of hair, big tits, and usually pretty nice noses once they had them fixed. He told Stick he'd been out with plenty of Jewish girls, including the little starlet in L.A. Stick said he wasn't sure if he ever had. He asked Frank if it was all right to mention the word *Jew* in front of them or refer to them as being Jewish in any way. Frank said, "You dumb shit, that's what they *are.* Don't you think they know it?"

There was a schoolteacher named Karen who didn't talk or look like a schoolteacher. Stick didn't think she looked Jewish either. Karen said some funny things about her sixth-graders being sex-crazed and how the little girls stuck out their training bras for the horny little boys. Frank started taking Karen out and sometimes he spent the night at her apartment. Stick didn't think she seemed too impressed with Frank, though. She was off all summer with nothing to do.

There was a dental hygienist by the name of Donna who had a boyfriend but wasn't going to marry him until he made as much as she did. She told them how much a dentist with a good practice could make and referred to net and gross a lot. Donna was way down at the bottom of Frank's list of things to do.

Sonny, the photographer's model, was the winner of the group. But she was unresponsive to drink offers. She seldom came up to their apartment with the others. She'd lie there behind her big sunglasses and hardly ever laugh when they said something funny. Frank said she was battery-operated. You pressed a little button on her can and she'd say, "Hi, I'm Sonny. I'm a model. So fuck off."

Stick noticed that Frank watched her, studied her, more than he did the others. Sonny was the only one Frank had trouble talking to.

There was a girl in the next apartment—a career lady but not one of the group—who they found out was a pro. Stick called her Mona because sometimes, through the wall, he'd hear her in there with a guy, saying things to him and moaning like she was about to die it was so good. Frank called her what's-her-name. He was polite to her but not interested. He said a guy would be out of his mind to pay for it at the Villa Monterey. Stick never mentioned it to Frank, but he liked her. He liked her straight dark hair parted in the middle. He liked the calm expression in her eyes and the quiet way she talked, though she never said very much. She was fragile-looking, a thin little thing with bony shoulders sticking out of her sleeveless blouse. When he'd see her outside he couldn't believe she was the same girl he'd hear moaning and carrying on through the wall. Maybe sometime, when Frank wasn't around, he'd get talking to her in private and find out which one was the real Mona.

They both liked the cocktail waitress, Jackie, who worked at a place called the Ball Joint and wore a kitty outfit with little ears and a tail. Jackie wasn't the smartest girl there, but she was very friendly. Also she had the biggest pair at the Villa Monterey, even when they weren't pushed up by her kitty outfit. She showed the group one time, in her bikini, how she placed drinks on a table, bending her knees and keeping her body straight so they wouldn't fall out. Frank said if they ever did and hit somebody, they'd kill him. Jackie worked nights and usually didn't drink in the afternoon, but was liable to bang on their door when she got home, 2:30 in the morning, if she saw a light on and heard the hi-fi playing. It wasn't unusual.

Their apartment had become a little social center, with the best-stocked bar in the building. Frank started it, inviting people up, especially on weekends. After a while they could count on people dropping in whenever there was a sign of something going on.

There'd be a good selection of career ladies.

There might even be some of the young married set. Frank would lure them away from their cookouts with Chivas Regal and talk about car prices and inflation with the husbands while he appraised the cute little housewives.

There might be two or three young single guys, somebody's date, and Barry Kleiman for sure. The career ladies called Barry the Prince. Stick thought because he looked like Prince Valiant with his hair, but that wasn't the reason. Barry was successful, owned a McDonald's franchise, wore bright-colored sport outfits with a white plastic belt and white patent-leather loafers, and was only about twenty pounds overweight. Barry would stand with his elbows tucked in close and his wrists limp and say, "Listen, when I was a kid, the neighborhood I grew up in? It was so dirty I'd sit out in the sun for two hours and get a nice stain." Then he'd wait for their reaction with an innocent, wide-eyed expression. Karen said he used to do Jerry Lewis imitations.

"Not a bad guy," Frank said. "He could be a pain in the ass, you know? But he's not a bad guy."

"You go for Barry, you must really like the place," Stick said.

Frank seemed surprised. "Yeah, I like it. You don't?"

"It's all right, I guess."

"All *right?* You ever had it like this, pouring cement?"

No, he'd never lived in a place with a swimming pool and had a party going most of the week with two guns in the closet and fifteen hundred bucks in an Oxydol box under the sink. It was funny, he never had.

When Frank recited his line—"Well, here we are"—instead of saying, "Are you sure?" he should say, "Where, Frank? Where exactly are we? And for how long?"

It was like getting excited and moving to Florida and having the Atlantic Ocean down the street and palm trees and a nice tan all year and wondering, Now what? Sitting in a marina bar, watching gulls diving at the waves and seeing the charter boats out by the horizon, it didn't make the beer taste better. He'd tell himself this was the life and go home and have to take a nap before supper.

He wondered if he missed working, putting in a nine-, ten-hour day driving the big transit mix and pouring the footings for the condominiums that would someday wall out the ocean from Key West to Jacksonville Beach. There was plenty of work down there. It was on his mind a lot and he wasn't sure why, because the thought of going back to hauling cement bored the shit out of him.

He'd say to himself, What do you want to do more than anything?

Go see his little girl.

All right, but what do you want to do with your *life?*

He'd think about it a while and picture things.

He didn't see himself owning a cement company or a chicken farm or a restaurant. He never thought much about owning things, having a big house and a powerboat. He didn't care one way or the other about clothes. He'd never been much of a tourist. The travel brochures made it look good and he could see himself under a thatched roof with a big rum drink and some colored guys banging on oil drums, but he'd end up thinking, Then what do you do? Go in and get dressed up and eat the American Plan dinner and listen to the fag with the hairpiece play his cocktail piano and get bombed for no reason and go to bed and get up and do it over again the next day. He could picture a girl with him, on the beach, under the thatched roof. A nice-looking, quiet girl. Not his ex-wife. He never pictured his ex-wife with him and he never pictured the girl as his wife.

Maybe, Stick told himself, this was the kind of life he always wanted but never realized it before. Hold up one or two places a week, make more money than he could spend, and live in a thirty-unit L-shaped authentic California apartment building that had a private swimming pool and patio in the crotch of the L and was full of career ladies laying around waiting for it.

It sounded good.

Didn't it?

Yeah, Stick guessed it did.

6

They liked supermarkets. Get a polite manager who was scared shitless and not more than a few people in the store, that was the ideal situation, worth three or four gas stations even on a bad day. The only trouble with supermarkets, they were big. You never knew who might be down an aisle somewhere.

They hit the Kroger store in West Bloomfield early Saturday morning.

It looked good. No customers yet. The checkout counters were empty. The only person they saw was a stockboy stamping prices on canned goods. Stick asked him for the manager, saying he'd been called about a check that'd bounced and he wanted to cover it. He followed the boy to the back and waited, holding the swinging door open, seeing the manager back there talking to a Budweiser deliveryman and a few of the checkout girls drinking coffee. When the manager and the stockboy came out, Stick let the door swing closed. And when the manager said, "May I have your name, please?" Stick said, "No sir," taking the Smith from inside his jacket, "but you can give me your money."

The manager said, "Oh, my God," and the three of them paraded up to the front where Frank was waiting. Frank got the cash register key from the manager and headed for the checkout counters. Stick and the manager and the stockboy went into the cashier's enclosure, Stick bringing a Kroger bag with him.

The manager kept saying, "Oh, my God." He told Stick he'd only been manager here one week. Stick said well, he was getting good experience, wasn't he? The stockboy was a heavy-boned, rangy kid who kept staring at him, making him nervous, until Stick told him to lay on the floor, face-down. He told the manager to clean out the cash drawer and open the safe. The manager had to get a piece of paper out of his wallet with the combination written on it, then kept missing numbers as he turned the dial and would have to start over again; but finally he got it open and pulled out a trayful of bills and personal checks. When he started to count the bills, Stick told him never mind, he'd do it later. The manager thanked him.

"What about these?" the manager said, picking up the checks.

"Keep 'em," Stick said.

"I appreciate that very much," the manager said. "I really do."

"Just the bills," Stick said, "no change. You can keep that, too."

"Thank you," the manager said. "Thank you very much."

Frank was at the third checkout counter, digging the bills out of the cash register and stuffing them in a Kroger bag. He looked up to see a woman with hair curlers pushing a cart toward him. He was taken by surprise and his hand went into his jacket for the Python. He'd looked down the aisles and hadn't seen anyone in the store. The woman began unloading her cart—coffee, milk, bread, and a few other items—not paying any attention to him. Frank brought his hand out of the jacket. The best thing to do was get rid of her, fast. He said, "How're you this morning?" and began ringing up the groceries, not looking at her. She was a pale, puffy woman with a permanent scowl etched in her face. And the hair curlers—in case anyone thought she wasn't ugly enough she had light-blue plastic curlers wrapped in her light-blue hair.

The woman squinted at him. "You're new."

"Yes, ma'am, new assistant manager."

"Where's your white coat?"

He was going to say that a jacket and sunglasses was the new thing for assistant managers, you cluck, you dumb, ugly broad, but he played it straight and told her they were getting him a white coat with his name on it. He punched the total and said, "Four sixty-eight, please."

The woman was digging in her purse, looking for something. She took almost a minute to bring out a piece of newspaper, unfold it, and hand it to him.

"Coupon for the coffee," the woman said. "Twenty cents off."

Frank took the coupon and looked at it. "Okay, then that's four forty-eight. No, wait a minute." He noticed the date on the coupon. "This offer's expired. It's not, you know . . . redeemable anymore, it's no good."

"I couldn't come in yesterday," the woman said. "It's not my fault. I cut the coupon out and there it is."

"I'm sorry," Frank said. "It says, see? Thursday and Friday only. Big letters."

"I've been coming here fifteen years, using the coupons," the woman said. "My husband and I. We buy all our groceries, our dog food, everything here. I'm one day late and you're going to tell me this is no good?"

"I'm sorry, I wish there was something I could do about it."

"Yesterday Earl took the car, had Timmie with him. All day he's gone, didn't even feed Timmie the whole while, and I had to sit home alone."

"All right—" Frank said.

"After all the money this store's made off us," the woman said. "I could've been going to Farmer Jack, Safeway. No, I come here and then get treated like I'm somebody with food stamps."

Frank was about to give in, but he changed his mind. He looked right at the lady now and said, "I got an idea. Why don't you take the coupon—okay?—and the one-pound can of Maxwell House coffee and shove 'em up your ass."

When they were in the stolen car, the Kroger bags on the floor, turning out of the parking lot, Frank said, "That fucking Earl. He stays out with their car all day, their dog, his old lady gets pissed off and makes life miserable for everybody. Jesus."

Stick wasn't listening. He was anxious. He waited for Frank to finish and said, "The manager, you know what he says when I'm leaving? Honest to God, he says, 'Thank you very much, sir, and come back again.' "

"That poor fucking Earl," Frank said. "I sure wouldn't want to be him."

They got a little over seventeen hundred at Kroger's. The story in the paper said, "about three thousand." Typical. Four days later, to show you how it could go, they hit a place and didn't get anything. The guy wouldn't give them the money.

It was a good thing it didn't happen on their first job. They would have quit. The guy was Armenian, a little bald-headed, excitable Armenian who ran a party store. No liquor, but imported beer and wine and expensive gourmet items, and the store was in a good location, out North Woodward near Bloomfield Hills. They went in on a Saturday night at ten. Frank took out his Python and Stick turned the OPEN sign around to CLOSED and pulled the shade down on the glass door.

Right away the little Armenian said, "What do you want to do this to me for? I never done nothing to you. I never saw you before." He stood there with his hands raised in the air.

Frank said, "Sir, put your hands down, will you?"

"I don't want this happening to me," the Armenian said in his high, excitable voice. "Since I move out here it never happen before. Never. Good people live out here. Why aren't you good people? You don't have to do this to me."

"It won't hurt at all, you do what I tell you," Frank said. "You understand? Now put your fucking hands down!"

Stick found the guy's wife in the back room, a little dark-haired lady with a moustache, clutching her hands in front of her like she was praying. Stick said, "Everything's going to be all right, mama. Nothing to worry about." He moved her into the toilet compartment, closed the door, and poked around the storage room that was stacked high with beer and soft-drink cases.

Frank looked up from the cash register when Stick came back out.

"He's got a safe or he hid it somewhere."

Stick shook his head. "Not out there."

"Thirty-eight bucks and change," Frank said. "For tomorrow. He's cleaned out the drawer."

Stick went over to the Armenian, turned him around to face the shelves, and felt the pockets of his white store coat.

"Nothing."

"It's somewhere," Frank said.

"All the money I have, in the cash register," the Armenian said to the shelf of canned smoked oysters and clams. "I don't have no more than that."

"Hey," Frank said, "come on. All day you make thirty-eight bucks? Where is it? You hide it someplace?"

"I took it to the bank."

"No, you didn't. You been here all day."

"My wife took it." His voice went higher as he said, "Where is my wife—what did you do to her!"

"This guy here raped her," Frank said.

Stick made a face like he was going to get sick.

"Now *I'm* going to rape her, you don't tell us where the money is."

The Armenian didn't say anything. He was considering whether he should give up the money or let his wife get raped again.

"Come on," Frank said to him, touching the back of the Armenian's head with the Colt Python, "where is it! You don't get it out by the time I count three, I'm going to blow your bald head apart. . . . One."

"Do it!" the Armenian said in his high voice.

"Two."

"Kill me! You take my money, kill me!"

"Three."

Frank clicked the hammer back with his thumb. The Armenian's shoulders hunched rigid and held like that. Stick waited, feeling his own tension.

After a moment Frank said, "Shit."

There was no point in wasting any more time. They could tear the place apart and not find anything.

Frank said to the Armenian, "You're lucky, you know that? You're dumb fucking lucky, that's all."

After they left and were driving away, Stick said, "Shit, we forgot the thirty-eight bucks."

There weren't any textbooks on armed robbery. The only way to learn was through experience.

They found out gas stations weren't as good as they looked. Hand the kid a twenty and watch him go over to the manager or owner who'd take the wad out of his pocket and peel off change. But it didn't amount to that much: a bunch of singles and fives. There were too many people using credit cards now. Also, the high-volume service stations, where the money would be, always had five or six guys working there, using wrenches and tire irons, some hard-looking guys, maybe not too bright, who might see the gun pointing at them and decide to take a swing anyway. In their three gas station hits they went in and got out fast, the best take seven-eighty, which they figured was about as good as you could do.

They crossed off gas stations and altered a couple of their ten rules for success and happiness, finding it was all right to be polite, but you still had to scare the guy enough so he'd know better than to try and be a hero. It was all right, too, to dress well, look presentable. But they realized they'd better not become typecast or pretty soon the police would be writing a book on the two dudes who always wore business suits and said please and thank you. So they wore jackets sometimes, and raincoats. Stick had a pair of coveralls he liked he'd bought at J. C. Penney. They were comfortable and no one seemed to bother looking at him. Frank liked his pale-tan safari jacket with the epaulets. Very sharp, big in California. He liked the way the Python rested in the deep side pocket and didn't show. Usually, after a job, they kept the guns locked in the glove compartment of the T-bird. Stick thought they should put them away somewhere, hidden. But Frank said it was better to have them handy; they saw a place they liked, they were ready. Keep them in the apartment, some inquisitive broad could be snooping around and find them. Ho ho, what're these two business types doing with loaded firearms? Stick wasn't convinced, but he couldn't think of a better place to keep them.

Speaking of rules, Stick said maybe there was one more they should add. Number Eleven. Never try and hold up an Armenian.

They had taken in, so far, close to twenty-five thousand, spent a lot, but still had ninety-six hundred in a safe-deposit box at the Troy branch of Detroit Bank & Trust and about fifteen hundred or so spending money in the Oxydol box under the sink. They didn't divide the money. Except for major purchases—like the car and an eight-hundred-dollar hi-fi setup Frank picked out for them—the money went from the bank safe deposit to the Oxydol box, usually a thousand at a time, where it was available to both of them for pocket money and personal expenditures. There was no rule as to how much you could take; it was whatever you needed.

Two months ago, when they'd moved in, Stick had questioned the arrangement. He'd see Frank dipping in every day or so for fifty, a hundred, sometimes as much as two hundred. Finally he'd said, "Don't you think it'd be better, after a job, we divvied it up?"

Frank said, "I thought we were partners."

"Equal partners," Stick said. "We divvy it up, then we know it's equal."

"Wait just a minute now. You saying I'm cheating you?"

"I'm saying it might be better to split it each time, that's all. Then we know where we stand, individually."

"You know where the dough is," Frank said, "right? Under the sink, that's where we keep it. And you know you can go in there and take as much as you need, right? So how am I cheating you?"

"I understand the arrangement," Stick said. "I'm only asking, you think it would be better if we each took care of our own dough?"

"What're you, insecure? You want to hide it?"

"If half the dough's mine, why can't I do anything I want with it?"

"Jesus," Frank said, "you sound like a little kid. Nya nya nya, I got my money hidden and I'm not gonna tell you where it is. What is this shit? We partners or not?"

Stick let it drop.

From then on, he took two hundred dollars a week out of the Oxydol box, over and above what he needed, and put it away in his suitcase.

7

Stick was on the balcony, looking down at the empty patio. It was quiet, the pool area in shadows. He turned when he heard Frank come out of his bedroom and watched him walk over to the bar in one of his new suits and finish a drink he'd made and forgotten about.

"You taking the car?"

"No," Frank said, "we're going to walk. Broads love to get taken out to dinner and have to walk. You going out?"

"How?"

"What do you mean, how? You going out?"

"I mean *how*. What am I supposed to do, hitchhike?"

Frank took his time. He said, "It seems to me I remember I said maybe we better get two cars. You said, 'Two cars? Christ, what do we need with two cars?' You remember that?"

"How come you figure it's yours?" Stick said. "Take it anytime you want."

"Jesus Christ," Frank said, "I don't believe it. You want a car, steal one. You want it bad enough, *buy* one, for Christ sake. Take it out of the bank thing."

"Have a nice time," Stick said.

Frank was shaking his head, a little sadly, patiently. "Sometimes, you know what? You sound like a broad. A wife. Poor fucking martyr's got to sit home while the guy's out having a good time."

"I'll wait up for you," Stick said. "Case you come in, you fall and hit your head on the toilet when you're throwing up."

"How long you been saving that?"

"It just came to me, you throw up a lot."

"You're quite a conversationalist," Frank said. "I'd like to stay and chat, but I'm running a little late." He went out.

There was a junior executive group at the Villa, a few guys with friends who were always coming over. Sometimes in the evening, after they'd changed from their business outfits to Levi's and Adidas, they'd sit on the patio and drink beer. If Stick was out on the balcony he'd listen to them, see if he could learn anything.

Usually it was about how stoned one of them got the night before. Or the best source of grass in Ann Arbor. Or why this one guy had switched from a Wilson Jack Kramer to a Bancroft Competition. Or how a friend of one of them had brought back eight cases of Coors from Vail. Then he wouldn't hear anything for a minute or so—one of them talking low—then loud laughter. The laughter would get louder as they went through the six-packs, and the junior executives would say *shit* a lot more. That was about all Stick learned.

This evening he didn't learn anything. They had two beers and decided to go to the show. Stick wondered what Mona was doing. Frank was gone. It'd be a good time if he was going to do it. He liked her looks and could picture her clearly in his mind, but he couldn't see her making all those sounds.

He wondered how much she charged.

He went out past the Formica table at the end of the living room to the kitchen and got a can of Busch Bavarian, came back in, sat down on one of the canvas chairs, and stared at an orange-and-yellow shape on the wall, a mess of colors, like somebody had spilled a dozen eggs and framed them.

He put the beer on the glass coffee table, went over and got Donna Fargo going on the hi-fi. He listened to her tell how she was the luckiest girl in the U.S.A., how she would wake up and say, "Mornin' Lord, howdy sun," and studied himself in the polished aluminum mirror on the wall. He looked dark and gaunt, a little mean-looking with his serious expression. Howdy there. I'm your next-door neighbor. I was wondering—

Going out the door and along the second-floor walk, he was still wondering.

I was wondering, if you weren't busy—

I was wondering, if you were free—had some free time, I mean.

He said to himself, Shit, let her do it. She knows what you want.

He knocked on her door and waited and knocked a couple more times. Still nothing, not a sound from inside the apartment. Stick went back to his own place, picked up the can of Busch, and walked out on the balcony. It was still quiet, with a dull evening sky clouding over. A lifeless expanse of sky, boring.

But there was somebody down there now. In the swimming pool. A girl doing a sidestroke, trying to keep her head up and barely moving. She was actually in the water, and Stick couldn't recall any of the career ladies ever actually swimming before. He thought she had on a reddish bathing cap, then realized it was her hair—the redheaded one with the frizzy hair the guy in the silver Mark IV came to visit a couple of times a week. That one.

Arlene saw him standing there with her purple beach towel as she came out of the pool in her lavender bikini, her beads, and her seven rings. She said, "Hi," and laughed.

Stick handed her the towel, asked her how she was doing, and learned, Just fine.

He said, "Your friend coming over tonight?"

"He's tied up," Arlene said. "Had to go to Lansing." She began drying her wiry hair, rubbing it hard, and Stick couldn't see her face for a while. He watched her little boobs jiggling up and down. They were small but well shaped, perky. She had freckles on her chest. Stick figured she was a redhead all the way.

"What're you supposed to do when he doesn't show," Stick said, "sit around, be a good little girl?"

She answered him, but he couldn't hear what she said under the heavy towel.

"Do what?"

She peeked out at him through the purple folds. "I said he never told me I had to sit and twiddle my thumbs."

Stick gave her a little grin. "Don't you like to twiddle?"

Arlene grinned back and giggled. "I don't know as I ever have, tell you the truth. Is it fun?"

"You're from somewhere, aren't you?" Stick said. "Let me guess. Not Louisville. No, little more this way. Columbus, Ohio."

"Uh-unh, Indianapolis," Arlene said.

"Close," Stick said. "You take Interstate 70 right on over to Indianapolis from Columbus. Used to be old U.S. 40." He wasn't going to let go of Columbus that easy.

"I was Miss NHRA Nationals last year," Arlene said. "You know, the drag races? I was going to go out to California—a friend of mine lives in Bakersfield—but I was asked to come here instead, to do special promotions for Hi-Performance Products Incorporated. You know them?"

"I think I've heard the name."

"They make Hi-Speed Cams. That's their main thing. Also Hi-Performance Shifters. Pretty soon they're going into mag wheels and headers."

"It must be interesting work," Stick said.

"You'd think so. But what it is," Arlene said, "it's a pain in the ass. Those drag strips are so dirty. I mean the dust and grease and all. The noise, God. The first thing I do I get back to the motel is dive in the pool. I love to swim."

"I noticed, I was out on the balcony there," Stick said, glancing up at the apartment. "You're like a fish in the water."

"I love it, the feeling, like I don't even have a body."

"I guarantee you got a body," Stick said.

Arlene laughed, raised closed eyes to the dull sky, and shook her wiry hair. It barely moved.

Stick was looking at her mouth, slightly open, her slender little nose and the trace of something greenish on her eyelids.

"I was thinking," he said, "after all that swimming, how'd you like a nice cool drink now to wet your insides?"

Arlene loved the apartment. She said it was cool, it looked like it would be in California. Stick thought Arlene looked pretty cool, too, on the bamboo barstool in her little swimming suit, bare feet hooked on the rung and her legs sloping apart. He fixed her Salty Dogs, once she told him how, kept the vodka bottle handy, and sipped a bourbon over ice while she told him what it was like to put on a little metallic silver outfit with white boots and pose for camshaft promotion shots, with the hot lights and all. She said it wasn't any picnic and Stick said he bet it wasn't. He watched her rubbing her eyes and blinking, but didn't say anything about it until she'd put away three Salty Dogs and was working on number four.

He said, "It's that chlorine in the pool. What you ought to do is go in and take a shower."

"You mean here?"

"What's the matter with here?"

"But I don't have anything to put on after," Arlene said, "except this wet swimming suit."

If that was all she was worried about, Stick knew he was home. He said, "I'll get you a robe or something. How'll that be?"

That was how he got her in the shower. He put her drink on the top of the toilet tank, adjusted the spray nice and warm, and went out, closing the door.

Stick didn't own a robe. Maybe Frank had one, but he didn't

bother to look. He went into his bedroom and got undressed, put his shoes and socks in the closet, hung up his new pants and shirt, got down to his striped boxer shorts, thinking he could have taken her to dinner, spent twenty bucks. He could have taken her to a movie and then to a bar, hear some music, then coming home ask her if she wanted a nightcap at his place. He could have gone through all that and then have her say thanks anyway, she was tired. Find out first, then take her out after; that was the way to do it. He couldn't figure out why he had hesitated going to Mona's, trying to get the words right. Mona was a pro, whether she looked like one or not. Arlene was a—what? Hot-rod queen. A flake. Part-time camshaft model and kept lady. But he really didn't know her or how she'd react.

She might scream. She might say, Now wait a minute, or, Get the hell out of here, or threaten to call the police, or be so scared she couldn't say anything.

What Arlene did say, when he pulled the curtain back and stepped naked into the shower with her, was, "Hon, get me another Salty Dog first, will you?"

They were in bed, dried off and smelling of Mennen's talcum powder, when Mona started.

That faint sound through the wall, a caressing sound without words.

Stick hadn't heard her come in. Probably while they were in the shower. He was on an elbow right now, half over Arlene with a leg between hers, giving her a little knee, feeling strong with his gut sucked in, giving her nice tender kisses and feeling her hands moving over the muscles in his back.

Arlene opened her eyes.

"What's that?"

"What?" He put his mouth on hers to keep her from talking.

"Like somebody's in pain."

"I doubt if it's pain," Stick said. He got back to it and Arlene began to squirm and press hard against him.

Mona, in another bed in another room, said, "Oh, Jesus. Oh, God. Oh, Jesus."

Arlene's eyes opened again. "Listen."

"Oh please—"

Arlene slid around him and sat up. "Where's it coming from, next door?"

"I guess so."

"Who lives there?"

"The one—I don't know her name."

Arlene frowned. "The mousy one with the straight hair?"

"I don't know as she's mousy. A little plain maybe. Not what you'd expect—"

Arlene stopped him. "Listen."

She got out of bed, carefully climbing over him, and followed the faint murmuring sound to the wall where the dresser stood. Stick watched her crouch there—a naked redhead who looked especially naked to him because her skin was white and didn't show tan lines—her face alert, pressed to the wall, her perky little boobs hanging free.

"You want to learn how it's done. Is that it?"

"Shhhhhhhh."

"I thought you knew. You seemed to be doing all right."

Arlene didn't look over or change her expression. The room was silent. Stick could hear the sound again.

After a moment Arlene said, "Oh ... *now*, please. Oh, please, please, please," keeping her voice low.

"I'd be glad to oblige," Stick said.

Arlene was fascinated, glued to the wall, her eyes alive and mouth slightly open.

"Give it to me. Give me everything, oh, please. Oh, God, Jesus."

"Maybe what she's doing," Stick said, "she's saying her prayers."

"Uh-unh. She just said the word."

"What word?"

"I can't say it out loud. God, now she's saying it over and over."

"Spell it," Stick said.

He got a Marlboro off the night table with the Chinese figurine lamp and sat up in bed to smoke and watch Arlene and tried to imagine what was going on in the bed on the other side of the wall. He could picture Mona's face, her eyes closed; but he couldn't picture her saying anything or picture the guy with her. He didn't want to picture the guy. Arlene's eyes opened a little wider. It wouldn't be long now. Arlene looked good. He wondered if he could like her seriously. Studying her he realized she was very pretty. Delicate features. Slim body. Flat little tummy. Not at all self-conscious about standing there naked. But she couldn't say the word.

Arlene must have been thinking about it, too. When she came back to bed and crawled over him she said, "I could never say that. I can do it, God, no trouble at all. But I can't say it. Isn't that strange?"

Stick said, "I was thinking, why don't you take your rings off? So nobody'll get hurt."

8

The bar in Hazel Park was on Dequindre, only a few blocks from the racetrack. They had been in once before and watched a couple of big winners buy rounds for the house. They weren't sure if bars were worth it and picked this one as a good place to find out.

When they went in at 1:30 A.M., a half hour before closing, it was filled with the sound of voices and country music playing on the jukebox. The bar section was still very much alive, though the tables were empty now and the waitress was standing by the service station counting her tips.

Once they pulled their guns, Stick would cover the people at the bar and put them down on the floor while Frank concentrated on the bartender, a woman, and got her to empty the cash register. Before Frank could get his Python out, Stick touched him on the arm.

"Let's sit down."

They got a table. The waitress brought them a couple of draft beers and left.

"The guy with the hair," Stick said, "at the end of the bar."

The guy was at the curved end nearer the door, facing the length of the bar: thick hair over his ears, big arms and shoulders in a dull yellow-satin athletic jacket. Frank drank some of his beer as the guy's head turned toward them.

"What about him?"

"He eyed us when we came in. Watch him, keeps looking around."

"Maybe he's waiting for somebody."

"Or maybe he's a cop, staking the place out. You read about it? They been doing that."

"A cop," Frank said. "He looks like a bush leaguer never made it."

"Cops put on these outfits now, play dress-up," Stick said. "You never know anymore."

"If you don't feel right about it," Frank said, "let's go. Maybe it's not a good idea anyway. Six, seven, nine with the waitress, that's a lot of people to keep track of."

"Wait," Stick said. "I think he's leaving."

They watched the guy in the yellow-satin jacket slide off the stool and pick up a leather case that must have been leaning against the bar on the other side of him.

"He's got pool cues," Frank said. "I thought he was a jock. He's a pool-hall cowboy."

"Going to the can," Stick said.

There was an inscription on the back of his jacket. They watched it go into the men's room.

"Port Huron Bullets," Stick said. "He's one of the famous Port Huron Bullets. You ever heard of them?"

"We'll wait'll he leaves," Frank said. He finished his beer. When he took a cigarette out Stick did, too, and got a light from him.

Dolly Parton was singing on the jukebox. Stick had been in love with Dolly when he used to watch the "Porter Waggoner Show" and paused to listen before he said, "You want to do it, huh?"

Frank looked at him. "What's the matter, you nervous?"

"No more than usual. You bring a bag?"

"Shit, I forgot," Frank said. "They probably got something behind the bar. Wrap it in the broad's apron or something."

"She doesn't have an apron on."

"We'll put it in *some*thing, okay?"

"I don't know," Stick said. "I don't feel we're a hundred percent this time. You know what I mean?"

"When're we ever a hundred percent sure?"

"I don't mean sure. I mean ready, wanting to do it. We come in, right away we hang back."

Frank was looking past him. "Here he comes."

Stick saw the change in Frank's expression and heard him say, "Jesus Christ," softly, with a sound of awe. He heard that and heard Loretta Lynn now saying they didn't make men like her daddy anymore, as he turned and saw the guy in the yellow-satin jacket and the door of the Men's Room behind him, the guy raising a pump-action shotgun level with his waist.

"Don't nobody move! This is a holdup!"

The guy shouted it, drowning out Loretta Lynn. "I'll shoot the first one moves!"

When he swung the shotgun at their table, Frank and Stick were looking right at him about fifteen feet away. "You two—don't make a move. Don't anybody. I'm warning you. I'll shoot to kill."

"Wants everybody to know he means business," Frank said.

They watched him move hesitantly toward the bar, telling people who were looking over their shoulders at him to turn the fuck around. Loretta Lynn was finished and it was quiet in the place now as he got around behind the bar and moved down to where the woman bartender was standing at the cash register.

"How come he doesn't make 'em lay on the floor?" Stick said. "You believe it?"

"He doesn't know what he's doing," Frank said. "Dumb pool-hall cowboy. Tells everybody on his jacket where he's from."

"That shotgun'd be a pain in the ass," Stick said, "wouldn't it? You imagine carrying a shotgun around?"

"Keep your hands on the bar!" the guy shouted at somebody.

"He's pretty nervous," Frank said. "Maybe it's his first time."

"He's more nervous than I am. Look at him wave that scattergun," Stick said. "Doesn't know where to point it."

"What he ought to do," Frank said, "is put it on the waitress. Tell 'em he'll blow her off if anybody moves, or if the broad doesn't give him the money."

"Yeah, get 'em laying down first, they don't see where he's at." Stick shook his head. "Dumb cowboy, I wouldn't be surprised he had a horse outside."

"Runs out in the street waving his shotgun," Frank said. "Or you suppose he puts it back in the case first?"

"He goes in the toilet," Stick said, "and comes out again pretending he's got pool cues in it. Now he's getting the change off the bar. What'd she put the money in? The broad."

"Looked like her purse."

"Runs out with a shotgun and a purse," Stick said. "That'd be a sight, wouldn't it? How much you think he got?"

Frank was silent for a moment, watching the guy as he moved carefully toward the end of the bar.

"He isn't out of here yet."

Stick looked at Frank, then back to the guy, who was coming around the bar and now backing toward the door.

"It's an idea, isn't it?" Stick said.

"If we see the chance."

"I think when he goes to open the door," Stick said.

The guy seemed more nervous than before. He glanced over at their table but was concentrating on the people at the bar. "Don't nobody move," he said. "I go out, I'm liable to come back in to make sure. Anybody I see moved gets a load of twelve-gauge, and I *mean* it."

"He talks too much," Stick said.

The guy turned to the door, raising the shotgun barrel straight up in front of him, and started to push it open.

"Drop it," Frank said.

The guy hesitated, his back to them and the shotgun upright against the door. He had a moment, but when he finally turned, it was too late. Both Frank and Stick, standing away from the table, ten feet apart, had their revolvers on him, aimed at arm's length.

"Come on," Frank said, "put it down."

When the shotgun was on the floor, Stick walked over to the guy and took the purse from him.

He said, "Much obliged, partner. We appreciate it."

The story in the *Detroit News* the next day described how for six hours the would-be holdup man and the bar patrons were locked up together in a storeroom where all the liquor and bar supplies were kept. When they were found the next morning, the newspaper account stated, the would-be holdup man appeared to have suffered a severe beating, while the bar patrons were in a festive state of intoxication.

"Can you see it?" Stick said. "The Port Huron Bullet comes out, blood all over him, can't open his eyes. Hasn't got any idea what happened to him. Keeps asking himself, over and over, 'What went wrong?' "

"A customer comes out," Frank said, "absolutely fried. Cop says to him, 'Sir, you want to tell us how much you had stolen? Any valuables?' The guy, the customer, looks at him with these bleary eyes and says, 'Who the fuck cares?' "

They got a kick out of the Hazel Park bar robbery, plus a little better than eleven thousand in cash.

They decided they didn't like bars, though: too many people and too unpredictable with booze involved. So they crossed off bars along with gas stations and would concentrate on other types of establishments.

9

Three of the career ladies were at the pool when Frank and Stick came down: two of them lying face up, eyes closed—Mary Kay, the skinny nurse with the wide hips, and Jackie, the cocktail lounge kitty—and one on her stomach, face hidden in an outstretched arm. Frank knew by the short, dark hair and deep tan it was Karen, the schoolteacher. Karen had her bra strap unfastened, out of the way, and there was no line. Her brown skin glistened with oil, smooth and bare all the way down to where the little bikini bottom almost covered her can.

Stick, with his towel and a rolled-up magazine, eased into the first empty lounge he came to, near the edge of the grass.

Frank made a production of it. He stood with his gold beach towel over one shoulder, looked at his watch, checked the angle of the sun, then dragged a lounge chair around—with the sound of aluminum scraping on cement—to catch the direct rays.

Without opening her eyes Jackie said, "Frank's here."

"I'm sorry, honey, the chair wake you up?" He brought a tray table over for his towel, his watch, and for the drinks he'd have later on.

"You're supposed to lift it," Jackie said. "It leaves marks."

"Yeah, I always forget."

Karen's face rose from her arm.

"Frank, while you're up, you want to do my back?"

"I'll force myself," Frank said.

Stick had his magazine, the last issue of *Oui*, folded open. He had looked at the pictures already, the boob and crotch shots. Now he was reading about Alex Karras and what Alex thought about Howard Cosell and doing NFL color on TV. Looking over the top of the magazine, he watched Frank sit down on the edge of Karen's lounge.

The nurse, Mary Kay, was watching them, too. Mary Kay usually didn't say much. She listened; sometimes she laughed.

Stick wondered what she thought of them. Probably nothing. She probably saw so many weird things up in that nut ward nothing down here would shock her.

"Cut it out," Karen said.

"What am I doing?"

Stick looked over there again. As Frank's hands caressed her back, one of them slid into the space between her arm and body.

"*Fra*-ank!"

"What's the matter? I'm not doing anything."

"That's enough."

"Little more right . . . *there.*"

"Frank—"

As he stood up and moved about idly, wiping his hands on his chest and stomach, Stick said, "Sure is full of the devil, isn't he?"

Frank looked up at the sun, raising his arms and stretching. "Oh, man. Perfect day, isn't it? Sun, the sky's clear, little breeze so it's not too hot . . . Jackie, you got a perfect navel, you know that? Anybody ever tell you?"

She pressed her chin to her chest to look down at it. "What's so different about it?"

"It's round," Frank said, "like a bullet hole. Pow, right in the navel."

"I don't know, Frank," Jackie said, "sometimes I wonder about you."

"What do you wonder?"

"If you're all there."

"I'm all here. Hey, look at me. Jackie, look. You see anything missing?"

"The exhibitionist," Karen said. "You ever see him go out with his raincoat on? Sunny day, he's wearing a raincoat. We heard about guys like that, Frank. Our moms told us a long time ago."

Frank looked over at Stick, and Stick said mildly, "He's insecure is all. Wears drawers under his pajamas, and socks to bed."

"See, I'm right," Jackie said. "He's a little strange."

Frank liked it there in the center of things, playing around with the career ladies. He looked over at the nurse, to get them all involved.

"Mary Kay, honey, you got room for me in your psycho ward? Maybe I better have some tests."

"We're overcrowded," Mary Kay said. "We don't have enough beds the way it is."

"How about if I stood up?"

Stick felt sorry for her—put on the spot and not having a smart-ass reply ready. Everybody had to be a smart-ass, get a laugh and make it look easy. It wore you out, thinking, just staying in a conversation.

He said to Mary Kay, "How about giving him a shot, then, to quiet him down? Case anybody wanted to take a nap?"

Mary Kay smiled but didn't say anything.

Stick let it go. It looked like too much of a job to bring her out. And if he got her out, then what? There had to be something better to do. He went up to the apartment, poured a half bottle of vodka and a quart of tonic into a plastic pitcher, threw in some limes and ice and carried it down on a tray with a half dozen plastic poolside glasses.

Arlene was in his lounge chair, looking at the magazine. She didn't notice him right away. Frank was talking to Karen.

"It's funny nobody ever asked before. What'd you think we were, retired?"

"Are you kidding?" Karen said. "We thought you were out of work."

Frank looked up at Stick and moved his towel, making room on the table next to him.

"You hear that? She thought we were out of work."

"It just looks like it sometimes," Stick said. He picked up the glasses as Frank poured them. Mary Kay shook her head and said no thanks. Jackie took a sip and made a little sound of appreciation. Karen was snapping her bra and he had to wait for her to take the glass. Arlene smiled at him. She said, "Here, there's room. Come on."

Stick sat down on the edge of the chair, feeling the aluminum tube beneath his thighs. He saw Mary Kay watching and then look away.

"What we are," Frank said, "we're sales motivators. We go in a place, say a car dealership, okay? We motivate the salesmen, get them off their cans, by actually showing them how to cultivate prospects and close deals. I demonstrate what we call the *frank* approach, how to appear open and sincere with customers, sympathetic to their needs. Then Ernest here, better known as Stick, shows them how an *earnest*, confident attitude will close the sale every time."

Arlene gave Stick a little poke. "You must travel a lot. You ever been to California?"

Frank answered her. "Many times. Write us care of the Continental Hyatt House, Sunset Boulevard."

"I'd love to go out there," Arlene said. "I've got a friend in Bakersfield."

She went into the pool after a while and Stick got a chance to stretch out again with his magazine, half listening to Frank bullshitting the ladies. Finally he heard Frank say, "Which reminds me, partner. We got a sales meeting this afternoon." As Stick got up Frank was telling the ladies they hated to leave but would see them again real soon. Stick kept trying to think of something to say, something a little clever.

Walking away from the patio with the pitcher and tray and magazine under his arm, he glanced back and said, "You all be good now."

10

There was a six o'clock wedding at the Shrine of the Little Flower, on Woodward in Royal Oak. Stick took a Chevrolet Impala that was parked in line at the side of the church—washed, key in the ignition, ready to go.

Frank was waiting in the T-bird, in the lot behind the Berkley Theater on Twelve Mile Road. They changed from their suit coats to lightweight jackets, took off their ties, and got their revolvers out of the glove box. Frank put on sunglasses; Stick, a souvenir Detroit Tiger baseball cap. They left their suit coats and ties in the T-bird, got in the Impala, and drove over to the A&P on the corner of Southfield and Twelve. On the way, Stick said he almost took the car with the pink-and-white pompoms all over it. He didn't because he was afraid Frank might feel a little funny riding in it.

It was a good-looking A&P, in a high-income suburban area. But Frank didn't like all the cars in the parking area. Too many.

They drove back to a bowling alley–bar on Twelve in Berkley to kill some time and had a few vodkas and tonic in the dim, chrome-and-Formica lounge. Sitting in a bar in the early evening reminded Stick of Florida. He didn't like the feeling.

"I was thinking," Stick said, "you could tell them the truth and nobody'd believe it. Girl says, 'What do you do for a living?' And you say, 'Oh, we hold up stores, different places.' And Jackie or one of them would say, 'I believe it.' Only she wouldn't. None of them would."

"You think that'd be funny, huh?" Frank said.

"You'd think it was funny if you'd thought of it," Stick said.

"You heard what Karen said about wearing the raincoats?"

"She thinks you're queer, that's all."

"That's what she does," Frank said, "thinks. She's got those big knockers, she's got nothing to do all day, she sits around and thinks."

When they got back to the A&P, there were only about a dozen cars in the lot. Stick pulled up, almost at the front entrance, where there was a NO PARKING—PICKUP ONLY sign.

"I'll see you," Stick said.

Frank slid over behind the wheel when Stick got out. He lit a cigarette and took his time smoking it, five or six minutes, then left the motor running and went into the store.

The manager was inside the cashier's enclosure. Frank could see his head and shoulders through the glass part of the partition. Stick wasn't in there.

Another employee, maybe the assistant, was working the Kwick-Check, eight-items-or-less, counter, where several people were lined up waiting. Only one other checkout counter was open. A woman was unloading a cart with a week's supply of groceries while a checkout girl in a red A&P smock rang them up.

The assistant, or whoever it was at the Kwick-Check counter, looked over at Frank, then down at the counter again.

Frank got a cart and pushed it down to the end of the store, turned left at baked goods, stopped at dairy products for a wedge of Pinconning cheese and some French onion dip, found the potato-chip counter, and was two aisles over before he ran into Stick.

Stick was putting two boxes of Jiffy corn bread mix in his cart. He already had lettuce, cucumbers, tomatoes, a sackful of potatoes, and four cans of Blue Lake mustard greens.

"Hi there," Frank said. "It certainly does save to shop at A&P, doesn't it?"

"It saves your ass if you got your eyes open," Stick said. "You see the guy at the counter?"

"I thought he might be the assistant."

"He might've been," Stick said, "if he hadn't gone into police work instead."

"You sure?"

"There's one just like him over in produce weighing tomatoes. You know the look, their face, when they look at you? Like they see clear through and can tell you what color drawers you got on."

"I don't know," Frank said. "You thought the guy in the bar was a cop."

"I could be wrong," Stick said, "but I got no intention of finding out if I'm right. I think we ought to get out of here."

Frank shrugged. "Well, if you don't have your heart in it, I guess that's it."

"Go over and look at the guy in produce," Stick said. "Big, hardheaded-looking guy. He might just as well have his badge pinned on his apron."

"I'm not doubting your word," Frank said, "you want to go, let's go."

"I'll be right behind you." Stick turned his cart around and started back up the aisle.

"Where you going?"

"Get some salt pork for my mustard greens."

They cruised down Southfield looking for another store and passed two shopping centers, one with a Wrigley, the other with a Farmer Jack, before Frank said anything.

"You didn't like either of those?"

Stick was driving. "I don't know. The parking, all the stores there, it looked congested. I see us trying to get out and some broad in a Cadillac's got everything fucked up."

"How about over there?" Frank said. "Nice neat little post office." It was a red-brick Colonial with white trim. "You ever hear of somebody knocking down a post office?"

"There's a good reason," Stick said. He saw determined-looking, clean-cut guys in narrow suits who never smiled. "It's called the Federal Bureau of Investigation."

Frank looked back as they passed it. "It might be an idea, though. U.S. Post Office. Save it for around Christmastime when business's up."

Stick didn't bite. He realized now what Frank was doing.

Coming to Ten Mile Road, Frank said, "Hey, there we are. What do you say?"

Stick looked at the bank on the southwest corner. Michigan National. He didn't say anything.

"You don't like it?"

"I like it," Stick said. "It's just I don't love it."

"How about the Chinese place? All right, you guys, give me all your fucking egg rolls. You like egg rolls or you love them?"

"The next one," Stick said, "I think I might go for."

It was a Food Lanes supermarket. Stick turned in and pulled to a stop facing the building. He liked the location, the alley running next to the store, the ample parking on two sides. Or they could park across the alley at the Chinese place. That might be better.

"It's up to you," Frank said. "Go in and look it over. I'll wait here."

He was still playing his game. Stick didn't say anything. He went in and took his time walking around the store and bought cigarettes. Frank had a bag of potato chips when he got back in the car and drove out.

"You still like it?"

"Not bad," Stick said. "The only thing, you notice the doors? The cashier's place's in the front, in the corner, and there's doors on both sides. Two doors to watch. Also there's a magazine rack. So from the cashier's place you can't see much of the store."

Frank put a potato chip in his mouth and crunched it between his teeth.

"But no cops in there dressed up like grocery boys?"

"Fuck you," Stick said.

"You want a chip? Lay's. They dare you to try and eat just one."

"You didn't like the looks of the guy any more than I did," Stick said. "I said he looked like a cop, you agreed."

"I said you also thought the guy in the bar looked like a cop, with the fucking shotgun."

"You're trying to make it look like it's my fault we didn't hit the place," Stick said. "Like I'm chicken or something. You want to hit the post office? How about that bank there. All that shit."

"Watch the road," Frank said.

"Watch your ass. You don't like the way I drive, get the fuck out."

"You know, it's funny," Frank said, "you come on as a very easygoing person. Then bang, no reason, you get a hard-on like you want to kill somebody."

"No reason, no, none at all," Stick said.

"I was being funny, for Christ sake, you get pissed off. Like the other day you're pissed off at me using the car. Think about it," Frank said. "You got this down-home, you-all delivery like nothing in the world bothers you, but you know what? I think you could be a pretty mean son of a bitch underneath it all."

Frank was turning it around again, making it all his fault. There was no sense arguing with him when he did that. Stick kept his eyes on the road and didn't say anything. It always irritated him and he would begin to think about how he'd got into this and wonder if he should get out, now, while he still had a choice and walk away.

But he had to admit they were doing better than he'd expected, and maybe it was natural for two guys as different as they were to rub each other the wrong way sometimes. So what, right? He could live with it, as long as they kept the jobs simple and didn't overextend themselves.

Frank offered the potato chips again and he took some.

"You want to do one or go home or what?"

"Well, as long as we're out," Stick said, "we may as well. You got a hundred on you?"

The hundred-dollar bill usually worked. It was something they had thought of after the experience with the Armenian and could save a lot of threatening and gun waving. Make a purchase and hand the guy the bill. He would always hesitate, then look in the cash register, then hesitate again. Then, with Frank standing there looking prosperous and honest in his suit, the guy would fish a roll out of his pocket or say, Just a minute, and step into the back room. Stick would come in and they'd find the guy taking his excess cash out of a safe or wherever he kept it hidden.

They stopped by the T-bird to put their suit coats back on, cruised around for a while and found a drugstore with a liquor department. Frank bought a bottle of J&B and handed the guy the hundred-dollar note. This led them back to the prescription department where the pharmacist was making change out of a drawer. Stick tied up the clerk and pharmacist with Ace wraps and one-inch adhesive—the same tape he had used to do his ankles before a basketball game—while Frank hit the cash registers and the secret drawer for sixteen-fifty, their all-time record drugstore take.

They stayed out, had dinner, and closed the bar at the Kingsley Inn, singing along with the piano player, talking and making friends but not seeing anything worth picking up; all too old. Driving home, going through the business section of Birmingham, they noticed an appliance store holding its Annual Twenty-four-Hour Marathon Sales Spectacular. They looked at each other, full of drinks, and grinned.

The two guys who ran the store were dressed up in flannel nightshirts, still smiling and friendly at 2:30 in the morning. Frank and Stick each got a free-gift yardstick with the store's name on it for coming in. They looked around for a few minutes. Then Frank picked out a couple of ice trays that were sale priced at $2.98 each and handed the hundred-dollar bill to the cluck behind the counter in his nightshirt. The cluck looked at Frank and at the bill and finally shook his head and said gee, he was sorry but he didn't have enough cash in the store to make change.

Walking out, Frank said, "Bullshit."

Stick said, "You cheap bastard, why didn't you pick out a radio or something?"

"Don't worry," Frank said.

A half hour later they met the cluck down the street, at the local bank's night-deposit box. They pressed a free-gift yard-stick into his back, relieved him of a little more than seven hundred in cash, and left the cluck standing there in his nightshirt.

Frank could be a pain in the ass sometimes, but they usually had a good time and it was a pretty interesting way to make a living.

11

The time before he had looked for Mona and found Arlene. Tonight it was the other way around.

Arlene wasn't in her apartment. He went there twice and knocked and waited.

Frank was out for the evening, with the car and probably Karen. Stick didn't bring up the car again. If he wanted a car he'd get his own. He didn't feel like going out, though. He made a drink and went down to sit by the pool for a while.

He liked the darkness and the lights beneath the clear water and the sound of crickets in the shrubs. The bourbon was good, too. It was nice, sitting by himself having a drink and a cigarette.

It could be his own private patio and swimming pool. He wondered if he'd enjoy it any more if it was.

Mona appeared out of the darkness, without a sound, and sank into a lounge chair by the deep end of the pool. He wondered if she had seen him, the glow from his cigarette. She sat with the backrest up, her legs stretched out, staring at the illuminated water. She didn't move. He wondered if her eyes were closed, staring at the water but not seeing it.

Stick said, "How you doing?"

Mona looked over.

"Hi. How're you?" She said it quietly, without putting any thing extra into it.

She reminded him of somebody. Her face was pale in the reflection of the underwater lights. Her hair seemed darker. It was her nose and her mouth and the way her hair hung close to her face. She reminded him of somebody in the movies he used to like.

He almost told her that—bringing the aluminum chair over next to her lounge—but it would sound dumb, like he was making it up. It didn't make sense, did it? Trying to think of something to say to a hooker that wouldn't sound dumb. Hooker or call girl or whore, prostitute, whatever she considered herself. That might be something to talk about—if there was a difference between them. Get in a conversation about it, like he was making a study. When did you first consider turning pro? First accept money? What do you think got you doing it? Is it true whores really don't like guys? And all that bullshit.

He had been with whores in Toledo, Findlay, Ohio; Columbus, Fort Wayne, Terre Haute, Rock Island, Illinois; Dubuque, and Minot, North Dakota. Most had been nice, a few had had no personality at all. But he had never met a whore with a nose and mouth like Mona's. And he couldn't look past her nose and mouth and see her as a whore. Also she seemed too small and frail to be a whore—even though he had read that women were better than men at withstanding pain or punishment. He pictured her taking her blouse off, no bra, and asking for the money; then imagined a guy punching her in the mouth, threatening to do it again, and getting it for nothing. It could happen, a guy who didn't have any feeling. It must be a pretty tough life. He wanted to get into it with her, but didn't know how.

What had he said to all those other whores from Toledo to Minot? He'd said, "How much?"

He said to Mona, "You want a drink? I can get you one."

"No, thank you, though."

"How about a sip then? It's bourbon."

She hesitated. "All right."

As she was taking a drink he said, "No trouble to get you one. Salty Dog, anything you want."

"No thanks." She handed the glass back. "I'm going up in a minute."

He wanted to say something so there wouldn't be a silence, but it came. She was staring at the pool again.

"You know, you remind me of somebody. I can't think of who it is."

"Is that so?"

"Somebody in the movies."

He said it and it didn't sound as bad as he thought it would.

"My dad used to say I reminded him of a Labrador retriever we had. His name was Larry. The dog, I mean."

"You sure don't look like a Labrador retriever," Stick said. "Maybe the hair."

"It was when Larry was a puppy. I think the feet had something to do with it," Mona said. "We both had big feet."

Stick looked at her legs, at the white sandals pointing out of her white slacks.

"They don't look very big."

"Seven and a half quad." She looked down at them and wiggled her toes. "I have trouble getting fitted, except sandals, something like that."

There was a silence again.

"You sure you don't want a drink?"

"No, I think I'll go up."

"I still can't think of who it is you look like."

"Somebody in the movies, huh?"

"Dark hair, really pretty."

"Oh, it's a girl?"

"Sure it's a girl. She was in—I know she was in one John Wayne was in."

"I don't know who it could be," Mona said. "I don't go to the movies much."

"It was on television. I think the Monday night movie about a month ago."

"I guess I was out."

Stick hesitated. "Working?"

"Could've been."

"How much you charge?"

"Fifty," Mona said. "How's that sound?"

Mona squeezed her eyes closed and said, "Oh, God. Jesus."

Stick said, "Hey, don't do that, okay? Unless you really mean it."

12

Stick didn't know why he expected her to be different. He realized now the person in there, behind the calm expression, was predictable and he'd met her before, many times. She wasn't a mystery person at all; she was really kind of dumb. She had never heard of Waylon Jennings or his hit record *Midnight Rider*. She hadn't even heard of Billy Crash Craddock or Jerry Reed, the Alabama Wild Man. She liked Roger Williams and Johnny Mathis. She also liked Tab with Jack Daniel's. Stick was disappointed, then relieved. He fixed himself some greens with salt pork and ring baloney and Jiffy corn bread mix, fell asleep watching the late movie, woke up, and went to bed. He didn't know what time Frank got in.

The way he knew he was home was seeing the colored girl in the kitchen the next morning.

He got the paper in and came into the kitchen in his striped undershorts, scratching the hair on his chest, reading a headline about Ford and not sure which Ford they were talking about. A pan of water was boiling on the range. The colored girl was looking in the refrigerator. She had on a bra and panties, that's all, and was barefoot.

She looked over at him and said, "I don't see no tomato juice."

Stick saw her as she spoke and maybe he jumped, he wasn't sure. It was pretty unexpected. Good-looking colored girl standing there in her underwear, he walks in the same way, like they were married or good friends. He felt funny, aware of his bare skin.

"What'd you say?"

"Tomato juice." She was relaxed, like she was in her own kitchen.

"In the cupboard," Stick said, "if we got any."

He watched her open the cupboard, look over the shelves, and reach for the gold can of Sacramento: slim brown body and white panties very low, legs stretched, on her tiptoes. He really felt funny. He didn't know if it was because she was black or because she was in her underwear. He tried to seem at ease and sound casual.

"You the maid?"

"Yeah, the cleaning lady," the girl said. "But I don't do floors or any ironing."

"LaGreta," Stick said. "Are you LaGreta?"

The girl turned and looked at him. "You know somebody that name?"

"I don't know her. I think I heard of her."

"Uh-huh. Where's your opener, love?"

"In the drawer there."

He watched her get it out and pry two holes in the top of the can.

"You and him work together, huh?"

"You left me," Stick said. "I thought we were talking about LaGreta."

"She's my mother."

"Oh." Stick nodded.

"You see it now?"

"Well—not exactly. You might think we're somebody else you heard about, I don't know."

"Yeah, that's it," the girl said. "You're somebody else."

"You and . . . my friend, you meet each other at Sportree's, I bet."

"Hey, baby, don't worry about it. Just tell me where I can find the vodka."

"I'll get it." Stick went out to the bar, still holding the newspaper in front of him, still not at ease talking to the girl. Young little colored girl, and he felt awkward. He came back in with a bottle of vodka. The girl was lacing a glass of ice with Lea & Perrins and Tabasco.

"He like it hot?"

"Probably."

"I hope so. It's the only way I fix it." She took the vodka bottle, poured in a couple of ounces, and filled the glass with tomato juice.

"You work with your mamma?"

"I told you I was a cleaning lady."

"Come on, really. What do you do?"

"I suppose you'll learn sooner or later anyway," the girl said. "I'm a brain surgeon." She moved past him with the Bloody Mary.

Stick watched her tight little can cross the living room and go into the hall, then heard her voice.

"Come on, sport. Time to open those baby blues and face the world."

Stick made bacon and fried some eggs in the grease.

When the girl came out again she was dressed in slacks and a blouse and earrings, a jacket over her arm. She didn't care for fried eggs, asked if they had any real coffee and settled for freeze-dried instant. Stick got up the nerve to ask her a few questions while she drank her coffee and read Shirley Eder and Earl Wilson. Her name was Marlys. She was twenty years old, not a brain surgeon, she worked in the office of a department store as a secretary.

Marlys grabbed her jacket and purse, yelled into the bedroom, "See you, sport," and was gone.

When Frank came out in his jockeys with the empty glass, looking like he'd been through major surgery the night before, Stick said, "What's Rule Number Nine?"

Frank said, "For Christ sake, lemme alone."

He looked terrible first thing in the morning, his hairdo mussed up and needing a shave, sad, wet eyes looking out of a swollen face. Stick could understand why the colored girl was anxious to leave. Frank's bedroom probably smelled like a sour-mash still.

"Don't feel so good, huh?"

"I'm all right. Once I have some breakfast."

"You throw up yet? Get down there and make love to the toilet bowl?"

Frank didn't answer. He turned the fire on under the pan of water.

"Rule Number Eight," Stick said. "Never go back to an old bar or hangout. You go to Sportree's."

"An old hangout. I've been there twice, three times."

"Rule Number Nine. Never tell anyone your business. You pick up a broad, her *mother* knows what you do."

"She doesn't know me," Frank said, "not by name. We never met."

"Never tell a junkie even your name," Stick said. "The place is a dope store, full of heads. Rule Number Ten—you want another one? Never associate with people known to be in crime. Your friend Sportree—into many things, right? beginning with dope—and probably everybody else in the place."

Frank jiggled the pan of water to make it boil faster. "The guy's a friend of mine. I talked to him for a while, then Marlys came in, we been getting to know each other."

"Marlys," Stick said. "I thought you went out with Karen."

"I went out with Sonny, since we're keeping records. I ran into her coming in, waited an hour while she changed into an identical outfit, and we went out, had dinner."

"Yeah?"

"Yeah what?"

"What happened?"

Frank looked over from the range. "It's a long, boring story. For your record, Sonny doesn't kiss and hug on the first date. Maybe not on the second or third or fourth, either. Maybe she never does. Maybe not even if you married her."

"What'd you do, try and rape her?"

"I bought her dinner. Forty-eight bucks with the tip. She takes a couple of bites of filet and leaves it. We come back here, it's nighty-night time, that's it."

"What'd you talk about?"

"Her. What do you think? She's in a couple of Chevy ads, you'd think she was a fucking movie star. I told her I'd been there already, used to take out a girl was in the movies. She isn't even listening. You tell her something, she's thinking about what she's going to say next about herself. It's not worth it. Forty-eight bucks—I say, You want to go somewhere else, hear some music? No. How about, I know a place we can see some interesting characters. No."

"So you went alone."

"I couldn't find anybody and it was just as well I didn't," Frank said, "since I ran into Marlys."

"She must be pretty good."

Frank looked over again as he took the water off the fire.

"Buddy, it's all good. Like chili, when you're in the mood. Even when it's bad it's good."

"I guess so," Stick said. "Matter of degree." He waited a moment, then said it. "I never done it with a colored girl."

"Or a Jewish girl, as I recall," Frank said. "Only white Anglo-Saxon Protestants."

"No, my wife was a Catholic at one time, when we first got married. There was another girl I used to go with when I was about eighteen, she was a Catholic, too."

"That's interesting," Frank said. He poured a cup of instant and took it over to the table. "You certainly talk about interesting things." Stirring the coffee, he began looking at the morning paper.

"You want to see something interesting," Stick said, "page three. Another guy shot knocking down a liquor store." He watched Frank turn the page.

"Where?"

"Down near the bottom. Bringing the total to six in the past week. You see it? Six guys shot, four killed, in attempted robberies. What does it tell you?"

Frank was looking at the news story. "The cop, it says Patrolman William Cotter, called out, 'Freeze! Police officer!' The suspect, Haven Owens—a jig," Frank said, "you can tell by the name—pointed his revolver at Patrolman Cotter, then turned and attempted to run from the store. He was shot three times in the back . . . wounds proved fatal . . . pronounced dead on arrival at Wayne County General. I like that wounds proved fatal—hit three times in the back with a fucking thirty-eight."

"What does it tell you?" Stick said. "Doesn't come right out and say, but the cop's waiting there, isn't he?"

"Of course he is. I know that. Christ, a little kid'd know it."

"So you go in a place now, since they're cracking down," Stick said, "how do you know it isn't staked out?"

"Because we don't work in Detroit. These suburban places, Troy, Clawson, for Christ sake, they don't have cops for stake-outs."

"You know that for a fact?"

"Hey, have we seen any? I don't mean feel it, as you say, imagine it, like the A&P. Have we actually seen any stake-outs?"

"All we need is one," Stick said. "We won't see any more for ten to twenty-five years."

13

The bright green repainted Chevy Nova stalled three times before they were out of the shopping center.

"The idle's set too low," Frank said. "I don't want to seem critical but how come, all the cars, you pick this turkey?"

"I think what sold me was the key on the visor," Stick said. "It's just cold."

"*Cold?* It's seventy degrees out."

"It was probably sitting there all day. Belongs to some kid works in one of the stores." When they were stopped at a light and the engine stalled again, Stick said, "Or else the idle's set too low."

It was 8:20 now, almost dark. Stick turned onto Southfield and eased over to the right lane, in no hurry, the store would be waiting.

Frank said, "You go any slower, this thing is going to roll over and die."

Stick didn't say anything. Maybe he was putting off getting there and that's why he didn't mind the car stalling. They were both stalling. He'd watch the approaching headlights, then shift his eyes to the rearview mirror. Police cars were black and white with blue-and-red bubbles. Oklahoma State Police were also black and white. And Texas. Texas Department of Public Safety. Black and white with three flashers on top—count 'em, three—in case anybody didn't know they were cops. He thought of something else, what an old boy from Oklahoma had said. "Do you know why there's a litter barrel every mile going down the highway in Texas?" "No, why?" "To dispose of all the shit they hand you in that state."

In Missouri they were cream-colored.

They drove past the bank, parked on the dark side of the Chinese restaurant, and walked across the alley to the Food Lanes supermarket.

Stick went in the front entrance and took a shopping cart as he moved along the aisle past the checkout counters—only two of them busy with customers. He'd circle through the store before coming back to the checkouts.

Frank went in the side door. Past the magazine rack Stick had mentioned, he looked toward the brightly lighted produce department, then glanced over at the cashier's enclosure and saw two heads, one bald, one a tall blond beehive.

Frank walked through the empty produce department to the back of the store, to the double doors with the little glass windows, and looked into the storage area. A couple of stockboys were loading cases onto hand trucks. By the time Frank got back to the front, Stick was at one of the checkout counters with a few grocery items in his cart, waiting behind a customer. A man in a sport shirt was standing at the magazine rack. He picked out a copy of *Outdoor Life* as Frank walked past him, to the cashier's window.

Frank looked over his shoulder. The guy was leafing through the magazine. He turned to the window again and the blond girl with the beehive, a two-hundred-pounder, was waiting for him.

"Can I help you?"

"Yes, you can," Frank said. He took the Python out of his safari jacket and rested it in the opening. "You can unlock the door if you will, please, and let me in."

Stick watched him go around, wait by the door a moment, then slip into the enclosure. He could see three heads in there now, the blond one higher than Frank's and the bald one. No one else seemed to have noticed Frank. The two checkout girls looked tired and probably wouldn't give a shit if the place caught fire, long as they got out.

Stick's turn came and the checkout girl began ringing up his groceries, a few things they needed anyway.

She said, "You like these buckwheat flakes?" pausing to study the box.

"I sure do," Stick said. "They're honey-flavored."

"I'll have to try them," the checkout girl said. She tore off the tape and gave him the total: $4.09.

Stick opened his poplin jacket and showed her the Smith sticking out of his pants. Like a dirty old man in front of a little kid.

"You see it?"

"Oh, my," the checkout girl said. She was in her forties and seemed like a friendly, easygoing person. "I've never been held up before. Lord, this is the first time."

Stick was pretty sure she wouldn't do anything dumb. "Something to tell your friends about," he said.

"I sure will." She tensed up then. "I mean I won't if you don't want me to."

"No, it's okay. Put the money in a bag. Just the bills." He got his own bag from the end of the counter and put the groceries in it while the checkout girl emptied the cash register. "Then get those other ones down there," Stick said, "the other cash registers."

The checkout girl at the next counter was busy with a Jewish-looking lady who was unloading a cart piled with groceries and telling the girl how a hundred dollars a week used to take care of everything, her hair and her cleaning woman, and now it barely covered food the way prices were, but she wasn't going to cut down or skimp because her husband insisted on only prime sirloin, filets or standing rib and also liked his snacks and that's where the money went, on meat like it was from sacred cows and the snacks, pastries, ice cream, he loved peanut brittle, something sweet to snack on watching TV.

The checkout girl was concentrating on ringing up the items, then would pause and lay on a buzzer for a few seconds to get a carry-out boy who never appeared. She probably didn't hear anything the woman said. That was fine, she was busy and had things on her mind.

"I'll tell you what," Stick said to his checkout girl. "On the other cash registers, take out the tray inside—you can carry four—and take them over to the cashier's place." He picked up his groceries and the shopping bag with the money in it. "I'll be right behind you."

If the Jewish lady ever finished and left, he'd come back for that cash register. He hoped he wouldn't get involved with her and have to tell her to lie down on the floor or something. The woman looked like she'd scream. The last thing he wanted was a screamer. That's why he liked his checkout girl—following her along the front of the counters as she stepped into each one and collected the cash register tray—she was excited and naturally scared, but she was probably already thinking how she was going to tell it after, the biggest thing that ever happened to her.

Stick noticed the guy at the magazine rack, half turned away from it. He wondered if the guy had looked down, just then, at his magazine.

Frank opened the door to the cashier's enclosure. Stick and the checkout girl stepped inside with her trays.

"Come on in," Frank said. "Mr. Miller here's having a little trouble with the safe."

The manager was down on his knees, fooling with the dial of the safe built into the counter. The big girl with the beehive was watching him, biting her lower lip.

Stick handed the checkout girl the bag of currency. "Put everything in here, will you? Except checks and silver." He touched Frank on the arm then and nodded toward the magazine rack.

"I saw him," Frank said.

The big girl glanced over.

"Honey, get down there by Mr. Miller, will you, please? Tell him he doesn't open the safe right now, I'm going to cause him pain and suffering."

"The guy just looked over," Stick said.

Frank's head rose. He studied the guy, not saying anything.

"He knows something's going on," Stick said. "Five people in here having a convention."

"Take it easy," Frank said.

Take it easy? Stick looked at him. He was taking it easy, his voice was calm, what the fuck was he talking about, take it easy.

Frank was stooped over the manager again, touching the big Python gently to the man's head.

"I'm going to count to three, Mr. Miller."

"I can't help it," the manager said, "I'm trying. I can't see the numbers with these glasses, they're my old pair. My regular glasses that I use, the frames broke—"

"Okay," Frank said.

"—and they're in being repaired. I was supposed to have them the next day, but they didn't have the frames—"

"Hey," Frank said, "I believe you, no shit, I really do. Just get out of the way." He glanced at the big girl's name tag. "Let Annette get in there. Give her the numbers."

Stick watched the guy close the magazine and put it under his arm. The guy hesitated but didn't look over. He got himself ready and started for the side entrance.

"Hey—" Stick said.

Frank looked up. The guy was going through the door, hurrying now as he moved through the breezeway to the outer door.

"He saw us," Stick said.

"Mr. Miller," Frank said to the manager, "a guy just walked out with a magazine without paying for it—the cheap son of a bitch."

"We better move," Stick said.

Frank looked at him. "Take it easy, okay?"

It got to him again, hooked him. Stick waited, making sure his voice would be calm, and moved closer to Frank.

"The guy's out, and if he's got a dime in his pocket we're going to be seeing the fucking colored lights in about three minutes."

"Or maybe he didn't notice anything," Frank said. "We're here, man, we're going to get what we came for." Looking down again: "Annette, would you mind, please, opening the fucking safe?" Saying it calmly, for Stick more than for the big blond girl.

Stick knew it. He had to keep himself in control again. It was crowded in here, the checkout girl staring at him then looking away quickly, he wanted to take what they had right now and get out. But the big blond girl was saying something. She had the safe open and Frank was stooped down next to her, holding the grocery bag. Stick looked at the clock on the wall.

Frank told everybody to lie down and not move and if he saw a head raise up he'd blow it off, giving them the farewell address in his cool-gunman voice. Stick took the bag from him. Going out, he glanced at the clock again. The Jewish-looking lady was still there, the checkout girl loading bags and buzzing the buzzer. Stick wasn't sure how much time had passed since the guy left with the magazine. Enough, though. He didn't see the guy outside anywhere. He didn't expect to. He kept a few steps ahead of Frank, who was holding back on purpose walking to the car. Fucking games.

They got in the Nova. Frank slammed his door, it didn't catch and he had to open it and slam it again.

"I hope it starts," Frank said, "and doesn't konk out. You think it's cold?"

Stick didn't say anything. He pushed the accelerator down halfway, held it, and snapped on the ignition. The engine caught at once with a good, heavy roar. Stick gave it a little more gas to be sure and listened to the idle. It was fine. But there was another sound, far away, a shrill, irritating sound that went *who-who, who-who,* and kept it up, getting louder, scaring the shit out of anybody sitting in a stolen car with a grocery bag full of money, scaring them way more than the old standard siren ever did.

Frank said, "Let's get out of here." Not quite as cool as before.

The blue-and-red flashers were coming down Southfield, weaving through the traffic, still a couple of blocks away. They saw the flashers as they came out of the shadow and turned in front of the Chinese place. Stick glanced and saw enough, looked away to figure out where he was going, and saw the man coming out of the restaurant, the man with a magazine running out across the drive, then stopping dead as he saw the green Nova and the two guys inside. He was about five feet away from them when he ran back into the restaurant.

The red-and-blue flashing squad car with its awful *who-who* wail almost lost it taking the corner, got itself straightened out passing the bank and the Chinese place, and swerved into the Food Lanes parking lot as Stick eased the Nova around the far corner of the restaurant, cut through the open blacktop area behind the Michigan National Bank, and hit Southfield already doing thirty, not fast enough to attract attention but enough to get them out of there. Stick could picture the guy running over to the squad car, waving the magazine at them and pointing. *A green car!* Or if he knew anything, *A green '72 Nova! Went that way!* Shit.

Frank was hunched around, looking back. "Nothing yet." He spotted the flashers a half mile back as they were going through an amber past Michigan Bell. "There they are."

Stick edged over to the left and followed the curving ramp that led to the Lodge Expressway. He didn't take it, though. He ducked out on the spur that connected with the Northland service drive, followed it to the first overpass, crossed the expressway, and two minutes later was weaving through the mile-long parking area on the east side of the Northland shopping complex.

Stick felt better.

There was no hurry now, no red-and-blue flashers in sight. They were hidden among rows of shining automobiles, protected by the mass of the department store, Hudson's Northland, rising above the arcades of shops and stores and neon lights that formed a wall against the darkness and the police, wherever they were, over there somewhere.

Stick felt pretty good, in fact, realizing he was in control and had been in control from the time the cop car came fishtailing around the corner. He had used his head and timed it and got out of there without squealing the tires or doing anything dumb. That was a good feeling, once it was over and he could look back at it. Frank, Mr. Cool, was still tense, watching for cops.

Stick glanced at him. "How about a J&B?"

"How about a couple?" Frank said. He paused and got some of his calm back. "Since we got nothing else to do."

14

The dining room was paneled and brightly lighted. Not in there, Frank said. In the cocktail lounge that was marble and velvet and dark wood, with imitation gas lamps and waitresses in French-maid outfits. Stick said, "You think we're dressed all right?"

Frank said, "Relax."

He was getting it all back now.

"It's the same booze in the bottles," Frank said. "The rest of the shit is overhead. But not bad, huh? I used to come here."

He called the waitress with the dark-dyed hairdo and rosy makeup "dear" and ordered doubles, scotch and a bourbon. It was funny, Frank was at ease now and Stick felt awkward, sitting in the booth with his poplin jacket on and the Food Lanes shopping bag next to him—the groceries in with the money, maybe two grand or more in there—afraid the manager or somebody was going to come over and ask them to leave because they weren't dressed right.

"Here's to it," Frank said. He raised his glass and took a drink. "You were right about the guy with the magazine. You see him outside?"

"See him—I almost ran over him."

"You should've. Teach him to mind his fucking business."

"Another half a minute," Stick said, "we wouldn't be here."

Frank sipped his drink. "Adds a little color. Otherwise it'd be routine, like a job. Same thing all the time."

"It was close," Stick said.

"Sure it was close, in a way it was. We're looking in the fucking whites of their eyes. But we did it. Suck in a little, let them go by, then take off. It's called timing. We don't have to put it down as a rule because we've got it, instinctively."

"You telling me you like it?" Stick said. "The flashers, that sound? That's a terrible sound to hear coming at you."

"It's part of it. You don't have to like it, no," Frank said. "You accept it, the possibility, and when it happens you keep it together."

"What're the odds?" Stick said. "One close one out of what, thirty? That's not bad, but maybe we've been lucky and it's starting to catch up."

"No, if you know what you're doing, each one is like the first time only better, because you've been there. Incidentally, it's thirty-one."

"But things can happen," Stick said. "In the grocery, I tell you the guy saw us. No, you're playing some fucking game, you're going to stay there till you get the safe. That's not going by instinct or rules or anything, that's so fucking dumb it's stupid."

"We're here, right? And we got what was in the safe."

"We're here—you want to do it like that every time?"

"All right—" Frank paused and lit a cigarette, then motioned to the waitress to do it again. "You're saying don't take unnecessary chances. I agree, up to a point. But the nature of the business, you play it as you come to it. The rules are basically good, *but* what I'm saying, you can't fit them into each and every situation."

"You're the one made them up," Stick said, "ten rules for success and happiness. Now you want to throw them out."

"Did I say that?"

"It's the same thing."

"Look, we start with the rules, fine. We obey them like the fucking Ten Commandments, nothing wrong with that, we're just starting out. But we also have experience now, instinct. We know as much about it, maybe more than anybody in the business."

"I don't know," Stick said, "thirty in a row—thirty-one in a row—maybe it's time to rest a while. It doesn't seem like much at the time, but it's hard work, it takes it out of you."

"That's right, it's not the kind of work for somebody with a heart condition. Hernia, it doesn't matter. Picking up money never gave anybody a hernia. It's hard work but not hard labor." Frank paused. "Actually, the amount of effort to pick up one or two grand, it doesn't take any more to lift twenty or thirty or, say, fifty grand. You follow me?"

"I'm ahead of you," Stick said. "I can see it coming."

"Don't start shifting around, listen a minute. I'm talking about what if we do the same thing practically we've been doing, only we pick up, say, fifty times more. What's wrong with that? One shot, we take a trip, we don't work for months."

"It seems to me we discussed banks one time, savings and loan," Stick said. "What're the odds, fifty-fifty?"

"I'm not talking about a bank."

"You going to tell me, or I have to guess? I remember this other time we're in a bar you get me into a quiz game. What's the best way to make the most money? The simplest way."

The waitress came with the drinks, giving Frank a chance to sit back and take his time. He waited until she walked away.

"I've been giving this a lot of thought," he said. "I'm not talking about some half-assed stunt like we walk into the downtown branch of the National Bank of Detroit. This one's real."

"Okay, it's not a bank. How many more guesses do I have?"

"I wasn't going to tell you about it till I thought you were ready. I'm still not sure you are." Frank paused, but Stick didn't say anything. "I'm talking about your attitude," Frank said. "I want to lay something on you and be able to discuss it like I'm talking to a pro, man who's been there. But if this thing tonight shook you up, then I don't think you're ready and maybe it's possible you never will be."

"I drove the car," Stick said.

"Yeah, you drove the car." Frank waited.

Stick took a drink. He could see a couple of kids arguing. Unbelievable. You were the one was scared, I wasn't. You were, too. I was not. Were, too. Maybe not in those words, but it would be the same thing.

He said, "All right, when you think I'm ready. Then again, if you don't think I'll ever be ready, you know what you can do with your great idea."

"I'll tell you something else," Frank said, "since you're in a nice open frame of mind. There'd be some other people involved."

Stick shook his head, very slowly, watching Frank, the two of them staring at each other in the gaslit cocktail lounge.

"You're trying different ways—why don't you come right out with it?"

"With what?"

"You want to knock off this twosome shit, split up. All right, that's fine with me, any time you want."

"I say anything about splitting up?"

"You haven't said anything at *all* yet. Everything is what you *didn't* say, for Christ sake. You want to say something, say it, and quit jerking around."

"I'm considering something," Frank said.

Stick had the urge to punch him out, go over the table and give him one. The son of a bitch, sitting there doing his cool number.

"I've got a proposition," Frank was saying, "but I don't want to spring it on you prematurely. I want to be sure you've got the balls for it before I tell you the whole thing."

"Leak out a little at a time. That's what you're doing, trying to get me to bite."

"Uh-unh, getting reactions."

"Why don't we talk about it again," Stick said, "sometime when a flasher's coming up behind us and you're pissing your pants."

Frank looked up at Stick as he slid out of the booth, the Food Lanes shopping bag in his hand.

"We're a little edgy, huh? I must've said something hit you where you live."

Stick was tired of it and didn't want to play anymore. "You going to stay or what?"

"No, I'm ready. I'll get the bill, you get the car." He looked for the waitress, then at Stick again. "A different one, right? In case they spotted that green turkey out there."

"I had that in mind," Stick said. His voice was calm, he wasn't going to let Frank rattle him anymore, not tonight. "You want any particular make or model?"

"One that doesn't stall'd be nice," Frank said. "See what you can do."

There was valet parking, but no board with keys on it by the entrance. The attendants probably parked the cars in the shopping plaza lot as close to the restaurant as they could and maybe even put the keys under the seat.

Stick rolled the top of the grocery bag a little tighter in his hand and walked out past the people waiting for their cars.

It would be easy to take one. If he didn't have to wait for Frank or swing back and pick him up—and see the owner of the car running out yelling for him to stop. Gee, I'm sorry, sir, is it yours? I guess I got the wrong one. And go through all that.

Frank complicated things. If he'd knock off the shit and stick to the rules, they could do very well in a year, shake hands, and dissolve the partnership.

He had told Frank about where he'd be, down toward the end of the lot, past the light poles and the car bodies shining in the darkness, and maybe over a couple of rows. He'd probably have to use the clips, do some rewiring under the dash. There were enough cars, a good selection, but he was tired and didn't feel like concentrating and getting himself into a calm-alert frame of mind. He shouldn't have let Frank bother him like that. He shouldn't have said he'd get a car, asking him what kind he wanted. That was dumb, playing Frank's game with him, like a little kid. Two kids playing chicken. Frank acting, talking about the big hit, fifty grand and some other people involved, trying to get a rise out of him with the big mystery bit. What he should do maybe, call Frank on it. Say, Come on, sure, I'm ready, let's go. Except the dumb shit might think he had to quit talking about it and do it and they'd walk in someplace for the big hit playing I-dare-you and get their fucking heads blown off.

He looked back, glancing over his shoulder, to see if he was far enough away from the restaurant.

Someone was coming along behind him.

Not Frank or a parking attendant, he was pretty sure. A guy taking his time. About thirty feet back, keeping pace, a thin, elongated figure against the lights of the restaurant. Not anyone he had noticed in front. He had a feeling the guy was black, and it tightened him up a little. The feeling just came, a reaction. There was no reason to be suspicious of the guy. The guy was going to get his car. A car he owned. That was kind of funny, he was out here to steal one, commit a crime, and he was worried about being robbed.

Stick moved through the rows of cars on his left, parked in two rows front end to front end, to the next aisle. He looked back. Nothing. He continued on toward the end of the lot. There were streetlights beyond the darkness and the sound of cars. When he looked back again, the guy was in the aisle, thirty feet behind him.

The second guy stepped into the open directly in front of him and stood waiting. Stick could see he was black. Tall like the one behind him, a couple of basketball players with easy moves. The guy's arms were folded, his hands beneath his biceps. He could be waiting for his friend, the guy following him.

Which was about as likely as waiting for a streetcar.

Stick moved out to walk around the guy, and the guy stepped out with him. He had to stop then or keep going and say excuse me or turn around and run. He stopped.

The black guy unfolded his arms so Stick could see the revolver in his hand. He was pretty sure it was real. The black guy said, "How you this evening?"

"Pretty good," Stick said. "Well, no, I take that back." He grinned to show the guy he was easy to get along with.

"Where your car at?"

"You might not believe this," Stick said, "but I don't have one."

"You don't, huh? You out for a stroll?" His gaze shifted as the tall, skinny one who'd been following came up on Stick's left. "He say he don't have a car."

"Put your arms out," the skinny black guy said.

Stick did it, holding the grocery bag extended in his left hand. He felt the guy pat him down, his jacket pockets and then his hips and back pockets. The guy's hands didn't go around to the front. He lifted Stick's wallet, took out the money, and dropped the wallet on the pavement.

Stick said, "Thank you." It just came out. He thought of the manager at the Kroger store who'd thanked him and told him to come back again.

"Twenty and three singles," the skinny black guy said. "Man, where your keys?"

"He left them in the car," the black guy with the gun said. "Come on, man, show it to us."

"I'm telling you, I don't have a car. I got to get one myself."

"You going to steal it?" the skinny black guy said. He sounded amused.

Stick looked at him, at his sweatshirt with the sleeves cut off, showing his long, stringy muscles. Six-three or four, with a nice outside jump shot and tough under the boards. They could go to some schoolyard with lights and play one-on-one.

"If all you want's a car, shit, help yourself," Stick said. "What one you want?"

"We'll take yours, man, anything you got," the black guy

with the gun said. "What's in the bag? You got some booze?"

"Buckwheat flakes," Stick said. "Cereal, a few other things."

The guy motioned with the gun. "Hand it to him."

Stick turned a little to face the skinny guy, backing away and bringing the grocery bag up in front of him with both hands on it. He felt the rear bumper of the car behind him, against his legs.

He said, "You guys want groceries, why don't you go to the store, help yourself?"

The black guy with the gun said, "Man, what you got in there you don't want us to have?" He motioned to his partner. "See what he's got."

Stick's right hand went under his jacket and closed on the butt of the .38. That was as far as he got. Before he could pull it or jerk the grocery bag out of reach, the skinny black guy got a grip on the bag, pushed him, grunted something, and threw a quick, hard jab into the side of his face. The grocery bag tore open between them, ripped apart, as Stick fell against the car, rolled to keep his balance, and held onto the trunk lid. He was dazed, his face numb, but he was still gripping the .38 under his jacket, like he was holding his stomach.

Both of the black guys were looking at the pavement, at the money scattered in a little pile with the cereal and the bread and boxes of Jell-O. The skinny black man stooped down and began to pick it up, saying, "Man, look, man, look at the motherfucking money the motherfucker's got, man, *look at it*"—scooping it up as fast as he could and stuffing it in the torn remains of the grocery bag.

The black guy with the gun looked from the money to Stick lying against the trunk of the car. He said, "Man, you robbed some place, didn't you? Shit." He began to grin, looking at the money again, and laughed, getting happy-excited about it, like finding money in the street.

"Man *robbed* a place, put it in a bag—"

He stopped—because if the man was a holdup man, if he was an armed robber—

Stick had the .38 out, extended, pointed at the guy.

The black guy with the gun said, "Shit," the excitement

gone out of his voice. He had his revolver in front of him but pointed at a down angle and away from Stick.

The skinny black guy hadn't looked up. He was down there, getting it all back into the torn-up bag, saying, "Look at it. Man, will you . . . look . . . at . . . it."

"Turn around," Stick said to the guy with the gun, "and let's see your arm. Throw it down there as far as you can."

The skinny black guy stopped talking and looked up from the pavement.

Stick could see him but kept his attention on the guy with the gun. When the guy didn't move, Stick said, "I don't know what you got, some Mickey Mouse piece. This one's a thirty-eight Smith. It'll go clean through you and break some windows down the street. Now turn the fuck around and throw it away."

The skinny guy crouched on the pavement said, "They two of us, man. How you going to get us both?"

Stick turned toward him a little but kept the .38 on the other one. "You worried about it," he said, "I'll do you first."

"Buuullshit. You ain't going to do nobody." The skinny guy got to his feet, holding the torn sack against his body. His free hand went into his pocket and came out with a clasp knife. Watching Stick, he opened the blade with his teeth.

"Shiiit, come on, man, hand me that thing. Let's cut out the bullshit."

"Do what he say," the black guy with the gun said. He was careful with the gun, not moving it, but he seemed confident again. It was in the tone of his voice.

Neither of them moved. The skinny guy waited, his hand extended with the knife in it—five, six feet away—patient, sure of himself. He said, "Man, you ever shoot that thing? You know how? Come on, give it to me. We let you go home with your buckwheat flakes."

Stick wasn't sure if the safety was off.

He wasn't sure which one of them he should look at.

He wasn't sure if he could fire the gun at either of them. He didn't like the guy's sound, the skinny black guy holding the money, but he didn't know if he could shoot him. He had had them for a moment and now he was losing it. He knew it and could feel it and he couldn't think of anything to say.

If he had had a little more time to make up his mind, maybe he would have said it wasn't worth it, shit no, and handed over the gun and taken his groceries and gone home. Maybe he looked like he was wavering, scared. Or he looked so easy the skinny guy couldn't resist going for him.

That's what the guy did, rushed him, pulling his knife hand back to throw it into him.

Stick shot him, not more than a yard away, and heard his scream with the heavy report of the gun.

The other black guy was caught by surprise, not ready until it was already happening, hurrying to get the revolver on the man, firing once, too soon.

Stick shot him twice, he was pretty sure in the chest. The guy fired again, wildly, a reflex action, and made a gasping sound, like the wind was knocked out of him, as he fell to the pavement.

The skinny black guy was running, holding the grocery bag against his sweatshirt. Stick heard himself yell at the guy to stop, to hold it right there, seeing the guy running and knowing he was going to keep running, and he fired almost as he yelled it, one shot from the .38 that caught him in the middle of the back. The skinny guy bounced off a car and hit the pavement face-down.

Stick didn't roll him over or feel for a pulse. He pulled the torn bag out from under him, in a hurry to get it, knowing he was leaving some bills but not caring about them, not wanting to touch the guy. He remembered that. He remembered the sound of someone running on pavement, coming this way, a dark figure against the restaurant sign, the way the skinny black guy had appeared when he first saw him. That seemed like a long time ago. Some other night. But he had talked to the guy less than a minute ago and now the guy was dead. The black guy with the gun lay on his back with his eyes open, staring at nothing. Maybe he could've talked to them a little more. Said, Look, you know how it is. I went to a lot of trouble for this, man. You want some, go get your own. Talk it over with them, couple of guys in the same business. No, a different type of business, but they'd understand things he did. He felt like he knew them. Couple of guys, shoot some baskets, play a little one-on-one, have a few beers after. The sound of the running steps was close, almost on top of him. He could hear someone breathing, out of breath.

"Jesus Christ," Frank said. He looked at the two black guys on the pavement and at Stick holding the .38 tightly against the grocery bag, and said it again, "Jesus Christ."

15

It was in the *News* the next afternoon. Frank went out for beer and brought back a paper. He read the story through, twice, and had a beer open for Stick when he came out of the shower and sat down in his striped shorts.

Stick lit a cigarette first and drank some of the beer. He was anxious, but at the same time he wasn't sure he wanted to read it. Maybe it would be better not to know anything about the two guys.

"Nobody saw us?"

Frank shook his head. "Uh-unh. I figure we were in the cab before anybody found them."

"It say who they were?"

"Read it."

Stick looked down at the paper.

"Man, you did a job," Frank said.

There was a quiet tone of respect in his voice Stick had never heard before.

The one-column story referred to it as "The Northland Slaying" and related how Andrew Seed and Walter Wheeler, both residents of Detroit, had been found shot to death in the parking lot of the shopping plaza, victims of an unknown assailant. Police were proceeding with an investigation, though there were no witnesses to the shooting or apparent motive other than attempted robbery. Both victims were known to the police.

Seed had been arrested several times on charges of robbery, felonious assault, and rape, and had served time in both the Detroit House of Correction and the Southern Michigan Prison at Jackson. Wheeler had a record of narcotics arrests and a conviction in addition to a list of assault and robbery charges. Both were also described as having been outstanding athletes while in high school, seven years before. Both had won All-City basketball recognition, first team, and All-State honorable mention.

"I knew it," Stick said. "It was a funny feeling, the way they moved or something, I knew they'd played and I wondered, What're they doing out here trying to hustle somebody?"

"You played," Frank said. "What were you doing, trying to steal a fucking car?"

"I wasn't that good, All-City. Those guys made All-City, All-State honorable mention."

"You were good with the Smith," Frank said. "Jesus, I couldn't believe it. Bam, bam—that's it, no fucking around. I wish I could've seen their faces. They're going to pull this easy hustle in a parking lot. Guy comes along with a bag of groceries, going home to mom and the kids. Yeah? That's what you think, motherfuckers. Man, next thing they know, they're fucking dead. That time just before, that few seconds, that's what I'd like to have seen. You should've waited for me. I'd have helped you."

"You could've done the whole thing," Stick said. "Any time. Listen, I think about it, I don't even believe it happened. I see the guy running away, I can still see him—this light-colored sweatshirt on with the sleeves cut off—I yelled at him to stop and I shot him, I mean I killed him."

"Because he wouldn't stop," Frank said. He sounded a little surprised. "What were you supposed to do, let him get away? He's got our twenty-three hundred, forty-eight bucks. Guy's a fucking thief."

"You don't kill somebody because he steals something."

"Bull*shit*, you don't. What do the cops do? They shoot you, man. You don't stop, they shoot you."

"I don't know," Stick said. "This is different."

"He was taking our money. You're supposed to let him take it? Sure, go ahead, any time. Bullshit, you're protecting our property."

"Frank, we stole it."

"Right, and that makes it ours. They weren't taking it from the store, going to all that work and getting their nerves stretched out, no, they think they're taking it from some meek, defenseless asshole who isn't going to do anything about it. Well, they made a mistake. And one's all you get."

Stick drew on his cigarette. He could see the skinny black guy running with his shoulders hunched. He should have gotten in between some cars, but he ran instead, already with one bullet in his side. The guy had nerve. He was holding all that money and he was going to keep it. Stick wondered if the guy was married and had a family. He wondered if he'd be listed in the death notices and if there'd be a funeral and if many people would attend. The two guys must've had friends. They'd gone to school in Detroit. He imagined a lot of black people at a cemetery. He thought about his little girl for some reason and wondered what she was doing.

"Maybe we ought to rest a while," he said to Frank.

"What're we doing?" Frank said. "We're sitting down, we're resting. I was thinking we ought to have a party."

"I mean knock it off for a while," Stick said. "Make sure they don't have something on us."

"The police? How could they?"

"They said there weren't any witnesses, but they wouldn't

say if there were, would they? I mean maybe there's a way we can be traced."

Frank shook his head. "No way. No car, no gun. We got the cab at least, what, a mile away from there. Nobody saw us or even knows it was two guys, right? And if there's no way they can even begin to trace us, we're clear."

"We're clear," Stick said, "but I still killed two guys."

"You sure did," Frank said. "Man. Listen, forget everything I said, we were talking in the bar, I said maybe you weren't ready for this thing I had in mind? I take it all back. You're ready."

"In the bar—you mean just before?"

"I told you I'd been working something out?"

"Yeah, I remember."

"Couple of days we'll know."

Stick wasn't sure he was following. He hadn't slept very well. All night he kept waking up and hearing the .38 going off and seeing the two black guys, not dreaming it but thinking about it, especially seeing the one who'd tried to run.

"Couple of days we'll know what?"

"Whether or not we can set it up. It's going to take a little doing."

"*We,*" Stick said. "You mean more than just you and me. You mentioned in the bar, you said, since I was in a nice, open frame of mind—"

"That was a little smart-ass of me," Frank said. "I take it back. Forget it. But yes, there would be a few other people involved, because of the nature of the job. Couple of helpers, guys to watch more than anything else. And one on the inside. She's already there. In fact, it's because of her I got the idea. We've been talking it over."

Stick was listening, paying close attention now. He knew Frank was serious.

He said, "You mean one of the broads lives here?"

"No, no, those broads, Christ," Frank said. "This one's got it together and she likes the idea. You understand, she wouldn't be in on it, involved directly, so to speak, but she'd give us all the inside information we'd need."

"If she doesn't live here—" Stick said. He stopped then. "You mean the colored broad? What's her name? Marlys?"

"That's right, you met her. I forgot," Frank said. "Very smart and grown up for her age."

Stick could see her again, in the white bra and panties. Cute little black girl, yes, very grown up.

"She said, I think she said she worked downtown, in an office."

"She works at Hudson's," Frank said. "Up on the fifteenth floor."

Stick frowned. "That's a department store."

"You bet it is," Frank said. "The biggest one in town."

"You're crazy," Stick said, "Jesus," and shook his head.

Frank waited.

"You're out of your fucking mind. Hudson's."

"The J. L. Hudson Company," Frank said. "You know how many cash registers they got in the store?"

"I don't want to know," Stick said. "I don't give a shit if they got a thousand."

"You're close," Frank said.

16

At one point in the evening there were fifteen people in the apartment. Frank found most of them; others dropped in. They'd come and go.

The way it started, Frank went out for a couple of hours in the afternoon—Stick didn't ask where—and when he got back he brought four of the career ladies up from the pool, Karen, Jackie, Mary Kay, and Arlene, and started making them drinks. Stick got out the grapefruit juice for the Salty Dogs and Arlene came over to help him. Even Mary Kay said she'd have one. It was strange to see four girls sitting around the apartment in swimming suits. Frank said they dressed up the place. Stick thought it looked like a Nevada whorehouse, the way he imagined one would look. Frank had had a few—wherever he'd gone—and was already a little high. He told Stick to come on and quit moping around. Stick decided, Why not? He'd have some fun and quit thinking about the two colored guys.

Then Frank told him Marlys was going to try and stop by later, and winked, and Stick thought about the two guys again. He wondered if Marlys knew them.

A little later Stick asked Mary Kay, didn't she have to go to work? And was surprised when she told him she was going to call in and say she was in bed with the curse. It was amazing, one and a half Salty Dogs.

Still a little later Frank went down to the ice machine, ran into Barry Kleiman in his white belt and white loafers talking to Sonny the Model and one of the young married couples, the Kaplans, and got them to come up. Frank went in and put on his safari jacket and wore it with a chain he borrowed from Arlene, no shirt. Barry Kleiman said, "Hey, cool."

They weren't sure when Donna, the dental hygienist, and her boyfriend came in; but they were there and after a while seemed like they'd always been there. Donna's boyfriend, Gordon, was working on his Ph.D. in something that had to do with clinical psychology and he spent a lot of time with Karen.

Every time Stick looked around, Arlene seemed to be watching him. That was the feeling he got. Like he was committed to her. She seemed to want to talk and finally steered him toward the balcony. But when they were out there, he spotted three of the junior executives down on the patio drinking beer and yelled at them to come up and be sociable.

The junior executives came in cautiously, like gunfighters in their tight Levi's, and slouched around a while; but pretty soon they were mixing it up with the others and Stick was glad he had invited them. It didn't hurt to be friendly. He told Arlene to be nice to them. The poor assholes were giving their lives to IBM and the Ford Motor Company and they deserved a little fun.

They were good-looking young guys with families in Bloomfield Hills, two of them named Ron and one named Scott. Ernest Stickley, Jr., could see them jogging through life in their thirty-dollar Adidases, never knowing it was hard. But he didn't hold it against them. He didn't give a shit, one way or the other, what they did.

One of the junior executive Rons went down to his apartment and brought back a Baggie of grass and a pack of yellow cigarette paper. He said it was Nicaragua gold, which impressed Karen and Jackie. Karen named a couple of other kinds she had smoked. Ron got a few joints going and pretty soon everybody was taking drags. Stick tried it. It was all right, but he didn't feel anything from the two drags and he didn't like the smell at all. Frank said, "Man, you know what we used to call this, this kind of scene? Reefer madness." Ron, rolling the joints, said you could call it anything you wanted, but why get mad? Stick asked him if they let you smoke grass out at the Ford Motor Company. Ron looked at him and said, "Ford Motor Company? I'm with Merrill fucking Lynch, man. How's your portfolio?"

Frank was cruising on scotch and reefer. He'd poke Stick and say, "Hey, are we having a party or we having a party?" Like he was celebrating something. Stick would say yeah, they were having a party.

Arlene was following Stick's instructions, being nice to the junior executive named Scott. She looked small and frail sitting next to him on the floor. Scott was studying the hammered silver pendant that hung between her breasts. Arlene told him it was a Navajo love symbol or else a sheep spirit, she'd forgotten which, and Scott was nodding, showing his interest in primitive art.

Stick went over to the eight-hundred-dollar hi-fi and put on a Billy Crash Craddock while he picked out a Loretta Lynn, an Olivia Newton-John, and a brand-new LP by Jerry Reed, the Alabama Wild Man.

Mary Kay said, "You like that music?"

He looked up to see her standing close to him with a smudged empty glass in her hand, blue eyes looking at him that he bet were blurry inside. Nice, clean-looking girl letting go. Why did that surprise him? Or what did clean-looking have to do with it?

Stick put the LPs down, took Mary Kay by the arm, and said some of the words along with Billy Crash Craddock, telling her perfect love is milk and honey, Captain Crunch, and you in the morning.

Stick said, "To answer your question, it's not one of my top ten favorites, but I guess I like it pretty well."

Mary Kay said, "I think it's a bunch of shit. Perfect love, milk and honey, and all that. It's a lot of bullshit."

A voice told Stick to get out, quick. If he hesitated, she'd tell him how she was the oldest girl in a family of ten kids and how she had to do all the housework and pay her own way through Blessed Sacrament because her dad drank and sat around the house in his undershirt reading paperbacks, and how she went to mass regularly, prayed for a vocation, worked hard, always did what she was told, and how she was a registered nurse with her own apartment, a savings account, and five doctors who wanted to get her in bed. If he didn't listen to the voice, he'd ask her, What's the problem? and she'd say, What's the *problem?* What good was all the hard work and being good? *This?* Then they'd get in a half-assed discussion about the meaning of life and maybe he'd get her in bed and maybe he wouldn't. Talk about bullshit. Mary Kay was just learning.

Stick said, "Listen, let me get back to you, okay? I think we need some ice."

He got out of that one, for the time being, but missed the scene with Frank and Sonny, which he'd have gotten a kick out of.

Sonny had had a glass of milk all evening; nothing else, no potato chips and dip or Pinconning cheese. She was out on the balcony with Barry Kleiman and one of the junior executives, the quieter of the two Rons. He and Barry were standing with their fingers in their tight pockets, posing with the poser, very cool and serious about it.

Frank had nothing personal against Sonny. He kind of liked her style, the fashion model put-on and all that. He liked it even though it pissed him off. Look at her. She was skinny, no tits to speak of; bony hips; long, thin, dumb-looking hair she liked to get out of her eyes with a lazy little toss of her head. No personality, no real person in there Frank could see. She stood around with her box pushed out like she was daring anybody to make a grab for it. That's what got him the most.

When Frank walked up to them Sonny handed him her empty milk glass.

"How about another one?" he said. "If you think you can handle it."

"No thanks." She didn't look at him. She turned to Barry and said, "I've got to get going," like it was his place and he was the host. "Have to be at the studio by seven tomorrow. I think we're doing some Oldsmobile stuff."

"Listen," Barry said, "what we were talking about. How can I help you? Tell me."

She gave him a little shrug. "I don't know. Talk to your agency."

"I mean it," Barry said, "you'd be terrific. I don't mean behind the counter, one of the broads there in the uniform. I mean a customer . . . high fashion, a very chic chick. You bite into this quarter-pounder. Your eyes are saying mmmmm, great. And here's the part. You get some mustard right here, on the corner of your mouth. Jesus, you'll have every guy watching TV wanting to lick it off."

Sonny was nodding, picturing it. "That's earthy," she said. "Or how about, just the tip of my tongue comes out?" She demonstrated. "In a tight close-up."

"Ter-*rif*ic."

"With kind of a down-under look." Sonny lowered her head slightly and gazed up with a sleepy, bedroom look in her eyes. "What do you think?"

Frank said, "You mind if I ask you a personal question?"

Sonny made it seem an effort to turn and look at him. "I think not, if it's all the same to you."

"What do you mean, all the same?"

"If you don't mind, then."

"But I mind. That's why I want to ask you something."

"All right, what is it?"

"You ever been laid?"

Sonny's composure held. She said, "Have you?"

"A few times."

"Good for you." She looked at Barry again. "You mind walking me down?"

"Do I *mind?* Does a bear—no, strike that." Barry held out his hand to Frank. "Man, it was fun, I mean it."

Frank said, "You going to try your luck?"

Barry frowned, a quick expression of pain. "Hey, come on, let's keep it light, okay?"

"He'll be right back," Sonny said. "Unless he's going home."

Frank looked at the quiet, good-looking Ron with his big shoulders and golf shirt.

"You following this?"

"Am I following it?"

"What's going on. The principle involved. The great truth. You know what it is?"

The quiet, good-looking Ron shook his head. "I guess you lost me."

"It's called," Frank said, "the myth of the pussy."

"Hey, what?" Barry was grinning. "Come *on.* The myth of the—what?"

"The myth of the pussy," Frank said again, solemnly. "It seems like a simple little harmless thing, doesn't it? Something every broad in the world has. But you know what? They sit back on their little myth and watch guys break up homes over it, go in debt, mess up their lives. It can make an intelligent man act like a little kid and do weird things . . . this idea, this myth that's been built up. Girls say, You're bigger and stronger than we are, buddy, but we got something you want, so watch it. They use the myth to get you to open doors and give them things and pick up checks. And some use it more than others." He looked at Sonny. "Some think it's really a big deal, and you know what? They don't even know what it's for."

"That's wild," Barry said, a little awed. "It really is."

"No, what it is," Frank said, "it's a fucking shame."

A little before eleven they drove over to Woodward to find a liquor store open. They needed scotch, vodka, and beer.

"And grapefruit juice," Stick said. Stick had got to the car first and he was driving. "All the broads I think're drinking Salty Dogs. You taste one?"

"They're having a good time," Frank said. "Everybody is. I think there's only one turd in the bunch and she left. No, maybe there's two, I don't know."

"Who do you mean?"

"That Irish broad, the nurse."

"She's all right. She's going through her first change."

"I'll check it out," Frank said. "That cute little housewife, I think she's another sleeper. Her husband's busy with Jackie, looking down her kitty outfit. Or I could steer him over to Karen. Yeah, I could do that. She'd keep him busy. Christ, her appetite, she'd eat him up."

Stick glanced over. "You wouldn't mind that?"

"What do you mean?"

"You wouldn't care if he got her in the sack?"

"Why should I?"

"I just wondered."

"Karen's all right," Frank said. "You know, nice build and all. Maybe a little bigger than she looks. I'd say she goes about one thirty-five. But she's kind of bossy. You see her there? Like she's the hostess, getting Jackie to pass the cheese and crackers. That's the way she is. In the sack she says, 'Okay, that's enough of that, now do this. Yeah, that's it right there. A little more. No, a little up. That's it, good. Okay, the other thing again. All right, let's try this.' It's like doing it by the fucking numbers." Frank put his head back on the seat cushion, relaxed, comfortably high. "It's something," he said. "All that scratch in one place. You believe it?"

"You don't say that anymore," Stick said. "Now you say, 'Well, here we are.' "

"That's right. Well, here we are. And you say, 'You sure?' Say it."

"You sure?"

"You bet your ass I'm sure," Frank said. "That's a quiz show on TV. It isn't really, but those dumb broads, they believe anything you tell them. Hey, am I sure? You better believe it I'm sure, because we got it fucking knocked and it's going to get even better. I don't know what happened to Marlys. I saw her this afternoon, I told her stop by, she wasn't doing anything. What's tomorrow?"

"Sunday."

"All right we'll wait'll Monday, we'll go down there, I'll show you around. It's not worked out yet, you understand, but

I want you, I think you ought to start to get the feel of the place."

"I've been to Hudson's, Frank. Lots of times."

"Upstairs, where the offices are?"

"I think so."

"End of the day," Frank said, "they leave fifty bucks in the cash registers, everything else goes upstairs."

Stick was a little high but alert, moving along in the night traffic on North Woodward, watching for a liquor store that was still open. He didn't want to get in an argument with Frank or even a discussion with him now. It would be pointless. Frank would start yelling and wouldn't remember anything.

Stick said, "You look on your side."

He saw it then, in the next block across the street, the neon sign and the lights inside, and felt himself relax again.

"There's a place, Frank. It's still open."

They parked in front. Going in, Frank said, "What do we need? J&B, vodka?"

"Grapefruit juice," Stick said. "I don't think they'll have it. Maybe."

He asked the clerk behind the counter, a neat little gray-haired man with rimless glasses, and the clerk said, "Yes sir, right over there. All your juices."

Stick got four big cans and brought them to the counter. Frank was ordering the liquor. Stick went over to the cooler and pulled out a case of Stroh's, the brand the young executives were drinking. Walking back to the counter with it, where the clerk was waiting, he saw Frank up by the front of the store.

"We got everything?"

"I'll be right back," Frank said. He went out the door.

There were three bottles of J&B and three top-priced Smirnoff on the counter. The clerk was putting them one at a time into an empty liquor case.

"That be it?" the clerk said.

"I guess a couple bottles of tonic," Stick said. He got potato chips and Fritos from a rack, a can of mixed nuts. The clerk was coming back with the tonic. He stopped, his eyes wide open behind the rimless glasses. Stick looked around.

Frank was coming toward the counter with a grin on his face, his Colt Python in one hand and Stick's Smith & Wesson in the other.

"What the fuck," Frank said. "Right?"

Stick almost said his name. It was right there—*Frank, you dumb shit.*

But they were into it already and it wasn't something you could call off and say, "Oops, just a minute, let's start over." Or tell the guy you were just kidding.

No, he had to take the poor scared-shitless clerk into the back room and tie him up with masking tape and paste a strip of it over his mouth, while Frank, the dumb shit, was out there cleaning the cash register. Stick didn't say a word to the clerk. He laid him on the floor and patted his shoulder, twice, telling the guy with the touch to be calm and not to move.

He still didn't say anything out in the store again. He picked up the cardboard case and took it to the car, got in and waited while Frank brought out a case of scotch and a case of Jack Daniel's and put them on the back seat.

Leaning in he said, "You think while we're at it we should grab some more beer?"

Stick, waiting behind the wheel, said, "Get in the fucking car."

When Frank's door slammed, Stick took his time pulling away from the curb and working the T-bird into the stream of traffic, his eyes going to the mirror to watch the headlights coming up behind them.

"I'd say we got five, six hundred," Frank said. "You missed the wad in the guy's pocket. I got it, I went back there for the cases. Let's see, plus a couple hundred worth of booze, just like that. Not bad for a quick trip to the store, huh?"

Stick didn't answer.

"You're not going to talk to me now?" Frank said. "Is that my punishment? For Christ sake, you saw the guy, the place is empty. You can't pass up something like that, it's too good."

"We're in a car," Stick said, "in your name. The registration, the plates."

"All right—this one time, it's an exception. There it is, you got to make up your mind that instant. So it's done and nobody saw us."

"How do you know?"

"Because I didn't see anybody. You got to see somebody for them to see you."

"Somebody could've been coming in," Stick said. "They see Twogun in there, for Christ sake, and they get out. But the car's sitting there, right? And they could've gotten the number."

"All right—we get home, we report it stolen."

"Frank, a dozen witnesses up there, they know we went out. The guy in the store, it'd take him one second to pick us out of a lineup."

"Hey, Ernest," Frank said, "don't be so fucking earnest, all right? It was a spur-of-the-moment thing. It's over, it's done. You want to live by the book all the time, is that it?"

"You wrote the book, ten rules for success and happiness," Stick said. "I didn't."

Neither of them said anything else until they reached the apartment building and Stick turned into the private parking area.

"There's a spot, right by the door."

"I already saw it," Stick said. He eased the T-bird into the space, turned off the ignition and the headlights.

Frank opened his door and paused. "You know something?"

Stick waited. "What?"

"I been thinking. I bet we end up with Karen and Jackie," Frank said. "I mean if Marlys doesn't show."

"That's what you been thinking, huh?"

"Yeah. Which one you want?"

17

There weren't as many people, though it was still smoky and smelled of incense and the noise level was high. Somebody had taken off Loretta Lynn and put on one of Frank's Montavanis. The quiet, good-looking Ron had passed out on Stick's bed, smelling like he'd thrown up. Stick came out to the bar and looked around as he made a drink.

Arlene wasn't there. Or the junior executive who'd been admiring her jewelry.

Frank came over to make a drink. "The place's thinning out. We'll have to get it going again."

Stick didn't say anything. He wasn't angry, he was tired. He wasn't upset about the guy passed out on his bed, he wanted to go sit down someplace where it was quiet. He thought of Arlene again. He'd like to get with her and fool around a little. Except she wasn't here.

"I don't think Marlys's coming," Frank said. "We better get a couple before they're all taken." He looked around the room, his gaze going past Mary Kay on the sofa. "I don't know, it's getting pretty thin."

He knew Sonny had left. He didn't see Donna or Arlene. Jackie was smashed. Karen—maybe.

Gordon, Donna's boyfriend, came over with two empty glasses.

"Where's Donna," Frank asked him, "in the can?"

"She left," Gordon said. "I told her I'd be down in a little while. It's my Saturday, but I'm having a very interesting conversation with Karen."

"It's your Saturday?"

"Every other Saturday I spend the night with Donna," Gordon said.

"What if you felt like doing it on a Tuesday night?"

Gordon was intently measuring an ounce and a half of vodka into each glass. He used the stainless-steel shot glass and had been measuring ounces and a half for over four hours.

"Sometimes Tuesday night," Gordon said, "if there's a special reason. See, Donna doesn't work on Wednesday."

"She rations it, huh?" Frank said. "She afraid she's going to run out?"

"No, she's got an idea about not overdoing anything. See, Donna's very parental. Usually she's into her critical parent. She uses *should* a lot. You *should* do this, you *shouldn't* do that. Then on Saturday, every other Saturday, she allows herself to get into her nurturing parent. Now Karen"—Gordon looked over to where she was sitting on the floor against a pile of orange and yellow pillows, still in her bikini—"Karen is very visceral. She feels and acts instinctively and has quite a lot of natural child in her."

"You're going to find out," Frank said, "she's got a lot of mama in her, too."

Gordon held the can of grapefruit juice poised over the glasses. He seemed interested and a little surprised.

"Are you into transactional analysis?"

"Uh-unh," Frank said, "but I've been into Karen." He looked around to get Stick's reaction. Stick wasn't there.

* * *

There were two Arlenes looking at him, the one holding the door partly open, wearing a man's white shirt over her bikini, and a life-size cutout of her on the other side of the room, the one Arlene pouting, the other smiling in her silver Hi-Performance Cams outfit and white boots.

Arlene said, "I don't know if I want to talk to you. I don't see you all week, you don't call—"

"I came by here, twice, you weren't home," Stick said.

"You don't pay any attention to me, you're busy talking to the other girls, putting your arms around them."

"How about you and the guy on the floor?"

"You told me to be nice to him."

"Is he here?"

"He got sick."

"Arlene," Stick said, "I haven't been feeling too good myself all week. I went to see a doctor, he checked me over, gave me a prescription—"

Arlene was showing a little concern. "What's wrong with you?"

"I went to the drugstore, gave the prescription to the pharmacist?"

"Yeah?"

"He said, 'You want this filled?' I said, 'No, it's a holdup note in Latin, you dumb shit.' "

She laughed and he was in.

Sitting down next to Mary Kay, alone on the sofa, Frank said, "Honey, you cook any good?"

Mary Kay looked at him with filmy eyes.

"Why?"

"I'm making conversation. You tell me what you like and I'll tell you what I like. Move over a little." He pulled an LP out from under him and sailed it at the hi-fi.

"If you want to talk, why don't you talk about something real," Mary Kay said.

"Okay. How do you like that Montavani? Nice, uh?"

"It sounds like cafeteria music."

"What do you like, then?"

"Nothing you've got, I looked. Country-western and Montavani."

"What're you," Frank said, "you get a little high, you like to argue?"

"I'm not arguing, I'm telling you what I don't like."

"You're a nurse, RN. I thought you were very sympathetic, got along with people, like to make them happy and all."

"Where'd you hear that?"

"Really," Frank said quietly. "I bet you are sympathetic . . . kind. I can see it in your eyes, you care about people."

"I tried," Mary Kay said. "I used to knock myself out being nice. And you know what you get? You get stepped on. If you're nice to people, they're nice to you? That's a lot of crap. They use you, give you the worst jobs. 'Sullivan, take care of One-oh-four—' "

"Who's Sullivan?"

"I'm Sullivan. 'Right away, Sullivan. One-oh-four's painting his wall with shit again.' That's what I get all night, things like that."

"This person," Frank said, "actually paints with it?"

"Smears it on the wall. Sometimes he eats it."

"Jesus," Frank said. He took the smudged glass from her hand. "Here, let me freshen you up." He fixed both of them a drink—Mary Kay's in a clean glass—came back and sat down again, close to her.

"You forgot the salt."

"You shouldn't use salt. It's not good for you." Frank laid his arm along the back of the couch and let his hand fall lightly on Mary Kay's shoulder.

"Listen, let me tell you something," he said, using his quiet tone again. "People who care, people who feel, are nice to one another. They make each other happy."

"I heard that," Mary Kay said. "All my life I heard it. And if you don't mind my saying, or whether you mind or not—"

"Wait, don't say it, Mary Kay." He turned her face gently and stared at her with his nice-guy expression. "All right?" Her lips were parted; there was a fresh pimple scar at the corner of her mouth. "You have to trust people, Mary Kay. No matter what kind of deals you've been handed, you have to go on trusting and believing."

"In what?"

"In yourself, in your own right to . . . have a good time and enjoy life. People need people." Frank paused, trying to think of the words to the song. "People who need people . . . lonely people needing people—" He was improvising now. "You know what I mean? They share their loneliness and find something."

"I get so tired of it," Mary Kay said.

"I know," Frank said. He was pretty tired himself, but he moved in closer. "I know."

"Why do I have to smile all the time and be nice when I don't feel like it?"

"You don't, honey. You should do what you feel like doing."

She snuggled against him, closing her eyes. "God, I get tired. The same thing all the time. Sometimes my face aches from smiling when I don't even want to."

"Listen, Mary Kay, how'd you like to stretch out and get comfortable?"

"Hmmm?"

"Go to your place, where it's quiet. What do you think?"

"I don't know if I could make it down the stairs, I'm so tired."

"Well, I guess I could help you," Frank said.

Mary Kay sighed. "You're a nice person, you know that?"

"I try to be," Frank said.

There was one picture Stick especially liked, Arlene kneeling with her back arched, winking as she kissed the knob of a Hi-Performance Four-Speed Shifter. There were shots of Arlene at the Nationals and at hot-rod shows and conventions. Arlene said the SEMA show was her favorite. Stick said he guessed it would be. He didn't ask her what See-Ma meant. He fixed them a couple more drinks and brought them over to the couch where Arlene was holding open the big album and got to see pictures of her posing with "Big Daddy" Don Garlits, Tom "Mongoose" McEwan, and Don "The Snake" Prudhomme.

She pointed them out and named them. She said she also had their autographs on a pair of her panties as a joke, if he wanted to see them. Stick said he'd look at anything she showed him.

All right, then.

The second album she got out wasn't as big as the first one and there weren't any shots of Hi-Performance machinery in it or silver outfits or white boots, either. It was Arlene in her birthday suit, skinny hips, perky boobs, and all, like a little girl posing for exotica. Stick said they were really cute pictures of her and found out her friend was a camera nut and owned three Nikons that cost about a thousand dollars each.

He wondered if she showed him the nude pictures on purpose. Whether she did or not they were working.

When she went in the bathroom to take a leak—that's what she said, "Be right back, I got to take a leak"—Stick picked up the two drinks and headed for the bedroom. He heard the toilet flush and the door open and then Arlene's voice out in the other room.

"Hey, where are you?"

He let her find him, lying on the bed in his striped shorts with the two drinks on the night table. Arlene said, "I suppose you want me to take my rings off."

The next thing she said was, "You always perspire a little, don't you?"

"Not always," Stick said. "Sometimes I do, I don't know why. It doesn't have anything to do with, you know, the enjoyment of it."

"I wondered."

Then neither of them said anything for a little while, lying next to each other in the darkness, touching but not holding. The light from the hall reached the bed, and if he turned his head he could see their outline, in shadow, on the wall close by. He liked her. He liked the way she moved, skinny little thing. She was funny. And she was smarter than she sounded. She sounded goofy, but it was just that she let it come out and didn't try to act or be someone else. He liked her a lot.

Arlene said, "I wondered, it made me think of it, something else."

"What?"

"If you were sweating that time—in the bar."

"What bar?"

"In Hazel Park."

"I don't remember any bar—" He stopped.

"The one a couple of blocks from the Hazel Park track."

Stick sat up. He knocked a glass off the night table getting the light on. She was looking up at him, eyes wide open, her hands clutching the sheet to her tightly.

"Oh, God, I shouldn't have said anything, should I?"

"Wait a minute, I'm not sure what you're talking about. Some bar I was supposed to've been at? You thought you saw me?"

"I saw you," Arlene said. "You and Frank, you took the money from him, I thought, God, they're cops. And then you locked us in the room."

"You were at the bar?"

"I had on this scarf, over my hair? You looked right at me once, I thought sure, I thought, Oh, God, but I guess you were busy, you looked right at me but didn't see me. I didn't know whether to say anything or not. Then in the room"—Arlene started to smile and she giggled—"it was really funny, everybody was opening bottles and drinking and the woman was trying to stop them. She kept hitting the poor guy—"

"Who were you with?"

"Just my friend."

"Arlene," Stick said, as gently as he could, "did you tell him you knew us?"

The telephone rang in the living room.

She frowned. "Who's that? I know he's out of town." She was up, climbing over him—

"Arlene—let it ring."

—running naked out of the room.

"Arlene—"

He listened and heard her saying, "Really? But isn't it kinda late? . . . No, but it's pretty short notice."

She'd been in the bar, seen the whole thing, and admitted it to him. Christ almighty.

"No, no, I didn't mean *that.* Hon, you know I'd love to

come. . . . Yeah, okay. . . . God, I'll have to move. . . . Okay, 'bye."

Arlene came back in the room, hurrying, not looking at Stick.

"I'm going to Chicago. Calls up practically in the middle of the night—gets the big urge, I *have* to come. He's sending the company plane over."

"Arlene," Stick said, "hold still a minute, okay?" He watched her come out of the closet with a suitcase and clothes over her arm.

"He's at the APAA convention. God, I didn't know it was the APAA. Who's he had in the booth? Some girl, must be from Chicago. But what would she wear?"

"Arlene, did you tell him about me and Frank, that you knew us?"

She looked at him briefly. "You got to get out of here, I'm being picked up. Why didn't he take me when he went? The prick. No, I shouldn't say that, he's been very nice to me."

"I'll drive you," Stick said. "We can talk in the car."

She was in the closet again, getting a green pantsuit and the shiny silver costume. "One of his hot-rodders is on the way over. God, the way they drive. He doesn't believe anybody should get to the airport more than ten minutes early. It means they don't have anything to do."

"Arlene, did you tell him our names?"

"Why would I do that?"

"Say yes or no, will you?"

"No, of course not."

He felt a little relief, just a little. It was funny, in a way, watching her run around the room naked, taking things out of the dresser and throwing them in the suitcase.

"Did you tell anybody else?"

She was out of the room again.

"Like the police!"

He heard the bathroom door close and lock and the water turned on. Stick put on his pants and shoes. He couldn't believe it. Carrying his shirt he went into the hall and stood close to the bathroom door.

"Arlene?"

"Hon, I can't talk now, I'm doing my eyes."

"You didn't tell anybody else?"

"God, I almost forgot. Look in the front closet, see if there's something hanging there, from the cleaner's."

Stick hesitated, then went into the living room, putting his shirt on.

The front doorbell rang.

Almost immediately the bathroom door opened.

"Get in the bedroom."

Her eyes, vividly lined and framed in silver-green, were wide open. She ran in and put on the green pantsuit before running back out to open the door. Stick waited.

He heard her say, "Larry, hi, you're a doll." She laughed at something Larry said. "No, no, get in the car, I'll be right out."

Arlene came into the bedroom with a dry cleaner's plastic bag, finished packing in less than half a minute, and picked up the suitcase.

"Arlene—"

"I'll talk to you when I get back," Arlene said and rolled her eyes at him. "God."

The front door closed and there was silence. Stick made himself a drink, Canadian Club, because her friend didn't have bourbon. He drank it and smoked a cigarette and went back to Arlene's bed for the night.

18

"I put a stack of plastic glasses on the bar," Frank said, "they use the good ones, have to go and *find* them so they can put their cigarettes out in the glasses—plastic ones're sitting right there."

Stick passed him, going out to the kitchen with a couple of ashtrays.

"I'm surprised you got anything in there at all," Frank said and picked up a glass. "Look at the cigarette butts. Potato chips all over, ground in the carpet, drinks spilled—like they're raised in a fucking barn."

Stick came out of the kitchen. He felt like moving, doing something, and kept picturing Arlene running around naked, packing the suitcase.

"Next morning always looks depressing," Stick said. "Especially with the sun out." He could remember hangovers in the Florida sun. He went through the open doors to the balcony and began gathering empty beer cans. "Nobody's down at the pool yet."

"And they aren't at church," Frank said. "Where you suppose all the partygoers are?"

"Throwing up," Stick said. "Hugging their toilets."

"You get the guy out of your bed all right?"

"He opened his eyes, didn't know where he was."

"You didn't come back, huh?"

"This morning," Stick said, "about half past seven." He didn't want to mention Arlene just yet—Arlene seeing them in the bar—so he said, "I noticed you weren't home."

"You want to know where I was?"

"With the nurse," Stick said. "I figured you were both about due."

He came in and dropped beer cans into an open grocery bag on the floor. "She any good?"

"The quiet ones," Frank said. He was resting, taking a break with a beer and a cigarette. "You know what they say about the quiet ones."

"I know what they say," Stick said, "I just don't know as it's true."

"Take my word, buddy."

"You promise to marry her?"

"We're engaged," Frank said. "I notice you went out, you must've made some arrangements."

Stick brought in more beer cans from the balcony. He didn't say anything. He let Frank believe whatever he wanted.

"Well, let's see," Frank said. "Karen was with the talker. Jackie was smashed. If you got her kitty outfit off, you might as well've put her jammy-jams on, she was through for the evening, and I can't see you doing a number on some broad's out practically cold, at least I hope you wouldn't. Arlene was already gone when we got back—was it Arlene?"

"You got another cigarette?"

"Last one. Look on my dresser. It must've been Karen, then. She got rid of the talker and you met her at her place."

Stick went into his bedroom; he might as well get his own. He was thinking maybe he should wait until Arlene got back and talk to her again. He didn't know what she really thought about it. Say she didn't tell her friend who they were, fine; but what did she think about it, seeing two guys she knew holding up a bar? She was nutty. It was hard to imagine what she might think. She might even think it was cute.

He could hear Frank in the living room.

"How you like doing it by the numbers? Now the other. Do the thing with the boobs. That Karen—she's too much. Now the one where we stand on our heads."

Stick got a pack of cigarettes from his dresser.

Tell him, he was thinking. You got to tell him sometime.

He opened the pack going out to the front room.

"She too much?"

"I wasn't with Karen," Stick said. "Arlene."

Frank raised his eyebrows, a little surprised. "Arlene—yeah? Not much there but I can see it could be very active, a good workout. Right?"

"She's a nice girl," Stick said.

"Almost all of them are," Frank said. "But is she any good?"

"What're you asking me something like that for?"

"You just asked me the same thing, for Christ sake."

"Okay, let's drop it," Stick said, "get the place cleaned up."

"You hear that? Honest to God," Frank said, "the way you think. You don't sound like a broad, but—I don't know—it's like you think like one, with a broad's mentality. I don't mean that as an insult—"

"You don't, huh?"

"No, it's just you've got a different way of looking at things."

"Wait'll I get a beer," Stick said. "We can sit down and argue for a change."

"We're supposed to be at Sportree's, four o'clock," Frank said.

That stopped it. Stick looked at Frank sitting there with his beer, Frank staring at him, waiting, sort of a little challenge in his expression.

Stick thought, Well, screw him. And then he thought, No, why fight about it?

He said, "What's that, the cocktail hour? Drinks are half price?"

"He's arranged a meeting, a special presentation," Frank said, "I think you're going to be quite interested in."

"Shop at Hudson's and be happy," Stick said. "Am I warm?"

"That's all you are," Frank said. "Shop at Hudson's and make enough to be happy for a year is the way it goes. It's all worked out. He's going to show you how we knock down the biggest department store in town and find happiness. Show you how it's no more trouble than a supermarket."

"Nothing to it, huh?"

"Not if you know what you're doing."

Stick said to himself, I'm not going to get pissed off. I'm not going to get in a dumb argument. I'm not going to say anything, no, nothing at all about Arlene.

He said to Frank, "Okay, let's go, then."

"One more thing," Frank said. "They're all going to be black. At least I think they are. Now, it's okay to call a Negro a Negro. Like with Jewish girls, they know what they are. But don't refer to them as niggers, okay?"

Fuck you, Stick said to himself. He said to Frank, "I'll try not to."

19

They were in Sportree's apartment, upstairs over the bar, and Frank was telling them how Stick had shot the two muggers in the Northland parking lot.

Stick was uncomfortable, he didn't like it at all. Three colored guys and a colored girl listening to Frank describe how he'd killed two other colored guys, not telling it the way it actually happened but making him sound like a gunman: The two guys come up and try to take the bag, my partner here doesn't say a word, fuck no, pulls out his piece, .38 chief's speccial, and blows the two guys away.

Blows them away—Christ, he shot one of them in the back.

Sportree would nod as he listened and sometimes smile, but you couldn't tell what he was thinking. Or sometimes what any of them were thinking. There was Sportree in some kind of funny loose open shirt and trading beads. Marlys cool in a bare midriff, showing a dark little navel. And the two guys Sportree had brought in for the job.

Leon Woody, with a beard and moustache, looked like an Arab. He sat quietly, with one leg crossed over the other. He'd smile a little with a gentle gaze that held as long as he wanted it to. Leon Woody reminded Stick of Sportree. There was something African, mysterious, about them. Nothing was going to hurry or surprise them.

The other one, Carmen Billy Ruiz, was Puerto Rican. His eyelids were heavy with scar tissue and his mouth looked puffy and sore drawing on his Jamaican tailor-made. A long time ago he had been a welterweight with a seventeen-and-seventeen record, then a sparring partner for Chico Vejar, then for Chuck Davey after Davey whipped Vejar. In 1955, in Detroit, he shot and killed a store clerk during a holdup and spent the next seventeen years in Jackson. (Carmen Billy Ruiz said *diez-y-siete* was a bad fucking number; don't mention it in front of him.) He resented the fact Stick had killed two men and said through a smoke cloud, while Frank was telling the story, "What is this shit? He put away a couple of kids." Leon Woody and Sportree looked at each other—Stick noticed this—and Leon Woody said, "Billy, be nice and let the man finish. Then you can tell how many you put away."

Stick was glad, God, he was glad he wasn't going to have any part of this. They could say anything they wanted. He'd listen and nod and seem to go along, and when they were through, that was it. He didn't know these guys or owe them a thing. Be nice, like the man said, and play along.

He nodded yes, he'd have another bourbon, yes please, when Marlys picked up his glass. Marlys was doing the drinks and constructing big Jamaican cigarettes with four pieces of paper each for Billy Ruiz and anybody who wanted one. The redheaded black girl who played the piano wasn't around. Unless she was in the bedroom. Or Sportree could've gotten rid of her for the meeting.

There wasn't any doubt Sportree was in charge. He sat on the couch with Marlys next to him, looking over his shoulder, and sheets of drawing paper on the coffee table that showed the floor plan of several different sections of Hudson's downtown store—including the administrative offices, with dotted lines leading to exits—and a plan of the exterior with adjacent streets indicated.

"We start with the outside," Sportree said and looked at Stick. "You—you here on Farmer Street on the back side of the building, in the bar, right here. You see the Brink's truck turn in the alley that run through the building. You know what I'm saying?"

"I know the alley you mean," Stick said. "It's like a tunnel."

"That's right," Sportree said. "They come in off Farmer, alley bends in there, they pick up the load and come out on the south side the building. Before that, soon as you see it coming, you make the call."

"What's the number?"

"You get the number when I'm through."

Sportree looked at Frank. "You by the telephone outside the men's room, north end of the toy department, fourteenth floor. You been there to see it?"

Frank nodded.

Sportree's gaze moved to Leon Woody. "You watching Frank. You got the doll box, huh, in the Hudson bag."

"Little Curly Laurie Walker's box," Leon Woody said.

Sportree began to smile and shook his head. "Come on, shit—Curly Laurie Walker. That her name?"

"Little redhead girl, three foot tall, she do everything but bleed," Leon Woody said. "Billy try to jump her. I give her to my little girl so she be safe."

"What was that?" Billy Ruiz said. "What'd you say?"

Marlys was laughing and slapped her leg. "I can see him doing it, stoned on his herb."

Billy Ruiz was frowning, puzzled. "See what?"

"Man, let's pay attention," Sportree said. "Okay? You got one minute. Bang on the door the men's room, Billy comes out in his uniform." He looked at Ruiz. "We get that tomorrow, bus driver suit, I know where we can get one. With the holster it be good enough, get you in the office. Okay, so the three of you take the stairs, here, by the exit sign. You go up to the office floor."

"How long's it take them, the Brink's guys?" Frank asked.

"About five minutes," Sportree said. "It varies."

Marlys looked up from the drawings. "You know the man down at the door, he's like a porter? He calls up the office when they come, then we know to expect them in a few minutes. He doesn't call and some dudes walk in with uniforms on, we know they not from Brink's."

"So we get to the office just before the Brink's guys," Frank said, "giving us, say, four minutes."

"Say three," Sportree said, "to get in and get out. They see Billy in the bus driver suit and the gun, they open the door. You two go in behind him, put the people on the floor, take the sacks, put them in the doll box, and get the fuck out, down the stairs to the toy department. You go in the stock room and put the box on the shelf where all the curly what's-her-name little jive-ass doll boxes are, in the back. The box is already marked." He looked at Leon Woody. "You been in there?"

"Yesterday."

"And they still got enough little curly-ass doll boxes?"

"Whole shelf full. I put it there and see Billy get out of his bus suit."

"All right," Sportree said, "about that time the bell's going to ring and they'll be security people all over the store, at every door and exit. The police, First Precinct, could be there before you get to the ground floor, and then it's time to be cool. First thing, dump your pieces in a trash bin, someplace like that. Then split up and circulate. They want to search you going out, that's fine, you just a dumb nigger, you don't know what the fuck is going on at *all.* They let you out, you go home. Two days later, this man here"—he looked at Stick—"goes up to the stock room and gets the doll box with the mark on it. He goes because nobody's seen him before, clean-looking white gentleman. Tell me you see something wrong." He waited.

Frank and Leon shook their heads.

Billy Ruiz said, "How much we going to get?"

"No way of knowing," Sportree said. "I told you, I give you a guarantee, five K off the top. You said beautiful. You want something else now?"

"I want to be with him, carry it out," Billy Ruiz said. "I don't want somebody giving me some shit later—we didn't do so well, here's a hunnert bills. Fuck that shit, man, right now."

Stick saw Sportree and Leon Woody look at each other again. "Hey, we trust each other," Sportree said to Billy Ruiz. "Nobody going to cheat nobody. You hear Frank saying anything? Leon? No, we all in this."

"This guy, he picking up the money, I don't even know him," Billy Ruiz said.

"He don't know you, either." Sportree looked over at Stick and back to Billy Ruiz. "You saying you want to pick it up, Billy? You don't trust nobody?"

"I go with him," Billy Ruiz said.

Stick saw the exchange between Sportree and Leon Woody again, their gaze meeting, each one knowing something.

"All right, Billy," Sportree said. "You go with him."

After that they sat around a little while. Sportree went out to the kitchen for something and Frank followed him. Marlys went over to the hi-fi and picked up a record sleeve. Stick looked over at Leon Woody sitting there quietly with his legs crossed. There was something he wanted to ask him. It wasn't important, but if he got the chance, if the guy happened to look over.

Billy Ruiz said to Marlys, "Hey, Mamma, play some of that Al-ton for me, okay?"

Marlys, reading the record sleeve, had her back to them. "You want some Alton Ellis and his Caribbean shit? I'll give you some Stevie," Marlys said. "Be grateful."

"He's all right, his soul," Billy Ruiz said. "It's very close."

"Close about a thousand miles," Marlys said. "Stevie can fake that reggae boogie shit better than Alton can do it straight."

Leon Woody was smiling, listening to them. Stick didn't know what they were talking about. He waited until the music came on. Leon Woody looked over at him, maybe to see what he thought of it.

"You have a little girl?" Stick said.

"Yeah, little eight-year-old. She small, not much bigger than the doll." Leon Woody smiled faintly. "Sportree has trouble with that name, don't he?"

"I got a little girl seven," Stick said. "She's going to be in the second grade next month."

"Is that right? Yeah, they cute that age, aren't they?"

Stick said yeah, they sure were. After that, he couldn't think of anything to say.

It was getting dark when they left. Frank drove. He was up, excited about what they were going to do. He tried to appear calm, but it showed in the way he took off from lights and wheeled the T-bird through traffic.

Stick said, "That Carmen Billy Ruiz—where'd he get a name like that?"

"He's Puerto Rican," Frank said. "He was a fighter once. Fought Chuck Davey—you remember him?"

Stick said, "What I meant to say—where'd they get him, for Christ sake. He could get you in trouble, not even trying."

Frank said, "Don't worry about it. Sportree's going to handle him."

"Is that what he's going to do?" Stick said, "because I'll tell you something, I don't see him doing anything else."

"He's been going down there—he's the one put the whole thing together." Frank looked over at Stick. "Now that you've seen it, what do you think?"

"What do I *think?* I think it looks like amateur night."

"Come on—"

"Come on where? You got a guy with a little girl used to steal TV sets. You got a crazy Puerto Rican living on dope and a guy runs a bar telling you what to do. A bus driver's suit—you imagine that crazy fucking guy walking in in a bus driver's suit? Is he going to have one of those change things on him?"

"He knows what he's doing," Frank said, "Sportree. Listen, that's why I took it to him. Everything he gets into, it goes. He doesn't touch something he doesn't make out."

Stick said, "What's he touching? He's sitting home watching the fucking ball game while you clowns are running around the store with a doll box. I thought you said it was your idea."

"It was, the basic idea, yeah, when I find out Marlys's working in the office. But it was Sportree worked it out. You got any doubts or questions, talk to him about it."

"I'm talking to *you.* I don't even know the guy, what do I want to talk to him for, like I work for him now or something? We got a nice thing going, two grand a week, we can't even spend it all, you want to go hold up a department store."

"You know for how much?"

"He said you didn't know."

"He told Billy we didn't know. We're talking about a minimum, I mean *minimum,* a hundred grand."

"You're crazy," Stick said. "It's all charge accounts there, and checks."

"Uh-unh, not the downtown store. Half the people go there are colored. You think they all got charge accounts?"

"I don't know—" Stick said.

"I know you don't. Listen, fourteen floors of cash registers, every floor the size of a city block. People come in, buy all kinds of things, some on charge, some pay with a check, and a bunch of them, man, a bunch of them, have to pay strictly cash, because that's all they've got."

"Anybody ever do it before?"

"Not the whole thing," Frank said, "that any of us can remember. Ten years ago, maybe more than that, a guy got twelve hundred from a cashier on the mezzanine. All small stuff."

"Small stuff like what we've been doing," Stick said, "and getting away with. Now all of a sudden you want to do the whole fucking thing at once."

"I'll talk to you when you calm down," Frank said. "It's staring you in the face and you can't even see it."

"Relax, huh?"

"Right. Relax and think about it. We walk in—it's waiting there in little gray sacks—and pick it up. Christ, you're outside, what're you worried about?"

"I'm outside—till I go in with that crazy Puerto Rican."

"I told you, what're you worried about him for? I talked to Sportree, he said, 'Don't worry about Billy.' "

"I'm not worried, because I'm not going to have anything to do with it," Stick said. "Nothing."

20

Stick lined up four pay phones on Farmer Street, behind the J. L. Hudson Company.

He did this after he'd given in and told Frank okay, but this was the last one, and found out this part of the plan hadn't been thought out at all. What if he went in the bar to call and some guy was using the phone? What if he went in the doughnut shop or the drugstore, the same thing? What if all of a sudden the Brink's truck comes and everybody around there decided to make phone calls? Sportree hadn't planned it at all. He'd gone through the motions. If they made it, fine; if they didn't, well, it wasn't his ass, he wasn't out a thing.

Stick didn't like relying on other people he didn't even know.

He didn't like Arlene knowing about them—Christ, just to add a little more to it—and not knowing where Arlene was and what she was thinking. She hadn't been home all week and he hadn't told Frank about her yet.

He told himself he was dumb. He should've stayed out of this, not learned anything about it. If he wasn't afraid of Frank and he didn't owe him anything, then why was he doing it?

Maybe he felt he did owe him something. Frank could've put him in jail, but he didn't. Shit no, Frank needed him.

He should've left for Florida. Right after shooting the two black guys, the next morning, he should've left and not said a word to Frank.

Now he was into something with three more black guys. Christ, everybody on the street, half the people anyway, seemed to be black. He wondered where everybody was going—if they had someplace to go. Or if they were out of work and just walking around downtown. It was a nice day, mid-seventies, the sky fairly clear. Maybe because some auto plants were shut down. What do you want, a job or a clear sky? He looked across at Hudson's—old, dark-red building filling the block and rising up fifteen floors, then narrowing into a tower that went up another five stories. He wondered where they kept the flag they displayed across the front of the building on some of the U.S. holidays, the biggest American flag ever made.

The Brink's truck was coming south on Farmer, the way Sportree had said it would. Stick went inside the bar on the corner. Nobody was using the phone. He stepped into the booth and made the call.

When the phone rang, Frank turned from the wall, ripped off the sheet of paper that said OUT OF ORDER, and picked up the receiver.

"Toy department."

That was all he said. A moment later he hung up and nodded as he turned.

Leon Woody was playing with a game called Mousetrap, watching the little metal ball rolling through a Rube Goldberg contraption that set off a chain reaction of things hitting things that finally dropped a plastic net over the mouse. Leon Woody left the counter, carrying a big greenish Hudson's shopping bag with a doll box inside, and walked down the main aisle to the Men's Room.

Frank watched him go inside. He started down the aisle.

Leon Woody came out of the Men's, followed by Carmen Billy Ruiz in the Air Force–blue bus driver's suit and peaked cap. Frank was ten feet behind them when they went through the door beneath the exit sign.

The stairway took one turn to the fifteenth floor. None of them said anything; the sound of their steps filled the stairwell. Leon Woody opened the door and stepped back to let Billy Ruiz go ahead of him. Billy hesitated.

Leon Woody said, "Take out the piece, hold it flat against your leg, you dig? Go past the elevators, down on the right side. That's this hand here. You see the door, credit department. Don't say nothing. Nod your head, they say anything to you."

Frank, waiting on the stairs, watched Billy Ruiz take out the gun he had given him, Stick's .38 chief's special. He could feel his own, the big Python, in the pocket of his safari jacket. The store was air-conditioned, but it was hot in the stairwell. Leon Woody glanced back at him and went through the door.

Frank hurried to catch it before it closed—like he didn't want to be left behind. He went out on the fifteenth floor, cutting diagonally across the main aisle, past the bank of elevators. Billy Ruiz was thirty feet ahead, taking his time. Leon Woody paused by the optical department to look at glasses frames. Frank came up next to him.

"What's he doing?"

"He's all right," Leon Woody said. "Be cool."

They moved on, past theatrical display boards and ticket windows, past the travel service and portrait studio. There were no customers anywhere. Billy Ruiz turned into the credit department. They were fifteen feet behind him now. A face appeared at a teller's window. The door next to the window opened. Billy Ruiz went through. Leon Woody sprinted the last few yards and caught the door. Frank went in behind him, pulling the Colt Python.

He heard Billy Ruiz say, "Turn around, everybody. I mean *everybody,* get down on the floor."

Frank saw their faces briefly, their eyes with the startled expressions, two older women and a young man. Marlys wasn't in the room. They got down on their hands and knees, the women awkwardly, and lowered themselves to the carpeting. Billy Ruiz covered them, holding the .38 straight out and down. Leon opened the doll box without taking it out of the shopping bag and set it on a table against the wall where five gray-canvas sacks were waiting. Leon looked at them a moment, then walked over to a door with a frosted-glass window and opened it a little at a time, looking in.

Marlys's eyes rose from her typewriter, but her fingers continued to move over the keys for another few moments. The door beyond her desk was open to an office where a man sat half turned from his desk, talking on a phone and gesturing with his free hand. They couldn't hear his voice. Leon Woody stepped away from the frosted-glass door. Marlys came out, closing it behind her, and Leon nodded toward the sacks.

Frank watched her walk over to the table. She paused, then touched three of the sacks and looked up at Leon Woody. When Leon nodded, she walked back to her office, went in, and closed the door. Like that, not a word.

Leon dropped two of the sacks into the doll box, then the three Marlys had indicated. Frank watched him, not understanding. What difference did it make which ones went in first? He wanted to touch Leon's arm, get his attention, frown at him or something.

He heard Billy Ruiz say, "Jesus!" Like he was sucking in his breath.

Frank looked over and saw him raising the .38—it didn't make sense—raising it up to an angle above his head.

Leon Woody yelled at him, "Hold it!"

And Frank didn't know what was going on, until he looked up, in the direction the .38 was pointing, and saw the window above the row of file cabinets and the guy outside, strapped in a safety harness with a cloth over his shoulder and a squeegee in his hand, standing on the window ledge.

The guy had been there all the time and they hadn't seen him, concentrating on the three people getting down on the floor. The guy standing there, leaning out away from the window, trying to get away from it, fifteen floors up and no place to hide.

Frank wanted to run—seeing the guy staring at them scared to death—get the hell out of here and keep running, forget it, call it off, the whole thing, like it hadn't happened.

Leon Woody said, very quietly, "Shit . . . man seen the whole show. I don't know where my head's at." And he shook it from side to side, almost as if to make sure he was awake. He said then, "Billy—"

Billy Ruiz shot the guy twice, through the glass, shattering the pane, and they saw the red spots blossom on his white T-shirt and his head snap back, maybe screaming—there was a sound, a woman screaming—the guy straining against the harness before his feet slipped from the ledge and his legs and hips dropped away and they could see only the top half of him in the shattered window, his head hanging forward, motionless. The woman inside the room was still screaming.

Billy Ruiz went for the door and Leon said, "Walk, man, don't run. Same way we came." Frank was right behind him, then stopped as Leon shoved the Hudson's shopping bag into his arms and took the Python in both hands.

"Let me have it."

"What for?"

"I'll get rid of it."

"Where you going?"

"Hey, be cool, we all going together."

Frank didn't understand, but he couldn't argue. He let go of the gun and held the Hudson's bag in front of him, his arms around it. It wasn't as heavy as he had thought it would be.

There were a few shoppers down toward the end of the aisle, by display cases. None of them seemed to be looking this way. The rest of the aisle was empty.

The three of them were close together going through the exit door to the stairway. Then Frank had to stop. Holding the box in front of him, he almost piled into Leon Woody standing at the top of the stairs looking down, waiting. Past him, Frank could see Billy Ruiz reaching the landing where the stair made its turn.

"Go on, for Christ sake."

Leon Woody didn't move or say anything. He raised the Colt Python, aiming it down, and shot Billy Ruiz between the shoulder blades, the explosion filling the stairwell as Billy Ruiz was slammed against the wall and slid partway down the rest of the stairway.

Leon Woody moved now. Frank watched him, his profile, bending over Billy Ruiz. He told himself to drop the box or throw it at him and get out, back through the door. He knew he wouldn't make it, though. Leon Woody was looking up, the Python in his hand pointing at him but not aimed at him.

"Come on, man," Leon Woody said, "what you waiting for? You know where to put it, back behind. It's already marked. Then go down the fourth floor, get the escalator. Maybe I see you outside."

Frank watched him go through the door to the toy department. By the time Frank got there, stepping over Billy Ruiz, not looking at him, Leon wasn't anywhere around.

The voice inside Frank Ryan wasn't in condition; it had gone to fat and was pretty weak when it told him he had fucked up and the whole thing was an awful mistake. The voice did get through, and in those words, but Frank barely heard it and it didn't take much to smother the voice completely. A couple of scotches on the rocks.

Stick said, "Well?"

Frank stood at the bar, between two of the bamboo stools, holding onto the drink. He heard the faint sound of a girl laughing, coming from the patio below, then silence again.

"Well what? It's done."

"I never saw so many police cars," Stick said. "I would say within ten minutes of the time I called, no more than that, they're all over the place, completely around the store, and these guys are running in with their riot guns."

"Don't tell me," Frank said. "They're waiting at the bottom

of the escalator, four of them with their guns out. Anybody looks suspicious, 'Would you mind stepping over here?' They're going through packages, searching people, even women."

"How'd you get out?"

"How'd I get out? I walked out. What're they going to find on me? 'Hey, what's going on, Officer?' And they give you something about a routine investigation—five hundred cops in the place, shotguns, riot outfits, everything, it's a routine investigation."

"You ditched your gun all right?"

"Leon took care of it."

"How come Leon?"

Stick was sitting forward in his chair, holding a can of beer between his hands. He watched Frank go over to the coffee table to get a cigarette.

"Weren't you carrying it?"

"I carried the doll box," Frank said. Lighting the cigarette gave him a little time. He walked back to the bar and took a drink of scotch.

"Yeah? So you gave him your gun?"

"We had a little problem." The whole thing would be in the evening paper—Frank realized that—still, he wanted to tell it the right way, like there was really nothing to it, or Stick was liable to go through the ceiling.

"What kind of problem?"

"Billy shot a guy."

"Jesus—I *told* you."

"Wait a minute, a witness," Frank said. "A guy washing the window."

"Christ almighty—"

"We look up, the guy saw the whole thing, sees Marlys, so Billy had to shoot him."

"I told you. Christ, didn't I tell you? That guy's going to fuck the whole thing up, not even trying?"

"Will you wait a minute?" Frank said. "Take it easy, okay? and listen." He paused to make sure his voice would sound calm. "Billy pulled something else."

Stick was staring at him, waiting.

"He tried—we're going down the stairs—he tried to grab the box from me. See, he wants the whole thing, probably had it planned all the time and that's why he was going to settle for five. He shoots a couple times and misses, luckily, Christ, and Leon, he's got the Python, he shot him and that was it."

"You left him there?"

"He was dead, for Christ sake."

Stick shook his head slowly and let his breath out and shook his head again. He said, "Oh, boy—well, how do you like the big leagues?"

"We still did it," Frank said. He was being earnest now. "We got the money, five sacks, waiting there in the stockroom."

"Hey, Frank, come on—"

"I'm not shitting you, we got it, it's there. Everything went according to the book except the thing with Billy Ruiz. Okay, Billy's out of it, put his five K back in the pot, you never liked the guy, anyway."

"Frank, you got two dead men—you want to go back in there for the walkie dolly box?"

"I look at it this way," Frank said, getting into it and feeling more at ease, in control. "Whether two guys are dead or not, the money's sitting there waiting. The two guys don't change anything—you think Sportree, Leon Woody's going to say, Yeah, well let's leave it, then? Bullshit. This is armed robbery, man, and you know what I'm talking about, you go in with a gun and sometimes you have to use it or else you'd carry a fucking water pistol, right? When it's you or him, buddy, you know who comes first or you're in the wrong business. Listen, I saw you blow away two guys in that parking lot. You ought to know what I'm talking about better than I do."

"It's different now," Stick said. "We're not talking about armed robbery, ten to a quarter, we're talking about murder, maybe life."

"I can't argue with you," Frank said, "or quibble about the degree. Yeah, it's different now. But the odds, the odds are the same. You go in, look around, take your time. You don't like the feel, you smell something isn't right, you walk out. Nobody's going to blame you for being careful. You don't like it, get out. If it looks okay, pick up the box. Anywhere along the line something doesn't look right, dump the box, get the fuck out. But remember one thing, my friend, Ernest Stickley, Junior, there's over a hundred grand in the box and it's no heavier than you're carrying the doll in it, a present for your little girl."

There was a silence. Stick took a sip of beer. "I'll think about it," he said.

"What's there to think about? Your part, what you said you'd do, hasn't changed any."

"I said I'd think about it."

Frank put on an act of being calm, in control. He said, "Take your time. But if you turn chickenshit before day after tomorrow, let me know, okay? I'll go get it myself."

Leon Woody came in while Frank was at Sportree's, the two of them sitting in the living room upstairs. Frank saw Marlys in the doorway for a moment: she looked in, didn't nod or say anything and kept going down the hall. Leon Woody said, "How you doing?" and sat down. Frank frowned, looking over at Sportree sitting there in his Afro-Arabian outfit and a big Jamaican smoke held delicately between his fingers.

"She upset about the man wash the windows," Sportree said.

"How upset?"

Sportree shook his head. "Uh-unh, little girl's fine."

"I can't keep up with you," Frank said. "Last week, no, the week before, it was the redheaded girl plays the piano."

"Yeah, she still playing, she happy," Sportree said. "The one I'm worried about is your friend, if he's got his shit together on this thing."

"Well, you say don't worry about Marlys," Frank said. "It's the same thing, you don't have to worry about Stick. I remind him he said he'd get it and he will, I'm sure of it."

"I like a man like that," Sportree said. "Can take his word. I mean if it's true."

"I don't know, I'm saying the same thing to him all the time. I'm in the middle of you two guys, I trust both of you, naturally, so I just assume you trust each other."

"You like him," Sportree said, "hey, then I like him. You

give me a Stick, I give you a Leon Woody." He looked over at Leon, who nodded but didn't say anything.

"And take away a Billy Ruiz," Frank was saying. "That was a setup, wasn't it? You knew he wasn't coming out."

"No, he could've made it. It was up to Leon. I told Leon to use his judgment."

"But what for? I mean if you don't trust the guy, what'd you bring him for?"

"Let me explain something to you," Sportree said. "See, Billy's fine for how you use him. Say to him, Billy, here two hundred-dollar bills. You keep one, if you can make that policeman over there eat the other one, tied on your hog. He'd try it, think it was easy money. But see, Billy was very, very dumb. He could go one two three four, no trouble. But something happen he had to go one three seven five, shit, you don't know what the man was going to do. So I told Leon, Hey, you come to where you got to travel light, then dump the excess baggage, man. See, another thing, if Billy was picked up, you got to hold your breath all the time he in there. They could punch him, he wouldn't say a word. As I told you, I trust him. But that man, he so fucking dumb they be getting things out of him he don't even know he telling."

"I guess so," Frank said, "but Christ, killing him like that—I wish we could've got rid of him some other way, put him on a plane to San Juan or someplace."

"Not easy, is it?" Sportree said, in his Afro-Arabian robe, the Jamaican toke between his fingers, watching the gray smoke curl up. "Sometime we have to make sacrifices."

Leon Woody was at the window, watching Frank's T-bird pull away, making sure. Sportree was smoking. He yelled out, "Hey, baby!"

Marlys came in behind the three-foot doll box she was carrying, smiling back there, and placed it on the coffee table by Sportree.

"Little Curly Laurie. You want to know how much she got in her box?"

"Tell us," Sportree said.

"Exactly eighty-seven thousand four hundred and twenty-five."

Sportree smiled in his Jamaican smoke. "You have any trouble?"

"Walked out with it in the bag, Leon's waiting," Marlys said. "I didn't see anybody giving me looks, but I wouldn't want to do it again."

"Divide three into eighty-seven," Sportree said, "you would."

Leon, coming over from the window to sit down, said, "Now this Stick goes in tomorrow, comes out with the box still there, marked. Frank pick him up, they come here all smiling—what do we say then?"

"We say—they open the box," Sportree said, "two sacks in there. Two? Open them, checks. Checks? What's this shit, checks? Where the money sacks? He looks at us, huh? We look at Frank. Hey, Frank? You put the box there the day before yesterday? Frank say yeah, he put it there. He start to look at his friend. His friend start to look at him. One put it there, the other pick it up. But what do they have? Bunch of checks made out to the J. L. and Hudson Company. Somebody begins to say—they looking at each other—Hey, fuck, what is this? What's going on, man? They don't know shit what's going on."

"So maybe they go after each other," Leon Woody said. "One say, You put it there, five sacks in it, or not? The other say, You pick it up, but you don't come out the store with everything."

"That's the way I like to see it," Sportree said. "Now after a while, sometime, they going to look at us. We can look back at them, our eyes saying what is this ofay shit going on? Somebody trying to fuck somebody? Or we can look back at them and not say anything. Frank say to me, You wouldn't be pulling something, would you? Not wanting to come right out and accuse me, you understand? Finally I say to him, Frank, maybe everybody better forget about the whole thing and not think of hurting each other, because if anybody gets hurt, you know who it's going to be. And none of us can go to the police, can we? Because we all in it. So why don't we quit talking about it, dig? And you all go home."

Leon said, "You think he do it, huh, go home and be good?"

"Why would a man want to die at his age?" Sportree said.

Stick got two sets of Michigan plates off cars parked on the roof of the Greyhound bus station and wrapped them in the morning edition of the *Free Press* that ran two follow-up stories on Hudson's robbery.

There was a graduation-looking photo of a smiling, dark-haired guy, the window washer, and a twenty-year-old shot of Carmen Billy Ruiz in a boxing pose, on the front page, wrapped around the license plates. On page three there was a photo of the window washer's wife and two small children, and on the sports page a column devoted to Billy Ruiz's seventeen-and-seventeen record and how he had been Chuck Davey's sparring partner. Davey, now of the Chuck Davey Insurance Agency, Southfield, recalled that Billy Ruiz liked to eat ice cream—he ate ice cream all the time—but was not much of a puncher.

The two sets of license plates went in the trunk of the T-bird to be transferred to Stick's suitcase. He might use them on the way to Florida, he might not, but extra plates were good to have. He'd pick up a car that afternoon sometime.

He'd decided, finally, to tell Frank his plan and Frank had said, Wait'll you see your cut and you're holding it in your hand before you start talking about leaving.

Stick said don't worry, he was taking his cut, he wasn't going up to the toy department for nothing; but this was the end of it. After, he'd go home get his bag and if Frank would drop him off at a shopping center he'd appreciate it.

Frank said, "What about your share in the bank deposit box?" Stick said, "We can pick it up after, or you give me the same amount out of your cut from the Hudson's deal and keep all what's in the bank." That was all right with Frank. He said, "All right, if that's what you want to do. You'll get down there, play on the beach with your little girl, and I'll probably see you in about a week." He said, "If I'm in Hawaii or Acapulco or someplace, I'll leave word with the lady, the manager." Frank was in a pretty good mood.

That was about all that was said between them that morning in the apartment and driving downtown. It didn't seem like much after being together three months. Frank drove up to the rooftop parking lot over the bus station and waited for him while he got the license plates. Then drove him around to the Woodward Avenue side of Hudson's and said, "I'll see you in about fifteen minutes."

That was the last they saw of each other for six days.

Stick took an escalator up as far as he could and then a local elevator to the fourteenth floor. It still took him less than five minutes. He located the stock room first, in an arcade that connected with another section of the store. He roamed through the toy department then for a few minutes. There were only a few customers around—one guy very intently fooling with some kind of a target game, a young guy in jeans with fairly long blond hair—and hardly any salespeople.

He watched the stock-room door another couple of minutes. Nobody went in or came out. He said, "Okay," let his breath out slowly, walked over, and pushed through the door.

Frank had said the third aisle over. But he hadn't said which side. The sectioned metal shelves reached almost to the ceiling and it looked like there were boxes of dolls on both sides, all the way down to the end.

America's Little Darling, Baby Angel, Playmate for a Princess, Baby Crissy, Crissy's Cousin Velvet, Jean Marie, Tender Love . . . Christ, Shirley Temple . . . Rub-a-Dub Dolly, Saucy, Wendy, Cutie Cleaner, Cathy Quick Curl, Peachy and her Puppets, Beautiful Lee Ann the Dancing Doll . . . there, Little Curly Laurie Walker. She wasn't bad-looking.

The one he wanted had a little red dot near the bottom of the box. Which wasn't on any of the ones in front. He had to pull them out one at a time to look at the boxes in the row behind. Then two at a time, Christ.

It was in the third row, the fifth one. Stick got it up to the front and shoved boxes in to fill the space. He picked it up.

Frank was right, it wasn't heavy at all. He wondered if he should look inside, make sure.

That was when he glanced to the side.

It was strange, recognizing the guy in the quick glance and wanting to do something with the box, not knowing the guy, but knowing who he was—even if he did have long hair and jeans on—and knowing, shit, it was too late.

"Drop it and put your hands on the shelf, man, right now."

The guy had a big gun like Frank's, some kind of a mag, the same guy who'd been fooling with the target game.

Stick didn't have anything to lose. He said, "What's going on? What is this, a holdup?"

"It sure looks like it to me," the guy said. He had a little leather case open in his other hand, showing a badge.

Another guy, in a suit, came around the corner from the other side, at the end of the aisle, and that was it.

Stick said, "I was in here looking—I thought it was the Men's Room."

"You piss on dolls?" the young man said. "Man," and whistled. "Hey, Walter, he says he thought it was the Men's Room."

The one in the suit was next to him now. He said, "I can see why he'd think that. All the toilets."

"No, I mean I was looking for a doll for my little girl. Then I had to go to the Men's Room. I came in here, I saw it wasn't, of course"—Stick was giving the young guy a nice grin he knew already wasn't going to do him any good—"but then I saw these dolls, see, and started looking at them . . . for my little girl."

"You like the one with the red dot on it best?" the young guy said.

"You can read me my rights if you want," Stick said, "I'm not saying another word."

21

Stick remembered a time once in Yankton, South Dakota, standing around back of the chutes at a rodeo, watching the contestants drawing the bulls they'd ride.

He remembered one especially, a skinny guy with his big scooped-brim hat and tight little can, spitting over his hip and saying, "If I cain't ride 'im, I'll eat 'im." He lasted about three and a half seconds on a bull named Candyman and came back through the dust limping and hitting his big curly hat against his chaps.

The young guy, the cop, reminded him of one of those bull riders or a saddle bronc rider. Long hair, no hips, faded jeans, boots. It was the badge and the foot-long .44 mag under his left arm that made him something else, a Detroit police officer.

Frank had said it, you couldn't tell the cops from the hackers and stalkers anymore.

Stick kept his eyes on the young guy while they were at the First Precinct police headquarters, but didn't say anything to him or answer any of his questions. Shit no, he was standing mute. He didn't say anything getting fingerprinted and photographed and the only thing he said at the arraignment was not guilty. They set a bond of five thousand dollars and asked him if he wanted it. He said no. They asked him if he had counsel. He said no. They asked him if he wanted the court to appoint counsel for him. He said no. He'd sit it out and take his chance at the examination. If he didn't say anything, if he didn't call anyone for bond money, if he didn't talk to a lawyer or to the young guy even about the weather, he knew they couldn't do a thing to him—not for picking up a doll box, even if it did have a red dot on it.

Stick sat in the Wayne County jail with all the colored guys awaiting trial. He had never seen so many colored guys. He didn't say much to them and got along all right. The place smelled—God, it smelled—and the food was awful, but he'd been here before. He'd make it.

It was funny, sitting in jail he remembered the ice machine at the motel in Yankton and the sign on it that said: WE CANNOT PROVIDE ICE FOR COOLERS. He remembered thinking at the time, But how do they know if they don't try?

He remembered going into the place next to the motel, walking up to the two girls at the bar, and saying, "Good evening, may I buy you ladies a drink?" One of them said, "You dumb bunny, we work here." He said, "Oh, then would you bring me a drink?" And she said, "Certainly, sir, what would you like?"

Sitting in the Wayne County jail. He remembered telling Frank, coming out the last time, they didn't serve cocktails in there.

Most of all a Porter Waggoner song kept going through his head, about a hurtin' behind his left eye and a tiny little bee buzzin' around in his stomach. Porter was all tore down because of too many good, good buddies and bad, bad gals.

Stick didn't know about the gals, but the buddies were something to think about.

Every once in a while he'd think about the doll box, too. He had only held it a moment, but he remembered, in that moment, the box was a lot lighter than he'd expected it to be.

And he kept thinking about the cop who'd arrested him, the young guy. He could tell the guy was eager.

The young cop's name was Cal Brown.

Once he said to a superior, "But look, I've learned that already. I know it. Responsi*bil*ity? Having people under you? Giving them paychecks and shit? I had sixty guys under me and I kept them fucking *alive.* I've done that, man, what, when I was twenty-three."

He had been a combat infantry officer in Vietnam and had been with the police department seven years, since trying out with the San Diego Chargers as a free-agent wide receiver and ruining one of his knees before the season started.

Today he was having lunch at the Hellas Café on Monroe with Emory Parks, the young little fat black assistant from the prosecutor's office. Cal Brown ordered the stuffed grape leaves, feta cheese salad, and a glass of retsina. Emory Parks ordered roast lamb and lima beans and hot tea. They were waiting for the food to come. Emory Parks was fooling with his tea bag. Cal Brown was hunched over the table on his elbows.

"You read up on it yet?"

"I haven't had time, man. I probably won't read it till we're in court."

"You met the guy before, three months ago. Three and a half."

"Refresh my memory."

"Ernest Stickley, Junior, auto theft. Charge dropped at the exam, no positive ID."

"Shit," the little prosecutor said, "you know how many Ernest Stickley, Juniors, there are?"

"This one was in on the Hudson's thing."

"You'd like to believe that."

"His roomie," Cal said, "the guy he lives with in a four-hundred-and-fifty-dollar-a-month apartment out in Troy—listen to this part—is the same guy who was the eyeball witness to the auto theft and lost his memory."

Emory Parks stopped fooling with his tea bag. "Is that so?"

"Interesting?"

"Where's this boy Stickley now, out?"

"In. Passed on the bond, passed on the free lawyer. He gives you his name, rank, and serial number and raises his hand when he has to go to the bathroom."

"What's he arraigned on?"

"Larceny from a building. Conspiring."

The little prosecutor frowned now. "Larceny? Shit, you got a murder in there, haven't you?"

"Murder? We got two murders. We got all fucking kinds of numbers going. That's why we're talking. Listen—the gun used on the window washer? Same one killed the two guys out at Northland. In the parking lot."

"Well, you don't need him for that. Man did the community a favor, as I recall."

"That's not my question. Right now I'm giving you facts, okay? One of the guys killed at Northland—I don't remember which one—had a piece of grocery bag in his hand, and a few bills. From a store that'd been knocked over about an hour before. But the guys that knocked over the store weren't black."

"This one, Stickley—you show his picture out there?"

"With the Southfield police. Manager says no, he never saw him. One of the checkout girls, she cocks her head, well, maybe. She couldn't say for sure."

"So you got to stay with Hudson's, which is better anyway."

"Not necessarily," Cal said. "Yes, it's better, but I mean there're other possibilities, at least two dozen robberies out there, all armed, same everything, two guys come in, very polite, but no bullshit. We can go that way, right? Follow it up and probably get a conviction."

"You mean hand it to all the little police departments out there, they ain't cutting their grass they can work on it, and the first one off his ass and gets an ID gets an armed robbery bust. That saves you some work, doesn't it?"

"Look," Cal said, "since I'm buying the fucking lunch, don't tell me things I know, okay?"

"Excuse my friend," the little prosecutor said to the waitress putting their plates in front of them. "He likes to talk dirty, he wasn't insulting the food."

The waitress looked at him but didn't change her expression. She either didn't know what he was talking about or didn't care. It was 1:30 and the place was crowded.

Cal didn't look at his stuffed grape leaves. He said, "We can send this clown out to the country. There're a dozen circuit courts he can get lost in."

"Or?" Emory Parks was starting on his lamb and lima beans.

"Let me tell you the rest. A different gun was used on Billy Ruiz. We found it in a trash thing, a Colt Python three-five-seven."

"Belonging to whom?"

"Guy out in Bloomfield Hills. Registered—you listening?"

"I can eat and still listen, Calvin. It's a trick I learned."

"The Colt's registered to this guy and"—Cal paused—"you ready? So is the thirty-eight they used on the window washer."

"That's impressive." Emory Parks nodded, chewing his lamb. "You're keeping it neat, but you're still out in suburbia with the two guns."

"They were stolen three and a half months ago, in May," Cal said. "Stickley was acquitted in May. The two dozen or so robberies that all smell alike go back to May. Two guys get in the business, liquor stores, supermarkets, doing pretty well—you follow me?"

"And they decide it's time to go big time."

"And they get greedy, right? and go for the big banana."

"Bring some friends in."

"Bring *some*body in. A white guy and two gentlemen of the Negro persuasion go into the Hudson's office. Not Stickley, though, an unknown male Caucasian, Billy Ruiz, and another black gent with an unhappy childhood. One of whom shot Billy Ruiz in the back on the way out. Why?"

"Shit, anybody'd shoot Billy Ruiz in the back if they got the chance. That's not the question. Ask the right one," the little prosecutor said. "No, let me ask you one. How'd you know the money was still there, in the box?"

"Not the money, checks. Just checks."

"Not the money?"

"Let me tell it," Cal said. "We're looking all over the fucking store, top to bottom, and we find a little something—this is the next day—in Billy Ruiz's street clothes. They're in another trash thing, on the same floor we found the Python."

"Something in his clothes."

"In a pocket. A little toy soldier, thing's two inches high, costs nine and a half bucks. No sales slip. Where's it from? The toy department. One floor below the office. What was Billy Ruiz doing in the toy department? We start looking, two o'clock in the morning—this is the second day after, now—we found the doll box with the checks in it."

"The question," the little prosecutor said, "what would he want with just checks?"

"He comes in the *second* day after," Cal said. "Keep that in mind. What if he thought the money was there, too?"

"I see that," the little prosecutor said. "Like maybe somebody's fucking somebody over."

"Like maybe somebody came in the day before," Cal said, "and picked up another dolly box with a mark on it, but they don't tell Mr. Stickley. He's supposed to come out, they open the box and they say, Yeah—giving him the dead eyes—now where's the real stuff? But he doesn't come out. He looks around and he's got a forty-four mag in his ass. He doesn't know he wasn't picking up the money, because he doesn't know what was in the box."

"And you haven't told him."

"Not yet. That's why we're having the lunch."

The little prosecutor paused. "The store, they haven't released the news yet that any money is missing."

"They don't want to advertise for any repeat business."

"How much?"

"In the neighborhood of eight-seven."

The little prosecutor smiled. "And you got this boy for larceny from a building, which I doubt will even get to trial. He says, 'I didn't know what was in the box besides a doll,' and you didn't let him look, or walk out with it."

"We figured, we were *sure* he'd be identified in the office."

"You haven't mentioned what his roommate was doing that day. What *do* they do, both of them?"

"Yes indeedy," Cal said, "how do these two pay the rent? Stickley, unemployed, drives a cement truck when he isn't behind the wheel of a stolen vehicle. Frank J. Ryan, that's his roomie, is a car salesman. Last place of employment, Red Bowers Chevrolet. You ready to hear it again? Three and a half months ago."

"You got a sheet on him?"

"Frank's been a clean liver up to now, or else he's never been caught. He's a dude, with the hair and the mod suit and shit. I present myself at the apartment with a search warrant and tell him his buddy's been arrested. 'Oh, my,' he says, 'I don't believe it. Stick? But he's a nice guy.' I'm thinking, Not Johnny, he was always such a good boy, good to his mother."

"What'd you find?"

"The search revealed nothing unusual or incriminating other than nine hundred bucks under the sink in an Oxydol box. Clever? Ryan goes, 'Gee, how did that get there?' I said to him, 'Don't you ever do the dishes?' He goes, 'Oh yeah, Stickley won it at Hazel Park, but he never knew where he'd put it.'"

The little prosecutor kept his plate neat and didn't let anything touch. He moved a few lima beans away from his mashed potatoes before slicing off a piece of lamb. He said, "Why don't you have the Hudson's people take a look at him?"

"Because the only one they saw—the only face—was Billy Ruiz. The other two, all they're sure of, one was black, one white."

"Well, maybe there's some liquor store and supermarket people out there can identify Ryan as well as Stickley."

"That could be," Cal said, "but then I wouldn't have anything, would I?"

"Your grape leaves are going to get cold."

Cal started eating and neither of them spoke while Emory Parks finished his roast lamb and poured himself more tea. He said, "I agree we should save them for the Hudson's job and get a murder conviction, besides find the money. We're building a new Renaissance Center, getting downtown all fixed up, we can't have this kind of shit going on. Doesn't look good, does it?"

"It fucks up our image," Cal said, "not to mention people getting killed."

"All right, you got two male Caucasians," Emory Parks said, "but no lead on the brother. What I've been wondering, if somebody might've bankrolled this deal."

"Bankroll? What's to bankroll? They get a secondhand bus driver suit from the Goodwill."

"How about the people in the office?"

"That's a possibility. They knew when to walk in. Two, the check sacks were sealed, hadn't been opened. So we assume they knew the money sacks from the check sacks. I don't want to sound racially biased, Emory, but there's a cute little black chick up there that's sort of caught our eye."

Emory Parks was thinking again.

"You didn't tell me where this Frank Ryan was the day of the robbery."

"He said he was home sleeping, but he thinks Stickley went out for a while in the morning. That afternoon, they got three broads can swear they were out sitting by the pool."

"Must be nice to be unemployed," Emory Parks said. He looked thoughtful again.

"I talked to the broads," Cal said, "asking them what they knew about the two guys. Every one of them: Oh, they're business consultants. They have something to do with sales training or something like that. Nice guys, and they throw keen parties. I go back to Ryan. What's this I hear you're a business consultant? He says oh, that was just a little patio bullshit they handed the girls one time. They didn't want the girls to know they were unemployed. Oh, is that why you throw these big parties? He said they'd bought a lot of stuff one time and had a little bit left. The little bit, two cases of booze. There was one girl"—he took a small notebook out of his pocket and turned a few pages—"Arlene Downey. I asked her if she knew the two guys. Yeah, she knew them, but just slightly. I asked her if she knew what they did for a living. Right then, just for a second, her expression—like the light went on and her mother caught her doing it on the couch. Then she was evasive, had been out of town a lot, hadn't seen much of them."

Emory Parks was smiling a little. "Right there, aren't they? But you can't quite reach them. I think . . . what you're going to have to do . . . first thing, tell Ryan his partner needs somebody to post his bond. I think, playing Mr. Innocent Nice Guy, he'll run down there and do it."

"Yeah," Cal said. "I think he would. He knows I know he's got some money. Yeah—"

"Then you got the two of them looking at each other, the one guy facing a conviction. What's the other guy going to say to him?"

"He's going to say, Jesus, it's a shitty deal, but hang in there, man. It's like, Gee, I'm sorry you got leukemia, but there isn't anything I can do about it."

"And what's Stickley thinking, feeling his temporary freedom? He's already served time, he knows what it's like in there."

"He's thinking, Why me and not them? See," Cal said, "the trouble is I can't mention the money to him, let him know he's been fucked over. We can't let that out yet to anybody."

"You don't have to tell him," Emory Parks said. "His buddies, maybe his roommate if he's one of them, they don't know what's in Mr. Stickley's head. They don't know what he knows or doesn't know. He was in jail, they couldn't touch him, they hold their breath. But if he's out—can they take a chance letting him go to trial? Won't the cops try and plea-bargain with him? They already shot poor Billy Ruiz. They going to take a chance on this cat telling stories about them?"

"It's interesting," Cal said.

"It's not only interesting," the little prosecutor said, "it's all you got. Unless you find out one of them's been jumping that cute little black chick in the office. Then you got a lead on something else."

"Listen," Cal said, "I think I've got enough to work on for a while. Yes sir, I believe this could open it up."

"If you plant a little seed with this Stickley before you turn him loose."

"Yeah"—Cal was nodding—"make sure he realizes what a shitty deal he's getting."

"Not only a shitty deal, make him realize life can be dangerous out there. Man disappears for a time, they find him in the trunk of a car out at the airport. Say to him he ought to be very careful where he goes, where he meets his friends."

"Yeah," Cal said, "get him to reconsider who his friends are, who can do him the most good."

"That's it." Emory Parks smiled then. "You're going to take all this back to Thirteen hundred and Walter's going to say, 'You've been talking to that fat little nigger again, haven't you?' And you'll say, 'Well, I just picked at his brain a little.' "

"Your ass," Cal said. "I'll tell him I figured it all out myself. You got a free lunch, you fat little nigger, what more do you want?"

22

"Why don't you just not say anything?" Stick said. "If you don't talk for a while, it's okay with me."

"Look, I'm sorry," Frank said. "You think I'm blaming you, for Christ sake? I'm trying to find out how it happened."

"How it *hap*pened? I reach for the box and the guy, the cop, puts a fucking gun in my face is how it happened. They're waiting there—this great idea—they know exactly where it was."

"But how could they?"

"How do I know? They found out or somebody told them—shit, I don't know. This fucking great idea—I should be in Florida right now, I'm facing a robbery conviction."

"Conspiring to commit larceny from a building," Frank said.

"At the moment. But the cop, you know what the hotshot

cop says? 'Maybe at the exam we'll change it to robbery armed. And if we do that, we might as well go all the way to murder, right?' "

"The guy's blowing smoke up your ass. I think they'll go in on the larceny thing and get it thrown out."

"Yeah, well I'll tell the judge that, you don't think I'll get convicted. I'm facing the fucking thing and you're sitting home with your nice thoughts."

They walked along in silence, away from the Wayne County jail building down St. Antoine toward the parking structure. It was four in the afternoon, warm and sunny. They had walked down this street once before—it seemed a long time ago—on their way to the Greek place, the Bouzouki.

Frank said, "You want a drink?"

"I want to take a shower and change my clothes," Stick said.

Frank was silent again. Everything he said came out wrong, not the way he intended it, or Stick would turn it around. He didn't know what to say to him, but he kept trying anyway. Walking along in silence, Stick next to him, was worse.

"There was a cop, a hippie-looking guy," Frank said, "he was out a couple of times. Came with a search warrant the first time. I said, You don't need that, we got nothing to hide. He found the dough under the sink. I told him it was our nest egg, we'd won it at the track."

"He talk to anybody else there?"

"He talked to everybody. The ladies told him we're consultants."

"How about Arlene? He talk to her?"

"I don't know, I guess so."

"She was away," Stick said, "in Chicago or someplace."

"She's back now. I've seen her a couple of times."

"But you don't know if he talked to her."

"You afraid he told her something? What's the guy know? There's one little piece in the paper about you. It said you'd been arrested, but it was only speculated, in connection with the Hudson's thing. See, they're not playing it up because they don't have a case against you. They start bragging they got the guy and then you walk out, they don't look so good."

"Who'd you talk to?" Stick said. "I mean the girls there."

"I talked to Karen and I talked to Jackie. They say, What's this with your buddy? I told them it was all a dumb mistake. You walk in, you're going to buy a doll, send to your little girl, they think you look suspicious for some reason and they arrest you. They get it cleared up, you'll be out, we'll all be laughing about it," Frank said. "Don't worry about the girls, they don't know anything."

"Arlene does," Stick said.

"What? There's nothing anybody could tell her."

"I'm saying Arlene knows about us."

It took Frank a moment. He almost came to a stop. "Wait a minute, you mean *you* told her something?"

"I didn't tell her anything," Stick said. "The bar in Hazel Park, we took the money from the guy? She was there."

"Come on—"

"Sitting at the bar with her friend."

"Jesus Christ—you sure?"

"Am I *sure?* She told me, she's sitting there. We push her in the room with everybody, we didn't even see her."

"But—she didn't go to the cops?"

"I think we'd of heard."

"Then what's she doing? She want something?"

"I don't know. I'm going to have to talk to her."

"You don't *know?* You discuss this with her—when was that?"

"Just before she left. I haven't seen her since that night."

"Jesus Christ," Frank said. "That's all we need."

Stick felt a little better. Frank wasn't his calm, casual self anymore.

"Latest development," Detective Calvin Brown said into the phone, "I didn't get to him soon enough. While we're having the lunch, his roomie put up the bond."

He took a sip of coffee as he listened to the little prosecutor and put the cup down on the metal desk in the little gray partitioned room that was called his office: Criminal Investigation Division, fifth floor, 130 Beaubien.

"It could be all right," the little prosecutor said, "if the man's been thinking and he realizes they could be worried about him and that's why they wanted him out. But you don't know, do you, the extent of his imagination."

"I don't know," Cal said. "He sounds like a country boy, but I really don't know."

"You don't want to find him dead before he has a chance to learn who his true friends are, do you?"

"No, I sure don't."

"Then you better see about talking to him pretty soon. Maybe go so far as to mention some money being taken. I've been thinking about that."

"I have, too," Cal said. "I just wanted to hear you say it."

"This other Ryan, man used to work with me a long time ago," Leon Woody said. "His name was *Jack* Ryan. We work for this man was in the carpet-cleaning business? Get in a house, we see some things we like, we have a window unlocked, come back at night. He was a nice boy, Jack Ryan."

Sportree came in from the kitchen with a drink in each hand. Frank Ryan thanked him as he took his and waited as Sportree handed the other drink to Leon Woody and went out again.

"No, I don't think I ever heard of him," Frank said.

"He wanted to be a baseball player."

"Is that right?"

"Play in the major leagues. Nice boy, but he couldn't hit a curve ball for shit."

"I guess it's pretty hard," Frank said, "you don't have an eye."

Sportree came in with a drink for himself and sat down.

"See, what I'm thinking," he said, "man was in the joint once, he sure don't want to go back."

"There's no reason he will," Frank said, leaning forward now, sitting on the couch. "All they got on him, he might've been *think*ing about robbing the place. How do they prove he knows there's money in the box?"

"I'm thinking I don't know what he's thinking," Sportree said. "Maybe he believes they can put him away. He does, he might want to tell them things, give them some names, huh? And they tear up his piece of paper."

"He wouldn't tell them *any*thing," Frank said. "I know he wouldn't."

"Thing that bothers me most," Sportree said, "man was in the joint. See, he think different after that. He finger his mama to stay out in the fresh air."

"Look," Frank said, "if they had something on him, it'd be different. If they were really going to hit him and he saw he was going to take the whole shot. But he knows if he waits them out, keeps his mouth shut, they're going to have to let him go. All he did, he picked up a box."

"*The* box."

"Yes, and they assumed things too quick, he'd been in on the hit and somebody in the office would identify him. Otherwise they'd have let him walk out with it and then nailed him. But they were too eager, little too sure of themselves."

Sportree looked over at Leon Woody.

"That'd be nice he don't say nothing," Leon Woody said, "and they say to him, Thank you, we sorry we bothered you, man, let him go. That'd be nice. But the way I see it, they going to take him down in the basement and whip the shit out of him and pull his fingernails out 'less he start to talk to them."

"Come on," Frank said, "they don't, they can't get away with that stuff anymore."

"Hey shit, they don't," Leon Woody said. "If he the only one they got, they going to do something with him, drop him out a window on his head, he don't start to talk to them. Say he try and run away."

Frank looked at Sportree. "How about I bring him around, you talk to him?"

"Might be an idea."

"I think you should," Frank said. "You got any doubts at all, talk to him. You trust me, don't you?"

"You not arrested," Sportree said. "Not yet."

"I mean wouldn't you trust me? If it was me instead of him? It's the same thing. I give you my word the guy won't talk."

Sportree said, "He knows about Billy getting hit, don't he?"

"I told him Billy wanted it all for himself and it was something had to be done."

"You make up a story, you not too sure of him either."

"No, it was so he'd go in and get the box, not change his mind."

Sportree and Leon Woody sat in silence, staring at him.

Frank shook his head. "Hey, come on, what're you thinking about? You're not sure you can trust the guy, you want to kill him, for Christ sake?"

"Frank," Sportree said, "we known each other a long time, longer than you known him. He start mentioning names, your name's going to be on the list, too. Everybody's name. Next thing, they got us in there for murder. Something a dead man did, and we didn't even make it, did we? Got nothing. But nothing is better than being in there for murder, and the only way we can have some peace of mind is to know your friend isn't going to tell them anything. You agree?"

"But he won't," Frank said. "I give you my word he won't talk."

There was a silence, and again they stared at him. Leon Woody took a sip of his drink. Sportree's fingers fooled with his trading beads.

"I'll bring him here," Frank said.

Sportree nodded. "I be anxious to see him."

23

"I thought we were coming right back," Arlene said, "but we went to St. Louis for the Gateway Nationals and I spent three days in the courtesy trailer passing out beer and soft drinks. Least it was air-conditioned. God, it was so hot and dusty at the track you wouldn't have believed it. But the only times *I* had to go out was when they gave out an award and I'd pose with Larry Huff and Chuck Hurst and Bob Amos and those guys. I got a lot more pictures. Oh, God, but there was a terrible accident. This pro stocker went out of control about nine hundred feet down the track, went through the guardrail, flipped over—fortunately there weren't many people in the stands that far down—"

"Arlene."

She stopped.

"Have you told anybody about seeing us?"

"What?"

"You know what I mean."

"I shouldn't have mentioned that to you, should I?"

"You did," Stick said. "I've been a little anxious wondering if you told anybody."

"I haven't. Honest to God, I haven't told a soul."

She was afraid of him and afraid of showing it. He saw it in her expression again, in her eyes, as he had seen it, momentarily, when she had opened the door and he was standing there. Then covering up quickly with a smile that must have ached: Come on in, stranger. Gosh, it's been a while, hasn't it? And getting rapidly into what she had been doing the past two weeks. Busy, God, she'd never been busier.

They were alone in her apartment in the quiet of a sunny afternoon. Arlene had come up from the pool a few minutes before—Stick had watched her from the balcony—and she was still in her lavender little two-piecer with her beads and rings and damp, tight-curly red hair, looking fragile and afraid. He wanted to touch her, put his arms around her, and feel the calm settle in her body as she realized there was nothing to be afraid of. But he knew he had to approach her gradually, that if he raised his hands she might scream and run from him.

"I believe you," Stick said. He tried a little smile and meant it. She was still tense but trying not to show it, standing in the middle of the room with the photographs and the life-size cutout of her in her silver Hi-Performance Cams outfit. They were both awkward standing there, not knowing what to do with their hands. Arlene touched a Maltese cross hanging from a thin gold chain and held on.

"How about the guy you were with? You didn't tell him you knew us?"

"Honest to gosh, I really didn't."

"Why not?"

"I don't know. . . . Well, I knew he wouldn't want to get involved, and you know, his wife finds out he was there with somebody. So I didn't say anything."

"Why didn't you tell the police? Leave him out of it."

"Well"—she made a face, frowning—"it's hard to explain. You want to sit down and have a drink or something? I don't know why I told you before. Maybe because I'd had all those drinks and wasn't feeling any pain, but I could sure use one now."

Stick made her a Salty Dog and then changed his mind and fixed one for himself, something to sip on. They sat down on the couch, Stick anxious but covering it pretty well, showing her she didn't have anything to worry about. He remembered telling Frank about Arlene knowing. It popped into his mind with the realization, an instinctive feeling, he shouldn't have; he should have waited at least, talked to Arlene first. Dumb, telling Frank because he had wanted to give him something to worry about. Would Frank tell the others? He said no, there wasn't any reason for him to tell them. But it continued to come into his mind, wondering about it and not being sure. Arlene sitting there, not knowing—he wanted to hold her.

"I liked you," Arlene said. "I mean I *like* you. The way it happened, it was funny, and it wasn't like you were robbing the bar, you were taking it from, you know, taking it from the one who did rob the place, like it was his then, and taking it wasn't a bad thing, it served him right. It was *fun*ny." She smiled a little. "God, I can still see it."

"Well, did you wonder," Stick said, "if we did it all the time? I mean, if that was what we did?"

"I didn't think about it."

"You must've, a little."

"I didn't. I said it wasn't any of my business. I thought—this may sound funny—I thought if you wanted to tell me, it was up to you."

"But if I had, then what would you think?"

"Well, I'd think that . . . you trusted me. You felt close enough that you could tell me something like that and know you didn't have to worry about it."

"You mean you wouldn't care?"

"Well, it isn't I wouldn't care. It's—see, I *have* thought about it and I always think, well, there's a reason. Like you have to have money for something. You need it desperately and nobody'll loan it to you, so you're just doing it for, whatever the reason is, and you're not going to do it anymore after."

"Arlene, I've held up a lot of places."

"Don't tell me, okay?"

"See, I can say I did need the money, as desperately as anybody needs it who doesn't have any. But I stole it."

"Why do you keep saying that? I don't want to know, okay?"

"You know about the Hudson's robbery?"

"Oh, God. Don't." She squeezed her eyes closed with an expression of pain.

"I was in on it," Stick said. "That's why I got arrested. It wasn't a mistake."

He told her about it, describing what he did, his part in the robbery, trying not to minimize or make excuses, telling it quietly and seeing her eyes open to watch him with an expression that gradually lost its tension as her face, with its delicate features, became composed and her eyes took on an expression of calm awareness, as though she were looking into him and seeing more than a man involved in a robbery, someone else inside the man. He was aware of this as he spoke, feeling an intimacy between them that was different, softer yet stronger than what he had felt making love to her, and he knew why he was telling her about himself. He needed her.

He said, "I don't know what to do."

She moved to him on the couch, still looking into his eyes, and took his face in her hands and kissed him, then put her arms around him and drew him against her body.

They were in the darkness now, in her bedroom, lying beside each other. He had slept and was awake, staring at the ceiling, at a faint reflection of light from the other room.

He said, "Can you go away for a while, till we see what happens?"

"Why?"

"Maybe some race or a convention coming up?"

"I'm not going to do that anymore." She sounded a little mad and surprised. "God, what do you think I am?" When he reached over and touched her she waited a moment and said, "Don't you love me?"

"I really do."

"Say it."

"I love you." He made his voice softer and said, "I love you—I never loved anybody so much."

He felt funny hearing himself and felt her breath come out in a little sigh as she turned to cling tightly against him and that part was good. He could feel her and knew by the touch who it was, the firm little body against his. He felt good. But God, he ought to take one thing at a time and save the best, put it someplace where it wouldn't get hurt. He knew he loved her. Like waking up and being somewhere else. He could hardly believe it.

"I'm not going to stay here," Arlene said. "I'll move out tomorrow, the stuff's not mine anyway. But I'm not going away—unless you want to and we go together."

"I got to stay for the pretrial thing, I can't jump bail. You get brought back with handcuffs on and they got you cold."

"Okay, I'll get another apartment then," Arlene said, "something cheaper. I've got enough to live on for at least a month."

"I can help you out there."

"No, I'll get another job if I have to. Tell you the truth, I'm awful sick of that silver outfit." She paused a moment. "It's funny, I just feel different with you."

"Everything could work out," Stick said. "They drop the charge and we get out of here and that's it. Clean living from now on. I'm liable to even get a job, too."

Arlene laughed, a muffled sound close to him that he liked. "That'd be nice of you," she said.

They held onto each other in the darkness. Pretty soon he'd get up and see if the car was downstairs. If it wasn't, he'd pick up a car somewhere, one last time. Everything could work out, that was true, it was possible.

As long as he stayed alive.

When Emory Parks walked into Cal Brown's drab gray partitioned office on the fifth floor, Cal looked surprised first, then turned on a little grin, and Emory knew he had something good to tell him.

"I saw Walter downstairs."

Cal's grin faded. "He told you?"

"He was in a hurry. He said, 'Stop up and see the boy if you get a chance.' All right, boy, what you got?"

Cal was happy again. He said, "The guy out in Bloomfield Hills with all the firearms? He got broken into again last night."

"They know where to go, don't they?"

"Maybe not *they* this time," Cal said. "One gun was taken, a Walther P-38, nine millimeter. The family was upstairs sleeping, didn't hear a thing."

"It could've been somebody else."

"You want to bet?"

"You're going to assume it's one of the whities. All right, if it makes you happy, but which one?"

"I like Mr. Stickley."

"That's a good first choice," the little prosecutor said. "But what if Mr. Ryan's in with the brothers—assuming there's more than one brother, which I'm inclined to believe—"

"Me, too," Cal said.

"—and they say to him, 'Hey, man, he's your roomie, you do it.' Then Mr. Ryan might have to get himself a weapon."

"I don't like it that way," Cal said. "Then it isn't divided up right. I want to see Frank and Ernest on the same team. I mean if the brothers are going to fuck over one of them, why not both?"

"You know what?" the little prosecutor said. "I believe you just said the magic word. *Both.* Why not? It wouldn't be any harder to take two whities as one, would it?"

Cal smiled. "But the whities have a gun now. Somebody's been doing some thinking and I like it."

"You talk to them yet?"

"It's on my list of things to do," Cal said. "I want to talk to one of the young ladies out there, too, Miss Arlene Downey, the one that was a little edgy. I've been looking into their friends and acquaintances through the computer, a nifty little machine, and you want to hear a it's-a-small-world story? Miss Arlene Downey, we find, was a witness to a holdup a month ago, the Saratoga Bar in Hazel Park. And the Saratoga Bar? Why it's on the list of twenty-five or so that fit the style of our friends Frank and Ernest."

"It certainly is a small world," the little prosecutor said. "You don't suppose she's working with them?"

"I don't know," Cal said, "but I'm sure anxious to find out."

24

"I go down to get the car last night," Frank said, "it's not there. I thought maybe I forgot where I parked it. I looked all over. Christ, I thought, I parked it right in front, it's gone. I thought somebody stole it and I got to call the police."

"You call them?"

"No, I go back out this morning, it's there. This afternoon it's gone again. Then just now—I don't know what the hell's going on."

"I had the other set of keys," Stick said.

"Why didn't you tell me? I'm thinking, Am I going crazy or what?"

"I got to get permission?"

"Save me some trouble, that's all. Where'd you spend the night?"

"With a friend."

"I didn't know you had any." Stick didn't smile and Frank said, "I'm kidding. What's the matter with you?"

"I didn't think it was funny."

"How about this one? We were so poor when I was a kid if you didn't wake up Christmas morning with a hard-on you didn't have anything to play with."

"You been talking to Barry."

"I just saw him outside. He was asking about you."

"How about Sportree, he been asking, too?"

He slipped it in and caught the startled look on Frank's face.

"Well, sure, he asked about you. He called me, in fact. He said, Why don't you make the bond on your friend? You want him sitting in jail?"

"Wanted me out, huh? In case I start getting too friendly with anybody? I can hear him: 'We don't know your friend, man. We don't know where his head's at on this thing.' He wants to talk to me?"

"Naturally he's concerned," Frank said. "Right, because he doesn't know you. But listen, I was the one suggested the two of you have a talk. He wasn't anxious or anything, he said maybe that was a good idea."

"I'm supposed to go down there? He must think I'm out of my fucking mind."

"As a matter of fact," Frank said, "put your mind at ease, he's not too hot on you coming to his place. And he's not going to come here, for obvious reasons, or anywhere the police or somebody might see you together."

"How about down by the fucking river late at night?" Stick said. "Jesus, he must think you're as dumb as I am. Or you think the same way he does, I don't know."

"I'm standing in the middle," Frank said. "I know both you guys, but I can't convince either of you to trust me, take my word. He doesn't care where you meet. He said you name the place you want to. He doesn't care at all, long as it's, you know, private, away from where you could be seen."

"You going to be there?"

"If you want me to, sure."

"I mean does Sportree want you to come along or am I supposed to show up alone?"

"*I* suggested it. I said *I'd* bring you. Why? What difference does it make?"

"I'm trying to find out what side you're on," Stick said.

"What *side* I'm on? For Christ sake, what're you talking about *sides*, there aren't any *sides*."

"Frank," Stick said quietly, "the guy wants to kill me."

"Come on—"

"Listen to me!" Stick waited, getting himself in control again. "I say two words, Sportree . . . Leon, they're in the can for murder, maybe life. He can't take a chance."

"What about me? I can say the two words. He want to kill me, too? He could've done it. I was with him."

"Maybe you are with him," Stick said. "Or he knows you stand to lose as much as he does, or he doesn't give a shit. I don't know, but I'm the one going to trial. I'm the one stands to lose if they can build something against me, and I'm the one stands to gain if I was to mention names."

Frank waited, staring at him. "They make you an offer?"

"Not yet, but I can see it coming. I wasn't in on the hit, they know that. So maybe they reduce it to some kind of accessory or shoplifting or throw it out altogether. They want somebody for murder, Frank. And they know I know who did it."

"Are you saying—let me get this straight." Frank walked over to the bar and poured himself a scotch. "Are you saying you're willing to make a deal with them? Cop down to shoplifting or some fucking thing?"

"No, I didn't say that," Stick said. "I'm going to ride it and keep my mouth shut and not get anywhere near that witness stand and I think I have a pretty good chance of making it, if they stay with the larceny thing. If they don't, well, tough shit, I've thought it over, I went in with my eyes open, nobody forced me, I still won't say a word. But Sportree, Leon, they're not going to hold their smoke in waiting to see what I do. Leon shot Billy Ruiz, you were standing there."

"He tried to take it all, sure, Leon didn't have any choice."

"Frank, don't shit me. A very reliable source, that hot-dog

cop, one of the first things he told me, Billy Ruiz was shot in the back. They didn't need him anymore and it's that simple. You make up a story he tried to take the goods, why? Frank, you're either with them or your head's all fucked up and you don't know what you're doing."

Stick watched him drink his scotch and pour another one.

"I don't know," Frank said. "I have some doubts, yeah. It's, well, it didn't work out. It looked easy, but things happened, things you couldn't plan on. You said we should've left it alone, stay with what we're doing. Okay, I have to agree with you, it got all fucked up and complicated. But it *could*'ve worked and we could've had an awful lot of money."

Stick said, "It never had a chance, Frank. You know why? Because you thought you knew this guy, but you don't."

"Take my word," Frank said, "okay? You don't trust him, then trust me."

"No," Stick said, "you take *my* word. Tell Sportree and Leon I've already shot two colored guys, so I know how to do it. They're always saying, Be cool. Well, tell them to be cool."

Arlene did a dumb thing. She was expecting some glossies taken at the Gateway Nationals and she wanted them, just to have, the last shots of her taken in the silver outfit. So she rented a box in the Royal Oak post office and told the lady manager of the Villa Monterey to forward her mail there. She thought it was safe because she'd just be a number, with no name.

That's how Cal found Arlene, in three steps, from the manager to the post office to the name and apartment address in Clawson.

Arlene opened the door, thinking it was Stick. She could feel her expression change. God.

Cal smiled and said, "How you doing, Miss Downey?" He had his notebook open in his hand and looked down at it.

"There's something here I wanted to ask you. About this holdup you were a witness to?"

25

The young guy, the cop, was straddling the leg-rest part of the lounge chair with his boots on the cement deck. Hunched forward in skinny faded Levi's and a corduroy sport coat and tie. Stick couldn't tell where he was carrying his gun.

He was relaxed, his hands folded in front of him, facing Frank, and seemed to be interested in whatever Frank was saying. Frank was lying back in his chair scratching his belly, being cool, his sunglasses raised to the hot four o'clock sky.

Stick watched them from the balcony. He went into the living room and walked to the Formica table and back to the balcony a few times, pausing to look down over the railing. They were the only ones at the pool. On the fifth pass, Stick said, "Shit," and went into his bedroom. He could either hide under the bed or put on his new bright blue swimming trunks. He put on the trunks.

"I believe you two know each other," Frank said. He'd had enough to drink to be relaxed or able to fake it; or else the guy, for some reason, wasn't scaring him. "He was just mentioning a friend of ours," Frank said to Stick walking up to them, "Arlene Downey."

"I thought she moved," Stick said. He pulled a chair around and sat down facing Cal Brown, showing him he didn't have anything to hide.

"That's what I told him," Frank said. "I haven't seen her around."

"Yeah, she moved," Cal said. "She's got an apartment in Clawson. But see, that's not the point. I'm not looking for her, I already talked to her. About twenty minutes ago."

Stick had his knees up in front of him, a barrier between him and the policeman.

"How's she doing?"

"She'll be okay, I think. The thing that's bothering her is that holdup she saw in a bar not too long ago. It's stuck in her mind."

"I don't believe I heard about that one," Frank said. Stick kept staring at the guy. It was coming now.

"She said it was two guys. They take the bills off this first guy that went in with a shotgun. Weird, huh? A shotgun."

"What're you trying to say?" Stick said.

"Okay." Cal straightened up a little, looking over at Stick. "Everything I say is off the record. Everything you say, same thing. No recorders, no bullshit. You know who I am, I know who you are. Let's talk things over."

"So talk," Frank said.

"All right, first thing," Cal said. "We could bust you on a couple dozen robbery armed. Listen, shit, just the cars you used could get you a hundred years apiece."

"What's he talking about?" Frank said.

"The two spades in the Northland parking lot, you can have them," Cal said. "It reminds me of an old saying, Don't ever shit a shitter. Don't ever try and hustle a couple of ace hustlers either, especially right after a job. But what I don't understand, on the Hudson's thing—"

"What Hudson's thing?" Frank said.

"The J. L. Hudson Company Hudson's thing," Cal said. "Is why you want to take just checks. What're you going to do with them? You got some guy named Hudson you're going to lay 'em off on?"

Frank didn't move. His face remained raised to the sky. But his eyes were open now behind the sunglasses.

"That's all they got in that one, just checks?"

"That's all your buddy was picking up," Cal said. "Two Brink's sacks in the doll box."

He waited, letting the silence lengthen.

"This was the second day after, right? What I been wondering, a theory of mine, is what if somebody went in there the next day, right after, and switched some other sacks to another box? Boy, that would sure fuck over the guys left with just the checks, wouldn't it?"

"I didn't read in the paper," Frank said, "about it being just checks in the box. I think—I believe it said whatever was stolen was recovered."

"Well, they don't like to publicize anything that'd make them look bad, or look dumb, you might say."

"You mean there's some money that was stolen, hasn't been found, recovered?" Frank said.

"Well, actually, I'm not at liberty to say. Normally there'd be seventy-five, a hundred thou in the cash sacks. And considerably more than that in checks." Cal grinned. "But the checks aren't worth shit in comparison, are they? And if you don't even have the checks, you ain't got nothing at all."

Stick said, "You want to come right out and say what you're trying to say?"

"I can spell it for you," Cal said. "It's a-s-s-h-o-l-e-s. That's what your associates, your black buddies, are making you look like."

"This is wild," Frank said. "Shit." He was sitting up now, pulling himself up and taking off his sunglasses to look at the guy. "You give us all this like we're supposed to know what you're talking about. Our black *buddies*—what black buddies?

Who? Give us some names. Shit, you start to make accusations give us some proof. What? You're talking about the Hudson's thing?"

"Frank—"

Stick waited. He looked from Frank to the policeman and said, "What's the deal?"

Cal Brown took his time. He put on a pleasant, innocent, sort of a surprised expression as he looked at Stick. He said, "Deal? Who's talking about a deal? I'm just telling you how I see it. The question is, do you want to go to Jackson for a while or do you want to take a chance on getting shot in the head by your buddies? It's entirely up to you, man."

There was a silence. Cal waited. He said then, "Well—" and got up to go, starting to move off, timing it, stopping and looking at Stick.

"I almost forgot. Your pretrial exam's been moved up."

It caught Stick by surprise. "How come nobody tells me?"

"I'm telling you," Cal said. "Day after tomorrow, nine o'clock. Frank Murphy Hall of Justice."

Frank was still in his trunks, pacing now, following the route from the balcony to the Formica table and back again. Stick had on a shirt, unbuttoned. He sat at the table with a cup of coffee, looking at it, looking at the wall, looking at Frank when Frank got in the way. Frank had a scotch on the bar and would stop off there every few minutes. He had two cigarettes going, one on the bar, one in an ashtray on the balcony he'd forgotten about.

"You didn't look in it at all?" Frank said.

"I didn't have time," Stick said. "I told you I thought it felt light."

"Five sacks went in the box, I saw them. Marlys came out—" Frank stopped. "Jesus, I'm standing there—Marlys *told* him. She pointed to three sacks, he put the other two in first. I watched him do it. The whole thing was set up, Billy Ruiz, everything. Leon, Marlys, somebody goes in the next day, takes out the three sacks, leaves the ones with the checks—Jesus."

"The cop spelled it right," Stick said, "didn't he?"

"We show up the next day," Frank said, "we got checks, that's all we got, checks. Sportree says, 'What's this shit?' Turns it fucking around on us. We say—we don't know what to say. We can't believe it."

"Your old buddy," Stick said. "He gives it to you, he puts it in all the way, doesn't he?"

"The son of a bitch," Frank said. "Like we're a couple of little kids. I'd like to have that Python right now—or get my hands on one."

"Don't do anything dumb," Stick said. "They're not going to let you walk in there with a gun. Take it easy. As your old buddy would say, be cool."

"I'm going to cool him," Frank said, "the son of a bitch, sitting back, all that time blowing smoke at us."

"Sitting back ready. I'm not trying to talk you out of anything," Stick said. "I'm saying you got to be careful and do it right. Put yourself in his place. If he's smart enough to pull this deal, he's not going to let you walk in and take it away from him. One advantage, he doesn't know what we know and he must think we're pretty dumb to begin with. I'm saying put yourself in his place and look at it as he sees it before you run out and do anything dumb. See, that's what's bothering you right now. You don't like the idea of him laughing at you, thinking you're dumb. Like when I swiped the car from you out there. You don't want to prove he's right, so let's think on it a while."

"We walked into places thirty times," Frank said, "no problem. How about once more? What's the difference?"

"The difference, they were guys in aprons and A&P coats. This guy's a pro. He's into, Christ, probably everything you can think of. He has people *killed*."

"And he thinks we're a couple of hicks," Frank said. "That's what I keep thinking about."

"I know you do, and maybe there's a way to use it, if you know what I mean. But it's something we'd have to give some thought to. Remember, I'm going to court the day after tomorrow and I might not be around for a while. We'll have to wait and see." Stick got up from the table and took his cup into the kitchen. When he came back in he said, "I'm going to see Arlene. Hang onto that scotch bottle till I get back."

He spent the night at Arlene's, patting her, saying, "Come on, it's okay," telling her as calmly as he could not to worry, the cop didn't know anything—that's the way they were, they showed their badge and were very official and serious and tried to scare you into admitting things, but it was all fake. Arlene said she hadn't told the cop anything. Good. Thank God, good, she hadn't slipped him anything, not knowing she was doing it. He got Arlene calmed down and lay there in the dark most of the night staring at the ceiling, hoping Frank was in bed and not out looking for a gun. He had a pretrial exam to face that could be the first step to putting him away and he had to worry about Frank and Arlene and the jazzy colored guy that had really fucked them over and they hadn't even felt it. It was a terrible mess, but it was also kind of interesting, exciting. He was getting to the point, feeling it, that he didn't have much to lose and maybe a lot to gain. What he had to do, lying there in the dark, was consider his options. Like:

Run.

No, don't run. Maybe don't move at all. Don't even look around. Forget about the money, somewhere between seventy-five and a hundred grand, the cop had said, implied. He believed the cop. So write it off.

To what?

The principle: Don't ever do business with a colored guy, especially one who's smarter than you are.

The funny thing was he still kind of liked the guy, Sportree—Maurice Jackson, his real name—Sportree in Detroit's black ghetto "Valley" and out on West Eight Mile. He admired him, the way he pulled it, and really didn't blame him. Why not? Sportree didn't give a shit about them one way or the other. Shit, if you're going to knock down a department store, get involved in murder, what was surprising about fucking over a couple of poor dumb white boys? Sportree didn't owe them anything.

They owed him something, though.

He sure hoped Frank was in bed.

He knew how Frank felt because he felt the same way. You could admire a guy's method, but you didn't have to grin and look dumb when the guy was putting it to you. You could *act* dumb, yes, if it helped the cause. And the cause was him and Frank, nobody else anymore. Except Arlene, but that was different.

All right, the options.

Sit tight. Don't say a word. Hope the larceny charge is dropped and go back to pouring cement and drinking beer and watching TV. Thank God you made it through and promise never to do it again.

Or, go for the prize. Get the fucker, sitting there blowing his Jamaican smoke.

Take the Luger P-38 and put it in the guy's face and say, "Give me the money, man. Be cool, man." All that *man* shit. "Be cool or else you're a dead nigger."

That sounded pretty good lying in the dark. Next to him, Arlene moved and he could hear her breathing.

Make sure Leon Woody was there and give him some of it. See it? The Luger, a good-looking, mean-looking, no-bullshit handgun. "Hey, man, you know what we do down in Oklahoma to guys like you?"

No, keep it straight. Who gives a shit where you came from or what they do in Oklahoma? He didn't even know what they did.

Keep it personal. He liked both of them. Leon Woody, too, with his little girl, he seemed like a nice guy and couldn't picture him shooting Billy Ruiz in the back.

He respected them.

But he also wanted them to respect him. And that was the whole thing. His only option.

It was about 4:30 in the morning by the time he figured out a way to do it that might work.

At 7:30 he woke up Arlene and said, "Come on, you're moving to a motel. And this time don't leave a forwarding address, okay?"

* * *

"They're sitting there in their swimming trunks taking a *sun*bath," Cal said. "These two assholes, it hadn't even entered their heads something was funny."

He was talking to his superior now, Detective Lieutenant Walter Shea, in the lieutenant's office at 1300.

"How about the stolen gun?" Walter said. "Somebody's been doing some thinking."

"I'm pretty sure it was for protection," Cal said. "Stickley's. In case the blackies came after him. But now things are different, a little more interesting."

"You didn't search his place, then."

"What do I want to find the gun for? I'd have to arrest him."

"I'm grateful you're telling me all this," Walter said, "so I won't feel my twenty-seven years were wasted."

Cal nodded politely. "Yes, sir, I can use all the experienced advice I can get."

"Emory suggest you go for a deal?"

"What's to make a deal about? I think they realize now they don't have anything to sell. Names, yes. Except that if Frank Ryan starts naming names, somebody's going to name his name right back. Because I'll bet you eighty-seven thousand bucks he was in the office when the window washer got it."

"So where are we?"

"Still watching," Cal said. "But I think the clowns are about ready to come out and put on a show."

26

"You tell him my court date's tomorrow," Stick said, "so if he's worried and wants to talk, it's got to be today."

"You were right there, you should've picked up two of these." Frank was sitting hunched over, examining the Walther, hefting it, feeling its weight, looking at its Luger profile in his hand. The box of cartridges was on the coffee table.

"Why would I get one for you?" Stick said. "I don't even know what fucking side you're on. I believe you told me more'n once you knew him a hell of a lot longer than you'd known me."

"That's what we should do," Frank said, "get in an argument. It just seems like, I don't know, we need more time to get ready."

"If he's setting up a hit on me, it's got to be today," Stick said. "Tomorrow I'm on the stand, you know that."

"But he doesn't know it," Frank said.

"Right. That's why he's going to have to move fast once you tell him and he finds out, I mean if he still wants me. I'll tell you something else I've been thinking," Stick said. "If he wants me, I bet he wants you, too. Why not? He's not going to split with you, he's already jacked you out of a cut. But if you found it out—he doesn't know what you'd do. So if he sets me up, why not set you up, too? Two birds. Two dumb fucking dumb white birds. I bet he says he wants you to be there."

Frank called Sportree and told him about Stick's court date.

Sportree said, "Yeah? Hey, yeah, I'd like to talk to him, as I told you. Let me get back to you."

Frank hung up.

Stick said, "He calls back, then we wait, then we call him back."

Frank said, "Jesus, I hope it works."

Stick said, "You hope it *works?* If it doesn't work, we're fucking dead."

"He didn't say anything about me being there."

"Wait," Stick said.

Sportree called back in twenty minutes. He said, "How about I meet both of you—"

Holding the phone, Frank looked over at Stick.

"—but I prefer you didn't come here, your friend going to court and everything, you understand?"

"Where?" Frank asked.

"How about—I mean you sure you can do it, nobody following you—how about this motel, call the Ritz Motel, out Woodward near that hospital, almost to Pontiac. Look for Leon's car, light blue '74 Continental. Make it nine o'clock."

"Just a minute." Frank put his hand over the mouthpiece and looked at Stick. "He wants to meet at a motel out by Pontiac, tonight."

"We walk in and Leon or some jig steps out of the can shooting," Stick said, "while Sportree's home watching Redd Foxx. I thought he was going to say some back alley, or an empty building. Tell him we'll meet him in front of the police station, talk in the car."

"Come on," Frank said. He was nervous holding the phone with Sportree on the other end.

"Tell him we'll think it over and get back to him. That's good enough."

Frank told him.

Sportree said, "Hey, don't be too long. I send somebody to pick you up."

Frank hung up. "He says he'll send somebody for us."

"I bet he will. One thing we know," Stick said, "no, two things. He can't take a chance doing it at his place. He's got too much going on there. And we're not going to get in with a gun. So you see any other way?"

"No, I don't guess so."

"Let's get going, then."

"Okay," Frank said. He laid the Luger on the coffee table and got up. "What're you going to wear?"

A half hour later Frank called him again from the Graeco-Roman lobby of the Vic Tanny on Eight Mile Road, almost directly across from Sportree's Royal Lounge.

"We decided it'd be better if we came to your place," Frank said.

"I *told* you," Sportree said. "Man could be followed, he bring 'em here. You want to get me in the shit? Frank, hey, use your head."

"No, we decided," Frank said. "Get Leon there so he can listen. We'll leave now and be very careful of tails and be there in about a half hour."

"Frank, listen to me—"

Frank hung up. He reached into the big pocket of his safari jacket for a pack of Marlboros.

"He doesn't like it."

"I bet he doesn't," Stick said. Stick was wearing his light green sport coat he'd bought in Florida. The right side hung straight, tight over his shoulder, with the Luger filling the inside pocket. They lighted cigarettes and stood by the showcase window, looking out across the parking lot and the flow of traffic on the wide, parkway-divided lanes of Eight Mile. It was a long way over there to Sportree's and the traffic was getting heavier. They concentrated on the cars that, every once in a while, pulled into Sportree's side lot.

A young guy with a build came over from the counter in his tight Vic Tanny T-shirt and tight black pants and asked them if they were members. Frank said they were thinking about joining but were waiting for a friend. The Vic Tanny guy invited them to make themselves comfortable and when their friend came he'd be happy to show them around and describe the different membership plans.

"It might not be a bad idea," Frank said. "Work out two, three times a week, get some steam or a sauna."

"I could never do push-ups and all that shit," Stick said. "I don't know, it sounds good, but it's so fucking boring. The thing to do, just don't eat so much."

"I don't eat much," Frank said.

"You drink too much. You know how many calories are in a shot? What you put away, those doubles, it's a couple of full meals."

"What do you do, count my drinks?"

"I can't," Stick said. "I can't count that fast."

"Jesus—" Frank said and stopped, looking out the window. "There we are. Light blue '74 Continental. Son of a bitch, how does he afford a car like that?"

"Maybe he lives in it," Stick said.

They watched the car pull off Eight Mile into Sportree's parking lot. A half minute later Leon Woody appeared, coming around front to the upstairs entrance, and went in.

Frank said, "What if there's a guy in the lot parks the cars?"

"I haven't seen anybody," Stick said, "but if there is, we go home and think of something else quick—"

"Maybe we should give it a little more time. I told him a half hour." Frank looked over at the Vic Tanny guy behind the counter, talking on the phone now. "Let's let him give us the tour. Maybe there's some broads in the sauna."

No parking-lot attendant, no one coming in behind them or going out. There was nothing to it. Frank pulled the T-bird into an empty space next to Leon's light blue Continental. They got out. Frank waited, standing by the rear deck of the T-bird.

Stick walked around the right side of Leon's car and opened the front door. He looked at Frank.

Frank nodded.

Stick took the Luger out of his coat pocket, felt under the seat to make sure it was clear and there was enough room, and slipped the Luger under there, carefully, and closed the door. He opened the rear door and reached in to feel under the front seat, closed the door and nodded as he walked out to where Frank was waiting.

"You're sure?" Frank said.

"You can reach it from both sides."

"I mean that we'll take his car. Shit, or if we're going anywhere."

"I can't see Sportree driving, exposing his plates," Stick said. "I can't see him letting us drive, meet them. What if we made a stop at the hardware store?"

"If we go anywhere," Frank said. "That's the big *if*."

"No, we're going somewhere," Stick said. "That's the only thing I'm sure of. Probably after it gets dark. And we're going to make it easy for him by acting as dumb as he thinks we are, playing into his hands and giving him a *reason* for taking us out, so he won't have to use force."

They were walking out of the lot toward the front.

"There's an old Indian saying," Stick said: "You can't judge a guy until you've walked a mile in his moccasins. I haven't been able to do that, but last night, all night long, I imagined being in that fucker's red patent-leather high-heel shoes, remembering everything I could about him—the way he talked, the way he moved, how he's kept himself out of the whole deal. He's not going to have a lot of noise in his place and get blood on his carpeting. We're going somewhere."

"And I'm supposed to offer to drive," Frank said.

"Don't forget that."

"And what if they say okay?"

"We're fucked," Stick said.

* * *

Leon Woody opened the door. He said, "How you doing?" and stepped inside. Sportree was in the doorway leading to the kitchen, pointing a pump-action shotgun at them.

Frank said, "What're you doing?" getting fear and amazement in his voice and not having to fake much of it.

"I want to make sure we still friends," Sportree said. "Leon's going to check you out, if that'd be all right."

"I don't get it," Frank said. Stick liked the dumb look on his face.

Leon did a good job. He felt every part of them where a gun or a knife could be hidden, and felt their coats, under the arms and the lining as well as the pockets. They let him, not saying anything, Frank staring at Sportree.

"Look like they still friends," Leon said.

Sportree turned with the shotgun and went into the kitchen. He came back out with two bottles, glasses, and a bowl of ice, saying, "Since you all're here." When they were sitting down and had their drinks, Sportree looked over at Stick.

"What kind of deal they make you?"

"As a matter of fact," Stick said, "they haven't said a word about a deal. They haven't made an attempt, physically, to get anything out of me either. The way it stands, I'm going to the exam tomorrow with no reason to say a word about anything that's not any of their business. All they got on me, I lifted a doll box off a shelf. If I was conspiring to walk out with it, they have to prove it."

Sportree got a Jamaican out of a gold-leaf box and lit it, looking at Stick.

Leon Woody said, "They know you part of something else."

"They got to prove that, too," Stick said.

"They ain't going to let you go."

"Then they'll have to make up something, and they'd still have to prove it."

"You saying you pure and they ain't nothing to worry about?"

"I'm saying I've played this straight so far," Stick said, "but I'm not saying you don't have anything to worry about. There seems to be a discrepancy in how many Brink's sacks were in the doll box originally and how many were there when I picked it up."

"Say what?" Leon Woody sounded a little surprised without changing his bearded African expression.

"Five went in," Stick said. "Three came out sometime before I got there."

"How you know that?" Sportree asked him.

"Because I can add and subtract," Stick said. "I think two from five is three. There were two sacks in the box when I looked in it, right before they stuck the gun in my face."

"This comes as something new," Sportree said, at ease with his cigarette. "You never mention it before."

"I wasn't there," Stick said. "I didn't know how many sacks went in. Frank and I are talking yesterday, not till yesterday he mentions five. I said, 'Five? There were only *two.*' "

Sportree smiled and shook his head, his gaze moving to Frank.

"What'd you think, Frank, he said that?"

"What'd I *think?*" He had a good on-the-muscle edge to his tone. "First I couldn't believe it. Then I thought, Shit, somebody's fucking somebody. Guy I thought was a friend of mine."

"Oh, my," Sportree said, shaking his head again. "It can get complicated, huh? People get the wrong idea." He looked at Stick. "What the police think?"

"I don't know what they think," Stick said. "They didn't discuss it with me. Maybe they think it's still in the store somewhere, I don't know. The thing is, we know it isn't." He kept his gaze on Sportree.

"Yeah, maybe they think it is," Sportree said, squinting in the smoke, thoughtful. "But I doubt it. See, that's why we have to be so careful—you coming here—man, they could be watching every move you make."

Frank said, still on the muscle, "I think we're getting off the subject, how we got fucked by a guy I thought was a friend."

"Frank, did we know Stick was going to get arrested?" Sportree waited, patient, like he was speaking to a child.

"No."

"So he'd come up here with two sacks, wouldn't he?"

"Yeah."

"What do you think I was going to do?"

"I don't know—shit, I don't get it at all. But you took the three sacks."

"As a precaution," Sportree said. "Marlys walked out with them in a box the next day. This was something I thought of after. If she can do it, fine. If they too many cops around, we wait to do it like we planned it. But see, then we have two chances and two's better than one."

"How come," Frank said, "you didn't call us after, say you had it?"

"Frank, you never give us your number till the other day. Unlisted, right? Marlys went out there to look for you. Said she couldn't find you. Probably out with those chicks."

"Shit."

"Come on, Frank, ain't no scam. We get it, man, we busy counting. Shit, you want to know what eighty-seven thousand look like? You and him supposed to come by the next day. Only he get arrested."

"*I* came by," Frank said, "the day after. You never mention it. Shit, we're sitting here talking, you already got it."

"Hey, man, listen to me. I'm telling you now, ain't I? Because I know I can trust him. But he's in jail, good friend of yours, I don't know what he's going to say. I don't know you two been talking or not. So I keep quiet till the smoke begin to settle and I see where I'm at, see where you and him are at. Okay, now everything's cool. He don't say a word tomorrow, he walk out and we split the kitty."

"Not tomorrow," Stick said, "right now. I can still go to trial. I could get ninety days, shit, a year, I don't know. I don't want to come out and not find anybody around."

"We be here," Sportree said. "Man, nobody's going nowhere."

"Today," Stick said. "Right now. I take care of mine, you take care of yours."

"I'd just as soon do it now," Frank said. "I get nervous

thinking about that much money sitting someplace, not making any interest."

Sportree grinned. "How you know it's not in the bank?"

"Shit," Frank said. "Where is it, under the bed?"

Sportree's finger caressed the little bebop growth on his chin, thinking, making up his mind. He looked over at Leon Woody.

"You can understand they want to see it."

Leon didn't say anything.

"Well, we might as well drive out there, make them happy. All right with you?"

"They own as much of it we do," Leon said. "I feel better, though, we wait till it gets a little dark. People won't see us walking in and out of places."

Sportree looked over at Frank. "We can relax here a while, have something to eat—"

"Where we going?" Stick asked.

Sportree grinned. "We all going together, man. You'll see."

27

In the parking lot, walking past the cars, Frank and Stick were following Leon Woody. Stick thought Sportree was right behind them. But when he glanced around, Sportree wasn't there, he hadn't turned the corner.

Leon was walking toward his light blue Continental. Frank said, "Hey, Leon, I'll drive."

Leon looked around. "How you going to drive, man, you don't know where we going?"

"You tell me," Frank said.

Stick was thinking, Shit. He wanted Sportree to be here.

But it was all right. Sportree came around the corner, some kind of coat or jacket over his arm. Leon waited for him. He said then, "Frank say he want to drive."

Sportree looked happy, going out for the evening to have a

good time. He said, "Shit, Leon drive. Then we come back, have a drink, get your car. Frank, you ride up with Leon, me and the Stick here will sit in the back."

Stick saw it, Sportree and Leon looking at each other, quick little look in the dreamy African eyes, telling each other something. They never let down, Stick thought.

They went on North Woodward as far as Norwalk Freight Lines, past the semi's lined up in the dim-lighted yard, and U-turned around the island and came back south a few blocks to the Ritz Motel, VACANCY in orange on the big, bright-lighted Las Vegas sign. There were heavy-duty truck cabs in there, Macks and Peterbilts, and a couple of vans and a few new-model cars with Michigan plates. The swimming pool was lighted and empty in the half rectangle; most of the units were dark. Leon Woody let the Continental glide quietly into a parking space in the far corner of the rectangle, in front of Number 24, away from the motel office. Leon cut the ignition.

Sportree said, "Hey, shit, listen." And Leon turned the key back on so Sportree could hear the radio.

Leon got out, taking the motel key out of his pocket. Frank got out. Stick waited in the back seat with Sportree.

" 'Feel Like Making Love,' " Sportree said. "Bob James, hey, shit. Idris, listen to Idris, huh?" Sportree sat there listening. Stick sat there. Sportree wouldn't get out of the car. It was pretty good, it melted over Stick with a nice beat, but it wasn't Merle Haggard and Stick wasn't sure how long he could sit there.

Sportree said, "That's a number, you know it? Man used to arrange for Aretha." He opened the door and finally got out of the car, then reached into the front for the key and turned off the ignition.

Stick waited.

Sportree looked back at him. "You coming? You don't seem too anxious."

Stick said, "What? I dropped my cigarettes."

When Sportree turned, Stick reached under the seat. Jesus, where was it? His hand touched the grip and he got it out, stuck it in the waist of his pants, and pulled the jacket down over it.

They went inside, into Number 24, a big room with a double bed and two twins and a refrigerator that had a cooking range and sink on top. Stick knew it wasn't going to take too much time. There wasn't anything to talk about, nothing to look at, no faking anything. No, it'd be done quick. Sportree had the poplin jacket over his arm. He looked around, as if picking a place to sit down, but he didn't. Frank was standing there, too, waiting for it. Leon Woody went into the bathroom and closed the door.

Stick said to himself, Here it is.

In the bathroom, Leon Woody took a Colt .45 automatic out of the medicine cabinet and wrapped a towel around it loosely. He flushed the toilet.

Stick was ready. When he saw Leon come out with the towel wrapped around his hand, around something in his hand, Stick pulled the Luger, pointed it at him, at the white, surprised look in Leon's eyes, and shot him in the face. Stick turned the Luger on Sportree and shot him twice in the body, dead center, above the jacket falling away and the revolver in Sportree's hand. Sportree made a grunting sound, the wind going out of him, and fell back against a chair, turning it over and going down as he hit the wall.

Stick said to himself, I don't believe it. You've killed four colored guys.

"Jesus Christ," Frank said. "Holy Christ almighty."

Stick got down on one knee over Sportree and took the car keys and another ring of keys from his side pocket. Frank was saying, Jesus Christ.

"We'll leave them," Stick said, "we might as well. And take Leon's car."

"We got to get our car," Frank said.

"You bet we do," Stick said, "and that ain't all. It's got to be in his apartment someplace."

Marlys was in the bedroom with the air conditioning going, lying on top of the bed in a short little slip she used for a nightgown, reading *Viva* and listening to Stevie coming out of the bedroom speaker. She heard the door to the apartment open and close and looked over the top of the magazine, waiting.

"Hey, I'm in here. Where you been?"

She was looking at the magazine again when Stick came in, the Luger in his hand, not pointing it, holding it at his side. He saw her slender dark legs extending from the slip, her ankles crossed.

"Hey—"

Marlys jumped and sat up quickly, swinging her legs over the side of the bed.

"What you want?" Not about to take anything from him.

"A doll box," Stick said.

"Where's Sportree? You come walking in here—what kind of shit is this?"

They heard Frank call from the other room, "I found it. Come on." He appeared in the bedroom doorway with the Little Curly Laurie Walker box under his arm and smiled at the girl. "Hi, Marlys."

"I think you better put that back and talk to Sportree," Marlys said. "I mean if you have any sense at all."

"I think he'd want us to have it," Frank said.

Marlys frowned at him. "What you talking about?"

"You're going to find out anyway," Frank said. "He died. And you know something? You could, too."

They didn't say anything walking out to the parking lot or while Frank dropped the doll box in the trunk of the T-bird—not until they were driving away from the place, in the night traffic on Eight Mile.

Stick said, "Slow down."

Frank said, "Jesus, the steering wheel of Leon's car, you had your hands all over it."

"I wiped it off," Stick said, "the keys just in case, the door handles, different places we might have touched."

Frank kept watching the rearview mirror. He said, "I'm trying to see how we could've messed up. What do you think?"

"I think we're halfway home," Stick said. "But we got to make one stop."

"You think she'll do it?"

"She said she would."

"I don't know—bringing her in."

"You got somebody else in mind?" Stick looked over at him. "I think we're lucky the way it's working out. She's a good one, which is pretty nice, since we sure as shit can't take it home and that hot-dog cop drops in to visit again. I don't see any other way."

28

Stick was at the Frank Murphy Hall of Justice, fifth floor, before nine the next morning, and found out examinations would be held in Judge Robert J. Columbo's courtroom. He told the clerk who he was and sat in the seats with the waiters and spectators two and a half hours, listening to examinations: a rape, a complicated dope-related shooting, and a felonious assault, watching the little fat black prosecutor, whom he remembered from the time before. The judge didn't say much; he seemed patient, sitting back in his chair against the light wood paneling, but would interrupt in a relaxed way when the defense attorneys took too much time, and he kept it moving.

When the judge took the envelope from the clerk and called Stick's number, he walked in through the gate and was sworn in, gave his name, sat down at the table facing the witness stand, and didn't say a word after that.

The young guy, the cop, took the stand, told about arresting Ernest Stickley, Jr., in the storeroom of the J. L. Hudson Company toy department, and identified Stick as the one. There was no mention of the holdup. After Cal Brown had testified, was questioned, and stepped down, the little prosecutor talked to the judge for several minutes in conference, then turned and walked away from the bench shaking his head, knowing it was going to happen, but making a show of being surprised after His Honor asked him if he actually wanted to bring this one to trial; he had said yes, and His Honor had said he didn't. He dismissed the charge and called a noon recess.

Frank was there in the audience, getting up now with the rest of the people, starting to move toward the door. Stick was coming through the gate to join the crowd. Frank was grinning as he caught Stick's eye, and Stick grinned.

Cal Brown was waiting. He held the gate as Stick swung it open and said, "Be good now." He was grinning, too. Everybody seemed happy.

Cal watched them move out through the courtroom doorway, seeing their Caucasian heads among the pimp hats and naturals.

The little prosecutor came over to watch, too. He said, "Now, about the real business."

Cal said, "Their place was searched while they were here. I was hoping we'd come up with a P-38, like the one caused the death of the brothers and was stolen from that guy's house in Bloomfield, and of course I was hoping we'd find the eighty-seven. Nothing."

"What if they run out on you?"

"We got somebody watching their place. The two guys' clothes, the money still there in the Oxydol box and about a grand in an old beat-up suitcase—they run, they're going home first."

"You hope."

"That's all I got is hope," Cal said, "that somebody fucks up."

Stick called Arlene from a phone booth on the first floor of the Frank Murphy Hall of Justice. When she answered he said,

"I'm out. No shit, it's all done, no trial. . . . Okay, call Delta, it'll have to be that five-something flight, five forty-five, I think, nonstop to Miami. Make the three reservations—your name, Mr. E. Stickley, Mr. F. Ryan. . . . Sure, you can use real names, we haven't done anything. . . . No, you won't have any trouble this time of year. Find out how much and take enough out of the box to cover it and fifty or a hundred for yourself, for magazines and gum and. . . . Right. Take a cab out to Metro. Pick up, pay for all three tickets but only pick up your own. Leave the other two at the Delta counter with our name on it. You got a suitcase that'll hold it? . . . Good, put it all in the suitcase, nothing else in with it, and burn the box. . . . In the bathtub, I don't know, someplace you won't burn the goddamn motel down. Then, listen, check the suitcase through with your own stuff. Don't carry it on, you know, they look at everything. . . . That's right. . . . No, we'll see you in the Miami airport. You get there, check the suitcase in one of those boxes, you know, and meet us in the bar in the Miami airport near the Delta counter. It's way down at one end. At Metro, waiting for the plane, you see us, don't say anything or act like you recognize us at all. . . . No, shit no, we won't be sitting together. . . . I know. . . . Listen, I can understand, I'm a little nervous, too, but don't worry. There isn't anything to worry about. . . . Right, a few more hours it'll be over. . . . I do, too. . . . You'll hear me say it plenty. . . . All right. Arlene? I love you. . . . 'Bye."

Frank dropped his cigarette and stepped on it. "It took you long enough."

"I wanted to go over it again."

"She got it cold?"

"I don't see how we can miss," Stick said.

"I don't know, I think maybe we ought to put it in the car and just go."

"How far?" Stick said.

Burning the doll box made a mess, left a tubful of black ashes that dissolved under the shower spray but left a dark, smeary-looking stain in the tub. Arlene wished she had some Ajax. The bath soap just seemed to smear it around more. The maid would probably think she'd been awfully dirty, greasing a car or something.

The money—God, $87,000 and a little more, in all kinds of bills—was stacked neatly in the small light blue suitcase, with a few inches to spare. She thought about laying one of her photograph albums on top—it would fit perfectly—but she remembered what Stick had said. Just the money. So she'd have to jam her albums and manila envelopes of photographs in with her clothes.

You don't need them anymore, she thought.

Or the silver costume.

The pictures would be fun to look at later, years later. Here's mommy when she was a model. Here's mommy at the Indy Nationals. Cute?

The NHRA Grand Nationals were going to be in Los Angeles this year. September 5-6-7. She could picture it on posters and in ads that ran in hot-rod magazines. They'd get some other girl. In Los Angeles that probably wouldn't be hard at all.

The silver costume didn't take up any room; it didn't even have to be folded, it was so skimpy. The boots were soft and rolled up and could be stuck down at the corners.

The life-size cutout—smiling at her—God, what was she going to do with it?

She had made Stick bring it along with all her stuff. He'd said, Why? What did she need it for? She remembered she had been surprised at him asking and had said she just wanted it, that's all.

She would have to leave it now and she wondered what they'd do with it and if they'd be mad. Well, they could just throw it out. She saw her life-size reinforced cardboard image cracked and folded in a trash can, her face looking out. She was glad she was getting out of here. She hated being alone and thinking so much. God, how did a person stop thinking when they wanted to?

Arlene finished packing, called a cab, and paid the motel bill. When the cab came she walked out with her purse, following the driver carrying the two suitcases, and closed the door on the smiling life-size cutout in the silver costume.

The lady, the manager of the Villa Monterey, said she wished she could take a vacation sometime. Frank said well, they'd been working pretty hard and needed a chance to take it easy and recharge the old batteries. The lady, the manager, said she'd have thought they got enough rest sitting around the pool every day. Sitting, yes, Frank said, but they were always thinking, and thinking was hard work. He paid her four-fifty in advance for the next month, September, and she smiled and said she hoped they had a nice time.

Stick, waiting there, was glad she wasn't a talker. He was starting to get awful antsy.

Cal Brown had volunteered and taken over the watch. Surveillance of suspects.

He was parked across from the Villa Monterey and down a hundred feet in a dark brown Chrysler Cordoba they had taken off a smack dealer the week before. Cal was in love with the car, his first time in it, and he was trying to think of ways to keep it for his own personal-official use.

He watched them come out of the Villa Monterey with their suitcases and open the trunk of the white T-bird. The one guy, Stickley, with a cardboard suitcase, looked like he was going somewhere to pick sugar beets. The other one, Ryan, had on a suit that glistened in the afternoon sun.

Well now, Cal Brown said to himself. Hit them now or wait? He had warrants in his pocket for search or arrest, with the dates left blank.

Is the eighty-seven in the suitcase?

No. Probably not.

So why hit them now?

Are they going to pick it up and keep going?

Probably. Yes.

Might you need more help than just yourself, rather than maybe blow it and get your head cut off, not to mention other parts?

Bet your ass.

But he did not turn on the newly installed radio until he had followed the white T-bird for fifteen minutes and finally they hit the Southfield Freeway, going south.

He said into the mike, after describing the cars and their location, "Get me some very quiet state police backup. Give them my code and let me have theirs. We could be heading for the Ohio line, but I got a feeling we're going to turn off on Ninety-four."

That's what they did, south of the Veterans Hospital, took the off ramp down through the tight curve to the right, past the sign that said AIRPORT. It was about twenty minutes from here, out the old Willow Run Expressway.

Cal got on the mike again. "We'll need two men at each terminal, International, North Terminal, and West. Give them descriptions. They're to watch for the suspects and keep them under surveillance, but are not to collar them unless they attempt to put their luggage on a flight. I'm going to be right behind them—but just in case."

The T-bird crept along in the dimness of the cement structure, past the lines of cars that seemed to extend without end, up one lane and down another, from the first to the third level.

Stick was driving. He said, "Come on, let's go up on the roof."

Frank said, "I don't *want* to park it on the roof. Twice I parked up there, I come back, my wheel covers're gone."

"They can take the wheel covers anyplace you park," Stick said. "Right in front, in the no-parking zone, they can take your fucking wheel covers."

"There's more chance up there," Frank said. "Sitting up there away from everything a couple of weeks."

Stick said, "You worried about the car, then come back in a couple of days and get it. How long you think it'll take us to make the deposits? Say eight banks, North Miami to Lauderdale. You drive it in a half hour, less."

"Maybe we'll want to rest a while. *Maybe?* Christ, I'm tighter now than when I went in that fucking store."

"What I'm really saying," Stick said, "what difference does it make how long we leave it or if it gets stripped or not or even gets stolen, so what? Buy a new one."

"I like this one," Frank said. "I don't want to see it get damaged."

"Then come back tomorrow." Stick paused. "Wait a minute. What're we arguing about?"

"I don't want to park it up on the roof," Frank said.

Arlene paid the cabdriver and turned around to see a porter picking up her two suitcases. The porter asked her, What airline, ma'am? Arlene said thank you, but she'd take the bags herself, they weren't heavy. The porter, without a word, set them down and turned away as she picked them up. Arlene was afraid to let the bags out of her sight. She had never been so tense. She went through the automatic doors that opened in front of her, beginning to angle toward the right as she entered the terminal, knowing Delta was over there, the counters running the length of the right wall. She had come in and walked over that way before, going to Atlanta and Daytona Beach for NASCAR races.

But this time Arlene stopped.

Directly in front of her, high above the American Air Lines counter, was a giant black rectangle with white lighted letters and numbers that listed departures. It was strange the way her gaze saw, not a list of flight numbers and cities, but only one.

LOS ANGELES.
FLIGHT 41.
5:30 P.M.
ON TIME.

She looked over at the clock high above the Delta counter. A quarter to five.

Arlene thought of her friend in Bakersfield. She thought of the Grand Nationals coming up, the week after next. She thought of Hollywood. That was strange, Hollywood. She thought of the silver costume. And she thought of her age, twenty-six. In a month, twenty-seven. Why'd she think of that?

Arlene walked over to the American counter.

Frank and Stick came across the enclosed overpass that joined the parking structure to the main entrance that was on the second level of the West Terminal, Detroit Metropolitan. They had walked from the parked T-bird, carrying their bags, about two hundred yards.

Frank said, "You got the keys?"

Stick said, "What keys?"

"The *car* keys."

"Jesus Christ," Stick said.

Maybe he wouldn't be coming back with Frank in a couple of weeks. Let him get the car by himself, he loved it so much.

They crossed the roadway and passed the cars being unloaded and the porters and the hand trucks—none of the porters offered to take their bags—and entered the terminal through the automatic doors.

"I don't see her around," Stick said.

Frank's gaze followed Stick's, studying the people walking around and waiting, most of them waiting at counters, some sitting down in the rows of seats. The place didn't seem very busy.

There were several lines at the Delta counter. Frank picked the shortest line, behind two people. Stick waited with him a minute, then stepped over to a line of three people. Frank gave him a look. Ten minutes later Frank was still behind the two people. Stick was at the counter. Frank came over. He said to the reservations clerk, "Mr. Ryan and Mr. Stickley. I believe you're holding a couple of seats for us. The Miami flight."

The clerk stepped over to a machine, punched a few keys, waited while the thing clicked back at him, and punched a few more. He did it again and stepped back to them saying, "Yes, you're confirmed on Flight Eleven-eighty, departing at five forty-five from Gate Twenty-nine. Will you be checking your luggage through?"

"Yes, we will," Frank said.

Behind him, Stick said, "I don't see her anywhere."

Frank said, over his shoulder, "She's probably at the gate already, picking her seat."

The clerk was holding up an American Air Lines ticket envelope, looking at it. He said, "I see this was left for you. It has your names on it." He handed the envelope to Frank.

Stick saw the names, written in ink, as Frank took the envelope. *Mr. E. Stickley, Mr. F. Ryan,* one above the other.

The clerk said, "If you'll put your luggage up here please—" He was holding the luggage tags.

Frank shoved the American Air Lines envelope into his inside coat pocket and reached down for his suitcase. Behind him, Stick was picking up his ratty-looking bag. Behind Stick, somebody said, "Just a moment, please."

They both looked around. Frank said, "What?"

There were two of them, thirty-year-old guys in neat summer-weight suits, no hats. They looked like pro football players. No they didn't, they looked like cops.

One of them had his badge case open already, giving them a look at his shield. He said, "State police. I'd like you, please, to pick up your suitcases and go around the counter over there to that door you see marked AUTHORIZED PERSONNEL ONLY."

"What is this?" Frank said, indignant. "What for?"

The state policeman said, "Pick up your bag, buddy, *now.*"

"I just want to know what's going on, for Christ sake. I mean what is this? You accusing us of something, or what?"

Frank stopped as Cal Brown came in and walked up to the two state cops and showed them his credentials. They nodded and said something to him.

Stick was watching. He said mildly, "I hope this doesn't take too long. We got a flight to make."

Cal Brown turned to them sitting at the metal table in the bare, brightly fluorescent-lighted room, and gave them a nice smile.

"You got a flight, I got two warrants," he said, taking them out of his jacket, giving them a flash of the mag holstered under the jacket, and holding the warrants up for them to see. "This one's for search. You mind?"

"If we miss the flight, you got to pay for it," Frank said.

"No, the airline'll put you on another one free of charge," Cal said. "I mean if you're going anywhere."

Stick said, "If you want to look in our bags, go ahead. I mean maybe if we hurry up, we can get it done. What do you think?"

They watched as the two state cops came over and opened their suitcases and began going through them, taking out each item of clothing separately and feeling it.

Frank sat back and lighted a cigarette. He said, "I hope, when you're through, you guys put it all back the way it was."

Stick said to Cal, "You mind I ask what you're looking for?"

"Yeah, I do," Cal said.

They unrolled socks and looked inside shoes and studied their toilet kits very closely. The one going through Stick's bag took out a wad of bills and looked over at Cal. Cal shook his head. Frank stared at the money, then at Stick, but he didn't say anything to anybody, not until the two state cops were finished.

"Is that it, Officers?"

Cal Brown said, "Now if you'll stand up please, gents, and empty your pockets—lay whatever you have on the table."

"Come on," Frank said, "pat us down if you want. You think we're carrying guns, for Christ sake, on an *air*plane?"

"Get up," Cal said.

Stick took out his wallet, the car keys, a pack of Marlboros, matches, and a comb.

Frank started with his coat. He took his sunglasses case and the American Air Lines envelope out of his inside coat pocket. He pulled out his wallet and a clean, folded handkerchief.

Cal looked at the American envelope. Why, if they were flying Delta— He picked it up.

Stick was watching him. Frank was digging for loose change in his pants pocket.

Cal took a piece of paper out of the envelope. He unfolded it and a locker key fell to the table. He looked down at the key, then at Stick, then at the piece of paper for a moment, and handed it to Stick.

Stick looked at the two words written in ink in the neat, slanting feminine hand.

I'm sorry.

He kept looking at the words.

Cal handed the locker key to one of the state cops, who studied the number on it as he walked out.

Frank was frowning, not knowing what was going on.

"What's it say?"

Stick handed him the note. He said to Cal, "Maybe somebody left that, we got it by mistake, you know?"

"With your names on it?" Cal said.

Walking through the terminal, the two state cops were behind them carrying their bags. Cal was right in front of them, holding tight to the small, light blue suitcase. No one they passed stopped or turned around or seemed to notice that the two in the middle were handcuffed together.

They went through the automatic doors and down the sidewalk, away from the entrance, to wait for the police car to pull up.

Frank said, half whispering against his shoulder, trying not to move his mouth, "Of all the ones, all the broads that'd jump at the chance, I mean *jump,* you pick that turkey. Christ, and I let you, I go along. What'd you say, the great judge of broads? 'She's a good one.' Your exact words, 'She's a good one.' "

"She didn't mean this to happen," Stick said. "It's not her fault."

"Whose fault is it, mine? What'd I say? Let's put it in the car and go, take the swag and run, man, and not get anybody else in the act. Remember that? Hey, remember the rule? Don't tell anybody your business. Nobody. Especially a junkie. Shit, especially a broad. One you pick."

The police car was pulling up to them.

"What do you think I went to the trouble to think up all those rules for? You remember the ten rules? We act like businessmen and nobody knows our business. You remember that?"

Stick said, "Frank, why don't you shut the fuck up?"

STICK

7

Stick said he wasn't going if they had to pick up anything. Rainy said no, there wasn't any product in the deal; all they had to do was drop a bag. Stick said, "And the guy's giving you five grand?"

"It makes him feel important," Rainy said, "it's how it's done. Listen, this's the big time, man, I'm taking you uptown."

Rainy told Stick he didn't even have to say a word unless the guy Chucky asked him something. Which he probably would, Chucky liked to talk. He was a you-all, he talked real nice and easy, real slooow, slower than you, Rainy said. Stick said he could hardly wait to meet the guy, thinking: Rainy and Chucky ... like they were hanging around the playground.

You go out to Hialeah, Calder, Rainy said, everybody out there, the cocktail waitresses, everybody, they call him just Chucky. But you go down on Southwest Eighth Street, around in there, or some places down in South Miami where they used to know him on the street, anybody down there they still call him Chucky Buck, Rainy said. It was like his street name before he moved up to his top floor condominium. Yeah, Chucky Buck. Now, he went to his country club, any place like that, he used his real name again, Chucky Gorman. He was about forty but tried to act young. Big guy. Not real fat, but he had a weird shape for a guy, like a woman. Maybe he was even kind of a weird person, some people thought he was a switch-hitter. But a nice guy. You could jive with him, say anything you want, Chucky never got bummed or nothing.

Rainy's real name was Rene Moya: light-skinned Puerto Rican and something like one-eighth Haitian from his mother's side. He drove van loads of marijuana from Miami up the Interstate to Toledo and Detroit. He weighed a hundred and thirty and wore a neat little waiter mustache.

Stick's name was Ernest Stickley, Jr. He was forty-two years old, born in Norman, Oklahoma, but raised in Detroit where his dad had come to work at Ford Rouge. Stick looked like he was from another time: dustbowl farmer turned hobo. He was at a low point in his life.

He and Rainy had met in Jackson, Michigan, when both of them were staying at 4000 Cooper Street, gateway to the world's largest walled prison: Stick doing seven to twenty for armed robbery; Rainy three to four, possession with intent to deliver, after they told him, "You walk you talk," which meant probation, and he turned them down, hung in and did the full three. Rainy got out a few months before Stick's release date. He told Stick to come down to Miami and get some sunshine, some fresh air, man, meet some chicks. Stick said he was going down there anyway to see his little girl; he hadn't seen her since she was seven.

What they were doing now was not recreation; it was to make a buck.

Stick kept looking at the girl-bartender because she was so fresh and clean looking she could be in an orange juice or a suntan lotion ad. She had a glow to her, perfect tan, perfect white teeth, a tall girl with nice easy moves, natural. She wore a little nameplate that said her name was Bobbi.

They had come up from Miami to Lauderdale in Rainy's new van to meet this guy Chucky and run the errand for him.

The place they were in was called Wolfgang's, a marina bar on the Intracoastal at Sunrise. Outside, every half hour a bell would start dinging and the bridge would go up to let a few cruisers and sailboats go by. Inside, then, somebody down at the end of the bar would blow what sounded like a foghorn, a baritone moan and everybody, all the late afternoon fun-seekers, would break up. There was a terrace outside with an awning where you could sit and drink and watch the boats go by. Otherwise, it was like a lot of bars with rose-tinted mirrors and high-gloss wood-grained plastic. A Happy Hour bar.

Everybody was sure working at it.

Didn't these people have any problems?

Even Rainy Moya seemed happy, feeling the beat and giving the oval edge of the bar funky little finger slaps like it was a fifty-foot bongo. Stick thought it was disco, the music coming out of turned-up speakers somewhere. He mentioned the word disco and the guy on the bar stool to his right—maybe the only guy in the place older than Stick, a hairy bald-headed guy wearing mirror sunglasses and a nautical blue-with-white-piping beach outfit—said disco was out, nobody discoed no more. Stick didn't like the guy looking at him, hanging on everything he said to Rainy. He asked what people did now if they didn't disco and Rainy said they fucked. Rainy said man, you been away too long, you got to get caught up with the scene. The music still sounded like disco. Latin disco. Rainy said no, man, it's fusion, it's rock, it's a lot of beats. Where you been?

Stick thought he had kept up. Eleven Block, for honor inmates in maximum security, had its own lounge area on the floor of the cellblock with a color TV. But maybe he had missed a few important events and passings. Nobody had told him when Warren Oates died last spring. He had heard about Belushi but not Warren Oates. He subscribed to magazines . . . He did a hundred pushups and situps a day the first year and toward the end of the seventh year . . .

Rainy and the tourist in the beach outfit were talking past Stick, vouching for each other, the guy saying everything was different now and Rainy saying that's right. The guy saying especially the broads. Rainy saying that's right, nudging Stick and saying listen to him. The guy saying he was married twice but not now, all the stuff around, a guy would have to be out of his mind to get married. Stick glancing at the guy—thinking no way, never, not this guy—and seeing two of himself, his face distorted, sickly, in the guy's mirror sunglasses; he looked a little better in the tinted glass behind the bar, but the girl-bartender, Bobbi, giving all the loudmouths a nice natural smile, meaning it, not putting it on, made him feel old. Why was she happy, working in this place, watching people get smashed? . . . Rainy was saying that's right, man, you don't have to waste no time buying drinks you don't want to; you see a chick you ask her she want to do it, man; she don't, okay, no problem, man, you go ask the next one.

Stick left his bourbon and went to the men's room. He was tired of hearing guys talk, guys wanting you to believe they were street, guys saying *man* all the time. He shouldn't have called Rainy. Well, maybe call him and have a drink, but he shouldn't have promised him anything. Stick washed his hands with the fragrant pink soap that came out of the dispenser, washed them good and stared into the clear mirror at his features. Pale, solemn. Who was that? Like looking at someone else. Back in another life before Jackson he could narrow his eyes at his reflection—hard-boned but not bad looking—and say, "That's it, huh? That's all you got?" Then grin and catch a gleam in there and know that if common sense, intelligence, caution, all the straightarrow stuff ever failed him there was always bullshit to fall back on, live by your wits and a tight sphincter. But there was no gleam today. White skin, white shirt, he looked like he just got off the bus with a cardboard suitcase. He came back from the men's room and nothing had changed.

Sliding up on the barstool, he said to Rainy, "Is he coming or not?"

Rainy looked at the clock face in a miniature ship's wheel behind the bar. Five-forty. Rainy said, "He don't get here by six, man, we go to his place. It's right there, across the bridge." He nodded toward the sunlight out on the terrace—across the waterway that was like a wide canal—to the dock and sloping lawn of a condominium.

The tourist turned to look as Stick did, giving Stick the back of his mangy head, bare on top, sunburnt, oily strands of hair hanging over his terrycloth collar. Stick heard Rainy say, "Bobbi? . . . Hey, Bobbi . . ." and now Stick caught a glimpse of his two faces in the mirror sunglasses as the tourist turned this way again, the tourist keeping his nose right in there. The tourist saw Rainy trying to get the good-looking girl-bartender's attention and called louder than Rainy did, "Hey, Bobbi!" She looked up, capping a strainer over a martini shaker, pouring, raising the shaker up and down, twisting off that last drop. "Get your ass down here," the tourist said. "We need you." He said to Stick, "I wouldn't mind some of that. How about you?"

Stick looked at the guy hunched over the bar, hairy arms, big hand wrapped around a gin and tonic. Stick said, "You got short eyes? That your problem?"

The guy's forehead creased. "What?"

Stick turned away. The girl was coming over to Rainy now. She looked like Cybill Shepherd, tall, that type, but younger. She was about the healthiest-looking girl Stick had ever seen. Outdoor looking in a pink knit shirt with a little alligator on it, one of those polo or golf shirts—but not like the other girl-bartender who wore hers tight with her breasts sticking straight out, encased—no, Bobbi wore hers loose with a natural sexiness in the way it hung and the way it strained against her when she made certain moves. She seemed almost too young to be working in here.

Stick's daughter was fourteen. He hadn't seen her yet. He'd called, spoken briefly to his ex-wife . . .

Rainy was saying to the girl, "Chucky been in?"

She shook her head. "Haven't seen him." She said, "No, so far it's been a perfect day."

"I wasn't sure he stuck his head in and we might have missed him," Rainy said.

She said, "Are you serious? How could you miss Chucky?"

Stick liked her tone, the easy confidence. He'd bet she was aware and didn't miss much. She said, "You guys want another one?" looking from Rainy this way, directly at him now. Stick shook his head. Her eyes lingered a moment and he felt a lift and wanted to say something to her.

The tourist said, "You can do me. Fact I'd let you do just about anything you want to me."

She said, "Big deal."

The tourist said, "Honey, it might be the biggest deal you ever saw. If you get my meaning." He reached over to pat her hand, resting on the bar.

She raised her eyebrows and began to say something as Stick said to the tourist, "Keep your hands off her."

The tourist looked over. "What?"

Bobbi said, "The way it goes, don't touch what you can't afford."

Rainy was off his stool. He came around with his hand moving across Stick's back. He said, close to him, "Hey, come on, man, let's take it easy."

Stick said, "Short eyes . . . Look at him."

The guy said, "The hell's he talking about?"

Rainy, still close to Stick, said, "For who, man? We're in a bar."

"Look at him," Stick said.

"All right, it's all right, man, we got to leave anyway. It's time to go." Rainy kept his hands on Stick's shoulders, turning him away from the tourist, getting him down from the stool.

The tourist took off his sunglasses, squinting, sitting up straight. "What'd he just say?"

"It's okay, we got to go," Rainy said and looked at Bobbi, who hadn't moved. "Lemme have the check. No, we'll be back. I'll take care of it later. Okay?"

Stick heard the guy say, "Jesus Christ, some kind of weirdo . . ." but didn't look at him or at the girl. He was strung up and had to get out of here.

They left the van in the parking lot and walked across the bridge with the traffic moving toward the ocean, tires humming on the metal grid. Stick breathed in and out. He could feel the sun on his back and could feel the Atlantic ocean two blocks away, beyond the mile-long public beach with its blue cabanas stacked up for the day. He began to come down.

"Man, I see your face," Rainy said, "I know I got to get you out of there."

Stick said, "You hear him, what he said?"

"What did he say? He's jiving her a little. He has some drinks and goes back to the Holiday Inn. Has to sit there and look at his old lady."

"He told you he wasn't married. Didn't you hear him?"

"Hey, listen to you. What difference does it make? He's got an old lady or he don't, nobody cares." Rainy reached up, laid his hand on Stick's shoulder. "Man, you were the one taught me how to be cool, you remember? Showed me how to make it, not take everything personal, you remember that? Serious things, yeah, you go all the way, but not bullshit things. It's the same out here, man. You got to tell the difference, right? You didn't have to prove nothing. What was that in there—little bullshit play with the girl Bobbi? She don't care. She gets that shit all the time."

Stick didn't say anything.

"You're out with the civilians now," Rainy said, "you dig? It's a free country out here, man." He poked Stick's shoulder and let his hand drop. "Buy some new clothes and get laid a few times you feel better."

They moved into the shade of the fifteen-story condominium and started up the drive. A Cadillac stood by the entrance; two guys in suits, sportshirt collars sticking out, were talking to the doorman, looking this way now.

"They work for him," Rainy said.

The two guys were watching them come up the blacktop grade, both with hands in their pants pockets, giving them dull stares. Stick could see them standing in a cell-block yard in work clothes, down jackets. You could wear anything you wanted at Jackson—if you could keep it and not have to give it to some colored guy with a knit cap down on his eyes. Walk in cherry they would try to take your clothes first, if your clothes had any style, then get around to trying for your body. Most of the cons there were black. Still, you saw the tough white guys with the solid bodies and dark hair. That type, they all had the thick dark hair and stood like they were daring you to move them out of the way. The difference here, Stick realized now, these dark-haired guys were probably Cuban. They were serious mean looking, but not as big as the dark-haired guys he was used to.

"You know them?"

"Maybe," Rainy said. "I'm not sure. He's got plenty of people hang around him."

"What's he scared of?"

"Are you kidding me?" Rainy said.

2

If he had to make a decision over the phone as opposed to just shooting the shit, Chucky liked to take the call in his den where he had a conference speaker system on his eight-foot desk and, over by the door to the living room, a hat-tree loaded with different kinds of hats and caps. He'd put one of them on—the salty yachting cap or the big straw cowboy hat, the hardhat if somebody was trying to give him a hard time, the long-peak fisherman's cap if he was being philosophical—and move around while he carried on the phone conversation.

When he was moving, Chucky believed, it was like he felt his mind and body on "high" and fully alert, his neurons flashing, making the right connections. It went back to when he was hyperkinetic as a little kid: ten, eleven years old, Christ, he went through something like four dogs, ran the ass off them; they'd come dragging into the house, their tongues hanging out, gasping. He said when he got to running full out even hounds'd throw it in, fuck it, look up at him with those sad eyes.

Chucky said he mellowed out quite a bit since he'd grown up, found a plateau he could live on in peace. The steps: flunked out of Wake Forest prelaw. Reached an incredible screaming high in Nam, seven months in-country to a time, two hundred days compressed to a time he couldn't move to save his mind, had no way to release the panic short of killing himself and tried to, tried like hell . . . and was brought down with Thorazine at the VA hospital in Memphis. The final step, Miami, where Charles Lindsay Gorman III passed through his Chucky Buck phase, hustled, got rich and found happiness on a maintenance dosage of Valium and 'ludes: before meals or whenever his motor got stuck on high idle.

The effect of his medication was like swimming under water, only without any water. Floating in lights. He still moved, felt the urge, but he wasn't moving kinetically now, he was floating. He'd load up and let the mood move him along. Cock the straw boater on the side of his head and do a soft shoe on the parquet floor of the den, shuffle stiff-legged to this draggy Kool-and-the-Gang beat he'd turn on softly in his head. Just float, experiencing hundreds of thousands of colored lights popping inside his head like trip flares, only without a sound. See, Chucky said, your hearing gets so acute you have to soundproof your head, turn the decibels way down.

For some reason he had found himself explaining this phenom to the young guy working for the Cubans, Eddie Moke—the person he was talking to right now on the phone—and Moke had said, "That's what you do, uh, float? I think you got brain damage, man. I think you ought to check it out." With that frozen sound Moke had, barely moving his mouth. The boy was a study, trying hard to effect the grungy look of a heavy-metal rock star, the headband, the illustrated disco shirt open all the way . . .

He should never have told Moke about floating and doing the soft shoe. The only reason he had was because of the way Moke sat on his spine, giving himself curvature, practically lying in whatever chair he was in, and Chucky had asked him how he could stay like that without ever moving, like he mainlined cement. You would say things to Moke and he wouldn't respond unless he had to and then would barely move his mouth. And Chucky would take another swing at it, yes, just like trying to bust cement. The Latins dressed up and posed and gave you snappy TV lines—"What's happening, man?"—but this Moke, he'd lock his jaw like a stoned rocker and give you dreamy slit eyes. Hardest thing in the world, trying to talk to him on the phone . . .

Chucky said to his conference system, "You still there?"

Moke's voice, a nasal twang partly hidden in there, said, "Yeah, I'm here."

"Well, what do you think?"

"I think you better pay the man."

Chucky, circling his desk, ran stiff-curled fingers through his hair—the wiry blondish waves kinking back on his head—made a glide over to the tree and put on his orange hardhat, set it low over his eyes.

"I'm *going* to pay him. That's not the question I asked you, boy. Have I ever said I didn't intend to pay?"

The speaker system remained silent.

An idea edged its way into Chucky's brain. What if the boy kept his mouth shut because he felt alone, like some redneck manure-spreader among all the Latin dandies? What if the boy was simply self-conscious? It had occurred to Chucky there was another image that would fit him better. A bronc-stomper was what Moke should be playing, not some candy-ass rocker.

But that analysis would have to wait.

Chucky continued circling the desk. "To answer the question, no. I told Nestor that. I told *you, you* told *him*." Keep the record straight. "He gets delivery tonight. Two-hundred thousand paid in full. In hundreds—Lionel says he got all used hundreds and a Samsonite bag tested by a four-hundred-pound gorilla, so we know it won't come open, right? Blow away. But giving him a *person* along with it . . . that's pretty weird shit we're talking about there, you know it? I think it slips Nestor's mind he's living in Miami, Florida, now. You know what I mean? Mention to him if you would, we're part-civilized here. Our gods don't think much of human sacrifice."

"They don't?" Moke's voice said.

The boy could be dry if you fed him lines. Chucky moved from his desk toward the balcony, then remembered something and changed his direction. At the door to the living room he removed his hardhat and pressed in close to the door panel to look through a peep hole.

The girl sat at the near end of the sofa, giving Chucky her left profile from about fifteen feet. More than pleasant looking though not sensational. She sat paging through his latest copy of *Shotgun News* with some degree of interest. Sandals, slim legs crossed, she'd go about a hundred and five. It looked like a beige sundress under the white cotton blazer, the sleeves pushed up a little on her arms. Nice tan. No jewelry except for the Cartier-style watch with the leather band. Blond-streaked hair to her shoulders, cut off he would say abruptly, a manageable style, simple—rather than all swirly curly the way Chucky liked a girl's hair. She didn't look anything like he'd been picturing her since talking to his friend Barry and arranging the date. No, she looked like somebody's sister, like she'd smile a lot with healthy uncapped teeth, hands folded in her lap and say, "Gee, Mr. Gorman . . ." She also looked, from here, about eighteen years old. He'd see in a minute if she was any good.

Chucky swapped the hardhat for the snappy yachting cap he tilted low over his eyes. Moving back to the desk he said, "Tell Nestor . . . tell him before he starts freebasing this evening, gets to trembling and becomes devilish . . . I expect a call."

The phone speaker remained silent.

"Tell him we have customs, too," Chucky said. "Gringo customs. We kill a chicken, we eat it, we don't shake beads and sprinkle its blood around. He wants a life for a life, he has to ask for it himself. It has to come from on high, not told to me by some messenger boy."

Silence. Though Chucky knew this one wouldn't last.

Moke's voice said, "I expect you realize how much you need him, you want a good source."

"Like I need a three-foot yang-yang," Chucky said. "The man comes through, why not, all the dough he's making. But I'll tell you, the association is far from comfortable. Nestor, all he has to do is see *The Godfather* on TV, he goes freaky for a week. The point here is, he *knows* I wasn't playing that tune. I *didn't* set him up. I made an honest mistake . . ."

"You made a dumb mistake."

"Which I'm paying for. But you tell him, hear? I'm sitting on the cashbox till he calls me."

Silence.

"You got it? Grunt once for yes, two for no."

"You threaten him you know what he'll do."

"Tell me," Chucky said. "Keep talking while your mouth's still open."

"He'll cut off your product or your *cojones*, one."

Chucky said, "Do you know how many times in the past ten years I've been cut off, sold out, fucked over, picked up, jerked around one way or another and yet, look-it here, who's still king of the shit pile?" Pink warning lights began popping before his eyes and he paused to let them settle, melt down, wanting to use only a portion of his energy. He said, "It's dumb to get mad at the help for what the master's doing. I got a young lady waiting out'n the living room wants to proposition me . . ."

Moke's voice said, "You calling that little piss squirt my master? Jeez-us Christ."

It stopped Chucky cold. He cocked his head, looking at the telephone machine on his desk.

"There may be hope for you yet," he said, beginning slowly. "I've seen white boys, fine young men, take on that greaseball strut, that curl to the lip, and land in a federal correction facility for showing off. Isn't anything the DEA despises worse'n a white boy turned spic or hippie on 'em. You worked for me I'd dress you up, Mr. Moke."

"Thank the Lord Jesus I don't," Moke's voice said, still not hiding that unruly twang.

Push him some more. "You believe," Chucky said, "I can't change your life or even bring it to a close?"

"I would like to see you step up and try," Moke's voice said, with enough pure bottomland in it to make Chucky break into a grin as he stepped over to the tree and exchanged the yachting cap for the big straw cowboy hat.

He reached back in his mind and across the river then—take Crump Boulevard from the VA hospital—all the way over to West Memphis to get more of a shitkicker edge to his tone and said, "Tell me something, I'm curious. Where you from? I'm going to say

. . . you ready? I'm going to say inside of fifty miles of some snake bend in the Red River. Am I right or wrong?"

There was a long hesitation before Moke's voice said, "How'd you pick that out?"

"I'm right, huh? Where you from?"

"Texarkana."

"You don't mean to tell me. Come on," Chucky said, "I was going to *say* Texarkana and I chickened out. I just had a strange feeling."

"You did?"

"Listen, tell me something else. What's a cowboy like you doing working for a pack of breeds?"

"Making wages," Moke's voice said.

Chucky waited a moment, holding himself still. "I bet you've never been turned loose, kicked outta the chute, so to speak. You know what I'm saying? Allowed to show what you can do."

"I bet I haven't neither."

"You don't take part in that weird *santería* shit, do you?"

"They start painting chickens I go on over to Neon Leon's have a cold beer."

Chucky waited again. It was hard.

"Hey. I just had a thought. What would you say to coming by here for a few cold ones, tell some lies? Say tomorrow? I got a hunch about something."

"What's that?"

"I don't want to talk about it over the phone. Let's wait till tomorrow."

"I suppose I could stop by," Moke's natural voice said.

"Fine," Chucky said. "Yeah, hey. Tell that weird Cuban I need a word with him. You suppose you could do that for me?"

"I'll see what he says," Moke's voice said.

"Shake her easy," Chucky said.

He sighed, worn out, switched off the system. Like trying to get a little girl back in olden times to take off her panties. It was hard labor, what you had to do to cover your ass and stay ahead. Work work work:

Moke did strongarm chores for the Cuban. Moke would be a dandy choice—dumb, eager and right there—to take the Cuban out should the need arise.

3

Shotgun News, Kyle McLaren learned, offered a lot more than shotguns. It was a tabloid-size catalogue of military weapons and gear: rifles, handguns, nasty-looking submachine guns, knives, machetes, steel whips . . . steel *whips*? . . . Dutch army helmets, mustard gas in a handy ten-ounce aerosol container . . .

It occurred to her she might have to do a double check on Mr. Gorman, ask around, learn a little more about his life-style. *Shotgun News* did not go with the brocade draperies, the formal, traditional furniture, the huge Hudson Valley landscapes in the heavy gilt frames. Or did it? Maybe his mother had decorated the place. Maybe Chucky Gorman was hardline NRA, ready to defend his property against Communists, Cubans, Haitians or citizens of Miami in general; living thirty miles north might not be to him a safe enough distance.

There was a phone with extension buttons—one of them lit—on

the marble coffee table, no ashtray, no other magazines. *Shotgun News* was it.

How about a nice MIA-E2 semiautomatic rifle with matching handguard, sling and bipod? Set it up on the table and get them coming over the rail of the fifteen-story balcony.

It occurred to her, also, to move from the sofa. The sliding glass doors to the balcony were directly across the room, the draperies pulled back all the way, so that she faced sun-reflected sky flat on the glass, a west exposure. If Mr. Gorman sat across from her she wouldn't be able to read his expression. But as Kyle waited and the sky paled, lost its fire, her mind changed with it.

Why bother to move? To begin with, she was almost certain she was wasting her time, that she would not be able to relate to a grown man who went by the name "Chucky." She could recall only one person in her whole life named Chucky and he was a little kid back in New York, a spoiled little pain in the ass, in fact; so there you were. The profile she had on this Chucky described a man:

Thirty-two who looked at least forty. Originally from Georgia, a well-to-do family that milled cotton for generations, carried Chucky on a remittance for a time—he'd had some kind of mental problem—then cut him off, disowned him. It didn't matter though, because Chucky did all right on his own: invested, bought real estate, belonged to a good club . . . But what did he do exactly?

Her friend Barry Stam, who was also a client and had indirectly arranged this meeting, said, "Ask him. See what he says." Barry, with his put-on innocence, eyebrows raised. "I'll be interested to hear your impression, what you think of him."

"Does he have money? I mean a lot."

"Wait and see," Barry said, deadpan. "He's an unusual type. Colorful, you might say."

She waited, all right . . .

Almost a half hour before a door finally opened and there he was.

As for Kyle's instant impression—as Chucky came in with his shirt hanging out, wearing untied sneakers, baggy pants and a straw cowboy hat, grinning—she had to believe this Chucky wasn't much older or much different than the other Chucky she had once known on East Thirty-first Street in New York. This one was a great deal larger and in his heart, beneath all that bulk, he could be a *Shotgun*

News freak, a hardline conservative, an eccentric with Old South connections, but he sure wasn't anyone's image of a serious businessman.

Look at that sweet young thing.

Chucky believed he loved girls who were sweet and wholesome, without guile or wile, because he didn't know any. But here was one right in his own living room. He felt alive.

Then felt the cowboy hat perched on his thick crown and raised his eyes to make sure that's what it was. He said to the sweet girl, "Whoops, you caught me playing." He pulled off the hat as he walked back to the den, sailed it inside and slammed the door closed.

"Now then . . . So you're Kyle McLaren." Sounding like he couldn't believe it. Which was true, though he gave the words more amazement than he actually felt. "I enjoyed the newsletters you sent. You write all that stuff in there?"

She said, "Yes, it's part of the service." But seemed just a bit vague. Now getting her neat mind in order.

"And you come all the way down from Palm Beach to see me? I appreciate it."

She said, "Well, I get around—"

"Hey, I bet you do."

"I travel quite a lot," Kyle said. "So I don't consider the drive from Palm Beach a major effort."

That sounded pretty neat and orderly. Chucky slipped over next to the coffee table to look down at her, get a closer view. Delicate girl features—a touch of blush, lip gloss maybe, just a speck—but with a backpacking outdoor look about her. Her right hand rested on a straw handbag next to her.

"You don't have a little mini tape recorder in there, do you?"

He heard her say, "No, I don't. Why, do they inhibit you?" as he turned and walked a few steps toward the balcony. Stopped and turned back to her with his grin in place.

"I know people these days'd have you patted down before they'd say a word. Which doesn't sound like too bad an idea." He paused, catching her solemn expression, and said, "I hope you know when I'm kidding."

Kyle said, "Why don't you give me a call sometime when you're not"—picking up her handbag—"and I happen to be down this way."

Chucky said, "Hey, come on, I'm serious now. Look-it how serious I am."

But she glanced toward the door and so did Chucky at the sound of three light raps. Chucky said, "Yeah? Who goes?" and one of the double doors opened.

Lionel Oliva, in a pale-blue double-breasted suit and silky gray sportshirt, stepped in from the hall. He said to Chucky, "Rainy is here. What should I do with him?"

"Jesus, Rainy," Chucky said, "that's right. Put him in the den."

"There somebody with him. Rainy say is a friend of his."

Chucky squinted. "You got one of my shirts on."

"You gave it to me," Lionel said.

"Yeah, I guess it's all right," Chucky said. "Rainy's insecure." He started to turn away and stopped. "Lionel? You ever see the guy before?"

"No, it's somebody he met, you know, where he was up there."

"Yeah, I guess it's okay," Chucky said. The door closed as he turned back to Miss Kyle McLaren .

All eyes. Look at her looking at him, the little broad from Palm Beach in her pure and spotless sundress, clean undies and a light cotton blazer, perfect for business or casual wear, for that cocktail at the Everglades Club with an important client or maybe even Mr. Right . . . He could see a shot of her and this clean-cut bozo in *Town & Country.*

"What can I get you?"

"Nothing, thanks."

"You don't drink?"

She said, "I don't care for anything." Sitting on the edge of the sofa. "Why don't we try to do this another time?"

"No, look, you're here," Chucky said. "Let me ask you one question, we can play it from there. Okay?"

She nodded. "All right."

"What do you think of gold?"

"Right now? I like Swiss franc futures better."

"Come on, how do you see it as an investment? What I want to know is, you going to give me a straight answer or a lot of words?"

"Well, first of all"—she sounded vague again—"you don't invest in gold, you speculate. The British fleet moved on the Falklands last spring and the price rose twenty-three points the first two days . . ."

"There. That's what I mean by words," Chucky said, moving in on the coffee table again. "Now you're going to tell me about uncertainties in the world market, devaluation of the pound, all those Wall Street words. Right?"

"And as the fleet sailed," Kyle said, settling back into the sofa but not taking her eyes from his, "*Evita* was still playing in the West End. If you find that interesting maybe you'd like to back a Broadway play. It offers about the same risk as grain futures, but it's way more fun. Or, if you like movies, I can show you a film offering that doesn't look too bad."

Chucky's grin this time was honest, sincere. "Ve-ry clever. Movies, I never thought of movies. You know what the last one I saw was?"

"*Gone with the Wind*," Kyle said. "Do you do much trading?"

"In what?"

"I mean are you active in the market."

"Well, you know, now and then. But hey, listen. If I invested in a movie, would I get to meet any starlets?"

The girl just stared at him.

"I'm serious," Chucky said. "Something like that, that sounds interesting. But let me tell you where I'm at, okay? The particular problem I run into . . . No, first you tell me a few things. See if you're the type of expert I need."

She said, "What do you want to know, my background, business experience?"

"Yeah, where you been, how old you are . . ."

"I'm thirty-one," Kyle said. "I started out as an analyst at Merrill Lynch, moved to Hutton to handle accounts . . . came down here and opened my own office two and a half years ago . . ."

"You married?"

"No."

"You fool around?"

"Mr. Gorman, I have to tell you something."

"Please, Chucky. Everybody calls me Chucky, even the help."

She said, "Chucky," carefully, as though she was trying it out. "All right ... Chucky." She bent her head down and up, brushed short bangs across her forehead. "I'm getting a kink in my neck, looking up at you."

"Hey, I'm sorry." He took several steps back. "How's this?"

"Why don't you sit down?"

It was as though the idea hadn't occurred to him. He said, "Yeah, I could do that, I guess." And came around the coffee table to sit sideways on the sofa, arm extended, his hand resting against the high rounded back.

She said, "Can I ask you something?"

Her eyes surprised him. A soft blue. Calm. No gee-whiz expression lurking in there. Ah, but the hands were folded in her lap.

"Ask anything you want."

She said, "What are you doing?"

Chucky stared, see if she'd look away. But those calm eyes didn't move. There was a slight bump in her nose. That and the shoulder-length hair cut off abruptly and without any swirls gave her the outdoor look. Her mouth, very yummy, lips slightly parted ...

He said, "I think I'm falling in love. No, what was the question? You want to know what I'm doing. You mean right now as of this point in time? I'm interviewing you."

She said, "Oh," and nodded with a thoughtful expression.

"Aren't I?"

She said, "Do you know what I do?"

"Yeah, you're like an investment counselor. Right? Tell people what to do with their money."

She nodded again. "That's right. But I specialize, you have to understand, in private placements, growth opportunities, usually going into new companies that need equity capital."

Chucky said, "Yeah, but why do I have to understand it as long as you do?"

"I want to make a point," Kyle said, "so that we understand one another."

Quiet voice to go with the quiet eyes. No girlish tricks. Yes, a first. Chucky was sure of it.

"I spend most of my time," she said now, "finding the opportunities. I'll look into as many as fifty companies to find one or two with what I consider above-average potential."

"How do you find 'em?"

"Leads from people I know. Bankers, lawyers, stockbrokers . . . So you can understand that if I were to show you a limited partnership opportunity that looks promising, or a start-up company that's about to go public, I've already put a lot of time into it. And time is money, isn't it?"

"I've heard that."

"So when you say, at this particular point in time, you're interviewing me, you have to understand something else."

"I do? What?"

"That the chances of my turning you down as a client are far greater than your not accepting me as your financial advisor."

"Jesus," Chucky said, "and you look like such a nice sweet girl."

"I am a nice girl," Kyle said. "Sweet? I don't know. If you mean passive, submissive—"

"No, I understand," Chucky said. "What you're saying is you don't take any shit from anybody, or at least your clients."

"There you are," Kyle said, and gave him a nice-girl smile. "Should we try to be serious, or would you rather not?"

"What do you do," Chucky said, "you scare the shit outta your clients? I have to say, I heard a lot of good things about you."

"From whom?"

"Well, Barry Stam, one. Some others at Leucadendra. I get down there to play golf once in a while." He paused and said, "I don't know if I should be telling you that?"

"Why, because Barry's a client of mine?"

"Let me put it this way," Chucky said, "if you're going to ask Barry about me, then I might have to open my soul, tell some secrets so as to give you the straight dope"—he grinned, turning it on and off—"so to speak. Yeah, we're friends, play golf, fool around. But Barry, whether you know it or not, is very impressionable. He likes to—well, he has a certain image of himself and likes to associate with people you don't ordinarily, you know, find in country club circles. You know what I mean?"

"Tell me," Kyle said.

"He likes to think he's on the inside, knows where the action is.

That's why he hangs around the Mutiny, Wolfgang's, places like that. You follow me?" She seemed to nod. "Anyway, I heard a lot of good things about you; though I don't know if you can help me out any. See, I've talked to advisors, financial planners. These guys, they come in here in their dark-blue three-piece suits, the alligator cases, graphs, all kinds of statistics, and you know what they do? They blow smoke at me. That's bad enough, trying to understand what they're talking about. Then, when I go to tell them about my particular situation, explain my plight, so to speak—"

The phone on the coffee table rang, a light showing.

Chucky got up. "I have to take that."

She seemed surprised he didn't pick up this phone.

"Would you like me to leave?"

"No, stay put," Chucky said, walking away. "I won't be but a minute."

Kyle watched him slide open the glass door, step out on the balcony. There was another phone on the metal patio table. He picked it up and turned to the railing as he began to speak, hunching over now in the privacy of the fifteen-story drop, his shape clearly defined now against the sky. A very strange-looking guy. Big all over, high waisted, narrow through the shoulders, the broad hips of a woman . . . and a sagging crotch. Chucky was a picture.

She could imagine this Christmas sitting around the table with her dad and her two older brothers—"I've got to tell you about Chucky. You won't believe it"—her mom and her brothers' wives in the living room while Kyle and the boys talked about stock gambits, swindles, high rollers, placed bets on the Super Bowl, raked over Reagan, David Stockman, the Federal Reserve Board, made fun of dogmas and people in high places and would laugh until her mom stuck her head in the door with her look of quiet amazement. Her dad had been on Wall Street since she was a baby and remained, he said, because he didn't know how to do anything else. She would never tell him she made more money than he did, with her snobby Gucci-Cartier approach to investment counseling; though it was her dad who'd told her rich people loved to be pushed around—as long as they believed they were being pushed exclusively. Her dad was dry, the cynic who'd never cheered, screamed or cried until her brother Jim moved up to the Red Sox from Pawtucket, had a 12–2 record by the All Star break his first year, pitched three scoreless innings and finished the season 18–8. Jim was a stockbroker, now, still in Boston. Her brother Mike had made it through Columbia Law and was now an agent in the New York office of the FBI.

She pictured telling Chucky about "my brother the Fed" and had to smile. He could be tiresome, but at least he was different. She might go with Chucky.

4

Stick tried the leather chair behind the giant desk, swiveling slowly from side to side as he stared at the phone system, at the dull orange glow in one of the extension buttons.

He said, "I bet what's his name, Chucky's talking to somebody. You want to listen in?"

It brought Rainy away from the glass doors, coming over with his shoulders hunched like he was tiptoeing, not wanting to make any noise.

"Come on, man, don't fool around."

"I haven't touched it."

"He's got phones all over this place," Rainy said. "You know how many phones he's got?"

"Four," Stick said. "Five?"

"Five, shit. He's got . . . I think he's got one, two, three, four . . . five, six, seven"—Rainy seemed to be picturing them as he counted, punching the air with one finger, giving it short jabs—"eight, nine, he's got like twelve phones up here."

"That's a lot of phones," Stick said. "He must like phones, huh?"

"He has to have them," Rainy said. "Chucky owns the whole top floor up here, the apartments like connected together. Cost him, I hear, a million dollars. Shit, that's nothing to him. Some of his guys stay here. That one, Lionel Oliva, he's like his bodyguard. Chucky has an apartment he keeps a broad in when he's got a broad here, you know, staying. I don't know if he's got one staying here now or not. Chucky goes through broads, man. They don't stay too long. He gets rid of them or they get nervous being with him and have to leave. Some guys—did I tell you that? They say he's a switch hitter, but I never seen him with anything but a broad.'

Stick said, "No chicks, huh?"

Rainy said, "What?"

"Nothing," Stick said. He'd think about it, see if there was a distinction between a chick and a broad. Or ask Rainy about it sometime. He got up from the desk where he was making Rainy nervous and looked around the paneled den. The wood walls and floor made the room seem bare.

Stick went over to a row of framed color photographs of groups of men in sporty attire. A group with golf clubs. A group standing by a row of sailfish hanging by their tails. A group having drinks on the fantail of a yacht. The name, lettered in gold on the stern, was *Seaweed.* This one interested Stick because there were two girls in string bikinis standing among the soft-looking guys in their Easter-egg outfits, the girls acting coy, trying to appear surprised, their mouths saying *Ohhh* to whatever the guys were doing or saying to them. Stick looked a little closer. One of the girls wore a gold slave chain around her bare middle—yeah, and the comedian next to her with the wide-eyed who-me? look had his hand behind the girl and was pulling the chain tight so that it dug into her nice flat belly.

"The one in the pink shirt on the boat?" Rainy came over and pointed. "That one. That's Chucky."

Stick didn't say anything right away. His first impression, Chucky was one of those poor miserable slobs everybody picked on when they were kids, washed his face with snow, and he'd slink off rubbing his tears and snot, to go eat some candy.

"Is that Chucky's boat?"

"I don't think so. If it's his he never ask me to go for a ride."

"Nice-looking broads."

He said it to see if Rainy would correct him, tell him no, they were chicks. But Rainy didn't say anything and Stick turned away from the photographs.

There was a dartboard hanging on the wall, the paneling around it gorged with tiny holes.

There was a TV set. At first Stick thought there were two standing side by side but then saw the smaller one was a home computer. Seven years ago he remembered computers as big metal boxes. Now little kids were playing with them. He had not played any of those games yet himself; they looked complicated.

He picked up from the floor a straw cowboy hat with a big scoop brim and looked inside it. The "Crested Beaut" model, with the initials CLG engraved in the sweatband. Stick placed it on the hat-tree that was piled with hats and caps of all kinds. Different-colored golf caps, a yachting cap, an orange hardhat, a straw boater, a red military beret, a long-billed fisherman hat, a New York Yankee baseball cap, a tennis hat. The guy seemed to like hats and telephones.

Stick walked over to the glass doors, slid one open and Rainy said, "Lionel told us to wait here, man."

"I won't go too far," Stick said.

It was warmer outside than in and felt good. He'd have to get used to air conditioning again. The sun was going fast now, laying off beyond where the Everglades would be, just the top part of it showing now, fiery red, but you could look right at it. You could almost see it going down.

Directly below, on the waterway, it seemed hours later, already getting dark down there, the boats showing their running lights, and there was a string of dull amber bulbs along the awning of Wolfgang's outside terrace. Stick was looking almost straight down at it and could hear the music, a faint pulsing beat he would swear was disco. They'd have to remember to go back after and pay the tab. He could picture Bobbi, the friendly bartender, the easy way she had with the young guys coming in high-fiving each other, making loud remarks. Rainy was right, he had to lay back and get with the rhythm of it again. Loud remarks that could get you stabbed in Jackson didn't mean a thing outside. Just guys showing off, trying to act like studs. That Bobbi was sure nice looking . . .

Stick straightened from the metal railing, looking down the length of the balcony, and saw a heavy-set guy with his shirt hanging out, maybe thirty feet away, and it took him by surprise. At first he thought the guy was throwing up, the way he was leaning over the rail; but now he straightened and did a little pivot and Stick saw he was talking on the phone. It had to be Chucky. Even without the pink shirt he had on in the boat picture, yeah, that would be Chucky. He didn't look like the type of guy who owned the whole top floor of a condominium. He looked to Stick like a guy, if he was ever in Jackson, would be somebody's live-in old lady before he ever got out of R and G.

Chucky was saying into the phone, "I'm not holding out on you, don't say that. You and I been doing business . . . Come on, you know goddamn well I would never . . . What? . . . *No.* Why would I want to cut off my source, for Christ sake? Look, we been all over that. I goofed, okay? I got taken in same as you. Listen, I even had his plates run on the computer, they didn't show . . . What? . . . Okay, yeah, you're right . . . Nestor? . . . Hey, Nestor, come on, it's done, it's over with . . . Yeah, I'm sorry. I told you that, Christ, how many times? All I want to know—and I appreciate your calling—I was wondering now you've had a chance to think it over, you know, calm down some, how about I pay you the two hundred and we call it square?" Chucky leaned over the rail again, concentrating as he listened to the heavily accented voice. Finally he said, "Hey, if it's that big a deal with you . . . No, but I got to tell you it's weird." Chucky straightened again, looking out at the very top curve of the sun, all that was left. "Am I arguing with you? I'm saying it's weird, that's all, but how you see it, amigo, that's up to you . . . What? No, as far as I'm concerned it's out of my hands once I send the man with the cash. Like any other drop . . . No, I don't want to hear any more about it. How you tip the boy is up to you . . ."

Kyle watched him replace the phone and straighten very slowly to pause and look out at the sky. Different now—he'd been animated during the phone conversation, shoulders hunching, arm extending, gesturing, his big rear end swaying as he leaned over the rail. For several moments he stood noticeably still.

Now he was moving again, wound up, coming back in with a painted-on smile, shaking his head.

"How about stock in a bulletproof vest company? Jesus, the way things are getting around here . . ."

He seemed to want a response to that, waiting, the grin turning to a little-boy sly look.

Kyle said, "There's a U.S. affiliate of an Israeli company that makes bulletproof ski jackets, jumpsuits, mostly casual wear. They come in nylon or corduroy with removable panels of a Du Pont protective fiber. I think Kelvar Twenty-nine." And waited to see if that impressed him.

Chucky stared back at her. "Guy I was just talking to, he's looking for U.S. investments, loaded, wants me to find him something. But you know what I get from stockbrokers, the investment experts?"

"Tell me," Kyle said.

"They say things like—you ask 'em about the market, they say, 'Well, it's due to take a fairly dynamic upturn if prevailing uncertainties related to interest rates and the price of bullshit futures can be resolved during the coming quarter. . . .' I don't like uncertainty," Chucky said, moving again. "It upsets my tummy-tum and when I eat I get constipated, I get cramps. But you know where I'm coming from, don't you? I don't have to spell it out."

"No, I would just as soon you didn't," Kyle said. "An interest in bulletproof vests and—how did you put it?—'the way things are getting around here,' and by that I take it you mean down in action-packed Miami."

"See?" Chucky said. "You know."

Kyle hunched forward, leaning on her knees. No, it wasn't going to work with Chucky standing up. She sat back again, brushing at her bangs with the tips of her fingers.

"You see, Chucky, when a client comes to me with nervous disorders, popping Gelusils and so forth, I tell him first of all I'm not a doctor. And second, if the deals I suggest are keeping him awake nights, then he should be in treasury bills or money-market funds. Beyond that . . ." Kyle shrugged.

"No, my problem . . ." Chucky said and hesitated.

Kyle came forward again, slowly. ". . . Is getting someone to sympathize with your problem. Isn't it?"

"There," Chucky said, "you know exactly where I'm at. They come in here in their dark-blue three-piece outfits, the black wingtips, guys they look like they shower and shave about four times a day. I tell them I got a very special problem . . ."

Behind Chucky, on the balcony, a man in a white shirt looked in as he walked past the open sliding door. Kyle saw him briefly, there and then gone.

"No, that's not true," Chucky said. "I don't say anything about a problem. It *becomes* a problem when they start fooling with their glasses and these tight little knots they've got in their prep ties like they never heard of dealing in cash before. It's like, I go in Holy Cross over there for a few days, see if I got ulcers, gastritis, whatever. Have the upper and lower GIs, the barium enema . . . You know you get to look at your insides on TV now? The doctor goes, 'Go ahead, take a look.' I tell him, 'You outta your mind? I want to see my bowels, for Christ sake?' . . . I go to pay, the cashier, she doesn't see any hospitalization written down on my papers, she goes, 'Don't you have Blue Cross?' No, I tell her I'm paying cash. Her mouth drops open down to here. 'But you owe four thousand three-hundred and eighty-two,' something like that, '*dollars* and fifty-three cents.' I go, 'Yeah? What's the problem?' She doesn't know how to handle it if you pay in cash. Same with these guys in the dark blue suits . . ." Chucky was moving, turning.

Just as the man in the white shirt, on the balcony, was passing the doorway again, glancing in as he went back the other way.

"Hey!"

Chucky stopped him as Kyle watched, surprised.

"You mind telling me what you're doing here?"

"I'm with Rainy," Stick said.

"You don't look like you're with Rainy to me," Chucky said. "You look like you're walking around my home taking in the sights. What're you, an appraiser?"

Stick turned to walk away.

"Wait a minute," Chucky said. "Wait just a goddamn minute there. I asked you a question. You're walking around my place like somebody invited you—in you see anything you like?"

Kyle watched the man stand awkwardly for a moment, as though he didn't know what to do with his hands or didn't know how to answer. Though his expression, staring at Chucky, seemed at ease. It caught her by surprise when he stepped into the doorway. He looked around the living room, taking his time. He looked directly at her.

Then looked at Chucky again. He said, "No, I guess I don't," and walked away.

Chucky turned to Kyle. "You believe it? Jesus Christ." He started for the balcony but turned again, doing his pivot step, and said, "The hell with it. I'll get it straightened out."

Kyle said, "You don't know him?"

"I never saw him before in my life." Moving again. "We're having a time here getting down to business." He turned to her, rubbing her hands together. "You don't want a drink, huh?"

Kyle shook her head. "No, but go ahead."

"You see why I get ulcers, people walking in. I don't mean as a habit, but I tell you, I get involved now and again with some weird folks," Chucky said. "Did Barry—you mentioned he's a client of yours—did he tell you much about me?"

"He said, 'Wait till you meet him,'" Kyle said, "and gave me that sidelong look over his glasses with his eyebrows raised."

"I can see him," Chucky said. "Well, the gist of it is, I got funds looking to go to work and I don't know where to put 'em. Not only because I don't read *The Wall Street Journal*, but like I mentioned not having Blue Cross–Blue Shield, people don't know how to act you say you deal in cash. You get away from condos, which I'm sick to death of, getting jacked around by the developers, having to discount my dough—I don't even like condominiums, I don't know what I'm doing living in one." He paused. "But it's safe up here, you know it? It's pretty safe, usually."

Kyle said, "You don't have to bare your soul. In fact, I would just as soon you didn't."

"Anyway, what's my goal, the American dream," Chucky said. "What else? Put money in some gimmick everybody *has* to have, get rich and retire. No more worries, no more looking over your shoulder. So the boys in the dark-blue three-piece suits come up here, the wingtips, I start talking, they start pulling at their little ties. I think I ever showed them the actual funds, emptied out the suitcases and the ice coolers, piled it all on the table, they'd strangle to death."

Kyle was nodding, trying to be objective about it and discovering that she was accepting Chucky's problem without too much trouble. It surprised her that she felt no aversion. But then money was simply money. It had no intrinsic moral value. It passed from hand to hand . . . and a one-hundred-dollar bill in Miami today could be in Minneapolis tomorrow, one of a thousand others just like it buying a Bridgeport milling machine.

She touched her throat. "Well, I'm not wearing a necktie."

Chucky looked at her with a gleam. "No, you're not, are you?"

"I'll tell you right now though," Kyle said, "I don't do laundry."

Chucky grinned. "That's cute. But how does it help me?"

"Well, I don't see why I couldn't advise you," Kyle said. "Get you into an equity situation that looks promising. I've got several. Barry bought into a beautiful little company in Dayton last month. They make instrumentation to measure analog and digital signals."

"I see high-tech in my future," Chucky said. "Computers. That's where I understand it's at." He saw Kyle staring at him, waiting. "*I* read. You think I'm not up on all this shit?"

"By the time you read in *Time* magazine about a trend," Kyle said-, "it's over. That's when you sell short if you're going to do any trading at all. Don't worry, I'll find you something. If they want your investment bad enough you can deliver it in one-dollar bills in a wheelbarrow. So don't worry about that either . . . As long as you pay my fees by check. Can we agree to that?"

"No problem," Chucky said. "Boy, you're fun, you know it? You're so girlish and yet . . ." His expression began to change, the gleam becoming smug. "It's not going to bother your, let's say, your propriety any, doing business with me?"

"You have a lawyer, don't you?"

"You kidding? I got a law *firm*."

"And they charge you fees."

"Up front, a retainer . . . Yeah, I see what you mean." Chucky grinned, still with that smugness. "So I won't worry any about your personal ethics." He winked. "Just kidding."

Kyle said, "Good, and I won't worry about your drug habit." She gave him her nice-girl smile. "And I'm not kidding."

Lionel came in with the suitcase and laid it on the desk. It seemed to Stick like a ceremony: all of them standing around waiting, Rainy taking the suitcase now, bringing it down to his side and hefting it. "Tested by a four-hundred-pound gorilla," Chucky said, "so we know she won't come apart on you."

Rainy was grinning. "You always say that."

Stick waited, nothing to do. Lionel was looking at him with a sleepy expression, heavy features slack. Rainy had said Lionel's name was Oliva, a Cuban; all the guys, he said, that worked for Chucky were Cuban. He had five or six of them hanging around this place, some others when he needed them. Stick tried staring back at Lionel, not giving it much, and Lionel held on for about five seconds before looking away. Chucky had hardly looked at him at all since coming in from the living room, alone. The girl must have left. She had seemed out of place here. She looked like a social worker with money, if there was such a thing as that. Or a tennis pro. She had looked at him: she had those eyes that knew things but didn't tell you what she was feeling.

Rainy was saying, "I was thinking we should have a gun. One of us."

It took Stick by surprise. He wanted to get Rainy's eye and shake his head at him. But maybe he didn't have to. Chucky was saying, "You tell me you're bringing Bozo here with you 'cause there's nothing to it, he's going for the ride. So what do you need a gun for?"

Rainy said, "You always give me one before. Like Brinks, man, for just in case. Why is it different this one?"

Chucky said, "You want the job? You want the job, get outta here . . . Lionel?"

Lionel went over to the door and stood waiting to see them out as Rainy said, "How about the pay? Five grand you said."

"We'll take care of that tomorrow," Chucky said. "I'll be here, you know I'm going to be here . . . Now go on, get out . . ."

* * *

Chucky punched out a number on his phone system, walked over to the hat-tree and set the "Crested Beaut" model over his eyes. When Moke's voice came on, Chucky said:

"Delivery's on its way."

Silence.

"You hear me?"

"I ain't deaf, am I?"

Just dumb, Chucky thought. He said, "For the other part of the deal, instead of Rainy, how about you take the bozo that's with him? You think you could do that?"

"It don't matter none to me," Moke's voice said.

Chucky said, "Hey, partner? See you tomorrow."

Moke was starting to work for him already and didn't even know it.

5

Rainy, behind the wheel of the Chevy van, would glance at Stick as he spoke and from Stick back to the four lanes of freeway and the red taillights moving in the dark.

"The way I understand it, Chucky owes the money because it was his fault Nestor Soto had to put up a bond, the two-hundred thousand, to get one of his guys out. Then when the guy left and went to Colombia it was okay with Nestor because he say Chucky has to pay him. See, Chucky knew a guy from New York or some place he thought was a good guy. He see him in the Mutiny, different places, he knows the guy is buying product, right? Now this guy tells Chucky he wants to make a big buy—I don't know how many kilos, man—I'm talking about coke. So Chucky is thinking okay, no problem. He'll broker the deal, put the guy in touch with Nestor Soto and make about five–ten percent from the guy, everybody's happy, right? Except what do you know, this guy from New

York, man, he turns out he's a deep narc, man, from the BNDD. Sure, he put it together, they raid this place Nestor has down in Homestead on the canal, kill one of his guys, bust the other one—that's the two-hundred-thousand bond—take all his shit, man, and Nestor believe Chucky put the stuff on him. What else is he going to think? Nestor is crazy anyway. Sometime they call him El Chaco, from some wild place where he was born. El Chaco. He believe in *santería*, man, like voodoo. He start free-basing, he kill these animals as a sacrifice, with a knife. It can scare the shit out of you, you see something like that. Chucky explain it to him, no, man, he was surprised as Nestor the guy was a narc. He say, ask anybody at the Mutiny, they tell you. Nestor, he finally say okay, but Chucky has to pay him for the bond, you know, that Nestor lost."

"Forfeitted," Stick said.

"Yeah, forfeit. The court don't give it back. So that's it, man, in the suitcase. He always say that, Chucky? About the gorilla." Rainy grinned. "Oh, man . . ."

"Why'd he pick you?"

"What, to take it? He ask me."

"He's got all those guys—why didn't he send one of them with it?"

"I tell him I need a job, some money. So . . ."

Stick thought about it, trying to accept Chucky doing Rainy a favor. "What's he on?"

Rainy glanced over. "Who, Chucky? 'Ludes, man. You can tell, uh? How he moves?"

"Like he's walking in mud," Stick said.

Following 95 through Miami, Stick couldn't believe all the cement that had been poured since he was last here, when he was married and living here . . . He had begun thinking about his former wife, Mary Lou, when Rainy had to brake hard in traffic not watching his lane, and Stick felt his bucket seat slide forward and had to plant his feet. His wife's Camaro had had a seat like that. He would adjust it, there, but it would break loose within a few days and give them something to discuss when his wife wasn't complaining about the hot weather, about not seeing her friends, about her mother driving her crazy . . . till they moved back to Detroit and she began complaining about the cold, busing, about the colored taking over the shopping malls. Now she was back here again, Stick believed, because she missed bitching about her mother. They were a great pair, with their mouths turned down and set that way for all time. He hoped it wouldn't hurt his little girl, always hearing the negative side of things. His little girl's name was Katy. She had sent him handmade birthday and Father's Day cards, her school pictures some years, and twenty letters during the time he was in prison; more than half of them written when she was twelve. He'd call tomorrow . . . get a present for her . . .

They left the freeway and after that Stick didn't know where they were, somewhere in South Miami; all the streets, up-down and across were numbers. Finally Rainy turned a corner at Southwest Seventy-Third Street and pulled up in front of a place with a sign that said Neon Leon's. They had to meet a guy here, Rainy said, who would tell them where to go. A guy name Moke.

Stick said, "Why don't you give him the bag? Get it over with."

"I have to give it to Nestor Soto or his father-in-law, a guy name Avilanosa, nobody else," Rainy said. "Nestor don't advertise, I have to find out where he is . . . Lock your door."

Stick watched Rainy go into the place—a lounge or a restaurant, it looked new, whatever it was, flashy. *Neon Leon's.* Hot shit. Places like this and Wolfgang's made Stick tired thinking about them. He was getting old. Getting on and nothing to show for it. He'd earned five dollars a week in Jackson as a clerk-porter in the Guidance Center office, filing, mopping floors, cleaning toilets, and managed to come out with 680 dollars. A hundred and a half to get to Florida; a week paid in advance at the Hotel Bon-Aire on South Beach . . . he had about three hundred left. He'd go as high as a grand from Rainy for sitting here in the dark guarding Chucky's suitcase with almost a quarter of a million in it. Christ . . .

Moke came out, let go of the door and Rainy had to catch it. Stick watched him approach his side of the van as Rainy came around and got back in.

"He's going with us."

When Stick opened the door Moke said to him, gesturing with his head, hair to his shoulders, "Get in the back." He seemed stoned, half asleep, holding his left arm, the elbow, pressed in. He had on an old worn-out leather jacket zipped partway up, nothing under it but bare skin. Stick would bet he had a couple of tattoos on him somewhere, crude, threatening artwork.

"I got to get out," Stick said, "before you get in, don't I?" Wanting him to move back.

Moke said, "I guess if you're stupid."

Rainy was patting the inner side of his seat. "Through here, man. Just come through here."

Stick edged around between the seats to the rear compartment, hearing Moke say, "Where'd you find him at?" in that lazy, know-it-all tone so familiar, a twang of pure ignorance.

Moke climbed in and slammed the door. Then looked around at Stick. "Let me have the suitcase. Make sure you assholes aren't pulling any shit here."

The compartment bare, Stick was about to sit on the case. He got it up in front of him, kneeling on the carpet, and thought about shoving it hard into Moke's face. He could feel his heart beating.

Moke took the suitcase, laid it on his lap and fooled with the clasps until he got the top half raised. Rainy glanced out the side windows, then switched on the interior light. Stick raised up on his knees. He saw neat rows of banded one-hundred-dollar bills filling the suitcase. Moke picked up one of the packets and riffled through it, picked up another one, raising it to his ear and did it again. "Yep, it's all there." Rainy started to laugh. Moke half-turned to put dull eyes on Stick.

"The fuck you looking at?"

Rainy said, "Hey, where we suppose to go, man? Let's get the show on the road."

Stick got a good look at those sleepy eyes before Moke straightened around again, told Rainy to go on over to 87th Avenue and head south.

He could still feel his heart beating.

What he had to do was tell himself, keep telling himself, he had nothing to do with this, he was along for the ride. Take a moment to think, realize where he was now and not just react to things.

That guy he had read about last winter, the one who wrote the book inside and they got him a parole, that guy hadn't stopped to think. Maybe the other guy, the guy working in the luncheonette who told him there was no place for customers to go to the bathroom there, the health department or something didn't allow it, maybe he had said the wrong thing and the guy just out had felt his heart beating. That was understandable. But out here you didn't use a knife on somebody who said you couldn't take a leak. Inside you would have pissed on the *guy*. But outside—he shouldn't have even had the knife on him. He shouldn't have been *out* to begin with after they knew he had killed inside and didn't think anything of human life and after he had spent all that time in the hole. They could've read the guy's book and known they shouldn't ever let a guy like that out. It was so different out . . . All the lights, for one thing, all the headlights and streetlights, the neon lights, all other people's lights that had nothing to do with you. But inside you all lived together in the same fluorescent light or lights in metal cages without shades. You were in the same kind of light together all the time. If a guy like Moke ever gave you that look or tried to lean on you various ways, everybody was watching and you better back him off or else sew up your asshole because if you gave the guy the first inch he'd take the rest any time he wanted.

You were lucky in there, Stick began to think. Jesus, you were lucky. You know it?

He had backed some of them off, the hot-shit guys in the wool-knit caps, but he wouldn't have backed them off the whole seven years if he hadn't been lucky and found a six-four, 240-pound soul-buddy by the name of DeJohn Holmes. One moment thinking he was going to die against that cement wall. The next moment DeJohn's face grinning, showing him glints of gold and a pink tongue, DeJohn saying, "Man, you my frien'. Don't you know that?" Stick shaking his head, still thinking he was going to die, and DeJohn saying, "Man, I hear you the one did the motherfucker put me in here. Tell me your pleasure, you want weed, you want shit, tell me what you want . . ."

Moke had been saying, "Turn here, hang a left the next corner," saying, "I got a Two-eighty Z'd put this fucker on the trailer in reverse." Saying, "About a Hunnert and fifteenth. It's before you get down to Montgomery . . ."

Now he said, "Past the school."

"I don't know where in the hell I'm at," Rainy said.

"Go on around the other side . . . Yeah, see the drive? In there."

Rainy said, "We going to school? I think it's closed."

They moved along the side of the old building, a playground or athletic field extending off to their left.

"Park along here," Moke said, "facing out. Turn your engine off."

"I can't see nothing," Rainy said.

They sat in silence.

"You got any weed?" Rainy said.

Moke didn't answer him.

"How about some music?" Rainy said. Then said, "Here comes somebody. Man, I hope it ain't cops."

Stick kneeled up. He saw headlights coming across the field toward them, creeping, coming out of darkness. In the beams now he saw a baseball diamond.

Moke said, "Pop your lights on and off . . . I said *off,* asshole!"

Stick remained quiet, watching as the headlights came to a stop maybe fifty or sixty feet away, along the third base line. The headlights went off. Then came on again glaring, switched to high beam.

Moke said, "Okay, get out," and watched as Rainy opened his door and stepped down. Moke shoved the suitcase at him. "Wait now. I want this boy to take it over," glancing around at Stick.

Rainy said, "Man, I got it, I'll take it. What's a difference?"

Moke said, "This boy here's suppose to take it's what I'm saying to you."

Rainy said, "No, man, I'm the one," backing away from the van with the suitcase.

Stick was looking at Moke's face, eyelids heavy in the light beams. He said, "Why would I do it? I come along for the ride."

He heard Rainy, outside, saying, "I'm going, okay? I want to say hi to Nestor. I haven't seen him."

Moke was shaking his head. "Jeez-us Christ—hey, come back here, will you!"

Stick saw interior lights go on as a door opened behind the headlights, giving shape to a full-size American car. A figure appeared at the right front fender. Rainy was in the beams now, out in front of the van. He called out, "Nestor? . . . Who is that?" Raised the suitcase in one hand and gave it a pat with the other. "I got it, man!"

Moke said, "Well, shit, I don't care."

All that was happening was there in front of Stick, watching from a second-row seat. He saw Moke's right hand dig inside the worn-out jacket.

Moke saying, "We'll make 'er a two-for-one special, today only."

Stick yelled out, "Rainy!"

Through the windshield he saw Rainy look back. Saw the figure by the headlights raise something in his hands and saw the muzzle flash as he heard the burst of gunfire, a hammering sound out in the open. Saw Rainy, outside, stumble and saw nickel-plate gleaming inside, the big revolver coming up in Moke's hand.

Stick lunged hard with his hands and shoulder into the back of Moke's seat and felt it rush on its tracks and stop dead and heard Moke's grunt as his head slammed against the windshield. Stick didn't wait, stop to look. The headlight beams lit up the compartment, showed him the rear-door latch. He banged through the doors and left the van running, digging hard, that hammering sound chasing him until he was around the corner of the school building.

With no idea of direction he walked residential streets of tile-roofed bungalows concealed in shrubbery, aroused a few relentless dogs, came out to commercial lights again, finding South Dixie Highway without knowing where it was. He waved down a taxi, let the driver look him over, told the driver South Beach and didn't say another word after that. They had to leave city streets and traffic, break free onto MacArthur Causeway before he opened the window to feel the breeze coming off the bay and to stare at distant solitary lights out in the Atlantic ocean, listening in his mind to Moke saying, *This boy here's suppose to take it . . .*

Suppose to die.

They sold nickel bags inside for seven bucks, they sold regular cigarettes, shampoo, all that kind of stuff; they sold shine made from potatoes, spud juice at ten bucks a gallon, or let fruit juice stand till it turned and drank that. Stick's former partner, Frank Ryan, died of the potatoes in the prison hospital.

DeJohn Holmes said he could have anything he wanted. A sateen jacket? Blue and gold with his name on the back? *Stick.* Look nice, be a man of fashion.

Here was the strange part. It wasn't any of the colored guys in the wool-knit caps he had to watch.

No, out of five thousand eight hundred and something losers shuffling around, hanging out in the yard, getting high, chasing sissies, it was a white guy named Luther doing two to five who stared at him a few weeks, circled in and finally told Stick he was going to kill him. Why?

(Just like, why would he have thought he had to watch Moke? He wasn't mixed up in that business.)

It didn't make sense: sitting there in the Big Top, the dining hall, one morning with his cold scrambled eggs and having this stone-eyed asshole biker chewing with his mouth open telling him he was going to put a shank in him when he least expected. The colored guys—Christ, he got along fine with the colored guys and they knew all about him, from DeJohn Holmes.

DeJohn was one of the "mayors" at Jackson and ran a section of the yard, taking cuts on the card games and numbers and renting out weight-lifting equipment by the quarter hour when he wasn't using it. "Stay by me when you need to," DeJohn told Stick. "I'll show you how to jail, not lose any good time mixing up with crazies."

But why did Luther want to kill him?

"'Cause he see you talking to me when you should be hanging out with the white boys. Start with that," DeJohn said. "Man like him, he don't even know how to brush his teeth. You watch him 'cause you don't know when the bug is going to go out on him and he turn hisself loose. Maybe he thinks in his stone mind you somebody else or you remind him of somebody stepped on him one time. Or he like to be like you and he can't. He say he going to shank you and you say watching the motherfucker eat is enough to turn you sick to death anyway. But see, he so slow in the head he has to think, man, to blink. So I get him assigned the meat shop and let him see he fuck with my frien' Stickley what can befall him."

Pure luck. Getting next to DeJohn, being discovered by him. DeJohn's story:

"A man point at me in Recorder's Court, City of Detroit, say yeah, that's him, that's him. Say I'm the one come in his place with a gun and cleaned out both his cash registers. Yeah, that's him. I draw thirty to life for the third and final time around. Now that man that pointed—not because I took his cash receipts but took his woman, *one* time, *one* night only and she love it—that man was Sportree, who died of gunshot at the hand of my frien' Ernest Stickley, Jr.," DeJohn said. "They some details missing, but it was some funny business following when you and Frank robbed the J. L. Hudson Company in downtown Detroit and got ate up."

Stick was careful. He said he was doing his time for a grocery store in Oakland County, not any homicide or robbery in downtown Detroit.

DeJohn said, "I know that. It's cool." He said, "Believe me, my man. You my man and it's cool. But it don't change you did Sportree and the dude was with him."

Stick said, to DeJohn only, okay, but it was unavoidable.

DeJohn said, "They all unavoidable when you have to do it. Like the two brothers in the shopping mall, in the parking lot, I believe was Northland."

Stick said yeah, that had been unavoidable too, the two brothers wanting to *mug* him, for Christ sake, take his groceries.

DeJohn showed his gold and his pink tongue. "Groceries, yeah, shit"—enjoying it—"and the cash underneath the Wheaties from the store where you and Frank did your shopping." DeJohn said, "What they say, you could have got a hundred years just for the cars you used on those jobs. You take the fall on the grocery store, but they got Frank on the big one, didn't they? The Hudson's store."

Stick wondered how he knew all that.

DeJohn said, "You famous, baby."

When Luther made the move it was at a time when Stick was playing basketball in the yard. He left the game wheezing, out of shape, put on his work jacket and sat bent over on a bench trying to get his breath. He felt the wet on his back and thought at first it was sweat. He began to smell something . . . Christ, gasoline, and heard it when Luther dropped the match on him and *wouf* the back of his jacket went up in flames and he dove head-first over to land on his back on the cement and roll from side to side grinding in that hot sting . . . seeing the guy standing there with the Windex squirt bottle of clear liquid watching him.

DeJohn said it was the man's style and they should've known. "But the man lied to you, didn't he? Say he was going to shank you."

Three days later there was an accident in the butcher shop. Three witnesses in wool caps and white aprons swore Luther was splitting pork ribs with a cleaver, missed and cut off his left hand.

DeJohn said, "Man was lucky, wasn't he? He could have been seriously hurt and bled to death." He said, "I told him that, too."

There was all kinds of luck.

Stick sat on the cement porch of the Hotel Bon-Aire, listening to elderly people with New York Jewish accents complain about high prices, about Medicare and how Reagan had betrayed them. The hotel was light-green stucco, four stories, and seemed more like a retirement home than a hotel. Stick could feel the old people staring at him; one asked if he was with the government, looking things over.

August, no tourists, but still a lot of people on South Beach.

He crossed the street always lined with cars and went out on the sand past the clumps of sea grape and the Cuban families cooking over charcoal, eating at the picnic tables, and lay in the sun listening to bits of voice sounds coming to him in Spanish. They sounded like they were arguing but looked like they were having fun. Try and figure out Cubans. He would lie in the sun not moving and think about going up to Stuart or Daytona, or maybe over on the west coast around Naples, work construction. He could always drive a transit-mix, he'd done enough of that before.

With the hot glare pressing on his glasses and his eyes closed tight he would try to look into the future to a place where a man forty-two, starting over, could find something interesting and make up for lost time. If he was going to work he'd have to stay in Florida and get back in construction. Not around Miami, though. Or Detroit. People up there with seniority were drawing unemployment. He didn't look so far ahead that he pictured himself an old man on the street, he pictured himself *now;* but he couldn't, no matter how hard he thought, see himself *doing* anything.

He still hadn't spoken to his ex-wife or his daughter. Now, the way things were, he wasn't ready.

He was going to buy some clothes and get lucky there. The manager of the hotel, an old bent-over guy, showed him laundry packages of stuff a guy had left in his room Stick could have for thirty bucks. Different-colored shirts with little polo players on them, nice pants just a little tight, a couple light jackets, everything clean and neatly folded, fairly new stuff but without that brand-new look, which Stick liked even better. The manager said this young fella that left the clothes was here in May, went off to Key West for the weekend and never came back. The manager settled for twenty. Stick went out and bought a pair of sneakers with blue stripes on the sides.

They were the most comfortable shoes he'd ever owned. In the early evening he'd walk up Collins Avenue from Seventh Street as far as Forty-first sometimes, up around the big hotels, and on the way back find a nice quiet bar, have a few bourbons over crushed ice, suck on that good stuff and feel himself, after a few evenings of it, beginning to settle down and get his confidence back. He burned the first day in the sun. But by the fourth day he looked like he was working construction again, getting tan faster than he ever had before. His hair even looked different, lighter; he let it fall in its natural bent instead of combing it back behind his ears. Four days and he looked like a regular Florida native. Next he would be going to discos, doing those slinky numbers with the ladies. There were enough of them around, he had a waitress or two hitting on him every night; but he wasn't anxious to move in that direction yet. He had to make up his mind about something, take one thing at a time.

He bought a post card to send to DeJohn that showed a bunch of alligators, one with its mouth wide open, next to a kidney-shaped cement pool. He would sit with his bourbon and stare at the empty white message side of the card, thinking:

Dear DeJohn, My luck almost ran out on me the other night . . .

Dear DeJohn, man, could I use you right now . . .

Dear DeJohn, Rainy asked me to go with him on a deal that was supposed to be a Sunday drive . . .

But if he was going to go into all that, he'd have to put it in a letter. Tell what happened. Tell what he was going to do about it.

Well, the way it looked when he first started thinking about it, nothing.

Because there was nothing he *could* do. And because it was none of his business, it was Rainy's. Rainy knew there was always a risk, that kind of business, but it was how he made his living. It didn't matter what the deal was and it didn't do any good to think about it, because he didn't know all the facts.

Chucky owes a Cuban money. Chucky makes the payment. The Cuban takes the money—you assume that—and has Chucky's bagman killed. Why? Because as Rainy said, the Cuban was crazy, that's all. You were dealing with people, they weren't just weird, they had machine guns.

What he tried to do during the day, lying on the beach, taking walks along the surf, was think only about his future. Look at it in bright sunlight. Here it was, the world. What did it have to offer? All he had ever seen was one shady part of it. He found his thinking would come to: pick up a car and take off—And then his thinking would start jumping all over the place.

But in the evening, settled down, feeling himself again, he was able to narrow his view, look at pieces of what had happened and come to a conclusion that had a hole in it but still made enough sense. He believed, first:

They didn't kill Rainy because he was Rainy. They didn't seem to care who they killed. Either one, he or Rainy would do. Moke said, "Shit, I don't care." Or both of them. Moke said, "Make it a two-for-one special."

But Rainy wasn't the first choice.

Stick could see Moke looking at him and saying, "*This boy here's suppose to take it.*"

He had to squint hard trying to understand this part.

Maybe he'd heard it wrong. Or Moke had decided on his own to send him out there with the suitcase; so in Moke's mind he was *suppose to take it* and it was that simple.

Because if he'd heard it *right*, the way it sounded, then somebody had given Moke instructions. Send out the guy with Rainy. And who even knew there was going to be a guy with Rainy? Except Chucky.

So the second thing Stick came to believe:

Chucky was giving the Cuban somebody to kill. Part of doing business. Rainy said Chucky owned the Cuban money. Rainy didn't know he owed the Cuban a lot more than that, he owed the Cuban a life, too. Maybe Rainy didn't serve enough time to learn how those things worked. Stick knew.

He could sip his bourbon and know exactly why Chucky had picked him. Because he had crossed the line, walked where he shouldn't have walked. Because he had given Chucky a look. Because he had inspected Chucky's home, a room in it, and said he wasn't impressed.

"You see anything you like?"

Asking for it. What was he supposed to say, yeah, I love it? Ask him who his decorator was?

Once Stick reached this conclusion he could look back at what had happened, including Rainy's murder, and accept it. He wished he could have helped Rainy. But Rainy and all these people were in the same life. It was how they dealt with one another. To them, inside or outside eighteen-foot walls with gun towers, the life was the same. So if in time Stick could put Jackson out of his mind he'd be able to forget about this business too. Begin by walking away from it.

Except that he began thinking about Chucky now and the one hole—a question mark, really—in his conclusion.

Chucky might have set them up, but a fact still remained. The suitcase tested by the four-hundred-pound gorilla had been delivered. Didn't Chucky owe somebody five thousand dollars?

On the post card with the alligators on it he sent to DeJohn, the message read:

Dear DeJ:
So far you aren't missing a thing not being here—as you can tell from that bunch of girls hanging around the swimming pool (over). Listen, I'd even take your old lady, Antoine, before I'd pick one of them. UGGGG!!! Tell the brothers disco is out and

Soul is in. God bless you and take care of yourself. I'm going now to seek my fortune. Wish me luck.

Stick

He put on the lime green polo shirt, a pair of khakis faded almost white that didn't need a belt and matched the poplin jacket; he put on his new sneakers with the blue stripes and stuffed the rest of his new wardrobe into a white canvas bag with blue handles. Well, look at sporty, he said to the dresser mirror, liking his color especially, his tan face smiling at him.

For seven years he had worn state clothes. He told DeJohn, turning down offers of sateen athletic jackets and sportshirts, he was reminding himself he was a con and would not pretend to be something else until he was out of there.

Now what was he?

He'd find out pretty soon.

6

He wondered why you could walk into a bar and smell it when it was empty or there were only a few people but you couldn't smell it when the place was crowded.

He wondered why there were more cars in the parking lot than people inside the place.

Coming in from sunlight with his canvas bag Stick opened and closed his eyes in the dimness, saw only a few tables occupied, a couple of guys in hardhats sitting at the bar. It was so quiet he thought at first it was the wrong place. As he stood there the bell rang outside for the bridge to go up but nobody blew the foghorn. Maybe this was the time to come. He wasn't feeling old, he was still feeling pretty good; a little tired maybe. It had taken three and a half hours and seven rides to thumb his way up US 1 from Miami to Lauderdale and to walk to the beach from federal highway.

No, it was the right place. The girl-bartender, Bobbi, was serving the two hardhats.

Stick went down to the other end of the bar where it was still afternoon, sunlight filling the wide opening to the terrace. A good spot. He could swivel a quarter turn on the stool, look across the Intracoastal and see the front of Chucky's building, the blacktop drive curving up to the entrance.

When Bobbi came down the bar in her loose pink-knit shirt and said, "Well, hi, how're you doing?" giving him a cocktail napkin, Stick was sure she recognized him. He said just fine and ordered a Michelob draft. But when she brought the beer and he placed a ten and a five on the bar she said, "What's that for?"

"The other day, remember, I was in here with Rainy?"

She said, "You were?"

"You held the tab 'cause we were coming back later."

It took her a moment. "That was last *week.*' She seemed to study him, cocking her head. "You were with Rainy?"

"Remember the hairy guy? Made a pass at you?"

"That was you?"

"No—guy in a beach outfit, long hair. He grabbed your hand."

Her mouth opened. She said after a moment, "The one, you called him . . . short eyes?"

"Yeah, I might've."

She was nodding, thoughtful. "Yeah, I remember." Then frowned. "What's it mean? Short eyes."

"Well, usually, I guess it refers to a child molester."

She didn't speak right away, putting something together in her mind. Then seemed to have the answer, sure of it.

"You were with Rainy, weren't you? Up in Michigan."

"Jackson," Stick said. The beer tasted good; it was one of the things he had missed the most.

"I used to write to him," Bobbi said. "Well, I wrote a couple times. Yeah, I remember now when you said that I thought, it sounds like something you'd hear, you know, where you and Rainy were."

"In prison," Stick said. "It's all right to say it. We were in prison together."

"But why'd you call him that?"

"That's what he looked like to me. At that time. I know—it wasn't any of my business."

"I'm used to it. You should see some of the old farts come in here, try and make out. Bunch a dirty old men."

"I can believe it," Stick said. He didn't feel old at all this time. He felt in shape, the way she was looking at him, confiding. He saw her with him in brief flashes, a balcony on the ocean, her eyes smiling in amber candlelight, wine glasses, soft bossa nova, a dreamy look as she stretched, reached behind her and slowly pulled off the pink shirt. She said:

"Where's Rainy? I haven't seen him."

Stick shook his head. "I haven't either."

"I don't think he's been in since the last time, when you were here." She smiled then. "Yeah, I remember you now. Boy, have you changed." She seemed at ease with him, like they were old friends.

"It's nice to be remembered," Stick said. "Sometimes, anyway." He pushed the glass toward her. "Why don't you give me another one of those."

She drew several more for him while he watched the boats go by and saw, finally, the dark-haired Cuban-looking guys in their tight suits and sportshirts across the way ... and began to think of another time in another bar, in Detroit, sitting with Frank Ryan while Frank told him his rules for success and happiness in armed robbery. And Stick, fresh out of the Wayne County jail, feeling as lucky and confident as he did right now, had listened. He could have walked away from Frank and saved himself seven years.

He could walk away from this place . . .

A heavyset dark-haired guy in a pale blue suit and blue print shirt came in from the terrace, passed behind Stick and stood at the empty bar a few stools away. He rapped on the rounded edge of the bar with a car key and said, "Hey, Bobbi!"

Stick turned to look at his profile. It was Lionel Oliva. Lionel ordered a rum and tonic. As he waited, lightly tapping his key on the bar, he called out to Bobbi, "Turn a music on. This place is dead."

Stick said to him, "How's it going?"

Lionel looked at him, stared a moment with no expression of interest and shrugged. He turned back to wait for Bobbi.

Stick felt himself relax more as he sipped his beer.

He could walk away clean. Go out to the parking lot. He'd noticed when he came in a Mercedes, a couple of Cadillacs, a brand-new Corvette he could get five grand for easy, even without a delivery order . . . and not have to go up to the top floor of that condominium, try and talk Chucky out of it and worry about getting thrown off a fifteen-story balcony.

The prize out in the parking lot was a Rolls Silver Shadow, light gray, that was about fifteen years old and in show condition. Though the 'Vette would be easier to move. Get some plates off another car, drive up to Atlanta and unload it. Fly back tomorrow night, see his little girl . . . Except a 'Vette, the new ones, they say you had to punch a hole through the steering column and it was easy to butcher. The old-model Rolls would be a lot easier to get into and take off.

Lionel walked past him with his drink, going out to the terrace. He didn't look back. And they had stared at each other in Chucky's place.

Bobbi came over. He thought she was going to mention Lionel, but she said, "That tab you were asking about? I remember, it's taken care of."

"Who paid it?"

"You were suppose to meet Chucky that time?" Stick nodded. "Well, when you didn't come back I put it on his charge. Is that all right?"

"That's fine. You can put these on it too, you want."

"Chucky always forgets to sign, so we have a pen that writes just like his."

"I'll have to thank him," Stick said.

"That was his bodyguard was just here. So Chucky'll probably be in."

"Yeah? What's he need a bodyguard for?"

Bobbi said, "I make drinks, but I'm not dumb. You know as well as I do if you're a friend of Rainy's, and that's all I'm gonna say."

"I don't blame you," Stick said.

He watched her walk away and began thinking of his partner again, Frank Ryan: sitting in the bar telling Frank he was going to Florida to see his little girl—Christ, almost seven and a half years later he still hadn't seen her . . . No, he'd listened to Frank tell him that in the area of taking money that didn't belong to you—as opposed to lifting goods you had to fence—the method that paid the most for "percentagewise" the least amount of risk was armed robbery. He'd said, big deal. After all that buildup. And Frank had said, "Say it backwards, robbery comma armed. It can be a *very* big deal," and had even quoted actual statistics, saying they could follow his rules for success and happiness in armed robbery and make three to five grand a week, easy. That was when he should have walked out, right at that moment, when he didn't have a dime, but was calm inside. Confident, reasonably happy. And most of all, free.

He caught Bobbi's eye. Coming over she said, "Same way?"

Stick shook his head. He said, "No, I think it's time to check out." He hesitated and said, "I'm going to see my little girl."

Bobbi said, "Oh?" and sounded surprised. "How old is she?"

"She's fourteen now," Stick said. "You remind me of her. You sort of look alike."

He walked out feeling absolved, almost proud of himself. Though he couldn't help catching another glimpse of her taking off that pink shirt in amber candlelight, the waves breaking outside in the dark . . .

Barry came off the *Seaweed* with its port side still three feet from the dock, engines rumbling low, inching the fifty-eight-foot Hatteras gently in to berth.

Chucky and a girl named Pam and Barry's friend Aurora stood by the deck chairs in the stern watching Barry, wanting to stop him. Not wringing their hands exactly, but caught in a tableau of surprise: Chucky in a striped red-white-and-blue T-shirt down over his hips, the two girls in skimpy little nothing bikinis.

Chucky said, "You coming back, what?"

Aurora, dark hair shining, voice whining, said, "Bar-*ry*! Will you wait, *please*!"

Barry was pointing to the stern line his deckhand had thrown onto the dock, Barry gesturing, saying something to Lionel, who stood there in his light blue suit and didn't seem to know what to do. Barry's captain sat up on the flying bridge of the *Seaweed* observing, unconcerned behind his sunglasses, as the deckhand ran forward and jumped dockside with the bow line.

Barry looked up, squinting. He said to the boat, "Rorie? Chucky's going to run you home, babe. Okay? I gotta run."

Chucky said, "I am?"

Aurora, pouting, said, "You promised we're going to have dinner."

"I got a call," Barry said. "Didn't I get a call? I was on the goddamn phone—how long? You saw me."

Aurora said, "You're always on the goddamn phone."

Barry said, "Call you later, babe."

Aurora tried once more to stop him. "Bar-*ry*!"

But he was gone.

Bobbi's face brightened, broke into a big smile as she saw him coming. Then tried to turn it off but couldn't and a small grin lingered as Barry came over to the bar, his expression blank. Not grim, not serious; blank.

He made a gun of his right hand, index finger extended, and cocked it at Bobbi's face.

"What's the last thing that goes through a bug's mind as it hits the windshield?"

Bobbi said, "I don't know, what?"

"Its asshole . . . Where're the keys?"

"What keys?"

"The car keys. Cecil was here, right? Tell me he was here."

"He was here."

"And he gave you the keys to the Rolls."

"Uh-unh. He tried to give me a hard time though."

Barry put the palm of his hand to his forehead, said, "Oh, Christ," and did a half turn before looking at Bobbi again. "He was drinking?"

"I don't know why you ever hired him in the first place," Bobbi said, serious, with innocent eyes.

Barry said, "Hey." He paused for emphasis. "I'll take care of Cecil. Okay? You say he was drinking?"

"He had a few."

Barry shook his head, then leaned on the bar, weary. "He leave the Rolls? I don't know what good it'd do me, but tell me at least he left the car."

"I wouldn't know," Bobbi said. "He came in, sat down right there. Didn't have his uniform on . . ."

"It's his day off."

"Had four Chivas with a couple of beers and left, pissed."

"Pissed off."

"That's what I said."

"There's a difference," Barry said. He slapped the bar and said, "*Shit.*" Then glanced toward the terrace at the sound of Chucky's voice—Chucky coming in with the two girls. They were wearing short beach covers to their hips, looking nude underneath. Barry said to Bobbi, "They sit around drinking, it's Chucky's party, not mine. Don't give Aurora any martinis; she'll lay every guy that comes in." He looked toward the terrace again as he moved down the bar. "Rorie, I'll see you later, babe. Call you as soon as I can."

He heard her say, "Bar-*ry*!' but kept moving down the length of the bar, out.

Stick watched the guy in cut-off jeans and plain white sneakers—he had very hairy legs—coming tearing out of the place and run over to the Rolls-Royce. He tried the door. Locked. He bent over to peer into the car, shielding his eyes with his hands. Then started yanking on the door, trying to tear the handle off. Then straightened up and banged his fist on the roof of the car, swearing, saying Jesus Christ and goddamn it. Really mad. Having a little tantrum. Stick wondered—assuming the guy had locked his key in the car—what there was to get so excited about.

Stick was sitting on Wolfgang's front steps under the awning, at a point where he'd decided this was not the place to pick up a car, not in daylight—he'd have to go to a shopping mall or a movie theater parking lot—when this little guy in the cut-offs came flying out. Dark hair down over his ears. At first Stick thought the guy was Cuban, all the Cubans around. But then decided no, no Cuban who could afford a Rolls was going to run around in cutoffs and a yellow alligator shirt hanging out. No, the guy was probably Jewish, a rich young Jewish guy in his early thirties. He reminded Stick of Frankie Avalon, the hair, or a young Tony Curtis.

Stick said to him, "You need a coat hanger?"

Barry looked over at Stick for the first time. With hope, or surprise. Then seemed to lose it and put his hands on his hips, shoulders rounding, though he seemed to be standing up straight.

"No keys. It wouldn't do me any good even if I got in."

"You lose 'em?"

"My asshole driver's suppose to drop the car off, leave the keys at the bar. Sounds easy, right? Take the keys out, hand 'em to the girl? Totally wrong."

"Can you give him a call?"

"Where? It's his day off. Wherever he is he's smashed by now. That's it for Cecil. No more of this bullshit, I'm telling you . . ."

Stick got up. He brushed at the seat of his new faded khaki pants. Smoothed the front of his lime green shirt with the little polo player on it. He was going to pick up his canvas bag, then decided not to, not yet. Look interested, but casual about it.

He said, "Maybe I can help you."

Barry said, "What, get in the car? All I had to do was get in the car I'd break the goddamn window. I got to get *in* and I got to be in Bal Harbour"—he looked at his Rolex— "shit, in less'n forty minutes. And I need stuff that's *in* the car and I gotta make about five phone calls on the way."

"You got a phone in the car?"

"I got two phones. Channel Grabber in the car, another one in a briefcase in the trunk."

"What year's the Rolls?"

Barry paused. "Sixty-seven. Silver Shadow, man. They stopped making 'em not too long after."

Stick nodded. He said, "I bet you I can get in and have it started in . . . fifty seconds."

Barry paused again. "You kidding me?"

"Bet you a hundred bucks," Stick said.

Barry said, "You're *not* kidding, are you? Jesus Christ, you're serious."

He watched Stick hunch down over his canvas bag, zip it open and feel around inside. Watched him take out a coat hanger. Watched hin feel around again and take out a length of lamp cord, several feet of it with metal clips at each end.

Barry's mouth opened. He said, "What're you, a car thief? I don't believe it. Jesus, you want a car thief—you think there's ever a car thief around when you need one? Honest to God, I don't believe it—right before my eyes." He paused a moment. "What were you going to do, swing with my car?"

"Hundred bucks," Stick said, bending out the coat hanger without looking at it.

Barry stared, his expression grave. "The Polack runs in this place, he says, 'Gimme a coat hanger quick. My wife and kids're locked in the car.'" He raised his arm to look at his Rolex, paused and said, "Go!"

Stick wasn't going to appear hurried. He walked over to the Rolls and had the coat hanger ready by the time he reached the car door, worked it in over the top of the window and lowered the hooked end to the door handle without fishing, got an angle on it and tugged, twice, three times. Pulled the coat hanger out and opened the door. He said to Barry, "Now pop the hood."

"The bonnet," Barry said. "With the Rolls Silver Shadow, man, you get a bonnet."

Stick got in under the hood, Barry watching him with interest, seeing how he clipped one end of the lamp cord to the battery and the other end to the ignition coil. Stick bent the coat hanger into a U-shape then touched the solenoid activator terminal with one end, the battery terminal with the other. The starter whirred, the engine came to life in a roar and idled down. Stick turned his head to Barry. "How long?"

Barry looked at his watch. "You just made a hundred bucks. About . . . four seconds to spare. Not bad."

Stick lowered the hood, the bonnet, and brushed his hands together. "One problem, though. You're going to burn out the ignition you run it this way. You have to get a ballast resistor put on."

Barry said, "What do I have to worry about my ignition I got you, the phantom jumper. Get in the car, you can tell me all about yourself . . . your record, how many convictions, anything you want. *You* drive."

Stick was still at the front end. "I wasn't planning on going to Bal Harbour."

"What're you talking about?" Barry said. He was by the door on the passenger side now. "The engine dies I'm fucked, right? You have to jump it again. Come on, you got me into this, you got to make sure I get home."

Stick said, "Bal Harbour? That where you live?"

"You'll love it," Barry said. "Get in the car."

7

At first Stick thought he was talking about cars to whoever it was on the phone, saying, "No, long term I'm only looking at convertibles now," like he was going to buy a fleet of them. "Short term, yeah, I'll listen." But then, Stick realized, he was talking about stocks and bonds and probably had a stockbroker on the other end of the line. The guy asking about "capital-gain potential" and "default risk."

Here they were cruising south on 95, traffic beginning to tighten up, following the same route he and Rainy had taken last week.

The guy, Barry Stam, had the phone wedged between his cheek and shoulder as he wrote words and figures on a yellow legal pad, scrawled them on a slant with a gold pen. The guy sitting there in his cut-offs and sneakers, *The Wall Street Journal* and dark-brown alligator case on his hairy legs. It was a picture, something Stick had never seen before. Driving away from Wolfgang's, the guy said,

"Barry Stam," offering his hand. Stick took it, saying "Ernest Stickley." And the guy said, "But they call you Stick, right? What else."

He was saying into the phone now, "Gimme it again. Parkview? ... Yeah, million and a half at, what was that, eight and a half? ... Eight point seven ... Yeah, I got it. Due when? ... What? ... I know it isn't, for Christ sake, it's a municipal. Listen, I may help you out, Arthur. Gimme a minute to ponder, I'll get back to you."

Stick kept his gaze straight ahead in the traffic, down the length of that pearl-gray hood, squinting a little against the afternoon glare. It was cool and quiet inside, nice feel to the leather seat.

"You got to keep it working," Barry said, punching a number on the phone system. "We sleep, you and I, right? But money never sleeps, man. Play golf on the weekend, the money's still working its ass off. Work work work ..."

Stick said, "You talking about it earning interest?"

But Barry was on the phone again. "Hi, babe. Me again ... No, the boat's in Lauderdale, I'm on my way home." Relaxed now, comfortable, a warmth to his tone that wasn't there with the broker. "I just talked to Art. I mean Arthur please, what's the matter with me. He's got a tax anticipation note, million and a half at eight point seven due in July ... Parkview public schools." A police car screamed past them, lights flashing. "What? The fuzz're after some poor asshole ... *No,* not me, for Christ sake. You know I'm an *ex*cellent driver."

Stick looked over and Barry was waiting, gave him a wink. With his thick dark young-movie-star hair down over his ears and forehead the guy looked like he was acting into the phone.

"Yeah, due in July, the fifteenth." He paused, listening. "Why June?" Writing something on the legal pad now. "Yeah, okay, I'll see what he says. Hey, Kyle? ... Love you, babe." He listened for a moment, a grin forming. "Hey, come on. Don't say it less you mean it." He listened again. "Wait. When do you get back? ... Then why don't you come into Miami? Save some time. I'll pick you up ... Sure, no problem ... Okay, babe, have a nice trip. I'll see you."

He rang off and punched another phone number. "Lemme have Arthur." Waited and said, "Arthur? Gimme a June fifteen come-due on the Parkview note I'll do you a special favor, take the whole load." He waited, but not long. "End of June I'm into"—he searched over the yellow pad with his pen—"housing or some goddamn thing. Or is it soy bean futures? I don't know, I can't find the . . . What?" He listened and then said patiently, "'Cause the funds're promised, Arthur, earmarked. Out of this into that. It never sleeps, man. It doesn't even stop to fucking catch its breath. Don't you know your business, for Christ sake?" Glancing at Stick, but getting no reaction. "Yeah, all right. Lemme know." Near the end now, trailing off. "No, call me at home . . . Hey, Arthur? No more government securities. Keep that shit to yourself for a while . . . Yeah, all right."

Stick let him make a few notes and put the yellow pad in the case before he glanced over.

"You do a lot of investing, uh?"

"You want a simple yes or no or an in-depth answer?" Barry said, reaching around to drop the case and the newspaper on the back seat. He crossed his legs then, got comfortable. "What you should ask is what I do when I'm not investing, trading or speculating in this and that. And the answer is, nothing. 'Cause whatever I'm doing, I'm also at the same time investing, trading or speculating. It's like it's my life force. You understand what I mean? Like you're breathing while you're doing other things, but if you weren't breathing, man, you wouldn't be doing *any*thing." He seemed mildly pleased with himself. "That answer your question?"

Stick wondered why he'd asked it. He gave Barry a nod. Barry was looking at him, staring.

"What do you do? When you're not hot-wiring cars."

"Same as you," Stick said. "Nothing. Only when I'm doing it I'm not investing, trading or speculating. When I do nothing, I believe in doing nothing."

"How many cars you steal in your career?"

"Somewhere between three and four hundred."

"There any money in it?"

"I don't know, I don't do it anymore," Stick said. "That was a long time ago."

"You just happen to have the jump-wire in your bag."

Stick didn't say anything to that. Why bother.

"Lemme try an easy one," Barry said. "You live here? In Florida?"

"I used to."

"You do any time?"

Stick kept his eyes on the road. "Some."

"Raiford?"

"No. Up north. You ever hear of Jackson?"

"No shit," Barry said, impressed. "That's heavy duty."

Stick glanced over at him.

"For car theft?"

"Robbery."

"What kind? From a building? Little B and E?"

"Armed."

"No shit. Don't tell me a bank . . ."

"No banks," Stick said, beginning to warm up, not caring what he told the guy, or maybe wanting to impress him. "Banks are for thrill-seekers."

"How many convictions?"

"I did a bit in Milan before. Wasn't much, ten months."

"What's Milan?"

"Federal. It's up near Detroit."

"UDAA?"

"No, but I got probation on one of those. The next one I went to Milan on. You go, normally, from joy-riding to unlawfully driving away; then you go big-time, transporting across a state line and you get the feds after you. Familiar?"

"Why do you say that?"

"Well, before you started not doing anything while you're playing the stock market," Stick said, "I think you were a lawyer."

"That's very perceptive of you," Barry said. "I practiced a couple years, picked up on contracts, all that corporate bullshit, how to avoid paying taxes . . . So you had two raps up in Michigan, you come down to where the action is . . . You going for three?"

"I came here to visit my little girl."

"Really? I love it— an early Robert Mitchum. Nice guy gets fucked over . . . 'It's a bum rap, I didn't do it, I swear.'"

"I did it," Stick said.

"And now you're sorry for all your past sins?"

"Most of 'em."

"Most of 'em," Barry said, "the ones you got nailed for. I love it. How'd you make out in the joint?"

Stick looked over. "How'd I make out?"

"You have to take a lot of shit?"

"There isn't anything else they offer."

"But you made it okay? Got rehabilitated?"

"Yes sir, I've learned my lesson."

Barry said, "You want a job?"

Stick glanced at him. "Doing what?"

"What you're doing. Driving."

"You mean be a chauffeur? I've never done it."

"Well, if you've driven three, four-hundred different cars, right, that's what you said? You must have a pretty good feel for it."

Stick was watching the green freeway signs. "Bal Harbour, where do we get off?"

"Hundred and twenty-fifth. It's the next one. Goes over to Broad Causeway."

"What happens when we get there?"

"What do you want to happen?"

"I mean if I don't take your offer? You going to give me bus fare or what?"

"Jesus, you're already into me for a hundred bucks."

"You owe me a hundred, but I haven't seen it yet," Stick said. He looked at the rearview mirror and began edging over, into the lane to his right.

Barry said, "Don't worry about it, you'll get it."

Stick got over to the far-right lane, followed the exit ramp off, descending, turned left on 125th Street and moved along slowly—in more traffic than he could ever remember, it seemed everywhere you went down here—until he was able to swing in next to the curb at an Amoco station and set the hand brake.

He turned to face Barry now. "When?"

"When what?"

"When do I get the hundred?"

"Jesus Christ," Barry said. "You don't trust me?"

"I don't know you," Stick said. "You could've come in first in the bullshit finals and I didn't hear about it. Last week I was in a deal with a friend of mine, we didn't ask for our pay up front and we missed out. My friend, I can't tell you how *he* missed out. Now, I don't know. It wasn't the kind of deal you can take the guy to court, you know, and sue him."

Barry seemed amazed and Stick wasn't sure if he'd been listening.

"You don't trust me . . ." Barry said.

"If I did I'd have to trust everybody I meet, wouldn't I?"

"You're the one did time, for Christ sake, not me!"

"That's right," Stick said, "and I'll tell you how it works in a place like that. You owe somebody you better fucking pay up as quick as you can. You make people wait in there or they get the wrong idea about you, your mom gets a letter, you passed away in surgery. The way it works here, I get out of the car, take my jumper and go home."

"Hey," Barry said.

"What?"

"It's cool." Giving him the level-eye look now. One of the boys. "You want me to pay you right this fucking instant? All right, I'll pay you. I thought, I guess it was my presumption, you understood." Very serious now. Rolling to one side as he spoke, digging into his back pocket to bring out a fold of currency in a silver clip.

"Where I'm coming from. Understood what?"

"That my word—when I give my fucking *word*, when I tell a guy on the phone I'm putting up a million and a half for a tax anticipation note it means I'm going to come across with a million and a half and he *knows* it. I don't have to sign anything, he *knows* it. You follow me?"

"I should've upped the bet," Stick said.

"I say I owe you a hundred, here . . ." Barry snapped off a clean new bill and extended it. "Here's the hundred. Are we all right? We square?"

Stick took the bill. He said, "Thank you very much." Put the Rolls in gear and they continued west on 125th Street, followed the causeway across the upper neck of Biscayne Bay, passed through Bay Harbour Islands and came to the Atlantic ocean at Collins Avenue, a much different Collins Avenue from the one down in South Beach— a fifteen-minute ride from the Amoco station on 125th and neither of them opened his mouth, made a sound, until they were looking at the ocean and Barry said, "Left."

Now they were in Florida postcardland, surf and sunny sky, lush tropical greenery. Stick took it all in, watched it get better and better. They turned left again, off Collins, and came to a gatehouse. A guard in a white shirt with epaulets and a blue pith-helmet—the guy was *armed*—waved the Rolls through, not even ducking down to look in, and now it got even better than before, though with a manicured look: a maintained tropical park of white walls and high trimmed hedges, palm trees against the sky, all kinds of flowering plants, occasionally a black-topped drive and a glimpse of wonderland . . . worlds away from a bleached house in Norman on an oil lease or a flat on the west side of Detroit, playing ball in sight of railroad switchyards and the stacks at Ford Rouge.

"Next one on the right," Barry said, "we're home."

Stick turned into the drive, 100 Bali Way, followed the blacktop through a patch of jungle and came in view of the house, white with a whiter roof; it reminded Stick of a mausoleum, neat and simple. Barry said, "Around back." They came to a turnaround area of cobblestones, four garage doors, a covered walk leading to the house and Stick couldn't believe the size and sprawl of the place. Like an assortment of low modules stuck together, open sides and walls of glass set at angles, the grounds dropping away from the house in gradual tiers, with wide steps that might front a museum leading down to the terraced patio and on to the swimming pool. A sweep of manicured lawn extended to a boat dock and a southwest view of Biscayne Bay, downtown Miami standing in rows of high-rises beyond. On the far side of the swimming pool, past shrubbery and palm trees, Stick saw a red tennis court with a red striped awning along one side and beyond that a second house that was like a wing of the main house, a module broken off and moved two hundred feet away. Stick's gaze came back to the row of garage doors.

"How many cars you have?"

"Four," Barry said, "at the moment." He got out, then stuck his head back in and reached for his attaché case. "It's all right to be impressed. I am and I own the joint."

Stick sat behind the wheel taking it in. He saw a woman in a green robe standing on the terrace, looking this way, brown hair with gleams of red in the sunlight.

Barry yelled at her, "Babe, how you doing!" Then ducked into the car again and glanced at Stick as he got his *Journal*. "The lady of the house. You'll have to drive her around too, but usually just over to the club. Leucadendra. It's in Coral Gables, if you don't know where it is. I doubt if she knows how to get there. But I'm the one you have to impress. You're not an alcoholic, are you?"

"I never thought about it," Stick said.

"That's a good answer. Cecil'd say he was going to an AA meeting and come back smashed. Well, you get a guy out of a rehab center you take your chances."

Stick said, "Why do you want to hire me?"

Barry stood slightly bent over, looking in. "What do you mean, why do I want to hire you? I'm offering you a job. You're sitting in the car already, I don't have to go to the service."

"What's the job pay?"

"Jesus Christ," Barry said. He straightened and bent over again. "Two bills a week, room and board. All you can eat—got a great cook. But no fucking the maids, they're nice girls. The broad that comes in does the laundry, that's up to you. What else you want to know? . . . Clothes, I buy the uniforms."

"I have to wear a uniform?"

"Jesus Christ," Barry said, "what is this? Yeah, you wear a uniform. A three-button, single-breasted suit. You wear a black one, a dark gray or a light tan, depending. That sound okay to you?"

"Where do I live? I have my own room?"

"I don't believe this," Barry said. He half-turned, nodding toward the garage wing. "There's a two-bedroom apartment in there you share with the houseman but, yes, you have your own room. Now, you want the job or not? Jesus . . ."

"Let me explain something so you understand," Stick said. "See, I did seven years straight up day to day in a room six and a half feet wide by ten feet deep. I know I have to overcome stumbling blocks, bad luck of all kinds and a tendency now and then to take shortcuts, you might say, or I could go back there or a place like it. But while I'm out, and as long as I stay out, I can choose where I live. So why don't I look at the room and then I'll let you know. How'll that be?"

Barry said, after a moment, "Sure." He didn't seem to know what else to say.

8

Chucky waited outside. Because when he mentioned Wolfgang's on the phone Kyle said she didn't do business in bars. Not snippy about it, fairly low key, in her natural style. Stating a fact. She said she was going to be down this way and wanted to drop something off. Or, if he liked the looks of the stock offering he could sign a letter of intent.

He told her lay it on him, he'd sign on the dotted line. Told her he had a pressing engagement and *had* to be at Wolfgang's and if she'd make an exception this time he'd never let it happen again.

What he wanted was for Kyle McLaren to meet Eddie Moke, and say something nice to him. A small favor to ask. Also he wanted to impress the boy. He wanted Eddie Moke in his pocket as an Anti-Cuban Protection Guarantee. A white-boy buffer between Chucky and the crazies. Somebody who thought American but worked for the chickenkillers. Chucky did not intend to make any more quarter-million-dollar offerings for honest mistakes.

He stood there in his size 44 red-white-and-blue striped T-shirt, boat freak or patriot, talking to the parking attendant who'd come on for Happy Hour, talking about cars. The young-kid attendant, seeing the gray Porsche roll in, said, "Now there's my idea of wheels. Shit, a Nine-twenty-one."

And Chucky *knew* it was going to be Kyle. Dove gray Porsche with a stylish faint orange pinstripe. She was her own girl, wasn't she? Palm Beach, stock portfolios and high-performance iron. Mom and dad'd trip over each other getting to her. He got his smile ready and there she was:

In pale yellow, plain dark sunglasses, a zip-up case in one hand, brushing at her bangs with the other. He liked her hair better this time, it was blonder in outside light, yes, had a nice outdoor look that was *her.* A good-looking broad with brains. He wondered if Pam and Aurora had finished their drinks yet . . .

Aware of everything at once moving around in his head, floating in and out of his mind's vision, pictures and now live action in the pale yellow dress. Ready?

"Kyle!"

She flipped up the sunglasses coming over, then removed them. She said, "Chucky," almost matching the intensity of his greeting. But immediately her expression relaxed, again composed. She said, "Well, are you ready to become a corporate shareholder?"

Chucky said, "If I don't have to read any small print. Hey, come on inside, I want you to meet some people." Going up the steps, his hands lightly touching her back, he said, "Would you do something for me?"

She looked at him but didn't seem surprised.

"What?"

"Tell this boy I'm going to introduce you to that you like his hat."

Chucky brought a chair over to the table, waving at people, asking how they were doing. Both of the girls, Pam and Aurora, made room; but the young guy drinking beer out of the bottle, introduced simply as Moke, didn't move.

Very serious, with that official American-cowboy funneled brim curving down on his eyes. Grim. While his body tried to appear casual- the indifferent stud.

Kyle said, "I like your hat. It has a lot of character."

Moke stirred. He looked at her, looked past her, came back to her, then stretched to look out at the room, showing her his pointy Adam's apple, vulnerable white throat. He might not have heard what she said, with the rock beat, a bell dinging outside, a foghorn blaring inside among cheers and forced laughter—poor timing.

She leaned close to the table. "I said I like your hat."

And got a reaction this time. Moke touched the brim, moved it up and then down on his eyes again. The strands of dark hair to his shoulders didn't move.

"It's an original Crested Beaut," Chucky said.

"I like your shirt, too," Kyle made herself say, though she wasn't sure why. The shirt was light blue with dark-red roses across the yoke, pearl buttons open almost all the way down the front, bony chest showing. "Are you a cowboy?"

"Moke's from Texas, the real article," Chucky said. "Hey, Moke?"

Moke shrugged, like it wasn't anything.

"I believe it," Kyle said. And that was enough of that. She wondered what Chucky was doing. If he was putting on a show. If he felt the need to have people around him.

The girl named Pam, Kyle assumed, was Chucky's. She had more hair than Kyle had ever seen before on a human head. Ash blond. More than all of Charlie's Angels put together, making her face seem tiny, hiding in there. Her hand, bearing a diamond solitaire, rested on Chucky's arm. She yawned but seemed content.

The other girl, Aurora, was dark-haired, cat-faced, with bedroom eyes, languid moves; she wore rings on seven of her fingers, a diamond, an opal, intricate designs in gold. She didn't yawn, she wound the straw from her collins around her thumb, pulled it off and wound it again.

Chucky said, "We were out with Barry earlier today, cruised up from Dinner Key. Little boat party."

"I know," Kyle said. "He called me as I was leaving home."

Pam said, "Every time we go out'n the boat"—she spoke slowly, dragging her words—"and then come in here after and go, you know, to the ladies' room? I wash my hands and all, comb my hair. And then, whenever I look at myself in the mirror after we've been out on the boat? My zits look bigger."

"They are," Aurora said.

Chucky said to Kyle, "You work out of your house, uh?"

"I have an office there."

"These two work out of their house, too," Chucky said.

Pam slapped his arm. "What's that suppose to mean?"

Aurora said to him, "I thought you were going to take me home." The whine in her voice surprised Kyle; she had expected a purr. She heard Chucky say, "You want to leave, call a cab." And the whine again: "You big shit, Barry said you're suppose to take me." They weren't bedroom eyes, they were joyless, at best sleepy.

Chucky said, "Hey, when'd I start working for Barry? You want to go home, go home. You want to wait'll we're through here, I'll take you. Now you be a good girl."

Aurora said, "Well, why can't Lionel take me?"

"'Cause Lionel's busy."

Moke said, "Doing what, eating? I ain't seen that sucker do nothing else." Moke grinned, his eyes slipped over to Kyle to get her reaction.

She smiled, an act of courtesy, and regretted it.

Encouraged, Moke said, "Yeah, Lionel, he gets his snout in the trough he'll feed all day you let him. Won't he?"

Chucky said, "Well, he is a size, all right."

Moke said, "He was mine I'd keep him out'n a feed lot."

"Why don't I leave this with you," Kyle said, setting her case upright on her lap. She zipped it open and brought out a printed binder and a few loose papers. "You can take your time, read over the prospectus and give me a call . . . not this week, though. I'm going to be in New York."

"I can't wait," Chucky said. "Let's get 'er done now."

"He can't read, is what his trouble is," Moke said. "Can you?"

Kyle kept her eyes on Chucky. "You want to do it *here*?"

"It'll be a first," Chucky said. "The only legit deal ever made in this place."

Kyle said, "Well . . ." and placed the bound prospectus in front of him. "It's a software company, been in business two years."

"Software," Moke drawled, "they make that toilet paper don't hurt none when you wipe yourself?"

Pam said, "God, you're sickening."

Kyle didn't look up. "They've developed a series of programs for personal computers." She glanced at Chucky. "You wanted to get into high-tech."

"Love it," Chucky said. "I got a computer myself. I show it to you?"

Kyle shook her head, surprised. "No, you didn't."

"I don't know how to operate it," Chucky said. "I got a fourteen-year-old kid comes in when I need him, name of Gary. Gary can key into Dade and Broward County, both their systems. I ask him to run a license number? Gary can tell me in about ten seconds if it's on a county or government vehicle or belongs to a pal. All the time popping his bubble gum."

Moke said, "You shitting me?"

"Ask it the birth date of your favorite trooper," Chucky said, "case you want to send him a card with a little something in it."

Kyle said, "Well, you only plug into Dow-Jones with this one. They're specializing in programs for mailing lists, forecasts, cost analyses, budgets, word processing. They've somehow organized an eighty-eight-thousand-word dictionary inside ninety-three K bytes of disc space, if that excites you . . ."

"Dig it," Chucky said. "What else?"

"Well, the market," Kyle said, "is definitely there. It's been increasing by a third each year, while this particular company has tripled its revenue over the past two years and they're now reasonably sure of a three-hundred-percent annual growth rate through at least 'Eighty-five."

Aurora said, "How do you know all that?"

Kyle looked up to see the dark-haired girl frowning at her. "I'm sorry. What?"

"How do you know about all that kind of stuff?"

"I read," Kyle said. She placed a typewritten letter before Chucky that was addressed to an investment banking company in New York, then went into her case again for a pen. "That's the subscription form. Sign where you see your name at the bottom and you'll be a one-and-a-half percent shareholder in Stor-Tech, Inc."

Aurora said, "I mean but how did you *learn* all that?"

"She's smart, what she is," Moke said. If anybody wanted the answer.

"I've got an idea," Kyle said to poor puzzled Aurora frowning at her. "I'll give you a lift home and tell you all about it on the way. How's that?"

Chucky said, "Hey, come on, you're not leaving us, are you?"

"Have to," Kyle said. "Isn't that the way it is, just when you're having fun . . ."

Bobbi raised her arm straight up, called to Chucky going out to the terrace and waved the check at him. She watched him come back through the customers standing around by the opening, Moke right behind him in that stupid cowboy hat.

"You want to sign or pay for it?"

"I'm a signer," Chucky said. "Gimme your pen."

Bobbi had to go over to the cash register to get it. Lying there on the back counter was the drink check her boss wanted verified, so she brought that with her and held it out to Chucky with the ballpoint.

"Gabe says I have to show you this one I signed your name to. From last week."

Chucky took the check, looked at it. "You write just like I do."

"I try to save you the bother, but Gabe can tell the difference."

"Just come straight out from the loop and put a little tail on it. This one here you can almost read," Chucky said. "You didn't give yourself a tip."

"'Course not. You think I'm trying to rip you off?"

"Not my sweet girl," Chucky said, still looking at the check. "Who was I with? I don't remember."

"Well, actually," Bobbi said—she was afraid he was going to ask that—"you weren't here but Rainy said put it on your tab"—Chucky looking up at her now—"'cause he and this guy he was with were supposed to meet you, but you didn't show up."

"Last Thursday?" Chucky said, his big pupils staring right at her now.

Moke was in close to him, leaning on the bar and looking at the check past Chucky's shoulder. Bobbi raised her hand to smooth her hair in back, fooling with it for something to do and saw Moke, the creep, staring at her armpit. Moke was weird. He'd sit at the bar sometimes and just stare, hold his beer bottle by the neck in his fist, never taking it away from his mouth, and giving it a little flip with his wrist when he wanted a sip. When he was being funny he'd ask for a straw with the beer and wait for her to laugh. He was going to wait a long time, the stupid shit. What a 'tard.

"He say I was coming in?" Chucky asked.

"Who, Rainy? Yeah, you were supposed to meet 'em here," Bobbi said. "Rainy and this friend of his. He was here about an hour ago, I just saw him."

"Rainy was?" Chucky seemed confused.

"No, not Rainy. His friend."

"While I've been here?"

"I don't know. Maybe. I didn't notice."

Chucky had straightened. "Not while I been here." He turned to Moke. "You see him?"

"See who?" Moke said.

"The guy, the one that was with Rainy last week. You know, went with him . . ."

Now Moke straightened up from the bar. "He was in here? When?"

"She says just a while ago."

"I don't know," Bobbi said, instinct telling her to back off, "maybe it was a couple of hours ago." She didn't like the look on Moke's face. Or Chucky's, for that matter.

"Musta just missed him," Chucky said. "What'd you say his name was?"

"I don't know his name. Only he's a friend of Rainy's."

"Slim fella, with brownish hair," Chucky said.

She had never seen Chucky so intent, serious. A moment ago she was going to say something about how much Rainy's friend had changed, his appearance, like he'd been sick and now was all better, but changed her mind and said, "Just ordinary looking, I guess."

"Where's he staying?" Chucky asked her.

"I don't know." With irritation now, to show she was getting tired of this. "Ask Rainy."

Neither of them said anything.

Moke seemed about to, then raised his eyebrows and grinned. Then rubbed his hand over his mouth and looked away, like TV actors did, acting innocent. Immature or stupid—Bobbi believed you could go either way with Moke and be right. Even stoned he was a simple study.

Chucky said, "Well, it doesn't matter." He bent over to sign the check.

And Moke said something that would stay with Bobbi for a long while after. He said, "It was dark time I seen him, but I'd know that sucker again, I betcha anything." With an eager sound to his drawl.

She was glad she didn't tell them how much Rainy's friend had changed. She wondered if he'd come in again. She wondered what she'd say to him, if he did.

They were on the walkway of the bridge, crossing toward Chucky's condo, Lionel trailing behind. Moke said, "Girl says ask Rainy. That'd be some deal. Get one of them air tanks you put on your back for diving, pair of flippers . . ."

"I don't want to know anything about that," Chucky said.

"Well, you better see about this fella. I tell Nestor he's gonna say find him and take him off the street."

Chucky wiped at his face with the palm of his hand. He wanted to run. Run home, run up fifteen flights of stairs, that elevator was so slow, and pop some caps; when he was wired he had to move right *now.* He said, "She must've made a mistake. The guy wouldn't be hanging around here, so don't worry about it."

Moke took hold of Chucky's arm, bringing him to a stop in the middle of the bridge walkway, people giving them looks as they had to step off the curb to go around. Lionel came up but Moke didn't pay any attention to him or the people, saying to Chucky, "You're the one sent the fella with Rainy. *I* saw him run off. Avilanosa's standing there with his Mac-ten smoking, man, *he* saw him run off. Avilanosa goes, who was that? I tell him, beats a shit outta me. Some guy Chucky wanted taken out."

Chucky, trying to keep his jaw tight, said, "The guy was with Rainy. I didn't even know him. Listen, I gotta go."

"Yeah, you said to me on the phone, take the bozo with Rainy. You recall that?"

"I might've at the time," Chucky said, moving, twisting his shoulders, wanting to snap his fingers. "It doesn't matter if I said it or not, right? I'll take care of the matter. The guy's around I'll find him."

Moke said, "You fuck Nestor again, man, he'll send Avilanosa. And there won't be nothing in the world I can do about that or want to try—no matter how many goddamn hats you give me, partner . . . Hey, you hear me!"

Chucky was running with the appearance of jogging, just in time moving to hold back the panic beginning to seep through his nervous system. If Moke touched him now, if Moke tried to stop him . . .

He felt exactly the way he had felt when he was twelve years old and had killed the dog with his hands.

9

The houseman, Cornell Lewis, said, "Does it please you?" Making it a point, maybe, to show Stick he had manners, but not putting him on.

Stick didn't expect a double bed with a view of palm trees out the window. He said, "I think I'll take it."

"I bet you will," Cornell said. "So, we got the bathroom between us, tub and shower . . ." He moved off and Stick paused to take a look at the bathroom: the clean tile, the seat on the toilet. "We got us our rec room I like to call it, with the color TV . . . refrigerator and stove over there . . . if we don't want to eat in the kitchen with the help."

"You cook?"

Cornell looked at him. "Yeah, I cook. Don't you?"

Stick said, "I cook probably better'n I fix cars—he's going to find out."

"Nothing to fix on his," Cornell said. "They break down he trade it in, get a new one . . . Come on, I'm suppose to show you the rest. The master want you to be acquainted where everything's at. He yell to you, 'Hey, Stickley, bring me a phone out the morning room.' You know which one's the morning room no matter what time of day it is. You dig?"

"Yeah, but I don't work inside."

"He like his driver to be versa-tile, do things around the house, help out when they have company. 'Cept Cecil. Cecil broke things, generally fucked up and didn't give a shit. Beautiful human being. So Mr. Stam kept him out of the house. Shoulda put him on a chain."

"I haven't heard anything good about Cecil," Stick said. "You get along with him?"

"Get along with Cecil you need a whip and a chair, or one of those cattle prods? First place, he don't like black folks and in the second place he hates 'em. He should be back any time, pick up his mess."

Stick said, "He doesn't even know he's fired, does he?"

Cornell made a face, an expression of pain. "Not yet."

It seemed more like a museum than a place where people lived: all marble and glass or wide open, full of hanging plants and flower arrangements, potted palm trees. Looking across some of the rooms or down a hall it was hard to tell what was outside and what was in.

The living room was like an art gallery: two steps down to a gray marble floor and a sectional piece in the middle, pure white, where about a dozen people could sit among the pillows and look at the paintings and pieces of sculpture that didn't make any sense at all. The room was pale gray and pink and white except for a black marble cocktail table. There were white flowers on it—no ashtrays—and several copies of a magazine, fanned out, called *Savvy.*

Stick went down into the living room, stood before a canvas about ten feet by five, gray shapes that could be parts of the human body, organs, bones, scattered over a plain white background.

"What is it?"

Cornell said, "Whatever your imagination allows."

He stood on the marble steps taller than Stick: a light-skinned black man of no apparent age but with the body of a distance runner: as neat as the decor in pressed gray trousers, black suspenders over a white dress shirt open at the neck, polished black loafers with tassels: the houseman nearly ready for evening duty.

"You have to do any of the cleaning?"

"The maids," Cornell said.

"Well, they do a job," Stick said.

"No trash, no dust," Cornell said, "or cold drafts coming in broken windows." He paused. Stick was looking at him now. Cornell said, "You from the block, aren't you?"

Stick came back toward him, still looking around, pausing at a polished stone that could have been an owl if it had eyes. He said, "I think you're guessing."

"I might have been," Cornell said, "but you answered the question, didn't you?"

"Well, as they say . . ." Stick said.

"What do they say where you were?" Cornell seemed even more at ease, ready to smile. "I come out of Raiford, then some trusty time at Lake Butler four years ago and found my new career."

"Jackson," Stick said.

"Mmmm, that musta impressed him. Yeah, Jacktown, have riots and everything up there."

"I think he liked it," Stick said.

"What the man likes is to rub against danger without getting any on him," Cornell said. "Make him feel like the macho man. You know what I'm saying?"

"He goes," Stick said, "'How'd you make it in the joint?' Like he's been there. He sounds like a probation officer."

"I know it . . . Come on." Cornell turned and they moved off. "I know what you saying. He ask how you make it like he knows what it is you have to make. I try and tell him, start with the doors clangin' shut. Every place you go the door slide open, the door clang shut. Go in the cell, *clang*, you in there, man. He act like he knows . . . That man ever took a flop there people would pass him around, everybody have a piece."

"Dress him up in doll clothes," Stick said, "and play house. But he wants you to think he knows all that."

"Wants you to think he's *baaad*, what he wants you to think. You understand what I'm saying to you? Yeah, like he's the one knows and he's testing to see if *you* know, 'cept he don't know shit less you tell him." Cornell was looser now, coming at Stick with that quick clipped black way of street talking. "You see by some of the rough trade he associates with what I mean. People he has in his *house*, man, you see their picture in the paper, some state attorney investigation, that kind of thing. It's why he hired you—why he hired me. See, he sits there at the club with his rich friends? Say, 'Oh yeah, I go right in the cage with 'em. They wouldn't hurt me none. No, I know how to handle 'em, how to treat 'em.' He tells *every*body. You understand? So there happen to be a fugitive warrant out on you someplace—you know what I'm saying? You best fly your ass out of here."

"I did it straight up," Stick said. "I'm done. For good."

"You hope to Jesus."

Stick said, "He get you out of a halfway house or coming through the window?"

"Shit," Cornell said. "You know how he found me? Man didn't know nothing about me, I was doorman at a place down the beach, this big private condominium. He comes driving up—place is full of cars on account of this reception somebody's having. See, I didn't park cars, I have to stay there by the door. But Mr. Stam, he slide his window down, his hand riding on it, he got this ten sticking out from between his fingers. He say to me, 'You got room for one more, haven't you?' and shove the bill at me, like go on, take it. So I do, I tuck it in my shirt. I say to him, 'No, sir, we full up,' and walk away. He gets out of the car and comes over to me, stands right here." Cornell held the palm of his hand straight up in front of his face. Then lowered it to his chin. "No, more like here. Like he's the little manager and I'm the umpire. You know what I'm saying? Right here. He say, 'What are you, some kind of smartass?' I go, 'You offer me the money, shove it at me to take it. Wouldn't I be a fool not to?' He turn and come back and he's got his lip like pressed against his teeth? He say, 'You got nerve, kid. I like a kid with nerve.' Takes a c-note out of his pocket from a roll, hands it to me and says in his natural voice again but real loud, 'Now park the fucking car!' I go, I scratch my head, I go, 'Oh, tha's what you wanted.' We doing this skit, see? He go in the party, come out a little later, I'm still there. He say, 'What do you do, man, when you not impersonating a doorman?' See, I know the man's crazy, likes to fool, so I tell him the truth figure he'll think I'm giving him some shit. I go, 'Well, I hustle, you know, I deal, I steal, sell TV sets and silverware out the back door.' Man love it. He say, 'You polish the silverware 'fore you fence it? You know how to do that?' Coming on to me now. 'You the cool cat with the hot goods?' All that kind of shit. Now it's part of his routine. They have company, I come in with a tray of canapés to serve the guests? He'll say to one of the ladies, 'Watch your purse, Sharon, here comes Cornell.' Then what I do, I grin and chuckle."

"Doesn't bother you?" Stick said.

"Bother me how? Put on the clown suit, man. Grin and chuckle. 'Yessuh, Mr. Stam.' Say to the lady, big blond lady name of Sharon, 'Oh, that Mr. Stam, he *ter*rible what he say.' Put on the clown suit and they don't see you. Then you can watch 'em. Learn something . . ."

He seemed thoughtful. Stick said, "Learn what?"

"I don't know. *Some*thing," Cornell said. "There must be *some*thing you hear listening to all these rich people can do some good."

"Something they don't know they're telling you," Stick said.

"Yeah," Cornell said, dragging the word. "You got it."

"Only you don't know what you're listening for."

"Not till I hear it," Cornell said. "But when I hear it—you understand me?—then I'll know it."

"You been listening for four years?"

"What's the hurry?" Cornell said.

Right, and if he never heard magic words of opportunity what was he out? Cornell was playing his grin-and-chuckle game with himself, Stick decided. Which was all right: he'd probably admit it if you held him down. On the other hand listening and being ready, not sitting back on your heels, there could be something to it.

He wondered where the man was.

"Phoning," Cornell said. "When you don't see him he's phoning. When you *do* see him he's phoning."

"People with money like phones," Stick said.

"Love 'em," Cornell said. "It's a truth you can write down, memorize."

"I met a guy has twelve phones," Stick said.

"Twelve's nothing," Cornell said. "Mr. Stam's got seven in the garage part counting the ones in the cars. Must be fifteen in this house and the guest house and four, five outside." He said, "Here, look in as we go by the den."

Sure enough, there he was on the phone, sitting at a black desk in a room painted black, sitting in a cone of light from the ceiling, holding a red phone. Stick caught glimpses of gold and red. What stopped him was the blown-up black and white photo of Barry, about six feet of him from cut-offs to yachting cap, eyebrows raised in innocence, his expression saying *who, me?* The black and white Barry behind and above the real Barry on the phone.

Why was it familiar? The expression.

Cornell said, "Hey," in a whisper and they moved on. Now Cornell was saying the man liked black 'cause it was restful, kept him calm swinging the big deals. Loved a red phone with the black.

Stick, listening, kept seeing that *who, me?* expression in his mind. The man had not looked familiar in the car, not someone he'd seen before . . . until he thought of another photo in a group of photos on the paneled wall of a den . . . all the guys in their Easter-egg colors and the two girls on the aft end of the yacht . . . the exact same *who, me?* expression on the guy next to the girl with the gold chain digging into her tan belly, *yes*, the guy next to her. Who, me? I'm not doing anything.

Jesus. Barry and Chucky . . .

He could be wrong. The same expression, but two different guys that looked somewhat alike, the same type.

"Now the man's wife, Miz Diane Stam," Cornell was saying, "she something else. You see her here, you see her there. What the man says she does, she putzes. Putzes around the house trying to think up things to be done. Then she give you a list. Man loves phones, the woman gets off on lists. List say put all the books in the library in alphabet order by the author's names. List say put red licorice Jelly Bellies in the black den, put mango and marzipan Jelly Bellies in the morning room . . . There she is. Grape ones in the living room."

They were coming through a pantry into the kitchen.

The woman still had on the green robe, a thin, silky material. She was talking to the cook. Cornell waited. Stick would bet, judging from the way the robe hung, she had those round white breasts that looked full of milk and showed little blue veins. She was about thirty, a good age. When she turned to them Cornell said, "Miz Stam, I like you to meet your new driver. Stickley."

She was looking at him but could have been thinking of something else. Vague brown eyes, pale complexion, thick brown hair pulled back and tied with a piece of yarn.

"Stickley?"

"Yes, ma'am."

The kind he thought of as a soft, comfortable woman, slow moving, passive—they always had that pale white skin.

"Stickley . . . is that English?"

The kind if he saw her alone in a bar he'd feel his crotch come alive and then he'd be anxious, nervous, going through the opening remarks and was sure he sounded dumb.

"Yes, ma'am, it's English," Stick said. Though he had never considered himself or his people from anywhere but the Midwest.

"That's nice," Mrs. Stam said. "Well then . . ." Stick waited, but that was it. She walked out of the kitchen.

He met the cook, Mrs. Hoffer, a bowlegged old lady in a white uniform: strong-looking woman, she swiped at Cornell with her neck towel when he patted her behind, but Stick could see she liked it. He told her he was glad to meet her and she said, "You too, kiddo."

Cornell put an arm around her shoulders. "This lady makes super blintzes, don't you, mama? Makes knedlachs, piroshkis, what else, kugel, all that good stuff. I'm showing her some gourmet tricks, like how to save her bacon grease and pour it in with the collards."

The kitchen was a pretty friendly place. Stick met Luisa Rosa and Mariana, the maids that Cornell called the Marielita Twins from Cooba. They smiled and stayed fairly close to one another, both in yellow uniforms with white aprons. Cornell said he was teaching them to speak American, how to say, "I'm feeling depressed because of my anxieties," and "Have a nice day."

No—Stick decided—Cornell wasn't listening for magic words. He was home.

After supper, coming back along the breezeway to the garage, he began thinking of that big blown-up *who, me?* photo again—wondering if he could stick his head in the den, take another look—and a strange thing happened. He saw a yacht tied up at the dock now. Big sleek-looking cruiser that had to be fifty feet long. He went down to the dock, began pacing it off from the bow, counted twenty strides and looked at the stern.

Seaweed. And beneath it, *Bal Harbour, Fla.*

He walked back to the apartment in the garage, now relating Barry's *who, me?* expression to the cruiser in the photo in Chucky's den, but still not sure of something.

Cornell was wearing a pearl gray tie now with his gray trousers, slipping on a lightweight black blazer.

"You going out?"

"Man, you think I wear this to go *out*? Look like the undertaker."

"There's a boat tied up at the dock."

"*Boat?* That's a halfa million dollars worth of cabin cruiser, the *Seaweed.* The man makes some of his great escapes on it."

"I thought maybe somebody stopped by."

"We got company coming, but not by sea." Cornell buttoned his blazer, turned sideways to the dresser mirror to look at himself. "You a lean, handsome motherfucker, ain't you?"

"He has parties on the boat, uh?"

Cornell turned from the dresser. "What you trying to find out I might help you with?"

"Our boss, I wondered if he's got a friend by the name of Chucky."

Cornell's face broke into a smile. "Chucky? You know Chucky? You do, there some things you haven't told me."

"They pretty good friends?"

"They play together sometime. How you know Chucky?"

"There was a fella name Rainy Moya at Jackson, used to work for him."

Cornell shook his head. "Don't know any Rainy Moyas. But Chucky, shit, Chucky's the head clown, our man's star attraction, his *in* with the bad guys, the wise guys, all those guys . . . What you looking at?"

Stick waited.

Cornell said, "Yeah," taking his time, "there some things you have not told me."

"I got to talk to somebody," Stick said.

"Don't get me into nothing, man, I'm clean, I'm staying clean."

"I need to find out something . . ."

"I got to go to work."

"Wait a minute, okay? I want to ask you a question, that's all. I think," Stick said, and hesitated. "I practically *know*, Chucky set up a guy, the one I mentioned. Rainy. Sent him to drop a bag knowing he was going to get whacked. Guy steps out of the car with a gun big enough to kill Jesus. But you tell me Chucky's the head clown, lot of laughs." Stick waited.

Cornell said, "Yeah? What's the question?"

"Is he or isn't he?"

"I got to go to work," Cornell said.

Stick fell asleep. He wasn't sure for how long. He was watching a James Bond movie on television, sitting up in a comfortable chair, but when something touched him he jumped and the news was on.

Cornell said, "Didn't mean to scare you . . . Mr. Stam would like you to come out to the patio."

Stick had to look up at him. "That all you going to tell me? How should I dress?"

"You fine like you are."

"What's the problem?"

"Cecil," Cornell said. "Cecil come home mean and ugly. Don't like the idea he's fired."

"I been waiting for him to come and get this stuff out of there,' Stick said, "so I can go to bed."

"Well, he's here now. Mr. Stam want you to have a talk with him."

"I didn't fire him, *he* did."

"Then come tell Mr. Stam that."

"What's the guy think, I took his job?"

"Ain't any way to know what Cecil thinks."

"Yeah? What's he like?"

"Cecil? He's an ugly redneck mother*fucker* is what he is. And he don't *like* nothing."

"Wait a minute," Stick said. "I get into this—then he's got to come here and pick up his *clothes*? After?"

Cornell said, "Man, what can I tell you?"

It was an informal get-together. Friends over for a few drinks, some cold shrimp and crablegs: Barry's lawyer, his internist and his yacht broker and their wives in casual dress, light sweaters over shoulders, their faces immobile, softly illuminated by patio lights buried among rows of plants, candles on the buffet table and a circle of torches burning on black metal poles.

Barry and Diane wore white caftans, Diane among the guests while Barry stood in his robe, in the ritual glow cast by the torches, to face Cecil, who hung against the portable bar.

Cecil would shift his weight and the cart would move, the bottles chiming against each other. He would reach behind him, take a bottle by the neck and swing it backhand to arc over the heads of the guests—no one moved—and splash in the swimming pool. Several bottles floated almost submerged in the clean glow of underwater lights.

Barry held his elbows in, palms of his hands extended flat, facing up. He would gesture as he spoke, then return to this palms-up pose of resignation.

"Cece? . . . What can I tell you?"

"You already tole me, asshole. If I heard you right." Cecil was drunk enough to stumble. He would cling to the cart as he raised a bottle of Jack Daniel's to his mouth.

"That's what I mean. What more can I say?"

"You can say it ain't so, pussyface. We'll talk her over."

Barry was solemn. "Cece, you're not giving me much reason to even listen to you." He glanced off into the dark. It looked like someone was coming. Finally. "I don't want to call the cops, Cece, but I don't know. I press charges you've got a parole violation. Right?" Barry looked at his guests, picked out his lawyer. "David? Wouldn't you say he's on dangerous ground?"

The lawyer stirred, sat up straighter. He said, "Well, I suppose it's possible . . ."

The figure, coming from the general direction of the garage, was cutting across the slope of lawn now. Carrying something at his side. A bucket? Something round, with a handle. A second figure, Cornell, trailed behind.

Barry said, somewhat louder, "Well, Cece, it's up to you. I'm going to ask you once more to leave quietly."

"And I'm own ask you to bite this," Cecil said, palming his crotch. "Little pussymouth Jew-boy, you might be pretty good."

"That's it, all she wrote," Barry said. "You're paid up and your replacement's right here, so get the fuck out. *Now.*" He stepped back toward his guests, looking at Stick coming into the torchlit patio . . . The hell was he doing? Carrying an old two-gallon gasoline can . . .

Stick walked past Cecil without looking at him, not wanting to. He'd seen enough of Cecil already: that hard-bone back-country type, cords in his neck and pale arms, big nostrils—Christ, hearing the guy blowing air through his nose to clear it. You did not talk to the Cecils of the world drunk; you threw a net over them if you had one. Cops and prison guards beat their brains in and they kept coming back. Stick walked over to the buffet table. He placed a glass on the edge, unscrewed the cap on the gooseneck spout of the gasoline can and raised it carefully to pour.

Cecil said, "The fuck you drinking?"

Stick placed the can on the ground. He picked up the glass, filled to the brim, turned carefully and came over to Cecil with it. Cecil stared at him, weaving a little, pressing back against the cart as Stick raised the glass.

"You doing? I don't drink gasoline, for Christ sake. Is it reg'ler or ethyl?"

Stick paused, almost smiled. Then emptied the glass with an up-and-down toss of his hand, wetting down the front of Cecil's shirt and the fly of his trousers.

There was a sound from the guests, an intake of breath, but no one moved. They stared in silence. They watched Cecil push against the bar, his elbow sweeping off bottles, watched him raise the fifth of Jack Daniel's over his head, the sour mash flooding down his arm, over the front of his shirt already soaked. He seemed about to club down with the bottle . . .

Stick raised his left hand, flicked on a lighter and held it inches from Cecil's chest.

"Your bag's packed," Stick said, looking at him over the flame. "You want to leave or you want to argue?"

He was making his bed, changing the sheets, when Cornell came in, leaned against the door frame to watch him.

Cornell said, "I don't know what you worried about Chucky for . . . Mr. Stickley."

Stick looked over at him. "I don't know if I am or not. You never answered the question."

"Hospital corners," Cornell said. "Know how to do all kinds of things, don't you? You about scared the shit out of the guests. They all had a double Chivas and went home to bed." Cornell came into the room, looking around at nothing; the walls, painted a light green, were bare. "You ask me is Chucky a clown or what. Could he have had your friend killed? Ask Mr. Stam, no. Chucky's the funky white Anglo-Saxon cocaine dealer, weird, but wouldn't hurt a soul. Ask on the street, that's another something else. They speak of Chucky, say bad things about him. Set up his own man, set up his mama, wouldn't make no difference. Works with de Coobans and stays zonked on the 'ludes. Way you want to never never be."

"He come here to visit?"

"Time to time," Cornell said. "But as I say, man know how to play with fire shouldn't have to worry none."

Stick brought up the green plaid bedspread over the pillows, then pulled it back down again and folded it across the foot.

"You want to know what was in the can?" He looked up at Cornell. "Water."

Cornell said, "Sure, 'nough?" His grin widening, "Shit . . . you telling me the truth?"

"Where was I going to get gasoline?" Stick said. "Drive all the way over the Amoco station?"

10

When was the last time he had a choice and picked out his own clothes?

He wore state clothes. He wore sporty clothes left by the guy who went to Key West and didn't come back. Now he had a black suit, a gray one and a tan one a tailor in the Eden Roc Hotel had chalked, altered and delivered in three and a half days as a special favor to Mr. Stam. Two seventy-five a copy.

The last time would have been in '76, but he couldn't remember the clothes, outside of a Hawaiian shirt that had sailboats and palm trees on it.

He was to wear a white or light blue shirt, black regular tie. He was to wear the black suit with the black Cadillac, the gray suit with the Rolls, the tan suit with the beige Continental. He could wear anything he wanted when he drove Mrs. Stam; usually she took the green Mercedes.

Stick said, "In the morning when I get up, do I sit around in my underwear, wait till I find out what car we're taking?"

"That's very funny," Barry said. "No, you don't sit around in your underwear, I tell you the night before." His eyes serious, questioning. Like he might be having a few doubts. "You keep the cars washed, gassed, ready to go, either for a time I tell you or within ten minutes of my call. You think you can handle that?"

Saying it to a man who had never been in the armed forces but had recently taken seven years of penal shit and was full up. Stick waited a moment, as though he was getting it straight in his mind but concerned about something. He let himself ease back and said, "Yes, sir. But if we have to synchronize our watches we're in trouble. I don't have a watch."

He would remember Barry's solemn eyes staring at him. Where were the one-liners?

He asked Cornell about it later on: the guy seemed different from one day to the next.

Cornell said, "What's wrong with you? I explained, didn't I? The man's top bill. *We* don't say the line, the man says the line. What we do, *we* grin and chuckle. Shit, I told you that."

Stick said, "Yeah, but he gave me a watch to use."

"Sure he did," Cornell said. "The same time he wants you to respect him he remembers you coming with that gasoline can . . . Man wants you to be stupid but happy."

They took the Cadillac limousine to Leucadendra. Barry sat in back and made phone calls. He talked to his broker, Arthur, told him he'd get back to him. He dialed three numbers asking for someone named Kyle, was unable to find her and was short with Arthur when he spoke to him again; he'd get back. Then spoke to a girl who was "Rorie" at first—Barry laying down a field of soft snow about how much he missed her—then "Aurora" as he explained almost deal by deal how busy he was, why he hadn't been able to see her. Stick, all dressed up in his black suit, would glance at the rearview mirror and see Barry in his tennis whites acting into the phone, telling the girl he was on his way at this very moment to a meeting with his lawyers, but hey, how about meeting on the boat later, around six or so.

He said to Stick, "You know the difference between a wife and a mistress? . . . Night and day, man."

Stick looked at the rearview mirror. "That's right, isn't it?" With a note of appreciation, but not giving it too much.

"Sometimes you ask yourself," Barry said, "is it worth it?" He waited for Stick to look at the mirror again. "Bet your ass it is."

Stick looked at the mirror again and nodded. Why not?

They drove into the grounds of Leucadendra past fairways to the tennis courts that were off beyond the stucco Spanish clubhouse with its red tile roof. Getting out, Barry pointed to a side entrance that went into the men's grill and told Stick to "park over there somewhere and hang out, I'll be an hour or so."

Barry walked off carrying three tennis racquets in an athletic bag, a sweater tied around his shoulders. Stick watched him from the air-conditioned car. It was about ninety degrees out there, the sky almost cloudless. He put the Cadillac in "drive" and swung it around.

Park and wait. All right.

But wait a minute . . .

It startled him, something he had failed to consider: that on a job like this he could spend more than half the time doing nothing, waiting. Twenty minutes from Bal Harbour to Coral Gables, now he'd be "an hour or so." Did that mean more than one hour but less than two? If Barry played tennis and then had drinks and maybe lunch in the men's grill . . . Stick realized he could be hanging around here for two hours at least. Or even three hours . . . Driving, he was doing something, he could shut himself off from the man in the back seat. But waiting, he was waiting for the man to come and set him in motion again. Wind him up. He could wait all day and have no right to complain—"Hey, you said you were going to be an hour or so"—because waiting was part of the job. Chauffeurs waited. There were some right here, standing by their cars lined up in the circular drive. Three uniformed chauffeurs. Older guys, all of them in their late fifties or early sixties.

Watching him from the shade. They'd know the Cadillac from the vanity plate, BS-2. The Rolls was BS-1, the Continental BS-3. Mrs. Stam's Mercedes bore a conventional number. Stick got out and walked up the drive. Yeah, they were at least in their sixties. All three wore dark uniforms, white shirts, glasses.

The one wearing a chauffeur's cap, cocked a little to one side, said to him, "Looks like Cecil finally got let go." Stick nodded, coming up to join them—a younger look-alike in his uniform, the new guy—and the one in the chauffeur's cap glanced at the other two. "I told you. Didn't I tell you?" Then to Stick again, "He got looped once too often, didn't he?"

"I guess so," Stick said.

They shook their heads talking about Cecil and it surprised Stick that they seemed disappointed. They told their names: Harvey with the cap, Edgar and John, who didn't say much, and told who they worked for as though Stick would recognize the names. They smoked cigarettes with one hand in their pants pocket and referred to other club member names that Stick realized he was supposed to know. He saw that you acquired a casualness in this job: Yes, you knew all those people and nothing anyone said surprised you. Though Stick let what they said surprise him when they got around to Cecil again, talking about his memory, how ignorant he was but had this knack for remembering things. While Owen, who was Mr. Stam's driver before Cecil, Owen would jot things down he couldn't remember The three talking among themselves about Cecil and Owen, Stick listening.

Until Harvey turned to him and asked, "How's Mr. Stam doing on that deal he's got in California, that seed company?"

"I don't know anything about it," Stick told him but paid closer attention now. These old guys were taking their time but gradually moving in on him, the new man.

Harvey said, "You play the market?"

Stick said no and the three of them acted mildly surprised. "Gee, that's a shame," Harvey said, "sitting where you area, right there in the catbird seat."

Stick knew he was supposed to ask Harvey what he meant, so he did.

"Working for Barry Stam," Harvey said, sounding surprised.

"We ask him, what looks good, Mr. Stam?" Edgar said, "and he tells us. Gives us some pretty good tips."

The one named John smirked, said, "Not bad a'tall."

Harvey said, "You know, over-the-counter stuff mostly, companies nobody knows anything about."

Edgar said, "Or some hasn't reached the counter yet. Some of those brand-new stock deals he gets into."

Stick said, "Well, I hear him talking on the phone. It's about all he does."

Harvey said, "That's right. Now Cecil, he'd recall the names and numbers for you from mem'ry. Owen, he'd have to jot 'em down. But Cecil, he was like a jukebox. You put a coin in him and he played you a tune. Look off at number two fairway there, get a squint on his face and go right down a list of stocks, tell you the bid and the ask."

Edgar said, "He did pretty well, too."

John said, "*Well*? He cleaned up."

Harvey said, "I betcha he was making a hundred a week, easy."

Stick said, "Cecil played the stock market?"

"No, from tips," Edgar said.

"Don't confuse the man," Harvey said. "Cecil'd give us a stock tip and get the regular kind of tip back. But I'm not talking about a buck or a five. A good one, like a new company Mr. Stam was going into? That could be worth fifty bucks."

Stick said, "You guys must do all right, you can afford a fifty-buck tip."

Harvey looked at Edgar and back to Stick. "I work for a lady who don't know shit but what her broker tells her and her broker don't know shit either outside of what's on the Big Board. You follow me? Ten years ago Barry Stam was a little smarty kid'd get mad and hit his tennis racquet down on the pavement, bust about two a week. Today little Barry could buy this whole club they ever wanted to sell it. He started out with a rich daddy like everybody else around here, but he passed his daddy by—I mean he could buy his *daddy*, he wanted to. Started in real estate but makes all his money from stock investments now, mostly the last few years. He's the man with the touch a gold. So if I give old Mrs. Wilson a tip sounds good to her, she gives *me* a tip and then I turn around and split it with Cecil.

You see how it works? And not just with me or Edgar or John. You can work it with pretty near any one of the fellas you see here."

"Waiting around," Stick said.

"Yeah, right here."

Stick said, "Doesn't it bore the shit out of you?"

Chucky was looking at a ton and a half of next to top-grade Colombian marijuana that had a street value of almost two million dollars. Nestor Soto had bought it in Santa Marta for forty dollars a pound, brought it up from Colombia by sea and air and delivered it to Chucky for two hundred dollars a pound. Now Chucky would turn it over to jobbers and dealers in odd lots—eating extra pills for the next two days—and double his investment.

It was pressure time in the old horse barn—off NW 16th Avenue, out past Hialeah—waiting to move the grass. Dishonest people in the business could hear about it and rip him off. Or somebody could cop to the DEA or the FBI or the BNDD or Dade County Public Safety and they'd confiscate the load, smoke it up in the municipal incinerator and he'd still have to pay Nestor six hundred grand. Within forty-eight hours, that was the deal. Nestor could even steal it from him, sell it again to some other dealer.

Chucky had guys with shotguns in the stables, out in a stand of scrub pine and down NW 16th in a car with a PREP radio. Lionel carried a radio hooked to his belt, his suitcoat hanging open. Chucky wore his hardhat and a long white lab coat, his duster, that he left here on a nail or draped over the handle of a pitchfork.

He said to Lionel, "What I should do, I'm thinking seriously, get out of the wholesale end, work strictly as a broker. I didn't have to stockpile I could be a normal human being." Looking up at the bales, seeing daylight through the rickety boards. He imagined a wind raising dust across the yard, swooping in to blow away the barn, rip the lab coat from his back and he'd be standing here with his stacked bales, exposed. "I brokered I could do it all on the phone. Or having my dinner where people stop in. Way I used to do it. What do you need?—see Chucky Buck, the first booth there."

"Sounds good," Lionel said, "but you don't make no money. Five, ten bucks a pound."

"I'm talking about just the weed. What's this load worth if I brokered it? I wouldn't make the deal for less'n thirty grand, on the telephone, never have to look at it. Okay, take the thirty and buy half a kilo of good Peruvian flake. You see what I mean? Look at this pile of horseshit—look at it."

"I'm looking at it," Lionel said.

"Cost me what, six hundred grand. Same as ten kilos of Peruvian. Only you don't have to lease a fucking barn to stockpile coke. Listen, this stockpiling—I didn't have to sit on it and wonder who in the hell knows about it outside of enough people we could have a dance we all got together, I wouldn't have this pressure. Right here's where I feel it," Chucky said, slipping a hand inside his white lab coat to touch his abdomen. "Locks up the intestines, man. Every night I'm watching the late news I have a vodka and citrate of magnesia . . . You saw they found Rainy. You see it? It was on the news and this morning's *Herald* had it, way in the back."

Lionel shook his head. "I don't think so."

"You don't *think* so," Chucky said. "You mean—here it's about the same guy you handed a suitcase to goes out and gets shot six times and maybe you saw it, maybe you didn't?"

"No, I don't guess I did."

"They pulled him out at the Bay Front yacht basin. Cause of death gunshot. And they identify him 'cause he's got his wallet in his pocket with the driver's license. You believe it?"

"Yeah, well, it's too bad. I like Rainy okay," Lionel said. "I work for a guy three years ago; man, I didn't like to work for him at all. He got shot, too. I was very happy about it . . ."

Chucky wondered if Lionel was going to make some kind of point, but never found out. Lionel's walkie-talkie squawked and began speaking to them in Spanish. Lionel unhooked it from his belt and spoke back to it in Spanish, Chucky waiting.

"He say it look like Nestor's car coming. The white Cadillac."

Chucky straightened. "How many?"

"He say only three. It look like Moke and Avilanosa with him."

Chucky said, "Shit," and stepped over to the barn opening to see the car already approaching, its dust trail blowing into the pines that bordered the road in from the highway. Coming past the stables the car drew two of Chucky's men from the shade to follow along behind, one of them with a pump-action shotgun.

Moke, getting out, glanced back at them unimpressed. He had on his cowboy hat, the front of the brim bent down on a line with his nose. He said to Chucky, "Brought somebody wants to visit with you, partner." Moke wearing his new shitkicker image for all to see.

Avilanosa, coming from the driver's side, was another type entirely and Chucky felt no vibes from that direction. He saw Avilanosa as primitive man in a plaid sportcoat: the cane cutter, with his big hands, his big gut, his bowed legs, who served as Nestor's bodyguard and current father-in-law. A Cuban redneck. Chucky found it hard even to say hi to him. Though he did, with a grin.

"Well, how you doing?" Saving his concentration for Nestor, hoping to read the wooden-face little dude before he surprised him with some new demand.

Nestor got out of the back seat of the Fleetwood Cadillac to stand gazing about through tinted glasses as though he'd never been here before. It was typical of him—the sandbagger—he'd distract you while he crept up, get you looking the other way. He raised his hand now in a limp gesture of recognition and gold gleamed, a diamond flashed in dusty sunlight. The little king with gigolo hair and mahogany skin. Nestor passed himself off as Spanish Cuban; but there were people who said he was part Lengua Indian from the wild, miserable Chaco country of Paraguay originally—raised on the alkaline flats and fed spider eggs. Which had made him evil and mean. Another primitive passing for a South Miami dude. Chucky felt he should be trading him beads instead of crisp new cash.

He said, "Nestor," grinning, "you're some kind of rare exhibit, you know it? You're a fucking floor show, man, all by yourself, and you don't even have to perform."

Nestor seemed to like that. He smiled and said, "Chucky," coming into the barn shade, his dark-brown suit losing some of its silky sheen. He looked at the bales of grass, nodding. "You got it okay, uh? It's very good grade Santa Marta. You like it?"

"It's all right," Chucky said. "If I'm lucky, I don't get ripped off or busted I'll make a few bucks . . . You hear about Steinberg? You remember him?"

"Yes, of course," Nestor said, "but I don't see him for, I think, five years."

"Right, he was busted in 'Seventy-eight and ran out on his bond.

I just heard they picked him up again out in California. But you know how they found him? You remember that big goddamn St. Bernard he had?"

"Yes, of course. Sasha."

"Right. And you recall how many different names Steinberg used? I don't know what he was using out there, California, but he never changed the dog's name, Sasha. How do they find him? Through the vet. Sasha's doctor."

He got a smile from Nestor, that's all. Not enough to loosen him up, if he needed it.

"The moral of the story," Chucky said, "the *punto*, any time you go a.k.a. you better be sure everybody with you does too. You had a goat, didn't you? Different animals?"

"They all die," Nestor said.

"Oh," Chucky said. With the awful feeling he'd said the wrong thing. He wasn't going to mention chickens.

Nestor said, "What is it you wear? You dress like you gonna kill something. This place a *carniceria*?"

Chucky held his arms out, showing off his lab coat. "Just one of my many outfits."

"You look like you gonna kill the *pollo*."

Shit. "Not me, Nestor." And couldn't help saying, "I like chickens." He felt Avilanosa come up on him and turned enough to see the pitchfork—Christ!—and tried to get out of the way, hunching. But Avilanosa only gave him tap with it, hitting the tines flat on top of his hardhat.

Nestor smiled. "Like that you kill the cow, yes?"

Avilanosa tapped him again, a little harder. Chucky felt the jolt down through his neck.

"Yes, for fat cows," Nestor said.

Avilanosa raised the pitchfork again and there was nothing Chucky could do but grin and hunch his shoulders playing pie-in-the-face straightman to the free-basing Cubans. But this time Avilanosa used two hands and brought the edge of the pitchfork down with force and Chucky was driven to his hands and knees, pole-axed, the hardhat cracked down the middle rolling away from him. He felt Avilanosa's foot jab him in the ribs to push him over, head ringing, an awful pain down the back of his neck. Now he saw

Avilanosa and Nestor looking down at him. He saw Moke, his arms folded. Turning his head he could see his bodyguard, Lionel, standing by the barn opening, two more figures behind Lionel against the sunlight. Now a bale was coming down on him and he tried to roll away but a foot held him. Another bale came down, more bales—his head was free, he could see the faces, but he couldn't move his arms or his legs, the bales piling on top of each other, some rolling off. The weight didn't hurt but he couldn't move. He tried. *He couldn't move.* He tried again, straining, looking at Nestor, pleading with his eyes. *He couldn't move*! And now he began to scream. . .

Because it was exactly the same as the time at Dau Tieng with the 25th Infantry—Easy Company—no place for a boy inducted drunk and living in-country stoned but not stoned enough—when they were overrun and he was in the ditch trying to press himself into muddy invisibility and the VC came down on top of him, blown apart by their own mortars: black pajamas and mud slamming down on him, lying on his back *and he couldn't move.* Pinned, wedged beneath all those bodies. The stump of a leg pushed against his cheek, his head lower than his body. Looking up at green tracers and the weedy edge of the ditch, the creviced sides coming apart, sliding down with the pounding noise, straining his neck to raise his head against the mud rising higher around his face *and he couldn't move*! This was when he began screaming to kill himself, to burst his lungs, rupture his heart, screaming so hard he saw lights exploding and didn't know if they were in the wash of sky or inside his head, screaming himself out of his body . . . to come back to life in Memphis, Tennessee, the VA hospital.

Avilanosa speared the pitchfork into the bale close to Chucky's face, inches from it, stooped down and said, "Hey!" So that when Chucky stopped screaming and opened his eyes he was looking through the tines of the pitchfork, imprisoned.

Nestor stood over him now, frowning as Chucky's eyes focused and he came back to them. "What's the matter with you? You can't be quiet for a moment? You always like to move when I tell you something. I want you listen, okay? I want this guy was with Rene. You tell Moke it's no problem for you, but I don't hear nothing that you find him."

Chucky seemed to strain to speak, out of breath. "We just heard it, few days ago."

"Yes, it's what I mean. A few days, you haven't done nothing," Nestor said. "But you busy, you doing business."

"With you!" Chucky began to cough with the weight and the odor of the marijuana.

"Try to be tranquil," Nestor said. "Breathe slowly. The man with connections, you can sell this in a day, but you can't find the guy was with Rene."

"Nobody even heard of him," Chucky said, coughing again. "None of Rainy's friends. Nobody." He breathed in and out, trying to calm himself. "All I know, Rainy asked me could the guy go with him. Some guy he did time with, but I never saw him before in my life."

"You don't know him," Nestor said, "but you want him dead."

Chucky said, "It was him or Rainy, so I picked him, that's all. I know Rainy. I told you, I send somebody with the money and it's out of my hands, you do what you want. So that's all I did. He got away from *you*, not me."

"Listen to you," Nestor said. He pinched the crease in each leg of his brown silk trousers to squat close to Chucky, resting his arms on his knees, balanced, his body erect. "You give me a lot of shit, you know it? You send a federal man to do business with me. You send somebody you don't know who he is for me to kill. You say you gonna find this guy, you don't do it. You say you gonna tell me places to put my money, make it clean, you don't do it. Tell me what good you do."

"I've been busy," Chucky said. "I just got into that myself, finding investments. Let me up, Nestor, come on, we'll talk about it."

"I don't want to talk about investment," Nestor said. "I want to tell you find this guy was with Rene. It's the first thing, it's the only thing you have to do."

"I gotta sell this weed, Nestor, or I can't pay you," Chucky said. "You know that."

"You sell it, I don't think about that. I think about this guy was with Rene, who he is, where he is. I think you better find him . . ."

"I'm trying—I'm doing everything I can!"

"Shhh. Listen to me," Nestor said. "You don't find him we gonna have to do the ceremony, make an offering to Changó and Elegua. I can do it, you see, because I'm *babalawos*, a high priest before I came here. I don't do it they get angry and I have some more bad luck. You understand?"

Chucky said, "Come on, Nestor, Jesus Christ," panic edging into his voice again, seeing El Chaco the medicine man looking at him from another century and another side of the world. "What you believe, man, that's fine. But I'm not into that, I'm an outsider, man, I don't know anything about it—*nothing*."

"We return a gift to the earth in sacrifice," Nestor said to the face beneath the steel bars of the pitchfork. "You understand? You find this guy was with Rene or we gonna bury you alive."

Moke, in the front seat of the Fleetwood Cadillac, looked back through the rear window at Chucky's guys standing by the barn opening, turning away from the dust blowing at them. They weren't going to try anything. He adjusted his Crested Beaut, loosening the sweatband sticking to his forehead and looked at Nestor sitting with his legs crossed, hands folded in his lap. Neat little guy, smart as hell.

"Old Chucky," Moke said, "isn't anything he's scareder of'n not being able to move. I don't know why, but it's true."

"There something wrong with him, in his head," Nestor said. "He's a man to pity. But I tell you something, he know how to move the product."

"He thought he was gonna get offered up right there," Moke said and looked at Avilanosa driving, his huge fists gripping the steering wheel. "Didn't he?"

"He believe it," Avilanosa said, almost smiling.

"Sure, he did," Moke said, being part of this Cuban business, looking at Nestor in the back seat again. "You pull that *santería* on 'em they start pooping apple butter, I swear."

"Yes, it's good to use," Nestor said. "Save you a lot of work. I find out a long time ago, gods can scare the shit out of anyone."

11

He waited three and a half hours counting lunch at the snack bar, a hot dog, listening to golfers in their Easter bunny outfits describing their lies and how they chipped out of trouble pin-high and blew a five-foot putt, becoming macho and obscenely emotional about it. All these people seemed to have their troubles.

Barry came out in his white shorts and a clean tennis shirt trimmed in blue and yellow. Jumping in back, slamming the door, he said, "Let's get outta here." As they drove through Coral Gables toward South Dixie he said, "They bug you for tips on the market?"

Stick looked at the rearview mirror. "Yeah, as a matter of fact. The other drivers there, they say you've got the touch. You only pick winners."

Voice from the rear of the air-conditioned Cadillac enclosed in tinted glass:

"Is that right? The touch, uh? The people those guys work for, the families, all their dough was handed down, they never had to lift a finger. It's a goddamn good thing, too. If their IQs were any lower they'd be plants, shrubbery . . . The touch, huh? . . . You know how you acquire the touch, Stickley?"

He'd see what it was like to say, "No, sir."

"You work your ass off, that's how."

"Yes, sir."

"They wouldn't know anything about that, getting up and going to work, man. They tell their drivers to hang out, try and learn something. It doesn't bother me, though. They ask you for anything in particular? Certain areas, like oil, high-tech?"

"They wanted to know about, I think one of 'em said over-the-counter stock."

"Yeah, new issues mostly, that's what they like. Tell 'em—I got one for you. Tell 'em to buy Ranco Manufacturing. Which I'm getting ready to unload. But don't tell 'em that. Tell 'em, buy Ranco. Whisper it . . . Shit, tell 'em anything you want, make a few bucks. Gen-uh-rul Mo-tors. You might have to spell it for 'em."

Stick said to the mirror, "How'd you know about the other drivers?"

"I happen to know things, Stickley. Stickley, old boy. My wife thinks you're English. What'd you tell her, you're from Jacksonshire? Oh yes, that's right next to Yorkshire . . . Stay on Ninety-five, we're going to Lauderdale . . . I know things that'd surprise the shit out of you, Stickley. I know, for instance, that fall you took up in Michigan wasn't half of it. I understand you and your partner were in something much bigger. You and your partner. What was his name? . . ."

"Who, Frank Ryan?" Stick said to the mirror.

"That was it, Ryan. You and Ryan had a deal going with some jigaboos that blew up in your face. But before you took your fall—I think while you were out on bond, according to my source, which is A-one reliable—you took out the jigs. True or false?"

Stick did not feel he could tell the story through a small rectangle of glass to a guy sitting behind him, even if he wanted to. He said, "Where'd you hear that?"

"I understand before the big one went down, you and Frank Ryan, there were a couple *other* spades you blew away. You got something against colored people, Stickley? I better tell Cornell to watch his ass."

Stick looked at the mirror, at the young millionaire trying to sound street. "You checking up on me?"

"You mind? Since I'm providing your bed and board?"

"I thought I was working for it."

"Now you seem bothered by semantics. You want me to rephrase it?"

The street tone didn't go with the words. Guy didn't know how to stay in character. "Who's your source? You don't mind my asking."

"Yeah, I mind. I don't think it's any of your business."

Trying to sound on the muscle now, a hard-nose. The guy should try out for the movies. See if in about a hundred years he could take Warren Oates's place. Christ. Why wouldn't he just relax and enjoy being rich? On the phone again, talking to his Rorie. The little asshole big-dealer sitting in the backseat of his limo in his tennis whites trying to sound like a hardass and coming off like Eddie Fisher doing Marlon Brando. The first thing he should do is get rid of all his phones except one. Maybe two. And drive his own fucking car.

Stick said, "You mind my asking where we're going?"

"I'm on the phone!" Then, sounding tired: "I'll tell you when we get there. Okay?" Indicating to Rorie the kind of shit he had to put up with from the help. Stick was silent, listening now to Barry telling Rorie babe he was sorry about the interruption. Telling her to take a cab and meet him. To be there in fifteen minutes. Voice rising now:

"Because I'm running late and I don't have time to pick you up. You now have exactly fourteen and a half minutes—got it? Be there or that's all she wrote, babe." He hung up.

For a minute or so Stick thought over the situation. He said, "Mr. Stam? When we get to where we're going—"

"Wolfgang's." Barry was dialing again.

"You going to want me to wait?"

Stick looked at the mirror for an answer that, at this moment, could be crucial.

"No, drop me off." He had his hand over the phone.

Stick said, not sure, "I don't have to wait around?"

He heard Barry say, "Go home. Do whatever you want." Heard him say, "Babe?" his tone mellowing. "I'm sorry. I had a bad day... Yeah, I know. Listen, you want to come home with me? . . . What?"

Giggling now. Stick watched him in the mirror. The guy was grinning with his shoulders hunched, giggling like a little kid.

"No, I mean on the boat. What'd you think? I'm serious, babe. Don't you know when I'm serious? . . . Fourteen minutes." He hung up.

"I'm not saying she's tough . . ." Barry said.

Stick looked at the mirror.

". . . but she's the only broad I know who kick-starts her vibrator."

Stick kept staring at the mirror until a horn blared next to him and he got back in his lane.

He was lucky to find an empty seat down at Bobbi's end of the bar. When she came over with the cocktail napkin she blinked her eyes at his suit and said, "Are you trying to confuse me or something?"

"I wouldn't mind talking to you," Stick said, "over a nice dinner somewhere. You ever leave this place?"

She made a face, disappointed. "I come on at five and work straight through. I'd love to some other time . . . You working?"

"No, I'm not a funeral director," Stick said. "You know a guy named Barry Stam? Has a boat here?" She was nodding eagerly as he said it. "I work for him."

"You work for *Barry*? Oh, my God—"

"What do you think of him? You like him?"

"Yeah . . ." though not sounding too sure. "He's cute. He's flaky but he's cute. He always zings me with a—not a joke really—a one-liner, every time he comes in. I see him coming and get ready. Yeah, he's a nice guy, basically, when he doesn't try so hard." She paused, raising her hand. "Ah, now I know what happened to Cecil." She glanced at a customer waving at her. "Be right back. Wait. What do you want?"

She brought him a bourbon, smiling. "And how's your daughter? You have fun with her?"

"Yeah, she's fine," Stick said, tried to think of something to add and was saved. Bobbi left him again. He watched her making drinks—unhurried but very efficient, no wasted motion, pleasant with the customers. He still had to call his ex-wife. He wondered if he was forgetting on purpose, putting it off . . .

Bobbi came back, placed another bourbon in front of him and said, barely moving her mouth, "I'll put it on Chucky's, the dumb shit."

"He isn't here, is he?" Stick glanced over his shoulder at the crowded room. It was packed, noisy, up-beat music and voices filling the place.

Bobbi said, "No, but somebody else is. Don't look around. He's coming back from the men's . . . Sitting down now, about the middle of the bar."

"Who?" Stick looked at the tinted bar mirror.

"Eddie Moke, the creep. He's a friend of Chucky's."

"I don't see him."

"About halfway down. The cowboy hat—God, you can't miss him."

He saw the hat—pale straw with a high crown, scooped brim—and recognized it right away. Or knew of one just like it. Hanging on a hat-tree with about a dozen different kinds of caps and hats.

"Every time he comes in he asks if I've seen you."

Moke stared straight ahead at his reflection in the rose-tinted glass. He raised his fist, holding the neck of a beer bottle, to his mouth. The hat didn't move.

"What do you tell him?"

"Nothing. There's nothing to tell," Bobbi said. "I might've done something dumb though. You know the last time you were here? And I didn't recognize you right away?"

"Yeah . . ."

"I was explaining to Chucky about signing his check—you know, when you were here with Rainy—and I told them you'd been in, like just a little while before. They started asking me your name and if I knew where you lived, I told them to ask Rainy . . . But I shouldn't've, huh?"

"No, that's all right."

"I don't even *know* your name."

"But you might know where I live, now."

He saw her eyes change, her gaze become flat. "Thanks a lot. You think I'd tell those creeps anything?"

"I didn't mean it that way. My name's Ernest Stickley and I live at One Hundred Bali Way. In the garage."

Her eyes became warm again. "Ernest?"

"Stick."

She did a little something with her eyebrows and her shoulders, putting on a dreamy look, and moved off to take care of a customer.

Stick finished his drink, left a five and walked down the bar to where Moke, in a body shirt striped black and yellow, skin tight, straddled his stool, hunched over his beer and a paper dish of peanuts: Moke throwing a few peanuts in his mouth, then taking a swig of beer before he'd begin to chew. Stick laid a hand on his shoulder, feeling bone. The hat came around and now he saw dull eyes staring at him from between the curved brim and the bony shoulder.

"You mind my asking," Stick said, standing there in his black suit and tie, "where a cowboy gets a hat like that?"

"Buy 'em at the store," Moke said, sucking bits of peanut from his teeth.

Stick narrowed his eyes at the hat, studying it, giving Moke time to look him over.

"I like that high crown. It stands up there."

"It's a Crested Beaut," Moke said.

"It sure is," Stick said. "You mind taking it off, let me have a look at it?"

Moke straightened, turned to the bar mirror as he lifted the hat carefully, passed it over his shoulder and began brushing at his hair with bony white fingers.

Stick took the hat, held it at various angles, turned it over to look inside. "There's something sticking out of the sweatband."

"Toilet paper," Moke said. "I put some toilet paper in there so'd fit me good and snug."

"Feels like a fine grade of straw," Stick said.

"The best," Moke said.

"Doesn't crease on you, get out of shape?"

"Can't hurt it none," Moke said.

"Let's see," Stick said. He dropped the hat on the floor and stepped on it, crushing the crown flat, grinding it against the polished vinyl tile. He picked the hat up then and placed it on the bar in front of Moke. "Thanks," Stick said.

He walked away. Along the bar, through the foyer and out the front door to the pavement. The parking attendant said, "Yes, sir," coming over, and Stick pointed. "It's right there."

Moke finally appeared. He stood at the top of the three steps, in the shade of the awning over the entrance, holding his crushed hat. He looked at Stick waiting for him. Stick took off his coat. The Cadillac came up next to him and the attendant jumped out. Stick threw the coat in on the seat. He gave the attendant a dollar, said something to him and the attendant walked away. He pulled off his tie and threw it in the car.

Moke came down one step in his cowboy boots, hesitated and stayed there. He said, "I've seen you someplace."

Stick walked toward him now, to the edge of the awning. Moke turned sideways, raised a boot to the top step again. He appeared uncertain, confused by a dude with a Cadillac coming on like a street fighter. He stared hard but was cautious and seemed ready to run back inside if he had to.

"You know me," Stick said, "or not?"

Moke didn't answer. Stick walked back to the car. He paused with his hand on the door to look at Moke again.

"I know you," Stick said.

He got in the car and drove off, west on Sunrise, Moke watching the Cadillac till it was out of sight.

Chucky could recover from anything, including great bodily harm, in a matter of a few minutes once he was home and got his caps working. Oh, my God—the sheer physical relief of coming down, able to move in slow motion again, at this moment bathed and naked beneath a gold lamé robe that brushed the parquet floor as he moved to the mood, gliding past the muted streaks of sunset outside the sliding glass doors. He heard a male French voice singing *La Mer*, up-beat, big band in the background, drummer pushing, driving Chucky to slip and slide, doing a funky soft-shoe in his sweat socks, his world turned upside down . . .

His natural state like being on speed or semi-blacked-out drunk, remembering things after and asking himself, did I do that? The only one remembered clearly was killing the dog. Twenty years ago, in the beginning. Picking up the little dog nipping at him, running home and choking it and throwing it against the brick wall. Yes. But others . . . Did I do that? Frag the Easy Company CO? The son of a bitch constantly on his back. Rolled the grenade into his hootch and Lieutenant . . . he couldn't even think of his name, was sent home in a bag. Did I do that? Run over the guy who wanted to argue about a parking place? Vaguely remembering the guy coming back toward the car with his short sleeves tight around his biceps, one of those. Took the guy out with a squeal of rubber and ripped off his door . . . Cut some Cuban hustler across the street from Neon Leon's with a steak knife? . . . Well, when he was young and full of the Old Nick maybe, hadn't yet settled down on the right amount of caps. "Brain scan your ass," he'd said to the neurologist, "it's down in my tummy where it starts."

He heard the door open, came around with the beat to see Lionel.

"Moke is here."

And stopped dead in ringing silence.

"Who's with him?"

"Nobody with him, he's alone. He's mad at something."

"You sure? If that cane cutter's with him—I see Avilanosa you're fired."

"What was I suppose to do?" Lionel said. "I couldn' do nothing."

"What good are you"—picking up Lionel's accent—"you couldn' do nothing? Guy's beating me on the head, you stand there."

"I don't know what you want us to do," Lionel said, "you don't say nothing."

"How could I? I'm on the *ground*—you're standing there watching."

"I didn't want to leave you," Lionel said.

Chucky did a slow turn with his arms extended like airplane wings, came all the way around and Lionel was still there, faithful servant who wouldn't leave him. "Send in Moke," Chucky said, holding his pose, ready to fly at the snake, buzz and confuse him. But it was Chucky who was caught by surprise. Moke stepped in and sailed his Crested Beaut hard in Chucky's direction to land on the floor upright, creased and cracked, the crown stove in.

"What'd you do?"

"Son of a bitch stomped on it."

"You let him?"

"Son of a bitch grabbed it, stomped it, run out and took off in his Caddy 'fore I could stop him. License BS-two." Moke looked over at Chucky's home computer. "Ask that thing whose car it belongs to."

Chucky took a moment—all this coming at once. He felt a warm glow rise through him, closed his eyes, pinched the bridge of his nose and said, "Black Cadillac, Florida vanity license plate BS-two. Owner, Barry Stam. Address . . . something Bali Way. The number isn't clear."

Moke was staring, mouth slack. Chucky thought for a moment of slipping over and kicking him in the balls. It brought a smile and he said, "You mean little Barry Stam took your hat off your head and did a dance number on it? Ah, Cecil was with him . . ."

"Wasn't nobody with him. He grab it and run out."

"Where was this, 'cross the street?"

"Wolfgang's. Nestor said hang out there and wait for the fella if he come back. And what do you know," Moke said, his ugly mouth curling into a grin.

Chucky frowned. "Wait. This guy we're talking about, he's around five-seven with thick dark hair, Jewish?"

When Moke didn't understand something he became mean. "You know what he looks like same as me. Thin fella, 'bout my size. Only now he's all dressed up, got a suit of clothes. I *knew* him. See, I knew him but I didn't. Till he goes, 'You know me?' I still wasn't sure 'cause it was dark in the van that time. Then he goes, 'Well, I know *you*.' And right then I knew who it was."

Chucky was trying to catch up, get the facts straight in his mind. "I thought he stomped your hat and ran. Now you say you talked to him?"

Moke got meaner. He said, "You hear what I'm telling you, fatass? It was the guy was with Rainy we been looking for, for Christ sake!" Quieter then. "Only with a suit on. Driving this black Caddy."

Chucky became a statue, wondering how long he could hold without moving.

Moke said, "Well, goddamnit, say something."

"Son of a gun," Chucky said.

12

Waiting again. This time at Miami International. Down under the terminal near the Eastern baggage claim area. This time in the Lincoln Continental, color coordinated in his tan chauffeur's outfit. While sporty Barry, in a starched workshirt and pressed faded jeans, had gone inside to meet somebody named Kyle McLaren, arriving from New York.

Did he dress like that, Stick wondered, so people would think he worked? Mistake him for a regular guy?

Regular guys didn't have color-coordinated chauffeurs.

Regular guys didn't keep their girl friends on a yacht tied up in the front yard 150 feet from where their wives walked around outside in flowing see-through robes.

How did they keep their faces straight?

A little more than an hour and a half ago he had walked from the garage to the pool in his tans, ready to go. Had waited for Barry, swimming his morning lengths, to come up the ladder in his briefs, lean, hairy, very dark, shaking water from limp hands, gold chain glistening. Had looked at his new watch as Barry slipped on a white terrycloth robe and announced it was 11:30. Barry said, "So?"

"You said the flight arrives at one?"

"I said one-oh-five."

"What time you want to leave?"

Barry looked out at the bay, the narrow sea at Miami's high-rise shore, and placed his hands on his hips inside the robe, if not defiant a little pissed off.

"Stickley, anybody gets to an airport more than ten minutes before a flight leaves or a flight arrives doesn't have anything to do."

Stick said, "I didn't know you were busy." Barry looked at him and Stick added, "Very good, sir."

He walked back to the garage to find Cornell standing just inside the door he'd rolled up earlier to bring out the Lincoln. At the edge of shade, holding binoculars to his face, Cornell said, "I knew it." He lowered the glasses after a moment and handed them to Stick. "Look out there at the boat. Tell me what you see."

Stick raised the glasses, adjusted the focus. "A seagull."

"Not that bird, another bird. *In* the boat."

He saw the superstructure dazzling white, the empty flying bridge moving with a slight roll, the yacht close in his vision, riding above the gray-weathered dock pilings.

"Toward the back end," Cornell's voice said.

He saw the figure now, a woman moving about in the cabin, wearing something white, a beach cover hanging open. A young woman with dark hair, long and full around her shoulders.

"See her?"

"Is that Aurora?"

"That's Aurora. The man's number one at the moment. Now look at the man . . . dying."

Stick edged the binoculars left, past trunks of palm trees, brought his vision down to the swimming pool. Barry was at the umbrella table with his morning papers, a silver service of coffee. He faced the bay, holding a section of newspaper folded lengthwise.

"Mr. Cool," Cornell said. "Love it. Love it . . . Uh-oh, here she come."

Stick cut his gaze back to the yacht.

"No, the terrace. Up on the terrace, man. Here come Miz Diane."

Stick made a quarter turn and put the glasses squarely on Mrs. Stam coming through the formal garden to the terrace steps: silky, see-through lavender negligee stirring, sunlight defining her legs as she descended, laying fire in her hair, glinting on sunglasses that concealed her expression.

"Saturday morning soap," Cornell said. "Better than *All My Children* put together. Lady of the house saying to the lady in the boat, 'He might be fucking you, girl, but I got it *all*.'"

Stick lowered the glasses. "She knows?"

"Course she knows. Last night she see him tippy-toeing out the house—she knows. He tell her he has to see Neil, that's his captain, Neil King, he drives the boat like you drive cars. She tell him, 'Neil ain't there, I saw him leave.' He tell her yeah, he has to get these important papers he forgot. Man leaves important papers wherever he wants to go. Now he like to sneak out there again, but Miz Diane's standing over him with the rolling pin."

Stick put the glasses on Mrs. Stam again, seated now on a lounge, lying back, the negligee coming open to show her bathing suit, two strips of lavender, her pale flesh, the inside of her raised thigh.

"She's going to get burned."

"Never tans, never burns," Cornell said. "She don't stay out long enough. Like shady places best."

Stick held the glasses fixed on Mrs. Stam and felt a stirring in his crotch. She didn't have a *Playboy* body, perfect measurements; it wasn't that. What her body did for him, it met requirements fixed in his mind a long time ago, a day of revelation: Back in Norman when he was ten and saw the full-grown woman friend of his mother naked one time, visiting, and had walked in their bathroom and saw that white skin and that thick patch of hair between her legs. Thinking thereafter that was the ticket when it came to a bare-naked woman, pleasure that would turn you inside out just to look at. He was thoughtful bringing the glasses down, squinting in the bright sunlight, wondering if he was a simple soul. But if he was, what was wrong with that?

He said, "What if Diane wants to go for a boat ride?"

"Make her seasick," Cornell said. "The man's crazy but he ain't dumb. This afternoon he'll say, 'Come on, who wants to go out on the boat?' He sometime he even begs her, say, 'You be all right, babe. It's calm out today.' Uh-unh, she won't set foot on it."

Stick looked toward the pool, at the woman's white body resting on the lounge. "What does she get out of this?"

"Anything she wants. Believe it."

"It's a show, isn't it?"

"It's cuckooland, what it is."

"Fun to watch," Stick said, "if you don't happen to be doing anything."

"'Specially if you listen," Cornell said. "Don't forget to listen."

First Barry was talking, animated, swinging a tote bag up over his shoulder. Now the girl—who would be Kyle McLaren—was giving it back, though with more controlled gestures, raising her hand as a point of attention and using it to brush her hair back from her face. She carried a straw purse and flat leather briefcase in her other hand. A skycap waited behind them with two bags. Stick had not recognized her yet.

He pulled the Continental forward, edging into the third lane from the curb, popped the trunk release and got out. Across the roofs of cars he could see Barry stretching, face raised, looking everywhere but directly in front of him. Stick went back to the trunk, raised the lid. When he looked over again they were coming toward the car, Barry in his starched work clothes, his hand on the girl's arm. She looked familiar . . .

Then recognized her, the girl in Chucky's living room, remembering the streaked blond hair, the girl he'd thought of as athletic, with the calm, knowing eyes. He moved around to the door and held it open.

The girl was saying, "I'm talking about a direct correlation between effort and results. The payoff, and I don't mean money—" She stopped. She was looking directly at him now, close enough to shake hands. "Isn't satisfying enough."

Barry said, "Everybody's got problems, babe. Get in the car."

Away from the terminal Stick's hand went to the rear-view

mirror—Kyle McLaren was sitting directly behind him—and adjusted the angle to her face. She was relating something about her father, that she'd felt impatient with him for the first time and wasn't sure why. Stick heard her say, "He's always gotten away with being a snob and a cynic because he's funny, with that dry delivery. But this time, I don't know why, it was tiresome and I thought, do I sound like that?"

"I want to call Arthur," Barry said. "Gimme the names, whatever you got for me."

"Today's Saturday."

"And tomorrow's Sunday—Arthur doesn't care. You kidding?"

"I'm trying to tell you something that concerns *me* for a change. Is that all right?"

"Hey, come on, I always listen. I better, I pay you enough."

"I told my dad about Chucky."

Stick looked up at the mirror.

Kyle was looking at the mirror.

Seeing each other's eyes.

Stick's gaze returned to the freeway. They were on 112 now, going toward the ocean in fairly light traffic. He heard her say, "I practically acted him out, and I do a pretty good Chucky, if I have to say so myself."

"You think I don't listen? You say something like that, it hurts me."

"Just shut up for a minute, okay? First I did Chucky paying his hospital bill with cash. The three thousand and something for his constipation problem. Then, Chucky carrying an ice-cooler full of hundred-dollar bills into First Boston, dumping it on their conference table, the board of directors standing there watching—"

"Where's Arthur's home phone?" Barry had his attaché case open on his lap. "I got it here someplace." He looked over, poked her arm. "Hey. I'm playing with you. Tonight do your Chucky for me. When we have time."

"You're exactly like my dad," Kyle said. "I tell him about Chucky and he says, 'How do you stand the humidity down there?' He's been here once. He took my mother to the Roney Plaza in 'Forty-seven. He could tell then it was a breeding ground for stuntmen and third-raters." Stick heard her say she was tired. She sounded tired, disinterested. He saw her unzip her soft leather case and take out a file folder.

He saw Barry with the phone now, dialing, handing Kyle a sheet of legal paper, saying, "Get Chucky—you want my advice—get him into commodities and lose his ass, or else he's going to drive you nuts. Here, take it." She was looking out the window and Barry had to wave the legal sheet in front of her. Stick looked away, approaching the 95 interchange, followed the gradual curve down and around to head north. It was a beautiful day, but neither of them had said anything about the weather. He thought of Cornell telling him to listen, maybe learn something.

He met her eyes again, briefly, as she looked up from the yellow legal sheet. She said, "Good, stay with cheap play for the time being. Few more months, anyway. I like Kaneb, I like Fleetwood . . ."

Barry was saying, "Whatta you mean, who is it? Cut the shit, Arthur, and turn on your recorder. I want to go with Kaneb Services"—he looked at Kyle and she held up her hand, fingers spread—"another five thousand . . . Right." He listened, saying "Yeah," then put his hand over the phone. "Arthur says put another ten in Automated Medical. Whatta you think? . . . Hey."

"I'm sorry. What?"

"Automated Medical Labs. I forgot what they do."

"Interferon," Kyle said, "the cancer treatment. They're also working on herpes."

"Jesus, you're kidding . . . Arthur, let's go ahead with Automated Medical . . . No, couple thousand shares . . . You bet." He listened again, nodding. "Let me think about it a minute." He turned to Kyle. "Wake up. Ranco Manufacturing—they were at twelve, they're up to seventeen. Arthur's been telling me all week it's time to get out. Whatta you say?"

It was a name Stick had heard before. Ranco. The one Barry had told him to give to the chauffeurs, but not before he sold his shares.

She was saying, "I'm going to sleep all week."

"Come on, Ranco. It's at seventeen. Sell or not?"

"What's your position?"

"Four thousand shares. It's one you gave me last year."

Stick watched her paging through her folder. He heard her say, after a moment, "Yeah, I remember now. It's a very thin issue."

"Come on, Arthur's waiting."

"The float's only three-hundred-fifty thousand. Ask him what the net earnings are per share. And predicted year-end."

Stick tried to make sense out of it. Barry spoke to Arthur, then put his hand over the phone. "Two and a quarter. Projected to go up another buck a share, but Arthur says we've heard that song before."

Kyle said, "What do they make? Something for the military, isn't it? Water tanks?"

"Right, portable tanks; they pull 'em behind a truck. And some other equipment, all government contract."

Stick saw her face as she looked up. She didn't seem interested. She said, "The P-E ratio for Ranco should be about twenty to one, at least. They're forecasting three and a quarter and the stock's only at seventeen?"

"Come on—do I sell?"

"With that skimpy float it'd be awfully easy to drive the price up. I think Arthur wants to keep it in the house."

"You sure?"

"Tell him you think it's going up," Kyle answered. "See what he says."

Barry: "What're you doing, Arthur, blowing smoke at me? That stock's going to the fucking moon . . . *Yes*, I believe it. You schmuck, what're you trying to pull?" He listened and said to Kyle, hand over the phone, "Arthur says it's volatile, very shaky."

Kyle: "I think Arthur's shaky. Tell him he can have it when it hits fifty, not before. Tell him you want five thousand more shares before it hits twenty or you're going to Hutton."

They turned off the freeway at 125th Street, Stick concentrating, committing to memory Kaneb, Automated Medical Labs, Ranco Manufacturing . . .

And now Kyle was reading from her file folder: "Titan Valve, two thousand shares at fifteen and a half . . . Delpha Health Services, twelve bucks a share, another two thousand." Biotech Systems . . . KMA Industries . . .

Stick added names to his list.

Barry: "Arthur says the market for IPOs is very mushy. Stay out of it."

Kyle: "That's what Arthur's supposed to say. They have to sell the board up before they try new issues. How many times've I told you that?"

Barry: "Arthur says the fringers aren't gonna make it."

Kyle: "I don't pick fringers."

Barry: "He says the bloom is off the energy rose."

Kyle: "I'm going to be sick in your car."

Barry: "He says high tech remains first in the hearts of investors."

Kyle: "Tell Arthur good-bye."

It was hard work, driving and listening. Trying to remember that Southwest Bell and British Colonial Hydro were corporate bonds that looked good. That you could make a killing on Firestone if the company was taken over and the possibility kept getting better. By the time they crossed over on the causeway and were approaching Bal Harbour Stick was sure of one thing: Barry would never be the chauffeur's hero without Kyle McLaren.

Barry never let up. As the car swung into the drive, home, he was talking about somebody named Howard Ruff, who—as near as Stick could figure out—was an investment expert of some kind, an economic forecaster. Barry sounded impressed. "Howard Ruff says buy all the gold you can and silver's even better."

"He'll tell you to buy his record album, too," Kyle said. "If you like the advice of a guy who sings *Climb Every Mountain* and *You Light Up My Life*, I can't help you."

It didn't matter that Stick had never heard of Howard Ruff. He was getting a pretty good idea who Kyle McLaren was.

He got her bags out of the trunk and carried them to the terrace where Kyle was talking to Diane Stam. Barry was heading for the morning room, ducking under the awning that shaded the arched openings in the wall. Stick hung back, watching the two ladies in polite conversation: one with slender brown legs, smiling easily, touching Diane's arm; the other a different type, soft and white beneath a striped robe. They were edging away from each other now but with pleasant expressions; they seemed to get along. Kyle glanced toward him, waiting with her bags. Diane turned away and he followed Kyle along the paved walk that led from the terrace to the tennis court. He had not been to this side of the property before, but Kyle seemed to know where she was going. She carried a tote slung over one shoulder and the briefcase under her other arm. They passed the line of palm trees and under the red-and-white-striped awning—there were deck chairs here and a small bar, empty now—crossed the red clay court and approached the guest house just on the other side, partly hidden in shrubbery. There was a door here; but Kyle walked past it, following the path around front to the bayside of the house.

Turning the corner she glanced back at Stick and said, "We'll let the producer have the sun in the morning. I'll take the room with the view."

He didn't know what she was talking about and was going to ask, what producer? But now they were at another entrance. One of the maids appeared in the doorway as they approached and Kyle said, "Luisa Rosa!" like she was glad to see her, the maid smiling. "How're the anxieties doing?"

"My depression is much better," the maid said, still smiling. "I'm very glad to see you again.'

Stick took the bags inside as they stood talking. He looked around the living room, which seemed to be all yellow and white with rattan furniture, fresh-cut flowers everywhere, a bottle of champagne in a silver bucket on the cocktail table with three glasses. He wasn't sure what to do with the bags. The entire front wall was glass, facing the bay, Barry's cruiser tied up off to the right. He wondered if the girl was still aboard. He heard Luisa Rosa laugh. He heard her voice, with its pleasant accent, say, "Have a nice day."

"You can put those in the bedroom," Kyle said, "if you will, please."

There were twin beds pushed together with yellow spreads, screens that opened onto a patio and a somewhat different view of Biscayne Bay. The guest house was bigger than any house he had ever lived in. As he came out she was unslinging the tote, dropping it with her briefcase onto the sofa.

He paused, not sure of the procedure, wondering if she was going to offer him a tip. He hoped not.

She said, "I've been curious about something for the past—I guess it's been about two weeks. Do you remember my being at Mr. Gorman's, in Lauderdale? We were in the living room and you walked by on the balcony."

"You know I remember it," Stick said. She did, too. He could feel it between them. "You want to know what I was doing there?"

She said, "If I'm not being nosy. I'm curious, because Chucky didn't seem to have any idea who you were, in his own apartment."

"I was with a friend of mine. He was waiting to see him."

"Do you recall what you said?"

"He asked me—what, if I was an appraiser?" He smiled as he saw her smile, familiar with each other, and knew what she was going to say.

"Yeah, but the best part"—her eyes smiling now—"he asked if you saw anything you liked, and you looked around, not the least bit hurried, and you said, 'No, I guess not,' and walked away."

"You remember that."

"Your timing was great."

"Thank you. Can I ask you one?"

"What was I doing there?"

"No, I figured that out. You tell people like Barry and Chucky what to do with their money. Barry comes off as the boy wonder, but you're the brains."

She raised her eyebrows. "You got that on the way from the airport?"

"I got more than that. You put up with him, but you're getting tired of it. He only listens when you're talking about business . . ."

"That's amazing."

"No, it isn't, that's what you told him. *I* listen. But I think there's more to it. You kept telling him you're tired, I think you're tired of what you're doing. *You* feed and he scores the points, makes all the money."

"You're close, but that's not it." Those gentle, knowing eyes stayed on him and she seemed about to say more, perhaps confide. But she eased away from herself, saying, "You don't sound quite—well, like a man who wears a chauffeur's uniform."

"One of the help. No, ordinarily I'm self-employed. I'll try this another week or so."

"You don't like to drive?"

"I don't like to wait for people."

"I don't either. What do you usually do?"

"Well, I sold cars for a few years. Used ones. I drove a truck now and then . . ." He said, "What I wanted to ask you—that time at Chucky's a couple weeks ago, you only saw me for about a half a minute . . ."

"Yeah, about that."

"How did you recognize me today?"

She said, sounding a little surprised, "That's a good question, you don't even look like the same person. But I knew you as soon as I walked up to the car."

13

Cornell Lewis was sitting in a pair of red briefs watching television, his bare feet up on a chair he'd pulled over. He didn't look up as Stick came in.

"What's going on?"

"Chuck Norris, man. Look-it him do it to the gooks."

"I mean what's going on *here*?"

"Nothing—resting up for the evening. I'm off, man."

"There some kind of a producer gonna be staying here?"

"Next week he's coming. Monday, I think."

"Movie producer?"

"Look-it Chuck. Shit, huh? Yeah, the producer gonna show the man and some of his friends how to get into show biz. As I understand it. Gonna have a few people over for the day."

"We just picked up a girl at the airport—"

"Yeah, Kyle. She's nice, huh? That Kyle is the only reason I know of I'd ever want to be white and I don't even think she'd care."

"She work for Barry?"

"No, she work for herself, like an advisor. Tells the man how to invest his hard-earned bread."

"She didn't seem too anxious in the car. Or she was tired."

"Man bugs her. No, see, she specializes, tells the man what different businesses he should go into. But, see, he's in *every*thing. You know, with his stocks and bonds? You know what I'm saying? See, she *knows* all that stockmarket shit better than he does, even though it's not what she specializes in. So he like *uses* her every chance he can."

"Yeah, that's what it sounded like."

"Ah, you listening, huh? Look at this one, man." Nodding at the TV set. "Hawaiian Punch, with little Donny and Marie. They cute, you know it? Look-it 'em."

"She live in New York?"

"Who, this girl?"

"Kyle McLaren."

"She live in Palm Beach. I think she used to be in New York when she was a stockbroker. First time she come here she was telling me all about it. She's got a brother that's in the FBI."

"Jesus, you kidding?"

"Not here. I think in New York. Look-it little Donny and Marie. Yeah, baby, I give you a punch. Shit, I'd punch him too, he's so cute."

"Why's she staying here?"

"Who's that?"

"Kyle McLaren." He liked her name.

"Man wants her to be here for the producer, the show biz pitch and then spend some time with him. But not the way you thinking. I seen the man, he's half in the bag one time start to hit on her? No deal. She put him down quick, but very nice about it. No strain, no pain. Man say she don't take no shit offa *any*body. One of these millionaires—don't matter who it is, she don't like him she don't do business with him."

"She married?"

"I don't believe—no, she live by herself. Got a condo up there on Lake Worth."

Stick took off his coat and tie, walked into his room to drop them on the bed and came out again.

"How's Aurora doing?"

"What are you, the question man? She still out'n the boat. Man run in and talk to her on the phone soon as you got back. Could almost hear her yelling from outside. Got this voice sound like she crying."

Stick said, "So they'll be going out for a cruise."

"Uh-unh, not today. Mama fixed him, she called some people and made a date to meet at the club for cocktails and dinner . . . little dancing to that ricky-tick club jive. Yeah, they gonna have *fun*, man. Big evening at the country club with all the beautiful folks."

"I guess I drive, uh?"

"Said tell you the black suit."

He watched Chuck Norris lay out several Orientals with chops and kicks but without changing his expression. He was surprised Chuck Norris was a little guy. Chuck and Chucky . . .

Chucky and Barry and all the hotshots who made it look easy. He said to Cornell, "What's the most you ever made on a job? Before you got sent away."

"You mean in my other life?"

"Yeah, what's the most you scored?"

"Was from a liquor store. I had a piece I picked up on a break-in one time? I went in there . . . had to do speed to get me in the door. I took eleven hundred and sixty dollars and could never do it again sky high. Why you asking?"

"I was just thinking," Stick said, "that making a phone call to your broker in the back seat of a Cadillac doing sixty miles an hour with the air conditioning on is an awful lot easier than going in someplace with a gun, isn't it?"

Cornell looked away from the television screen for the first time. "You just finding that out?"

"I got a few things to learn," Stick said.

The chauffeurs were not watching with purpose, though they were looking out of darkness toward the source of the music, across flower beds and shrubbery to the club patio strung with paper lanterns where ladies in long skirts danced with men in blazers and pastel trousers to medleys of show tunes: some barely moving, some moving as though they were following footprints, some of the ladies discoing with studied abandon while their men, with glazed expressions, glasses reflecting the lantern glow, hunched their shoulders and sometimes snapped their fingers.

The sound of elevator music filled the night. Stick had never seen a country club dance before.

He'd dropped off the Stams and Kyle McLaren an hour ago, raced up to Southwest Eighth Street to find a bar and had several bourbons over shaved ice while Cubans stared at him in his black suit. Or would have stared at him anyway. Stick didn't mind. He was free, taking a timeout; he bothered no one and they left him alone. Now he was back at Leucadendra.

Harvey saw him, adjusted his chauffeur's cap and came away from the others: a half-dozen drivers over there, along the edge of light coming from a window in the working part of the clubhouse. One of the drivers looked like Lionel Oliva, but it was too dark here to be certain. Faint moonlight through the palm trees, the sound of a kitchen fan blending with the melodic rush of the five-piece dance band, *The Man I Love* turning into *A Stranger in Paradise* as Harvey, chauffeur's cap cocked like a fighter pilot's, came over to him.

"How's it going? Or should I say, what do you hear from the back seat these days?"

"That heavyset guy over there," Stick said, "his name Lionel?"

"That's him, the Cuban." Harvey turned his back to the group, standing in close. "Says his boss's been in there in the locker room rolling Indian dice since this afternoon and Lionel ain't had his dinner yet."

"Why doesn't he leave and come back?" Stick wasn't sure if he wanted Lionel here, or if it mattered.

"He'd drive off and there'd be Mr. Gorman looking for him," Harvey said. "Don't you know that's how it works?"

Stick said, "I guess I'll learn, if I stay at it long enough." The bourbon was glowing inside him and Lionel's presence, he decided, didn't matter. Though it gave him something else to think about: still another chance of running into Chucky Gorman. He had walked into a new, tight little world down here and had not yet walked out the other side. But he was learning a few things.

Harvey was holding back, trying to appear casual. He said, "Look at all that money out there dancing. Not a care in the world."

It seemed enough of an opening. Stick said, "On these stock market tips you mentioned? . . ."

Harvey said, "Yeah, how we doing there?"

"Well, I wondered if you have a certain procedure you follow." He saw Edgar coming over now.

"You tell us what Mr. Stam's playing," Harvey said. He shrugged, hands in his pants pockets.

Stick waited. "That's it?"

Harvey said to Edgar, "He wants to know is there any procedure giving us, telling us about any interesting stocks he might've heard about."

"What procedure?" Edgar said.

Stick said, "What if I give you a good one and you pass it on and then come back and tell me your boss already has that stock? You know what I mean? How do I protect myself?" He saw Harvey and Edgar catch each other's eye as he looked off toward the strains of *Alley Cat*, Jesus, hoping they'd rush it faster than the others or he'd have to get out of here. It was the only song he knew that made him want to break something.

Edgar said, "You mean like if Mr. Harrison accepted the tip but told me he already had it?"

"I'd be out of luck," Stick said, "wouldn't I?"

"But Mr. Harrison would never pull anything like that."

"How do I know? You guys say it, but, hell, I don't know Mr. Harrison." He shot a glance at Harvey. "Or Miz Wilson. You know as well as I do rich people can be funny. They're not always generous." Stick shook his head, tired. "Boy, he was on that phone with his broker all the way from the airport. His financial advisor— you know who I mean? . . ."

Harvey said, "Miz McLaren?"

"That's the one, yeah. She was with him, see, telling him what to buy and then he'd pass it on to his broker. On the phone the whole time. See, she just come in from New York and I guess she had all these hot tips."

Edgar said, "Yeah? What were some of 'em?"

"Well, that's why I asked about a procedure," Stick said. "I got these companies"—he patted his side pocket—"fact I wrote 'em down right after we got back so I wouldn't forget. I remember you mentioning somebody did that."

Harvey said, "Over-the-counter stocks, huh?"

Stick said, "Well, I suppose you could say that." Not having any idea what Harvey was talking about, though he had heard it before. *Over the counter.* Harvey was squinting at him and Stick said, "I got one they say is about to take off and hit the moon and it's only seventeen bucks at the present time."

"Jeez," Edgar said. "Gonna take off, huh?"

"When they get done driving it up," Stick said. "It'll go at least to fifty, you can bet on it. Probably higher."

Harvey said, "They gonna drive it up, uh? What kind of stock is it?"

"You mean what kind of company?"

"Yeah, what do they do? What's the product?"

"Something for the military. I guess it's one of those top-secret deals, you know . . ."

Edgar said, "Musta heard about a big government contract, what it sounds like. That's the way you make it, get the inside poop. You in?"

"You better believe it," Stick said.

Harvey said, "I thought you never play the market."

"I do now," Stick said.

"How'd you make a buy on Saturday?"

"Well, I haven't actually done it yet, no. But I called this friend of mine, bartender, plays the market all the time. He'll take care of it first thing Monday. I told him buy all he can. This mother's gonna fly."

Edgar said, "Going from seventeen to fifty? That's—"

"Thirty-three hundred dollars a hundred," Harvey said. "About a three-hundred-percent kick," Harvey said. "I don't know, sounds fishy."

Stick edged out on unfamiliar ground. He said, "Not when you take into account the P-E ratio." Harvey was staring at him hard. "Figure twenty to one," Stick told him, eye to eye. "Based on"—shit, he dug in his mind for the words—"you know, what they're making, the profit."

"Earnings per share," Harvey said.

"That's what I said. See, forecasted up to like three and a quarter. So what's that tell you?"

"Jeez," Edgar said. "What's the stock?"

"We're back to procedure," Stick said. Christ, they were still bouncing relentlessly through *Alley Cat.* "I gotta go." He started off.

"Whatta you mean you gotta go?" Harvey said. "Wait a minute."

"I got to move around. I stand in one place too long—I got a bad knee, an old basketball injury starts acting up."

"We can walk with you," Harvey said. "Where you want to go? How about the men's locker room? I think we can promote us a cup a coffee in there."

"I was thinking of going for a drive," Stick said. "Mr. and Miz Stam oughta be a while yet."

Harvey said, "Wait now, you can never be sure; they're liable to come out any minute. Let's talk about this procedure idea, how you see it might work. Say just for this stock you mentioned."

"The seventeen-dollar one going up to fifty?"

"That one," Edgar said.

"Only way I see it," Stick said, "is cash up front. Two bills gets you the name of the stock. Monday the price goes up to three, and if I see the stock take off right away the price might go up even higher. How's that sound to you fellas?"

Harvey said, "You're crazy, or you think we are."

Stick said, "Then forget I mentioned it. You want to take your money home to bed with you, Harve, that's up to you. I personally believe money should never sleep . . ."

One A.M. the drivers brought their cars out of darkness now to gleam in lamplight, creeping them up the circular drive to the front entrance. One-twenty, Barry appeared like a playboy with a girl on each arm, his wife and Kyle. Stick got out of the car, came around.

But Barry wasn't holding them; they were guiding him along, keeping him in check. Barry was drunk, glassy-eyed. His mouth looked wet. He did not appear to Stick to be a fun-loving drunk. He looked, right now, like a high school kid ready to fight. He pulled his arm free of Diane's grasp, roughly. She smoothed the gauzy, peach-colored material of her dress, layers of it, touched her pearls.

Barry pulled open the front passenger-side door and said to Stick for all to hear, "Get inna car. I'm gonna drive."

Stick tried an easy smile. "You sure you want to?"

"Get inna fucking car, will you?"

Diane seemed paler than usual, face drawn. She turned as though to walk off, saw the dressed-up club members standing on the steps watching and turned back to the car again, not knowing where to look. Kyle, still holding Barry's arm, said, "If you drive, buddy, I walk."

Barry said, "Buddy? What's this buddy shit?"

"I mean it," Kyle said.

"Then walk, for Christ sake. You want to walk, walk."

Stick touched his boss's arm. "Mr. Stam?" Still pleasant. "I'm the one with the driving suit on."

Barry stared up at him with his boozy eyes, pink shirt open, necktie gone. He said, "Stick? Shit, I know why they call you that. Got nothing to do with Stickley, huh?" Barry getting a shrewd-drunk look now, crafty eyes. "You stick people up is why they call you Stick. Isn't that right?"

Stick made a gun of his hand, pointing it at Barry, saying, "Yes, sir, you got it right," crowding him into the front-seat opening, staying close, jamming him, so that Barry was forced to get in, Stick's head and shoulders following. Now with his back filling the doorway, in there with Barry, away from everyone outside watching, Stick said, "You little fucker, you say another word I'll punch you into the back seat. I drive. You can fire me tomorrow, but tonight I drive. You got it?" He waited. Barry stared straight ahead, rigid. His face bore a strained expression now that made his nose appear larger, vulnerable. But he didn't move or make a sound.

Stick came out of the car. He opened the rear door, turned to Diane and Kyle and said, "Ladies . . ."

Barry's expression had turned to stone. He refused to speak. He walked with exaggerated care along the hallway, brushing the wall with his shoulder, turned into his bedroom and fell across the bed. Stick looked in from the hall at Barry in his brown-canopied sultan's bed, a royal tent, the sides gathered up with gold roping. The poor little guy.

He waited for Diane to come out. "I'll undress him if you want. Put him under the covers . . . tuck him in."

She said, "He'll be all right," not smiling but calm once more, brown eyes impassive. "But if you would, please, go down to the boat . . ." She hesitated. "I want to be sure the key isn't there."

"I'll be glad to."

"If you don't mind." The voice so quiet and soft.

Not wanting to leave he wondered what would make her smile. Or show any kind of emotion. Her eyes seemed to daydream, looking at him and giving him the feeling he was in the dream. Letting him look at her . . . at the pearls lying against her skin, lips slightly parted and the eyes again, reflecting . . . what?

"Is there anything else I can do?"

Hesitant. "I don't think so . . ."

"Can I get you something?" He said it knowing it made little sense. Yet she seemed to accept it without question. He felt that if he took her by the hand and led her through the house and out the garage, to his room, she would follow along without a word, without making a sound. Her gaze lulled him.

"Well, if you need me . . ."

He turned to go and she said, "I'll be up for a little while."

He paused. He nodded. He couldn't think of anything else to say. "All right . . ."

She turned the light off in Barry's room, looked at him once more and walked past him and across the hall to a bedroom door, pushed it open and went in. A slanting patch of light appeared on the hall floor. The door closed. He didn't hear the lock click. A narrow line of light remained on the polished marble. It took him several moments to move away.

Kyle was waiting on the terrace, holding her arms—her brown arms and shoulders bare in the blue cotton shift—looking up at the sky. She turned as Stick approached, coming down the steps.

"Is he all right?"

"He passed out."

"What did you say to him in the car?"

The pool lay behind her in light green illumination, darkness beyond.

"I told him to behave himself."

She narrowed her eyes—for fun, it didn't matter. "I'll bet."

"You want, I'll walk you home."

"Fine." And started off, as though she was expecting it: crossed the patio toward the walk that led to the tennis court, Kyle telling him Barry was a terrible drinker and knew it and didn't get smashed very often. Booze wasn't that important to him.

"Like making money," Stick said.

"Barry's last day on earth he'll spend on the phone with his broker," Kyle said, "but not because he wants to make more money . . ."

"He just likes to talk on the phone."

"No—he gets his thrill playing with the money, risking it. He's got more than he'll ever be able to spend, but when he plays the market and *wins*, then he's outsmarted the game and that's his satisfaction, his accomplishment."

"But if he loses," Stick said, "what's he out? It's not like betting the farm. Is it?"

She said, with realization, "I should be telling you about taking risks . . ."

Stick said, "Oh," with his own sense of realization, that Barry had been talking about him. "I forgot I'm one of his exhibits now."

"You said you sold cars . . ."

"Used ones."

"You didn't mention you stole them first, and you were about to take off in Barry's Rolls when he came out and caught you."

"Is that how he tells it? He caught me? No, I helped him out, that's all, and he took a liking to me."

"I'm never sure when you're serious." They walked along the white squares of cement. "You want to know what he said?" Her tone changed to a mild street-sound imitation of Barry. "Jesus Christ, I got Aurora on the boat and Diane pacing up and down on the terrace and I got a new driver who was in prison for armed robbery and I don't know which one of my cars he's gonna steal . . . This was before we left for the club, waiting for Diane. She takes longer to get dressed than anyone I know."

"He say prison?"

"No, you're right. He said, in the slammer. Then at dinner he started in again, about you. Diane seemed interested and kept him going . . ."

"She did?"

"But you don't have to urge Barry when he's on. Which is almost all the time. The way he was drinking, I think it was for dramatic effect, so I'd think he's pining for Aurora. Or he wanted Diane to ask him what was wrong and he could say, oh, nothing. But she didn't. So he talked about you—you're right, with all the words—because he can get into the part and sound tough."

"He sounds like the Bowery Boys at Miami Beach," Stick said. "Why's he do that?"

They had crossed the tennis court and were following the walk that led to the front of the guest house. He saw the pale length of the cabin cruiser, windows dark—wondering if Diane wanted him to find somebody aboard and come running back to tell. Or if she wanted him to report back, tell her no, the key wasn't in the ignition. But no hired skipper was going to leave the key and she'd know that.

Kyle was saying that maybe Barry acted tough because he was insecure. "Maybe as a kid he was a little smartass and got beat up all the time. Barry loves to start fights in bars."

"He does?"

"Yes, but only when he's sure somebody'll stop it. You know, before they come to blows. Barry's got a problem."

They were coming to her front steps now.

Stick said, "Well, I've done some dumb things, I guess, trying to do it the hard way, but I haven't been in a fistfight since about the eighth grade."

"You sound just like my brother."

"You kidding? The Fed?"

She turned to him in the amber glow of the light by the door. "Barry tell you that?"

"Cornell. He says he'd change color for you."

"God, he's funny. I wish he were a client, instead of most of the ones I have. I could listen to him all day." She meant it, too, her eyes smiling. "No, you remind me of my other brother, the stockbroker. He used to pitch for the Red Sox."

"Jim McLaren, that's your brother?"

"Ah, you're a baseball fan."

"Sure, I used to watch him, when the Sox came to Detroit. He was always accused of throwing spitters. Right?"

"Or, as they say, doctoring the ball with a foreign substance. Jim used to say sweat isn't foreign, it's mine."

"What'd he do on a cold day?"

"Well, his pitch, he had a forkball and a gorgeous slider that broke down and in on a right-handed batter. Otherwise, Fenway Park, he could've gotten killed."

"That short left-field porch," Stick said. "So Jim McLaren's your brother, that's something. I always admired his nerve—the skinny southpaw with the high leg-kick. He isn't very big, is he?"

"About your size. He's heavier now."

"That was about, what, ten years ago."

"'Seventy-one was his last year. I was going to school in Boston, so I got to see him all the time."

"Lemme guess—Harvard Business School."

"Nope, I was at Boston U. In sociology, then I switched to speech therapy. But I left school, decided not to fight it and got a job as a market analyst. My dad's a stockbroker, he was pushing me toward Wall Street as far back as I can remember."

"You don't have to have a special degree?"

"No . . . You can't be dumb, but just selling stock you're usually no more than an order-taker anyway. You learn the words. I sold options for a few years, then got into commodities . . ."

"I don't understand any of that."

"Well, in that end of the market the next stop's Las Vegas. I got out of trading, came down to Palm Beach, the big bucks, and opened an office as an investment counselor. Anyway, you remind me a lot of Jim."

"When he's throwing spitters or selling stock?"

"You sound like him. But I didn't think of it till this evening, when Barry was talking about you. That's why I remembered you, I guess."

"You have fun at the club?"

"It was all right. Except for the music. As soon as I heard them swing into *Alley Cat*, God . . ."

Stick said, "Yeah? . . ."

"I was going to get up and leave. I can't stand that insipid goddamn song."

Stick said, "How about *Climb Every Mountain* and *You Light Up My Life*?"

She began to smile, those knowing eyes looking right at him. "How about a nightcap? We've got scotch, champagne and Gatorade."

"You drink with the help?"

"I'm help, too, aren't I?"

He said, "I have to do something for Mrs. Stam. How about if I come right back?"

Her expression didn't change; though the amused look in her eyes seemed different somehow. She said, "Well, if you make it, fine."

She went inside, leaving it up to him.

14

He wasn't sure if he should sneak aboard the docked cruiser or make noise. Either way he could scare hell out of the poor girl, probably waiting below. *A Prisoner of Love.* Perry Como, 1950-something. His mom's favorite. He had the feeling, ducking into the main cabin, even the guy's boat was bigger than any house he'd ever lived in. There was a light on below . . . down a short ladder . . . he felt his way along and came to a stateroom with—he couldn't believe it—a double bed. The spread—a blue, red and yellow rainbow design—was mussed, the rainbow pillows pulled out from beneath the cover. He heard a noise, a pumping action, water running . . .

The girl came into the room with her head down. She wore a man's turtleneck sweater and was holding the bottom of it with her wrists, bunched up, while she buttoned the waist of her white shorts, rings on all her fingers.

Stick said, "Aurora?"

She jumped with a strangled sound, drawing back.

"It's okay. I'm a friend."

"Who *are* you?" All eyes.

"I work for Barry."

"Where is he?" About to cry, she seemed so frightened. "Did he tell you to get me?"

"He's in bed."

"In *bed*!"

"Shhhh. You don't want to wake up his wife."

"The hell I don't! You know how long I've been on this fucking boat?" She had the eyes of a cat now, a mean one.

"I know. I dropped him off yesterday to meet you. I'm his chauffeur."

"You're not Cecil."

"I wouldn't want to be. I'm the new one."

She seemed suspicious, but got over it right away. "Good. You can drive me home. That son of a bitch, I'm telling you . . ."

"I'm supposed to see if the key's here."

"What key?"

Was she scowling or pouting? Her lower lip stuck out.

"The one you start the boat with. Is it here?"

"How would I know? I don't want you to drive me home in *this*. I don't want to ever see this fucking boat again as long as I live. I mean in a car."

"I don't think I can do that."

"Why not?"

"I mean unless he tells me."

"You're driving me home," Aurora said. "I don't give a shit what Barry says. All I do is wait for him."

"You too, huh?"

She didn't hear him. Aurora was pulling the sweater up over her head and he was staring at her bare breasts. Two round red eyes staring back at him as she fought the sweater, trying to work the snug neck past her chin, her breasts swaying, bouncing up and down, big ones. When the sweater came off it left her hair sticking out in all directions. She was the wild woman of Bal Harbour now, the cat woman of Biscayne Bay.

"You too, huh?"

"What?"

"You said all you do is wait."

"*Wait*? You don't even know."

"Yes, I do," Stick said. He couldn't take his eyes off her breasts as she smoothed her hair now, not looking at him. They were beauties. They were show breasts. "I wait around till he wants to go out, then we go someplace and I have to wait around again, hours sometimes."

"The big shit," Aurora said. "Why does he have to be so mean?"

"Well, that's what he is," Stick said, "a meany. I'll tell you something though. I'd never make you wait." No, *sir*.

"You wouldn't?" She looked at him, caught him staring, hypnotized, but didn't seem to mind. "I've been all by myself since last night. Not *any*body came to see me." She was unbuttoning the shorts now, pushed them down, stepped out with one foot and kicked them across the bed with the other. She stood with hands on hips in narrow bikini panties, looking around the stateroom. "I don't know where I put my clothes."

Stick didn't know where to look. At her tiny white panties between tan tummy and thighs or at her big white breasts. It was better than a cellblock dream, beyond imagination. She came to the foot of the bed, bent over, aimed her can at him and picked up a pair of designer jeans, turned then and sat down on the bed with the jeans in her lap.

"I don't know what to do." That lower lip quivering a little, pushing out.

Stick knew what he wanted to do. He wanted to bite that lip off. First. He walked over to her, reached out carefully and put his hand on her shoulder. There, there. She didn't spook, draw back. He said, "Don't worry, I'll"—what?—"help you out. If I can." And saw those kitty eyes raised, peering out from among long dark lashes. He eased down on the bed, arm moving around her back. The poor little thing. She snuggled against him, laid her hand on the tight material across his thigh.

"He doesn't care about me. How I feel." Yes, she wanted to be comforted—this little girl all by herself. He brought his hand past those beauties to her bare arm and stroked it gently, saw her face raise in the lamplight, her sorrowful eyes. "I feel so lonely."

"I know . . ."

"Will you be nice to me?"

"I'll try— I mean I *will.* I'll be nice as can be to you."

She slid up around his black suit, cat turning to snake, arms going around his neck, acrobatic tan thighs twisting, uncoiling to straddle him, feeling her pushing and letting himself be pushed over to lie on the rainbow-design spread, her mouth coming down on his now, murmuring, "Will you take me home after?"

His mouth on hers made mmmmm sounds, like he was humming.

Did he sleep? Maybe for a minute, fading out and back again, opening his eyes to her lazy gaze, a tangle of dark hair spread over the rainbow pillow.

She said, very softly, "Boy, you're good. Whoever you are." She said, surprised, but still softly, "You still have your tie on." She said, sounding drowsy, eyes closing, "Would I love a glass of milk."

It sounded good, an ice-cold glass. But he chose a can of Bud instead, closed the refrigerator, light gone from the kitchen again, and popped the can. Aurora could have her milk in the morning, when she woke up. He wanted a cigarette. He hadn't had a cigarette in almost four years but he wanted one now. He could live on simple pleasures. Every once in a while accept one not so simple. When the sound came from the hall he thought of an animal; it was like a series of grunts, low snuffling sounds. Close.

He placed his beer on the counter and stepped over to the doorway to listen. Mrs. Hoffer, snoring. The cook's room was right there, a wing off the kitchen. The maids went home to Little Havana when they were through. Barry said they went home every night and brushed their hair, a hundred strokes, then they'd do the other leg.

A voice said, "Oh . . ."

He turned to see a figure in the hall, faint light from a window far behind telling him it was Mrs. Stam, a silhouette within a sheer cover that reached the floor.

"Did you hear something?" Her voice a whisper.

"I think it's Mrs. Hoffer."

"No, I mean outside."

"It could've been me. I just came in."

"No, it was something else. Would you look, please?"

She turned and he followed her, hearing bare feet pat on marble. She brought him out to the morning room past fat chairs finished in canvas and over to one of the arched openings. They stood at a border of flower pots, Stick behind her, hunching a little to see out past the awning at eye level. They looked out at the terrace in clear, cloudless moonlight, at the sweep of lawn beyond the pool, the bay like a little ocean and there it was in the night sky. He felt a warm rush, an irresistible urge and had to say it.

"Shine on my love and me."

Diane's head turned, chin to her shoulder, so that he saw her profile in soft illumination and caught the expensive scent of her perfume. She said, "What?"

"Moon over Miami," Stick said. "It's true. There it is."

She said, "Oh." After a moment she said, "Yes, it is." She stood without moving.

He said, "What are we listening for?"

"Wait." Quietly, a hushed tone.

She turned then very slowly, staring out at the terrace. Her shoulder touched his chest. She remained this way until her face came closer and she said, though not looking at him, "I'm frightened."

"Of what?"

"Would you walk out by the hedge?"

"What am I looking for?"

"I'm not sure. Whatever it is . . ."

"Whatever what is?"

"Please . . ."

He ducked under the awning, walked across the flagstones to the low hedge that bordered the top level of the terrace, looked across at the tiers descending to the pool. Looked the other way, past the sloping lawn to the turnaround by the garage. He came full circle, slowly, until he was facing the house again.

Diane stood within the oval arch, facing him in moonlight, waiting . . . that picture out of early memory more than thirty years ago of a bare naked lady with a bush of hair between her legs and it hadn't changed one bit, it was true and beautiful as ever, as real as that moon over Miami and he was a boy again in a grown-man's chauffeur's suit with the lady of the house ready to go for a ride . . . on fat canvas cushions on the floor, as it turned out. She nearly killed him she was so much moving female telling him to do it, do it, saying oh, God, oh, God, do it, that quiet woman set free, Stick wondering what kind of glittering phase of his life he was going through this woman so pleased she couldn't believe it, breathless the way he stayed with her and never let up till she was wrung limp and Stick was soaring to his own stars and said to her, cocky, "Now it's my turn . . ."

Kyle said, "You've changed. Good."

He followed her into the yellow living room softly lighted, set to music he couldn't identify but good stuff that had a George Benson sound with subtle percussion rimshots rocking it along. He had changed into his lime green knit shirt and laundered khakis, and brushed his teeth, and washed up here and there.

"I hope I didn't take too long. I was afraid you'd be in bed."

"No, I'm wide awake. You're the one looks tired."

"Been a long day," Stick said. And not over yet. "They keep me jumping, when I'm not waiting around."

Was she looking at him funny? She wasn't as tall as before; barefoot now, but still wearing the dress with little thin straps. Her tan skin glowed in the lamplight. The whites of her eyes seemed whiter. When they settled into the deep sofa with the scotch she poured, Kyle sat low with her legs stretched out, bare feet crossed on the cocktail table. She was a cushion away from him. He thought of her in the car this afternoon and said, "What's float mean? And P-E?"

She said, "Is that what you want to talk about?" The way she had sounded when she told Barry she was tired.

"No, but tell me some time. There a lot of words you have to learn?"

"No more than if you wanted to be a croupier. Or a car salesman. You probably know a lot of words I don't. So there you are." Now she sounded more relaxed than tired, her head turned against the cushion, looking at him.

Stick said, "I wondered—you don't mind I was in jail? It doesn't make you nervous?"

"No, it surprises me, you lived that kind of life. I know you're smarter than that, just talking to you."

"It looked easy," Stick said. "What do you have to know to steal a car? Get in and start it."

"What about the risk, was that part of it? The excitement?"

"I was making a living. I'd drive a cement truck, a transit-mix for a while, then go back to it. I don't know—maybe I thought I was getting away with something. I was a lot younger and dumber then. I did a little time for cars; then I was picked up again and thought I'd be going away for quite a while. But at the pretrial exam the witness got on the stand and said he made a mistake, he'd never seen me before. I couldn't believe it. Till after, I find out he has a plan of his own. Did Barry mention Frank Ryan to you?"

"Was that your partner?"

Stick nodded. "I never said a word about Frank, but he knew all about him, like somebody read him my sheet."

"Barry has a friend in the Dade State Attorney's office," Kyle said. "That's his source. His friend called the Detroit police."

"That's what I thought. Anyway, Frank Ryan was the witness. He was a car salesman. I mean a real one. So after I was let off Frank took me aside and told me his plan—his ten rules for success and happiness in armed robbery—and we went in business together."

"You're kidding."

"No, he had ten rules. I remember he wrote 'em down for me on cocktail napkins."

"Were you successful?"

"For about three months."

"Happy?"

"When I wasn't scared to death. It was a lot different than picking up a Cadillac and selling it down in Ohio for parts, but there was a lot of money in it too."

"What were some of the rules?"

"Well, like, always be polite on the job. Say please and thank you."

"You serious?"

"Keeps everybody calm. Never call your partner by name, when you're in the place. Never use your own car. Never flash money.

Never tell anybody your business . . . Like that, just common sense They worked, too."

"Then why'd you get caught?"

"We broke rule number ten. Never associate with people known to be in crime. We teamed up with some guys that Frank knew and . . . well, it didn't work out."

"Where's Frank? Still in prison?"

"He died in Jackson. Cirrhosis. He got hooked on moonshine they made out of potatoes. Toward the end his stomach was out to here, his liver . . . Dumb shit. I told him, he wouldn't listen. He never learned how to jail. You know, live in a place like that. So, he died."

"Were you good friends?"

"Well, we were together all the time. We had a nice apartment. Sometimes, it was like we were married, the kind of arguments we had. Over little picky things that didn't matter. But we had a good time for a while. It was different, I'll say that."

"What're you smiling at?"

"Nothing, really. I can hear him bitching, like an old lady."

"Do you miss him?"

"Do I *miss* him? No, I don't miss him, I re*mem*ber him, you know, I suppose we were pretty close at that. But it was a different kind of life and it's over."

She said, "Didn't you feel you were doing anything wrong? Stealing?"

"Sure, I knew it was wrong. And I knew I'd have to pay for it if I got caught. I accepted that. And that's what happened and now it's over with. Done. Now I'm going to get in the stock market, become a financial expert."

She said, "You probably could"—still with her head against the cushion—"if you wanted to. Why not? We could trade places. I'll get a designer chauffeur uniform."

"What's the matter with what you're doing?"

"I don't know—I'm tired of it."

"I think I mentioned that this afternoon."

"I know you did. But I'm not tired of it—as you implied, because I tell my clients what to do and they make all the money. Money doesn't have anything to do with it. I'm tired of this middle position, advising. There's no tangible satisfaction. What I'd like, I *think*, is to run a manufacturing business. Produce something, an end product, and not just deal in paper."

"How about portable water tanks?" Stick said. "I understand, you sell to the military there's a lot of money in it."

She said, just barely smiling, "You're kind of a showoff, aren't you? But very subtle. 'Do you see anything you like?' And before Chucky knows it he's your straight man, 'No, I guess not,' and walk away. You're an actor, aren't you?"

"Nope. I'm a very simple soul."

"What's the name of the water tank company?"

"Ranco Manufacturing."

"What're some other good buys?"

"Automated Medical Labs. Kaneb Services. Firestone, maybe, if there's a takeover."

"You're scary."

Stick eased over to rest his arm on the cushion separating them, leaning closer to her. "But I still don't know what a float is, or options."

She said, "I have a feeling you could learn everything there is to know in about two days."

"You want to teach me?" He touched her hand lying in her lap, finger tips tracing fine bones.

She said, "I don't know if I'm ready for you," though she turned her hand over, felt his callused palm and slowly laced her fingers into his, still with her head against the cushion of the backrest, eyes mildly appraising, perhaps curious. "I think I'm out of practice. I deal with people who read balance sheets and play business golf and go from the club to board-of-directors meetings."

"You don't have any fun?"

She said, "I have friends—we go to polo matches, we go sailing, we play tennis . . ."

"Yeah? . . ."

"When I'm home, but I travel quite a lot."

"You going with a guy?"

"No, not really. I see the same people most of the time . . . I go to dinner parties and sit next to recently divorced men, most of them very wealthy . . ."

"Yeah? . . ."

"And listen to them talk about themselves. Or real estate."

"You get to laugh much?"

"Politely. Nothing's that funny."

"It sounds like the whole show is."

"Yeah, if there was somebody else, you know, to nudge and say, God, listen to that pontificating asshole; but I feel like I'm alone, I don't fit in."

Stick worked up closer to her, laid his head against the cushion to face hers, only a few inches away. He said, "You poor little girl, you could be having fun and you're stuck with humbuggers. You need somebody to play with." Meaning to volunteer and wondering seriously if this was the evening he'd go for the hat trick.

Three goals, three different girls, this one with blue eyes becoming sad and a soft powdery scent—this one a giant step beyond the other two, a girl he could talk to and nudge and they'd give each other knowing looks. He was confident with the feeling he had engraved himself on her and she was attracted to him, for whatever reason.

She said, "I'm not sure what to call you."

What difference did it make? He said, "Ernest. That's my real name. I don't think of it much one way or the other. Stick I'm used to, it's all right. But now *Kyle*, that's a winner."

She said, "You want to know something?"

He said, "Uh-oh. What?"

"I made it up."

"Come on—you did?"

"You want to know my real name? . . . Emma."

He said, "Emma," rolled it around in his head and began to nod, slowly. "Emma. Emma Peel. What's wrong with it?"

"It sounds like enema. That's what kids used to call me."

He said, "But you're grown up now, Em," and raised his head enough to place his mouth on hers, kissed her with meaning while holding back a little, showing her he had restraint and was in control of himself, and so he would not look awkward if she twisted away. But she didn't. Her mouth began to work on his, gradually getting more serious about it—Stick keeping up, with no more glimpses of those other two, no more comparing or counting goals—until Kyle said, "I want to go to bed with you . . ."

He recognized Herbie Hancock working away in the living room now, the chorus telling them *Give It All Your Heart*, with drive, determination, but something had happened to his timing and across the bay the moon was gone, down behind Miami.

He said in the dark, "I don't know what's the matter."

She said, "It's all right. Let's go to sleep."

"I guess it's just one of those things. You never know."

"No, you don't."

"What does that mean?"

"I'm agreeing with you. It's just one of those things. Don't get mad at *me*."

"I'm not mad . . . You think I'm mad?"

"Why don't we go to sleep? All right?"

"Fine . . ."

15

The first thing Stick's former wife Mary Lou said to him after seven and a half years was, "Do you know what time it is?" Holding the door open with one hand, her robe closed with the other. She had three pink curlers sitting squarely on top of her head.

"It's about nine o'clock," Stick said. "Can I come in?"

"It's ten minutes of," Mary Lou said. "You woke me up—you know what time you woke me up?"

"I think it was about eight," Stick said.

"It was seven-forty. Because I looked at the clock. I could not imagine who could possibly be calling at seven-forty on Sunday morning."

Stick said, "What happened, I got a car to use right after I talked to you, if I'd drop somebody off in Lauderdale first. So I had to do it right away. Otherwise I'd be thumbing half the day and still might not get here."

She was looking past him toward the street. "That's the car? It's pretty old, isn't it?"

"A Rolls-Royce, Mary Lou, it doesn't matter how old it is." He glanced around at it, sitting out there on a street of cement ranch bungalows, bikes and toys on front lawns, where no Rolls had ever been before: Pompano Beach, a block off Federal Highway.

She said, as he knew she'd have to, "Did you steal it?" She had not changed one bit, still with that drawn look about the nose, like she was smelling her own bitter aura.

He said, "It's my boss's. We gonna stand here and talk or can I come in and see Katy?"

"She's sleeping," Mary Lou said, lowering her voice, but let him into the living room of shiny maple and blue-green plaid, Stick remembering living rooms like this, though not this particular one. He hadn't seen this maple set before. Or the electric organ. Or the grandfather clock. Mary Lou saying, "You didn't expect her to be up, did you?"

Stick said, "You go on with whatever you're doing. I won't bother you any." With a drawl to his voice he hadn't heard in years; as though being in the presence of this woman caused him to revert and he should go out and fix her car seat that was always slipping when she stopped.

She said, "I'm not going back to bed with you here," clutching that pink robe around her—more of the past coming back—like he might have a quick Sunday morning jump in mind. No thank you. He thought of Kyle and his spirit dipped. He would have to work his way back up and show her he was ordinarily fit and dependable. It was pride; but he was also fascinated by her and maybe a little bit in love. Really.

He said, "You sleep in curlers now?"

She raised her hand partway up but didn't touch her head. She turned and went out of the room.

Stick sat down to wait, careful of the crease in his pressed khakis. Looking around—there wasn't a piece of furniture or flowery print he recognized, here or in the dining-L. Everything looked new.

Mary Lou took till almost nine-thirty to return, wearing slacks now and a sleeveless print blouse, her dark hair combed blown up in a bouffant, cheeks rouged. He said, "Katy still asleep?"

"I didn't open her door to see."

"Why don't you wake her up?"

"Because she needs her sleep."

"You getting along all right?"

"You mean are we making ends meet without any help from you? Not one cent in over seven years? Yes, thank you, we're doing just fine."

"I sent you a couple hundred from Jackson."

"You sent a hundred and eighty-five dollars. Mr. Wonderful."

"I'm going to help out," Stick said. "In fact"—he dug out his wallet—"I got paid this morning. I even got a raise. I thought I was going to get fired for something I did, he gave me a raise. So I can let you have . . . here's three hundred. How's that?"

"In seven years," Mary Lou said, "I'd say it's pretty shitty. What would you say?"

He knew this would happen. "I'm going to give you something every week now, for Katy. Or every month." He laid the bills on the end table.

"You bet you are," Mary Lou said. "At least till you go to prison again. When do you think that'll be?"

It was hard not to get up and walk out. Stick said, "Not ever again. I've changed."

"Does the man you work for know you're a convict?"

"I'm an *ex*-convict, Mary Lou." The thought came into his mind that Mary Lou would make a pretty good hack at a women's correctional facility. Or even a men's. He said, "Tell me how your mother's doing."

She said, "Mama's dead." Giving him a withering look, as though he were the cause of it.

"I'm sorry to hear that, I really am."

"Why, 'cause you got along so well? You never said a kind word about mama in your life."

"I couldn't think of any," Stick said, seeing that tough old broad squinting at the Temptations on Ed Sullivan, saying, "Is that niggers?" Ready to turn off the set, miss her favorite program if they were. There was a twenty-four-inch console color TV set now. Plus the organ, all the new furniture . . . Looking around the room he said, "You must be doing pretty good over at Fashion Square."

She said, "Oh, you're interested in how we're getting by?"

He said, "Your mom left you fixed, didn't she? I know the last time I saw her she still had her First Communion money." It wasn't a good subject to stay with. He got off of it asking, "You dating anybody?"

She said, "I don't see that anything I'm doing is any of your business." She looked toward the front door a moment before Stick heard it bang open and there was his little girl:

Skinny brown legs and arms, coming in yelling, "Mom!" and stopping, looking amazed as she saw him on the sofa. He didn't want to say anything dumb. He smiled . . . She knew who he was, he could tell. But she glanced at her Mom for confirmation; got nothing. Mary Lou wasn't going to help.

When he stood up and said, "Katy?" she came to him, into his arms and he felt her arms going around his middle, the top of her head touching his mouth. He felt her clinging, meaning it. Heard her say against him, "I got your letter . . ."

But now Mary Lou was giving them a furious look.

"Where have you been!"

It pulled them apart. Katy said, "I told you I was staying at Jenny's." She seemed surprised. "Remember? And we're going to the beach today? They're waiting for me, I just came home to get my towel and stuff."

"Well," Mary Lou said, showing she was helpless, "your father finally comes to see you and you run off."

Katy said, "But I didn't know . . ."

"It's okay," Stick said, "go on. I just stopped by—I'll be around here, we'll get to see plenty of each other." He saw gratitude in the girl's eyes—more than that, recognition that they were in tune and would be at ease with one another. He said, "You look great. You're all grown up . . . How's school?"

"It's okay." She didn't seem anxious now.

"You like it?"

"Sorta. We go back, God, in two weeks. I can't believe it."

Mary Lou was moving to the front window. "Who's out in the car?"

"Just some kids. Jenny and David. And Tim. I told you we were going."

"Who's driving?"

"Lee." Surprised again. "I told you, his dad's letting him use the car."

"I thought his license was taken away."

"He got it back two months ago." She looked up at her dad, smiling. "How've you been?"

"Fine. I'll call you real soon, we'll go out for dinner. School's okay, huh?"

"It's all right." She was edging away.

"What's your favorite subject?"

"I guess typing."

"Typing," Stick said. "You any good?"

"Pretty good. I gotta go, okay?"

He watched her hurry out of the room, into the hall. "She spends the night out," he said to Mary Lou, "and you don't even know it?"

"I work. You should try it sometime."

"You work last night?"

"I was at services. You going to give me the third degree now? You should be quite good at it, all the experience you've had. Come out of prison and have the gall to start criticizing . . ."

She glanced away and Stick looked over to see Katy with a beach towel and a plastic bottle of suntan lotion, her expression vague, lost. Then came back into character with a look of innocence.

"I gotta go, okay? They're waiting." She came over and kissed him on the cheek and he kissed hers.

"I'll call you in a couple of days." He could see a reflection of himself in her, a little-girl version of his nose and mouth. More than anything he wanted to know what she was thinking. He watched her give her mother a peck on the cheek and start for the door.

Mary Lou said, "You have your towel, your lotion, you have your suit on?"

Katy pulled out the neck of her T-shirt and peered in. "Yep, it's still there."

"Don't stay in the sun too long."

"I won't."

"You'll get skin cancer."

"I won't."

"And don't be late. What time're you coming home?"

"*Ma*-om, I gotta *go*." She looked at her dad again, said, "See ya," and was gone.

Mary Lou remained at the window, sounds outside fading. He studied the round sag of her shoulders in the print blouse and felt a sadness and hoped she wouldn't say anything more to him. Her belly showed in the slacks, worn high, her hips broader than he remembered them . . . He would tell her she was cute as a bug and she would wrinkle up her nose at him and sometimes slap his arm . . . He was aware for the first time that she had no sense of style or color. He didn't want to talk to her anymore and still he asked, "How can she be out all night and you don't know it?"

Mary Lou turned from the window. "You've got a lot of nerve."

"We're not talking about me, we're on you for a change. Just tell me that one thing and I'll get out of your way."

"I knew she wasn't home," Mary Lou said. "I forgot for a minute, that's all. I went to services last night and when I got home her door was closed—it's always closed, I never know if she's in there or not. She's either in her room or on the phone."

"Services," Stick said. "You don't go to mass anymore?"

"I suppose you do?"

"Not too often."

She said, "Well, I attend the Church of Healing Grace now, since I've become acquainted with Reverend Don Forrestall . . ." Letting it hang.

So that Stick had to say, "Acquainted?"

"We're seeing each other. Reverend Don Forrestall has asked me to join his ministry as a healing assistant and I'm now studying for it. As soon as I heard him speak," Mary Lou said, "I had absolute certainty for the first time in my life."

A lie. He could never remember her being uncertain. She knew everything.

"I felt waves of love, which you would not understand, but it happened to me as he laid on his hands and Reverend Don Forrestall told me I had received the gift. He said, 'All things thou has seen the Lord do through me now shall be done through thee unto His praise and glory.'"

"He said that?" Stick said.

"In front of the congregation. I opened my mouth then and my fillings over here on this side"—Mary Lou hooked a finger inside her cheek—"had turned to pure gold. He's done it many, many times. Reverend Don Forrestall has cured thousands of severe toothaches, he's filled cavities with gold or silver, usually gold, he's corrected overbites, does wonderful things through laying on his hands and saying, 'In the name of Our Lord Jesus, let this mouth be healed that it may shout thy praise and glory.' It's all he has to do."

Stick said, "You mean Reverend Don is a dental faith healer?"

"Ailments of the mouth," Mary Lou said. "He does cold sores, fever blisters and inflammation of the gums also. Wisdom teeth . . ."

Stick said, "You had gold crowns put in there in 'Seventy-two. They cost a hundred and twenty-eight dollars."

"I never did. It was regular fillings and now they're gold, through the healing ministry of Reverend Don Forrestall."

"How much you give him?"

"Nothing. He doesn't *charge*, he does it in praise of the Lord Jesus."

"How much you contribute to the Church of the Healing Grace?"

"None of your business."

As soon as Aurora got home she called Pam at Chucky's, talked to her for almost a half hour about her experience and how she was going to tell off Mr. Barry Stam, the creep, who didn't think of anyone but himself. She said she wouldn't care if she never saw his big boat and his little pecker ever again.

Pam jumped on Chucky's bed, got him bolt upright and told about Barry's new driver taking Rorie home at eight o'clock in the morning for God's sake after being cooped up on Barry's boat for like almost two days. Chucky asked Pam what the new driver's name was and she said Aurora didn't know but she thought he was cute. Chucky called Moke, told him it would be worthwhile to go out and look for a gray Rolls returning to Bal Harbour, license number BS-one.

Moke sat in the blue Chevy van at the east end of Broad Causeway from ten-thirty to eleven-fifteen Sunday morning, wearing his brand-new forty-dollar Bullrider straw he'd bought with his own money. He smoked weed to help him wait and listened to WCKO playing nigger gospel. He said, "A-man and A-man," when he saw the gray Rolls come out of the chute past the twenty-cent toll gate. He followed after, turned in at the Bal Harbour shopping center and watched Stick get out of the Rolls and go into the drugstore. No suit on this morning, wearing khakis and a blue shirt, but it was the guy, no doubt of it. He had said to Chucky, why not call this fella Barry and ask him about his new driver? But Chucky said if they aroused suspicion the guy might take off; no, let's ease up close, Chucky said, not let on. Moke watched him come out of followed behind again and watched the son of a bitch drive in past the Bal Harbour gatehouse guard, giving him a wave.

Moke crept past in the van. Now should he call Chucky back, listen to him piss and moan? . . . Or call Avilanosa and get her done. Bright and clear, it was too nice a day to sit around smoking weed.

16

Stick pulled into the turnaround wondering what Kyle was doing, wondering what he'd say to her. Cornell was standing by the open garage door.

"You have a nice time with Rorie?"

"She never shut up all the way to Lauderdale." He pulled the Rolls into the garage and came out.

Cornell said, "Love the scene, sneaking her off the boat this morning. Man so hung over he could barely see to walk."

"Aurora says she's going to tell him off," Stick said. They were moving across the cobblestones toward the lawn.

"He's heard it," Cornell said. "Man will put up with just so much, then she be looking for another daddy. Speaking of—the lady was looking for you." Stick's gaze swung toward the pool and Cornell said, "Not that one, the lady of the house. I told her it was your day off. But she's gone now, went to the club to fool around, have a few salty dogs. How come you're back?"

"Why would I want to leave this," Stick said, his eyes moving across the slant of lawn again to the swimming pool: to Kyle on a lounge, motionless, long brown legs shining in the sun. Her suit, wide blue and white stripes, was cut high on the sides, almost to her hips. He wanted to walk up to her—say something to Barry first. Barry sat at the umbrella table with a pile of Sunday papers. Looking at Barry he felt sorry for him, or else it was a twinge of guilt; or an awareness that he might feel guilty if he thought about it long enough or hoped to be seduced again by the man's wife. But there would never be another night like that one. He'd keep it to bring out and look at now and then, close to his vest, knowing his amazement would be shaded with remorse once he got to the part with Kyle. Not because he'd failed but because he'd tried, because he'd included her in his personal record attempt. Dumb. Still, he could forgive himself. It wasn't that dumb. He didn't know on the guest-house sofa he was going to have a knot in his gut thinking of her the next day. There was no one to tell to get a reaction. All he could do was start again from scratch—something he'd had a lot of practice doing—and this time hope she'd feel he was worth waiting for.

Cornell said, "Was a man name of Harvey stop by, look like he was gonna be sick he didn't find you. Gave me a number said for you to call soon as you got back. Hey, you see your little girl?"

"I sure did." It picked him up, like that, thinking of her arms around him, saying close to him, *I got your letter* . . . It reached deep into him. He felt a sadness even while he smiled, telling Cornell about Katy, and asked, "How 'bout you, you have a good time last night?"

"Fell in love," Cornell said. "Again. Yeah, while you doing the chores."

"They keep you humping," Stick said.

"Man got good and smashed, uh? I hear him say he don't remember nothing. That's safe." Cornell looked off. "I think he's waving at me. Wants a bloody." Cornell walked to the edge of the grass, watched Barry beneath the umbrella waving his arms, gesturing. "No, don't want me, wants you."

Stick walked across the grass slope with his magazines and aftershave and toothpaste in the sack trying to get words ready and found he didn't have to. Barry was into the stock market again, throwing questions at Kyle lying motionless a few feet away, sunglasses covering her eyes, arms at her sides.

"How do you like Biogen? Raised forty million for research, their objective"—glancing at the newspaper—"to become the IBM of biotechnology."

Kyle said, not moving, "You're already into biotechnology."

"With what?"

"Automated Medical Labs."

"I want to cover my ass," Barry said. "This"—looking at the paper again—"recombinant DNA, you understand that?"

"Gene splicing."

Barry waited, Stick watching. "That's it, uh? Gene splicing?"

"Transplanting genetic characteristics from one cell to another. Cloning . . . mass-producing human hormones . . . all that stuff." She sounded sleepy.

"How do you know that?"

"You sound like Aurora," Kyle said, still not moving.

Barry looked up at the terrace, his gaze monitoring the area before settling on Stick. "Hey, buddy, how you doing?"

Kyle didn't look over. Stick said to Barry, "What can I get you?"

"Not a thing. Listen, I hope I didn't give you a hard time last night. I don't remember a goddamn thing from the time we walked outta the club. How was . . . my friend? She give you any trouble?"

"Not a bit. She was fine."

"Last time I got that drunk," Barry said, "years ago, I didn't know any better, I pick up a broad someplace—I mean I must've 'cause I wake up the next morning and there's this broad laying there. We're in a motel, that Holiday Inn over on LeJeune. I've got my arm out like this and the broad's laying on it with her head turned away from me? I lean up to get a look at her—I don't remember a goddamn thing from the night before—and, Jesus, I can't believe it. This is the ugliest broad I ever saw in my life. I mean that's how drunk I was. This broad was so ugly . . . Ask me how ugly she was."

Stick said, "How ugly was she?"

"She was so ugly I actually considered chewing my arm off rather than wake her up. You talk about an ugly broad . . ."

Stick glanced over. Kyle didn't move. Now Barry was looking at his newspaper again and Stick wondered if he was dismissed. He didn't want to leave, he hadn't learned anything yet.

Barry said, "I think Enzo Biochem's looking good. Up from six and a quarter to twenty-three." He turned to Kyle. "What do you think, babe?"

Kyle said, sleepy or bored, still without moving, "Nothing in the field of biotechnology has been brought to market. You're trading in names and numbers. They could be making cat food or you could be playing Keno for all it has to do with product." She said, even more slowly, "You don't need me for that."

Barry lowered his sunglasses and ducked his head looking over them. "Babe? What's the matter?"

"Nothing."

It seemed that was all she was going to say.

Stick said, "I heard about a dental faith healer, he straightens your teeth and fills cavities with gold in the name of Jesus. That come under biotechnology?"

Kyle opened her eyes.

"You're putting me on," Barry said. "Come on, you serious? A *den*tal faith healer? The age of specialization, man."

"At the Church of the Healing Grace," Stick said. He watched Kyle get up from the lounge.

"That's where you've been?" Barry said. "You get your teeth capped or what? Lemme see. Babe, you hear this? . . . Where you going?"

"Home."

"You mean *home* home?"

"No, my room"—waving him off with a tired gesture—"I'll see you later." Not looking at either of them as she walked around the deep end of the pool and headed for the tennis court. They both watched her. Barry said, "Look at those lovely long legs. They go right up to her brain, without any stops along the way."

Stick didn't say anything.

Kyle put on shorts and a tennis shirt and left the guest house with no purpose but to walk, feel herself doing something physical. She walked past hedges and walls that enclosed the wealth of the kind of people she counseled, walked east to the Atlantic ocean, a neutral ground, and took off her sneakers to wander an empty stretch of shoreline.

She had said to her dad, "The money's great, but there's no satisfaction. I want to *do* something, see tangible results." He told her to drop her start-up companies going public and get back on the Board quick, for the upswing. She said to her dad, "Do you know what I wanted to be when I was little? A cop . . . No, not ever a nurse or a nun." She had played guns with her brothers and baseball in Central Park and at school in Boston, the boys amazed she didn't throw like a girl. She side-armed snowballs at cops in '69 demonstrating on the Commons, knit scarf flying, nose running, perspiring in her pea-coat, drinking beer after and smoking pot; into living. Now: "There's no excitement anymore. I watch. I'm a spectator."

Her dad said get married, raise a family. When she felt like trading, pick up the phone.

"Who do I marry?"

Lot of bright young guys on the Street to choose from, share a common interest.

Like dating sociology majors at school: have something to talk about. Except that textbook conversations ran out of gas and when they took the Orange Line to Dudley Station and prowled through Roxbury she found she could not study "real people" statistically: they were in a life that made hers seem innocent make-believe. Still, she was drawn to the street, fascinated, feeling a rapport she didn't understand.

Kyle had brought that home from school and her dad said there was the Street and there was the street. One was neither more real nor unreal than the other. Kyle said, except one was concocted, invented in the name of commerce; while the other was concerned with existence, degrees of survival. She would talk about social and economic inequalities and watch her dad doze off in his chair.

Today there was still a distinction in her mind. Comparing her Street with the ghetto street—or with rural, suburban or industrial streets, for that matter—she felt insulated, left out of life. She dealt in paper, in notes, contracts, certificates, coupons, with a self-conscious feeling of irrelevance.

On her recent trip home Kyle said to her dad, "I think I want to get into manufacturing, make something."

"Like what?"

"I don't know, it's down the road. Maybe something in genetic engineering."

"Pie in the sky. You want to be realistic, buy a stamping plant in Detroit and go out of your mind that way."

"Or get into a service business that deals with people who need help on a survival level."

"The public defender complex. I thought you got over that in Boston."

"You've got an answer for everything, haven't you?"

"I hope to God I do," her dad said. "But if you're serious, why don't you make a lot of money in the market, then open a home for cute little nigger kids the Junior League ladies can dress up and take to the zoo? Would that make you happy?"

Her dad had not been entertained by the Chucky stories. Or, he'd refused to accept the fact his daughter had a drug dealer as a client, put it out of his mind without comment. Now, if she told him she'd gone to bed with a man who'd served seven years for armed robbery . . . (The failure to bring it off with skyrockets was beside the point.) On second thought her dad might accept Ernest Stickley the ex-con—once he knew him—and still disapprove of their sleeping together. It wasn't a subject you discussed with parents, at least not comfortably. She had lived with a premed student in Boston for a year and a lawyer on and off in New York for a year and a half; her parents had been aware of both, without a word of comment.

Getting involved with Ernest Stickley, Jr., from Norman, Oklahoma, by way of a state penitentiary—God—previewed what could be an entirely new experience. She liked him. She liked to talk to him and felt good with him. At this moment she missed him. He appeared to be predictable, but wasn't the least bit. The dental faith healer . . . She had left because she was tired of hearing Barry's voice and was certain he'd take over and do all the dental-faith-healer possibilities to death, without restraint. Which was one of Stick's strong points, his control, patience, without—thank God—putting on a show of being cool. They had been natural together in bed, both at ease, in sort of a dreamy nod. It was great. Until, *maybe*, he began to think too much and his male ego got him worrying about performing, being a star, instead of simply letting it happen. Her dad might call it the unfortunate stud syndrome, self-emasculation through anxiety. But that's all the analysis she was going to give it. Feeling good with him and close to him was enough for the time being. The boy-girl aspect could take care of itself.

What might require work would be getting him out of that chauffeur's uniform and into a business suit. But why not? He had the potential, he certainly caught on fast enough. Why not help him get started? Not think of it as rehabilitation, like she was going to straighten out his life. Though it was an intriguing idea: from armed robber to investment counselor. Forget the gun, Stickley, there's an easier way to make it. No, just help him out, gradually.

Her dad would call it latent motherhood.

Crossing Collins Avenue on the way back she noticed the van parked off the road by a clump of seagrape, standing alone. She could make out a man's head and shoulders through the windshield, a cowboy hat, and thought of Chucky's unbelievable friend Eddie Moke.

Kyle began to jog, just in case: in past the gatehouse and for several blocks, letting the perspiration sting her eyes, thighs aching now as she turned the corner and came along Bali Way. It was not until she saw the black limousine that she broke stride and slowed to a walk, catching her breath. The car stood at the entrance to Barry's driveway, a figure hunched over next to it. As she approached, the figure straightened, looking toward her. It was Stick. The car started up and came past her, a uniformed chauffeur at the wheel, alone in the car. Stick waited, starting to smile.

"You run in weather like this, Emma, you know what happens?"

"What?" She touched the sleeve of her T-shirt to her forehead. *Emma.* She had forgot about that part of last night.

"You die," Stick said. They started up the drive together, the blacktop soft underfoot. He said, "I just made nine hundred dollars. Not all from that one. The word's gotten around. He's my third customer; they call and stop by."

"I'm afraid to ask what you're selling."

"Guess."

"Not dope . . . Are you?"

"I never was into that. No, tips on the market. I'm a Wall Street tout, unless there's another name for it."

She said, "*Nine* hundred dollars?"

"Two hundred up front for a hot one about to take off, like Ranco. And I sold some over-the-counter stuff for fifty bucks each."

"*Nine* hundred dollars?"

"Cash, flat-rate deal, Em. I haven't figured out yet how to charge a percentage or if I should."

"Well, first you need a license." She was aware of the trace of amazement still in her voice. Now it was *Em*, like last night, familiar.

"I think I could even make up names of phony companies, they'd buy 'em. They've got that much faith in Barry. They think he's a wizard, up from boy wonder. They think you give him inside information, but he's the one who picks the winners. And you know what, he loves it. He said sell 'em anything you want."

They passed from sunlight into the shade of malaleucas and hibiscus lining the drive, the blacktop hard and firm now.

"So I guess what it comes down to," Stick said, "selling's pretty easy if you have what people want. Is that it?"

She was recovering. "They don't even have to want it," Kyle said. "They only have to believe they'd be fools to pass it up."

Barry called to them as they were crossing the terrace, walking away from the house. "Hey, where you going with my driver?"

He appeared out of a dark archway of the morning room—where his wife had stood in moonlight. Stick saw her again with a wince of guilt, a minor tug that was losing its edge.

Barry came out to the grass. "Stickley, I got a favor to ask. Guy's coming in from New York, five something. You want to go meet him?" Barry stood with one arm raised straight up, wrist bent, finger pointing somewhere beyond Biscayne Bay.

"It's my day off."

"I know it is. I'm not *telling* you to pick the guy up, I'm asking you."

"What if I wasn't here?" Stick said.

Kyle took a few aimless steps away and turned back, to be able to watch both of them.

"If you weren't here," Barry said, "then I'd have to pick him up myself or get Cornell, but you're here. I can see you, you're standing right there." Barry pointed. "That's you, isn't it?"

"Since it's my day off," Stick said, "I think it should be the same as I'm not here. Otherwise what good's a day off?"

"Jesus Christ," Barry said, "all I'm asking you to do is go to the fucking airport and pick somebody up. Take you maybe an hour and a half. Here—" He stepped back into the morning room and reappeared holding a rectangle of white cardboard, a shirt stiffener, that said in black Magic Marker MR. LEO FIRESTONE. "You hold this up as the passengers come off the flight. You don't even have to say anything."

Stick looked at Barry holding the sign against his chest. "I don't think I could do that."

Kyle said, "I couldn't either."

Barry said, "Whatta you mean you don't think you could do it? You don't *do* anything, you hold the fucking sign up, that's all."

Stick said, "You asking me if I want to do it?"

"As a favor, yeah."

"If you're giving me a choice," Stick said, "then I pass. I think you should handle it as if I'm not here. Okay?" He turned to Kyle. She shrugged and they started off across the terrace. Barry yelled at them, "I don't believe it!" but they kept going.

Kyle said, "Instead of trying to get fired, why don't you just quit?"

"I'm not trying to get fired." Stick seemed a little surprised. "You know him—he eats that up. Gives him something to tell his friends, act it out."

She said, "You're right, he'll work it into an I-don't-get-no-respect routine. But it's still chancy, meeting him head to head like that."

"You give in too easy. He picks your brain to pieces and you let him. You have to act like you don't need him."

"I don't," Kyle said, "but I like him. I'm not sure why exactly . . ."

"Well, you're in a position you know what you're doing, you can afford to let him take advantage of you. I'm still feeling around, learning a few things . . ."

"Fast," Kyle said.

"Doing some thinking . . ."

"Maybe I can help you."

"I bet you can, Em. Who's Leo Firestone?"

A horn blared loud behind the van parked in the seagrape and Moke jumped, lifted the curled brim from his eyes to check the outside mirror.

Nestor's car, the Fleetwood Caddy.

Well, now they were getting someplace. Moke got out and walked back on the driver's side, away from the road, hunching as the Cadillac window went down fast, automatically, and there was Avilanosa, with no expression but an odor of garlic that hit Moke in the face and he tried not to breathe.

"We going to take flowers," Avilanosa said.

"Shit," Moke said, "bust through the gate. All they got there's a rent-a-cop."

"We going to take flowers," Avilanosa said. "Nestor talk to Chucky, Chucky say he talk to the man lives there. He say the man is going to leave pretty soon."

Moke straightened, restless, fooled with his hat and hunched over again. "Why don't we just go *in*? Me and you."

"Listen to me," Avilanosa said. "The guy will be there alone he thinks, in the garage where he lives. We take him away from here to do it. They have business. You understand? So they don't want police to come and bother them."

"*Bus*iness? Jeez-us Christ, what's business got to do with it?" He saw the window start to rise. "Wait! You bring my piece?"

The window stopped for a moment. "I give it to you later," Avilanosa said, "when I come back."

17

Kyle gave Stick the prospectus to look over while she showered, telling him, "This is what a film offering looks like. It describes what you have to invest to become a limited partner and how you share in the profits, if and when."

"They all do it this way, make movies?"

"The independents do. Then they go to one of the major studios and try to make a distribution deal."

He sat on the guest-house patio turning pages, trying to get a quick idea of what it was about. There was a story synopsis—he read some of it—also names of actors he recognized; but most of it looked like a legal contract or a subpoena, or the kind of words you'd see in a small-print money-back guarantee and skip over.

The prospectus was spiral-bound, the size of a nine-by-twelve notebook with about sixty pages in it. The embossed plastic cover read:

FIRESTONE ENTERPRISES
PRESENTS A
LEO NORMAN FIRESTONE PRODUCTION
"SHUCK & JIVE"

He was interested but the legal tone stopped him and he didn't feel like concentrating. He would look off at the bright expanse of Miami—a postcard picture with sailboats and seagulls—but aware of Kyle's bedroom, its sliding glass doors right behind him. Kyle in there now where they'd been last night. Coming out of the shower, slipping on her skimpy white panties . . . Neither of them had mentioned last night. Everything seemed to be moving along fine, so he sure wasn't going to bring it up. The best thing to do with failure, put it out of your mind.

Kyle didn't take long. She came out in a sundress, barefoot, with a tray that held a bucket of ice, a bottle of Dewar's and glasses—this girl didn't fool around—and placed the tray on the patio table. She asked him what he thought of the movie deal, beginning to pour drinks.

"This isn't the tire company—buy now and look for a takeover, is it?"

"No, no relation. This is Leo Firestone, Hollywood film producer. It says. His credits are in there."

"I saw them. I mean I saw the list, but I must've missed the pictures when they came out. I never heard of any of them."

"You didn't see *Gringo Guns*? About five years ago."

"I was in prison."

"You were lucky. He did one of those, too. *Big House Breakout.* But he's best known for *The Cowboy and the Alien.*"

Stick turned to a page in the prospectus. "This *Shuck and Jive* . . . 'the hilarious escapades of a couple of undercover narcotics agents' . . . is he serious?"

"Two and a half million," Kyle said, "that's fairly serious. It's also zany, with riveting suspense and sizzling love."

He turned a few more pages. "Mostly, all I see is a lot of legal stuff."

"It describes the company, who the general partners are and their background, the risk factors, a budget estimate, a distribution plan . . ." She handed Stick a drink and sat down in a canvas director's chair with her own. "You'll see a tax opinion that runs about ten pages I think Leo Firestone's brother-in-law must've written. The story synopsis—you saw that—and some of the Hollywood stars Leo expects to sign."

"What you're telling me," Stick said, "this isn't your idea. You didn't bring Leo in."

"No, Barry ran into him somewhere, I think Bimini, and now Barry wants to be in the movie business. He thinks Leo is an extremely talented guy."

"Have you met him?"

"Not yet, but I can hardly wait. I told Barry months ago I'd shop a film venture for him if he was interested; they come along all the time. But the way Barry operates, he decides he wants to go *now*, he goes. He told Firestone he'd round up as many investors as he needed, with their checkbooks, and sit them down for the pitch. Leo must've kissed him."

"So if Barry goes in the others will too . . ."

"It's quite likely."

Stick turned to the first inside page. "It says a hundred and seventy-five Limited Partnership units at fourteen thousand two-eighty-five each . . . minimum purchase five units. That's . . . seventy grand to get in. Is that right? To raise two and a half million."

"You're close," Kyle said. "See, the offering's limited to thirty-five qualified investors. So the minimum you have to invest to get in is exactly seventy-one thousand four-hundred twenty-eight dollars and fifty-seven cents."

"And what does that get you?"

"Wait. That's the original prospectus you have," Kyle said. "Firestone, Barry says, is going to simplify the first couple of pages for the meeting tomorrow, sweeten the deal. Now the offering will call for ten investors to put in a hundred thousand each. A million bucks. Then Firestone will take that to the bank to leverage another million and a half on a note payable in five years. The limited partners put in a hundred thousand each for twenty percent of the picture, but they each get a tax write-off of two-hundred fifty thousand."

Stick said, "I'm not sure I understand that."

"How the tax law applies?"

"I don't think I'm ready for it," Stick said. "But the way it works here, Firestone makes his pitch and they walk up and they each hand him a hundred grand?"

"Right."

"How do they know he's gonna make the movie? Or if he does if it's gonna be any good?"

"In there under *risk* it states you should seek the counsel of an independent tax advisor," Kyle said. "Which these guys may or may not do. As I mentioned, if Barry goes in, the rest of them will probably follow."

"All that dough," Stick said, looking at the cover again, "for this."

"At least the title works," Kyle said. "I think the whole deal's shuck and jive."

Avilanosa made a U-turn, came around toward the van and pulled in behind it. Once he had backed into position the trunk of the Cadillac was only a few feet from the van's rear doors. Moke was out waiting, fooling with his Bullrider hat, setting it loose on his head. He looked at the Cadillac trunk as he heard it pop open but didn't touch it. Avilanosa, his belly sticking out of his summer-plaid sportcoat, came back and raised the lid, not looking at Moke. The trunk held a half-dozen pots of begonias.

"What'd you get so many for?"

"This is from Nestor and Chucky. I have the card," Avilanosa said. "Did the man leave?"

"Wasn't more'n a few minutes ago. Had his nigger driving him in the Rolls-Royce." Moke turned aside to spit into the sand. "Looks like an old woman's car."

"All right," Avilanosa said, his dark features closing in a squint as he looked off across the road, down the beach side of Collins Avenue. "What is that, what it says?"

Moke turned to look. "That's the Singapore Motel."

"Sing-apore," Avilanosa said, studying the sign.

"It's a place in China," Moke said.

"I know where it is," Avilanosa said. "All right, I'm going to leave this car over there." He looked up and down Collins, then reached into the trunk behind the red-flowering plants and brought out, wrapped loosely in a chamois, a 9-mm Beretta Parabellum that held fifteen rounds, blue steel with a wood grip. He raised the skirt of his coat and worked the automatic into the waist of his trousers.

Moke said, "Where's mine?" Avilanosa nodded to the trunk. Moke stuck his head in, felt around behind the flowers and came out with a High Standard 44 Mag Crusader with the long $8\frac{3}{8}$-inch barrel, a dull blue finish. Moke said with a whine, "Shit, I wanted my pearl-handle Smith for this one, my favorite."

Avilanosa pushed him, getting his attention, and said, "Put it under your clothes. And take off your hat. You don't look like somebody that brings flowers wearing that hat."

Stick said, "But there were some funny things that happened, too. There was an Armenian guy that owned a party store . . . That story Barry told about wanting to chew his arm off reminded me. You hear him tell that or were you asleep?"

"I've heard it before," Kyle said. "Barry calls it his coyote story."

"The guy, the Armenian, had thirty-eight bucks in the cash register and absolutely refused to tell us where he hid his money. This place had to be worth eight to twelve hundred, a Saturday night. So Frank sticks his gun in the guy's ear and tells him *I'm* gonna rape his wife if he doesn't get the dough out, quick. The wife's this dark, bent-over little old lady with a mustache I'd put in the bathroom. I want to say to Frank, not me, man, you do it. The guy, the Armenian, didn't say a word, nothing. Frank threatens to shoot him, counts to three and now the guy says, 'Kill me! I don't care—kill me!' So we left. And you know what? We forgot the thirty-eight bucks."

"You're right," Kyle said, pouring them another Dewar's, "you were in the wrong business. What you could do, though, maybe, is give Leo Firestone a pretty good story."

"Another time we're sitting in a bar, we're just about to make the move—a guy comes out of the men's room with a shotgun and holds the place up. Does it all wrong. Still, he got the dough. We waited till he was about to walk out and took it away from him. So we locked him in the storeroom where they kept the booze supply, cases stacked up—the guy and all the patrons that were in the place. The next day we read in the paper they were in there six hours. The cops open the door, everybody's smashed, having a great time and the holdup man, it said, appeared to have suffered a severe beating. I think he was in the wrong business, too." Stick shook his head. "I remember the guy was wearing a gold satin athletic jacket with *Port Huron Bullets* on the back."

She said, "Daring holdup pair get away with—how much on that one?"

"I don't remember. Our career only lasted a hundred days and it was over for good."

"But exciting, huh?"

"I'm not sure that's the word."

"I knew a couple of guys who sold commodities options, which is illegal, but not exactly dangerous," Kyle said. "And, I had a client who lost a hundred thousand in a real-estate swindle. I advised against getting into it and he said, 'But look who's investing, and named a very prominent local businessman. It turned out the *name* that lent so much assurance to this very shaky development was part of the scheme and the investors lost nine million dollars."

Stick said, "Without having to point a gun at anybody."

"You go to the same prison though," Kyle said.

Stick nodded. "That's the truth."

What it came down to every time if you lost: dirty drafty place with broken windows, awful food and dumb people, few you could talk to . . . far from Biscayne Bay sipping Dewar's on ice, watching the gulls and sailboats, the first red streaks of sunset. He felt at home here. He had felt at home down on South Beach, too, in that cheap retirement hotel. Strange? He hadn't liked that place any less. Maybe he didn't know where he belonged.

He said, "You know who else is from Norman? My old hometown?"

Kyle said, "Wait, let me guess."

He watched her thinking about it, that beautiful nose raised in the air, the delicate line of her nostril . . . looking at him again with clear blue eyes, interested.

"Is he a famous outlaw?"

"Uh-unh, James Garner. I wonder if they could get him for *Shuck and Jive.* My first choice would be Warren Oates, but he's gone."

She seemed surprised. "What happened to him?"

Stick didn't answer; he looked off, listening. "You hear a car door?"

"It's probably Diane," Kyle said. "Barry would be gone by now." She watched him get up, walk away from the patio.

Now Kyle got up. She followed him across the front of the guest house to the corner. It was nearly a hundred yards from here to the garage turnaround—beyond the tennis court, the palm trees, the terraced front yard—but they were able to make out the shape of the van, blue metal in the cavernous shade of old trees. A figure appeared from behind the van, carrying something that obscured him. Then another figure appeared. They were unloading plants.

Stick felt Kyle's hand touch him, stroke down his back. She said, "More customers for you?"

He shook his head. "I don't think so."

"If it's the same van," Kyle said, "it was parked out on the beach road when I came back. But there was only one person in it. This looks like a delivery."

"Did you get a look at him?"

"Not really. He was wearing a cowboy hat and reminded me of somebody. A very creepy guy who's a friend of Chucky's. If Chucky isn't creepy enough for you—" And stopped as Stick came around, taking her arm and she was moving with him back to the patio.

He said, "Put some shoes on."

18

From the off-side of the guest house they walked out toward the road, crossed the front of the property through stands of acacia trees and came all the way around to the driveway. Kyle asked questions and he told her to wait, not now. He told her to stay in the trees, he'd see about getting a car, if he could sneak one out of there.

But when he came to the corner of the garage and saw the van right there, the rear doors open, six pots of flowering plants standing on the cobblestones, he thought of taking the van and liked the idea. He didn't see Moke or the guy with him until they came out of the morning room and stood on the lawn to decide where they'd look next: go down to the cruiser tied up at the dock or over to the guest house. After a few moments they walked off toward the tennis court: a heavyset Cuban-looking guy, big hands hanging empty; Moke holding a long-barreled revolver at his side, but not wearing his hat.

The hat was on the driver's seat in the van. Stick reached in for it and saw the key in the ignition. He took the hat—glancing inside the crown to see the inscription, *Bullrider*, but no toilet paper in this one—and placed it behind the left front wheel, against the tire tread. He got up in the seat then and watched through the windshield. As soon as the two figures, way off now, walked around the front of the guest house and were no longer in sight, Stick turned the key. He let the engine idle low, backed up slowly, got the van turned around and looked out the window at Moke's Bullrider straw squashed flat on the cobblestones before heading down the drive, past the house to the trees in front. When Kyle got in she said, "When can I ask you what's going on?"

"While we're having dinner," Stick said. "Look in the glove box and see if there's a registration."

She said, "You like to know whose car you're stealing?" They followed Bal Harbour Drive to the gatehouse, followed the exit lane out and Kyle said, holding a plastic-covered registration, "Charles Buck, an address in South Miami."

Stick said, "Does that tell you anything? How about Chucky Gorman a.k.a. Charles Chucky Buck?"

They left the van in Bayfront Park, walked to a restaurant in Coral Gables, a favorite of Kyle's, where they dined in the seclusion of the garden patio and Stick told quietly how Rainy Mora was murdered.

Kyle did not interrupt. She seemed awed. When he had finished the story she asked questions, in turn, quietly. There was no hurry and she wanted to understand it and how he felt about it. They sipped wine, they ordered avocado and crabmeat . . . What was most difficult for her to understand was why he hadn't gone to the police.

Stick said, "The first thing you have to realize, the police aren't my friends." He said, "You're not only the best-looking girl I've ever known you're the smartest, by far, and I respect your judgment *but*—two things. Rainy's dead. He knew what he was doing, he knew what could happen to him, and it did. The other thing, I've already been to a correctional institution, I'm not going to put myself in a position like I'm asking to go back. I go to the cops with my record, tell my story, the first thing the state attorney'll do is try to get me to change it. He'll take the position, the only reason I'm talking to him I was working with the Cubans, but we had some kind of disagreement, so now I want to cop. The state attorney won't ever believe I was along for the ride or to keep Rainy company and make a few bucks. Why would I do that? I'd have to be crazy, guy with a record. But if I'm not, then they give you that business—if I'm smart I'll accept a plea deal, accessory or up as high as second degree, like they're doing me a favor, if I tell who pulled the trigger. Now I think I'd get off. But only after six months to a year in Dade County with a bond set around a quarter of a million."

"I know several good lawyers," Kyle said.

"Well, if they've had any experience along these lines they'd want ten up front and another fifteen if we go to trial. But even if I had the money I wouldn't give it to a lawyer."

"Don't worry about that part, the money."

"I appreciate it," Stick said, "but it's got nothing to do with lawyers. See—if I can explain it—you know Chucky deals, you know what goes on around here, the dope business. But you have to look at it from the inside maybe to understand what I'm talking about. I wasn't an innocent bystander, I was *there.* Rainy was there, too, but he didn't make it."

She said, "Don't you *feel* anything? How can you remove yourself from it?"

"You mean do I feel anything emotionally?"

"Yeah. How can you be objective?"

"Well, the only emotion that enters into it is fear—you see a guy with a submachine gun . . . I don't think I'm explaining it right. Am I *mad* at anybody?" He paused as though he had to think about it. "Yeah, I am. I'd like to kick Moke's teeth in. But then I think I would anyway, just knowing him. The guy with the machine gun, I don't know who he is but, yeah, I think the cops should take him off the street, for the good of mankind. Chucky, you know he's a bad guy—you want to see him go to jail?"

She said, "But he seems so harmless . . ."

"Does it have to be something personal? Like he kills a friend of yours? He didn't kill Rainy, he sent him to *be* killed. And me with him because I walked around his house and told him I didn't see anything I liked. Or maybe—give him the benefit—he told them to take me instead of Rainy because he didn't know me. But he sent the two guys in the van to Barry's house, we're pretty sure, because it's Chucky's van. And if they put me against the wall and you happened to be there, a witness . . . you see what I mean? That's your weird client you imitate and your dad doesn't think is very funny. I tend to go along with your dad. So, you want to turn Chucky in? What's he done you can give the state attorney to make a case?" He smiled at her. "I haven't had anybody to talk to before this. I keep going 'round and 'round."

She said, "I don't know how you've kept it in. You must think about it all the time."

"For a while I did."

"Why didn't you run, get as far away as you could?"

"I thought of that, too."

"But you stayed," Kyle said. She gave him an appraising look, thoughtful, as though to see into him and discover something he didn't understand himself. "Why?"

"I don't like to keep bringing it up," Stick said, "but I was into some heavy stuff and did time for it. I've met a lot of people with poor manners and ugly dispositions. Guys that chew with their mouth open. So it isn't like I'm new in the life. Something like this happens, the first thing you do is hide. Then you peek out. Then you come out a little way, look around. Come out a little farther. Finally you come all the way out, and in this particular situation a strange thing happened. Nobody recognized me."

"I did."

"Except you. I got to the point I was going to leave because I couldn't see myself going up to the top floor of Chucky's building, fifteen stories with a rail this high on the balcony, and demand anything. Like the five thousand for delivering the suitcase . . . Which he still owes. Then I go to work for Barry and find out he and Chucky are buddies, they double-date out on the boat. What's this, a sign? Maybe I should hang around, see what happens."

"What you're really saying," Kyle said, "you're not looking for a warm, safe place, are you? You like the action."

"I was in Las Vegas once," Stick said, "I was driving from L.A. to Detroit and I stopped in Las Vegas because I'd never seen it. I walked around all afternoon to the different hotels, lost twenty bucks, went back to the Travel Lodge and slept for a couple of hours. I went back out that evening, made the rounds again, had a warmed-over roast beef dinner at one of the hotels, lost forty bucks . . . Nothing had changed from the afternoon. The same people were playing the slot machines, there was the same litter and dust. There was a longer line now for the show at the Frontier, see Wayne Newton in his outfit. The place is all colored lights and chrome, red carpeting—you know what it looks like—but it's dirty, like a circus. Everything looks soiled. I couldn't get out of there fast enough. I drove straight through the night and most of the next day to Vail, Colorado. From all that phony glitter to Vail, where even the Holiday Inn sign is carved on a log; you have to look to find the name of the place. I go in a restaurant there, now it's all crepes and patty melts. People at the next table are ordering claret and soda, talking about the Woody Allen film they're going to see. And you know what? I walked around there half a day, the place bored the shit out of me, I had to get back to Detroit . . . You been to Vegas?"

"Couple of times."

"You like it?"

"How about cheap perfume covering up b.o.?"

"There you are. You been to Vail?"

"Once, in the summer."

"You like it?"

"It's all right. I wouldn't want to buy a place there and have to go all the time."

"Good, you know what I'm talking about," Stick said. "Could you live down on South Beach?"

"Well, it's an interesting area—yes, I could live there for a while."

"But you like Palm Beach."

"It's clean," Kyle said.

"See, I don't have a goal 'cause I don't seem to know what I want. Money, yeah, you have to have money. But I wouldn't want to be Barry, I wouldn't trade with him, live the way he does . . . You think I'm looking for action?" He seemed intent, wanting an answer.

"No, I said you like the action. You seem to."

"Maybe I do, to a certain extent. People race cars two hundred miles an hour, climb mountains . . . I tend to get in the way of people who carry firearms. Or I put myself in the way."

Kyle hesitated, staring. "I hate to ask, but . . . it's happened before?"

"As a matter of fact, twice."

"People have tried to kill you?"

"Well, two guys tried to mug me one time. One had a gun, the other a knife . . ."

"Yeah?"

"I shot 'em. I didn't feel I had a choice. The other time, two guys that Frank and I were doing business with set us up. We had a meeting, it was suppose to be a pay-off; but they came out with guns instead of money, so . . . I shot 'em. I've shot four people. I'm not the least bit prejudiced, I don't know if you happen to know that, but I'm not. But I've shot four people and all four happened to be colored guys. I mean it just happened that way. My closest friend in the can, outside of Frank, was a black guy. I get along great with Cornell Lewis, he's black . . . It's very strange."

Kyle said, carefully, taking her time, "Is there anything else you'd like to tell me? About yourself?"

"I think we're up to date now," Stick said. "I told you about my daughter . . ."

"A little."

"I hope you can get to meet her sometime."

"I'd like to."

"The only thing I haven't told you about is the tornado I was in when I was nine years old, in Norman. That was the scaredest I've ever been in my life, see a house blow away, gone . . . It was before we moved to Detroit."

She said, again carefully, "You accept what happens to you. You have the ability to detach yourself, look at things objectively."

He frowned. "You mean after or during?"

"I'm trying to find out what moves you."

"I thought I told you—being with you. But you don't believe me."

"You want to sleep with me, that's all."

He stared at her face in shadowed light, wanting to touch her.

"You're smarter than that," Stick said. "I know you're smarter than I am, that doesn't bother me. If I were the money whiz and you were, say, a bartender, you'd still be smarter only it wouldn't be as obvious. It doesn't matter who's what, we can talk without beating around. I could tell you I'm in love with you and you can be glad to hear it or you can clutch up and want to run, but there it is . . . What do you think?"

She hesitated. "Are you being romantic now?"

"I'm trying to tell you how I feel without exposing myself. You know what I mean."

"Playing it safe."

"I guess. I don't know."

She said, "I have a feeling you don't see us walking off into the sunset."

"In a way, that's what I *do* see," Stick said. "They kiss and it says The End. What happens after that is the part that's kind of hazy. Me coming home with cement dust all over my work clothes and pulling my pickup into the garage next to your Porsche."

She said, "Why not sell investments? I know you have the talent and I could help you get started."

"Well, it'd be better than you learning a building trade. And I would appreciate your help and pay attention. But I'd also be a little, well, uneasy."

"Why?"

"I'd be afraid—don't laugh, but I'd be afraid you'd try to make me over, into somebody else."

She didn't laugh; she was surprised. "Why would I do that?"

"I don't mean intentionally, I don't think you'd be aware of it. I think it's an instinct girls have, some girls, anyway. Like wanting to have a horse when they're around twelve. Young girls write to guys doing time; they think they can bring out the good person that's inside this mean, miserable son of a bitch that hates everybody. Or I'd start wearing suits and change on my own, become somebody else. You'd look at me and think, who's this guy? What happened to that nice, simple boy from Norman?"

She smiled a little as he did. "The nice, simple boy from Norman. That's how you see yourself? Come on, tell me the truth."

Stick shrugged. "Raised on an oil lease."

Looking right at him she said, "You know what you are, Ernest? You're a snob. You love the idea of living by your wits. Why would a slick guy like you want to work and lose your independence? Isn't that about it?"

He smiled again to see if she'd smile back. She did, staring at him with a glow in her eyes he would accept as mild admiration. They were having fun. He said, "You think I'm slick, huh?"

"*You* think you are."

"Uh-unh, I look in the mirror I see what's there, nothing else. But I learned in prison I can get along with myself and have a pretty good time without breaking my neck, or joining a club where you have to listen to *Alley Cat* . . . Rich people sure have fun, don't they?"

"You'd love to have money," Kyle said. "Don't tell me you wouldn't."

"Some. How 'bout you? How much you make a year?"

"Why?"

"Come on, how much?"

"I average better than a hundred thousand."

"And you live in Palm Beach 'cause it's clean."

"Don't oversimplify. I'm not tied to where I live or *how* I live. I can be as independent as you believe you are."

"But you're tired of helping people make money who don't need it and I come along, I look like a worthy cause. Help the underprivileged."

She raised her eyebrows and said, "That's not bad, Ernest, you may be right," and looked at him thoughtfully. "The deserving free spirit, just a regular guy, rehabilitated after a couple of trips to prison, and now . . . What's your game, Ernest? Tell me what you have in mind."

It surprised him. "You think I've been putting you on?"

"No, no, I think basically you're a straight-shooter—within your own frame of values . . ."

"I've told you things I've never told anybody."

She was nodding. "Yes, I know you have. Past things. But you haven't told me your plan."

"What plan?"

"How you're going to get Chucky to pay the five thousand he owes."

Stick let a silence fill in space between them, a pause while he smiled and admired those knowing eyes. When he felt time was up he said, "You got any ideas?"

They took a cab back. They walked through trees roundabout to the guest house and slipped inside while torches burned on the patio and faraway sounds drifted across the yard. Later, when they heard the door-chime and Barry's voice call "Babe?" they held each other without moving. They heard him bump something on the patio and held their breath.

Much later Kyle opened the draperies covering the glass doors and they had the bay and the nighttime sky to themselves. They whispered.

"There's nothing wrong with you, Ernie."

"Thank you."

"My polite lover."

Still later they heard doors bang, faint voices in the adjoining wing of the guest house. "Mr. Firestone," Kyle said. "It seems he's not alone." She left the bed and put on a light wrap.

"Hold a glass to the wall," Stick said. "You can hear what they're saying."

Kyle left the bedroom. A lamp went on in the living room. Stick lay without moving, neck bent against the pillow. Kyle came back. She stood in the doorway with a folder in her hands, looking at a sheet of paper that was attached to it.

"What's that?"

"The revised prospectus." She didn't look up. "And the guest list for tomorrow. Barry must've dropped it through the mail slot."

"I guess I'd better sneak off to my own room." Stick rolled out of bed and began looking for his shorts. "I'm suppose to help serve tomorrow, if you can picture that."

He heard her say, "You can't . . ." On his hands and knees looking under the bed.

"I'll try not to spill anything on you."

"*No*—you can't be here tomorrow."

Her tone brought his head up to look at her across the rumpled bed. "Why not?"

Kyle held out the sheet of paper. "Chucky's coming. Both of them, Chucky and his friend, Nestor Soto."

19

Leo Firestone told Barry he was a genius setting the morning room up for the conference: the long tables pushed together covered in bright yellow—dynamic color—the directors' chairs—very subtle—and right outside across the bay, Miami. "Where it's all happening," Firestone said with his glasses up on his bald head. "A cinema verité backdrop for the presentation. You weren't so fucking rich, Bare, I'd hire you for my art director."

As Stick and Cornell stood by Barry said, "It's your baby, Leo, but I do feel some responsibility. If the deal's got legs I don't want to see it crash and burn on account of something I neglected to do. Now how about the bar? You want it?"

Firestone began nodding with enthusiasm. "Yes, absolutely. I think the tone, the ambience we want should be very relaxed. I'm not making a pitch, I'm presenting a creative venture to a group of highly successful, intelligent men. I want them to understand they can let their hair down, say anything they want."

Stick watched him, fascinated. This was a Hollywood producer. This guy in the cowboy boots and tan cords, shirt hanging out: a strange, loose-fitting, ethnic-looking white shirt that some poor but clean peasant might wear, now on a fifty-year-old hipster. The guy's hair, brown and gray, hung from the circular edge of his bald, freckled crown almost to his shoulders. Stick had the feeling the guy liked the way he looked: tan, slim, not tall but with enough confidence he could slouch and not worry about his shoulders rounding on him.

Barry gestured to Stick and Cornell, waiting. "So bring the bar up. Set it in the arch there, be out of the way." He took Firestone down to the patio for coffee and Danish.

Kyle was at the umbrella table with Firestone's assistant, a tall, good-looking girl with dark hair cut short and hardly any breasts, though the ones she had were right there poking at her thin tank top. She wore her sunglasses up on her head, too. Cornell said her name was Jane, twenty-one years old. "The kind of girl you drop her off anywhere, I mean in the world, she'll find the man in charge and get next to him."

Stick said, "That mean you like her or not?"

"Means I have great admiration for the lady. I watched her last night serving them drinks and before that driving the car—thanks a whole lot . . ."

"It was my day off, he could've driven. Why didn't he pick 'em up?"

"Man was putting on his show. Called home twice, nobody answered. You and Kyle go someplace?"

"Went out to dinner."

"You walk?"

"Got a cab."

Cornell seemed to want to ask him more, but he said, "You watch this girl Jane. She still a baby, but that's the kind can go all the way, be a big name out'n Hollywood . . . While me and you gonna go down there and carry up the bar, get sweaty. Man, it's a bitch, ain't it, knowing enough to slip by, but not enough to make the run that will set you free."

"I don't think that way," Stick said.

Cornell said, "Yeah? Wait till I get you your white coat."

While they were setting up the bar, stocking it with bottles and glasses, Mrs. Stam came out with a bag of Jelly Bellies. She nodded to them. Stick watched her to see if she'd glance over, give him some kind of look. He hadn't seen her since they were both on the floor of this room early Sunday morning, a few feet from where she was pouring Jelly Bellies into a crystal jar. She was wearing a pale green sundress. Her legs from the knees down, Stick noticed, were straight but thick through the ankles; her instep seemed to puff out of her medium heels. When she was finished with the Jelly Bellies she asked them to come outside with her. Stick walked behind, watching Cornell talking to her, smiling and getting a smile back, watching her can roll from side to side. She wanted them to move the pots of begonias out of the drive, line them up along the edge of the grass overlooking the terrace. When they had finished she thanked them and walked away.

Stick said to Cornell, "You have any trouble talking to her?"

"Not too much."

"She looks at you," Stick said, "like she expects you to tell her something, but she never says anything."

Cornell said, "You got to say what she wants to hear, my man, then she'll talk to you."

"Got to push the right button, uh?"

Cornell said, dreamy, wise, "Got to find out where her interests lie, what activities please her most."

Telling the new man, the white boy.

"You could've fooled me," Stick said. "I thought all she liked to do was get laid."

He had on his white coat now over a white shirt with black tie and black pants. He believed he looked like a middle-aged busboy, a guy who had missed or blown whatever chances he'd had in life and was now on the way down. Which might not be bad. He certainly didn't look like a threat to anyone. He was at the bar slicing limes when Kyle came over. She surprised him.

She said, "I don't believe it." But without sounding serious, concerned.

"I don't either," Stick said, "but Barry'd rather have me over here than spilling stuff on people."

She said, "You know what I mean. You're still here."

"I think it's safer than out there somewhere, looking over my shoulder. If they're doing business with Barry they're not going to mess up his house, or get him involved. At least I hope."

"You might be right," Kyle said. "What're you going to say to Chucky?"

"Ask him what he wants to drink."

"Maybe you could poison him."

"Whatever anybody wants outside of whiskey and plain water they're taking a chance. I got limes, olives, cherries—what else do I need?"

"Balls," Kyle said. "But I guess you've got those, too."

The paring knife slipped on the tough skin of the lime Stick was holding, nicking the tip of his thumb. He said to her, "You're making me nervous."

By twelve-thirty the turnaround and upper end of the driveway resembled a Mercedes used car lot. There were six of them, the expensive BMW and two Cadillacs. Lionel Oliva and Avilanosa were the only drivers. They stood in the shade for a while, then wandered into the garage. When Cornell found them they were already inside the apartment, Lionel fooling with the TV set, Avilanosa looking around. Cornell said, "Oh." He said, "I spilled cocktail sauce on my pants, have to make a quick change." Lionel was tuning in a soap. "You all help yourself to beer and pop in the fridge, okay? But don't go in the bedrooms, if you don't mind, gents. Those are private quarters." Lionel said okay, sitting back, watching the soap. Avilanosa, looking into Stick's room from the hallway, didn't say anything.

Most of them were dressed casually and could be going out to play golf; two older men wore business suits. They all seemed to know one another, standing in groups, talking in loud, confident voices. Stick, behind the bar, decided the Cuban-looking guy wearing sunglasses and a brown silk suit that glistened and looked metallic was Nestor Soto. The man's expression never changed and he seemed to barely move his mouth as he spoke to Chucky. They stood apart from the others, Chucky waving the maids over to spear shrimp and hot meatballs from their trays. Stick saw Chucky glance over, chewing. Then Nestor was looking, staring at him.

Cornell, with a round tray, appeared before Stick to block his view.

"Two bloodies, a mimosa, two vodka tonic . . ."

"Wait a minute. What's a mimosa?"

"O.J. and champagne."

"Orange juice?"

"You got it. Two vodka tonic, then I want a Campari and soda . . ."

"Jesus Christ."

"That's the red one, underneath. And a salty dog."

"I quit," Stick said.

"Be cool. Tell me something—what did you mean, all she like to do is get laid?"

"Who, Diane?"

"Who we talking about? She come on to you?"

"Not in so many words." Not in *any* words. "No, I was kidding, I just think she's a little weird."

"She more like, formal about things . . . Listen, I make the salty dog. You make the bloodies, everybody will be happy."

"What do you put in it, tomato juice, what else?"

"Oh, shit," Cornell said.

After Cornell had moved off Stick saw Chucky looking over again. Chucky said something to Nestor Soto and started this way, coming around the conference table. But now Firestone's assistant, the girl in the tank top, stepped up to the bar.

"I guess Perrier."

Stick said, "Yes, ma'am," and poured her one. "Lime?"

"No, that's okay. It doesn't help it much."

"You don't like it," Stick said, "why do you drink it?"

She looked at him directly for the first time. Boyish from a distance this girl was a beauty up close, clean, precise features, perfect teeth. She said, "I thought all the cheeky help worked in L.A. Don't tell me you're an actor."

"I'm a chauffeur."

She looked at him for another moment, deadpan. "Well, you're not a comic, if you feel that's your gift."

Chucky stepped up next to the girl, laying a dozen used toothpicks on the bar. He said, "Honey, let me talk to this boy a minute, okay? Take your wah-wah someplace else."

The girl turned to Chucky with a pleasant expression, offering her hand. "Hi, I'm Jane, Mr. Firestone's assistant. You're Mr. Gorman, aren't you?"

Chucky took her hand. He said, "Jane, you want to be in show biz you ought to do some exercise, build up those pectorals."

Stick watched the girl smile as she shrugged, a nice lazy move. She said, "I work behind the camera, Mr. Gorman, so it really doesn't matter if I have tits or don't have them, does it?" She said, "Very nice meeting you," and walked away.

Chucky said, "How 'bout that?" looking past his shoulder. "That's a spunky girl, you know it?" He came back to Stick. "And you have to be some kind of spunky fella, hanging around here. We been looking all *over* for you."

Stick said, "How come?"

"Well, we thought you might be confused, what happened to Rainy . . ."

Barry's voice said, "Gentlemen, if you'll take a seat, we'd like to get started."

Stick leaned on the bar. He said, "Chucky?" and waited as he glanced around at Barry and then at Nestor. Chucky seemed anxious now. "I did time, twice, and made it, no problem."

"I heard that," Chucky said.

"Doesn't it tell you anything? Am I gonna go to Metro, give 'em a statement? They punch a button my sheet's on the screen. I say I was *there*, they gonna believe I was just watching?"

Barry's voice said, "Gentlemen . . . Chucky, hey, come on!"

Chucky said to Stick, "I'm not your problem, man. Nestor wants to talk to you."

"That's fine," Stick said. Chucky started to turn away and Stick said, "Hey, Chucky? I'm not a problem long as you pay what you owe me."

Chucky frowned at him. "You talking about?"

"Five grand," Stick said. "The suitcase was delivered, wasn't it?"

Chucky stared; he seemed about to say something, but Barry called his name again and Chucky walked over to the conference table.

Barry introduced Leo Firestone, who rose and said, "Gentlemen, when you're making love to a Jewish woman, you know how to tell when she reaches her climax?" He looked down the long table of impassive faces. "My dear wife Roz, the original princess, mother of two fine boys, Scott and Sherm, always blushes becomingly when I get to the punch line. Okay, from the top. You're making love to a Jewish woman—you know how to tell when she reaches her climax?" Firestone snapped his fingers. "Cue the blush from Roz. Punch line: she drops her emery board."

Barry raised his eyebrows. "It's true, believe me."

Firestone said, "What I want to do here is get you guys to drop your emery boards and realize this isn't another dry, boring investment proposal. It's an opportunity to have some fun for a change around a conference table. A profit opportunity to get those twenty million or more people who go to the movies every week to drop *their* emery boards, buy tickets and contribute to your financial stability. You with me so far?"

Jesus Christ, Stick thought.

From what he could see, behind the bar, Barry was with the guy. The others down the table seemed patient but that was about all. Each one of them had a prospectus at his place; some were open. Chucky leaned toward Nestor and whispered something, maybe translating; Nestor's face immobile, carved from dark wood. At the foot of the table Kyle sat next to the girl in the tank top, Jane; Kyle looking at the prospectus, Jane staring out at Biscayne Bay.

Firestone said, "I'm not going to go over the figures with you. It's all in the offering circular and you guys know far more about how limited partnerships are structured than I ever will, doing my number over on the creative side. But I want to mention something that's not in the prospectus I'll explain in detail later. And that is, even if this project doesn't get off the ground for one reason or another, I'll give you a tax write-off of two and a half times your investment. Gimme shelter is still the name of the tune, when you can pull it off."

Stick saw Kyle paying attention to that, making notes. The girl in the tank top was still looking out at the bay.

Firestone said, "So what we've got in Starsky and Hutch . . ." He grinned. "Testing you, see if you're paying attention. What we've got in *Shuck and Jive* are a couple of laid-back undercover operatives privy to, if you will, all the shit, all the scummy stuff going down in the Miami area. These guys might look like hippie bums to you gentlemen, but I want to relate to that vast fourteen to twenty-four audience out there. We'll see them cleaned up, too; but what I want to emphasize, these guys are pros. All the collars they've made down in Little Havana, I mean if you handcuffed them all side by side, lined them up, you'd have a spicket fence."

Stick watched Firestone, the dumb shit, look out over the audience. The man's gaze met Jane's and Stick saw her shake her head, twice, and nod toward the table where Nestor was staring at Firestone with his trancelike expression.

"If there's anyone here of Hispanic persuasion," Firestone said, "that's a bit of harmless levity along the lines I like to have a little fun with my Jewish ladies, God love 'em. No, we've been fortunate since the Bay of Pigs to receive into our land, our hearts, a great number of highly respectable and successful Spanish-speaking people. No, what we're talking about in *Shuck and Jive*, the film, is another element entirely. The garbage that has washed up on our shores, the gangsters, the murderers, who traffic in the sale of controlled substances with no regard whatsoever for human life."

Stick kept watching Nestor Soto. If he knew the guy and was sitting next to him, he'd give him a nudge with his elbow. Beautiful, sitting there listening to the bald-headed asshole from Hollywood.

"You read every day, I'm sure," Firestone said, "about the cocaine busts, the boatloads of marijuana confiscated, the gangland-type killings and murders. But, gentlemen, let me assure you it's only the tip of the iceberg you read about. If the papers even printed half the facts I've uncovered in my research it would literally curl your hair." Firestone patted the top of his head. "Fortunately I'm immune. I can look at the raunchy underbelly of the dope business, look at the vermin that live there with the eye of the artist and select its most dramatic elements for portrayal in a major motion picture." He held up the palms of his hands to the table. "But you ask me my source I'll plead the Fifth, so don't, okay? Believe me, you would not want to know these people."

Barry said, "Leo, let's move on to casting, okay?" Barry wide eyed, trying to appear innocent and interested at the same time.

Stick counted heads at the table. He believed Firestone had already lost three of his prospective investors—Chucky, Nestor and the guy who ran Wolfgang's, Gabe something—and might have to run for it before he was through. He sure seemed dumb for a Hollywood producer about to make another major motion picture.

Firestone moved to casting and told of several actors who had read the property and "flipped" and were under serious consideration. "You know," Firestone said, "what's his name. Tremendously successful recording star, plays Vegas." He looked down the center of the table.

And Jane said, "Neil Diamond."

"Right, Neil Diamond. He's perfect for the part of Jive, who plays cocktail piano as his cover . . . For Shuck we're considering . . . I have to tell you Sly Stallone turned it down—okay, that happens—due to commitments, but . . . what's his name, the guy that rides the motorcycle, the cop . . ."

"Erik Estrada," Jane said.

Jesus Christ, Stick thought. Warren Oates dead, you bonehead, could play it better than Erik Estrada.

"Erik Estrada is a real possibility." Firestone held up crossed fingers. "We're considering Laurence Olivier—Sir Laurence, I should say—for the role of Domingo, the wise old Cuban who turns snitch. It's a beautiful little cammie, could win Larry another best-supporting nomination. And for the female lead we're seriously considering . . . she was an answer on *Tic Tac Dough* the other night. The one that's emceed by my good friend Wink Martindale, reaches millions . . ."

"Linda Blair," Jane said.

"That's the girl, Linda Blair. Tremendously successful in . . . you remember, the kid throws up the pea soup?"

"*The Exorcist*," Jane said.

Firestone extended his arm, pointing to the back of the room. "My lovely assistant, Jane. If you wonder what I'd do without her . . . Listen, I'm going to open this up to the board of directors in a minute, you guys, and ask what you think of the story and what film stars you like that we might consider. There are a number of cameos I wouldn't be surprised one or two of you gentlemen"—looking at Chucky and Nestor—"might not fit perfectly. And don't tell me you'd turn it down. We're going to do this picture our way, gentlemen. Sell off foreign rights, TV, cable, which will more than recoup your investment before the picture is even released. Then let the majors bid for domestic distribution. I wasn't going to tell you this—but since I've got a handshake on it—listen up. Wherever David Begelman locates—and I know in my heart he'll be back in the thick of the action any day now—we'll cut a distribution deal. Take my word."

Stick poured a Jack Daniel's and stooped down to straighten the shelf beneath the bar while Firestone talked about bank loans and tax benefits, words that were hard to understand because they did not offer things to picture. By the time Stick finished his drink and stood up, Barry was saying, with his head cocked, "Yeah, I think I like it. I wouldn't mind seeing more broads in it. I think we could lighten the story up, show that *many* of the dealers are good guys that're only giving the public what they want. But on the whole I have to say, yeah, I think I like it very much."

Chucky said, "I think you're going to have to lighten it up considerably. I think you might even have to turn a few things around . . ."

Firestone winked and said, "That's the kind of input we want. Listen, we can write in walk-ons for any pretty faces you gentlemen might consider star material."

Barry said, "Okay, any questions about the investment itself, the risk, the tax angle? Anybody? Kyle, how about you? You have any questions?"

Stick watched her, seated with a pad of paper and the open prospectus on her lap. The girl in the tank top was watching her too, closely.

"Or any comments?" Barry said.

"Just one," Kyle said. "It sounds to me like a tax fraud."

Firestone pretended to do a double-take and then smiled, leaning over the table on his hands.

"I beg your pardon?"

Kyle said, "You want to raise a million here, a hundred thousand from each investor . . ."

"Very good," Firestone said, animated.

". . . take it to the bank and leverage another million and a half . . ."

"I think you've got it."

". . . and allow the investors to write off the bank loan even though they're not obligated to the bank. You are, but they aren't."

"By Jove, I think she's got it," Firestone said.

What an asshole, Stick thought. He wanted Kyle to let him have it. The girl in the tank top was sitting up straight, giving Kyle her full attention.

"I'm teasing you, sweetheart," Firestone said, "but you're right. We sign a recourse note to a bank payable in five years. So the guys each get to write off two-hundred and fifty thousand. Their hundred grand investment plus their share of the note, another hundred and fifty grand. *But* . . . here's the sweet spot of the deal. I give them each a signed memo that states they're not responsible for the bank loan. They've already written it off. And by the time the note comes due, in five years, the statute will have run out and the IRS won't be able to touch them. Now I think that's pretty cute, if I have to say so myself."

"Adorable," Kyle said. "Except the statute of limitations has nothing to do with it. When you forgive them a note that's due in five years—which they've already written off—then five years from now each investor will be a hundred and fifty thousand dollars ahead. Which is the same as income, and they'll have to declare it and pay tax on it. If you don't believe me, ask the IRS."

Firestone stared at her, half-smiling. "You serious?"

Kyle didn't answer him.

"Well," Firestone said, playing to the audience, giving the rich guys a palms-up, what-can-I-do shrug, "what it comes down to, really, is that age-old entrepreneurial question . . . who's to know?"

Kyle gave him her nice-girl smile and said, "I will, Mr. Firestone. That's why I say it's fraud . . ."

"Your interpretation . . ." Firestone said.

". . . and why I would advise any one of my clients to run if they ever see you coming."

Stick began to clap—four times before deciding he'd better knock it off. Kyle was smiling at him.

Cornell came over to the bar. "Three scotch, two vodka tonic. You learn anything?"

"Never open your mouth," Stick said, "when you're fulla shit. What happened—they're ordering regular drinks?"

It was interesting, everybody talking now, getting into it among themselves. Stick saw Kyle and the girl in the tank top in close conversation, the girl on the edge of her seat, nodding as she listened. While at the other end of the table Barry, shaking his head with a solemn expression—What can I tell you?—seemed to be finishing Firestone off, denying a reprieve.

Stick turned to watch Kyle and found Chucky standing at the bar, directly in front of him.

"Nestor's ready to talk to you."

20

They stood in acacia shade among expensive automobiles, Nestor looking him over, making no pretext of doing anything else, in control, letting Stick know it would be up to him.

Stick was not going to push him. There was a ritual of respect to be observed here, at the least a show of deference to the man who could order your death if he wanted it. Still, the way Stick saw it, he wasn't going to wait forever.

He said, "How long's it been? Three, four weeks? If I told Metro you'd a heard from them by now. Don't you think?" Trying not to get a plea in his voice. But the Cuban was not an ordinary-looking Cuban made up of black and Spanish parts going back four hundred years. This was an Indian-looking Cuban with a mask face he must have practiced for some time and could use now when he needed to scare hell out of people without saying a word. Who was he? What did he do on Sunday? Did he let his wife yell at him?

"What else can I tell you?" Stick said.

Chucky said, "You can tell me where a blue Chevy van's at for openers."

"Last seen in Bayfront Park," Stick said, "or impounded. You think I was gonna wait and talk to those guys? Moke's got his gun *out*, in his hand. The other guy, he didn't look like he even needed one. I left, that's all." He said to Chucky, "What would you do?"

Nestor kept staring at him.

Stick felt like pushing the Cuban. Let the Cuban take a swing and then belt him, crack the mask. He felt his stomach getting tighter and knew he would have to think, take his time before he said anything. But what was there to say? You didn't tell this guy anything, you listened. It tightened him up even more to realize that.

Nestor, staring, said, "I don't know . . ."

Stick asked him, "What do you want me to do?"

Nestor took his time. "You in the business?"

"No, I'm driving for Mr. Stam. That's all I'm doing."

"You were with Rene."

"That's right, I was with him, that's all."

"Got some action going, I understand," Chucky said, "selling tips on the stock market. I mean this is an enterprising guy," Chucky said to Nestor. "He came right out and asked me . . . You won't believe this. The suitcase Rainy had? He tells me he wants five grand for making the delivery. Right here, while he's working the bar."

"Well, it was delivered," Stick said, "and that's what you told us you'd pay."

Nestor's eyes moved, a momentary look of interest, mild surprise.

Stick saw it. He said, "What am I doing? Am I down at the state attorney's office? I'm standing here talking to you."

Nestor said, "You ever been to that office?"

"I don't even know where it is."

"By the courts, Northwest Twelfth," Nestor said. "They put a wire on you?"

"You want to feel me?"

"No, I don't feel you," Nestor said.

"He's not wired," Chucky said. "They wouldn't wire him for something like this, listen to all the bullshit. But he was a friend of Rainy's. How good a friend, that's what I want to know." Talking tough in front of Nestor.

Stick began to wonder which one was the problem, getting right down to it. Maybe it wasn't Nestor. Maybe he could talk to Nestor, but not in front of Chucky. It was a feeling and did not come from anything Nestor said or the way the man stared at him. It was like trying to decide who you would rather talk to: a man who might shoot you in the back, or a man who tells you to your face he's going to kill you?

This was in his mind now as he said to Nestor, not to Chucky, "I gotta go back to work. You want to talk to me sometime, give me a call. I'll be right here." Stick walked away.

It was Chucky who yelled after him, "Hey! I'm not done with you!" So he kept walking.

Chucky found Lionel and Avilanosa. While they were moving cars like parking attendants to work Nestor's Cadillac out of the turnaround, Chucky said, "What do you think?"

Nestor said, "It don't sound like *The Godfather*. I don't think this movie would be very good."

"I mean the guy," Chucky said, "Ernest Stickley. What do we do with him?"

"What do you want to do with him?"

"You were the one, I remember correctly, was so anxious to find him."

"Yes, and we did," Nestor said. "Now I don't worry about him so much. He ask a good question, what do you want him to do?" Nestor brushed at a fly close to his face, hand limp, diamond ring giving off a faint gleam. "He's here, he's not talking to nobody. I think what bothers you is what he wants ***you*** to do, uh? You promise Rene five thousand dollar?"

"I might have. Yeah, I probably said five to hook him. But you and I know it wasn't that kind of deal. Rainy's not coming back I'm not gonna pay him, am I?"

"Well, you made a deal and somebody come back."

"I didn't make it with ***him***."

Nestor smiled, a slight easing at the corners of his mouth. "He say to you, it was deliver, wasn't it?"

"See, that's what I mean," Chucky said. "Guy acts like he's got it coming. I didn't hire him, I hired Rainy."

"Yes, you keep telling me that. But it was deliver . . ."

"You think that's funny?"

"I think you can believe him."

"I'm not gonna give him five grand . . . Why would I give him anything?"

"I don't know," Nestor said.

"You think I should?"

"It's your business, not mine."

Chucky said, "But if I don't . . . I'm thinking out loud. A guy like that, you don't know what he might do. I mean something crazy. You know?"

"Then pay him."

"I don't owe him a fucking thing."

"Then get rid of him."

"What would you do?"

Nestor looked up at Chucky through his tinted glasses. "I don't know what I would do. I have no feeling about it, it isn't my business."

"I could argue that one with you. You're the one got the delivery. You were the other end of the deal."

"But I only promise to kill the delivery man, whoever it is," Nestor said. "And I keep my promise." He walked over to his car, Avilanosa holding the door open, and got in.

Big help . . .

Somebody had tossed his room. Emptied the drawers on the floor, pulled the bed covers apart, turned the mattress cocked half off the box spring. His magazines were still on the dresser. And the original prospectus Kyle had given him to read. The one in which thirty-five investors put in seventy-two thousand and something each and didn't involve the tricky bank loan part that Kyle said was a fraud. Stick took the prospectus over to his one bedroom chair—green plastic that was supposed to look like leather—sat down and began reading the film offering again, understanding most of it now and wondering why Firestone hadn't brought it out when Kyle shot down the other scheme. Except the story wasn't going to sell anyway. Christ, Shuck and Jive. Were they really that dumb out there?

Cornell said, "Oh, man," sadly, from the doorway. "I was afraid something like this might happen. Wasn't nothing I could do."

Stick looked over. "Who was it?"

"Nestor's man, his father-in-law. The big motherfucker looks like the bouncer at a live-sex show. He found out what he was looking for? Or shouldn't I ask?"

"Wasn't anything to find," Stick said. "Less he's trying to tell me something."

"Well, you cool about it. Didn't mess up your stuff too much?"

"No, it's okay." Stick wasn't interested in Nestor's father-in-law. He said, "The guy wasn't too quick, was he? Mr. Firestone."

"Man should be parking cars. He went to pack, gonna leave. Him and his little girl having an argument about something."

"She seemed pretty sharp."

"Has good instincts, but a few things to learn. I told you, she still a baby."

Stick straightened, smiled, and Cornell glanced over his shoulder at Kyle standing behind him and got out of her way so she could look in.

She said, "I don't know why, I thought you'd be neater than this."

"Somebody looking for the microfilm," Cornell said. "Did you know this man was a secret agent?"

She seemed concerned for a moment, but said, "I know he has secrets." Giving it a light touch.

They went into the sitting room, Stick telling her she was a star while Cornell popped open cans of beer. They put their feet up and did quick Leo Firestone sketches, recalling memorable moments—Firestone dumping on Hispanics right in front of Nestor—Stick saying he wouldn't have believed it if he hadn't seen it. Cornell saying, man, we should make the movie, put some real life in it.

"Chucky had the best idea," Kyle said, "but I don't think anyone heard him. He said lighten up and turn it around. I remember a story in the *Herald* about customs agents finding two hundred and thirty-six pounds of cocaine in a cargo jet—I think it said with a street value of a hundred and forty-seven *million*; but there wasn't anyone they could prove had knowledge of it. So all that coke's sitting in some storeroom."

"The Feds licking their lips," Cornell said. "I like the one, the customs plane chases the smuggler from Bimini, the man running out of gas and has to ditch, so he lands at Homestead, man, of all places, right at the customs *base*, where they keep their airplanes, and while they running around looking for him he goes in the office and steals the names and addresses of all the customs dudes. You dig it? Wait. Then—listen now—the man sends an announcement to all the customs dudes saying he's made it, he's quitting and, listen, invites them all to his retirement party in Nassau."

Stick liked it. "They go?"

"Would have to quit their jobs or sneak over to do it. No, the man said he would even send a jet plane over, pick 'em up. But the fools—you know what I mean? They could have gone over there, talk to the man drunk out of his mind celebrating and learn all his tricks. But no, the man in charge of the customs dudes won't let 'em go."

Stick said, "Instead of the guy taking the names and addresses—no, the one guy, Shuck, takes the names and addresses and Jive finds the two-hundred and thirty-six pounds of coke ... Except how's he going to lift it?"

Cornell said, "It ain't all in one cake, man, it's in bags. See-through baggies inside of burlap sacks; you know, inside something. They take it out, make two trips each, do it easy."

Kyle said, "I think the names would definitely have to go. Shuck and Jive. How about ... Stick and Cornell?"

"Frank and Ernest," Stick said. "But it doesn't have any punch, does it? Just lays there."

"Can't be too real," Cornell said. "Yeah, has to have some zip. Zip and Punch ... Sock and Pizazz."

"Sacco and Vanzetti," Kyle said. "How about Ron and Rick at the Seashore?"

"No, you know what the title is?" Stick said. "The two dopers rip off the Feds, walk away with a hundred and forty-seven million dollars worth of coke? Scam."

"That says it all," Kyle said.

"Yeah, Scam," Cornell said, grinning, dragging the word. "You want to hear a true story maybe we can work in? The gardener that comes here twice a week? Man's Colombian." Cornell still grinning. "You know what's coming, don't you? I had him put in a patch over the other side of the guest house among the hibiscus. Ain't Santa Marta, not the same kind of soil, you know? Won't make dreadlocks grow out of your head either. But it's fine domestic weed. What I'm saying, who wants some?"

Barry appeared. At first he looked surprised. Then sad, left out. Then waved his hand in front of his face and clutched his throat as though he couldn't breathe, wanting to be one of them. Brow furrowed, helpless, he said, "You know how far away you can smell this party you're having?"

Cornell, grinning: "Tell us, Mr. Stam."

"The Coast Guard station. I just saw a boat coming up from Government Cut . . . Gimme a hit."

Barry put his feet up with them. He said he should've held the meeting in here, get everybody zonked and decadent on a strong stone, get them good and banged—using all the words he knew—then present the movie deal. He said, "Leo Norman Firestone Presents told the emery board one, he should've started with the one, You know how to stop a Jewish broad from screwing? Marry her." He said to Cornell, "You like that one, huh? Little ethnic humor? You know how they know Adam was white? . . . You ever try to take a rib from a jig? I would've said black gentleman but it doesn't work as good. Okay?" He said to Kyle, "You ought to change your name"—Kyle and Stick giving each other a look—"to Hernia. Hernia, the ball buster. I say that, you understand, with affection, with deep admiration. Hernia McLaren. Try and con me, pal, I'll take your nuts home in my purse." He said to Stick, "Since this is not your day off, Stickley, and you're supposedly on the job I believe? Could I ask you to do something for me, if it's not too much trouble?"

Stick said, "It depends what it is."

Barry said, "He's not kidding. He makes it sound like he's playing along, but he isn't. I don't know—I think the help around here has more fun than the ... whatever the fuck I am. Sometimes I'm not too sure."

Cornell said, "You the master, Mr. Stam. The head dude."

"Thank you," Barry said, and looked at Stick again. "If you have time and it doesn't interfere with your plans too much ..."

Even with a buzz Stick was getting tired of smiling.

"... would you mind driving Leo Norman Firestone and his flat-chested assistant to the airport in about an hour?"

When Stick hesitated Barry said, "What're you doing, thinking it over?"

Stick said, "Mr. Stam, it sounds easy enough," and stared at him, straight faced. "But there's a mile of wire in a screen door."

He watched Barry nod with a thoughtful expression. It was good dope.

Eddie Moke picked up the black Cadillac, BS-2, coming out of Bal Harbour, identified Stickley driving—his window down as he went out the gate—but not the people in the back seat. Moke followed the limo all the way crosstown to Miami International ... goddamnit, where he had to be wide awake in all that airport traffic, not get faked out. It was coming on dusk, which was good, but made keeping the limo in sight harder.

Moke was operating on his own this trip, needing no orders or plan other than his will to get Mr. Stickley in a fix and shoot holes in him. He hoped then to find 105 dollars in Stickley's wallet. Forty for the Bullrider straw Stickley had run over and 65 for what he'd had to pay to get the van out of the Miami city pound. Chucky had asked him one time, "They ever let you out of the chute?"

Fat turd. There'd come a time he'd settle with Chucky. Most likely be told to and he'd take pleasure in it.

But this one now had become personal.

Wait till Stickley was alone going back. Run him off the road ... Or cut past him and open up, *yeah*, with the nickel-plate Mag and blow the sucker right out of his Cadillac saddle. If the chance didn't come he could always slip into that garage where he lived. Do it late at night.

Go on over to Nestor's after and tell him about it. Say, what else you need done? Nestor would be lost somewhere in his head or not believe it and him and Avilanosa would start laughing and speeling in Cuban and that's when he'd take the fellas ears out, wrapped in a hanky, and drop them on the table like a couple of dried apricots.

"You believe me now, señor?" Moke said out loud, looking through the windshield at the Cadillac parked with its trunk open, five cars ahead and two rows over in the traffic, by the Eastern sign. Then squinted and said, "The hell's going on?"

The man was walking away with his suitcase, shaking his head at a skycap. But now the skinny girl in the red undershirt was getting back in the car . . .

21

Jane sat in front with Stick on the way back to Miami Beach. He drove in silence, letting her come back down after the yelling match with Firestone all the way to the airport. The guy accusing her of not preparing him for the meeting, the spics. The girl actually telling him if he hadn't opened his mouth so ridiculously wide he wouldn't have been able to put his foot in it. Stick had kept his eyes on the mirror most of the way there.

He would still look at the mirror from time to time. They were on 112 heading east when Stick told her he'd kept waiting for the guy to fire her.

"He can't afford to," the girl said.

Whatever that meant. Did she have something on him?

She seemed relaxed now. She said, "You told me you were a chauffeur—remember, this afternoon? I thought you were trying to be funny."

"I don't think it's funny," Stick said, "at all."

"Well, some people are what they say they are," Jane said, "but not many. Especially in the industry. What they do, they talk on the phone, they take meetings and go to screenings and put down everything they see. They make wry, supposedly clever comments, but too loud and dumb to be clever. Because—you know why? They don't like pictures. If they didn't happen to be in the industry they wouldn't even go see them, ever. Bunch of fucking lawyers and business types . . . You know any lawyers that see pictures, actually go to a theater and buy a ticket?"

Stick said, "I've only known two and they didn't do me much good."

"The lawyers and the business types answer to the egomaniacs running the conglomerates that own the majors and none of them knows dick about film or has any kind of feeling for it," Jane said. "You want a development deal now you have to bring them a story that takes place on a giant pinball machine with a lot of flashing lights. Special effects, that's the name of the game. You don't have ten million bucks worth of special effects in the script you're fucked. You see *E.T.*?"

"Not yet."

"Mary Poppins goes electronic. Flying bicycles and Valley kids talking cute-dirty. I'd rate it right up there with that Velveeta cheese commercial, everybody's trying to promote a slice of cheese off this little boy and he won't give them any."

"I'll wait'll it's on TV," Stick said. He looked over at her sitting close to the door, tan bare shoulders slumped. She looked worn out. "Firestone a lawyer?"

"It's grossing three million a *day.* No, he's not a lawyer. Leo's problem, he doesn't have any talent. He makes rotten pictures. Did you see *The Cowboy and the Alien*?"

"I missed it . . . How come you work for him?"

"Because at least he makes pictures and I felt I could learn *some*thing, just being around. You ever read John O'Hara?"

"I might've."

"There's a character in one of his stories, an actor by the name of Doris Arlington. She works hard, she makes it, the studio finally gives her a contract that reflects her ability. Doris signs it, puts the pen down and says, 'There. I'll never suck another Jewish cock.' She isn't showing prejudice. She's saying she'll never again submit to people who have no understanding or feeling for her art. Well, I'm still submitting. I'll work on a picture I know is a piece of shit, because at least I'll be working."

"You like movies."

"I love them. I want to produce my own."

"Not *Shuck and Jive?*"

"Jesus . . ."

"How about—call it *Scam.* The two guys're dopers now. They walk into customs in the middle of the day and con them out of a hundred and forty-seven million dollars worth of top-grade cocaine."

"Starring Elliott Gould and George Segal," Jane said. "I saw it. Make it twenty-million dollars worth. Even with inflation it's a lot." She paused and said, "Considering some of the investors I think even Leo would've had a better chance of selling it."

"You think so?"

"He really blew it."

"How do you know some of those guys're into dope?"

"Nestor Soto? He practically wears a sign. And the pudgy one, Chucky. Barry hinted around he's a dealer."

"You like Barry?"

"I know a hundred and ninety-nine Barrys. They come with interchangeable one-liners."

"You think he deals?"

She turned enough to face Stick. "Is that what you're trying to find out? You're not really a chauffeur, are you?"

"Not in real life," Stick said, his gaze on Miami Beach in the distance, pale structures against the darkening sky. "Firestone said the Eden Roc, right? We natives call it just the Roc."

"What were you in real life?"

"That's a hard one. I'm still trying to decide what I want to be when I grow up."

"How about a cop?" She seemed to have hold of something and wasn't going to let go.

"Why do you say that?"

"You ask questions like a cop. Slip them in, no hurry, very

patient. What're you, a narc? . . . Well, it doesn't matter. You're not going to tell me if you are."

"Nobody's ever accused me of that before," Stick said. "Jesus, a narc . . ."

"I worked for a casting company when I first started. I'd make you any day as an undercover cop."

Stick thought for a minute, getting a glimpse of Biscayne Bay now, the little ocean before the big one. He said, "If I look institutionalized it's 'cause I just finished doing seven years for armed robbery. You want references, call the Detroit Police or the Oakland County Sheriff's Department. I'm not proud of it, but there it is."

She said, "Wow. Really? What was it like?"

"It wasn't like the movies, I'll tell you that."

"Did you get raped?"

"No, I had friends in the yard."

"Tell me about it."

"I have a feeling," Stick said, "if I was a narc you wouldn't be as interested."

"Probably not," Jane said. "What's the narc's motivation? It's a job. But an ex-con armed robber driving a limo for a millionaire who thinks he's a stand-up comic is something else. I mean if you do it straight though, not as a comedy."

"You think it'd sell?"

"I like it so far."

"Would you like it more if I told you we were being tailed?"

She turned half-around to look back over the seat.

"The van, blue Chevy. He's been on us since we left Bal Harbour."

"Who is it? Do you know him?"

"I have a good idea."

"But why is he following you?"

"I think he wants to kill me."

"Come on . . . Why?"

"I wrecked his cowboy hat. Two of 'em, in fact."

She sat back again to look straight ahead. They were on the Julia Tuttle Causeway now.

"I thought you were serious."

Stick said, "I've found that real life is weirder than the movies. But I like movies better, they're safer. You ever meet Warren Oates?"

"Yeah, once, at Dan Tana's. I was with a friend of his and he joined us for dinner. Why?"

"I just wondered. Was he a nice guy?"

"Yeah, I liked him. He was all right."

"How long you going to be at the Roc?"

"I guess a few days. I'm supposed to wait till Leo gets back from New York, but I'm going to make a few calls to L.A. and if I can find anything at all, *any*thing, I'm gone. If I have to hitchhike. Leo, the son of a bitch, hasn't paid me in over a month."

"Why you supposed to wait here?"

"Leo took a suite to use as a production office—he was so confident we'd be in business. It's cheaper to leave me here than take me to New York. While he makes another pitch and gets all the names wrong." She bit at her thumbnail, not so much anxious as impatient. "My problem, I've got plenty of self-esteem but no credits. I meet somebody like Kyle—very pro, a super lady—and it makes me want to *move*, get going . . . I loved the way she handled Leo, led him along with the questions—the asshole, with that condescending 'I think she's got it'—and then zapped him. It was a beautiful set piece, just beautiful."

"She knows what she's doing," Stick said.

Jane stared at him. "You've got something going with her, haven't you?"

Stick took his eyes from the causeway, the pavement rising gradually ahead of them. "I tell you I'm just the chauffeur . . ."

"Yeah, well, I caught a few looks passing back and forth between you," Jane said. "That's why I was sure you weren't *just* the chauffeur. Then I thought, Jesus, maybe *she's* a narc, too. Listen, the relationships around here are so weird I'd be willing to believe anything . . . starting with the butler, what's his name, Cornell, and the lady of the house. Is she in a nod all the time or what?"

"Yeah? You saw something there?"

"I could be wrong, but I'd bet even money they're fucking."

"Real life," Stick said.

"Yeah, you're right."

She looked around again as they came off the causeway and turned left onto Collins Avenue.

"Jesus, I think you're right. He *is* following us."

Stick cranked the wheel, pointing the Cadillac up and around the circular drive that rose to the Eden Roc's main entrance. He popped the trunk release as the girl opened her door. Then dug into his pants pocket before getting out and walking to the rear end of the Cadillac. A bellman came out, lifted the bag and tote from the trunk. Stick closed it, turned to see Jane looking down the ramp toward the street.

"He's parked back there. What're you going to do?"

"Maybe I can win his respect," Stick said. "Don't worry about it."

Her hand was extended now. "Well, it was fun. And I wish you luck."

Stick took her hand in both of his and saw her expression change, the lines through her jaw harden.

"What's this?"

"One-way fare to L.A. Or close to it."

She looked at the folded one-hundred-dollar bills in her hand, three of them. "For what?" With that hard edge, suspicious.

"You remember Chucky . . ."

"What about him?"

"The one told you to do breast exercises?"

"I know who you mean. Fatty."

"Suppose he calls you—"

"Bullshit—what're you *doing*? I thought you were a nice guy."

"Listen to me a minute, will you?" Standing here in his black suit arguing with a girl in a tank top, the liveried help watching. "What's the number of your suite?"

She hesitated. "Why?"

"Come on, just tell me."

"Fifteen-oh-three."

"When somebody calls, they want the production office, how do you answer the phone?"

"I say hello. What do you think?"

"What if you—just for the next couple of days when you answer, what if you said . . . Norman Enterprises? And sounded, well, happy and optimistic about it."

She said, "Norman Enterprises? . . ."

"Yeah. You like it? Good morning, Norman Enterprises. No, I'm sorry, Mr. Norman isn't in right now. You want to leave a message?"

She began to smile and looked like a little girl. She said, "Oh, wow," and sounded like a little girl.

"I'd really appreciate it," Stick said.

A cab driver came along the street toward the van, stocky old guy about sixty, pointing to the sign that said TAXIS ONLY, shaking his head. "You can't park here. Move it out." He didn't look Cuban to Moke, probably Italian. Wise-ass guy come down here from the Big City.

Moke had tied a lavender bandana around his head like a sweatband. He had on his old comfortable leather jacket that fit the bends and creases of his body, nothing under it but sweat and his big Smith & Wesson 44 Mag. It hurt, the better-than-eight-inch barrel digging into his groin and thigh but felt good, too. Moke rolled his window down, felt the rush of warm, humid air, rested his elbow on the sill.

He said, "Papa, you want to bleed out your ears? Keep talking to me."

The old guy stood his ground in the street but kept his mouth shut now, Moke getting a kick out of the geezer trying to give him an evil look. The next thing, Moke was sitting up straight, slipping the Hurst shifter into gear, ready to pop the clutch—and that old man better get out of the way.

Then got a surprise. The Cadillac had eased down the ramp and stopped, waiting for traffic to pass on Collins. Moke was sure it would turn right and head up to Bal Harbour. But the Cadillac turned *left*, came past him going south and Moke had to U-turn away from the cab stand to get on its tail.

Stickley had not looked at him going by. At least he hadn't seemed to, though it was hard to tell with those no-glare windows. Moke tailed the Cadillac back toward the causeway, then got another surprise when it turned left on Alton Road, staying on the island, crossed the narrow bridge over the inlet and now drove along Bay Shore Golf Course, darker in here with all the foliage, though the sky was still showing some daylight. When the Cadillac turned in at the club entrance Moke braked and held back. What was Stickley going in there for? It was a public course, they'd allow him, but it was sure too late to play any golf.

Moke drove past the entrance, scouting, saw rows of cars in the parking lot still. Two hundred feet down the road he turned around, came back and nosed the van into the lot past high shrubs and trees. The parked cars were scattered around. There was the Cadillac in the second row from the front, facing toward the clubhouse. There wasn't a soul around. Moke kept to the back of the lot before coming up slow behind the Cadillac, letting the van coast in neutral. He braked gently to stop a row behind.

Still nobody around. He rolled his window down. All he heard were crickets. He could sit and watch that Cadillac with its goddamn dark-tinted windows and Stickley might be in the car and he might not. He would have had time to get out and go into the clubhouse. Maybe have some drinks. Maybe he knew a waitress in there. Or he could be in that car waiting for somebody to come out, maybe picking up a waitress after work. If he *was* in that car, sitting there . . .

There was another car close on the driver's side of the Cadillac, empty space on the other.

Moke raised his door handle, pushed with his shoulder and slipped down off the seat. He pulled his 44 Mag, gleaming in the dusk, and his jeans felt loose on him. He did not have to check the loads; all he had to do was snick the safety off and he was ready. Tiptoe up on the passenger side of the Cadillac . . .

Which he did, concentrating on his game. Got all the way to the right-side door, eased in close, pressed his headband against the glass . . .

Empty.

The son of a bitch must have gone inside the clubhouse. It gave Moke little choice. He walked toward the clubhouse, looked over the near grounds, out at the fairways getting dark. Shit. He walked back to the van, got up behind the wheel and slammed the door. What difference did it make? Son of a bitch. He'd sat in here all day Sunday—his butt'd be growing into the seat pretty soon. He bent over and laid the Mag on the floor between his boots, handy.

It was when he straightened up again that the cord or whatever it was came over his head and around his neck—Christ!—yanked him back tight against the seat, making him gag, the cord or whatever it was digging into his throat, slick plastic-coated, and when he tried to pull it free his head was yanked back by the hair—Christ!—pulling his scalp, pulling his eyes open wide as they would go looking at the van ceiling.

Stick's voice, close, directly behind him, said, "You got a problem, son. How you're gonna hand me your gun without strangling to death."

22

Barry was going to kill him. The car telephone was still attached to one end of the cord. But he'd rather have Barry threaten and try than Moke, any day.

One fist clenched in a stringy handful of hair, the other twisting, pulling on the cord, keeping it taut, Stick did not want to let go. But he would have to give Moke some slack.

He said, "You think you can do it?"

Moke gagged, managed to say, breathless, "I can't breathe."

"I believe you," Stick said. "I want to see you reach down and pick up that piece by the barrel . . . Go ahead, try it." He rose on his knees, extending his arms to stay with Moke, saw the revolver, the clean mother-of-pearl grip. Stick let go of the telephone cord, took the solid weight of the Mag in his right hand and felt a world better. He pressed the tip of the barrel into the back of Moke's neck.

"Now your other one."

"I don't have no other one," Moke said.

Stick tightened his grip in Moke's greasy hair, yanked back hard and Moke screamed. Stick raised enough to look down into Moke's upturned face, into wide eyes rolled back, mouth open.

"You're gonna be bald-headed or dead, one. I want the piece you had Sunday."

"It's down underneath the seat."

"Let's see you bring it out the same way."

Moke found it, handed back the High Standard, and Stick released his hair to take it. He hefted the two revolvers; they felt of equal weight.

"Around eight pounds of heavy metal. You put on a show, don't you?"

"You gonna kill me?"

"I could. Save you doing time."

"Well, get her done."

Stick almost hit him with the gun, staring at the headband where he'd lay the barrel across Moke's skull. He put the High Standard down next to him, grabbed hold of Moke's hair again and got a howl from him as he yanked back as hard as he could.

He said, "Are you that fucking dumb? Is there something wrong with you?" Staring down into Moke's face, into those round dull eyes that knew nothing about him. "You think I wouldn't do it? I don't have the nerve? . . . I've *done* it."

He felt himself shaking. He had to let his body relax, sit back on his legs. He had to make a conscious effort to open his fist, release his hold on Moke's hair. Strands of it came away, twisted between his fingers.

Moke said, "Owww," a whine, and pulled himself up slowly, hunching, looking over his shoulder at Stick.

"We're going to get in the Cadillac," Stick said. "You're going to drive. You're going to take me to see Nestor."

Moke said, "Jeez-us Christ . . ."

"But don't open your mouth," Stick said. "I'm afraid I'd shoot you through the head, and I don't want us to have an accident."

Nestor dreamed of a jaguar that had walked down the deserted main street of Filadelfia, the town where he was born in the Chaco region of Paraguay. The street was deserted because of the jaguar, the people watching the wild animal from windows and from doors that were open a few inches. This jaguar was very likely the one that had killed several cows, a goat or two and an old horse; but no one threatened the life of the jaguar because of the wonder of seeing it in the street, in civilization. Walking past a truck, sniffing. Turning to look at a dog barking from a porch. Sniffing its way along the dirt street from one end to the other. Nestor was a small boy the day the jaguar came to town. He was there, but he wasn't certain now if his dreams came from what he had actually seen or what had been told to him many times and was able to see in his mind. It was winter, the dry time, and they said the jaguar was thirsty. They marveled at it and held children up to look at it. Then the men of the village—not the Mennonites who farmed here, but the men of the country who spoke Guaraní more times than Spanish—followed the cat out into the lifeless desert and on the second day the men shot it twenty times with their rifles and held a drawing, a lottery, for its skin.

Nestor dreamed occasionally of other places. He dreamed of Barranquilla in Colombia, of filth in narrow streets and the smell of fish. He dreamed of Cuba, of black smoke rising to the sky, fields on fire, the men going out to do battle with the cane. He could remember the fires clearly as well as dream about them.

But he dreamed most often of the jaguar in the Chaco, a place he could not recall from memory except for a few glimpses and smells. So if the jaguar was in his mind, coming uninvited as it did, it must be a sign.

Yes?

He told it to Stick on the backyard patio of the walled home in South Miami, the big revolvers lying on the stone table between them, the grass illuminated like a polo field, for security, the *santería* shrine against the cement wall, off in a corner, an altar to African gods that resembled an outdoor barbecue. Moke was gone. Sent home. Avilanosa brought them beer and left without a word. Nestor offered cocaine. Stick shook his head.

He said, "I wish I had a dream like that. I fall down steep, narrow stairs."

"What does it mean to you?"

"It means I'm not getting anywhere fast."

"Or there is danger up those stairs, uh? The sign being you shouldn't go there."

Stick thought about it. "Don't overreach. Don't bite off more than you can chew."

"Yes, of course."

"Or sometimes I see myself in a dream. I'm on a busy street, or I'm in a church . . ."

"Yes?"

"And I don't have any clothes on. I'm naked."

"It means you have nothing to hide," Nestor said. "I think it's good you tell me that. It's the same as with the jaguar dream. I see I don't have to worry about you. You come here . . . I see you, ah, isn't it something very unusual to see? How many men would do it?"

"But"—Stick wasn't sure how to say it—"the people of the town went out and shot the jaguar . . ."

"Yes, because it was their enemy again. The sign was over, the sign that you take with you and . . . *Como se dice, aplicar?*"

"Apply?"

"Yes, you apply it in your life to other things. I apply it to you. I think already I don't have to worry, you tell me you not going to the police or to the state attorney. All right, this afternoon I sleep, I have the dream. This evening, finally you come. Well, it's very clear to me then. You see it?"

"But if you never had the dream? . . ."

"I don't know. Shit. I get tired thinking. The dreams make it much easier to know things."

"Did a dream tell you to shoot Rene?" He said it quickly to have said it. Then knew it was all right.

Nestor smiled. "I wait for that. No, it was my intelligence told me. It was too bad. I know Rene, but he was the one Chucky sent. So, if I want to stay in the business, huh? . . . Not be ripped off, take to a cleaner . . ."

"I want to take somebody to a cleaner," Stick said.

Nestor smiled again. "The jaguar came looking for water. Now we find out what you come for."

"Permission," Stick said.

"How do you know to do this?"

"I was in prison. Or I just know, I'm not sure."

"You want that money from Chucky he promise you. Five thousand, uh?"

"Maybe more."

"Why not? If you can do it."

"But not if you say no. It wouldn't be worth it."

"It's your business with Chucky," Nestor said. "Only if you going to turn him in I say no. Because Chucky, they lock him in a room he start talking. He's very crazy, you know that. You give him to the police then I have to go to Colombia for a year or two and I don't want to do that. I like this place, this country, it's very good place to live."

"Make a lot of money here?"

"Yes, all you want."

"You pay income tax?"

"Some. But it's hard, I don't keep good records."

"Is Chucky dangerous?"

"Of course he is. The people he has, no. They're like waiters to him. He's afraid to have strong people, they throw him out, see they don't need him and take over his business. But Chucky himself, yes. Don't let him walk behind you."

"That's what I thought."

"If you know that, well . . . But he's not sitting there waiting to go to the cleaner. You have to know he would like you dead."

"He sent Moke to get me?"

"No, no one sent Moke. He like the shoot-them-up business. He wants everyone to think he's very bad. Sure, so Chucky, he try to buy Moke. And Moke, he's so stupid, from the country, huh? You can buy him for a cowboy hat. But he has no honor in remaining bought. Do you understand?"

"But you keep him around."

Nestor smiled. "Of course. Who knows when I have to send a—what is it, a *maleta*—a bag to someone in payment, huh?" Nestor shook his head, relaxed in his high-backed cane chair, hands hanging limp, diamond reflecting a cold spark of light. "I tell you, in this business, it's very difficult to find people of honor. Or people who have the custom of being generous. Chucky say you're . . . what is it? Enterprising. You sell information about the stock markets. You must be intelligent yourself to do that."

"It's only what I hear."

"Yes? What is it looks good these days?"

"Well," Stick said, "let me see. You know Chi-Chi's, the fast-food chain? It's at eighteen and a quarter. They say it should go up to thirty. Another one, Wendy's, looks good . . ."

Nestor took a pen from his shirt pocket, reached for an envelope among his mail lying on the stone table next to the two revolvers.

"How does it look, that one, McDonald's?"

"I think it's around seventy-five," Stick said.

"Yes, seventy-five and five-eights this morning."

"Yeah, well, I understand it should be up over a hundred pretty soon."

"I don't think so," Nestor said.

"Well, I got a thousand bucks, or will have," Stick said, "thinks it'll be a hundred or better by January."

He watched Nestor mark it down on his envelope.

23

Stick wrote on tablet paper: *Although Buck and Charlie are famous and experienced ~~trafficers~~ dealers, they are able to ~~get~~ be believed to be government agents, because of all the confusion there is among the different state and U.S. law enforcement groups that are falling all over each other ~~and~~ or not telling each other what they are doing in their work of trying to stop the ~~trafficing~~ dealing in controlled substances and apprehend the alleged . . .*

Jesus.

It was hard.

Why didn't he just say: *Since none of the feds know what the fuck they are doing, they believe that Buck and Charlie are . . .*

Cornell came out of his bedroom, sleep in his eyes. "You doing, writing to your mama?"

"Yeah, got to let her know I'm all right."

Cornell scratched himself idly, down to the bulge in his low-slung briefs. "I didn't hear you come in."

"I made a stop on the way home. Figured nobody'd be looking for me."

"They going out in the boat today. You suppose to meet them up in Lauderdale. I believe the man say five o'clock."

"What suit do I wear?"

"Didn't tell me that. Why don't you surprise him? Wear the tan suit with the black car and see if it freaks him any."

Stick thought of the telephone in the Cadillac, the cord ripped out of the box. He could see Barry picking it up his look of amazement . . .

He said, "Or the gray suit with the tan car?"

"Whatever your imagination tells you," Cornell said. "The maids call early this morning. You hear it?"

"Not a sound."

"They call *me* to tell the madam they don't have a ride today. The car won't start, like they know it ahead of time. Monday, the cook's day off . . . gonna be quiet around here. You got any plans? You could probably go someplace, you wanted to."

"You trying to get rid of me?"

"Man, free time, take it when you can."

It sounded good. Stick wrote two entire pages while Cornell made coffee and had his breakfast. When Cornell went into the bathroom Stick picked up the phone and dialed a number.

"Mary Lou? Hi, it's me . . . Come on—I want to talk to Katy . . . You sure? . . . The only reason I ask, the last time you thought she was sleeping she wasn't even home." He held the phone at arm's length while Mary Lou commented and he caught only some of the words, like, "Boy, you think you're so smart," and so forth along those lines. Stick brought the phone to his face again and said, "Mary Lou? If I have to get a court order I'm going to talk to Katy whether she's sleeping or what." Mary Lou hung up on him. He called her back and said, "I think we had a bad connection." Mary Lou said, "We sure did," and hung up again. Jesus. A lovely person. The mother of his only child. Himself forty-two and not too likely to have any more, unless . . . He dialed the number again. "Mary Lou? Could I ask you a special favor?" He heard her say, away from the phone, "Nobody," and heard his daughter's voice in the background. He yelled, "Katy!" loud. Very loud. He heard her voice in the background say, "But I want to talk to him . . ."

And heard her say into the phone, "Hi. What're you doing?" As though she really wanted to know.

Stick grinned. "Nothing. What're you doing?"

"Nothing."

"You want to do something?"

"Sure."

"You want to do some typing, take you about an hour maybe?"

"Sure. But I don't have a typewriter."

Stick said, "Honey, that's the least of our worries."

Kyle was having breakfast with Barry on the patio.

Stick watched them from the edge of the acacia trees, near the garage. He would like to avoid Barry this morning, but he wanted to see Kyle. He missed her. When he wasn't with her he imagined and believed she had already changed her mind about him. From the good feeling he saw in her eyes to no feeling. He couldn't hold on to the confidence he felt when he was with her. Was it a sign? He hadn't dreamed about her yet. But maybe she was at the top of the stairs he kept falling down.

Ask Nestor.

The cruiser *Seaweed* rumbled in out of the bay, stark, clean white, sunlight flashing on its glass and bright metal. Barry headed for the dock with his newspapers.

And Kyle was looking toward the house, the garage . . . Stick felt his confidence in place again, as though there had been no hollow feeling, doubts of any kind. He walked across the lawn and she was coming toward him now, coming so close he put his arms around her and was self-conscious for only a moment. It didn't matter if anyone was watching, they had to touch each other, renew the familiar feel.

He said, "Well, I got it straightened out."

"How?"

"I saw Nestor. We had a nice talk."

"Just like that," Kyle said. "You make everything sound easy."

She seemed relieved, though with a hint of suspicion, not knowing what he was doing; left out.

"You saw him last night?"

"I thought I might as well get it over with. I went to see him . . . He's scary, but you can talk to him."

"Ernest?" Looking up at him with those eyes. "Are you playing with me?"

"I would never do that. Spooky things're going on around us, but I think we're safe."

"I'm going home Wednesday or Thursday. After that I'll be in Boston a few days."

He said, "How'll we work it?"

She said, "When it's no longer convenient? I don't know, I'm going to leave it up to you."

He said, "Emma? . . ."

She took a moment to answer him. "What?"

"If I make a lot of money, will you tell me what to do with it?"

She said, "Any time. But I don't think you need me." And seemed to smile then, almost, and said, "I miss you, Ernest, and I don't know what to do about it."

Stick said, "We'll think of something."

He stood with Cornell and waved as *Seaweed* put out to sea. "It's the custom," the houseman said. "Wave some more. Like the man's going out to kill whales and won't be home till Christmas. Bye, bye. Have fun, y'all. Don't worry about us stay-at-homes . . ."

Cornell was watching television when Stick came out of his room, dressed to go, wearing his tan suitcoat, his gray trousers, a pale blue shirt and black tie. Cornell looked over and blinked.

"Gonna freak the man outta his head. What color car?"

"I haven't decided yet."

"Take the green Mercedes, the lady ain't going nowhere. Yeah, gonna freak him good. So where you off to?"

"The bank first. I want to open an account. I think over at Florida First National."

"That's a good one."

"Then I'm going up to Pompano, see my little girl."

"Beautiful. Have a nice day, man."

Stick felt like he was on display sitting by the big plate-glass window, people going by on Thirty-sixth Street—he felt them watching him as he filled out the application.

The assistant manager said, "That should do it. Now, let me give you a receipt." He counted the four fifties and the three one-hundred-dollar bills again. To make sure, Stick felt, he hadn't palmed one back in his pocket.

"And what type of business is it, Mr. Norman?"

"Mr. Stickley," Stick said.

"Yes, I beg your pardon." Looking at the application again. "Mr. Stickley, yes. And the company is Norman Enterprises. May I ask what you do?" Looking interested, leaning forward on the desk.

Stick said, "No, I don't think you better."

The assistant manager laughed politely and smiled and waited. Stick thanked him and left with his receipt.

Next—a pay phone.

It didn't occur to Stick until this moment that Chucky's number was not likely to be found in a telephone directory. He looked, before leaving the bank, and it wasn't. He tried Information and was told there was no listing. So he'd have to go back to the Stam residence and hope the number was somewhere in Barry's den. He said to himself, see? A simple thing like that. He'd have to get in the habit of writing down what he had to do. And then said, what do you mean, get in the habit? This was a one-shot deal.

Wasn't it?

Stick left the Cadillac in the shady part of the turnaround. He felt like a burglar walking into the house, not hearing a sound. It seemed empty and might be, though he had seen no one outside or expected to. Diane wasn't a sunbather and it wouldn't do much for Cornell to sit out there; though he could have deepened his color up at Butler, chopping weeds. Road gang tan. And look at us now—couple of former inmates walking around here where no hack would ever set foot, no probation or parole officer, none of those people on the good side.

He went into Barry's black den, almost all black but for rich touches of red and gold, the blown-up Barry in black and white looking down from the wall, innocent eyes open wide. Who, me?

Yes, you. Showboater.

But a nice guy, basically. If you had to work for anybody for any length of time and didn't want a boss-type boss.

Barry's leather-bound address book, red Morocco, sat on the black desk. Chucky was not among the Gs. No, he was with the Cs.

Chucky Gorman on Sunrise, Fort Lauderdale. Might as well do it now.

Stick dialed.

Lionel answered. He said wait.

When Chucky's voice came on it sounded strange, clear but distant, small.

Stick said, "You know who this is?"

"You want to appraise my furniture, my paintings?"

"I'd like to talk to you . . ."

"Yeah?"

"I mean in private. I can't talk here."

"You want to come up?"

"I was thinking someplace else."

"You can't get it any more private. I mean this is *private*, man."

"It's too high up."

"What're we going to discuss? If it's five grand and I were you I wouldn't come here either."

"No, I understand. I thought it was worth a shot."

"One, that's all. So tell me what we're gonna discuss you're afraid if I don't like it I'll drop you out the fifteen-story window?"

"All I can say—I mean over the phone—if you like it, fine. You don't, okay. Nobody's out anything. But it's the kind of deal could interest you. I happened to find out about it . . . I thought, well, I'll lay it on you. You like it, then you know I'm not holding nothing against you."

"You think I give a shit if you are?"

"You know what I mean. I can't explain it, I got to show you."

"You trying to sell me a stock tip?"

"No, it's not like that, but"—he dropped his voice—"it's from that source, if you know what I mean."

"Something Barry's into?"

"You got it."

"Where you want to meet? 'Cross the street?"

"That's fine. How about three o'clock? Around in there."

"I'll think about it."

Stick said, "That's all I ask, Mr. Gorman." Which might have been the most difficult thing he ever said in his life. He hated to lie.

A typewriter . . .

Right there, trim little Olivetti portable electric. He was not disappointed when he could not find the case; he walked out into the hall carrying the typewriter in front of him, and stopped.

What he saw was real. Cornell carrying a silver tray, silver decanter with a long, delicately curved spout, two silver goblets. He had come out of the hall from the kitchen, turned into this main, lateral hallway about twenty feet from Stick—turned before seeing him—and was now walking toward the bedroom wing.

What was unreal, Cornell wore a gold headband around his moderate natural and that was it. Otherwise the man was naked, showing a pronounced demarcation between back and buttocks, burnt sienna over caramel.

Stick followed—he would say he was unable to stop himself—drawn along with the typewriter to Diane's bedroom . . . cautiously through the room to a view of the atrium, the enclosed garden between the Stams' master bedrooms.

Stick remained inside the room, at the edge of drawn gold draperies, with a clear view of Cornell dropping to one knee, head bowed, offering the silver wine service to Diane, who sat on something Stick could not see, hidden by the folds of her transparent white negligee, her pale body naked beneath.

Diane said, "Arise, slave. And as you offer the cup, say how you will delight me with rites of barbaric pleasure."

Cornell rose, placed the tray on a low pedestal next to Diane. He poured champagne into the goblets, bowed as he handed one to Diane and said, "Yes, O Queen. What I am going to perform up one royal side of you and down the other, in the dark and savage land where I come from is called . . . the Freaky Deaky."

Diane said, "Let the rites begin."

Cornell turned and came into the bedroom. He walked past Stick to a stereo system, snapped in a cassette and turned it on. As the Dazz Band came out in full strength, began to funk its way through *Let It Whip*, he turned up the volume, started back to the atrium and stopped. Cornell looked directly at Stick holding the typewriter.

Said, "Come bearing a gift, huh? You want to be a barbarian rapist or a slave that gives pleasure?"

Stick said, "I got to go up the road . . ."

Cornell said, "It's cool. We catch you next time."

24

Stick got to Wolfgang's at ten after three, came into the dimness, the beer smell, with a thick manila envelope under his arm. He saw Chucky and Lionel right away, at a table in back talking to the guy who owned the place. Stick went up to the bar and waited for Bobbi to notice him. There—the big smile. This girl always made him feel good.

"Well, how you doing?"

"Not too bad."

"What're you up to now?" Nodding at his outfit. "You still working for Barry?"

"Yeah, for a while anyway."

"How's your daughter?"

"I'm glad you asked," Stick said. "You should see her type." He held up the nine-by-twelve manila envelope, placed it on the bar. "Fourteen years old, she could get a job in an office. Typed about ten pages for me, no mistakes. I offered to pay her"—he seemed both proud of this and surprised—"she wouldn't take it."

"Well, of course not. You're her dad."

"But I made her. Since I'm about seven years behind in her allowance."

Bobbi said, "Keep your shirt buttoned, Stickley, your heart'll fall out."

Lionel came over while Bobbi was pouring him a bourbon. He'd wanted to have a quick one or two first, but Lionel said, "What you doing? Chucky's waiting for you."

Stick turned on the stool with his surprised look. "Yeah? Where?"

Chucky was wearing his fishing cap that had an extra-long peak, tan cotton with the restful smoked-plastic visor he could pull down eye level and turn day to gray evening. He felt no pain or anxiety—he was moving product, already most of the load Nestor had delivered—and he did not see his life at the present time in abnormal danger. If he had to tell what he felt at the moment—watching Ernest Stickley coming from the bar in sporty tan and gray attire—he would say curiosity. With a little suspicion thrown in to keep him on his toes. Living in what Chucky believed was the rip-off capital of the world could do that to you. Make you squint at life.

"I'm sorry I'm late," Stick said, holding the envelope to his chest, his drink in the other hand.

He glanced around the room as he sat down. Chucky noted this and said, "Nobody here but afternoon drunks, a few tourists and maybe a sporty opportunist." Watching Stick closely, testing him with, "I called Barry this morning . . ."

Stick said, "Oh, shit," like all was lost.

"But he was gone," Chucky said, grinning now. He saw Stick nervous, leaning in close to the table, looking so different than he did that first time.

"Jesus," Stick said, "I thought you understood. Mr. Stam finds out about this I'm out of work."

"Well, let's have it," Chucky said. "Whatcha got?"

Stick had the envelope in front of him on the table. He pressed a hand on it as Chucky reached over.

"I don't think you better read it here."

"You picked this place."

"Well, just look at the first part. Okay?" He brought the prospectus out of the envelope and handed it to Chucky.

A familiar feel, familiar words, most of them. Chucky said, "You putting me on? This is the same shit as yesterday."

Stick shook his head. "Look at it good. Norman Enterprises . . ."

"Yeah?"

"You see the title? *Scam.* Turn to the next page. No, the next one. See how it works? Thirty-five limited partners putting in seventy-two five each?"

"Yeah?"

"It's *almost* the same deal. But it's different. They worked on it yesterday, Barry and Leo Firestone, till late last night. They got a different story now. About a couple of dealers named Charlie and Buck . . ."

"You don't mean to tell me."

"They pull the all-time Miami dope scam. Walk in and con the Feds out of forty million bucks worth of pure coke they'd taken off some Colombians. After a lot of action and sex, dirty words—be a minus R—they have a retirement party and invite all the narcs to it. It's a comedy, only based on real life."

"Charlie and Buck?"

"Cool guys. Witty. Barry wants a lot of sex in it."

"Yeah?"

"They did the story fast, you know. Leo says rough but inspired. It sounds pretty good to me."

Chucky flipped through pages. "Say the offering's different now?"

"They took the tax fraud out of it. Now it's a straight deal like any other offering. You put in seventy-two five and you and the other investors own half the movie. Not twenty percent like before, half. It's all in there. They put the investment money in Florida First National and if they don't make the picture you get it all back with interest."

"So when's Leo going to pitch this one?" He saw Stick glance around again.

"What do you think I sneaked it out for—give you a peek if you're going to see it anyway?"

"That was my next question."

"He's not going to show it, he's afraid to."

"Who is?"

"Leo Firestone—who're we talking about? He finds out who some of Barry's friends are yesterday, the guy's scared shitless. Won't have anything to do with anybody that's dealing or can't give him an authorized cashier's check on the investment without moving a kilo of flake. I mean the guy's scared to death at how close he came, talking about spics and scum . . . You heard him."

"Man didn't seem too bright."

"Yeah, well, his movies might be shitty but they gross big. All over the world. That's why Barry's so anxious to go in business with him. Have some fun and the dough keeps coming in for years. No risk at all the way Barry sees it."

"Yeah?"

"I suppose he's wrong sometimes, but, I don't know . . . So Barry had to promise Leo okay, he'd leave yesterday's group out of it. Maybe contact a couple of big shooters he knows, that's all. That's why they're using one of Leo's other company names. In case anybody hears about it. It gets in the paper nobody'll see it came out of the other deal."

"Fucking Barry . . ." Chucky said.

"He can't help it. See, Leo came down here as a favor to Barry, made the pitch. He wanted to raise the dough in New York."

"Leo did?"

"Yeah, so that's what he went back to do. He told Barry—I heard him—get your couple or three guys quick, 'cause I'm going to move on this right away, button it up."

"How quick?"

"From what I understand you got to get in right now. But that's only what I heard. It doesn't say anything about a time limit in there."

Chucky leafed through the prospectus. "It looks like the same one exactly. Most of it."

"Yeah, all the legal and technical stuff. What's changed is the story and the amount you invest. Barry says all the rest is boilerplate."

"Subscription application," Chucky said. "That part's different."

He pulled the bill of his cap lower on his eyes, saw Stick in a misty gray wash, most of the tables empty behind him, not many at the bar, the patrons still sober, quiet: a restful atmosphere conducive to clear thinking, spotting false notes and shifty moves. "What else?"

"What do you mean, what else? Read it, see if you want to go in."

"You just said the guy doesn't want me in. The fucker tries to sell a fraudulent deal, but he won't associate with certain types?"

"I think if you hand him the money," Stick said, "he's not going to turn you down. You know, once he sees he's not going to have any trouble . . . maybe."

"But he won't take cash. Didn't you just tell me that?"

"Write him a check."

"I don't write any in that amount. Seventy thousand."

"Seventy-two five."

"Never put more than nine grand and change in the bank. I'm referring to cash," Chucky said. "And they won't know how much you got."

Stick said, "It was an idea." He said after a moment, "Wait. Firestone's in New York, I took him to the airport this morning. But they have an office in the Eden Roc and I'm pretty sure his girl's there. You know the one?"

"The skinny broad."

"Take her the money, see what she says. The address and phone number are in there. I think the second page . . . Suite fifteen-oh-three, something like that. It's where you send the subscription agreement, Norman Enterprises Production Office."

Chucky leafed through the prospectus another moment or so before he got up and walked around the table.

"Where you going?"

Chucky completed his turn, providing his need for activity, motion, as his mind worked. He sat down again and said, "Something smells. I never heard of raising money and keeping it quiet or leaving people out . . ."

"If you got more people wanting in than units to sell," Stick began.

But now Chucky was saying, "How about Kyle? She know about this?"

"I don't recall she said much."

"These two guys are putting together a deal and she doesn't open her mouth? After she neutered Leo the day before?"

"She must've liked it."

"I better give Barry a call."

"You do," Stick said, "I'm back on the road."

Chucky grinned at him. "You believe I give a shit? I'm dying to know what you're up to."

Stick said, "Let's forget it." He picked up the prospectus. "I made a mistake."

Chucky squinted beneath the plastic bill. "I don't see what you get out of it. *Scam*, that's what it sounds like, all right, but I can't figure the angle . . . You pick up an old prospectus Leo tried to peddle when he was Norman Enterprises? My mouth is suppose to water, envy gets in my eyes, Barry running off with another winner, and for your trouble I let you have . . . what? You're still going for that five grand, aren't you?"

Stick said, "You ever do time?"

"'Nam. That's time and a half."

"You don't know what you're talking about," Stick said. "I'd have gone to Vietnam in a bathing suit. I know you can die in war, but worse things can happen to you in Jackson, Michigan. Sometimes you do favors for people so they don't defile you or piss in your food. Like a peace offering or buying insurance. You understand what I'm saying?" Chucky was looking away. "All I want is to be left alone."

"We'll get it settled," Chucky said.

He was looking toward the terrace at Kyle. She had come in from outside and stood there a moment before she saw them.

Stick said, "You're early. It isn't even four o'clock yet." He had the prospectus in the envelope again and was standing. "I'll get the car."

Chucky said, "Now don't rush off." He was up, pulling a chair out for Kyle.

She said, "We may be a while yet. Barry and Rorie are having a fight. And there's no possibility of it ending because they don't know what they're fighting about."

"Clash of personalities," Chucky said. "Where they, outside?"

"On the boat." She looked at Stick. "You might as well sit down." Then smiled at him. "You look nice." When he didn't smile back her expression changed. She glanced at Chucky, and Stick could see she was beginning to get the picture. Lionel brought Chucky a drink. Kyle shook her head saying she didn't care for anything, looking at Stick again. This time he gave her a weak smile.

Chucky said to her, "Well, how're you and Leo getting along? You make up?"

"He went back to New York," Kyle said. She glanced at Stick and he gave her another smile, on and off.

Chucky said, "Too bad that deal didn't work out. I think if they'd turned the story around, made the two guys like, oh, a couple happy hustlers . . . You know what I mean? Make it a comedy."

"And called it *Scam*?" Kyle said. "How about if they con the customs agents out of millions of dollars worth of stuff?"

Chucky was staring at her.

"And they stage a retirement party somewhere, Nassau, and invite all the customs guys . . ."

Chucky said, subdued, "That doesn't sound too bad . . . Change the offering to get the fraud out of it?"

"I would," Kyle said. "Maybe lower the price of the units . . ."

"Change the names of the two guys?" Chucky asked.

Kyle nodded. "Definitely. You want names that sound fun-loving but have character."

Chucky said, "How about Charlie and Buck?"

"Not bad." She was nodding again, giving Stick a look then as she got up. "If you'll excuse me . . . We've got a dinner engagement tonight and Barry's going to sulk all through it if he and Aurora don't kiss and make up. I'm going to see what I can do." She said to Stick, "You could get the car. Just give me a few minutes."

Stick sat back, watching that wonderful girl making her way through the tables. He was aware of more noise in the place, more people, music playing now.

Chucky said, "I pay her a consulting fee. She's suppose to advise me."

"I think she did," Stick said. "Look, I'm not going to beg you. You want Barry to have all the fun or it's too rich for your blood, forget I ever mentioned it." He pushed the manila envelope toward Chucky. "But if you want it you better move."

Chucky pushed his chair back to get up but continued to sit there. "Keeping it to themselves," he said.

"Trying to."

"I'd have to get them to take cash."

"Tempt 'em."

Chucky got up. He said, "Stay here," and walked out toward the foyer.

Stick went over to the bar and got another bourbon. Looking down the aisle, he could see Chucky out by the front entrance talking on the phone. The tricky part; all Stick could do was wait.

"Broad was very cagey," Chucky said, sitting down again.

Stick acted surprised. "You called the Roc?"

"She said Norman Enterprises and I asked for Leo. She goes, who is this, please? I told her I had spoken to Leo about investing in his new one, *Scam*, and she goes, oh, well I'm the only one here right now and would I like to leave my name. Very cagey."

"You tell her?"

"I hung up on her and called Florida First National."

"You did?"

"It's true, they got an account there."

"They move fast," Stick said.

"I'm thinking," Chucky said, "sign the subscription agreement, get it over to the Eden Roc . . . they see my name they might make up an excuse . . ."

"They might."

"But not if the money's already put in their account."

"Sounds good to me."

"I deposit cash, the bank reports it to the IRS, but it doesn't affect me any."

"I don't know anything about that," Stick said.

They saw Barry coming in now, his arm around Aurora's shoulder, Kyle following them.

Chucky said, "Possessive son of a bitch. Selfish. Spoiled rotten . . ."

They watched Barry walk up to the bar and point a finger at Bobbi. "What's the last thing goes through a bug's mind—"

Bobbi's smile faded; she tried to get it back looking eager, interested.

"I tell you that one? . . . I tell you about the Polack who think's Peter Pan's a wash basin in a cathouse? . . . The difference between erotic and kinky? Erotic you use a feather, kinky you use the whole chicken?"

Stick said to Chucky, "But he sure has fun."

Chucky said, "Jesus, get him outta here." Then said, "Wait a minute. On the subscription agreement? . . ."

"Yeah?"

"What should I put where it says 'Occupation'?"

"Put down Big Shooter," Stick said and saw Chucky actually consider it and shrug. It always surprised Stick, what you could tell people and they believed. Chucky was leaning over the table on his arms. He seemed relieved, as though now everything was all right between them: a couple of friends talking.

"I got to get out."

"I do too," Stick said. He put his hands on the table to rise.

"I'm pushing it now," Chucky said, confiding. "You can't stay in this ten years. Too many people, they start out they want a piece of you, then they want the whole thing."

Stick said, "Well . . ."

"People you deal with, you don't sign anything in this business, a subscription agreement . . ."

"I got to go," Stick said.

"You ask me if I did time? This's doing time, man. Same thing. You can't do what you want, you can't fucking *move.* Try and get some space—you know what I mean? To breathe in? You got to pay for it, buy people . . . I don't get out now, shit . . ."

Stick said, "So get out."

"They don't leave you alone. People like Nestor, Moke . . . I started out, I was quick, man. Now it's like . . . it's hard to explain. I'm still moving but it's like you cut off a snake's head, or a chicken, its body keeps moving, but its head doesn't know what the fuck's going on. It sees the body moving, flopping around, but it can't *feel* anything . . . You see a choice?"

Stick didn't say anything. Looking at him, hearing him, his tone, maybe beginning to understand Chucky for the first time.

"I got no choice. I stay in I get eaten up or I get picked up. Same thing. I get blown away by some crazy fucker like Moke or I get arraigned, sooner or later it'll happen, and they lock me up. You know how long I'd last? I wouldn't ever come up for trial. I wouldn't make it through—what is it, they can hold you like seventy-two hours? I wouldn't make it through the fucking *night*. They lock me up . . . I'd find a way. Bring in the kind of cap, man, concealed on you that'll set you free. There're ways . . ."

"Well, you been lucky so far," Stick said. "You must know what you're doing."

"I been lucky, sure. You got to be lucky. But I been stoking the fire, too, man, all the time stoking my fire . . . Well, it's burning out. I'm tired . . ."

Stick watched him straighten then, pushing back in his chair, his vacant gaze showing a faint gleam of hope.

"So I'm glad you came along," Chucky said. "You might not know it, but you're helping me get out."

Stick kept looking at him. He didn't know what to say. He didn't want to feel sorry for him. It wouldn't make sense to feel sorry for him . . .

He said, "I got to go."

He couldn't understand why people who lived in a place worth a couple million would go someplace else to enjoy themselves. He drove Barry, Diane and Kyle to Leucadendra in the Rolls and brought them home again at eleven, an uneventful trip both ways. When the Stams went inside Kyle walked out into darkness, to the seawall, and Stick followed.

She said, "So Chucky thinks *Scam* is for real. But what happens now?"

"What'd you tell me? Get 'em to believe they'd be a fool to pass it up?"

"You gave him a prospectus?"

"The old one, the one you showed me, but changed here and there."

She looked puzzled. "And he believes the investment's only five thousand?"

"Little more than that."

"How much more?"

"Seventy-two five."

"Seventy-two *thousand*?"

"I had to make it look real."

"My God, I'm helping you commit fraud!"

She was facing him, the lights of Miami behind her and he couldn't see her eyes, though in the tone of her voice there was something more than amazement.

"I thought, in the bar, you were talking about a few thousand, what he owes you."

"Yeah . . ."

"I could see what Chucky was doing, looking for some kind of verification, trying to be sly about it . . ."

"That's right."

"So I played along. What else was I going to do? You're sitting there in the middle."

"How does the amount change anything?"

It stopped her. "I shouldn't have come to the table. I saw you with him, I should've known."

"Sunday you wanted to help me."

"I know I did, but it was different then, exciting. Chucky was the bad guy . . ."

"He still is," Stick said. "He's so bad he'll never miss it."

"That's not the point. You're trying to swindle a client of mine out of seventy-two thousand dollars and I'm helping you."

"I appreciate it, too."

"But I *can't*. He pays me to look after his money."

"Well, he probably won't go for it anyway."

"I'm going to have to talk to him about it," Kyle said, "say *some*thing. Advise against it . . ."

"Why don't we just, for the fun of it," Stick said, "see if it works. If he pays up and you still feel sorry for him—"

"It isn't that at all, it's fraud."

"Okay, whatever the reason. If it bothers you too much I'll give it back. But let's see what happens."

"You promise?"

"On my honor," Stick said.

25

Chucky arrived at Florida First National, corner of Biscayne Boulevard and Thirty-Sixth, a few minutes past one. Lionel, carrying the suitcase, followed him in and waited as Chucky looked from the teller windows to the bank executives at their desks in the fenced-off area. He wondered how they could work, being out in plain sight like that, people walking by outside looking at them.

"We don't want to give it to a teller," Chucky said. "Won't have the right effect."

Lionel didn't know what he was talking about or that he was about to witness one of Chucky's fantasies come to life. Chucky took the suitcase now and Lionel followed him over to the assistant manager's desk, which was by the big plate-glass window.

Chucky said, "I'm here to make a deposit."

He snapped the suitcase open, turned it over as he raised it high, dumped banded packets of currency on the assistant manager's desk, all hundred-dollar bills, and gave him a big smile.

"Seventy-two thousand five hundred dollars, pay to the account of Norman Enterprises. We're in show business."

The assistant manager said, "Oh, really?"

"He wasn't too surprised," Chucky said to Lionel, crossing the Julia Tuttle on their way to the Eden Roc.

"We're in Miami," Lionel said.

They went up to Suite 1503, Chucky with his signed subscription agreement in a plain white envelope, and knocked on the door. He waited and knocked again.

"She's still at lunch," Chucky said. "Though to look at her you wouldn't think it would take long."

They went down to the lounge and had a few, returned in an hour to knock on the door again and waited in silence.

"I'll slip it under the door," Chucky said. "It might even be better if I do it that way."

They stopped at the main desk just to make sure. The clerk went to look, came back and said it seemed the party checked out this morning. Chucky said, "Gone on a trip to the Apple, huh? But they kept the suite, didn't they? The production office?" The clerk said no, checked out and didn't leave a forwarding address.

Chucky said to Lionel, "I want to go home right now."

He needed a secure atmosphere in which to think. Maybe scream, if he had to.

Avilanosa had some fun with Moke when he came to get his revolvers. He said, "Let the man take your pistols, huh? Why you do that?"

Moke would like to have gotten out without seeing Avilanosa today. See Nestor, pick up his guns and leave. But Nestor was resting, not to be disturbed—most likely in a deep nod—and his father-in-law was in charge of the house.

Moke said, "Come on, gimme 'em."

"What, these pistols?" Avilanosa said, offering them, then raising them over his head as Moke reached to take them.

"Come on, don't fuck around."

"Oh, listen to him, the *pistolero*," Avilanosa said, "who lose his pistols. Let them be taken away from him. Here."

Moke reached. Now, as Avilanosa raised the guns over his head, Moke shoved him hard. Avilanosa stumbled against the stone patio table, smiling, not appearing to be angry, playing with Moke. He said, "Here." But now Moke wouldn't take them, so Avilanosa placed the revolvers on the stone table and stepped aside. He waited for Moke to pick them up and work the barrels into his waist. At that moment he stepped toward Moke, chopped him with a backhand fist that was like a club, caught Moke across the face and sent him sprawling in the grass.

Moke came up with the nickel-plated Mag drawn and Avilanosa shook his head. He said, "You must not be feeling so good, you want to die. You should take some medicine, go to sleep."

Moke lowered the revolver to his side.

Avilanosa said, "You have the truck again you always lose? Man, you lose your pistols and your truck, uh? Get in that truck and go see Chucky."

"What for?"

"Scare him. Time to scare him so he don't forget to pay. You think you can scare him good?"

Moke walked away from Avilanosa, toward the door in the wooden gate that sealed off the driveway, Avilanosa's voice following him, pushing him: "Try see if you can scare him and not lose your pistols again . . ."

Barry told Stick that morning all four cars were ready for an oil change and lube; take them over to the Amoco station on 125th, he had a charge there. Stick said, "One at a time?" Seeing it as an all-day job.

Barry said, "No, you hook 'em end to end like a choo-choo, for Christ sake, of *course* one at a time. Get 'em gassed and washed, too."

It sounded like make-work, which could take two hours a car, easy. While Barry and Kyle spent the morning in his den shuffling through papers and doing figures. Stick began with the Lincoln, took it over, brought it back and they were still in there. He couldn't see a way to get Kyle alone. He called the bank around noon, gave his account number and said he wanted to verify his balance. The woman's voice said, exactly five hundred dollars and no cents.

He drove the Rolls over. They were busier now at the station and it took two and a half hours, round trip. He called the bank again, gave his number and said he'd like to verify his balance. A different woman's voice this time said, "Mr. Norman?"

"Mr. Stickley."

"Yes, that balance, Mr. Stickley, is exactly . . . let's see, seventy-three thousand dollars and no cents. Nice round figure."

He said, "Jesus Christ."

The woman said, "Pardon me?"

He had never had a feeling like this before in his life. He was worth at this moment seventy-three thousand dollars. He had thought up an idea with a little help, had talked to a guy for about a half hour selling him on the idea, and he was now worth seventy-three thousand dollars. The same thing they were doing in there in Barry's den, the same kind of thing, making money without working. It seemed the way to do it. He wanted to tell Kyle, but they were still at it.

He wanted to tell Cornell, somebody. But when he saw Cornell he thought better of it and tried to appear calm.

"Well, what're you up to today?"

"Cleaning silver."

"What is this, clean-up, fix-up day?"

"Got to keep us busy, man."

"Slave labor," Stick said.

Cornell grinned at him. "That slave duty can wear you down, man. But you get into it, it's kinda fun. You know what I'm saying? Lose yourself. Be anything you want."

"You do other . . . different things like that?"

"Mostly the queen and the slave."

"What's she the queen of?"

"Queen—I don't know exactly—queen of the afternoon with nothing to do. Queen of the Jelly Bellies. I never seen a lady wished so much she was a queen."

"Well," Stick said, "she looked like a pretty good one."

What he thought of doing, go in the den and tell Barry he was quitting. Except he had to talk to Kyle first. He took the Cadillac over to the station, thought of the movie girl, Jane, as he waited and called the Eden Roc.

Gone.

He hung up with the feeling it had been close. That if the timing hadn't been perfect he'd still be worth five hundred instead of seventy-three thousand. He said the number over and over again. He would like to sit down in a quiet, clean place without distractions, wrenches and tire irons hitting cement, and think about it. Prepare a speech. Hope that Kyle, later, would be in a realistic frame of mind. If she wasn't, deliver the speech: why it would be wrong . . . morally wrong to give dope money back to a dealer so he could buy more dope, corrupt more people and not pay any income tax on it. When on the other hand he would use the money wisely. How? . . . Christ, any way he wanted! Buy things. Buy a car. Buy things for Katy, clothes. Buy a truck, buy a business. Buy Wild Turkey instead of Early Times. There were wonderful ways to spend money that he and Frank had only begun to experience when their hundred days ended, abruptly.

Back and forth, the Stickley shuttle. He wanted to tell the Amoco guy with *Steve* on his shirt, but he didn't. It was nearly six by the time he got back with the Mercedes, the last one. Twenty-four hours since he'd pulled the deal of his life.

The Rolls was not in the garage.

He got out of the Mercedes, walked over to the edge of the grass. Barry was alone on the patio, sitting at the umbrella table with a drink and newspaper. Stick walked down there.

"All through."

"That wasn't too bad, was it?"

"No, sir, not at all." Why was it easier to say having seventy-three thousand dollars?

"I noticed the Rolls is gone."

"I let Kyle have it."

"Oh . . ." Could he ask? He had to. "Where'd she go?"

Barry looked up at him, frowning. "What?"

"I said, where'd she go?"

"That's what I thought you said. She went to see Mr. Gorman."

"When?"

"What's the matter with you?"

"*When?*"

"Little while ago. What *is* this?"

"Did he call her or she call him?"

"He called."

"And she left right away?"

"Yeah, soon after. The hell's wrong with you?"

Stick turned and ran.

Barry stood up and yelled at him. It didn't do any good. Stick was in the Mercedes now wheeling out of the drive.

26

Moke rode up to fifteen, all the way to the top, thinking: it was big time working for Nestor; but what did he get out of it other than a bunch of shit from Avilanosa? Thinking: if a turd like Chucky could have his own world up here, live how he wanted acting like a weird and nervous woman, then why couldn't Eddie Moke have it too? Or take what Chucky had from him?

Lionel opened the door and Moke opened his worn-out leather jacket to show the pearl grip of his 44.

"You see it?"

Lionel nodded. "You high, huh?"

"I been higher. Climb up another line or two. Nestor's coming to visit. He don't want none of you guys around here."

"It's okay," Lionel said.

"I'll watch Chucky he don't come to harm."

"I better tell him," Lionel said.

"No, I'll tell him. What's he doing?"

Lionel didn't answer. He said after a moment, "You going to kill him?"

It surprised Moke, made him curious. "What if I said that was the deal? What would you do?"

"Go to Miami, see my old woman," Lionel said. "When do we come back?"

"Later on tonight'd be okay."

"There's somebody in there with him. A woman," Lionel said.

"Don't worry about us," Moke said. "We be fine."

He stepped in, bringing Lionel out and closed the door on him. Moke knew the layout, enough of it. He walked down the front hall and turned left at the first door, Chucky's den with the phone deal and the hats . . . but no Crested Beaut or Bullrider hanging up there—the son of a bitch, the man's time was coming. Moke set the white yachting cap down on his eyes, strolled past the balcony glass catching some reflection to the living room door. He stooped to peer through the spy hole.

Kyle said, "Would you sit down? Please. And listen. You haven't heard anything I've said. You've got your mind made up."

Chucky moved. "You haven't said anything makes sense." And moved back, side to side, swaying. "You don't know anything about the deal, but you know what the story's about."

"No, I said it was a misunderstanding."

"Honey, I know when I'm getting fucked, I get this tingling sensation different than my other twitches and tingles . . ."

"Listen to me, okay? Just listen." She began slowly then. "He picked up an old prospectus, it was Leo's original offering, and thought we were going with it."

"Why would he think that?"

"He must've heard us talking about revising the story. It was a possibility . . ."

"You *told* me the story in the bar."

"I thought he was telling you what he'd heard. I was playing along. You know how you take a story and elaborate on it? . . . The way I understand it, he was trying to do you a favor, that's all."

Chucky glanced toward the door to his den and back to Kyle. "The first time you came here you said, you want to invest in a movie? You had it in mind *then.*"

"A movie, any movie. I wasn't talking about this one. Believe me, Barry's not involved in any kind of film project."

"Then I want to know what's going on . . ."

Moke slammed the door behind him to get their attention. He said, "I do, too. What're you people arguing about? Chucky, you're not suppose to fight with women." He nodded to Kyle on the sofa. "How you doing?" And looked at Chucky again. "I think you need your medicine."

Chucky said, "Who let you in? . . . You want to see me, wait in the other room. And take that hat off."

Moke adjusted the yachting cap over his eyes. He liked to see the edge of the peak squared straight across his vision. It meant the person had it together and was not prone to accept bullshit of any kind. He said to Chucky, putting his hand in the pocket of his jacket and bringing it out in a fist, "Yeah, it must be medicine time how you're acting." He opened his hand. Two white tablets dropped to the floor from the mound of pills he held.

"Got the real stuff here, the white tabs," Moke said. "Some reds, that bootleg shit . . . What're these blue ones for?"

Chucky started toward him. "Gimme those . . ."

Moke shoved his hand back into the pocket, left it there and pulled open his jacket with his other hand.

"See it?"

Chucky said, "I don't have time for you right now. Come on, gimme those."

"I cleaned out your pill drawer so you won't OD on me, have to take you to the hospital . . ."

Kyle stood up. She said to Chucky, "I'll see you another time."

"Stay there," Moke said. "We like your company." He said to Chucky, "They have to pump you out, man, it'd take a dredge, wouldn't it? Get way down there in your bottomland." Moke was having fun. He liked this smart good-looking girl as an audience. She looked right at him and listened, as she was doing now. It was fun to act up in front of her. Moke walked over to the glass doors to the balcony, flicked off the catch and slid one of the doors all the way open.

He had their attention.

"Sun going down, starting to cool, huh? Best time of the day."

Chucky said, "Tell me what you want, partner."

"Don't call me that less you mean it."

Chucky edged toward him and stopped. "Tell me."

"I want you to be healthy," Moke said, brought his hand out and looked at the pills. "I don't think you need these no more."

There were two Cadillacs and Barry's Rolls in the highrise circular drive, Lionel Oliva standing against the first car as the Mercedes came up the ramp toward him. Stick swung in past him and parked on the downgrade.

Lionel waited for him.

"You know Kyle McLaren? She upstairs?"

Lionel said, "You know Eddie Moke?"

Stick hesitated. "What's going on?"

"He's high, man. Got a funny look. He told me to get out."

Stick walked away from him toward the entrance, stopped and came back.

"I think he's going to kill him," Lionel said.

"You're his bodyguard . . ."

"No, it's not my business, this kind of thing."

"You have a key to the place?"

Lionel looked at him but didn't answer.

"Let me use it."

"You're crazy," Lionel said.

"Gimme the key."

Moke showed Chucky the three white tablets in the palm of his hand. "This the good stuff?"

Chucky shuffled, shook his head sadly and looked at Moke again. "You having fun?"

"How'd you know?"

"Take one. Mellow you down so you recognize your old pard."

"I got my old pard by the yang, ain't I?" Moke said. He stepped out on the balcony. "Watch." Closed his hand on the pills and threw them out over the rail.

Chucky moved a step toward him and Moke brought out the nickel-plated Mag in a practiced draw, effortless, a gesture.

"Like the policeman says, freeze, motherfucker ... Hey, you know what? I never said that before. Freeze, motherfucker. Maybe I ought to be a cop. A narc type, huh? Confiscate the dope"—digging into his pocket again—"and give it the deep six," flinging out his fist with a handful of caps and tabs, red, white and blue visible for only a moment, dots against the dull sky.

Chucky wanted to run. He felt he could run right through the wall, no problem, pull open his pill drawer ... there were some in the kitchen too. No, he'd eaten them. Ones in the bedroom, eaten. Bathroom, eaten. Down in the car, maybe. No, eaten. If there were no more in the pill drawer Moke had all he owned, a pocketful and dropping from between his fingers on the balcony, couple of red ones, the bootleg street, 'ludes. He tried to say to Moke as calmly as he could, as a statement and nothing else, "What're you picking on me for?" But it didn't sound at all the way he wanted it to. It sounded like he was starting to cry. Now Moke was saying it back to him the same way, whining, "What're you picking on me for?" With his ugly mouth curling, his ugliness oozing out of him. "What're you picking on me for?" He didn't want to scream. God, he didn't want to. But Moke's hand was coming out of the pocket again. He could see Moke making a habit of this once he started. Doing it any time he liked. Having fun. Doing it when he wasn't down at the dump shooting gulls. Doing it when he hadn't anything else on. He did *not* want to scream. He wished he could tell somebody, explain how he felt. But as Moke said something looking away—looking at what, it didn't matter—he did scream and rushed at him to grab that hand held in the air ...

A distraction—and Moke's attention was on Stick coming into the room like he was late for supper, then stopping dead as though he'd found himself in the wrong place or had busted into a surprise party. Look, there was surprise all over his face.

Moke said, "Well, look it here ..."

Then was instantly inspired, seeing his prize, and said like a happy give-away show emcee, "Well, come on down!" And felt air go out of him . . .

Chucky hit him with his body, arm raised reaching for the fist holding the pills. The force, the impact took them to the iron railing that came to Chucky's navel the times he leaned over it and stared at toy boats down on the Intracoastal. This time his side struck the rail, still reaching to grab the hand. But it was empty now, the hand clawing at his shirt, the other hand hitting at him with the gun barrel. Chucky screamed again or was still screaming without beginning or end, holding this squirming leather smelly thing, lifting Moke up, Moke twisting on him, and got Moke over the rail, his upper body and his head hanging down, hat gone, gun barrel banging on wrought iron now and somebody yelling at him—he heard the voice—somebody yelling to put him down. He had Moke by the legs and would put him down, all right, all the way down. He was between Moke's legs and saw the leather arm with the nickel-plate come through the iron bars, felt it against his shin and he raised his sneaker and brought it down hard to step on the gun, hold it against the floor. He raised the two legs, slippery, greasy jeans, cowboy boots up by his face and said down to Moke behind the bars, "Give me my pills!" Again, so different than he expected to hear it, breathless, on the edge of panic. He saw Moke's hand grope at the pocket, dig inside. He saw Moke's hand come out and saw pills falling in colors, pouring out of the upside-down pocket, Moke opening his hand to hold an iron bar and those pills going too, gone.

Somebody touched him on the shoulder. Chucky felt it. He twisted enough to see Stick on the balcony and yelled at him, "Get away from me!"

He heard Stick say, "Let me help you . . ."

Help him what? He yelled again, "Get away from me or I'll put him over!"

And didn't see Stick again.

He had to get his breath—in and out, in and out, slowly. It didn't do much good. He felt like he was running. He held Moke's ankles, raising them as he went down to his knees and sat back on his sneakers to look at Moke's upside-down face through the bars, Chucky breathing in and out, in and out.

He said, "How you doing, pard?"

Believing he was in control but hearing the words as a raw, breathless sound. It did him good to look at Moke, at Moke's eyes bugged out, face livid, straining, veins coming blue on his forehead. He wanted to tell Moke, "Don't move," and go get his camera. Lighten up the situation. But his shoulders and arms ached and what he wanted was to end it. He said, "You had enough?" He said, "You gonna be a good boy?"

Moke said, straining, but making the words clear enough, "Fuck you."

Chucky stared and began to experience a feeling of deep sadness, despair creeping over him. He was tired, his arms ached . . . What he should do was jump up, move—let's go!—grab a hat, psych himself, be somebody, *any*body. But with the sad feeling he knew that if he tried even to scream, to lose himself in the effort of emptying his lungs, the sound would come out a moan. He stared at Moke's upside-down face, hair hanging as though electrified. Looked into blunt eyes, unforgiving, that would never change. He thought, oh well. Raised Moke's legs above his head and gave a push.

Moke did it for him. Screamed.

They watched him eat pills he found on the floor of the balcony. They watched him pick up the revolver and come in, closing the glass door, closing out whatever was outside. He sat down in a deep chair, holding the gun in his lap.

Kyle waited. She swallowed to wet the dryness of her mouth; she felt her heart beating. She looked up, surprised, as Stick came over. He didn't say anything. It was like he was checking on her; yes, she was still here. She watched him walk over to Chucky, touch his shoulder, reach to take the revolver. But Chucky came alive for a moment, pointed the gun at him and Stick stepped away. She would remember him talking to Chucky, the quiet tone of his voice.

He said, the first thing he said was, "You have a lawyer?"

Chucky didn't answer. The room was so still.

"You have money to hire a good one?"

Chucky didn't answer.

"I owe you some. Soon as my checks come I'll pay you back. Seventy-two five. Man. Well . . . You want anything? Is there anything I can get you?"

Chucky didn't answer.

"I'd think about dropping the piece over the side. It's his, let the cops find it with him. He assaulted you, didn't he?"

Chucky didn't answer.

"I'll talk to them if you want. I'll talk to Nestor, tell him what happened . . . Let's call nine-eleven and get it over with. What do you say?"

Kyle watched Chucky look up. He said, "I'm not going to jail." He said, "I am not going to jail." She would remember looking at Stick then as he said:

"I don't blame you."

Stick came over to her and said, "Time to go." It was something else she would remember and come to realize how much more he knew than she did. Not, "Let's go." He said, "Time to go."

They were waiting for the elevator . . . The door opened. They heard the single gunshot. She heard her own sharp intake of breath and turned to go back in the apartment. But he held her by the arm.

When they were outside he said, "I'll take us back and get the Rolls later."

"I'm going home," Kyle said.

"All right. I'll drive you."

She said, "I'd rather you didn't. Tell Barry I'll return the car sometime." She paused. "But I should wait for the police . . ."

Stick shook his head. "They'll figure it out."

She said then, "I was right, after all. I'm not ready for you yet." Her eyes, still aware, could look into his and store pictures and feelings, but she would have to decide alone, another time, what to do with them. She walked to the Rolls and opened the door. Before getting in she looked at him again and said, "But call me sometime. Will you?"

"When I'm rich," Stick said.

27

Cornell was telling him to look around, man, look out the window at the sights, at the beauty of it, not to mention the food and the fringes, man, the fringes alone you couldn't even find anyplace else. All Stick could think of, he had seventy-three thousand dollars in Florida First National, Biscayne Boulevard and Thirty-Sixth. He told Cornell he was not into fringes.

"I'm not knocking 'em, don't get me wrong. As you say, whatever your imagination allows. This is wonderland, if you like it."

"You learned something," Cornell said, "didn't you?"

"I hope so. I know I can't hang around country clubs with guys that put one hand in their pocket and their foot up on the bumper and think they're smarter than the people they work for," Stick said. "I learned I can't wait around."

"You know where you going?"

"It doesn't matter." Not with seventy-three thousand dollars—

Jesus—in the bank.

"Well, you know what direction you going?"

"Straight," Stick said. "I may try Palm Beach."

"You got delusions . . . You give your notice?"

"First thing this morning. He said I'm not going anywhere till they count the silver. We talked it over, he said stop by sometime."

"I got to go take the man some fresh coffee."

"I'll see you before I leave," Stick said, packing his sporty outfits in the canvas bag, leaving the tan and gray and black suits hanging in the closet for the next poor guy.

Barry was at the umbrella table with the *Wall Street Journal* and assorted legal-looking papers. Stick put on his sunglasses, walked down with his bag.

"What's good this morning?"

"Tootsie Roll at thirteen and a quarter and I'm not putting you on. Earnings are up to a buck eighty a share." Barry looked toward the guest house, putting the paper down. "And where's my girl when I need her? Calls me last night, she's home doing her laundry. I said, how can you be home doing your laundry, your clothes're still here? I think she's getting spacey, hanging around with the help. Hey, and the phone in the Cadillac . . . I'm getting some stuff out of there—what happened to the phone, for Christ sake?"

"It broke," Stick said.

"You mean, it broke?"

Cornell was coming with the coffee.

"I don't know," Stick said. "Somebody must've been fooling with it."

"I thought maybe you called your lawyer," Barry said, "and got pissed off and tried to throw the phone out the window."

Stick said, "What? . . . I don't have a lawyer."

"Yeah, well, you better get one, quick . . . Here." Barry lifted the *Journal*, picked up three sheets of white, legal-size paper clipped together. "Here it is."

Cornell said, pouring, "Man come looking for you while you're taking your shower."

"What man?"

"A process server," Barry said.

Why did he seem to be enjoying himself all of a sudden? It tightened Stick up, looking at the legal papers Barry was holding. "What is it?"

"I couldn't help but notice," Barry said. "You've been presented with a motion, a show cause and a hearing date."

"For what?" Not sure he really wanted to know.

Barry held up the papers. "Circuit Court for the County of Broward . . . the plaintiff, Mary Lou Stickley, now comes before the court . . ."

"My ex-*wife*?"

". . . with a motion for immediate payment of child support in arrears etcetera and . . . this one, the court wants you to show cause why you shouldn't be held in contempt, Stickley, for being such a shitty dad and not paying any child support for the past seven years . . ."

"I just gave her three hundred bucks." He sounded amazed now.

"Well, she wants back pay, ten grand a year for the seven years since the divorce, which comes to—"

"Seventy thousand dollars," Stick said, so quietly they barely heard him.

"If you don't have it, you don't have it," Barry said. "I would advise you, though, to seek employment quick and keep mailing in those payments or you'll be going back to you know where . . . Hey! . . . Hey, where you going?" Barry looked at Cornell. "Where's he going?"

"I doubt he knows," Cornell said, and watched him cross the lawn to the driveway and pass from view around the corner of the garage.

There you are, Stick thought.

MR. MAJESTYK

1

This morning they were here for the melons: about sixty of them waiting patiently by the two stake trucks and the old blue-painted school bus. Most of them, including the few women here, were Chicano migrants, who had arrived in their old junk cars that were parked in a line behind the trucks. Others, the Valley Agricultural Workers Association had brought out from Phoenix, dropping them off at 5:30 A.M. on the outskirts of Edna, where the state road came out of the desert to cross the U.S. highway. The growers and the farm workers called it Junction. There was an Enco gas station on the corner, then a storefront with a big V.A.W.A. sign in the window that was the farm labor hiring hall—closed until next season—and then a café-bar with a red neon sign that said BEER-WINE. The rest of the storefronts in the block were empty—dark, gutted structures that were gradually being destroyed by the desert wind.

The farm workers stood around on the sidewalk waiting to be hired, waiting for the labor contractors to finish their coffee, finish talking to the foremen and the waitresses, and come out and point to them and motion them toward the stake trucks and the blue-painted school bus.

The dozen or so whites were easy to spot. Most of them were worn-out looking men in dirty, worn-out clothes that had once been their own or someone else's good clothes. A tight little group of them was drinking Thunderbird, passing the wine bottle around in a paper bag. A couple of them were sipping from beer cans. Two teenaged white boys with long hair stood off by themselves, hip-cocked, their arms folded over tight white T-shirts, not seeming to mind the early morning chill. They would look around casually and squint up at the pale sky.

The Chicanos, in their straw hats and baseball caps, plaid shirts, and Levis or khakis, with their lunch in paper bags, felt the chill. They would look at the sky knowing it was near the end of the season and soon most of them would be heading for California, to the Imperial and San Joaquin valleys. Some of them—once in a while for something to do—would shield their faces from the light and look in the window of the hiring hall, at the rows of folding chairs, at the display of old V.A.W.A. strike posters and yellowed newspaper pages with columns marked in red. They would stare at the photograph of Emiliano Zapata on the wall behind the counter, at the statue of the Virgin Mary on a stand, and try to read the hand-lettered announcements: *Todo el mundo está invitado que venga a la resada—*

Larry Mendoza came out of the café-bar with a carry-out cup of coffee in each hand—one black, one cream and sugar—and walked over to the curb, beyond the front of the old blue-painted school bus. Some of the farm workers stared at him—a thin, bony-shouldered, weathered-looking Chicano in clean Levis and high-heeled work boots, a Texas straw funneled low over his eyes—and one of them, also a Chicano, said, "Hey,

Larry, tell Julio you want me. Tell him write my name down at the top." Larry Mendoza glanced over at the man and nodded, but didn't say anything.

Another one said, "How much you paying, Larry? Buck forty?"

He nodded again and said, "Same as everybody." He felt them watching him because he was foreman out at Majestyk and could give some of them jobs. He knew how they felt, hoping each day to get their names on a work list. He had stood on this corner himself, waiting for a contractor to point to him. He had started in the fields for forty cents an hour. He'd worked for sixty cents, seventy-five cents. Now he was making eighty dollars a week, all year: he got to drive the pickup any time he wanted and his family lived in a house with an inside toilet. He wished he could hire all of them, assure each man right now that he'd be working today, but he couldn't do that. So he ignored them, looking down the sidewalk now toward the Enco station where the attendant was pumping gas into an old-model four-wheel drive pickup that was painted yellow, its high front end pointing this way. Larry Mendoza stood like that, his back to the school bus and the farm workers, waiting, then began to sip the coffee with cream and sugar.

The Enco gas station attendant, with the name *Gil* stitched over the pocket of his shirt, watched the numbers changing in the window of the pump and began to squeeze the handle of the nozzle that curved into the gas tank filler, slowing the rotation of the numbers, easing them in line to read three dollars even, and pulled the nozzle out of the opening.

When he looked over at the station he saw the guy who owned the pickup stepping out of the Men's Room, coming this way across the pavement—a dark, solemn-faced man who might have passed for a Chicano except for his name. Vince Majestyk. Hard-looking guy, but always quiet, the few times he had been here. Vincent Majestyk of MAJESTYK BRAND MELONS that was lettered on the doors of the pickup and made him sound like a big grower. Shit, he looked more like a picker than a grower. Maybe a foreman, with his khaki pants and blue shirt. From what the station attendant had heard about him, the guy was scratching to get by and probably wouldn't be around very long. Comes in, buys three bucks worth of gas. Big deal.

He said, "That's all you want?"

The guy, Majestyk, looked over at him as he walked past the front of the pickup. "If you're not too busy you can wipe the bugs off the windshield," he said, and kept going, over toward the school bus and the farm workers crowding around.

The gas station attendant said to himself, Shit. Get up at five in the morning to sell three bucks' worth. Wait around all day and watch the tourists drive by. Four-thirty sell the migrants each a buck's worth. Shit.

Larry Mendoza handed Majestyk the cup of black coffee and the two of them stood watching as Julio Tamaz, a labor contractor, looked over the waiting groups of farm workers, called off names and motioned them to the school bus. There were already men aboard, seated, their heads showing in the line of windows.

"We're almost ready to go," Mendoza said.

"Good ones?" Majestyk took a sip of coffee.

"The best he's got."

"Bob Santos," the labor contractor called out. "And . . . Anbrocio Verrara."

"They're good," Mendoza said.

"Luis Ortega!"

A frail old man grinned and hurried toward the bus.

"Wait a minute," Mendoza said. "I don't know him. He ever picked before?"

Julio Tamaz, the labor contractor, turned to them with a surprised look. "Luis? All his life. Man, he was conceived in a melon field." Julio's expression brightened, relaxed in a smile as he looked at Majestyk. "Hey, Vincent, nice to see you."

Mendoza said, "That's thirty. We want any more'n that?"

Majestyk was finishing his coffee. He lowered the cup. "If Julio's got any like to work for nothing."

"Man," Julio said, "you tight with the dollar. Like to squeeze it to death."

"How's my credit?"

"Vincent"—Julio's expression was sad now—"I told you. What do I pay them with?"

"All right, I just wondered if you'd changed your mind." He took a fold of bills out of his pants pocket and handed them to the labor contractor. "Straight buck forty an hour, ten hours' work for a crew of thirty comes to four hundred and twenty. Don't short anybody."

Julio seemed offended now. "I take my percent. I don't need to cheat them."

"Larry'll ride with you," Majestyk said. "He finds anybody hasn't slipped honeydew melons before, they come back with you and we get a refund. Right?"

"Man, I never give you no bums. These people all experts."

Majestyk had already turned away and was walking back to the Enco station.

The attendant with the name *Gil* on his shirt was standing by the pickup.

"That's three bucks."

Majestyk reached into a back pocket for his wallet this time. He took out a five-dollar bill and handed it to the attendant, who looked at the bill and then at Majestyk. Without a word he turned and leisurely walked off toward the station. Majestyk watched him for a moment, knowing the guy was going to make him wait. He walked off after the guy and followed him into the station, but still had to wait while the guy fooled around at the cash register, shifting bills around in the cash drawer and breaking open a roll of coins.

"Take your time," Majestyk said.

When the bell rang he turned to see a car pulling into the station: an old-model Ford sedan that was faded blue-purple and rusting out, and needed a muffler. He watched the people getting out, moving slowly, stretching and looking around. There seemed to more of them than the car could hold.

The station attendant was saying, "I'm short of singles. I'll have to give you some change."

There were five of them, four men in work clothes and a young woman, migrants, looking around, trying to seem at ease. The young woman took a bandana from her head and, raising her face in the sunlight, closing her eyes, shook her hair from side to side, freeing it in the light breeze that came across the highway stirring sand dust. She was a good-looking girl, nice figure in pants and a T-shirt, in her early twenties, or maybe even younger. Very good-looking. Not self-conscious now, as though she was alone with whatever was behind her closed eyes. Two of the men went to the pop machine digging coins out of their pockets.

Beyond the girl the blue-painted school bus passed the station and the state road intersection, moving east down the highway.

"Here you are," the attendant said.

Majestyk held out his hand and the attendant dropped eight quarters into his palm, four at a time.

"Three, that's four and five. Hurry back and see us now."

Majestyk didn't say anything. He gave the guy a little smile. He had enough to think about and wasn't going to let the guy bother him. When he turned to the doorway he had to stop short. The girl, holding the bandana, was coming in and their eyes met for a moment—nice eyes, brown—before she looked past him toward the attendant.

"Is there a key you have to the Ladies' Room?"

The attendant's eyes moved past her, to the four men outside, and back again. "No, it's broken, you can't use it. Go down the road someplace."

"Maybe it's all right now," the girl said. "Have you looked at it? Sometimes they get all right by themselves."

The attendant was shaking his head now. "I'm telling you it's broken. Take my word for it and go someplace else, all right?"

"What about the other one?" the girl said. "The Men's Room."

"It's broken too. Both of 'em are broken."

"See, we go in separately," the girl went on. "The men, they come out, then I go in. So you don't have to call the cops, say we're doing it in there."

"I can call the cops right now." The attendant's voice was

louder, irritated. "I'm telling you both toilets are broken. You got to go someplace else."

"Where do you go?" the girl said. She waited a moment, not looking around but knowing the four men were close to the doorway now, and could hear her.

The attendant said, "I'm warning you—"

And the girl said, "Maybe you never go, uh? That's why you're full of shit."

The migrants grinned, some of them laughed out loud and there were words in Spanish, though the girl continued to stare at the attendant calmly, almost without expression.

The attendant turned to a counter and came around with a wrench in his hand, his jaw set tightly. Majestyk reached over to put a hand on the man's arm.

He said, "When did the toilet break? Since I used it?"

"Listen, I got to do what I'm told." He pulled his arm away from Majestyk and lowered his voice then, though the tension was still there. "Like anybody else. The boss says don't let no migrants in the toilets. He says I don't care they dancing around like they can taste it, don't let them in the toilets. They go in there, mess up the place, piss all over, take a bath in the sink, use all the towels, steal the toilet paper, man, it's like a bunch of pigs was in there. Place is filthy, I got to clean up after."

"Let them use it," Majestyk said.

"I tell you what my boss said. Man, I can't do nothing about it."

"What're they supposed to do?"

"Go out in the bushes, I don't know. Mister, you have any idea how many migrants stop here?"

"I know what they can do," Majestyk said. He turned from the attendant to the nice-looking Chicano girl, noticing now that she was wearing small pearl earrings.

"He says for all of you to come inside."

"I want them out of here!"

"He says he's sorry the toilets are broken."

"They're always broken," the girl said. "Every place they keep the broken toilets locked up so nobody steal them."

Majestyk was looking at her again. "You come here to work?"

"For the melons or whatever time it is. Last month we were over at Yuma."

"You know melons, uh?"

"Melons, onions, lettuce, anything you got."

"You want to work today?"

The girl seemed to think about it and then shrugged and said, "Yeah, well, since we forgot our golf clubs we might as well, uh?"

"After you go to the bathroom." Majestyk's gaze, with the soft hint of a smile, held on her for another moment.

"First things first," the girl said.

"Listen, I don't say they can't use them," the attendant said now. "You think I own this place? I work here."

"He says he works here," Majestyk said.

The girl nodded. "We believe it."

"And he says since the toilets are broken you can use something else." Majestyk's gaze moved away, past the attendant and the shelves of lube oil and the cash register and the coffee and candy machines, taking in the office.

"What're you doing?" The attendant was frowning, staring at him. "Listen, they can't use something else. They got to get out of here."

Majestyk's gaze stopped, held for a moment before coming back to the attendant. "He says use the wastebasket if you want," and motioned to the migrants with his hand. "Come on. All of you, come on in."

As two of the migrants came in hesitantly behind the girl, grinning, enjoying it, and the other two moved in closer behind her, the attendant said, "Jesus Christ, you're crazy! I'm going to call the police, that's what I'm going to do."

"Try and hold on to yourself," Majestyk said to him quietly. "You don't own this place. You don't have to pay for broken windows or anything. What do you care?"

The phone was on the desk in front of him, but the Enco gas station man with *Gil* over his shirt pocket, who had never been farther away from this place than Phoenix, hesitated now, afraid to reach for the phone or even look at it. What would happen if he did? Christ, what was going on here? He didn't know this guy Vincent Majestyk. Christ, a cold, quiet guy, he didn't know anything about him except he grew melons. He'd hardly ever seen him before.

"How do you want it?" Majestyk said to the attendant.

Watching him, the migrants were grinning, beginning to glance at each other, confident of this man for no reason they knew of but feeling it, enjoying it, stained and golden smiles softening dark faces and bringing life to their eyes, expressions that separated them as individuals able to think and feel, each one a person now, each one beginning to laugh to himself at this gas station man and his boss and his wastebasket and his toilets he could keep locked or shove up his ass for all they cared. God, it was good; it was going to be something to tell about.

"Let them use the toilets," Majestyk said to the attendant. "All right?"

The attendant held on another moment, as if thinking it over, letting them know he was not being forced into anything but was making up his own mind. He shrugged indifferently then and nodded to two keys that were attached to flat pieces of wood and hung from the wall next to the door.

"Keys're right there," the attendant said. "Just don't take all day."

2

The girl rode with him in the pickup and the four men followed in the Ford sedan that needed a paint job and a muffler, heading east on the highway toward the morning sun, seeing the flat view of sand and scrub giving way to sweeps of green fields on both sides of the highway, citrus and vegetable farms, irrigation canals and, in the near distance, stands of trees that bordered the fields and marked back roads and dry washes. Beyond the trees, in the far distance, a haze of mountains stood low against the sky, forming a horizon that was fifty miles away, in another world.

The girl was at ease, though every once in a while she would turn and look through the back window to make sure the car was still following.

Finally Majestyk said, "I'm not going to lose them."

"I'm not worried about that," the girl said. "It's the car. It could quit on them any time, blow a tire or something."

"They relatives of yours?"

"Friends. We worked the same place at Yuma."

"How long you been traveling together?"

The girl looked at him. "What are you trying to find out? If I sleep with them?"

"I'm sorry. I was just curious, I didn't mean to offend you."

When she spoke again her tone was quiet, the hostility gone. "We go to different places, help organize the farm workers. But we have to stop and work to pay our way."

"You're with the union?"

"Why? I tell you, yes, then you don't hire us?"

"You sure get on the muscle easy. I don't care if you're union or not, long as you know melons."

"Intimately. I've been in the fields most of my life."

"You sound like you went to school though."

"Couple of years. University of Texas, El Paso. I took English and History and Economics. Psychology 101. I went to the football games, learned all the cheers. Yeaaa, team—" Her voice trailed off and she added, quietly, "Shit."

"I never went past high school," Majestyk said.

"So you didn't waste any time."

He looked at her again, interested, intrigued. "You haven't told me your name."

"Nancy Chavez. I'm not related to the other Chavez, but I'll tell you something. I was on the picket line with them at Delano, during the grape strike."

"I believe it."

"I was fifteen."

He glanced at her and waited again, because she seemed deep in thought. Finally he said, "Are you from California?"

"Texas. Born in Laredo. We moved to San Antonio when I was little."

"Yeah? I was at Fort Hood for a while. I used to get down to San Antone pretty often."

"That's nice," Nancy Chavez said.

He looked at her again, but didn't say anything. Neither of

them spoke until they were passing melon fields and came in sight of the packing shed, a long wooden structure that looked like a warehouse. It was painted yellow, with MAJESTYK BRAND MELONS written across the length of the building in five-foot bright green letters.

As the pickup slowed down, approaching a dirt road adjacent to the packing shed, the girl said, "That's you, uh?"

"That's me," Majestyk said.

The pickup turned off the highway onto the dirt road and passed the front of the packing shed. There were crates stacked on the loading dock, the double doors were open; but there was no sign of activity, the shed stood dark and empty. Next to it was a low frame building with a corrugated metal roof that resembled an army barracks. The girl knew what it was, or what it had been—living quarters for migrants. It was also empty, some of its windows broken, its white paint peeling, fading gray.

The farmhouse was next, another fifty yards down the road, where three small children—two boys and a little girl—were standing in the hard-packed yard, watching the pickup drive past, and a woman was hanging wash on a clothesline that extended out from the side of the house. The children waved and Nancy put her hand out the window to wave back at them. "Are they yours, too?"

"My foreman, Larry Mendoza's," Majestyk said. "That's my house way down there, by the trees."

She could see the place now, white against the dark stand of woods, a small, one-story farmhouse with a porch, almost identical to the foreman's house. She could see the blue school bus standing in the road ahead and, off to the left beyond the ditch, the melon fields, endless rows of green vines that were familiar to the girl and never changed, hot dusty rows that seemed to reach from Texas to California, and were always waiting to be picked.

"You must have a thousand acres," she said. "More than that."

"A hundred and sixty. The man that owned this land used to have a big operation, but he subdivided when he sold out. This is my second crop year, and if I don't make it this time—"

When he stopped, the girl said, "What?"

She turned to see him staring straight ahead through the windshield, at the school bus they were approaching and the men standing in the road. She could see the car now, a new model of some kind shining golden in the sunlight, parked beyond the bus. Beyond the car was a stake truck. At the same time she was aware of the figures out in the melon field, at least twenty or more, stooped figures dotted among the rows.

She said, "You have two crews working?"

"I only hired one," Majestyk said.

"Then who's out there working?"

He didn't answer her. He pulled up behind the bus and got out without wasting any time, feeling a tenseness now as he walked past the bus, past the faces in the windows, and saw Larry Mendoza's serious, concerned expression. His foreman stood with Julio Tamaz by the front of the bus, both of them watching him, anxious. Only a few of Julio's crew had gotten out. The rest of them were still inside wondering, as he was, what the hell was going on.

He was aware of the two men standing by the gold Dodge Charger that was parked on the left side of the road—long hair and Mexican bandit moustaches, one of them wearing sunglasses. A skinny, hipless guy with a big metal belt buckle, bright yellow shirt and cowboy boots, watching him, seeming unconcerned, lounged against the rear deck of the Charger with his arms folded. There was another guy he had never seen before standing by the stake truck that, he noticed now, had a horn-type speaker mounted on the roof of the cab.

"We get here," Larry Mendoza said, "this guy's already got a crew working."

Julio Tamaz said, "What are we supposed to do, Vincent, go home? Man, what is this?"

Majestyk walked over to the ditch, behind the Charger, and stood looking out at the field, at the men standing among the rows with long burlap sacks hanging from their shoulders. Only a few of them were working. All of them, he noticed, were white. And all of them, that he could make out clearly, had the same worn-out, seedy look, skid row bums taken from the street and dropped in a melon field.

But not my melon field, Majestyk was saying to himself. He turned to the skinny dude with sunglasses lounged against the car.

"I don't think I know you."

He watched the guy straighten with a lazy effort and come off the car extending his hand.

"I'm Bobby Kopas. Come out from Phoenix with some top hand pickers for you."

Majestyk ignored the waiting hand. "I don't think I've ever done business with you either. What I know for sure is I never will."

Bobby Kopas grinned at him, letting his hand fall. "'Fore you say anything you might be sorry about—how does a buck twenty an hour sound to you? Save yourself some money and they're already hard at it."

"I hire who I want," Majestyk said. "I don't hire a bunch of winos never slipped melons before."

Kopas glanced over at the bus, at Larry Mendoza and Julio and Nancy Chavez. "I don't know—you hire all these Latins, no white people. Looks like discrimination to me."

"Call them out and get off my land," Majestyk said.

"These Latins buddies of yours? What do you care who does the job, long as it gets done?"

"I just told you, I hire who I want."

"Yeah, well the thing is you want me," Kopas said. "Only it hasn't sunk in your head yet. Because everything is easier and less trouble when you hire my crew. If you understand what I'm saying to you."

There it was, a little muscle-flexing. Hotshot dude trying to pressure him, sure of himself, with two strong-arm guys to back him up. Majestyk stared at him and thought about it and finally he said, "Well, you're making sounds like you're a mean little ass-kicker. Only you haven't convinced me yet it's true. Then again, if you say anything else and I don't like it, I'm liable to take your head off. So maybe you ought to consider that."

Majestyk stared at him a moment, as Kopas began to say, "Now hang on a minute, dad—" but that was all. Majestyk turned away, ignoring him, looking out at the field again and began yelling at the winos.

"Come on, time to go home! Leave anything you picked or messed up and haul ass out, right now! Come on, gents, move it!"

The few that were working stopped, straightened, and now all of the men in the rows were looking this way, not sure what to do. Kopas saw them. He had to stop them before they moved. He turned to the guy behind him and nodded toward the stake truck. The guy took off. The other one, standing by the truck, saw him coming and quickly got into the cab.

"You hear me?" Majestyk yelled out. "Time to go home. Man made a mistake. You come to the wrong place." As he began to say, "Come on, move!" his words were drowned out by a blast of rock music, intense hard rock, the sound of electrified, amplified guitars wailing out over the melon fields.

Majestyk looked toward the truck, at the horn speaker mounted on the cab. His gaze shifted to Bobby Kopas. He saw him grinning and saw the grin fade as he moved toward him. He saw him get around to the side of the Charger, reach in through the open window and come out with a pump-action shotgun. Kopas put the gun under his arm, pointing down slightly, holding it with both hands, and Majestyk stopped.

Nancy Chavez, staring at Bobby Kopas, came away from the bus. She said, "Man, what're you going to do now, shoot us?"

"I'm gonna talk to him and this time he's gonna listen," Kopas said. "That's what I'm gonna do."

She was moving toward him, taking her time. "Buck twenty an hour—you going to shoot people for that? Man, you need another hit of something."

"He threatened me," Kopas said, "and all your people heard it. But I'll tell you, he ain't gonna threaten me again."

Staring at him, moving toward him, Nancy Chavez said, "I don't know—guy brings wine heads out, plays music for them. He must be a little funny."

Majestyk was past the trunk of the car, two strides from the muzzle of the shotgun.

"You say you come from Phoenix? What do you do there, roll drunks and hire them as pickers?"

Kopas kept his eyes on him, holding onto the shotgun. "I'm telling you, keep back. Stay where you are."

"Mean little ass-kicker like you," Majestyk said. "What do you need a gun for?"

"I'm warning you!"

Majestyk stepped into him as he brought the shotgun up, grabbing the barrel with his left hand and drove his right fist hard into Bobby Kopas's face, getting some nose and mouth, staying with him as Kopas went back against the car door and slammed the fist into him again, getting his sunglasses this time, wiping them from his face, and pulling the shotgun out of his hands as Kopas twisted and his head and shoulders fell into the window opening.

The other one with the hair and heavy moustache who had been with Kopas was coming back from the truck, coming fast, but not in time. He stopped and raised his hands, three yards away, as Majestyk put the shotgun on him.

The loud rock music continued, the wailing guitars wailed on, until Majestyk stepped into the middle of the road, raised the shotgun and blew the horn speaker off the top of the stake truck.

The sound stopped. Majestyk looked at the man with his hands half raised. He pumped a shell into the chamber of the shotgun and walked past him to the truck. When he opened the rightside door he could hear the radio music again, the rock guitars. The man sitting behind the wheel stared at him.

"Get those wine heads out of my field," Majestyk said, and slammed the door.

He came back to the Charger, nodded toward Kopas hanging against the door and said to the one with his hands raised, "Put him inside and get out of here." He waited, seeing the blood coming out of Kopas's nose, staining his yellow shirt, as the guy pulled Kopas around, opened the door and eased him onto the seat.

"You got the key?" When the guy nodded Majestyk said, "Open the trunk."

He had to wait for him again, for the guy to walk back and unlock it. As the trunk lid swung up, Majestyk stepped over, threw the shotgun inside and slammed it closed. He stood one stride away from the guy with the hair and the heavy moustache who was staring at him and maybe was on the verge of doing something.

Majestyk said, "Make up your mind."

The guy hesitated; but the moment was there and passed. He walked around to the driver's side and got in the car.

Majestyk walked up on the other side to look at Kopas holding a handkerchief to his face. He said, "Hey," and waited for Kopas to lower the handkerchief and look out at him.

"You want my opinion, buddy, I think you're in the wrong business."

3

He was arrested that afternoon.

Nancy Chavez saw it happen. She was crouched in the vines working a row, slipping the ripe honeydew melons off, gently turning the ones that would be ready in a day or two, pushing them under the vines so they would not be exposed to the sun. Her sack, with the rope loop digging into her shoulder, was almost full. A few more melons and she would carry it over to the road and hand it up to Vincent Majestyk in the trailer that was hooked to the pickup truck. Maybe they would talk a little bit while he unloaded the sack and she got a drink of water from the canvas bag that hung from the side of the trailer. He had been curious about her, admitting it, and she was curious about him. There were questions in her mind, though she wasn't sure she could come right out and ask them. She wondered if he lived alone or had a wife somewhere. She wondered if he knew what he was doing, if he could harvest a hundred and sixty acres within the next week, sort and pack the melons and get them to a broker. Even for a late crop he was running out of time.

When her sack was full and she looked up again, straightening, the squad car, with blue lights flashing, was standing in the road by the pickup truck. She saw the two policemen, in khaki uniforms and cowboy hats, talking to Majestyk in the trailer. When he came down and one of them took him by the arm, he pulled his arm free and the other policeman moved in close with his hand on his holster. What the hell was going on?

Nancy Chavez dropped the sack and started across the rows. Some of the other pickers were watching now and Larry Mendoza was coming out of the field, not far away from her. She hurried, but by the time she and Mendoza reached the road, Majestyk was in the squad car and it was moving off, blue lights spinning, raising a column of dust that thinned to nothing by the time the squad car reached the highway and turned left, toward Edna.

"What's going on?" Nancy Chavez said. "They arresting him?"

Larry Mendoza shook his head, squinting in the sun glare. "I don't know. But I guess somebody better go find out."

"Is there somebody at his house maybe you better tell?"

"No, there's nobody lives there but him."

"He isn't married?"

"Not anymore."

The squad car was out of sight but Mendoza was still staring in the direction of the highway. "Those were sheriff deputies. Well, I guess I better go find out."

"If there's anything you want me to do," the girl said, "don't be afraid to tell me. Go on, we'll take care of the melons."

The Edna Post of the County Sheriff's Department had been remodeled and painted light green. Everything was light green, the cement block walls, the metal desks, the chairs, the formica counter—light green and chrome-trimmed under bright fluorescent lights. They took Majestyk into an office, sat him down against the wall and left him.

After a while one of the arresting officers came back in with a file folder, sat down at a desk where there was a typewriter and began to peck at the keys with two fingers. The deputy's name was Harold Ritchie. He was built like a running guard, had served four years in the Marines, including a combat tour in Vietnam, and had a tattoo on his right forearm, a snake coiled around a dagger, with an inscription that said *Death Before Dishonor*.

Looking down at the typewriter, as if reciting the words from memory, he said, "This warrant states that you have been arrested on a charge that constitutes a felony, assault with a deadly weapon. You may choose to stand mute at this time and of course you have a right to counsel. You can call a lawyer or anybody you want. You are allowed one phone call—"

The deputy paused, looking up, as a man in a lightweight summer suit came into the office and closed the door behind him.

The man said, "Go on. Don't let me interrupt."

His tone was mild, his appearance slightly rumpled. For some reason he reminded Majestyk of a schoolteacher, a man who had taught high school English or civics for at least thirty years, though he knew the man was a policeman.

"After which," Ritchie continued, "you will be released on bond, if you choose, or held here till you're taken to the county seat for your pretrial examination."

The deputy looked up, finished. The mild-appearing man came over to the desk, his gaze holding on Majestyk.

"My name is Detective Lieutenant McAllen. Do you understand your rights under the law?"

"I can keep my mouth shut, and that seems about it," Majestyk said.

"You can tell your side of it if you want. Feel free."

"A man I never saw before tried to force me to use a crew I didn't need."

"So you hit him with a shotgun."

"I hit him with a fist."

"The complainant says he was offering you a business proposition. Instead of a simple no thanks, you assaulted him with a shotgun."

"It was his, not mine," Majestyk said. "Man was trespassing on my land."

"Lieutenant"—the deputy was holding the file folder; he handed it, open, to McAllen—"four years ago in California he got one to five for assault. Served a year in Folsom."

McAllen studied the folder a moment before looking up. "Vincent A. Majestyk. What're you, a Polack?"

Majestyk stared at him in silence. The lieutenant was looking at the folder again.

"He grows melons," the deputy said. "Generally keeps to himself. I mean he hasn't given us any trouble before this."

"But sometimes you like to mix it up," McAllen said. "You use a gun the time in California?"

"I was in a bar. A man hit me with a beer bottle."

"Sitting there minding your own business, he hit you with a bottle."

"We were arguing about something. He wanted to go outside. I told him to drink his beer."

"So he hit you and you hit him back. If it was your first offense, how come they put you away?"

"The guy was in the hospital a while," Majestyk said. "He came to the trial with a broken collarbone and his jaw wired up and some buddies of his that said I started it and kicked his face in when he was on the floor."

"But you never did such a thing."

"I've already been tried for it. You want to do it again?"

"Served your time and now making an honest living. You married?"

"I was four years. My wife divorced me while I was in prison."

"Run out on you, huh? How come? Didn't you get along?"

"You want to talk about my marriage? Find out what we did in bed?"

McAllen didn't say anything for a moment. He stared at Majestyk, then turned to leave, dropping the folder on the desk.

"I think you better talk to a lawyer."

"Lieutenant, I got a crop of melons to get in." He saw the man hesitate and turn to look at him again. "Let me get them picked, I'll come back right after."

McAllen took his time. "That's what you're worried about, melons?"

"I get them in and packed this week or I lose the crop. I'm asking for a few days, that's all."

"The court'll set a bond on you," McAllen said. "Pay it, you can go out and pick all the melons you want."

"Except if I put up bail I won't have any money left for a crew. And I can't pick a hundred and sixty acres by myself."

McAllen was thoughtful again, studying him. He said, "I don't know anything about you but the fact you've been arrested for assault and have a previous conviction. So I don't have any reason to feel sorry for you, do I?"

"I give you my word," Majestyk said. "I'll come right back."

"And even if I did feel sorry for you, if for some reason I believed you, the law doesn't happen to make any provision for your word," McAllen said. "That's how it is." He turned and walked out.

Larry Mendoza waited three and a half hours on the bench by the main desk, looking up every time one of the deputies came out of an office. They would stand around drinking coffee, not paying any attention to him. Finally they told him no, it was too late to see his friend now, he'd have to come back tomorrow. They told him the charge was felonious assault and the bond was set at five thousand, which would cost him five hundred, cash, if he wanted to go to the county seat and get a bondsman to put up the money. Or wait a couple of days for the examination. If the court set a trial date and appointed a lawyer, maybe the lawyer could get the bond lowered.

Christ, he didn't know anything about bonds or examinations. He didn't know what the hell was going on—how they could arrest a man for throwing somebody off his property who didn't belong there. It didn't make sense.

When he got back Julio had already picked up his crew and was gone. He asked his wife, Helen, and Nancy Chavez and the four men who were with her—the group of them sitting on the front steps of his house in the shade—if it made any sense.

Nancy Chavez said, "Cops. Talking to cops is like talking to the wall. They don't tell you anything they don't want to."

Of course not, it didn't make sense. Christ almighty, who ever expected cops to make sense? All they could do was keep working, do that much for him while he was in jail, then all of them tell at the examination, or whatever it was, what happened and maybe, if the judge listened, he would see it didn't make any sense and Vincent would get off. Maybe.

Helen Mendoza let Nancy use her kitchen and gave her some green beens and beets to go with the Franco-American spaghetti she fixed for her friends and herself. Larry Mendoza said why didn't they stay in Vincent's house while he was in jail. Vincent wouldn't mind. In fact he'd want them to. Nancy Chavez said all right, for one night. But tomorrow they'd get the migrant quarters in shape, clean up the kitchen and a couple of rooms and stay there. They had cots and bedding in the car. For a week it wouldn't be so bad. They'd lived in worse places.

Larry Mendoza went back to the Edna Post the next day, Saturday. They searched him good and put him in a little closet of a room that had a table, two chairs facing each other and a metal cabinet. He waited about a half hour before a deputy brought Majestyk in and closed the door. The deputy waited outside. They could see him through the glass part of the door.

"Are you all right? Christ, it doesn't make any sense."

"I'm fine," Majestyk told him. "Listen, what we got to think about's the crop. You're here visiting me, you should be working the crew.

"Man, we're worried about you. What if they put you in jail?"

"I'm already in jail."

"In the penitentiary. For something that don't make any sense."

"We're going to court Monday," Majestyk said. "I'll see if I can talk to the judge, explain it to him."

"And we'll be there," Mendoza said. "Tell them what happened."

"I'll tell them. You'll be out in the field."

"Vincent, you need all the help you can get. You got to have a lawyer."

"I need pickers more than I do a lawyer," Majestyk said, "and they both cost money."

"The deputy says the court will appoint one."

"Maybe. We'll see what happens. But right now, today and tomorrow, the melons are out there, right? And they're not going to wait much longer. You don't get them in we'll lose a crop, two years in a row."

Mendoza was frowning, confused. "How can something like this happen? It doesn't make any sense."

"I don't know," Majestyk said. "If it isn't a drought or a hailstorm it's something else. Skinny little dude comes along thinking he's a big shooter—"

"Bobby Kopas," Mendoza said. "This morning Julio says he saw the guy's car parked at a motel."

"Where?"

"Right here, in Edna. He's still hanging around."

"I can't think about him," Majestyk said. "I would sure like to see him again sometime, but I can't think about him. I do—I'm liable to get it in my head to bust out of here."

Mendoza reached across the table to touch his arm. "Vincent, don't do anything foolish, all right?"

"I'll try not to," Majestyk said.

4

Monday morning, early, they brought Majestyk and four other prisoners out of the jail area to a tank cell, near the back entrance, that was used for drunks and overnighters. There were no bunks in here, only a varnished bench against two of the light green cement block walls, a washbasin, and a toilet without a seat. The fluorescent lights, built into the ceiling and covered with wire mesh, reflected on the benches and waxed tile floor. For a jail the place was clean and bright; that much could be said for it.

The food wasn't too good though. A trusty, with a deputy standing by, slipped the trays in under the barred section of wall, next to the door. Five trays, for Majestyk, two Chicanos, a black guy, and a dark-haired, dude-looking guy in a suit and tinted glasses who hadn't said a word all morning.

One of the Chicanos passed the trays around and went back to sit with the other Chicano, probably a couple of migrants. The black guy was near the corner, where the two benches met. The dark-haired guy looked at his tray and set it on the bench next to him, between where he was sitting low against the wall and where Majestyk sat with his tray on his lap.

Stiff-looking fried eggs and dried-up pork sausage, stale bread, no butter, and lukewarm coffee. Majestyk ate it, cleaned the tray, because he was hungry. But he'd have a word for the deputy when he saw him again. The one with the tattoo. Ask him if they ruined the food on purpose. Christ, it was just as easy to do it right. Where'd they get the idea food had to be stiff and cold?

He looked down at the tray next to him. The guy hadn't touched anything. He sat with his shoulders hunched against the wall, smoking a cigarette. Long dark wavy hair that almost covered his ears and a two-day growth of beard. Striped collar sticking out of the rumpled, expensive-looking dark suit. Shirt open, no tie. No expression on his face behind the lightly tinted wire-frame glasses.

Looking at him, Majestyk said, "You going to eat your sausage?"

The guy drew on his cigarette. He didn't look at Majestyk. He moved his hand to the tray, behind it, and sent it off the bench to hit with a sharp metal clatter, skidding, spilling over the tile floor.

The two Chicanos and the black guy were poised over their trays, eyes raised, but watching only for a moment before looking down again and continuing to eat.

"You're not going to eat it," Majestyk said, "then nobody does, uh?"

The dark-haired guy was lighting a fresh cigarette from the butt of another, the pack still in his hand.

He said, "You want it? Help yourself."

"I guess not," Majestyk said. He looked at the guy as he put the pack of cigarettes in his coat pocket. "You got an extra one of those?"

The guy didn't say anything. He drew on his cigarette and blew the smoke out slowly.

"I'll pay you back when I get out," Majestyk said. "How'll that be?"

The guy turned now to look at him, and another voice said, "Hey, you want a smoke?"

The black guy was holding up a cigarette package that was almost flat.

Majestyk put his tray on the bench and walked over to him. They both took one and Majestyk sat down next to the black guy to get a light.

"Man, don't you know who that is?"

"Some movie star?"

"That's Frank Renda." The black guy kept his voice low, barely moving his mouth.

"He looks like an accordian player," Majestyk said, "used to be on TV."

"Jesus Christ, I said Frank Renda."

"I don't know—I might've heard of him."

"He's in the rackets. Was a hit man. You know what I'm saying to you? He shoots people, with a gun."

"But they caught him, huh?"

"Been trying to for a long time," the black guy said. "Other night this off-duty cop pulls up in front of a bar, some place up on the highway. He sees a man come out. Sees Renda get out of his car, walk up to the man, and bust him five times with a thirty-eight."

"Why didn't the cop shoot him?"

"Didn't have to. Renda's gun's empty."

"He doesn't sound too bright. Pulling a dumb thing like that."

"They say he wanted the man bad, couldn't wait."

Majestyk was studying Renda. Maybe he was dumb, but he looked cool, patient, like somebody who moved slowly, without wasted effort. He didn't look like an accordian player now. He looked like some of the guys he had seen in prison, at Folsom. Mean, confident, hard-nosed guys who would give you that look no matter what you said to them. Like who the fuck are you? Don't waste my time. How did guys get like that? Always on the muscle.

"They got him this time," the black guy said. "Gonna nail

his ass for ninety-nine years—you ask him is he gonna eat his sausage."

Because of Renda they brought the five prisoners out the back way to the parking area, where the gray county bus and the squad cars were waiting. Get them out quick, without attracting a lot of attention. But a crowd of local people had already gathered, along with the reporters and TV newsmen who had been in Edna the past two days and were ready for them. A cameraman with a shoulder-mounted rig began shooting as soon as the door opened and the deputies began to bring them out in single file, the two Chicanos first, startled by the camera and the people watching, then the black guy. They held up Renda and Majestyk in the hallway inside the door, to handcuff them because they were felons. A deputy told them to put their hands behind their backs; but the deputy named Ritchie told him to cuff them in front—it was a long ride, let them sit back and enjoy it.

When Renda appeared, between two deputies, the TV camera held on him, panning with him to the bus, and a newsman tried to get in closer, extending a hand mike.

"Frank, over here. What do you think your chances are? They got a case against you or not?"

Renda held his head low, turned away from the camera. A deputy stuck out his hand, pushing the mike away, and two more deputies moved in quickly, from the steps by the rear door, to stand in the newsman's way and restrain him if they had to. This left Majestyk alone at the top of the steps. He watched them put Renda aboard the bus. Four, five deputies standing now with their backs to him. He watched the newsman with the mike come around and mount the steps. The newsman turned, facing the bus, and the TV camera swung toward him.

Majestyk was close enough to hear him and stood listening as the TV newsman said, "Today, Frank Renda is being taken to the county seat for pretrial examination on a charge that will undoubtedly be first-degree murder. Renda, a familiar name in organized crime, has been arrested nine times without a conviction. Now, it would appear, his luck has finally run out. The prosecutor's office is convinced Renda will stand trial, be convicted of the murder charge, and spend the rest of his life in prison. This is Ron Malone with TV-Action News coming to you from Edna."

Majestyk walked down the steps past the newsman, came up behind the deputies standing by the bus door and said, "Excuse me."

The two deputies nearest him turned, with momentary looks of surprise. One of them took his arm then and said, "Get in there."

He got in, moved past the driver and the deputy standing by him, and took a seat on the left side of the bus, in front of the black guy, who leaned forward as he sat down and said over his shoulder, "You get on TV? Your mama'll be proud to see you."

Renda sat across the aisle, a row ahead of him. The two Chicanos sat together on Renda's side, two rows closer to the front. When the door closed and the bus began to move, circling out of the parking area with a squad car leading and another following, the deputy standing by the driver moved down the aisle to take a seat in the back of the bus. Both he and the driver, Majestyk noticed, were unarmed.

He said to himself, How does that help you? And settled back to stare out the window at the familiar billboards and motels and gas stations, the tacoburger place, the stores that advertised used clothing, *Ropa Usada.* Railroad tracks ran parallel with the highway, beyond a bank of weeds. They passed the warehouses and loading sheds that lined the tracks, platformed old buildings that bore the names of growers and produce companies. They passed the silver water tower that stood against the sky—EDNA, HOME OF THE BRONCOS—and moved out into miles of fences and flat green fields, until the irrigation ditches ended and the subdued land turned color, reverted to its original state, and became desert country.

Looking out at the land he wondered when he would be coming back. When, or if he would be coming back. He said to himself, What are you doing here? How did it happen? Sitting handcuffed in a prison bus. His fields miles behind him. Going to stand trial again. The chance of going to prison again. Could that happen? No, he said to himself, refusing to believe it. He could not let it happen, because he could not live in a prison again, ever. He couldn't think about it without the feeling of panic coming over him, the feeling of being suffocated, caged, enclosed by iron bars and cement walls and not able to get out. He remembered reading about a man exploring a cave, hundreds of feet underground, who had crawled into a seam in the rocks and had got wedged there, because of his equipment and was unable to move foward or backward or reach the equipment with his hands to free it. Majestyk had stopped reading and closed the magazine, because he knew the man had died there.

Prison was for men like Frank Renda—sitting across the aisle with his own thoughts, slouched low in his seat, staring straight ahead, off somewhere in his mind. What was he thinking about?

What difference did it make? Majestyk forgot about Frank Renda and did not look at him again until almost a half hour later, when the land outside the bus had changed again, submitting to signs and gas stations and motels, and the empty highway became a busy street that was taking them through a run-down industrial area on the outskirts of the city.

He noticed Renda because Renda was sitting up straighter now, stretching to see ahead, through the windshield, then turning to look out the windows as the bus moved along in the steady flow of traffic. The man had seemed half asleep before. Now he was alert, as though he was looking for a particular store or building, a man looking for an address written on a piece of paper. Or maybe he had lived around here at one time and it was like revisiting the old neighborhood, seeing what had changed. That was the feeling Majestyk had. He was curious about Renda again and continued to watch him and glance off to follow his gaze. Through the windshield now—to see the intersection they were approaching, the green light and the man standing in the middle of the street, caught between the flows of traffic.

Later, he remembered noticing the man moments before it happened. Maybe ten seconds before—seeing the man in bib overalls holding a paper bag by the neck, a farmer who'd come to town for a bottle of whiskey, guy from the sticks who didn't know how to cross a busy street and got trapped. He remembered thinking that and remembered, vividly, the man in bib overalls waiting for the lead squad car to pass him and then starting across the street, weaving slightly, walking directly into the path of the bus.

There was a screeching sound as the driver slammed on the brakes and the tires grabbed the hot pavement. Majestyk was thrown forward against the seat in front of him, but pushed himself up quickly to see if the man had been hit. No, because the driver was yelling at him. "Goddamn drunk—get out of the way!"

He saw the man's head and shoulders then, past the hood of the bus, the man grinning at the driver.

"Will you get the hell out of the way!"

The deputy who'd been in the rear was coming up the aisle, past Majestyk, and the driver was standing now, leaning on the steering wheel.

The man in the overalls, whose name was Eugene Lundy, was still grinning as he took a .44 Colt magnum out of the paper bag, extended it over the front of the hood, and fired five times, five holes blossoming on the windshield as the driver hit against his seat and went out of it and the deputy was slammed backward down the aisle and hit the floor where Majestyk was standing.

Lundy drew a .45 automatic out of his overalls, turned and fired four times at the squad car that had come to a stop across the intersection. Then he was moving—as the doors of the squad car swung open—past the front of the bus and down the cross street.

Harold Ritchie knocked his hat off getting out of the lead squad car, swinging out of there fast and drawing his big Colt special. He put it on Lundy, tracking with him, and yelled out for him to halt, concentrating, when he heard his partner call his name.

"Ritch!"

And he looked up to see the panel truck coming like crazy on the wrong side of the street, swerving around from behind the bus to take a sweeping right at the intersection. Ritchie jumped back out of the way, though the truck had room to spare. He saw one of the rear doors open and the bottle with the lighted rag for a wick come flying out and he was moving to the right, running hard, waving an oncoming car to keep back when the bottle smashed against the rear deck of the squad car and burst into flames. Five seconds later the gas tank exploded and instantly the entire car was on fire, inside and out.

Ritchie was across the street now, waving at the traffic, yelling at cars to stop where they were. He didn't see his partner or know where he was. From this angle he could see the second squad car close behind the bus and the driver-side door swing open.

In the same moment he saw the station wagon coming up fast from behind. He saw the shotgun muzzles poke out through the side windows and heard them and saw them go off as the station wagon swerved in, sheared the door off the squad car, and kept coming, beginning a sweeping right turn around the bus.

Ritchie raised his big Colt special, steadying it beneath the grip with his left hand and squeezed off four shots into the station wagon's windshield. The first two would have been enough, because they hit the driver in the face and the wagon was already out of control, half through the turn when the driver slumped over the wheel and the wagon slammed squarely into the burning squad car.

One of the men in the back seat of the wagon tried to get out the left side and Ritchie shot him before he cleared the doorway. But then he had to reload and the two who went out the other side of the wagon made it to a line of parked cars before Ritchie could put his Colt on them. He still didn't know where his partner was until he got to the station wagon, looked out past the rear end of it and saw his partner lying in the street.

Watching from the bus, Majestyk recognized Ritchie, the

one with the tattoo who looked like a pro lineman. He was aiming and firing at two men crouched behind a parked car—until one of them raised up, let go with a shotgun and they took off, running up the street past a line of storefronts. Ritchie stepped out from behind the station wagon, fired two shots that shattered two plate-glass windows, then lowered his Colt and started after them, waving his arm again, yelling at the people on the sidewalk and pressed close to the buildings to get inside, to get the hell off the street.

Now there were no police in front of the bus.

The moment Renda moved, Majestyk's gaze was on him, following him up the aisle past the two Chicanos huddled low in their seat. He watched Renda—who did not bother to look at the dead driver lying on the floor—reach past the steering wheel and pull a control level. The door opened. Renda approached it cautiously, looking through the opening and down the cross street a half block to where Eugene Lundy and the panel truck were waiting. He seemed about to step out, then twisted away from the opening, dropping to his hands and knees, as two shots drilled through the pane of glass in the door panel.

Majestyk's gaze came away and he looked down at the deputy lying in the aisle. He was sure the man was dead, but he got out of his seat and reached down to feel for a pulse. Nothing. God, no, the man had been shot through the chest. Majestyk was about to rise, then hesitated as he saw the ring of keys hanging from the deputy's belt. He told himself to do it, *now*, and think about it later if he had to. That's what he did, unhooked the ring and slipped the keys into his pants pocket. As he rose, turning toward the rear of the bus, he saw the black guy, only a few feet away, staring at him.

Neither of them spoke. The black guy looked away and Majestyk moved down the aisle to the back windows.

The second squad car was close behind, directly below him. He could see the deputy behind the wheel, his face bloody, talking excitedly into the radio mike. The next moment he was out of the car with his revolver drawn, moving around the back end of it to the sidewalk. Majestyk watched him. The deputy ran in between two cars that were facing out of a used car lot, then down behind the row of gleaming cars with prices painted on the windshields to where his partner was covering the door of the bus from behind the end car in the line.

Majestyk made his way back up the aisle in a crouch, watching the used car lot through the right-side windows. He saw both deputies raise their revolvers and fire.

With the closely spaced reports Renda dropped again away from the door and behind the first row of seats.

Halfway up the aisle Majestyk watched him.

Renda was looking at the two Chicanos now who were also crouched in the aisle, close to each other with their shoulders hunched.

After a moment Renda said, "Come on, let's go. We're getting out of here."

When they realized he was speaking to them the two Chicanos looked at him wide-eyed, frightened to death, and Renda said again, "Come on, move!"

One of the Chicanos said, "We don't want to go nowhere."

"Jesus, you think we're going to talk it over? I said we're going." Renda was reaching for them now, pulling the first one to his feet, then the other one, pushing them past him in the narrow aisleway.

The other Chicano said, "Man, I was drunk driving—I don't run away from that."

And the Chicano who had spoken before was saying, as he was pushed to the front, "Listen, please, they see us coming out they start shooting!"

"That's what we're going to find out," Renda said.

He crowded them, jamming them in the doorway, then put a foot behind the second man—as the man said, "Please, don't! We don't want to go!"—pushed hard and the two Chicanos were out of the bus, stumbling, getting to their feet, starting to make a run or it.

Majestyk watched the two deputies in the used car lot swing their revolvers over to cover them and was sure they were going to fire. But now the two Chicanos were running toward them with their hands raised high in the air, screaming, "Don't shoot! Please! Don't shoot!" And the deputies lowered their revolvers and waved them into the used car lot.

Renda was watching, crouched by the open door as Majestyk came the rest of the way up the aisle.

"Go out there, you give yourself up or get shot," Majestyk said.

Renda looked over his shoulder at him. He watched Majestyk step over the dead driver and slip into the seat, lean against the steering wheel and reach with both hands to turn on the ignition.

"What're you doing?"

Majestyk didn't answer him. He put the bus in gear, began to ease it forward a few feet, then braked and shifted into reverse.

The two deputies in the used car lot saw it happen. They moved the two Chicanos out of the way and returned their attention to the bus—in time to see it start up abruptly in reverse and smash its high rear end into the grille of their squad car. The bus moved forward—God almighty—went into reverse and again slammed into the car, cranked its wheels and made a U-turn out of there, leaving the radiator of the squad car spewing water and the two deputies watching it pick up speed, back the way they had come. They wanted to shoot. They were ready, but at the last moment had to hold their fire because of the people in cars and on the sidewalk, on the other side of the street.

Then the two city police cars were approaching the intersection from the south—off to the left—their sirens wailing, and the two deputies ran out to the sidewalk, waving their arms to flag the cars down.

Majestyk heard the sirens, the sound growing fainter, somewhere behind them. He headed west on the street they had taken into town, turned north on a side street, then west again a few blocks up. Finally he slowed down and eased the bus into an alley, behind a row of cinder-block industrial buildings that appeared deserted. He pulled the lever to open the door and looked around at the black guy.

"Here's your stop."

"Man," the black guy said, "you know where you going? If they don't shoot you?"

Renda was in the aisle, moving toward the black guy. "Come on, Sambo, move it. And take them with you."

Majestyk helped the black guy lift the bodies of the driver and the deputy and ease them out through the narrow doorway. Renda told them to hurry up, for Christ sake, but Majestyk paid no attention to him.

As he got behind the wheel again the black guy, standing outside, said, "Man, what did you do?"

Majestyk looked at him. For a moment he seemed about to say something, then closed the door in the black guy's face and took off down the alley.

Move out fast and try to get to high country before the police set up road blocks and got their helicopters out. That's what he had to do. Keep to the back roads, working north, get far enough away from the highway and find some good cover.

That's what he did. Found an old sagging feed barn sitting out by itself on a dried-up section of pasture land, pulled the bus inside, and swung the double doors shut to enclose them in dim silence.

Majestyk remained by the crack of vertical light that showed between the doors, looking out in the direction they had come, seeing the dust settling in the sun glare.

Somewhere behind him in the gloom Renda said, "You move, don't you? I figured you for some kind of a local clown, but you move."

Majestyk didn't say anything.

"What'd they bust you for?"

"Assault."

"With what?"

"A shotgun."

"Assault, shit, that's attempted murder. They were going to jam you the same as me."

"Maybe," Majestyk said.

"Maybe? What do you think you're going to do about it?"

"I got an idea might work."

"Listen," Renda said, "we get to a phone we're out of the country before morning. Drive to Mexico, get some passports, we're gone."

His back still to Renda, Majestyk pulled the deputy's keys out of his pocket. He'd almost forgotten about them, hurrying to get out of there, maybe hurrying too fast and not thinking clearly. He would have to slow down a little. Not waste time, but make sure he wasn't doing anything dumb. He listened to Renda as he began to study the keys and select one that would fit his handcuffs.

"I got friends," Renda was saying, "as you noticed, huh? It was set up in a hurry and they blew it. All right, I call some more friends. They get us out of the country, someplace no extradition, and wait and see what happens. I got enough to live on, I mean high, the rest of my life. It won't be home, shit no, but it won't be in the fucking slam either. I couldn't make that. Couple of weeks I'd be sawing my fucking wrists." He paused. "What're you doing?"

Majestyk didn't say anything and Renda came over to him, his face brightening as he saw the keys.

"Jesus, it keeps getting better. You not only move, you think. Give me those, hold your hands up." As he tried the keys in Majestyk's handcuffs he said, "Figure if you take a long chance, get me out of there, it'd be worth something, huh? Okay, you do something for me, I do something for you. Maybe fix it so you can go with me."

Renda snapped the handcuffs open. As Majestyk slipped them off Renda handed him the keys and raised his own hands to be unlocked.

"How's that sound?"

"I think you got it ass-backwards," Majestyk said, returning the keys to his pocket. "I'm not going with you, you're going with me."

He found an old hackamore that did the job. Looping it around the link of the handcuffs, he could pull Renda along by the length of rope, yank on it when Renda resisted, held back, and the cuffs would dig into his hands.

Leaving the feed barn, hauled out into the sunlight, Renda put up a fight, yelling what the fuck was going on, calling him a crazy insane son of a bitch. So he belted Renda, gave him a good one right in the mouth that quieted him down, and brought him along. But, God, he didn't like the look in the man's eyes. The man wanted to kill him and would probably try. So his idea had better turn out to be a good one and come off without any hitches.

All afternoon and into the evening he led Renda by the hackamore, forcing him to keep up as they moved through the brush country, following dry washes and arroyos that gradually began to climb, reaching toward the high slopes. Majestyk, in his work clothes and heavy work boots, had little trouble; he seemed at home here. He seemed to know what he was doing, where he was going. Renda, in his tailored suit and thin-soled shoes, stumbled along, falling sometimes, getting his sweat-stained face and clothes caked with dust. Majestyk judged the man's endurance and let him rest when he felt he was near the end of it. Then would pull him to his feet again and they would continue on, through brush and pinyon thickets, climbing, angling across high slopes and open meadows.

He brought Renda more than ten miles this way, up into the mountains, and at dusk when they reached the cabin—a crude one-room structure that was part timber and part adobe—he had the feeling Renda would not have gone another ten yards.

"We're home," Majestyk said.

Renda looked at the place with a dull, lifeless expression. "Where are we?"

"Place I use sometime. Mostly in hunting season."

Inside, he found a kitchen match on a shelf, feeling for it in the dark, and lighted a kerosene lamp that hung from the overhead.

"We got coffee and canned milk. Probably find some soup or some beans. I haven't been up here since spring."

Renda was looking around the room, at the two metal bunks with bare mattresses, the wooden table and two chairs, the cupboard with open shelves that showed a few cans and cobwebs, but were nearly empty. Renda went to the nearest bunk and sat down. Majestyk followed him over, taking the keys from his pocket.

"Hold up your hands."

The man sure looked worn out. Renda raised his arms slowly, too tired to move. But as soon as Majestyk freed one of his hands, Renda came off the bunk, pushing, chopping at Majestyk with hard jabs. It took him by surprise, Renda's fists stinging his face, and he had to back off and set himself before he could go after Renda, jabbing, feinting, then slamming in a hard right that stunned him and dropped him to the bunk. Majestyk put a knee on him and got him handcuffed to the metal frame before he could move again.

It took something out of him. Majestyk had to sit down on the other bunk and rest, get his breath.

There was a silence until Renda said, "All right. What do you call this game?"

Majestyk looked over at him. "You'll find out."

"Tomorrow night," Renda said quietly, "we could be in L.A. Stay at a place I know, get some broads in, booze, anything you want to eat or drink, get some new clothes. A couple days later we're in Mexico. Get a boat, some more broads. I mean like you never seen before. Cruise around, anything you want, it's on the house. You ever have it like that? Anything you want?"

"I been to L.A." Majestyk said. "I been to Mexico and I been laid."

"Okay, what do you want?"

"I want to get a melon crop in. That's what I want to do." Renda gave him a puzzled look and he added, "I grow melons."

"Hire your work done."

"I hope to. But I got to be there."

"I'll tell you something," Renda said, taking his time. "I've killed seven men with a gun, one with a crowbar, and another guy I threw off a roof. Five stories. Some people I didn't kill but I had it done. Like I can have it done for you, even if I get put away and they let you off. Any way you look at it, you're dead. Unless we go out of here together. Or, we make a deal."

"What kind of deal?"

"Put a price on it. You take the cuffs off, I walk away. What's it cost?" Renda watched him closely. "If you think it's going to be hot out there, all right, you'll have dough, you can go anywhere you want." He paused. "Or if you feel like taking a chance, turn yourself in, you can tell them I got away. Serve some time, come out, the dough's waiting. How much?" He paused again. "You don't know what your price is, do you? Afraid you might be low. All right, I'll tell you what it is. Twenty-five."

"Twenty-five what?"

"Twenty-five thousand dollars."

It was Majestyk's turn to pause. "How would we work it? I mean how would I get the money?"

"You call a Phoenix number," Renda said. "Say you got a message for Wiley. You say where you want the money delivered and where I can be picked up. It's all you have to do."

Majestyk seemed to be thinking about it. He said, "Twenty-five thousand, huh?"

"Tax free."

"Could you go any higher than that?"

Renda grinned. "Getting greedy now. Like what's another five or ten."

"I just wondered."

"Twenty-five," Renda said. "That's your price. A nice round number. Buy yourself a tractor, a new pair of overalls. Put the rest away for your retirement." He waited a moment. "Well, what do you think?"

"You say I call somebody named Wiley," Majestyk said. "What's the number?"

5

The Papago Trading Post was a highway novelty store in the desert, about three miles below and east of the hunting cabin. Big red-painted signs on and around the place advertised AUTHENTIC INDIAN SOUVENIRS . . . ARROWHEADS . . . MOCCASINS . . . HOMEMADE CANDY and ICE COLD BEER. There was a Coca-Cola sign, an Olympia sign, and a Coors sign.

Majestyk came down from the cabin about nine in the morning and approached the store from about three hundred yards up the highway, reading the signs and listening for the sounds of oncoming cars. Nobody passed him. He reached the store and went inside.

Beyond the counters displaying the trinkets and souvenirs, the Indian dolls and blankets, and sayings carved on varnished pieces of wood—like, "*There's only one thing money can't buy.*

Poverty"—he saw the owner of the place sitting at a counter that was marble and looked like a soda fountain. The man was about sixty, frail-looking with yellowish gray hair. He was having a beer, drinking it from the can.

Approaching him Majestyk said, "I got a flat tire a couple of miles back. No spare."

"That's a shame," the owner said.

"I wonder if I could use your phone. Call a friend of mine."

"Where's he live?"

"Down at Edna."

"That's two bits call Edna."

Majestyk watched him raise the wet-glistening beer can to his mouth.

"I don't have a spare. The truth is, I don't have any money on me."

"Have to trust you then, won't I?"

Majestyk smiled at him. "You trust me for a can of that too?"

When he got his Coors, a sixteen-ounce can, he took it over to the wall phone with him, looked up a number in the Edna directory, and dialed it. He kept his back to the man at the counter. When a voice came on he said, quietly, "I believe you have a Lieutenant McAllen there? . . . Let me speak to him, please."

He waited, looking over at the counter where the owner of the place was watching him, then turned his back to the man and hunched over the phone again.

"This is Vincent Majestyk. You remember we met a few days ago?" He paused, interrupted, then said, "No, I'm downtown in a hotel. Where do you think I am? Listen, why don't you let me talk for a minute, all right?" But he was interrupted again. "Listen to me, will you? I got Frank Renda . . . I said I got him. . . . You want to listen or you want me to hang up? . . . Okay, I got Renda and you got an assault charge against me. Drop it, tear it up, kick it under the rug, and I'll give you Frank Renda."

With the loud sounds coming from the receiver he held the phone away from him, covered the speaker with his hand, and looked over at the owner of the place.

"He's sore cause I took him away from his breakfast." He turned and put the phone to his ear again, waiting to break in.

"Yeah, well nothing's free in this world," Majestyk said finally. "You want him, that's the deal. . . . No, I'll deliver him. You come here you're liable to say you found us. But I bring him in it's me doing it and nobody else. . . . Yeah. Yeah, well it's nice doing business with you too."

He hung up, took a sip of beer, but didn't move away from the phone. "Put another call on there, okay?" he said to the store owner. "Phoenix. And maybe a couple more beers, to go."

He finished dialing, waited, and as he turned to the wall said, "I got a message for somebody named Wiley. You understand? All right, get a pencil and piece of paper and write down what I tell you."

It was a little after twelve, the sun directly above them, when the sports car appeared on the county road. They had been waiting since eleven-thirty, partway up the slope that was covered with stands of pinyon pine. In that time this was the first car they had seen.

"That's it," Renda said. He started to rise, awkwardly, still handcuffed.

Majestyk motioned to him. "Keep down." He watched the sports car, a white Jaguar XK, go by raising a trail of dust on the gravel road, finally reaching a point where it passed from sight beyond the trees.

"That's the *car,*" Renda said.

Majestyk continued to watch the road, saying nothing until the car appeared again, coming slowly from the other direction.

"All right, let's go."

By the time they reached the road the Jaguar was approaching them and came to an abrupt stop. An attractive young girl with short blond hair and big round sunglasses got out and stood looking at them over the open door.

Majestyk stared, taken by surprise. He hadn't expected a girl. The possibility had never entered his mind.

"Who's that?"

"That's Wiley," Renda said. He started toward the car and called to the girl, "You got the money?"

"I already gave it to him," the girl said. "God, Frank, you're a mess."

"What do you mean you gave it to him? Come on, for Christ sake, where's the money?"

She was frowning as she raised the sunglasses and placed them on her head. "I was told to stop at the store on the highway and pay the man three dollars and eighty-five cents, and that's what I did. It's the only money I was told to bring."

Renda turned to Majestyk, who was walking toward the Jaguar now, looking at it closely.

"What are you pulling? What kind of shit are you *pulling!* We made a deal—twenty-five grand!"

"It doesn't look like you'd fit in the trunk," Majestyk said. "So I guess maybe you better drive, Frank. Keep your hands on something. Wiley can squeeze in behind the seats." He looked at Renda then. "You can get in by yourself, or I can help you in. Either way."

"I must have missed something," Wiley said. "Is it all right if I ask where we're going?"

Majestyk gave her a pleasant smile. "To jail, honey. Where'd you think?"

Wiley was three years out of Northwestern University, drama school; two years out of Universal City, a little television; one year out of a Las Vegas show-bar, topless; and six months into Frank Renda.

Until recently she had been amazed that life with him could be so—not boring, really—uneventful. Living with a real-life man who killed people had sounded like the trip to end all trips. It turned out to be mostly lying around swimming pools while he talked on the phone. Frank was fun to watch. He was a natural actor and didn't know it. He played roles constantly, from cool dude to spoiled child, and looked at himself in the mirror a lot, like almost every actor she had ever known. It was interesting watching him. Still, it was getting to be something of a drag until, four days ago, when she fingered the guy in the bar for him. No, it wasn't exactly a finger job. What she did was sit at the bar, keeping an eye on the guy. When it looked like he was getting ready to pay his check, she got up and walked out of the place, letting Frank know the guy was coming, giving him a minute or so to get ready. She didn't know what Frank had against the guy; she didn't ask him. This was real-life drama. She stood off to the side and watched Frank calmly shoot the guy five times. Wow. From about ten feet away. The guy was a great dier. It was really a show, cinéma vérité. Until the cop came from out of nowhere and jammed his gun into Frank's back. She got out of there, took a cab back to her apartment and waited, the next four days, close to the phone.

More true-life adventure now, scrunched behind the bucket seats of an XK Jag, driving down a back-country dirt road, her handcuffed boyfriend with both hands on the top arc of the steering wheel, and a solemn-faced, farmer-looking guy staring at him, watching every move he made.

"Left when you get to the blacktop," Majestyk said. "That'll take us to the highway."

Renda braked. As he began to turn onto the county road he lost his grip and had to grab the steering wheel and crank it hard to keep from going into the ditch. Wiley was thrown hard against the back of Majestyk's seat. He glanced around as she straightened up, holding onto the seat.

"Hey, are you trying to put me through the windshield?"

Renda's eyes raised to the rearview mirror and the reflection of Wiley's face. Their eyes met briefly before he shifted his gaze to the road again. Perhaps a minute passed before he glanced at Majestyk.

"All right, you got a new game. What's it cost?"

"Three dollars and eighty-five cents," Majestyk said. "You paid and you're in."

"Come on, cut the bullshit. How much you want?"

"Nothing."

"I explained it as simply as I could," Renda said. "We make a deal or you're dead. I get sent away, you're still dead."

"I've already made a deal."

Renda glanced at him again. "You think the cops can keep you alive? They'd have to live with you the rest of your life. Can you see that? Never knowing when it's going to happen?"

When Majestyk didn't answer, Wiley said, "He's kind of weird, isn't he?"

Renda's eyes raised to the rearview mirror and met Wiley's gaze.

When he looked at the road he saw the curve approaching, waited, started into the curve and braked sharply to reduce his speed. Again Wiley was thrown against Majestyk's seat.

"Hey Frank, take it easy, okay?"

He glanced at her reflection. She was ready.

Coming out of the curve and hitting the straightaway, Renda accelerated to almost seventy, held it for a quarter of a mile, then raised his right foot and mashed it down on the brake pedal.

Wiley already had her hand on the latch to release the backrest of Majestyk's seat. It was free as the car braked suddenly and she threw herself hard against it, her weight and the momentum slamming Majestyk into the dashboard.

"Frank, under the seat!" She screamed it.

"Get it, for Christ sake!"

Renda was accelerating with his left foot, bringing his right foot up and over the transmission hump to kick viciously at Majestyk, jammed between the seat and the dashboard, as Wiley reached beneath the driver's seat, groped frantically, and came up with a Colt .45 automatic in her left hand.

"Shoot him! Shoot the son of a bitch, will you!"

"I don't know how!"

"Pull the fucking trigger!"

Majestyk pushed against the seat back, lunging at Wiley. Renda hit the brakes again, bouncing Majestyk off the dashboard. But he was able to push off from it, twisting around enough to get a hand on the girl's arm just as she fired and the automatic exploded less than a foot from his head.

Renda was kicking at him again. "Christ, shoot him!"

He kicked at Majestyk's ribs, got his heel in hard a couple of times, kicked again and this time his heel hit Majestyk's belt buckle, slipped off and hit the door handle as Wiley pulled his arm free and put the automatic in Majestyk's face. The door opened and she saw him going out, fired, saw his expression and fired twice again, saw the window of the swung-open door shatter, but he was gone, out of the car, and she knew she hadn't hit him.

The XK Jag was two hundred feet up the road before its brake lights flashed on. The car made a tight turn, backed up on the narrow blacktop, and turned again to come back this way.

Majestyk heard the sound of the engine. He was lying face-down on the shoulder of the road, propped on his elbows, dazed, staring at gravel and feeling it cutting into the palms of his hands. His vision was blurred and when he wiped his eyes saw blood on the back of his hand. He heard the engine sound louder, winding up, coming toward him. When he raised his head he saw the headlights and the grille, low to the ground, the nose swinging toward the gravel shoulder, coming directly at him.

With all of his strength he threw himself to the side, rolling into the ditch, as the Jag swept past. A moment later he heard the tires squealing on the blacktop and knew he had to get out of here, pushing himself up now, out of the weeds, climbing the bank away from the road and ducking through the wire fence, as the Jag made its tight turn and came back and this time stopped.

Majestyk was running across the open scrub, weaving through the dusty brush clumps, by the time Renda got out of the car and began firing at him with the automatic, both hands extended in the handcuffs. Majestyk kept running. Renda jumped across the ditch, got to the fence, and laid the .45 on the top of a post, aimed, and squeezed the trigger three times, but the figure out in the scrub was too small now and it would have to be a lucky shot to bring him down. He fired once more and the automatic clicked empty.

Seventy, eighty, yards away, Majestyk finally came to a stop, worn out, getting his breath. He turned to look at the man standing by the fence post and, for a while, they stared at one another, each knowing who the other man was and what he felt and not having to say anything. Renda crossed the ditch to the Jag and Majestyk watched it drive away.

It seemed easier to get out of jail than it was to get back in.

He got a ride in a feed truck as far as Junction, after walking a couple of miles, then sitting down to rest and waiting almost an hour in the sun. When the driver asked what'd happened to him he said he'd blown a tire and gone off the road and was thrown out when his pickup went into the ditch. The driver said he was lucky he wasn't killed and Majestyk agreed.

At Junction he went into the Enco station and asked the attendant, the one named Gil, for the key to the Men's Room. The attendant gave it to him without saying anything, though he had a little smile on his face looking at Majestyk's dirty, beat-up condition. In the Men's Room he saw what a mess he was: blood and dirt caked on his face, his shirt torn up the back, his hands raw-looking with imbedded gravel.

It was four-thirty that afternoon when he walked into the Edna Post of the County Sheriff's Department and asked the deputy behind the desk if Lieutenant McAllen was around. The deputy, ignoring his face, asked him what it was he wanted to see the lieutenant about.

"I want to go to jail," Majestyk said.

He waited on the bench thinking, Christ, trying to get back in. He was still sitting on the bench twenty minutes later when McAllen walked up to him and stood there, not saying anything.

"I had him," Majestyk said.

"Did you?"

"I guess you want to hear what happened."

"I think I can see," McAllen said.

6

Getting Renda to Mexico was no problem. A young guy who brought reefer in two or three times a month flew him down in his Cessna, landing on a desert airstrip not far from Hermosillo. Renda spent two nights in a motel while the rest of it was being worked out. On the morning of the third day an Olds 98 with California plates and a house trailer attached—with Eugene Lundy behind the wheel and Wiley curled on the back seat reading a current best-selling novel—pulled up in front of the motel. Renda, wearing work clothes and a week's growth of beard, walked out of his room and got in the trailer. The Olds took off and didn't stop again until they were on the coast road south of Guaymas and Lundy thought maybe Frank would want to get out and stretch his legs, exercise a little, breathe in the salt air, and throw a couple of stones at the Gulf of California. Wiley said to him, "You don't know Frank very well, do you?"

He didn't come out of the trailer or bother to look up when the door opened. He was sitting in back on one of the bunks, smoking a cigarette.

Wiley said, "Hey, do you love it? I think it's great."

Behind her, Lundy said, "Air-conditioned, you got plenty of vodka, scotch, steaks, and beer in the ice box and"—he took an envelope out of his pocket and handed it to Renda—"twenty-five hundred cigarette money."

Wiley was opening cabinets and doors. "There's a shower in the john. Even a magazine rack."

"Tonight we'll be in Mazatlan," Lundy said. "We can stay there or go on down to Acapulco, it's up to you."

Renda looked up at him. "Regular vacation. You having a nice time?"

"Listen, I think I could use a rest. That stunt, hitting the fucking bus, that took some years off me."

Renda watched him turn to the refrigerator and take out a can of beer.

"Where is he?"

"You want one?"

"I said where is he!"

Lundy, about to pop open the can, looked over at Renda. "The guy? He turned himself in. Last I heard they're still holding him at Edna."

Wiley came in to stretch out on the opposite bunk. "Kind of tight fit, but all the comforts of home."

"We're not at home," Renda said. "He is."

"He's in jail, Frank." Wiley's tone was soft, approaching him carefully. "You're free. We can go anywhere you want."

"There's only one thing I want," Renda said. "Him."

Lundy opened the can and took a swig. "He gets out, we can have somebody take care of that."

Renda shook his head. "Not somebody. I said *I* want him. I want him to see it and know it's me. Put the gun in his stomach and look at him. Not say anything, just look at him and make sure he understands."

"You still have to wait," Lundy said.

Renda didn't say anything. He was still picturing it, putting the gun in the melon grower's stomach.

"All right, let me ask you," Lundy said. "What do you do, walk in the jail, ask them for a visitor's pass? How do you get close to the guy?"

"You get him out of jail."

"You get him out. How?"

"Find the guy he hit," Renda said. "Tell him to drop the complaint. It was all a mistake, a misunderstanding."

"What if the guy doesn't want to drop it?"

"Jesus, I said *tell* him, not ask him."

"Maybe pay him something?"

"That's up to you. See what it takes."

"You mean you want me to do it? Go back there?"

"I'm talking to you, aren't I?"

"I just wanted to be sure."

"You're going to go back and set it up," Renda said. "Find the guy made the complaint and get that done. Get some people if you see we need them. Call me, I come up. We go in and get out fast. No bullshit screwing around. Arrange it, I walk up to him, and it's done."

Lundy took a sip of beer, getting the right words ready in his mind. "I keep thinking though, what about the cops? They'll be looking for you, watching your house, the apartment."

"Christ, you think I'm going to go home? We'll stay someplace else. Call Harry, tell him to arrange it."

"I mean right now, why take a chance?"

"I told you why."

"I'm not against it," Lundy said. "I'm just thinking, we're this far. Why change your mind all of a sudden?"

"I didn't change it. I hadn't made it up yet. But the more I think about it—I know it's what I'm going to do."

"I was going to lie on the beach," Wiley said, "and read my book."

Lundy waited a moment. "You know, Frank, there's a lot of guys'd do it. I mean guys the cops aren't waiting to flag."

Renda said, "Hey, Gene, one more time. I said I want him. I

never wanted anybody so bad and I'm going to do it strictly as a favor to myself. You understand? Am I getting through to you? *I'm* going to do it, not somebody else. Before I take any trips or lay on any beach I'm going to walk up to that melon grower son of a bitch, I'm going to look him in the eyes, and I'm going to kill him."

Harold Ritchie was a pallbearer at his partner's funeral. Bob Almont, good guy to ride with in a squad car, and god*damn* he'd miss him. Shot down in the street by some creepy son of a bitch. Ritchie hoped it was the one he'd shot coming out of the station wagon. He went to Bob Almont's house after the funeral, with Bob's close friends and a few relatives that'd come from Oklahoma. They sat around drinking coffee and picking at the casserole dishes some neighbors had brought over, while Evelyn Almont stayed in the kitchen most of the time or sat with her two little tiny kids who didn't know what the hell was going on. After a couple of hours of watching that, it was a relief to get back to the post.

The deputy at the counter tore off a teletype sheet and handed it to him. "What you asked for. Just come in."

He read it as he walked over to Lieutenant McAllen's office, knocked twice, and walked in. McAllen was sitting at his desk.

"You're right," Ritchie said, "Phoenix had a sheet on him. Robert L. Kopas, a.k.a. Bobby Kopas, Bobby Curtis. Two arrests, B and E, and extortion. One conviction. Served two years in Florence."

"I could feel it," McAllen said. "The guy's up to something."

"Changed his mind and dropped the charge. The way I read it," Ritchie said, "he's decided it'd be more fun to get back at the guy himself."

"Maybe. But is he smart enough? Or dumb enough to try it? However you want to look at it." McAllen paused. "Or did somebody put him up to it?"

Ritchie was nodding. "That's a thought."

"Yes, it is, isn't it?" McAllen said. "You got any more on Majestyk?"

"On my desk. I'll be right back." Ritchie went out and returned within the minute with an open file folder in his hands, looking at it.

"Not much. He lived in California most of his life. High school education. Truck driver, farm laborer. Owned his own place till he went to Folsom on the assault conviction. Here's something. In the army three years, a Ranger instructor at Fort Benning."

McAllen raised his eyebrows. "An instructor."

"Combat adviser in Laos before that," Ritchie went on. "Captured by the Pathet Lao, escaped and brought three enemy prisoners with him. Got a Silver Star." Looking up at McAllen he said, "Man doesn't fool, does he?"

"Well, he's a different cut than what we usually get."

"Doesn't seem afraid to take chances."

"Doesn't appear to." McAllen was thoughtful a moment. "Let's talk to him and find out."

He said to Majestyk, "You look better than the last time I saw you."

"Thank you, but I'd just as soon wear my own clothes." He was dressed in jail denims with white stripes down the sides of the pants. The scrapes and cuts on his face were healing and he was clean-shaven. "What I'd like to know which nobody'll tell me, is when I'm going to court."

"Why don't you have a seat?" McAllen said.

"I've been sitting for four days."

"So you're used to it," McAllen said. "Sit down."

He watched Majestyk take the chair then picked up a pack of cigarettes and matches and leaned over to hand them across the desk.

"Have a smoke."

As Majestyk lighted a cigarette, McAllen said, "I guess what you want most is to get out of here."

He waited, but Majestyk, looking at him, said nothing. "Well, I think it might be arranged."

Majestyk continued to wait, not giving McAllen any help.

"The guy you hit, Bobby Kopas?" McAllen said finally. "He dropped the charge against you."

When Majestyk still waited, McAllen said, "You hear what I said?"

"Why'd he do that?"

"He said he thought it over. It wasn't important enough for him to waste a lot of time in court. You think that's the reason?"

"I met him once," Majestyk said. "I can't say I know him or what's in his head."

"He's got a record. Extortion, breaking and entering. Does that tell you anything?"

"You say it, I believe it."

"I'm saying he could have a reason of his own to see you walking around free."

"Well, whatever his reason is, I'll go along with it," Majestyk said. "If it means getting my crop in."

"You can stay if you want," McAllen said.

"Why would I want to?"

"Because Frank Renda's also walking around free."

Majestyk saw him waiting for his reaction and he said, "Why don't you just tell me what you're going to anyway, without all the suspense."

McAllen looked over at Ritchie and back again. He said, "The eyeball witness who saw Frank Renda commit murder was an off-duty police officer."

"I heard that."

"He was a member of this department."

Majestyk waited.

"He was killed during Renda's escape. Shot dead. So there's no witness. The gun Renda used—is alleged to have used—can't be traced to him. That means there's no case."

"If you want him so bad," Majestyk said, "why don't you arrest him for the escape?"

"Because there's no way to tie him in with the attempt. His lawyer made that clear and the prosecutor had to agree. Technically—and tell me how you like this?—he was kidnapped. We can stick you with that if we want. Or let you go. Or, we can hold you in protective custody."

"Protective custody against what?"

"Frank Renda. What do you think he's going to do when he finds out you're on the street?"

"I don't know. What?"

"He might've already found out. Though right now we don't know where he is or what he's doing."

Majestyk took a drag on the cigarette and let the smoke out slowly. "Are you trying to tell me my life's in danger?"

"You should know him by now. What do you think?"

"Why would he risk getting arrested again? I mean just to get me."

"Because it's his business. Now you've given him a personal reason to kill," McAllen said. "And I can't think of anything that would stop him trying."

"You're that sure."

"He might even think it would be easy. Get careless again, like he did the last time."

"Something's finally starting to get through," Majestyk said. "You'll let me go if I'll sit home and act as your bait."

"Something like that."

"Maybe even you'd like him to shoot me, so you can get him for murder."

"That entered my mind," McAllen said, "but we'll settle for attempted."

"Attempted, huh? And if he pulls it off, you try something else then?"

"I believe you're the guy who wanted to make a deal," McAllen said, "so you could get your melons picked. All right, go pick them."

"And where'll you be?"

"We'll be around."

"He could send somebody else."

"He could." McAllen nodded. "Or he could wait a few months, or a year. Shoot you some night while you're sleeping. Or wire your truck with dynamite. One morning you get in and turn the key—" McAllen paused. "No, you're right, we don't know for certain he'll try for you himself, just as we can't guarantee we'll be able to stop him if he does. It's a chancy situation any way you look at it. But remember, you got yourself into it. So, as things stand, it's the best offer I can make."

"Well then"—Majestyk got up from the chair, stubbing out the cigarette—"I guess there's no reason for me to hang around, is there?"

It was still cool at 6:00 A.M., the vines were wet and darkened the pants legs of the pickers as they worked along the rows with their burlap sacks. Somebody said it was insecticide, the wetness, but most of them knew the fields had not been sprayed in several days and that moisture had settled during the night. Their pants and the vines would be hot and dusty dry within an hour. The sun, which they would have all day, faced them from the eastern boundary of the fields, above a tangle of willows that lined an arroyo five miles away. The sun seemed that close to them.

Larry Mendoza stood by the pickup truck counting the stooped, round figures in the rows. He had counted them before, but he counted them again and got the same number. Twelve, including Nancy Chavez and the ones from Yuma—

thank God for them. But he wasn't going to get any crop in with twelve people. Some of them had never picked before—like the two Anglo kids he'd been able to get because nobody else wanted them.

He saw one of them stretching in his white T-shirt, rolling his shoulders to work the ache out of his back, and Mendoza yelled at him, "Hey, how you going to pick melons standing up!"

He crossed the ditch and went out into the field, toward the white T-shirt that said *Bronco Athletic Dept.* and had a small numeral on it, 22, in a square.

"I was seeing how much I had in the sack," the white Anglo kid said.

"Fill it," Larry Mendoza told him. "That's how much you put in. Then you stand up."

"I'm getting used to it already."

A colored guy he had hired that morning, who was working the next row, was watching them. Mendoza said to him, "You need something? You want some help or something?"

The colored guy didn't answer; he turned and stooped over and went back to work. At least the colored guy had picked before, not melons, but he had picked and knew what he was doing. The Anglo kid, with his muscular arms and shoulders and cut-off pants and tennis shoes—like he was out here on his vacation—couldn't pick his nose.

"This one"—Mendoza took a honeydew from the Anglo kid's sack—"it's not ready. Remember I told you, you pick the *ripe ones.* You loosen the other ones in the dirt. You don't turn them so the sun hits the underneath, you just loosen them."

"That's what I been doing," the Anglo kid said.

"The ones aren't ready, we come back for later on."

"I thought it was ripe." The Anglo kid stooped to lay the melon among the vine leaves.

Larry Mendoza closed his eyes and opened them and adjusted the funneled brim of his straw hat. "You going to put it back on the vine? Tie it on? You pick it, it stays picked. You got to keep it then. You understand?"

"Sure," the Anglo kid said.

Sure. How do you find them? Mendoza asked himself, turning from the kid who might last the day but would never be back tomorrow. Walking to the road his gaze stopped on another big-shouldered, blond-haired Bronco from Edna and yelled at him, "Hey, whitey, where are you, in church? Get off your knees or go home, I get somebody else!" Christ, he wasn't paying them a buck forty an hour to rest. He yelled at the guy again, "You hear me? I'll get somebody else!"

"Like it's easy," Nancy Chavez said. She was going over to the trailer with a full sack of melons hanging from her shoulder. Pretty girl, thin but strong-looking, with a dark bandana and little pearl earrings.

"I may have to go to Mexico," Mendoza said. "Christ, nobody wants to work anymore. And some of the ones I got don't know how."

"Teach them," the girl said. "Somebody had tc teach you."

"Yeah, when I was eight years old." He went over to the pickup truck and got in. "Now I got to tell Vincent. He don't have enough to worry about."

"Tell him we'll get it done," the girl said. "Somehow."

Majestyk came out through the screen door of his house to wait on the porch. When he saw the pickup coming he walked out to the road. Larry Mendoza moved over and Majestyk got in behind the wheel.

"How'd you sleep?"

"Too long."

"Man, you need it."

Majestyk swung the pickup around in a tight turn. When they were heading back toward the field that was being worked, on their right now, Mendoza said, "I try again this morning, same thing. Nobody wants to work for us. I talk to Julio Tamaz, some of the others. What's going on? What is this shit? Julio says man, I don't have a crew for you, that's all."

"He can get all he wants," Majestyk said.

"I know it. He turn some away, says they're no good. I hire them and find out he's right."

As they approached the trailer, standing by itself on the side of the road, Mendoza saw the girl with the dark bandana and pearl earrings coming out of the field again with a sack of melons. He glanced at Majestyk and saw him watching her.

"That one," Mendoza said, "Nancy Chavez. She wasn't here, we wouldn't have any good workers at all. She got some more friends drove over from Yuma. She picks better than two men. But we got to have a full crew, soon, or we never get it done."

Mendoza got out by the trailer. He slammed the door and said through the window, "I hope you have better luck than me."

"Least I'll find out what's going on," Majestyk said. He could see the girl by the trailer, unloading her melon sack. That was something, she was still here. She didn't know him or owe him anything, but she was still here.

Harold Ritchie was leaning over the fender of the State Highway Department pickup truck, holding a pair of binoculars to his eyes. He was looking across the highway and across a section of melon field to where the dust column was following Majestyk's yellow truck all the way up the side road.

"It could be him this time," Ritchie said. "Hang on."

He was speaking to another deputy who was sitting inside a tool shed by a police-frequency two-way radio. It was hotter than hell inside and the door was open so he could get some air. The shed hadn't been built for people to sit in, but it was the best they could do. Besides the shed, there was a mobile generator, a tar pot, some grading equipment, a pile of gravel, a portable toilet that looked like a rounded phone booth without windows, wooden barricades and lanterns and a sign that said ROAD CONSTRUCTION 500 FT., though nothing was going on. The only ones here were Ritchie and the deputy operating the radio, both of them in work clothes.

"Yeah, it's him," Ritchie said now, lowering the glasses and watching Majestyk's pickup come out of the side road without stopping and swing onto the highway. "Jesus Christ, I could arrest him for that," Ritchie said. "Tell them he just drove out in his truck, yellow four-wheel-drive pickup, heading toward Edna. I'm getting on him right now."

Ritchie slid behind the wheel of the State Highway Department truck and took off after him.

Majestyk parked across the highway from the blue school bus and the stake truck and the old junk cars the migrants would return to later in the day. In the stillness he could hear the juke box out on the street. Tammy Wynette, with a twangy Nashville backup, telling about some boy she loved who was in love with somebody else.

Majestyk followed the sound of the music to the café-bar and had the screen door open when the State Highway Department truck slowed down at the Junction intersection and came coasting by. He gave the truck a little wave before he went inside.

A waitress was serving Julio Tamaz and another Chicano labor contractor their breakfast. They were sitting at a table, the only customers in the place. Another woman, wearing a stained white apron, was sweeping the floor, moving chairs around, banging them against the formica tables. The two men didn't look up as Majestyk approached them. They were busy with the salt and pepper and pouring sugar and cream. Julio was dousing his fried eggs dark brown with Lee & Perrins.

"Julio?"

He looked up then, with a surprised expression he had prepared as Majestyk walked over.

"Hey, Vincent. They let you out, huh? Good."

Majestyk pulled a chair out but didn't sit down. He stood with his hand on it, as though he had changed his mind.

"How come I can't hire a crew?"

"Man, you been away, in jail."

"Larry Mendoza hasn't. Last two mornings you turned him down. How come?"

"It's the time of the year. I got too much business." He poked at the eggs with his fork, yellow appearing, mixing with the brown. "Other people need crews too. They ask me first."

"All right," Majestyk said, "I'm asking you right now for thirty people tomorrow morning. Buck forty."

Julio kept busy with his eggs and didn't look up. "I got

crews signed more than a week. Vincent, you too late, that's all."

Majestyk watched him begin to eat his eggs before turning his attention to the other man at the table. He was already finishing, wiping the yolk from his plate with a piece of toast.

"How about you?" Majestyk said. "You get me a crew?"

"Me?" With the same helpless tone as Julio's. "Maybe in ten days," the labor contractor said. "I can't promise you nothing right now."

"In ten days my crop will be ruined."

"Like Julio says, other people ask first. We can't help that."

"What is this, stick-up time? You want more money? What?"

"It's not money, Vincent." Julio's tone was sad as well as helpless. "How can we get you people if we don't have any?"

Majestyk pulled the chair out a little farther. This time he sat down and leaned over the edge of the table on his arms.

He said quietly, "Julio, what's going on?"

"I tole you. I got too much work."

"You'd drive to Mexico if you had to. Come on, somebody pay you, threaten you? What?"

"Listen," Julio said, intently now, his voice lower, "I got to work for a living and I can't do it in no goddamn hospital. You understand?"

"I'm beginning to. You could help me though."

"I'm not going to say any more. Man, I've said enough."

Majestyk stared at him a moment. Finally he said, "Okay," got up and walked away from the table.

Julio called after him, "Vincent, next season, uh?"

That contractor at the table with him, eating his piece of toast, said, "If he's still around."

Coming out of the place into the sunlight he was aware of the State Highway Department truck parked across the street and the deputy sitting in the cab, watching him. Tell him you're going back home, Majestyk was thinking. Put his mind at ease. He started for the street, through the space between the back of the school bus and the stake truck, when the voice stopped him.

"You looking for a crew?"

He saw Bobby Kopas then, leaning against a car with his arms folded, a familiar pose, a tight lavender shirt; sunglasses and bandit moustache hiding a thin, bony face. The car, an Olds 98, was at the curb in front of the school bus. Someone else was inside, a big-shouldered man, behind the wheel.

"You want pickers, maybe I can get you some wine heads," Kopas said. He straightened, unfolding his arms, as Majestyk walked over to him. "You touch me, man, you're back in jail by lunchtime."

Majestyk stared at him, standing there close enough to touch. All he had to do was grab the front of that pretty shirt and belt him. It would be easy and it would be pure pleasure. But the deputy was across the street and Majestyk didn't have to look over to know he was watching them. He wondered if Kopas knew the man in the State Highway Department truck was a cop.

"You dropped the complaint," Majestyk said. "Why? You want to try and pay me back yourself?"

"I do you a favor—Jesus, after you like to broke my nose, you think I'm pulling something." Kopas gave him the hint of a grin. "Man, I'm being a good neighbor, that's all."

"What'd you say to Julio Tamaz and the other contractors? You pay them off or threaten them? How'd you work it?"

The little grin was still there. "Man, I hope nobody's telling stories on me, giving me a bad name."

"They didn't say it was you. I'm saying it."

"Why would I do a thing like that?"

"So I'll lose my crop."

"I think you must be a little mixed up," Kopas said. "Don't know where your head's at. Here you are standing in deep shit and you're worried about a little dinky melon crop."

"You've been talking to somebody," Majestyk said.

"Who's that?" Kopas said, giving him the grin.

"I can fix it you'd have a hard time smiling again."

Kopas tensed and the grin vanished. "Listen, I'm not kidding. You even make a fist, man, you're back in jail."

"Are you working for him?"

"Who's that?"

"He get you to drop the complaint?"

"I think I'm tired of talking to you," Kopas said. He moved to the car door and opened it, then looked back at Majestyk. "I'll tell you one thing though. Somebody's going to set your ass on fire. And I'm going to be there to see it."

The Olds started off as Kopas got in and slammed the door. Majestyk caught a glimpse of the driver's profile—looking at Kopas, saying something—and for a moment he thought he knew the man or had seen him before. But the car was moving away and it was too late to get another look at him and be sure. Big shoulders, curly hair. Maybe he was one of the guys who had been with Kopas a week ago, the day it began. Or a different one. The car was different.

What difference did it make? He had enough people to think about without bringing in new ones. Faces to remember. Frank Renda's. Telling him he was going to kill him. Now Kopas and Renda. The man had already started to make his move. He didn't waste time. He found Kopas and hired him. That was plain enough. Now they were beginning to play a game with him. Let him know they were coming. Give him something to keep him awake nights. He thought of telling the deputy in the State Highway Department truck. Get him after them, quick, before they turned off the highway somewhere. Maybe they would lead him to Renda.

But Renda didn't have any reason to hide. He was free.

And what does the cop do, arrest them? For what?

No, whatever's going to happen is going to happen, Majestyk thought. So go home and pick your melons.

8

"I'm not shittin' you," Kopas said. "I was thinking of dropping the complaint anyway, so I could take care of the son of a bitch myself."

Eugene Lundy wasn't listening to him. He was staring straight ahead, over the hood of the Olds 98, at the vacant land of dust-green mesquite and sun glare and bugs rising with the airstream and exploding in yellow bursts against the windshield. Like somebody was spitting them there.

"Load up the pump gun and wait for him," Kopas said. "Or stick it in his window some night. See him sittin' on the toilet. *Bam.* Scatter the motherfucker all over the room."

Lundy was counting the bug stains, more than a dozen of the yellow ones: some kind of bug flying along having a nice time and the next thing sucked into the wind, coming up fast over the hood and wiped out, the bug not knowing what in the name of Christ happened to him. Maybe they had been butterflies. Seeing the bugs suddenly, there wasn't time to tell what they were.

"I got to piss," Kopas said.

Lundy looked at the speedometer and up again. He was holding between seventy and seventy-five down the country road that rose and dropped through the desert, seeing no other cars, no people, not even signs.

"Man, I'm in pain," Kopas said. "All you got to do is stop the car."

"We're almost there," Lundy said. "I'm not going to stop twice."

"How long you think it's going to take me, an hour? All I want to do is take a piss."

"Hold it," Lundy said.

Maybe they were all different kinds of bugs, but all bugs were yellow inside. Like all people were red inside. Maybe. Lundy had never thought about it before. His gaze held on the stained windshield as he waited for a bug to come up over the hood.

He felt so good his eyes were watering, and kept going like he was never going to stop. Jesus, what a relief. Son of a bitch Lundy made him hold it twenty minutes, refusing to stop the car. He'd finally pleaded with him, Christ, just slow down, he'd piss out the window, but the son of a bitch wouldn't even do that. A very cold son of a bitch who didn't say much, sitting on two pieces under his seat, a Colt .45 automatic and a big fucking Colt .44 mag. He had asked the guy if he had been in on the bus job and the guy had looked at him and said, "The bus job. Is that what you call it?" And that was all he'd said.

Bobby Kopas zipped up his fly and walked around to the front of the Olds where Lundy was standing, squinting up at the sky.

"Hurry up and wait," Kopas said. "I never seen a plane come in on time in my life. Not even the airlines, not once I ever went out to the airport. Everybody sitting around waiting.

Go in the cocktail lounge you're smashed by the time the fucking plane arrives. You ever seen a plane come in on time?"

Staring at the sky and the flat strip of desert beyond the road, Lundy said, "Why don't you shut your mouth for a while?"

Christ, you couldn't even talk to the guy. Kopas moved around with his hands in his pockets, kicking a few stones, looking around for some shade, which there wasn't a bit of anywhere, squinting in the hot glare, squinting even with his wraparound sunglasses on. The glasses made him sweat and he had to keep wiping his eyes. Lundy stood there not moving, like the heat didn't bother him at all. Big, heavy son of a bitch who should've been lathered with sweat by now, like a horse.

They heard the plane before they saw it, the faraway droning sound, then a dot in the sky coming in low, the sun flashing on its windshield. The Cessna passed over them at about a hundred feet. As it banked, descending, coming around in a wide circle, Lundy finally spoke. He said, "Wait here," and walked out into the desert.

Kopas was excited now. He wanted to appear cool and make a good impression. He put his hands on his hipbones and cocked one leg, pointing the toe of the boot out a little. Like a gunfighter. So the guy was big time. He'd act cool, savvy, show the guy he wasn't all that impressed.

He watched the plane come to a stop about a hundred yards away. Lundy, going out to meet it, was holding up his arm, waving at the plane. Big jerk.

Renda came out first and then the girl—white slacks and a bright green blouse. Even at this distance she looked good. Blond, nice slim figure. Now they were coming this way and Lundy was talking to them, gesturing, probably telling Renda how the murder charge against him had been dropped. Renda wouldn't have known about it, though the pilot might have told him. As the plane started its engine to take off, the prop wash blew sand at them and they hunched their shoulders and turned away from the stinging blast of air. Lundy was talking again. Renda stopped and they all stopped. Renda was saying something.

Then Lundy was talking again. As they came up to the road Kopas heard Lundy say, "You could have rode up here bare-ass on a white horse, nobody would've stopped you."

"What about the bus thing?" the girl asked him.

She was something. Maybe the best-looking girl Bobby Kopas had ever seen.

"There's nothing they can stick you with," Lundy said. "The bus, nothing. They tried to, naturally. There're three cops involved and they don't like that one bit. But what're they going to stick you with? You didn't shoot the cops. You didn't take the bus. The guy did, Majestyk. But they don't even jam him for that. You see what I'm getting at?"

Kopas had never heard Lundy talk so much.

The good-looking girl said, "God, nothing like a little dumb luck."

"Luck, bullshit," Renda said. "Timing. Make it happen. And never run till you see you're being chased."

"With a fast lawyer available at all times," the girl said. She didn't seem to be afraid of him.

"They had to let him go," Renda said. "I could see that right away, the cops coming up with this great idea. Don't stick him with the bus, no, let him go so I'll show up and try for him."

"That's the question," Lundy said. "What're the cops doing?"

"No, the question is what's the guy doing? Is he sitting still for it or what?"

"He's around," Lundy said. "We just saw him."

Kopas stepped out of the way as they approached the Olds. He set a grin on his face and said, "Probably home by now waiting on you, Mr. Renda."

Renda looked at him. Christ, with the coldest look he'd ever gotten from a person. Like he was a thing or wasn't even there. Christ, he'd been arrested, he'd been in the can. He wasn't some lightweight who didn't know what he was doing.

He said, "Mr. Renda? I wonder if I could ask you a favor." Renda was looking at him again. "I know it's your party, but—after you finish the son of a bitch—you mind if I put a couple of slugs in him?"

Renda said to Lundy, "Who's this asshole?"

"Bobby Kopas. Boy Majestyk hit."

"You pay him to drop it?"

"Five hundred."

"Then what's he doing here?"

"He's working for us," Lundy said, "to see nobody works for Majestyk. So there won't be a crowd hanging around there. He knows the guy's place, back roads, ways in and out. I thought he might come in handy."

Kopas thought he could add to that. He said, "I been watching that Polack melon picker since they let him out. He doesn't fart that I don't know about it."

The girl said, probably to Lundy, "Is he for real?"

Kopas wasn't sure what she meant. He kept his eyes on Renda, who was staring at him, and tried not to look away.

"You're telling me you know him pretty well?" Renda asked.

"I know he's a stuck-up son of a bitch. Got a two-bit farm and thinks he's a big grower."

"How long's he lived here?"

Kopas grinned. "Not much longer I guess, huh?"

"I ask you a question," Renda said, "you don't seem to want to answer it."

Jesus, that look again. "Well, I'm not sure how long exactly he's been here. Couple years, I guess. I just got into this labor business recently, when I seen there was money in it."

"Show me where he lives," Renda said.

"Yes sir, any time you say."

"Right now."

"Frank," Lundy said, "your lawyer got the house, it's all set. Up in the mountains, nobody can bother you or know you're there. I thought maybe you'd want to go up to the house first, you know, take it easy for a while."

Renda said, "Gene, did I come here to take it easy? I could be home, not at some place in the mountains. But I'm not home."

"I know you're anxious," Lundy began.

"Gene, I want to see the guy's place," Renda said. "I want to see it right now."

* * *

The two Anglo kids in the white T-shirts quit at noon and Mendoza paid them off. That left nine. So Majestyk went out in the field and picked melons all the rest of the day with Nancy Chavez and her friends from Yuma. Maybe next year he could stand around and watch, or sit in an office like a big melon grower. Sit on the porch and drink iced tea. That would be nice.

He wasn't used to this. He could feel the soreness in his back, and each time he reached the end of a row it would take him a little longer to straighten up. All day, dirty and sweaty and thirsty—drinking the lukewarm water in the canvas bag. Tomorrow he'd get a tub of ice and some pop, cover it with a piece of burlap. He'd forgotten how difficult and painful stooped labor was. Around 5:30, after eleven hours of it, the pickers began to straggle out of the field and unload their last melon sacks at the trailer parked on the road.

Majestyk was finishing a row, finally, when Nancy Chavez crossed through the vines and came toward him, a full sack hanging from her shoulder.

She said, "I've been watching you. For a grower you're pretty good."

"Lady, I've picked way more'n I've ever grown." He got up with an effort, trying not to show it, and the girl smiled at him. As they moved off toward the trailer, where Mendoza and two of his small sons were emptying the sacks and stacking the melons, Majestyk said, "I meant to ask if you ever sorted."

"All the time. It's what I do best."

"Maybe you could start things going in the packing shed tomorrow. If you'd like to."

"Whatever you say."

"We ever get it done, I'd like to pay everybody something extra."

"You worried we won't take it?"

"I just want you to know I appreciate your staying here and all."

"Don't mention it. You're paying, aren't you?"

"Are the quarters all right? They haven't been used in a while. Couple of years at least."

"They're okay," the girl said. "We've lived in worse."

They were approaching the trailer and he wanted to say something to her before they reached it and Mendoza might hear him.

"You want to have supper with me?"

She turned her head to look at him. "Where, your house? Just the two of us, all alone?"

"We can go down the highway you want. I don't care."

They were at the trailer now. She handed up her sack to Mendoza before looking at Majestyk again.

"For a man needs a job done, where do you get all this free time? You want to pack melons, why don't we start?"

"You mean tonight?"

"Why not?"

"They'd keep working?"

"For money. You make it when you can." She said then, "If you don't want to ask them, I'll do it. We'll eat, then go to the packing shed and work another half shift. All right?"

"Lady," Majestyk said, "you swing that I'll marry you and give you a home."

She seemed to be considering it, her expression serious, solemn, before saying, "How about if I settle for a cold beer after work?"

"All you want."

"Maybe a couple."

She gave him a nice look and walked away, up the road toward the migrant quarters. Both Majestyk and Mendoza, on the trailer, stood watching her.

Mendoza said, "You like a piece of that, huh?" He looked down at Majestyk's deadpan expression and added quickly, "Hey, I don't mean nothing. Take it easy."

Majestyk handed him his sack. "You hear what she said? They'll start packing tonight."

Mendoza emptied the sack and came down off the trailer while his sons stacked the melons. "You must live right," he said. "Or maybe it's time you had some good luck for a change." He nodded toward the migrant quarters, fishing a cigarette out of his shirt pocket. "Those people, they're twice as good as what Julio brings up. Good people. They work hard because they like you. They don't want to see you lose a crop."

"I don't know," Majestyk said. "Maybe we can do it."

"We'll do it, Vincent. Don't get anybody else mad at you, we'll do it."

"We're coming to it now," Kopas said, over his shoulder. "On the right there. That's his packing shed."

Renda and Wiley were in the back seat. Lundy was driving, slowing down now as they approached the yellow building with MAJESTYK BRAND MELONS painted on the side.

"See," Kopas said. "Puts his name up as big as he can get it. Down the end of that road we're coming to his house. Way down, where you see the trees."

Renda was studying the road, then hunching forward to look across the field at the road, at the trailer and the figures in the road and the three old cars parked in front of the migrant living quarters.

He sat back again. "You said nobody was working for him."

"No crews," Kopas said. "He picked up a few migrants, that's all."

"They're people, aren't they?"

"Some claim they are. I don't." Christ, he knew right away he shouldn't have said it. It slipped out, talking smart again and not answering his question direct. He waited, looking straight ahead, knowing it was coming. But Renda didn't say anything for a moment, not until they were passing the sign that said ROAD CONSTRUCTION 500 FT., passing the barricades and equipment, the portable toilet and the State Highway Department pickup truck.

He said then, "Go up to the next road and turn around."

Lundy's eyes raised to the rearview mirror. "You want another look at his layout? That's all there is, what you saw."

"Gene," Renda said, "turn the fucking car around."

They had to go up about a mile to do it. Coming back, approaching the road repair site again, Renda said, "How long's that been there?"

Kopas wasn't sure what he meant at first and had to twist around to see where he was looking.

"That road stuff? I don't know, a few days."

"How long!" Renda's voice drilled into the back of his head and Kopas kept staring at the barricades and equipment as they approached, trying to remember, trying to recall quickly how many days.

"They been there as long as I been watching his place. I'm sure of that."

Now they were even with the site, going past it. Kopas was looking out the side window and saw the guy in khaki work clothes getting into the pickup truck. It was a close look at a face he'd seen somewhere before, but only a quick glimpse, and he was turning to look back when Renda's voice hit him in the head again.

"It's *cops!* Jesus, don't you know a cop when you see one!"

Kopas was turned, trying to see the guy, but it was too late. Looking past Renda, trying not to meet his eyes, he said, "You sure? I thought if there was any cops around I'd recognize them."

And he remembered as he said it and turned back around to stare at the windshield. Christ yes, the guy was a deputy. He'd seen him in Edna, at the station. He'd seen him in the pickup earlier today, across the street, when he was talking to Majestyk.

Kopas gave himself a little time, trying to relax and sound natural, before he said, "Well, I figure after a while they get tired waiting, they'll pick up and leave."

Nobody said anything.

"Then we can run off those Mexicans he's got. No sweat to that."

There was a silence again before Renda said, "Pull over."

Lundy looked up. "What?"

"Pull over, for Christ sake, and stop the car."

Lundy braked, bringing the Olds to a gradual stop on the shoulder of the road. They sat in silence, waiting for Renda.

"Hey, asshole. Get out of the car."

"Me?"

Kopas turned enough to look over his shoulder. Renda was staring the way he had stared before—as if not even seeing him—and he knew the man wasn't going to say anything.

"What did you want me to do?"

"Get out," Lundy said. "That's all you have to do."

Kopas grinned. "Is this a joke or something?"

Nobody was laughing. The girl had a book open and was reading, not even paying any attention.

Kopas said to Lundy, "I mean I left my car in Edna, where you picked me up. That's a six-mile hike just back to Junction."

Lundy didn't say anything.

Kopas waited another moment before he got out and turned to the car to close the door. He saw the window next to Renda lower without a sound.

"Come here," Renda said.

Kopas hunched over to look in the window. The girl was still reading the book.

"You hear me all right?"

"Yes, sir, fine."

"The way you come on," Renda said, "I don't like it. I don't know you a half hour you start talking shit out the side of your mouth. I say I don't want anybody working for him, he's got a dozen people living there. The cops set up a fucking grandstand to watch the show, you don't know they're cops. What I'm saying, I don't see you're doing me a lot of good."

"Mr. Renda, I been watching, seeing he doesn't run off."

"I'll tell you what," Renda said. "You go home, maybe we'll see you, maybe not. But listen, if it happens don't ever talk shit to me again, okay? Don't ever tell me what I'm going to do."

"I sure didn't mean anything like that, Mr. Renda."

But that was the end of it and he knew it. The window went up, the Olds drove off and Bobby Kopas was left standing there, six miles from Edna, feeling like a dumb shit who'd blown his chance.

9

Renda's lawyer was a senior partner in a firm that represented a number of businessmen and business organizations who shared related or complementary interests. Renda's lawyer looked out for his clients, helping them any way he could, and liked to see them help one another, too. For example, he had a client, a mortage broker, who was spending twelve months in the Federal Penitentiary at Lewisburg for willfully conspiring to defraud the United States government. All right, the mortgage broker had a hunting lodge–weekend funhouse up in the mountains that he wasn't using. Frank Renda, he was informed, wanted some solitude, a place to rest where no one would bother him. So Renda's lawyer arranged for Frank to lease the place from the mortgage broker for only six hundred dollars a week.

That was all right with the lawyer, Frank wanting a place in the mountains. But it wasn't all right if he was going to sit up there on his ass worrying about a 160-acre melon grower when he should be attending to his commercial affairs: his restaurant linen service, his laundry and dry cleaning supply company, his modeling service, and his string of massage parlors. That's where the money was to be made; not in shooting people.

The lawyer knew Frank Renda very well—his moods, his inclinations—so he knew it was sometimes hard to get through to him, once he had made up his mind. He began calling Frank at the mortgage broker's hunting lodge an hour after the Cessna was scheduled to drop him in the desert. There was no answer at the place until late afternoon, and then he had to wait another ten minutes before Renda came to the phone.

Wiley handed it to him, the phone and a scotch, and went over to a bearskin couch where her reading glasses and her novel were waiting.

Renda stood looking around the room, at the Navajo blankets and mounted heads of antelope and mule deer, the shellacked beams and big wagon-wheel chandelier, antique guns and branding irons. Christ, western shit all over the place. He had never met the mortgage broker friend of his lawyer, but he could picture the guy now: little Jewboy with a cowboy hat, string tie and high-heeled boots, and horn-rimmed glasses and a big fucking cigar.

He said into the phone, "Yeah."

His lawyer's calm, unhurried voice came on. "How are you, Frank? How was the trip?"

"Great, and the weather's great if it doesn't rain or snow. Come on, Harry, what do you want?"

"You like the place all right?"

"It looks like a fucking dude ranch."

"I called a few times this afternoon." The tone was still calm, unhurried. "Where've you been?"

"On the can," Renda said. "I come here to get away, I'm in the fucking place ten minutes and the phone starts ringing."

"I'm not going to bother you," the lawyer said. "I want to let you know how the situation stands."

"I thought I was clear."

"You are at the moment. Technically you're free on a five-thousand-dollar bond, pending your appearance at an investigation in ten days. It's a formality, something to inconvenience us. Though there is the possibility they'll try to dream up a lesser charge."

"No they won't," Renda said. "They don't want to touch me unless it's for the big one."

"I'm glad you understand that," the lawyer said. "So you know this is not the time to do anything"—he paused—"that would bring you under suspicion. Frank, they want you very badly."

"What else is new?"

"You must also have figured out why they released the melon grower."

Renda didn't say anything.

"All right," the lawyer said, "then let me mention that you have business matters that need your attention."

"Anything I was doing can wait."

"And you have business associates," the lawyer went on, "who may not feel like waiting. It's been my experience that the general reaction is one of impatience with anyone who puts his personal affairs ahead of the . . . common good, if you will."

"I've got something to do," Renda said. "I think they understand that. If they don't, tough shit."

"All right, you're saying you're going to do what you want," the lawyer said. "I want it on record that I'm advising you to wait—"

"You got your machine on?"

"Getting every word. As I was saying, I want it on record that I'm advising you to wait. I'm suggesting that any dealings you might have with the melon grower would be extremely ill-timed."

"Harry," Renda said, "don't fuck with me, okay? I need you, I'll call you."

He hung up.

Wiley rested her book on her lap and looked over the top of her reading glasses.

"What did he want?"

"The usual shit. Lawyers, they talk and talk, they don't say anything."

"I'll bet he told you not to do anything hasty," Wiley said. He didn't answer. She watched him sit down with his scotch and take a drink, sipping it, thinking about something.

She tried again. "After all, you pay him for his advice."

He looked over at her. "And you know what I pay you for. So why don't you shut the fuck up?"

"You don't pay me."

"It's the same thing."

She was starting to annoy him. Not too much yet, but she was starting. He had dumped a wife who had bored the shit out of him, talking all the time, buying clothes and showing them to him, and now he had a girl who was a college graduate drama major, very bright, who read dirty books. Books she thought were dirty. He said to himself, Where are you? What the fuck are you doing?

Five years ago it had been better, simpler. Get a name, do a study on the guy, learn his habits, walk up to him at the right time, and pull the trigger. It was done. Take a vacation, wait for a call, and come back. L.A., Vegas, wherever they wanted him. Now it was business all the time. The boring meetings, discussions, planning, all the fucking papers to sign and talking on the phone. Phones all over the place. He used to have one phone. It would ring, he'd say hello, and a voice would give him the name. That was it. He didn't even have to say good-bye. Now he had six phones in his house, four in the apartment. He took Librium and Demerol and Maalox and even smoked reefer sometimes, which he had never done before in his life or trusted anybody who did. A hundred and fifty grand plus a year to talk on the phone and sign the papers. He used to take a contract for five grand and had got as much as ten when it was tricky or the guy had a name.

That's what he missed. The planning and then pulling the trigger, being very steady, with no wasted motions. Then lying around after, drinking all the scotch he wanted for a while and thinking about how he'd pulled the trigger. He was good then. During the last few days he had caught himself wondering if he was still good and would be good enough to hit the melon grower clean. He hadn't hit the guy coming out of the bar very clean and that was probably why it was on his mind. He hadn't hit anybody in a while and had taken the job because he missed the action and had talked them into letting him hit the guy, who wasn't anybody at all to speak of. But he had been too *up*, too anxious to pull the trigger and experience the feeling again, and he hadn't blueprinted the job the way he should have. Christ, an off-duty cop sitting there watching. Empty the gun like a fucking cowboy and not have any left for the cop. Or not looking around enough beforehand. Not noticing the cop. Like it was his first time or like his fucking brains were in his socks. They could be wondering about him right now. What's the matter with him? Can't he pull a simple hit anymore?

No, they wouldn't be thinking that. They didn't know enough about it, how you made it work. They'd think it was dumb luck the cop was there and dumb luck the cop was killed and couldn't finger him. So the two canceled each other out and he was okay.

Except somebody had talked to the lawyer and that's why the lawyer had talked to him. It wasn't the lawyer's idea to call—he realized that now without any doubt. The lawyer wouldn't do anything unless he was getting paid to do it or somebody had told him to. Their lawyer, *they*, were telling him not to go after the melon grower. Because they thought he was wasting time or because it might involve them in some way or because they didn't have anything against the guy. The guy had not done anything to the organization. If he had, sure, hit him. They could pay him to do it and he wouldn't think any more about it. That was the difference. He *was* thinking about it and this time they couldn't pay him to hit the guy. He wouldn't take it. That was the thing. He couldn't get the melon grower out of his head he wanted to hit him so bad, and he wasn't sure why. Not because the guy had belted him a couple of times; though that could be reason enough. No, it was the way the guy had looked at him. The way he talked. The way he pulled that cheap cool shit and acted like he couldn't be bought.

How do you explain that to them?

Look, I *want* to hit the guy. I got to. I want him—listen, I never gave a shit about anybody before in my life, anybody I hit. It was never a personal thing before like this one.

Or try this.

Listen, if nobody gives a bunch of shit about this, if you let me hit him, then I'll give you the next one, anybody you want, free.

He said to himself, For Christ sake, you going to ask permission? You want the guy, do it.

And he yelled out, "Gene."

Wiley looked up from her book.

Lundy came in from wherever he had been with a can of Coors in his hand.

Renda said to him, "How many we got?"

Lundy wasn't sure at first what he was talking about, if he meant beers or what. But as he looked at Renda, he understood and said, "You and me for openers. I don't know when we're going, so I don't have anybody here. I thought after we talk about it, you know, see what you got in mind, I make a call and we get whatever we need."

"I think we need a truck," Renda said. "Good-size one. I'm not sure, but just in case we got to haul some people."

Lundy nodded. "Bobby Kopas's got one. Stake truck, open in back."

"All right," Renda said, then immediately shook his head. "No. Shit, I don't want him around. Get the truck tell him you're going to borrow it you'll bring it back, and get . . . four, five guys who know what they're doing."

"For when?"

"Tonight," Renda said. "Let's get it done before the fucking phone starts ringing again."

There was enough light in the packing shed to work by, but it was a dreary, bleak kind of light, like a light in a garage that didn't reach into the corners. A string of 100-watt bulbs, hanging beneath tin shades, extended the length of the conveyor that was bringing the melons in from the dock outside. The sound in the packing shed was the steady hum of the motor that drove the conveyor.

Most of the crew were outside, unloading the trailer. Nancy Chavez and Larry Mendoza's wife, Helen, did the sorting and were good at it, their hands deftly feeling, rolling the melons on the canvas belt, pulling out the ones that were badly bruised or overripe. Majestyk and Larry Mendoza were at the end of the line, packing the melons in cardboard cartons that bore the MAJESTYK BRAND label. Two other men in the crew were stacking the cartons, building a wall of them as high as they could reach.

By the time the trailer was unloaded it was almost ten o'clock. There were still melons on the conveyor, but Majestyk shut it down and said that was enough for one night, more than he'd expected they'd get done.

Mendoza came along the line to where his wife was standing and said, "I don't know, Vincent, but I think we're going to do it."

Nancy said, "If we can keep the grower working instead of goofing off, laying around in jail."

Majestyk was tired, but he felt good. He felt like talking to her and getting to know her. He said, "I remember—it seems to me somebody mentioned having a beer after work."

Nancy looked across the conveyor at him. "You still buying?"

"Sure, I'm going to be rich in about a week." He said to Mendoza, "Larry? How about you and Helen?"

"No, me and mama got more important things to do," Mendoza said, and slapped his wife on the can, making her jump a little and grin at them. "We're going to bed."

Nancy was still looking at Majestyk. "Maybe you'd rather do that." As she saw him begin to smile, she added quickly, "I mean if you're tired."

Majestyk said, "Come on, let's go get a couple of cold ones." He was still smiling at her.

Harold Ritchie watched the headlights of the pickup approaching the highway and said to the deputy over by the tool shed, "Now where in the hell's he going?"

"If it's him," the deputy said.

"I guess I'm going to have to find out, aren't I?"

Ritchie walked over to the State Highway Department truck, grabbed the door handle and looked around again. "'Less you want to this time. You been sittin' all day."

"You can talk plainer than that," the deputy said. "I'm about to go sit again. I think I got me some bad enchiladas or something."

He waited until Ritchie drove off before he went into the tool shed and radioed the Edna Post to let them know what was going on—which would be relayed to Lieutenant McAllen probably sitting home reading the paper or watching TV, a nice, clean, lighted bathroom down the hall from him, empty, nobody even using it.

Walking over to the portable toilet he was thinking, hell, he should've tailed the pickup this time, probably could've stopped at a gas station somewhere, or a bar. Unbuckling his belt, the deputy stepped inside the toilet and closed the door.

Less than a hundred yards east of the construction site three pair of headlights popped on.

The stake truck came first, followed by the two sedans, picking up speed, the truck reaching forty miles an hour by the time it got to the barricades, swerved in and sideswiped the portable toilet, the right front fender glancing off, scraping metal against metal, but the corner of the stake body catching it squarely, mashing into the light metal as it tore the structure from its base, carried it with forward momentum almost to the tool shed before it bounced end over end into the ditch. The stake truck kept going and turned into the road that led to Majestyk's place.

The two sedans, Lundy's Olds 98 and a dark-colored Dodge, came to a stop by the barricades, the Olds bathing the battered toilet in its headlight beams.

Renda and Lundy, and a third man with a machine gun under his arm, got out of the cars and walked into the beam of light. When Lundy got the twisted door of the toilet open, straining to pull it free, the third man aimed his machine gun into the opening. Lundy pushed him aside, reached in with one arm and when he straightened again looked at Renda.

"Dead."

"Must've got hit by a truck," Renda said.

* * *

Pushing open the screen a little, Mendoza could see the stake truck in front of the migrant quarters and hear the low rumble of its engine. Just sitting there. Nobody had got out of the truck. Nobody had come out of the migrant quarters. They were all inside or around someplace close by because their cars were there, the three old junk heaps. When the two pair of headlights came down the road from the highway and passed the migrant quarters, Mendoza moved away from the doorway. He was wearing only his jockey shorts—maybe he should hurry up and put some clothes on. But the cars weren't coming to his place. They kept going.

Behind him his wife whispered, "Who are they? Do you know them?"

He knew. He was pretty sure he knew. But he said to her, "Stay with the children."

When she stepped into the doorway to look out he pulled her back because of the slip she wore as a nightgown. It showed dull white in the moonlight and he was afraid they would see her, even though he knew they were all the way to Vincent's house by now.

She said again, "Who are they?"

"I don't know," Mendoza answered. "But they don't have any business with us and they're not friends I know of. Go to bed."

She lingered, but finally moved away from him. When he heard the springs and knew she was in bed again, he pushed open the screen door carefully and went outside, holding the door to close it, so it wouldn't make noise. On the steps of the porch, looking down the road, he could see the headlights of the two cars in front of Vincent's house. He didn't know if they were waiting or if they had gone inside. He said, God, why don't they leave? He's not there, they can see that, so go on, get out of here. Vincent was with a girl, talking, drinking beer. He could be gone for hours, having a good time; stay out late he could still get up early and work. They didn't know him.

He saw them in the headlights for a moment and faintly heard the car doors slam, then went into the house again as the cars came back this way. He was sure they were going to pass his house, leave, and when the cars turned in—coming straight at his house before stopping close to the porch—he couldn't believe it and began backing away from the screen door, but not soon enough. The headlights were blinding and he knew they could see him. He could hear the engines idling. Some men, three of them, dark shapes were coming up on the porch. When they came into the house he still couldn't see them because of the headlights.

One of them walked past him. He heard his wife's voice. "What do you want?" Frightened. He didn't hear the children.

Renda said, "Where is he?"

Mendoza thought of his wife and three children in the bedrooms, behind him. What was he? A guy standing in his underwear who just got waked up out of a sound sleep. How was he supposed to know what was going on?

He said, "I don't know. You mean Vincent Majestyk? Isn't he at home?"

He had never seen Eugene Lundy before and didn't see his features now, only a big shape that stepped up close to him. The next thing he knew he was hit in the mouth with a fist and felt the wall slam against his back. The man reached for him then and held him against the wall so he wouldn't fall down.

"Where is he?" Renda said again.

"I don't know," Mendoza said. "Believe me, I knew I'd tell you."

"He go into town?"

"I don't know," Mendoza said. "Honest to God, I thought he was home in bed."

Renda waited, knowing he was wasting time. The guy was probably telling the truth. He said, "Bring him along. And his wife."

They brought everybody out of the migrant quarters, pushing them to hurry up, making them stand in front of the place, in underwear or just pants, barefoot, squinting in the glare of the truck's headlights. Mendoza and his wife were pushed into the group by the men with guns in their hands who stood out of the light. The migrants waited, everyone too afraid to speak or ask what was going on.

Finally Lundy, who stood with Renda next to the truck, said to them, "We're looking for the boss. Who wants to tell us where he's at?" Lundy waited, giving them time. In the silence they could hear the crickets in the melon field. "Nobody knows, huh?" Lundy said then. "Nobody heard where he was going or saw him leave?"

Quietly, to Lundy, Renda said, "We got a dead cop and we're running out of time. Get rid of them."

Renda walked off into the darkness, toward the packing shed. He heard Lundy tell them, "You all've got two minutes to get in your cars and drive away from here and never come back." He heard one of the migrants say, a weak little voice with an accent, "We been working, but we haven't been paid yet. How we suppose to get paid?" And he heard Lundy say, "Keep talking, I'm going to start busting some heads. Now you people all get the hell out of here. Now."

The doors of the packing shed were open. Renda went up the steps to the loading dock and looked inside. He could make out the conveyor and the melons on the canvas belt. He was curious about the place—as if the place might be able to tell him something about the man who owned it. Feeling along the wall inside the door, he found the light switch. Outside there was a sound of engines trying to start and finally turning over.

Lundy and the one with the machine gun came in. Renda was staring at the wall of cartons, the melons that had been sorted and packed that evening.

"Man's been busy," Lundy said.

"I said to him what do you want?" Renda continued to stare at the wall of melon cartons and Lundy and the one with the machine gun looked over at him. "He said I want to get my melons in," Renda went on. "That's all he wanted. Get his melons in."

Lundy couldn't believe it when he saw Frank pull out his .45 automatic—Christ almighty—and start firing it at the stacked-up melon cases, firing away, making an awful racket in the place, until his gun was empty.

Renda looked at them then. He seemed calm. His voice was, and said, "What're you waiting for?"

Lundy always did what he was told. It didn't have to make sense. He took out his big magnum and opened up at the cartons. Then the other one with the machine gun let go and the din was louder than before. They tore up the cartons, lacing them with bullet holes. Renda took the machine gun from the guy, turned to the conveyor, and shot up all the melons left on the canvas belt, blew them apart, scattering pieces all over the shed.

Christ, Lundy thought. He hoped Frank felt better now.

Kopas had been told they'd probably drop his truck off later that night, somewhere near the county road intersection west of Edna, where there was that Enco station on the corner and the café. Kopas asked what time. Lundy said, when they got back. But if they had to take some people somewhere—and Kopas had a hunch he meant the migrants—then he wouldn't get his truck back until morning.

But the migrants had cars. They could run them off in their own cars and not have to take them anywhere. So Kopas was pretty sure the truck would be back tonight.

He hung around the café-bar that evening, going outside and looking up the highway every once in a while. Being sure they had gone to Majestyk's place, he was anxious to know if they had killed him. If they hadn't been able to for some reason—and if Renda was with them—he was anxious for Renda to see him again. Renda might decide he was a handy man to have around after all: he was alert, waited, did what he was told.

When Majestyk and the girl arrived, he was in the Men's Room of the café-bar. He came back into the room that was about half full of Chicanos and spotted Majestyk and the girl right away, sitting in a booth along the wall. He didn't see the two deputies at the bar—Ritchie and a deputy who had met him here—didn't notice them because they were in work clothes, and all Kopas was thinking about was getting out of there before Majestyk looked over. He glanced at the booth again as he went out the door—leaving the light and the smoke and the loud country steel-guitar beat inside—and saw Majestyk listening to something the girl was saying, giving her his full attention. Good.

He was more excited now than earlier in the day when he was out in the desert, the plane was taking off, and he was waiting to meet the famous Frank Renda. He saw Majestyk's pickup, parked a short way down from the café. He had a thought and began looking at the other cars, on both sides of the highway, and there it was, the State Highway Department truck. It was parked at the Enco station by the pumps; the station closed for the night.

Kopas started putting things together in his mind. They hadn't gotten Majestyk because Majestyk was inside. Also a cop was in there, or around someplace. He was more anxious now than ever. He went across the highway and across the county road to wait there at the intersection, moving around, wanting them to hurry up and come before the guy left. About fifteen minutes passed. He was so anxious for them to come that, when he saw the three pair of headlights approaching, he knew it was them and couldn't be anyone else. The thing now was he had to act cool and hold down his excitement.

Lundy, slowing down for the intersection, saw the figure on the corner. He recognized the shirt, bright in the headlights, and the sunglasses and the curled-brim Texas hat. He said to Renda, next to him, "There's Bobby. He looks like he's got to take a leak or something."

Kopas was there as the car came to a stop, hunched down to look in the side window. He said, as calmly as he could, "Mr. Renda . . . man you want's inside that place over there, having a beer."

Renda said, "Alone?"

"With a girl. One works for him."

"Where's the cop sitting?" Renda asked.

The good feeling was there and it was gone as he felt his confidence begin to drain out of him. Kopas straightened and, with a squinting, serious expression, looked over toward the State Highway Department truck parked at the gas station.

He said, "I'm not exactly sure yet, Mr. Renda. But you want me to, I'll find out."

He was not aware of the country music or the two deputies at the bar or the other people in the place. Not right now. His hand was on the bottle of beer, but he was not drinking it. He was looking at the girl's eyes, at the pearl earrings and the way her dark hair was parted on the side, without the bandana, and had a silver clip holding it back, away from her face.

Nancy said, "Do you mind my asking about her?"

"No, it's all right." Majestyk paused. "I don't know, I guess people change. Or else it turns out they're somebody else all the time and you didn't realize it. Do you think it's hard to know people?"

"Not always," Nancy said. "Was she blond, with blue eyes?"

"Most of the time blond. You put your hair up in rollers? You have very pretty hair."

"Once in a while I have. Why?"

"I picture my wife, I see her with rollers. She was always fooling with her hair, or washing it."

"You have any kids?"

"Little girl, seven."

"And you miss her."

"I guess I do. I haven't seen either of them in two years. They moved to Los Angeles."

A silence began to lengthen and Nancy said, "Are you thinking about them?"

"No, not really."

"What are you thinking about?"

"I'm thinking I'd like to know you better."

"Well, I'll fill out a personnel form," Nancy said. "Read it over, see if I pass."

"Always a little bit on the muscle." He was staring at her as he said, "You're very pretty."

"No, not very. But I suppose not bad-looking either. Not somebody you'd kick out of bed, huh, if that's what you've got in mind."

"Why don't you try and relax a little," Majestyk said, "and be yourself. Find out what it's like."

"You want to go to bed with me. Why don't you say it?"

"I'd like to hold you."

"See how close we can get?"

"Sometimes, hard as you try, you can't get close enough," he said. "You know that?" She didn't answer, but he knew by her expression, the soft smile, she was aware of the feeling. Wanting to lie very close to someone, holding each other, not saying anything, because they wouldn't have to use words to say it.

He said, "Let's go home, all right? Go to my house."

There was no need to make him wait. Or, as he said, to be on the muscle. She was aware that they knew each other, each other's feelings. She knew she could relax with him and be herself. Still she hesitated, she supposed out of habit, before saying to him, "All right, your house." She smiled then as he smiled. "But first I'll go to the Ladies'—if it isn't locked."

"If it is," he said, "I'll kick it open."

He watched her cross the room—and the men looking up at her as she passed their tables—to the little hall that led back to the kitchen and the rest rooms.

He saw a man come away from the jukebox and turn into the hallway and knew, even before the man with the hat and the sunglasses looked over his shoulder and grinned at him, it was Bobby Kopas. Majestyk started to slide out of the booth, rising. Then stopped, and sat down again as he felt the pressure of the hand on his shoulder.

"How you doing, buddy?"

Majestyk looked up, then past Renda toward the bar. "There're two cops sitting over there."

Renda took his time. He slid into the seat where Nancy had been and looked at Majestyk before saying, "If there weren't, you'd already be dead."

Majestyk's eyes went to the hallway again. Kopas was still there, watching.

"Leave the girl alone, all right? She doesn't have anything to do with this."

"I don't give a shit about the girl," Renda said. "As long as she stays in the can, out of the way. I got something to tell you. You probably already know it, but I want to make sure you do. I'm going to kill you."

"When?" Majestyk said.

"I don't know. It could be tomorrow. It could be next week." Renda spoke in a normal tone, quietly, without the sound of a threat in his voice. "You could hide in the basement of the police station, but I'm going to get you and you know it."

Majestyk raised the beer bottle and took a drink. Putting it down again his hand remained on the bottle and he seemed to study it thoughtfully before looking at Renda again.

"Can I ask you why?"

"I told you why. We make a deal or you're dead. The fact I got off has got nothing to do with it. You jammed me. You tried to, and nobody does that."

"I don't guess I can talk you out of it then, huh?"

"Jesus Christ—"

"Or there's anything I can do about it?"

"You can run," Renda said. "I'll find you. You can live at the police station. But you got to come out some time. There's no statute of limitations on this one. Whether I kill you tonight or a year from tonight, you're still going to be dead."

Majestyk nodded and was thoughtful again, fooling with the beer bottle. He said, "Well, I guess I got nothing to lose, have I?"

He raised the bottle in his left hand, but it was the right fist that did the job, hooked into Renda's face, in the moment he was distracted by the bottle, and slammed him back against the partition. There was no purpose in hitting him again or hitting him with the bottle. There was little satisfaction in it; but he was letting the guy know he wasn't a goat tied to a post. If Renda wanted him he was going to have to work for it.

The people at the next tables saw the blood and the look of pure astonishment on Renda's face. They saw the expression begin to change as he touched his face, a dead expression that told nothing, but stared at Vincent Majestyk as he got up from the table.

They heard Majestyk lean over, his hands on the table, and

say to the man he had hit, "Why don't you call the cops?" They watched him walk away as the man sat there.

Bobby Kopas didn't like it at all, what was happening now. Majestyk coming toward him. Renda, in the booth, who could stand up any second and start blasting the guy. The two cops at the bar, trying to see past the people at the tables who were standing now.

But nothing happened. Kopas stepped back as Majestyk came into the hallway and went past him—didn't even look at him—to the Ladies' Room. He didn't do anything. Renda didn't. Nobody did. Majestyk pushed open the door to the Ladies' Room and said to the girl who was standing there, "Let's go home."

It could have been a good night. Then there was no chance of it being even a pretty good night. They got back to the place to find no one there. Not even Mendoza and his family. Majestyk saw the flares and the flashing lights across the field, on the highway. The lights were there for some time before he went over and found out a deputy had been killed. Hit and run it looked like.

Harold Ritchie blew up when he saw Majestyk. He said, "Goddamn it, you're the one started this!"

Majestyk said to him, "Listen, an hour ago I had fourteen people at my place counting my foreman and his family. Now everybody's gone, chased off while you're sitting in a bar drinking beer."

"And a man was killed and we don't know who done it because I had to watch *you!*" Ritchie yelled at him.

There was no point standing on the highway arguing with a sheriff's deputy in the pink-red flickering light of the flares that had been set around the area.

Majestyk went home. He told Nancy what had happened, then told her to sleep in the bedroom, he'd sleep on the couch in the living room. When she objected he said, "I'm not going to argue with you. You're sleeping in there."

She didn't say any more and he didn't either. It wasn't until the next morning they found out what had been done inside the packing shed.

10

When Nancy came into the shed, Majestyk was opening the cartons that were stitched with bullet holes and stained where juice from the melons had seeped out. She looked at the open cartons scattered about the floor, at the chunks of melon, yellow fragments, on the conveyor line.

"If he can't have you, he'll take your melons," the girl said. "How does it look?"

"Some are all right."

He walked past her, out to the loading dock, and stared at his empty fields and the pale morning sky. Some were all right. Spend a half day to sort them, maybe have one load to deliver to the broker. Most of the crop was still on the vines. If he could get it in he would at least break even and be able to try it again next year. If he could get the crop in. If he could get a crew. And if Renda would forget the whole thing and leave him alone.

But that was not going to happen, so he'd sit here and wait and watch the crop rot in the field.

Unless you could finish it somehow, Majestyk thought, and had a strange feeling as he thought it. Instead of waiting, what if there was something he could do to get it over with?

When he saw the figure walking in from the highway he knew it was Larry Mendoza—the slow, easy way he moved—and went down to the road to meet him. As Mendoza approached he held up his hand, as if to hold Majestyk off, knowing what was in his mind.

"Don't say nothing, Vincent. I live here, I work here. I took my wife and kids to her mother's, so they'd be out of the way. Now, what are we doing?"

"They hurt you," Majestyk said, staring at Mendoza's bruised, swollen mouth. "I'm sorry, Larry. I should have been here."

"No." Mendoza shook his head. "Getting that beer was the best thing you ever did."

"They asked you where I was and you wouldn't tell them," Majestyk said. "So they roughed you up."

"Not much. I only got hit once. Nobody else was hurt."

"You don't know if Frank Renda was one of them?"

"No, I never seen him, picture or nothing."

"Did you talk to the police?"

"Sure, a cop stop me in town, take me in. They ask some questions, but what do I tell them? Some men come, I don't even know who they are. I don't even *see* them. They tell us leave or get our heads busted. That's all. Come on, Vincent, we got some work, let's do it."

"If you'll do one thing for me, Larry," Majestyk said. "I think we got enough good melons for a load. Take the trailer into the warehouse and leave it there. You can come back later sometime, and get your personal things, your clothes and stuff."

Mendoza frowned. "What the hell are you talking about? I'll

bring the trailer back, we'll pick melons and load it again. You retiring already, or what?"

"I can't ask you to stay here," Majestyk said.

"Then don't ask. I'll get the trailer."

As he started away Majestyk said to him, "Larry . . . it's good to see you."

When he returned to the packing shed Nancy had already begun the sorting, separating the undamaged melons and placing them in fresh cartons. She looked up as he came in.

"Lots of them are still good, Vincent. More than I thought."

"Larry's going to take a load in," Majestyk said. "He'll drop you off in town."

"What am I going to town for?"

He realized, by her expression, he was taking her by surprise. "To get a bus," Majestyk said. God, he sounded cold and impersonal, but went on with it. "There's no reason now for you to stay. I'll pay you, give you money for the others in case you run into them." She came to her feet slowly, as he spoke.

"Last night you want to hold me," Nancy said, "see how close we can get. Today you want me to leave."

"Last night—that seems like a long time ago." He still didn't like his tone, but didn't know what to do about it. "I must've been nuts, or dreaming," he said, "believe the man'd sit and wait for me to get my crop in."

"All right, if you feel he's going to come back," the girl said, "then why don't we both leave?"

"Run and hide somewhere? He'd find me, sooner or later."

"So face it and get it over with, huh?" There was a sound of weariness in her tone. "Big brave man, has to stand alone and fight, no matter what. Where'd you learn to think like that?"

"You're not going to be here, so don't worry about it."

"Now you're mad."

"I don t have time to worry about it."

She said then, "I'll tell you something, Vincent. I've been in a car that was shot at and the man sitting next to me killed. Another time, a truck chased a bunch of us down a road, trying to run us over. And once I was in a union hall when they threw in a fire bomb and shot the place up. I don't need anybody looking out for me. But if you want me to leave, if you don't want me here, that's something else."

He had to say it right away, without hesitating. "All right, I don't want you here."

"I don't believe you."

She was holding him with her eyes, trying to make him tell what he felt.

"I said Larry'll drop you off. Get your bag and be ready when he leaves." He stared at her, fought her eyes, until finally she walked past him, out of the shed.

They were lifting the battered portable toilet onto a flatbed truck with a hoist when Lieutenant McAllen arrived. He had them set the toilet back on the ground and looked at it, not touching it or saying anything until he turned to Harold Ritchie.

"How's it written up? Hit and run?"

"That's about all we can call it for the time being," Ritchie said.

McAllen nodded. "What're they going to do with it?"

"Scrap it, I guess. 'Less the road people want to bump it out."

"You think maybe it ought to be dusted first?"

"Well, we could. But there's people been handling it."

"I'm interested in the door," McAllen said. "Like maybe someone pulled it open, at the time I mean, to see if the man was alive or dead. There could be some prints along the inside edge."

"I guess there could be at that," Ritchie said.

"Let's bring it in and do it at home," McAllen said. "I think that'd be better than having a lot of people hanging around here, don't you?"

Ritchie was looking past McAllen, squinting a little in the glare. "Here comes his truck." As McAllen turned, Ritchie raised his binoculars. "Pulling a trailer load of melons. Going to market, like he didn't have a goddamn trouble in the world. No, it ain't him," Ritchie said then, as the truck reached the highway. "It's his hired man, Larry Mendoza, and looks like . . . some Mexican broad."

* * *

Mendoza paid attention to his driving, concentrating on it, and would keep busy looking at the trailerload of melons through the rearview mirror, because he didn't know what to say. The girl, Nancy, didn't say anything either—staring out the side window, her suitcase on the seat between them—but he was aware of her, could feel her there, and wished she would start talking about something.

He tried a couple of times to get it going, asking her if she thought she would run into her friends. She said probably, sooner or later. He asked her if she thought all the migrant farm workers would ever be organized and paid a living wage. She said again probably, someday.

It was too hard to make up something, to avoid thinking about Vincent and what was going on. So Mendoza didn't say any more until they crossed the state road intersection and he pulled to a stop opposite the café-bar.

He said then, "You don't mind waiting?"

"No, it's all right. I can get something to eat," she said, opening the door and putting a hand on her suitcase.

"Sure, get a beer, something to eat. The bus always stops there, so don't worry about missing it."

She said, "Thanks, Larry, and good luck."

"Good luck to you, too."

She closed the door and walked around the front of the truck. As she started across the highway, Mendoza said, "Nancy—"

She paused to look back at him.

"If he didn't have this trouble going on—"

"I know," she said.

"Come back and see us, all right?"

She nodded this time—maybe it was a nod, Mendoza wasn't sure. He watched her reach the sidewalk and go in the café-bar.

He drove on, into Edna, thinking about the girl and Vincent, the kind of girl Vincent ought to have. Especially Vincent. He didn't refer to Chicanos as Latins or look down at them in any way. It was easy to tell when someone looked down, even when he pretended to be sincere and friendly. Mendoza didn't busy himself with the trailerload of melons now, looking through the rearview mirror. He thought about Vincent and the trouble he was in, wondering what was going to happen. He didn't notice the Oldsmobile 98 following him.

Just past the water tower that said EDNA, HOME OF THE BRONCOS, Mendoza turned off the highway, crossed the railroad tracks, and drove along the line of produce warehouses and packing sheds. At a loading dock, where a man was sitting eating a sandwich, his lunch pail next to him, Mendoza came to a stop and said out the side window, "Where's your boss? Man, I got a load of top-grade melons."

The man on the loading dock wasn't in any hurry. He took a bite of his sandwich and chewed it before saying, "He's out to lunch. You'll have to wait till he gets back."

"What if I unload while I'm waiting?"

"You know he's got to check them first," the man on the dock said. "Go sit down somewhere, take it easy."

Well, if he had to. But he wasn't going to wait in the hot sun, or in the pickup that would get like an oven. And he wasn't going to sit with the guy on the dock and have to talk to him—he could tell the guy had it against Chicanos. So Mendoza got out of the truck and walked around the corner of the warehouse where there was a strip of shade about five feet wide along the wall.

He sat down with his back to it, tilted his straw down over his eyes and settled into a reasonably comfortable position. He pictured himself there as someone might come along and see him. Goddamn Mexican sleeping in the shade. Make him wait and then call him a lazy Mex something or other. He yawned. He was tired because he had gotten only about four hours sleep last night at Helen's mother's house, all of them crowded in there, two of the kids in bed with them. He wouldn't mind taking a nap for about a half hour, till the broker got back from his lunch.

His eyes were closed. Maybe he had been asleep, he wasn't sure. But when he opened his eyes he saw the front end of the Olds 98 rolling toward him—creeping, like it was sneaking up on him—from about thirty feet away.

Mendoza got up so fast his hat fell off. What the hell was going on? The whole wall empty and a car coming directly at where he was standing. Like some kind of joke. Somebody trying to scare him.

But he knew it wasn't a joke when he saw Bobby Kopas, the skinny, hunch-shouldered hotshot guy, coming along the wall toward him. He knew there would be another guy coming from the other side. Mendoza turned enough to look over his shoulder and there he was. It was too late to run. The car kept coming and didn't stop until it was only about three feet from him. Kopas and the guy on the other side came up to stand by the front fenders. He could smell the engine in the afternoon heat.

Kopas said, "Larry, I believe you were told to shag ass and don't come back. Ain't that right?"

"I was just helping out my friend a little bit, deliver some melons," Mendoza said.

"We give you a chance to run, you don't even take it."

"No, listen. I'm just doing this as a favor. I get rid of the load I'm gone, you never see me again."

"Larry," Kopas said, "don't bullshit me, okay?"

"Honest to God, I'm going to drop the melons and keep going."

"In the Polack's truck?"

"No, I told him I leave it here, so he can pick it up."

"Is that a fact? When's he coming?"

"I don't know. Sometime. Maybe tomorrow."

"How's he supposed to get here?"

"Hitchhike, I guess. He don't worry about that."

"Larry, you're shittin' me, aren't you?"

"Honest to God, ask the man in the warehouse, around on the dock. Come on, let's ask him. He'll tell you."

"You aren't going nowhere," Kopas said. "You had your chance, Larry, you blew it."

The man behind the wheel of the Olds 98 hit the accelerator a couple of times, revving the engine. Mendoza looked at the car and at Kopas again quickly.

"Listen—what did I do to you? I worked for the guy that's all."

He saw Kopas step away and knew the car was coming as he stood with his back against the wall and no room, no direction, in which to run. He had to do something and jumped up, trying to raise his legs, but the car lunged into him, the bumper catching his legs and flattening him against the wall, holding him against it as he screamed and fell against the hood and then to the ground as the car went abruptly into reverse. He remembered thinking—the last thing as he tensed, squeezing his eyes closed—now the wheels were going to get him.

The hospital in Edna had an emergency room and eighteen beds, but it was more an outpatient clinic than a hospital and looked even more like a contemporary yellow-brick grade school.

For almost a year Majestyk had thought it was a school. He had never been in the hospital before today—before the squad car picked him up and delivered him, blue lights flashing, to the emergency entrance where an ambulance and another squad car were waiting. Inside, the first person he saw was Harold Ritchie, the deputy coming toward him from the desk where a nurse's aide sat typing.

"Where's Larry?"

"Round the corner. I'll show you."

"What'd they do to him?"

"Guy at the warehouse—there was only one guy anywhere near where it happened—didn't see a thing. Not even the car."

"What'd they *do* to him?"

"Broke his legs," Ritchie said.

He was lying on a stretcher bed covered with a sheet, his wife with him, a curtain drawn, separating them from the next bed where a little boy was crying. A nurse, with a tray of test tubes and syringes, was drawing a blood sample from Mendoza's arm. Majestyk waited. Helen saw him then and came over and he put his arms around her.

"Helen . . . how is he?"

He could feel her head nod against his chest. Her voice, muffled, said, "The doctor say he's going to be all right. Vincent, you know what they did?"

He held her gently, patting her shoulder. "I know." He held

her patiently because she needed his comfort, letting her relax and feel him close to her and know she was not alone. He heard Mendoza say, "Vincent?" and went over to the bed.

"Larry—God, I'm sorry."

"Vincent, I left the melons there."

"Don't worry about the melons."

"That's what I was going to say to you. Staying alive is more important than melons. Did you know that?" He seemed half asleep, his eyes closing and opening slowly.

Majestyk leaned in close to him. "Larry, who were they? You know them?"

"I think the same car as last night, the same people. And your friend, Bobby Kopas, he was there. Vincent, they not kidding. They do this to me, they going to kill you." Mendoza's face tightened as he held his breath, then let it out slowly before relaxing again. "Jesus, the pain when it comes—I never felt nothing like it."

"You want the nurse?"

"No, they already gave me something. They getting ready, going to set my legs."

"Larry, you're going to be all right. The doctor said so."

"I believe him."

"You go to sleep and wake up, it's done. You'll feel better."

Mendoza kept his eyes open, staring at Majestyk. He said, "You want me to feel better, Vincent? Tell me you'll go away. Hide somewhere. There's nothing wrong doing that. Or, sure as hell, you going to be dead."

Harold Ritchie was in the waiting room, arms folded, leaning against the wall. He came alive when he saw Majestyk going past, heading for the door.

"Hey, what'd he say? He tell you anything?"

Majestyk kept going, pushing through the door.

Outside, he saw Lieutenant McAllen getting out of a squad car. He heard McAllen say, "Wait a minute!" And heard himself say, "Bullshit," not looking at the man or slowing down until McAllen said, "If you will, please. Just for a minute."

He waited for McAllen to come to him.

"Where you going?"

"Pick up my equipment."

"We'll drive you."

"I can walk."

McAllen paused. "I'm sorry about your hired man."

"He wasn't my hired man. He was my friend."

"All right, he was your friend." McAllen's tone changed as he said it, became dry, official. "I believe you know a deputy was killed last night, run over or beaten to death possibly, about the same time your migrants left. We'd like to locate them, talk to them."

"Why don't you talk to Frank Renda instead?"

"Because if we brought him in for questioning he'd be out in an hour, and we wouldn't be any farther ahead."

"Where does he live? I'll talk to him."

"You would, wouldn't you?"

"Right now. Soon as I get a gun."

"We'll handle that," McAllen said. "The Phoenix police are watching both of his places, his house, his apartment. So far he hasn't been to either."

Majestyk stared at him. "You mean you don't know where he is? Christ, I was sitting with him last night. So were two of your deputies."

"They had to stay with you," McAllen said. "They radioed the post, but by the time a car got there Renda was gone. We know somebody's given him a place to stay. Probably in the mountains. But who, or where the place is, we don't know that yet."

"You don't know much of anything, do you?"

"I know I have a warrant with your name on it, and I can put you back in jail if you're tired of this."

"Or I can sit home and go broke," Majestyk said. "Why don't you just keep the hell out of the way for a while?"

"We pull out, you know what'll happen."

Majestyk nodded, as though he was thinking about it. "Well, let's see now. So far he's run off my crew, shot up a week's crop of melons and broke my friend's legs. So please don't give me any shit about police protection. Keep your hotshots and their flashing lights away from my property and maybe we can get this thing done and I can go back to work."

McAllen paused, studying Majestyk, as if trying to see into

his mind, to understand him. He said, "Still worried about your melons. You're not going to get them picked if you're dead."

"And if I'm dead it won't matter, will it?"

"You want to bet your life against a melon crop—" McAllen paused again. "All right, you're on your own."

"I have been," Majestyk said, "from the beginning."

McAllen watched him walk off, down the drive toward the main street. He was thinking. The man seems simple, but he's not. He's easy to misjudge. He knows what he wants. He's willing to take risks. And he could already be planning something you haven't thought of yet. Mr. Majestyk, he was thinking, I'd like to know you better.

Ritchie had been waiting a few yards off to the side. He walked over now.

"We pulling out?"

"Let's let him think so," McAllen said, "and see what happens."

11

The broker acted like he was doing him a favor, buying the trailerload of melons and waiting around after quitting time while Majestyk unloaded the cases himself because the warehousemen had gone home. He asked Majestyk how his hired man was. Majestyk told him Larry Mendoza was his friend, not his hired man. The broker said it must've been an accident. Mexican sleeping there in the shade, car comes along doesn't see him, rolls over his legs. Those people were always getting hurt with broken beer bottles and knives, the broker said. Now they were getting hurt while they slept. Majestyk didn't say anything. It was hard not to, but he held on and finally the broker went into his office. Later, when he picked up the check, he didn't say anything either. It was getting dark by the time he got out of there, heading home with the empty trailer.

Home. Nobody there now. A dark house at the end of a dirt road.

As he turned off the highway onto the road he looked at the rearview mirror, then out the side window to see the car that had been following him for several miles continue on. An Oldsmobile, it looked like.

He could hear crickets already in the settling darkness, nothing around to bother them. The packing shed was empty, Mendoza's house, the melon fields—driving past slowly, looking out at the dim fields the way he had looked at fields and rice paddies from the front seat of a jeep a dozen years before, feeling something then, expecting the unexpected and, for some reason, beginning to feel it again, now.

Majestyk drove up to within fifty yards of his house at the end of the road, stopped, turned the key off, put it in his pocket and waited a few moments, listening. When he got out he reached into the pickup bed for a wrench and used it to free the trailer hitch, crouched down between the pickup and the trailer where he could inch his gaze over the melon rows and study the dark mass of trees beyond his house. Pine trees. He didn't know what kind of trees he had watched twelve years ago, lying in the weeds not far from a Pathet Lao village after the H-34 helicopter had gone down, killing the pilot, the mechanic, and the ten Laotian soldiers. No, the trees were different. Only the feeling inside him, then and now, was the same.

Lundy cut his lights as he turned off the highway, hoping to hell he didn't get hung up on a stump or something. Once the road got into the trees it was all right. It was so narrow brush and tree limbs scraped the car on both sides, and the ruts were deep enough that he could feel his way along in the darkness and not worry about going off the road. He came up next to the Dodge parked in the small clearing, got out, and moved through the trees to where Bobby Kopas was watching the house.

Hearing him, Kopas looked over his shoulder. "He just come home."

"Who do you think I been following?" Lundy said. "Where is he?"

"By the truck. See him?"

It was about forty yards across a pasture to the house with its dark windows, and about the same distance again down the road to the pickup truck and trailer. Lundy held his gaze on the front end of the truck.

"I don't see him."

"Unhitching the trailer. He *was.*"

"Well, where's he now?"

"Goddamn it, he was there a minute ago."

"He go in the house?"

"I'd have seen him."

Lundy looked around, getting an uneasy feeling. "Where're the others?"

Kopas pointed with his thumb. "Down there in the trees. So's to watch the side and back of the place."

"Later on," Lundy said, "we'll bring some more people in, seal him up." He looked at Kopas. "If he's still here."

"He's here. We can't see him is all. Down in behind the truck."

"I hope so," Lundy said. "You imagine what Frank would do to you if the man slipped out?"

He moved through the melon rows to the irrigation ditch and again, smelling the damp earth close to his face, experienced a feeling from the time before. It was easier this time because he wasn't carrying the M-15 and the sack of grenades. He wouldn't mind having the M-15 now, or the .30–.30 Marlin in the house or the 12-gauge Remington. The shotgun would be best, at night, at close range. He had thought of the gun when he thought of scouting the house and decided against it. He could be caught in the open too easily. It was better to look around first, make sure, and not approach the house until it was full dark. He reached the end of the irrigation ditch and came up behind the pump housing. From here, in the deep shadows he was able to walk into the trees.

It had been midsummer when the pesticide tank truck came in through the back road to spray his outlying fields. Studying the trees he had remembered the road. It was a point to reach and follow, to help him keep his sense of direction. He remembered the clearing, too, and approached it through the dense trees and scrub as he had approached the village, smelling the wood smoke from a hundred meters away. He stopped when he heard the voice.

"I mean the man's got to be around, hasn't he? His truck's here. How's he going to go anyplace less he's in his truck?"

He knew the voice. There was another voice then, lower, and the sound of a car door slamming.

"Hey, I forgot to tell you—this afternoon, right after I got back—"

The familiar voice was drowned out by the car engine starting. Majestyk moved back into the trees. He waited. When the Olds 98 rolled past him he was close enough to touch it.

The deputy at the road repair site, sitting by the radio in the tool shed, said to the Edna Post, "His truck's still over there. Haven't seen nothing or heard a sound, so I judge he's home safely."

"Harold's about to leave," the voice coming over the radio said. "He wants to know what you want on your hamburgers."

"Mustard and relish," the deputy said.

"Mustard and relish, out."

"Out," the deputy said and flicked the switch off.

He heard the car coming and waited until it passed before stepping outside with the binoculars. So he saw only the taillights of the Olds, the lights becoming little red dots before they disappeared. He raised the binoculars putting them on Majestyk's house, inching them over to the trees and back again. It was too dark to see anything. Dark already, the melon grower was probably in bed, and here he hadn't even had his supper yet.

There were five of them watching the house. He came on them one at a time as he circled through the trees, passing them, seeing dark silhouettes, hearing a muffled cough. The last man was looking out of the trees toward an equipment shed and past it, across the yard, to the back of the house, Majestyk knew he could take the man from behind if he had to, with his hands. But he told himself no, as he had told himself the time before, circling the perimeter of the Pathet Lao village and almost running into the sentry—a young man or a boy who wore a cap with a short visor and held a Chicom machine gun across his skinny knees. He remembered the profile of the boy's face in the moonlight, the delicate features, and remembered wondering what the boy was thinking, if he was afraid, alone in the darkness. He could have shot him, cut his throat or broken his neck with his forearms. But he backtracked into the rain forest and waded for miles through a delta swamp so he wouldn't have to kill the boy. Maybe he had lost too much time and it was the reason they captured him the next morning as he slept, opening his eyes to see the muzzle of the Chicom in his face. He wasn't sure it was the reason he was caught; so he told himself it wasn't. They were on patrol and had stumbled across him.

There had been five of them then, as there were five now. They tied his arms behind him with hemp and looped it around his neck, to lead him back to the village or to another village. He was filthy and smelled from wading through the swamp. At a river he remembered was the Nam Lec, he asked if he could wash himself. One of them untied him and took him, with his Chicom, to the edge of the water. The rest sat on the bank ten yards away and began rolling cigarettes, leaning in toward the match one of them held, and the one guarding him was turned to watch them. Almost in one motion he grabbed the man by his collar, pulling him into the river, chopped him across the face with the side of his hand, took the Chicom away from him and shot two of the Pathet Lao with a single burst as they scrambled to raise their weapons. The three that were left he brought with him, thirty miles to the fire post at Hien Heup.

They gave him a Silver Star and a seventy-two-hour pass, which he spent in the bar at the Hotel Constellation in Vientiane. He told the story to a friend of his, another combat adviser sergeant, saying it didn't make sense, did it? Fall asleep and have to work your ass off to get out of a bad situation and they give you a medal. He remembered his friend saying, "You think people set out to win medals? They're just guys who fuck up and get lucky, that's all."

He was still glad, when he thought about it, he had not killed the sentry.

The one here, watching the back of the house, was nothing to worry about. Majestyk came out of the trees fifty yards down from the man, crossed at an angle so that the equipment shed would give him cover, and reached the side of the house without being seen. Then over the rail to the porch, where he waited a good minute, listening, before going in through the screen door.

In the dark he moved across the room to the cabinet where he kept his deer rifle and automatic shotgun, placed them on a long table behind the sofa that faced the front door, and went back to the cabinet for shells and cartridges. He began loading the shotgun first, thinking, You could go out the same way and take them one at a time. Except Bobby Kopas would be last and he'd run. Get them all together somehow. And Frank Renda, get him out there. That would be too much to ask, to have Renda waiting for him in the woods and not see him coming.

The sound was faint, the squeak of a floorboard, but clear in the silence. He came around with the shotgun at his hip, almost in the same moment he heard the sound, and put it squarely on the figure in the bedroom doorway.

"Don't shoot me, Vincent."

Nancy. He knew it before she spoke, seeing her size and shape against the light from the bedroom window, though not able to see her face. Her voice sounded calm.

"How'd you get here?"

"On the bus. It was going by—I went up to the driver and told him to stop. I told him I forgot something."

"You must've forgot your head. You know what you walked into?"

She didn't say anything. She had never heard this tone in his voice. Not loud, quiet, but God there was a cold edge to it, colder than it had been when he told her to leave.

"There are five men out there," Majestyk said. "With guns.

They're not going to let me leave and they're not going to let you leave either. You got nothing to do with this, but now you're in it."

She said to him quietly, "So I guess you're stuck with me, Vincent."

After a moment, when he came over to her and put his hand on her shoulder, turning her in the doorway so that the light showed part of her face, she knew his tone would be different.

"Why did you come back?"

"I don't know," she said, and that was partly true. "Maybe see what it's like to be on the same side as the grower. That's a funny thing, Vincent. All my life I've been fighting against the growers. Now, this is different."

"You like to fight?" He kept watching her, making up his mind.

"You don't know me yet," Nancy said. "I like to do a lot of things."

He raised the barrel of the shotgun. "You know how to use this?"

"Show me and I will."

"How about a deer rifle?"

"Aim it and pull the trigger. Isn't that all you do?" She waited, looking up at him.

"I don't want you to be here," he said then, "but I'm glad you are. You understand what I mean?"

"You don't have to say anything. If I didn't know how you feel I wouldn't be here."

"You're that sure?"

She hesitated. "I hope so."

"You do have to leave yourself open, don't you? Take a chance."

"That's what it's all about."

"We'll have to talk about it again, when we have more time."

"Sure, it can wait." She smiled at him, even more sure of herself now.

"I'm going outside," he said. "Bring the truck up closer to the house—case they get it in mind to pull some wires."

"Are we going to make a run?"

"I don't know what we're going to do yet. First thing, I'll show you how to work the rifle." She followed him to the table and watched him as he began to load the Marlin. "If anybody tries to come in," he said, "shoot him. Don't say, 'Put up your hands' or anything like that, shoot him."

"All right, Vincent."

He handed her the rifle and picked up the shotgun again. "But make sure it isn't me."

Wiley was on the bearskin couch with her book. She looked up, over her reading glasses, at Lundy and said, "Gene's here."

Renda didn't pay any attention to her. He was on the phone again. Lundy had never seen a guy who was on the phone as much as Frank. The first time he ever met him—after doing seven on the robbery armed conviction and getting out and going to see him with the note his cellmate had given him—Frank was on the phone. It seemed like he had been on it ever since.

Right now he was listening, standing by the bar making a drink, the phone wedged in between his shoulder and his jaw. He put the scotch bottle down, picked up his drink, took some of it, then put the glass down hard and said, "What the fuck you talking about—I got back *yes*terday. Where's the wasted time? What if I was still in Mexico? You going to tell me everything would stop? Shit no." He listened again, moving about impatiently. "Look, it's a personal matter—you said so yourself. It's got nothing to do with the organization. I get it done and we get back to business. Not before."

He slammed the phone down and picked up his drink again. "Fucking lawyers. You don't know if they're working for you or you're working for them."

Wiley said, "I think your friends are worried you might get them involved."

"That's what I need, some more opinions."

She went back to her book as he turned to Lundy.

"What's he doing?"

"He picked up his trailer," Lundy said, "and went right home."

"Alone?"

"He *was.* But Bobby says there's a girl there. Come before he got back. I don't know," Lundy said, "man's waiting to get shot he's got some tail with him."

Put yourself in his place, Renda was thinking, and said, "The cops could've told him don't worry and he feels safe. Thinks, with all that's happened, I won't come for him right away."

"Whenever we do it," Lundy said, "we can't just walk in. The cops could be there waiting."

"You see any?"

"No, but they could've slipped in when it got dark. Be all over the place."

"I don't have time to fool around," Renda said. "They're starting to pressure me, give me some shit, tell me forget about the guy or hire it done."

Lundy agreed with them 100 percent, but he said, "You want to hit him yourself you got to wait for the right time, that's all."

"I don't *have* time! Can't you get that in your head?" He took a drink of scotch and calmed down a little. "How many guys you got there?"

"Five. In the trees by his place. There's a back road takes you in there." He watched Frank put his glass down and go over to a window that looked out on a dark patio and swimming pool.

When Renda turned to him again he said, "If it can take you in, nobody sees you, it can take him out, can't it?"

"If there's no cops in his house."

"All right, you watch his place. He tries to move during the night, stop him. We see who comes out in the morning. We don't see any cops around we grab him, put him in a car, take him out in the desert."

"What about the girl?" Lundy said.

"What girl?"

"The one with him."

"If she's with him she goes too."

Looking at the page in her book, Wiley wondered what the

girl looked like. She wondered if the girl knew she might get killed. Or if the melon grower knew it. Yes, he'd know it, but she wasn't sure about the girl.

Lundy was gone. Frank was at the bar again making another drink. He was drinking too much, taking more pills than he ever had before.

Wiley said, "Do you every worry about—that you could get caught by the police? Or shot? Or killed?"

"Are you going to give me some more opinions?"

"I was just curious. Is that all right?" He didn't answer her and she said, "The guy really didn't mess you up that much, did he? I mean is it worth it? All the trouble?"

He turned from the bar with a fresh scotch.

"Is your book any good?"

"It's different."

"Good and dirty?"

"Dirty enough."

"Then why don't you read it?"

"And shut the fuck up."

"Right," Renda said, "and shut the fuck up."

For several minutes Majestyk stood by the screen door, holding it open a few inches, looking down the road toward the migrant quarters and the packing shed. He thought he had heard a car, not an engine sound but a squeak of springs rolling slowly over ruts. Now all he heard were the crickets. He looked out at his fields, past the pickup, that was parked about twenty feet from the porch now, facing the dirt road and the highway at the end of it. With his shotgun he moved to a side window and looked out at the dark mass of trees. There was no movement, no sound. He left the window.

From the bedroom doorway he could see the girl's profile against the window and the barrel of the Marlin.

"Anything?"

She shook her head. "I have trouble concentrating, Vincent. What I'd like to more than anything is straighten this place up."

"How can you see it in the dark?"

"When I came it was light. I never saw so much stuff not put away. Don't you hang anything up?"

"I haven't had much time for housekeeping. With one thing or another."

"What's that, on the other side of the bed?"

"Don't you know a deep-freeze when you see one? I got it secondhand for twenty-five bucks. Keep deer meat in it."

"I mean what's it doing in here?"

"What's the difference? You got to put it somewhere."

"You need help, Vincent. Well, maybe it's good you have it. They come, we can hide in it."

"They come shooting," he said, "we won't get a chance to hide. But if they *don't* come, soon, I lose a crop. I been thinking. He can wait a week, a year, long as he wants. But I can't wait anymore. So, I figure, I better get it done myself."

"Like turn it around?" She sounded interested.

"If I could spot him, bring him out—"

"Call him up," Nancy said. "Ask him to meet you someplace." There was enough light that she could see his expression, the smile beginning to form, and she said then, "I'm just kidding. I don't mean really do it. Come on, don't. You're just crazy enough to try."

"If he's watching us," Majestyk said, "I don't have to call him. And if he doesn't come tonight—" He paused. "I've got a half-assed idea that might be worth trying."

"God, you are going to turn it around, aren't you? Go after him instead of him after you."

"It's a thought, isn't it? Something he might not expect."

"God, Vincent, sometimes you scare me."

He smiled at her again, feeling pretty good considering everything, and went back into the living room.

12

Bobby Kopas said, "We got him for you, Mr. Renda. Sure'n hell he's in there and there ain't no way he can get out."

Renda stared at the house, at the early morning sun shining on the windows, waiting for some sign of life, wondering what the man was doing, if he was in there. The place looked deserted, worn out and left to rot. He was thinking that it would be getting hot in there. The guy should open a window, let in some air. The guy should be doing something, open the door, take the garbage out, something.

"He tries to go out the road," Lundy said, "we got two people down there in the packing shed. Another boy's over behind that trailer, see it? Case he tries to take off through the melon patch. Two more round the back. We cut his phone wire. I'd say all we got to do is walk up the door and ring the bell."

"If he's there," Renda said. He looked at Kopas. "You seen him this morning?"

Bobby Kopas had been up all night, but he wasn't even tired. He'd been doing a job and hadn't made any mistakes. He said, "I figure he's locked himself in the toilet. Else he's hiding under the bed."

"I still have trouble, don't I," Renda said, "asking you a question?"

"What I meant, Mr. Renda, no, we haven't seen him yet, but he's in the house. His truck's right there. There's no place else he could be."

"And nobody's come by?"

"The girl," Lundy said, "yesterday. She's the only one."

Renda was staring at the house again. It wasn't Sunday. It wasn't a day off. The guy wasn't sleeping in. He should have come out by now. He should have been out an hour ago, working, doing something. So if he was in there he knew what was going on. He felt it or smelled it or had seen somebody.

"I don't like it," Renda said.

Eugene Lundy didn't like it either, not a bit; but it was a living that paid good money and gave him plenty of time to get drunk in between jobs. The thing to do was not think about it too much and just get the job over with. He said, "Well, we can stand here with our finger up our ass or we can go pull the son of a bitch out of there and get it done."

It was good to have people like Gene Lundy, they were hard to find. "That's what we're going to do," Renda said, "but I don't want any fucking surprises. I don't need surprises. Gene, what have we got? What it looks like we've got. The guy in the house. He's got a girl with him. One, maybe two cops over on the highway. Are there more cops somewhere? You say no. All right, then what are the cops doing? Maybe they pulled out. Maybe they said fuck him. Maybe they don't give a shit about the guy and they don't care what happens to him. Except there's still a cop over on the highway. Gene, you're sure, right?"

Lundy nodded. "I saw him go in the tool shed. He's got a radio in there."

"All right," Renda said, "they know I'm going to hit him, they're hanging around. But they're not hanging around very close, are they? What're they doing?"

"Maybe," Lundy said, "they don't give a shit about the guy as you say. I don't know. Maybe they figure you were here, you're not going to come right back, they got a little time. I don't know how they think, fucking cops, but maybe that's what they think."

Renda took a minute, staring at the house. He nodded then and said, "Okay, we'll bring him out. We'll be quiet, go in and bring him out. Walk him back here to the car. And the girl. We'll have to take the girl."

Bobby Kopas had started to think about it too, the actual doing it, and he said, "Mr. Renda, what if he's got a gun?"

"He does, we take it away from him," Renda said. "He tries to use it, then we got no choice." He looked at Lundy. "Do it in the house and get out." He looked at Kopas then. "What I think we'll do—you walk up to the door first, we'll come in behind you."

Bobby Kopas heard it but didn't believe it. He said holy shit to himself and grinned because, Christ, he had never been in this kind of a set-up before and he didn't know how to act, what kind of a pose or anything. He felt like a dumb shit grinning, but what else was he going to do? He said, "Mr. Renda, I never done anything like this before. You know what I mean? I mean I might not be any good at it." Still grinning.

Renda said, "You walk up to the door, we come in behind you."

Majestyk put the two suitcases by the front door and looked at Nancy.

"You ready?"

"I guess so."

"Both bags go in the back of the truck. Save you time, and we might need the one sooner than I'd like."

"All right."

"Once you start, put your foot on it. Don't stop or slow down. Somebody gets in your way, run him over. Five or six miles down the highway you'll see the Enco sign on the corner. The café's right past it."

"Vincent—"

"Listen to me. You get out, take your suitcase, and walk over to the café."

"Vincent, please, you can't do it alone. You need someone."

"Think about what you have to do," he said. "That's enough. More than I have a right to ask."

"Please take me with you."

"I'm not going to argue with you," Majestyk said. "We've discussed it. I'm not going to change my mind now. You get off and I keep going and that's the way it's going to be."

"All right," Nancy said, "but you feel something, Vincent, the same as I do. You can't tell me you don't."

He opened the door and stepped back from it, out of the way. He said, "It's time to go."

They watched her come out with the suitcases and swing them, one at a time, into the back of the pickup. When she got in behind the wheel Lundy said, surprised, "She's taking off in his truck."

"Two suitcases," Renda said. He had to make up his mind right now. Stop her or let her go. The guy could be making her leave, getting her out of the way. Or the guy could be pulling something. He said to Kopas, "She have a suitcase yesterday?"

"Hey, that's right," Kopas said. "She did."

"How many?"

"Just one. Yeah, walked all the way across the field with it."

They heard her voice as she called something to the house. Her arm came out of the window and waved. As the truck started to roll away from the house Lundy said, "She's leaving him there. You believe it?"

Right now, Renda was thinking. Stop her. Yell to the guy behind the trailer. Yell at him to stop her, pull her out of the truck. But even as he made up his mind and screamed it, "Get her! Stop the truck!" it was too late.

Majestyk was out of the house, running, chasing the pickup,

catching the tailgate with his hands and rolling over it into the box as the truck roared off, raising a trail of dust.

Nancy caught only a glimpse of the one by the melon trailer. He was stepping into the road, raising a gun, then jumping aside, away from the front fender, and she was past him, her hands tight on the vibrating wheel, wondering if Vincent was being bounced to death on the metal floor of the box. She wanted to look around, but she kept her eyes on the road, doing fifty now and suddenly seeing the car coming out from the side of the packing shed, coming fast and braking, skidding a little as it reached the narrow road and sat there blocking the way. Nancy cranked the wheel hard to the right, swerved around the front of the car, in and out of the ditch and back onto the road. In the rearview mirror she saw the car back up and make a tight turn to come after her. She was approaching the highway now and would have to slow down.

Turn left and race the five or six miles to Edna. Get out at the café and take her suitcase while he jumped in behind the wheel and before she could say anything he would be gone, leading them up into the mountains somewhere and she would never see him again.

He couldn't do it alone. He needed her. The two of them might have a chance, but he was stubborn and wouldn't listen to her. So she could be meek and do what she was told and never see him after he got in the truck and she walked across the street to wait for the bus. Or—she could forget his instructions, everything he had said, and help him, whether he wanted her to or not. It was simple, already decided. When she reached the highway she turned right instead of left.

He was pounding on the window, yelling at her, "It's the other way! Where in the hell you going?"

She looked over her shoulder and gave him a nice smile, mashed the accelerator, and saw him fall off balance, away from the window.

The deputy at the road construction site saw him raise up again, just as the pickup was going by, and press against the truck's cab, by the back window. The deputy knew it was Majestyk. But he didn't get a good look at who was driving. He thought it was the girl, but he couldn't be sure. The truck went by so fast—west, away from Edna. He was on the radio when the car came out of the road—dark green Dodge, two-door model—squealed out, turning hard, and there wasn't any question in his mind somebody was after somebody.

Thirty seconds later Harold Ritchie was in McAllen's office.

"Renda or some of his people are hot after him. Going east on the highway."

"Now you're talking," McAllen said. "Let's put everything we got on it."

He knew what she was doing now, and knew what he had to do. Lying on his side in the pickup bed he opened his suitcase, took out the stock and barrel of the Remington 12-gauge, got them fitted together and shoved in five loads. It wasn't easy; it took him longer than usual, because of the metal vibrating beneath him and the sway of the truck and the wind. It was hard to keep his balance, propped on an elbow, hard to keep the shotgun steady and the shells in one place.

The crazy girl was having it her way. He saw her face a couple of times, looking over her shoulder through the window, seeing if he was ready.

He needed more time to get the Marlin put together and loaded.

But the dark green car was coming up on them fast. The truck could do maybe eighty, the car a hundred and twenty probably, or more. It wouldn't be long before it was running up their rear end. He looked back again, as they reached the lower end of a grade, and now saw two more cars behind the green one, closing in from about a half to a quarter of a mile away.

Nancy's eyes moved from the outside rearview mirror to the road ahead, the narrow blacktop racing at her, a straight line pointing through scrub and pasture land. On the left side of the road was a stock fence, miles of wire and posts and up ahead, finally, there it was, a side road. Higher posts marked the road. And a closed gate hung across the entrance.

There wouldn't be time to stop and open the gate. She knew that.

There wouldn't be time to load the Marlin. Majestyk realized that now. He put it down quickly, across the open suitcase, and picked up the shotgun again. He had to get turned around, face the tailgate.

He was moving, keeping low, on his elbows and knees—and was thrown hard against the side of the pickup box as the truck left the road and its high four-wheel-drive front end smashed through the wooden gate, exploded through it with the sound of boards splitting, ripped apart by the high metal bumper.

By the time Renda's three cars were through the gate and had come to a sudden stop, the truck was bounding across the desert pasture, making its own trail, running free where the cars couldn't follow.

No one had to say it. The rocks and holes, steepbanked washes and scrub, would rip the underbody of an automobile, tear out the suspension. They sat staring at the dust settling and the yellow speck out there in the open sunlight—Renda in the front seat with Lundy, Kopas in back.

"There's a road over there," Renda said finally. "They got to be headed for something."

"Taking a shortcut," Lundy said.

"There is one," Kopas said, "if I remember correctly. About a mile, county road cuts through there, goes up in the mountains."

The three cars turned in a tight circle and went out through the gate the way they had come in, the dark green Dodge leading off.

Within five miles the county blacktop began to wind and climb, making its way up into high country.

Majestyk felt better now. He had a little time to breathe and knew what he was going to do. The girl had set it up for him, given him the time. She had said he needed her and she was right. When he signaled to her and she stopped, he got out of the box and came up on her side.

"I guess there's no way to get rid of you, is there?"

"I told you before, Vincent, you're stuck with me."

She was the one to have along all right, but he couldn't think about her now. He told her to hold it about thirty-five, let them catch up again. He got back into the rear end and that was the last thing he said to her for a while.

There were a few new melon cartons in the pickup bed, flat pieces of cardboard he put under him for some cushion, soften the damn skid strips on the floor. Then he put the two suitcases at the back end of the pickup box, against the tailgate, and rested the shotgun on them. Lying belly down they were just about the right height. He reached up and pulled the latch open on one side of the tailgate. The other one would hold the gate closed until he was ready.

When he saw the three cars coming again, they were on a good stretch of road, straight and climbing, a pinyon slope rising above them on the right and a steep bank of shale and scrub that fell off to the left, dropping fifty or more feet into dense growth, dusty stands of mesquite.

Now he would have to keep down and rely on Nancy. In the window he saw her look back at him and nod. That meant they were coming up fast. He could hear the car.

Nancy was watching it in the rearview mirror—catching glimpses of the other two cars behind it—letting them come, watching the first car closely to see what it was going to do and trying to hold the truck steady on the narrow road. The car was fifty, forty feet away, crawling up on the truck, overtaking it and beginning to pull out, as if to pass. She held up two fingers in the rear window, a peace sign.

Majestyk was ready. He reached for the tailgate latch, pulled the chain off. The gate dropped, clanged open and there was the dark green Dodge charging at him, a little off to the right. At twenty feet Majestyk put his face to the shotgun, fired three times and saw the windshield explode and the car go out of control. It swerved across the road, sweeping past the tailgate, hit the bank on the right side and came back again—as the two cars behind, suddenly close, braked and fishtailed to keep from piling into the Dodge. The car veered sharply to the left, jumped the shoulder, and dived into the brush fifty feet below.

He fired twice at the second car, the Olds 98, but it was swerving to avoid hitting the bank. The shot raked its side and caught part of the third car, taking out a headlight, as the car rammed into the left rear fender of the Olds, kicked it sideways and both cars came to a hard abrupt stop.

Majestyk gave Nancy the sign, felt the pickup lurch as it shifted and took off, leaving the two cars piled up in the road.

The first thing Lundy did, he went over to the shoulder to look down at the Dodge, at the rear end of it sticking out of the brush. There was no sign of the two guys. They were probably still inside. He couldn't see how they could be alive, but it was possible. Lundy was starting down the bank when Renda called to him.

"Gene, come on." Renda was walking away from the rear of the Olds. The other car was slowly backing up. He said, "We're okay. Let's go."

Lundy began to say, "I was thinking we ought to—don't you think we should take a look?"

"We're going to get in the car, Gene, and not waste any more time. Now come on."

"They could be alive. Hurt pretty bad, caught in there."

"I don't give a shit what they are. We got something to do, right now, before he gets someplace and hides."

Renda didn't say any more until they were in the car, following the road up through the pinyon, looking at side trails, openings in the trees where he could have turned off. But there wasn't any way to tell.

"That goddamn truck of his, he can go anywhere," Renda said. "He knows this country. He told me, he comes up here hunting."

"If he knows it and we don't," Lundy said, "it changes things."

"I don't know, is he running or what? The son of a bitch."

"If he's still on this road," Lundy said, "we'll catch him. Otherwise I don't know either."

There was a game trail nearby where he had sat with the Marlin across his lap and waited for deer: meat for the winter, to be stored in his twenty-five-dollar deep-freeze. He wondered if he would go hunting this fall. If the girl would still be here. If either of them would be here.

He sat with the Marlin now as he had sat before, this time looking down the slope, through the pine trees to the road, the narrow black winding line far below. The cabin was less than a mile from here. He wondered if Renda would think of it and remember how to find it. No, he wouldn't have picked out landmarks and memorized them. He was from a world that didn't use landmarks.

He said to the girl, "Did you ever shoot a deer?"

"I don't think I could."

"What if you were hungry?"

"I still couldn't."

"You eat beef."

"But I don't have to kill it."

"All right, I'll make you a deal. I'll shoot it, you cook it."

"When are we going to do that, Vincent?"

"In a couple of months. We'll have plenty of time. Sit around, drink beer, watch TV. Maybe take some trips."

"Where do you want to go?"

"I don't care. Anyplace."

"We going to get married first?"

"Yeah, you want to?"

"I guess we might as well, Vincent. Soon as we get some time."

Looking down the slope he said, "Here come a couple of friends of ours."

They watched the two cars pass below them on the winding road.

"Now what, Vincent?"

"Now we give them a kick in the ass," Majestyk said.

Renda's three men in the second car, following the Olds, were in general agreement that riding around in the mountains was a bunch of shit. That Frank Renda ought to take care of his own hit, if he wanted the guy so bad. That maybe they should stop on the way back—if they ever got out of this fucking place—and see about the two guys who went over the side.

Though they must be dead; nobody had yelled for help. They were looking out the windows, up and down the slopes, but if the guy wasn't still on the road they knew they weren't going to find him. How could they get to him?

The one in the back seat said, "There shouldn't be nothing to it. Wait for the right time you can set the fucking guy on fire, do it any way you want. This hurry-up shit doesn't make any sense."

"You know what the trouble is?" the driver said. "The guy, the farmer, he doesn't know what he's doing. He shouldn't even still be around."

"That's it," the one in the back seat said. "If he knew anything he'd know enough not to be here. It's like some clown never been in the ring before. He's so clumsy, does so many wrong things, you can't hit the son of a bitch."

"Fighting a southpaw," the driver said. "You ever fight a southpaw?"

"You get used to that," the one in the back seat said. "I'm talking about a clown. Hayseed, doesn't even own a cup."

"So you know where to hit him," the driver said.

"Shit, try and get to the guy."

Talking about nothing, passing the time. The one in the back seat looked out the side window at the dun-colored slopes and rock formations. They were getting pretty high, moving along a hogback, the spine of a slope. He half turned to look out the back window and said, "Jesus!" loud enough to bring the driver's eyes to the rearview mirror and the man next to him around on the seat.

The high front end of Majestyk's pickup was on top of them, headlights and yellow sheetmetal framed in the back window, the guy behind the wheel looking right at them, saying something, and the girl next to him ducking down.

Majestyk pressed down on the gas, caught up and drove the high bumper into the car's rear deck. He saw the car beginning to pull away, pressed the gas pedal all the way to the floor and caught the rear end again, stayed with it this time, fighting the wheel to keep the car solidly in front of him, ramming it, bulldozing it down the narrow grade, hitting a shoulder and raising dust, hanging with it, seeing sky above the car and knowing what was coming, foot pressed hard on the gas for another five seconds before he raised it and mashed it down on the brake pedal.

The car almost made the turn. It skidded sideways, powersliding, hit the shoulder, and went through the guardrail turned onced in the air and exploded in flames five hundred feet below.

Majestyk was through the turn, saw the Olds 98 on the road three switchbacks below him, came to an abrupt stop, turned around, and headed back the way they had come, aware of the smoke now billowing up out of the canyon. He was sure Renda heard the explosion and would be coming back. So he'd go up into the pines again and work out the next step.

In the quiet of the cab he heard Nancy say, "I hope you never get mad at me, Vincent."

The Olds 98 came to a stop in the shadow of a high, seamed outcropping of rock. The shadow covered the road that continued in dimness, reaching a wall of rock and brush before bearing in a sharp curve to the right.

Lundy got the map out of the glove box and spread it open over the steering wheel. It was quiet in the car, except for the sound of Lundy straightening the map, smoothing the folds.

Renda stared straight ahead, through the windshield. We haven't been out here an hour, he was thinking, and he's killing us. Do you know what he's doing? Do you see it now?

Bobby Kopas fidgeted in the back seat, looking out the window on one side and then the other, bending down to see the crest of the high rocks. It was so quiet. Sunlight up there and shade down here. Nothing moving.

"His hunting country," Renda said. "He brought us here."

"I see where we're at," Lundy said. "The lodge is only about six, eight miles west of here, but roundabout to get to. 'Less we want to go all the way back to the highway, which I don't think is a good idea."

Renda wasn't listening to him. He was picturing a man in work clothes and scuffed lace-up boots, a farmer, a man who lived by himself and grew melons and didn't say much.

"He set us up," Renda said. "The farmboy knew what he was doing all the time and he set . . . us . . . up."

Lundy said, "What do you want to do? Go back the lodge? I don't see any sense in messing around here." He waited, watching Renda stare out the window. "Frank, what do you want to do?"

He didn't know. He realized now he didn't know anything about the man. It was like meeting him, out here, for the first time. He should have known there was someone else, another person, inside the farmer. The stunt the guy pulled with the bus and trying to take him in, make a deal. That wasn't a farmer. He had been too anxious to get the guy and had not taken time to think about him, study him and find out who he was inside.

Lundy said, "There's no sense sitting here."

Renda continued to stare at the wall of rock ahead of them, where the road curved, thinking of the man, trying to remember the things he had said, trying to out-think him now, before it was too late. He didn't see the figure standing on the crest of the rocks, not at first. And when he saw him he was a shadow that moved, a dark figure silhouetted against the sky a hundred yards away, holding something, raising it.

"Get out of here!"

Renda screamed it, Lundy looked up and the rifle shot drilled through the windshield and into the seat between them with a high whining sound that was outside, far away. The second shot tore through the glass two inches from the first and Renda screamed it again, "Get out of here!"

Majestyk put four more .30–30's into the car before it got around the bend and was out of sight. He might have hit one of them but he doubted it. He should have taken a little more time on the second shot, corrected and placed it over to the left more. That's what you get, you don't hunt in a year you forget how your weapons act.

He walked away from the crest, back into the pines where Nancy was waiting by the truck, shaking his head as he approached her.

"Missed. Now I got to bird-dog him."

"Now?" She seemed a little surprised. "How can you catch up with him?"

"I can cross-country, he can't."

"You're really going after him?"

"We're this far," he said and watched her cock her head, then look up through the pine branches.

"I think I hear a plane," she said. "You hear it?"

He heard it. Walking back from the crest into the trees he had heard it. "You'll see it in about a minute," he said. "Only it's not a plane, it's a helicopter."

Harold Ritchie had radioed ahead to cars patrolling the main roads as far as thirty miles east of Edna. They reported, during the next half hour, no sign of a yellow four-wheel-drive pickup, with or without anybody chasing it.

So he must have taken them up in the mountains, Lieutenant McAllen decided, and called the Phoenix Police for a helicopter. Get more ground covered in an hour than they could in a week.

It didn't even take that long. McAllen and Ritchie had been cruising the highway and some of the back roads. They were at the road repair site when the chopper radioed in. There was static and the sound of the rotor beating the air, but the pilot's voice was clear enough.

"Three-four Bravo, this is three-four Bravo. I believe we got him. Yellow pickup truck heading south, in the general direction of county road 201, just west of Santos Rim, God almighty, or else it's a mountain goat. I thought he was on a trail, but there ain't anything there. He's bouncing over the rocks, flying. Heading down through a wash now like it's a chute-the-chute. Look at that son of a bitch go!"

McAllen and Ritchie looked at one another. They didn't say anything.

"On 201 now heading west," the pilot's voice said. There

was a pause. "Hey, we got something else. Looks like ... an Oldsmobile or a Buick, late model, dark blue ... about a half mile out in front of the pickup, going like hell. Let me get down closer. This is three-four Bravo out."

Lieutenant McAllen looked up in the sunlight, toward the mountains, then at Harold Ritchie. "You don't suppose—"

"I'd more likely suppose it than not," Ritchie said.

They heard the radio crackle and the helicopter pilot's voice came on again.

"This is three-four Bravo. Looks like they pulled a disappearing act on us. I don't see either one of them now. They must've turned off on a trail through the timber. Hang on I'll give you some coordinates."

"About how far away are we talking about?" McAllen asked Ritchie. "The general area."

"Not far. Take us twenty, thirty minutes, depending on the coordinates he gives us."

"Then we'd still have to find them," McAllen said.

"We get enough cars up there," Ritchie said, "we can do it."

"But can we do it in time?"

Ritchie wasn't sure what he meant. "In time for what?"

"In time to keep him from killing himself," McAllen said.

13

Wiley was bored. She had finished her book. There wasn't anything else to read in the place but business and banking magazines and a few old *Playboys*. It was a little too cold to go in the pool—which wasn't much of a thrill even when it was warm. She was tired of lying in the sun but not tired enough to take a nap. The whole thing, lying around swimming pools, waiting, was getting to be a big goddamn bore.

And the ice in her iced tea had melted. She put the glass on the cement next to the lounge chair, snapped her orange bikini bottom a little higher on her can as she got up and went into the lodge, or whatever it was, that Frank said looked like a dude ranch.

It did look like a dude ranch. All those Indian blankets and animals looking out of the wall. She turned the hi-fi on, got some rock music she liked but didn't recognize and was patting her bare thighs gently, keeping time, when Frank came in the front door. Frank and Gene and the new one, the little smart-ass carrying a shotgun. She hadn't heard the car drive up.

"Well, hey. What's going on?"

The three of them were at the front windows, not paying any attention to her.

"I never seem to catch the beginning," Wiley said. "Will somebody tell me what's going on?"

She moved over a little, her hips keeping time with the music, to be able to look out the window, past Frank and across the open yard to where the long driveway came in through the trees. She didn't see the Olds; then she did—over to the side a little at the edge of the trees, as if hidden there. They were waiting for someone to come up the drive and as she realized this her hips stopped keeping time and she thought of the police.

"You think," Wiley said, "I should start packing or what?"

"He's in the trees," Renda said.

"He could be," Lundy said, "if he saw us turn. But maybe he didn't."

Renda looked over his shoulder at Wiley. "Give me the glasses. Over on the table."

"Would you mind telling me something?"

"Give me the *glasses.*"

He raised the window and got down on his knees, took the binoculars as she handed them to him and rested his elbows on the sill. The trees were close to him now, dark in there but clearly defined as he adjusted the focus, scanned slowly toward the drive, held for a while, trying to see down the length of the dirt road, then back again, slowly. He stopped. From the side of a tree about twenty feet into the woods, Majestyk was aiming a rifle at him.

With the sound of the shot, the glass above his head shattered. Renda dropped below the sill to his hands and knees, in a crouch. There was a silence before he heard the man's voice, coming from the trees.

"Frank, let's finish it. Come on, I got work to do."

Wiley watched Frank crawl from beneath the window and stand up, turning to put his back against the wall. She expected him to yell something at the guy, answer him, but he didn't. He was looking at her with a thoughtful sort of pleased expression; not really happy, but relaxed as he drew a .45 automatic from underneath his jacket. She still didn't know what was going on.

Majestyk handed Nancy the rifle and picked up the shotgun, leaning against a tree, as he saw the front door open.

Wiley came out in her orange bikini. She seemed at ease, even though she was looking around, more curious than afraid. Coming across the lawn she said, "Where are you?"

"Over here," Majestyk said. He saw her gaze turn this way, but was sure she couldn't see him yet.

"Frank's not home," Wiley said. "You want to come in and wait?" He didn't answer now and she turned to go. "Well, it was nice talking to you."

"Wiley—"

She stopped and looked back. "Yeah?"

"Come here."

"I don't know where you are."

"Over here. That's right."

He waited until she was in the trees, more cautious now, and finally saw where they were standing. "What's he doing?" Majestyk said. "He want you to point to me so he can shoot?"

"I told you, he's not home."

"The car's over there."

"It belongs to somebody else."

"Wiley, tell Frank the cops are on the way. Tell him if he wants to settle it he hasn't got much time."

She hesitated. "Police, huh. Listen, this really hasn't got anything to do with me. I just happen to stop by."

"Who else is in there? How many?"

She hesitated again. "Just Frank . . . and two others. God, he's going to kill me."

Majestyk turned to Nancy. "Put her in the truck. Drive back to the road and wait for me there."

Wiley said to Nancy, "I really don't know what's going on. I don't have any clothes or anything."

"Don't worry, I'll give you a nice outfit," Nancy said, and looked at Majestyk again. "Vincent, wait for the police, all right?"

"If they come," he said, "but right now it's still up to him."

They couldn't see her now. There had been a spot of orange in the trees, but now that was gone.

"Where'd she go?" Kopas said. He didn't like it at all. Five people dead, the man out there waiting for them. The man must be crazy, all he'd done.

"He grabbed her," Lundy said. He was holding his big magnum, resting it on the windowsill.

Why would he? Kopas was thinking and said, "Maybe they left. He sees we got him, so he took her and cut out."

"He's there," Renda said, sure of it now, since he had begun to know the man, understand him. "Son of a bitch, we got to suck him out. Or go in after him."

Kopas said, "You mean walk out there?"

Renda looked at him. "If I tell you to."

Majestyk came up to the Olds 98 through the trees, keeping low, and there was nothing to it. The next part he'd have to do and not worry about and if they spotted him and fired he'd have to back off and think of something else. He opened the front door on the passenger side, waited a moment, then slid in headfirst over the seat and pulled the key out of the ignition. Coming out he looked at the backrest of the seat cushion, at the two bullet holes that were hardly noticeable. Just a little more to the left. He wished he'd taken a couple more seconds. It would have saved him a lot of trouble.

They could still come out the front while he worked around through the trees to the back, but it wouldn't do them any good now. They weren't going anywhere, unless on foot, and then it would be even easier.

That's what he did: cut across the open to the blind side of the house and stayed close to it as he made his way around to the patio.

It could work because they wouldn't expect him. Get up to a window or the glass door underneath the sundeck, shove the pump gun in, and wait for somebody to turn around. He moved past the lounge chair Wiley had been using a little while before, his eyes on the window. Even if he had looked down then he might not have seen the iced tea glass, it was so close to the chair. By the time he did see it he had kicked it over—hearing it like a window breaking—and all he saw were the broken fragments and a piece of lemon on the wet cement.

Renda turned from the front window. He stood listening, holding the .45 automatic at his side, then raised it as he started across the room toward the patio door. Lundy followed him.

Kopas waited. He wasn't sure he wanted to go over there. He watched Renda press against the glass panes to look out, trying to see down the outside wall of the house. Kopas knew he'd have to open the door and stick his head out to see anything. He wondered if Renda would open the door, if he'd go out. Christ, it would take guts.

He heard Renda say to Lundy, "You stay here. I'm going up on the sundeck. I spot him I'll yell to you."

Lundy nodded, holding the big mag, and moved in close to the door as Renda came back across the room. Kopas still didn't know what to do. He was sure, though, he didn't like being here with the guy right outside, the guy maybe poking a gun in a window any minute.

That is why he followed Renda to the front hall and up the stairs. The guy couldn't poke a gun into a second-floor window.

Renda went into a bedroom and over to the sliding glass door that opened on the sundeck. He glanced at Kopas as he went out, noticing him, but didn't say anything—like the other times, looking through him as if he wasn't there.

Kopas said, "What you want me to do, Mr. Renda?"

Maybe Renda hadn't heard him. He was out on the sundeck now, looking over the railing at the patio. Kopas raised his shotgun and moved to the open doorway. He didn't go out. He could see most of the patio and the swimming pool, the sun reflecting on the clear green water. He watched Renda go to his hands and knees, trying to see down through the narrow spaces between the deck boards. Renda crawled along this way, coming back to the door before he got to his feet again.

"Son of a bitch, he's under there," Renda said.

But where? Kopas was thinking. The deck was about thirty feet long. He could be right underneath them or he could be down a ways or hiding behind something. He watched Renda move to the rail again, then look over to the left, to where the patio door would be, where Lundy was waiting. He watched Renda lean over the rail and point the .45 straight down—and couldn't believe it when Renda suddenly yelled out.

"Gene, he's going around the side! Get him!"

Majestyk's eyes were raised to the sundeck above his head, his shotgun pointing straight up to where he was pretty sure Renda was standing—where he had heard the movement and where the glint of sunlight between the boards were blotted out.

He didn't know it was Renda, not until he heard Renda's voice, his words clear, startling. And heard something else. A door. Quick footsteps on cement.

He had time—at least three seconds, before Lundy, running alongside the swimming pool, saw him, came to a stop and swung the magnum at him—time to swing the shotgun down and fire and pump and fire again and see Gene Lundy blown off his feet into the swimming pool.

Renda saw that much and knew where the man was down below, knew close enough, and began firing the .45 automatic straight down at the deck boards, concentrating on a small area only a few feet to his left, fired and fired, splintering, gouging the stained wood, and kept firing until the automatic was empty.

He stood listening then. When the gunfire ringing in his ears began to fade, he could hear, very faintly, the sound of hi-fi rock music coming from the main room. That was all. He stepped into the bedroom to reload the .45, still listening, watching the patio—pulling out the clip and throwing it aside, taking another clip from his jacket pocket and smacking it with his palm into the grip.

"Go take a look," Renda said.

Kopas had backed away from the glass doors until the bed stopped him and he felt it against his legs. "Mr. Renda—" He stopped and started over. "The man wasn't running around the side. I was looking, I didn't see him. You told Gene that—you *used* Gene to spot the guy."

Kopas saw him turn and saw his eyes, not looking through him this time but right at him.

"Go downstairs," Renda said, "look out the door. If he's laying there, walk out on the patio. If he isn't laying there, stay where you are."

"I'm sorry," Bobby Kopas said. "I mean I don't even know what I'm *doing* here. I don't give a shit about the guy. Really, it's none of my business. I think I better just—split. You know?" He had to get out, that's all. Just get the hell out of here, though not make it look like he was scared or running. He said, "I'll leave this case you need it," and dropped the shotgun on the bed as he got around the foot of it and headed for the door.

Renda said, "Bobby—"

Kopas kept going.

He was almost to the stairway when Renda came out into the hall.

"Bobby!"

His hand was on the stair rail. Below him was the open front door and sunlight. He didn't hear his name again. He didn't care if he did. He didn't care now if Renda thought he was running. Just get *out*, that's all.

He got halfway down.

Renda shot him from the top of the stairs, hitting him squarely in the back, twice. Lowering the .45 he saw Kopas lying face-down in the front hall, a few feet from the door, and was aware of the hi-fi music again—a slow rock instrumental—coming from the main room.

All right, he'd go down, go through the room to the patio. Look outside.

Or he could go out the front door and walk around. If the guy was alive he wouldn't know which way he'd be coming from, wouldn't know where to look.

But the guy was probably dead. Or at least hit. He must have hit him. So it didn't matter. Renda moved down the stairs, holding his gaze on the archway below and to the right, that led into the main room. He was at the bottom, in the front hall, about to step over Bobby Kopas's legs, when the hi-fi music stopped. It stopped abruptly, in the middle of the rock number.

Renda waited.

There was no sound from the room. Animal heads looking down in silence at—what? Where would he be? Behind something. Renda could see only part of the room from where he was standing, the windows along the front wall. He would have to walk through the archway to see the rest, not knowing where the guy was. He had never done it like this before, walked in, the guy knowing he was coming. Guy waiting with a shotgun. There was a shotgun upstairs. But if he went up the guy could move again and he wouldn't know where. He knew the guy was in the room. But it was a big room. Or he could be outside again, with the shotgun sticking in the window.

He said to himself, This isn't a fucking game. *Get out.*

Renda went through the doorway, ran across the grass to the Olds 98 and got to it, pulled the door open and started to slide in.

The key wasn't in the ignition.

The fucking key wasn't in the ignition! Lundy had it. No, or it was on the floor . . . or on the dash . . . or on the sun visor. Somewhere!

"Frank?"

Renda came out slowly, turning a little to look over the top of the open door.

Majestyk was standing on the front steps of the house, the shotgun cradled in the crook of his left arm.

"You hear it?" Majestyk said.

Renda turned a little more, keeping the car door in front of him. He could hear it now, the faint sound of a police siren.

Majestyk waited.

Behind the door, below the window ledge, Renda shifted the .45 automatic in his left hand. He knew he could do it, hit the guy before he moved. Farmboy standing there not knowing it was over. He said, "You want to think about it?"

Majestyk shook his head. "Last chance, Frank."

Renda brought up the .45 automatic, at arm's length out past the edge of the door and fired, trying to aim now as he fired again.

Majestyk swung the shotgun on him and blew out the window in the door, watched Renda stagger out from behind it, still holding the .45 extended, and shot him again, the 12-gauge charge slamming Renda against the side of the car and taking out the rear-door window. Renda went down to his knees, hung there a moment and fell face-down.

Majestyk was sitting on the front steps with the shotgun across his knees. He watched the three squad cars come barreling in through the trees, watched them pull to nose-diving stops and the doors swing open and the deputies come piling out with riot guns and drawn revolvers. They stopped when they saw him and stood there looking around. Lieutenant McAllen walked over.

"You were right," Majestyk said. "That man was trying to kill me."

McAllen looked at him. He didn't say anything. He kept going and walked over to where Renda was lying, stooped down and felt his throat for a pulse. He looked over at Majestyk again.

But Majestyk was walking away, over toward the pickup that had come in behind the squad cars, where the girl was standing.

McAllen watched him put his hand on the girl's shoulder as he opened the door and heard him say, "We'll get us a couple of six-packs on the way home. Right?" And he heard the girl say, "Right." He watched Majestyk's hand slide down to the girl's can as she climbed into the cab and heard her say, "Hey, watch it!" He didn't hear what Majestyk said to her as he slammed the door, but he heard the girl's laughter.

Then Majestyk was walking around the pickup to the driver's side. He looked over and gave McAllen a little wave. McAllen didn't wave back or say a word. He heard the girl laugh again and watched the pickup drive off through the trees.

READ MORE IN PENGUIN

A SELECTION OF CRIME AND MYSTERY

Devices and Desires P. D. James

When Commander Adam Dalgliesh becomes involved in the hunt for the killer in a remote area of the Norfolk coast, he finds himself caught up in the dangerous secrets of the headland community. And then one moonlit night it becomes chillingly apparent that there is more than one killer at work in Larsoken . . .

Gallowglass Barbara Vine

When Sandor saves little Joe from the path of a London tube train he claims his life for himself. In adoration and gratitude, Joe willingly offers himself to him, becoming Sandor's *gallowglass*, servant to the chief. 'Of all living writers, she can enter most convincingly into the criminal, or even pathological, mind' – *Sunday Times*

Death among the Dons Janet Neel

'*Death among the Dons* is probably the best crime novel set in a women's college since Dorothy Sayers's *Gaudy Night*' – T. J. Binyon. 'Janet Neel sets her nerve-tingling plot in a wonderfully alive and intelligent collegiate milieu' – *Sunday Times*

Pleading Guilty Scott Turow

Gage and Griswell is a large law firm with an even larger problem: $5.6 million has suddenly vanished from the coffers of its largest client. 'Extravagant with danger, sex and especially money – and full of surprises to the end' – *Independent on Sunday*

The Big Sleep Raymond Chandler

Millionaire General Sternwood, a paralysed old man, is already two-thirds dead. He has two beautiful daughters – one a gambler, the other a degenerate – and an elusive adventurer as a son-in-law. The General is being blackmailed, and Marlowe's assignment is to get the blackmailer off his back. As it turns out, there's a lot more at stake . . .

READ MORE IN PENGUIN

A SELECTION OF CRIME AND MYSTERY

Paper Doll Robert B. Parker

Olivia Nelson had almost been a candidate for sainthood – perfect wife, perfect mother with a perfect home in the best part of Boston. Too perfect, perhaps. Because someone murdered her. But when Spenser sets out to solve the case, nothing – least of all the life and death of the victim – is what it seems . . .

This Way Out Sheila Radley

The thought of doing away with his mother-in-law would never have entered Derek Cartwright's head, if he had not begun to suffer from bad dreams – and if he had not met Hugh Packer. Sheila Radley's spine-chilling story traces the descent of an upright husband and citizen into blunder, nightmare and murder. 'Here is an author who can be bracketed with the best' – *Observer*

Fatlands Sarah Dunant

'Make way for Hannah Wolfe, one of the best private eyes, either sex, either side of the Atlantic' – *Daily Telegraph*. Hannah's latest brief is to mind teenage rebel Mattie Shepherd. But what began as a Knightsbridge shopping trip ends in an act of explosive violence.

Guardian Angel Sara Paretsky

When a friend of Mr Contreras, Vic Warshawski's loyal neighbour, claims that he has some information that will make him a rich man – and then turns up dead in the canal, Vic knows it's no coincidence. 'The richest and most engaging yet of Ms Paretsky's thrillers' – *The New York Times*

Berlin Noir Philip Kerr

Ex-policeman Bernie Gunther thought he'd seen everything on the streets of 1930s Berlin. But then he went freelance and with each case he tackled he became sucked further into the grisly excesses of Nazi sub-culture. And even after the war, amidst the decayed, imperial splendour of Vienna, Bernie uncovered a legacy that made the wartime atrocities look lily-white by comparison . . .

READ MORE IN PENGUIN

A SELECTION OF CRIME AND MYSTERY

Ripley Under Water Patricia Highsmith

Tom Ripley's past would not bear too much close scrutiny. But he has carefully covered his tracks as far as murder and forgery are concerned. Or so he thinks. 'Ripley is back, as polite and lethal as ever . . . he does what he wants and gets away with it. That's why we like him' – *Time Out*

Death of a Partner Janet Neel

His relationship with wilful girlfriend Francesca on the rocks, a harassed Detective Chief Inspector John McLeish is assigned to the case of missing Angela Morgan. An attractive, wealthy lobbyist, and fiancée to a high-ranking government minister, Angela courted success – and the envy of her detractors. When her badly decomposed body is found a week later, the shock waves ripple through Whitehall, and only the murderer knows why.

The Patience of Maigret Georges Simenon

They called it Maigret's longest investigation. For twenty years there have been a series of daring raids on Paris jewellers. The Superintendent has his suspicions about the organizer – but no proof. Then there is a murder that begins to provide the missing threads.

The Complete Richard Hannay John Buchan

From Scotland to Constantinople, rural England and the bloody battlefields of France, Richard Hannay's adventures in the pursuit of justice are classic, compelling reading. Collected here are: *The Thirty-Nine Steps*, *Greenmantle*, *Mr Standfast*, *The Three Hostages* and *The Island of Sheep*.

Pronto Elmore Leonard

'The American crime master moves to Italy and stays on top of his form in a cracking tale of small-time criminals' – *Independent*. 'Book by book . . . Elmore Leonard is painting an intimate, precise, funny, frightening and irresistible mural of the American underworld' – *New Yorker*

BY THE SAME AUTHOR

Killshot

'I shoot people,' the Blackbird said. 'Sometimes for money, sometimes for nothing.' 'A grip that seems casual at first and then tightens like a python' – *Daily Telegraph*. 'Probably the best Elmore Leonard book yet . . . this is naturalism carried out with a high degree of art' – *Independent*

Glitz

Underneath the Boardwalk in Atlantic City, a lot of insects creep. But the creepiest of all was Teddy. Devoted to his parrot-loving Momma, Teddy was a rapist-killer. And Teddy had a grudge . . . 'After finishing *Glitz*, I went out to the bookstore and bought everything else of Elmore Leonard I could find' – Stephen King

Pronto

Harry Arno thought he was pretty hip for a 66-year-old. He jogged, dated a woman twenty-five years his junior, and knew Vanilla Ice was a white guy. He also ran a gambling operation out of Miami Beach for another senior citizen named Jimmy Capotorto. Life was sweet.

But when he heard from a friendly cop that the FBI had started a rumour that he was skimming on Jimmy Cap, he knew it was time to put his long-prepared retirement plan into action.

BY THE SAME AUTHOR

'The king, the top crime writer anywhere, let alone America' – *Time Out*

LaBrava

Joe LaBrava came to Miami and met the girl of his dreams – Jean, a movie actress with a hangover from the fifties. And self-styled super-stud Richie Nobles, a security guard in love with his own hair and muscles. And crazy Cuban reject Cundo Rey, maniac in a million in a leopard jockstrap . . . And if you can believe the scam these three dreamed up, you're ready to read *LaBrava.*

Freaky Deaky

Freaky deak with someone else's woman, you could wind up hurt. Freaky deak with Robin, you could wind up all over the place. Literally. 'The best American writer of crime fiction alive – and perhaps the best ever' – *Newsweek*

Touch

'I bleed from five wounds and heal people, but I've never been in love. Isn't that something?'

They call him Juvenal, and he's a wanted man in downtown Detroit. The priests at the Sacred Heart Rehabilitation Center want him – to soothe the brows (and the DTs) of their alcoholic inmates. Bill (get-rich-quick) Hill wants him – to perform miracles and make money. And Lynn Faulkner, the record promoter, wants him – to love. But Juvenal's a normal guy who just happens to heal and bleed and work the odd wonder or two . . .

BY THE SAME AUTHOR

Rum Punch

For bail bondsman Max Cherry, control is slipping away fast. His ex just moved in with some Cuban artist, the mob is into his business, and he's broken the golden rule: never fall in love with a client. Especially one as smart as air hostess Jackie Burke. Ordell Robbie has made it semi-big with the women; Mercedes and attitude to prove it. For the giant leap to real wealth he's using a posse of cracked-up jackboys, and Jackie, the cutest sky smuggler he ever saw. But when Ms Burke gets grounded, all flights of fancy are up for grabs. Whose rum has the hardest punch?

'A brilliant and subversive book' – A. Alvarez in the *Sunday Telegraph*

Maximum Bob

'Welcome to the seriously weird domain of law enforcement, dope, lust and southern bigotry, which is the setting for Elmore Leonard's superlative stylish, black comedy *Maximum Bob* . . . This is a crime thriller with real, believable, if bizarre, crime and a spanking narrative pace' – *New Stateman & Society*

Get Shorty

Chili Palmer is a debt collector for the mob in Miami, but when one of his clients skips to Hollywood he decides to take a short working holiday on the Boulevard of Broken Dreams. Compared to the movie people, Chili is a small-time low-life. But, as the fat cats are about to discover, he is also tired of showing respect to people he thinks are assholes.

and

Bandits
Cat Chaser
City Primeval
Gold Coast
The Hunted
Split Images
The Switch
Unknown Man No. 89